THE RAVISHED EARTH

By the same author

Master of Morholm

THE
RAVISHED
EARTH

T. R. Wilson

St. Martin's Press

New York

Library of Congress Cataloging-in-Publication Data

Wilson, Timothy.
        The ravished earth / Timothy Wilson.
              p.   cm.
        Sequel to: Master of Morholm.
        ISBN 0-312-03919-0
        I. Title.
      PR6073.I4753R38   1990
      823′.914—dc20   89-24107
                    MAR   6 '90   CIP

First published in Great Britain by Grafton Books, a division of
the Collins Publishing Group.

First U.S. Edition

10 9 8 7 6 5 4 3 2 1

For Dorothy Harris

Many waters cannot quench love, neither can the floods drown it.

SONG OF SOLOMON

THE HARDWICKS OF MORHOLM

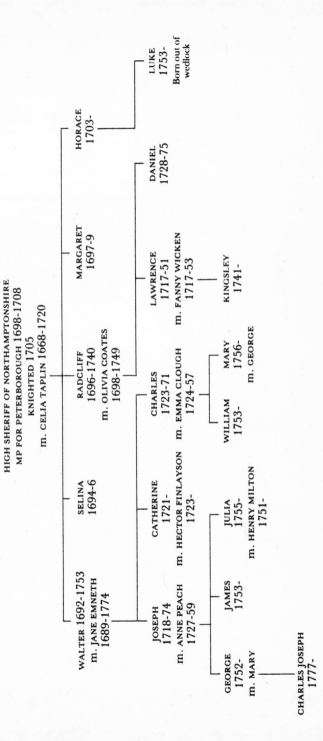

SIR ROBERT HARDWICK
OF MORHOLM
1661-1714
HIGH SHERIFF OF NORTHAMPTONSHIRE
MP FOR PETERBOROUGH 1698-1708
KNIGHTED 1705
m. CELIA TAPLIN 1668-1720

WALTER 1692-1753
m. JANE EMNETH
1689-1774

SELINA
1694-6

RADCLIFF
1696-1740
m. OLIVIA COATES
1698-1749

MARGARET
1697-9

HORACE
1703-

LUKE
1753-
Born out of
wedlock

JOSEPH
1718-74
m. ANNE PEACH
1727-59

CATHERINE
1721-
m. HECTOR FINLAYSON
1723-

CHARLES
1723-71
m. EMMA CLOUGH
1724-57

LAWRENCE
1717-51
m. FANNY WICKEN
1717-53

DANIEL
1728-75

GEORGE
1752-
m. MARY

JAMES
1753-

JULIA
1755-
m. HENRY MILTON
1751-

WILLIAM
1753-

MARY
1756-
m. GEORGE

KINGSLEY
1741-

CHARLES JOSEPH
1777-

BOOK I
December 1777

ONE

I

Rebecca Walsoken, riding into Stamford for the first time, thought for a moment the town must be in a state of riot.

It was cattle-market day, and though early frost had followed flood, so that the lower streets of the town were covered with ice, the occasion was noisy and vigorous as ever. Teeming with beasts and people, their numbers swollen by breedlings come in from the fen and out to make a day of it, the town communicated excitement. Rebecca had a hazy tantalising feeling of something about to happen, of a future densely crowded with possibilities.

She had been impressed by the spacious silence of the open landscape as they rode the eight miles from their new home to the town: she commented to her sister on how fresh the air smelt. Her father had pointed out the broad patches of ice and slush in the fields. 'The old enemy in this country,' he said. 'Such rich land, and so treacherous.'

Now as they left the bare fields and windmills behind and their horses clattered and slithered with nervous side-steps down St Mary's Hill into Stamford, a cacophony of human and animal voices greeted them. A herd of bullocks, driven by youths with reed switches in their hands, blocked the bridge at the foot of the hill. Rebecca's father, who had been here before, led the way beneath the arch sign of the great coaching inn, The George, and after he had seen to the stabling of the horses they warmed themselves before the fire in the coffee-room and drank a cup of spiced ale. There were several travellers here waiting for the Stamford Fly to take them to Lincoln, and from the taproom down the flagstoned passage came the sound of loud laughter and voices shouting in a strange harsh accent.

'It is an elegant town, and passing rich, though of course not as extensive as Norwich,' Mr Walsoken said, rubbing his hands over the fire. He puckered his black brows as there was a renewed yell of laughter from the taproom. 'Of course, on days such as this the fenmen come in, and they are known to be incorrigibly wild and uncouth. And godless. I have heard that, so isolated as they are out in the marshes, many of them live their whole lives without benefit of clergy.'

'Oh, pa, how shall we bear it?' said Sarah Walsoken, and her long face grew longer. Ever since they had moved into their new home, Bromswold, three days ago she had been peevish and homesick.

'Hush, child. In every part of the country there are men of all stations, each where God has seen fit to place them.' He beckoned the potboy over and gave him threepence for the ale. 'And though it is not a matter for worldly pride, here we shall move amongst the highest.'

Rebecca was warmed and revived by the ale, and restless to explore. 'Shall we move on, now, father?' she said, trying not to show her impatience, a sin he had often chided her for.

Mr Walsoken took a leather purse from his fob pocket. A large heavy man, there was a delicate slowness in his movements as he counted coins into Sarah's hand. 'Remember, my children, trades-men will soon observe you are strangers here, and hope to cheat you. Lawn handkerchiefs for your mother – plain, no colours – pay no more than two and sixpence each. Candles. Huckaback towelling – one and six a yard, no more. Castile soap, if it is to be had. And Dutch matting: that wing passage is draughty, and I fear for your mother's health. Do not be drawn into haggling. And do not loiter at vulgar entertainments. You will find me at Wiley's Bank, in Broad Street, when you are done.'

Sarah was still complaining as they crossed the bridge over the swollen river, but Rebecca had long mastered the art of making the right noises whilst not attending to her sister, and meanwhile she looked about her with interest. There seemed to be church spires everywhere: not squat and pebbled as in Norwich but soaring, built of a handsome grey stone, as were the elegant townhouses with their three and four storeys. Ladies picked their way across the cobbles in pattens, and had loops at their wrists to hold their gowns out of the dirt. Below the street level there were dark little workshops, for

12

tailors and dyers and tanners, and in one of these a wagon, squeezed by the thick traffic of carts and sedan chairs and coaches, had run its outside wheel down the steps and was stuck fast. The driver and the shopkeeper were having a fluent swearing match. Sarah, tripping on ahead of Rebecca, covered her ears.

The town lay between great farming regions, and marketing was a serious business: few paid any heed to the young women in cloaks and riding-hats threading their way across Red Lion Square. The elder of the two, Sarah, looked older than her twenty-four years, and had a sallow face lined by habitual anxiety. But there was something in the looks of the younger that made men spare her a second glance. She was unusually tall, and from under the cocked hat thick tawny hair tinged with copper escaped in a stream down her scarlet pelisse. The cold air had brought a high colour to her cheeks: and perhaps by force of contrast with the pinched demureness of her sister, there was something disconcertingly spirited about her long-legged walk and her frank dark eyes as she gazed about her.

'Why we must needs move I shall never understand,' Sarah said, as they stooped to enter the mercer's door. 'We were quite content where we were.'

'Content perhaps. But father wanted more,' said Rebecca. 'He's ambitious.'

'Rebecca!' Sarah greatly admired, and greatly feared Joshua Walsoken.

'Well, it's true!' said Rebecca, who did neither. 'You know he had always hankered to buy an estate. Deep down he thinks there is still something ungentlemanly about the mercantile, which is all non-sense, but he believes it. And now with mother's inheritance on top of everything, he is in a position to do it.'

'Oh, but such a place!' Sarah pointed a peremptory finger at a bolt of linen on the shelf behind the shopman. 'The house is almost falling down, and those dreadful fens stretching all around as far as the eye can see . . .'

'Father has plans for Bromswold, you'll see,' Rebecca said. 'Anyway . . . I like them. I think I shall like it here.' She peered through the little bottle-glass window across the square. The frozen flood water was rapidly melting and, churned up with mud and the countless cattle droppings, was becoming even more treacherous. Two bearers of a sedan chair, slush coating their legs up to the

13

knees, slipped and nearly fell, and the bewigged old gentleman they were carrying poked an indignant face out of the window.

Sarah was being finicky: she had already had several bolts of linen unrolled on the long deal counter. Rebecca slipped out of the shop and left her to it.

Rebecca had had no real regrets about leaving the old home in Norwich where she had spent her eighteen years. The rigidity of her father's rule over the household meant there were no friends to say goodbye to, no favourite scenes to leave, no fond associations to dwell on. Coming to this strange country suspended between endless sky and endless earth she felt only an excited sense of freedom.

She wandered at will: up Barn Hill where the proud faces of great townhouses looked down with distaste at the bustling sheep market: along Scotgate where smaller and meaner houses were shored up with wooden supports to prevent them tumbling into the street: along High Street, where there were fine shops with beautifully written boards: Woodroffe, Apothecary, where there were 'Drops and Tinctures to be had, prov'd to cure Rheumatism, Itch, Strangury and Stone, Rising of the Lights, and all manner of Distempers'; Geo. Bright, Peruke-Maker, Durable Wigs, Horsehair, Mohair, Copper Wire, Cork Wigs, also Sporting Wigs made of Drake-feathers; Sedgmoor and Milton, Booksellers and Printers; Thos. Fenney, Pipe-Maker. She hastened through the stink of the Shambles, where the guts of slaughtered beasts were thrown reeking into the gutters; and ignoring her father's warning, lingered around the entertainments in the square, the peep-shows, the man with no hands and feet who drew on the ground with chalks held between his teeth, the ragged ballad-singer and the man with a caged squirrel that rang a series of little bells in tune.

Admitting to herself at last that she ought to find Sarah, she came upon what was clearly the highlight of the morning's entertainment for a hooting crowd in Broad Street. The town magistrates had been meeting in quarter sessions, and one case had been sentenced to whipping at the cart's tail.

Rebecca had seen a public whipping before: in Norwich not long ago a man had been flogged in the market-place for selling poisonous simples that purported to bring on abortions. It was a woman here who was being whipped: she was tied by wrists and knees to the back of an open cart, but in the ankle-deep mire caused by the cattle-market the wheels had got stuck fast outside the Stag and Pheasant. A drunken crowd had issued from the inn with tankards in their hands to see the sport and were adding their voices to the jeering.

'What has she done?' Rebecca asked of an old man standing next to her.

'Whoring, they do say,' the old man said with a grin. ''Tis hard to credit, for who'd look at her? She got an arse like a Whittlesey cart-hoss!'

The woman must have been fifty. Her hair had been clumsily dyed red and she had few teeth, as was plain to see when she screamed at the lash. She had been stripped to the waist, and her grey-white breasts hung pendulously.

'Dear life, they'll wop her back abroad,' said an old woman nearby. ''Tis too much.'

There was a long sighing groan from the crowd as the gaoler administering the beating put up his whip and wiped his brow. Someone handed him a pot of beer and a constable stepped forward and made a hurried, inaudible proclamation. The woman had fallen silent and seemed half unconscious as her wrists were untied. A few men put their shoulders to the wheels of the cart to try to shift it. The crowd began to disperse.

Rebecca had turned to move with them when she saw the woman, her arms covering her breasts, walk unsteadily a few paces and then fall down. A ring of little boys with ragged trousers and bare feet danced round her: she saw one of them throw a stone and another aim a kick.

The boys, yelling with delight, were unaware of Rebecca's approach. She hit the first one across the head and knocked him down in the mud. Another spat and swore at her while a third began to kick at her shins, until a pair of big hands lifted him by the collar and hurled him bodily away.

'Little whelps, get away wi' you!' The young man waved his fist and the boys scattered. He looked at Rebecca and smiled and then bent to lift the woman who lay moaning on the ground. He heaved her to her feet with a rough gentleness. 'Come you up, mother.'

Rebecca stared at him until he noticed her expression and laughed. 'Oh, it's only a way of speaking, mistress. Doubtless you're not from hereabouts. She's no mother of mine.' He laughed again.

'Her back . . .' Rebecca said. The woman's bare back was raised in red weals, and there was mud and filth smeared where the skin had broken.

'Goose-grease you want for that,' the young man said. He took off his short serge coat and placed it carefully round the woman's shoulders. 'Here, cover yourself with this, old dear, and don't get caught next time.'

The woman accepted the coat without thanks and wiped at the dirt on her face. Her cheeks were pitted with pox. She looked from Rebecca to the young man suspiciously. 'Could do with a drink,' she said.

Rebecca gave her the sixpence from her purse. It was all the money she carried. Mr Walsoken allowed his daughters no more: if they wanted something they must come and ask him.

'That'll keep her in gin all day,' the young man said when the woman had gone limping away. 'She'll soon be set up again.' He looked at Rebecca with frank admiration. 'That was a rare treat to see you lighting at them younkers.'

She smiled, for his grin was infectious. He stood six feet tall, broad across the chest: with the coat gone he was dressed cleanly but not richly, with brown holland breeches and riding-boots, striped waistcoat and neckerchief. His hair was black and shaggy, falling over his brow and tied in a queue behind. 'And thank you for your aid,' she said. 'But now you have lost your coat.'

'Oh, I've sold me ten brace of fowl today. I can buy me a new one,' he said carelessly. 'But you want to have a care here, stepping in and robbing folk of their sport. They're like to turn on you instead.'

There was something very free in his manner which her upbringing, if not her inclination, told her she should resent. 'Poor sport I call it,' she said, drawing herself up with an attempt at haughtiness, so that her eyes were nearly level with his. 'Besides, I do as I please.'

'I'll bet you do, too,' he said, unabashed. 'Where are you from?'

'Norwich,' she said, abandoning the attempt and responding to his winning grin. 'We – my family – moved to Aysthorpe just a few days ago. I'm quite a stranger here.'

'I've been to Norwich once. Handsome place. And now – ' he made a mocking bow – 'you're no longer a stranger, for you've met your first true fenman. Luke Taplin, at your service. And you would be . . . ?' His dark eyes held hers, no longer laughing.

16

'Rebecca Walsoken,' she said. What would her father say if he could see her now? . . . She knew what he would say!

'I'm right glad to meet you – Rebecca,' he said, his voice soft now.

'Rebecca, what have you been doing?' Sarah's fractious voice broke in on them and her hand grasped Rebecca's arm. 'I've looked everywhere for you.' She gave the young man a glance, and then went on: 'Come along. It's time we met pa at the bank. What did you mean by taking off like that? Such a swindling villain as that draper was, I quite lost patience with him . . .'

Rebecca hung back, and said to the young man: 'I must go now. Goodbye . . .'

'I'm in to Stamford every market day,' he said urgently. 'Meet me, won't you? By the theatre. Next market day. Say ye will. Rebecca . . . ?'

'I – but . . . All right,' she stuttered, hardly knowing what she said, and turned and hurried after Sarah.

'Well, what's the matter?' Rebecca said impatiently at her sister's stare, aware that her cheeks were flushing.

'If pa were to know you'd been speaking to men in the street – and men of *that* class . . . !' Sarah was breathless with the enormity of it.

'Oh, that was nothing. Anyway it doesn't signify. Pa was born no better than he. Besides, who's to tell him?' She gave her sister a challenging look, and Sarah was silent.

Joshua Walsoken was waiting for them on the steps of Wiley's Bank, pale and erect and composed in his black suit and short bob-wig.

'You have been long about your shopping,' he said with his measured severity. Across the street there was a cheer as an old dame, soaked in cheap gin, hitched up her skirts and began an impromptu jig to the music of a hurdy-gurdy. Mr Walsoken pursed his lips. 'It would seem this occasion is given over to frivolity and drunkenness rather than industry,' he said. He gave an arm to each of his daughters. 'We shall go.' He led them at a brisk pace down Ironmonger Street, where smoke and smuts drifted from the cellar workshops. 'Is the money all spent, Sarah?'

'There is fourpence over, pa.'

Mr Walsoken took the change and put it with care in his purse. 'Good child. Now – oh, Mr Hardwick, sir!'

A man on the other side of the street who had been about to pass

17

them turned, then removed his hat and, stepping across the flooded gutter, came over to them.

'Your pardon, sir, do you recollect . . . ?' Mr Walsoken said. 'We chanced to meet in Aysthorpe when I was looking over Bromswold, a month or so ago.'

'The old Jarrett house, I remember perfectly. Mr Walsoken, how do you do? So, you have taken the house, I presume?'

'Just moved in. I have been so busy, I have been remiss in making myself known to my neighbours.'

The young man smiled. 'The house will be sadly in need of repair, I am sure. It has stood empty a long time.'

'Permit me to introduce you. These are my daughters: Sarah, Rebecca. This is Mr George Hardwick, children, of Morholm, the great house which you cannot fail to have noticed at the other end of Aysthorpe: principal landowner, and squire of our village.' Mr Walsoken rolled the information off his tongue with relish, as if he were describing himself.

'Dear me, you make me sound very grand.' George Hardwick was a good-looking man in the mid-twenties with a lean and distinguished and, Rebecca thought, rather preoccupied face. 'You have chosen an unfortunate day to come into Stamford, Mr Walsoken,' he went on. 'The town is not always so crowded.'

'Business cannot wait, Mr Hardwick. I have been dealing with Mr Wiley, the banker, to whom I have transferred my account.'

'My errand also. I hope you have left him in a good humour.' George Hardwick frowned up the street. 'I hope a certain public diversion is now over.'

Mr Walsoken lowered his brows and looked puzzled.

'Oh, I heard of a public whipping today,' said the young man. 'A spectacle the justices are kind enough to present frequently for our edification.'

'Yes, I saw it,' Rebecca said. 'An old woman. She was scarce able to stand afterwards.'

Her father gave her a silencing look, and went on with great seriousness: 'Are the local magistrates not conscientious in their duties, then, sir?'

George laughed wryly. 'In truth, I speak out of turn, for I am one myself, for the Soke of Peterborough. But my colleagues on the bench certainly do not lack zeal, that is for sure.' He looked at Mr Walsoken's sober bloodless face and coughed nervously. 'Well, I fear I must leave you, my time is short. I hope you will call on us at Morholm soon – er, that is to say, presently. The fact is my wife is daily expecting a confinement, so – '

'Oh, of course, sir, I quite understand,' said Mr Walsoken. 'Pray accept my good wishes for your wife's health, and if there is any service I can offer . . .'

'You are very kind. I look forward to our all meeting again.' He bowed, and Rebecca noticed again the worried lines in his face.

A keen wind was blowing from the east across the fens as they left Stamford and struck the rough road to Aysthorpe.

'How frequent are the markets in Stamford, father?' Rebecca asked, after Sarah, complaining bitterly of the cold, the damp, the wind and the distance, had talked herself silent.

'The main cattle markets are every three months, and there is a horse fair in February, I hear. But there is a general market in the town every Friday.'

A kestrel hung suspended over the black field below the road, motionless but for the rippling of the wind across its feathers.

'Why do you ask, daughter?'

'Oh . . . no reason, father . . .'

2

Luke Taplin left Stamford and set out for Holme Fen at four o'clock, when the sun was a brass disc a hand's breadth from the horizon. He rode his old, half-blind horse Royce, heading south on the Great North Road and then turning east across rutted boggy tracks. A horseman was unusual in the wet fens, where roads were so poor and few and the waterways more convenient. But in his chosen home Luke was unusual in many ways.

He had lingered about the town all afternoon. Having got a good price for his wild ducks, he had spent freely, as was his custom: drinking and swapping stories with a gang of old fen-tigers in the Eagle and Child, eating a weighty dinner of game pie at the Black Bull, buying a box of powders from the druggist to take back to old Sam, who had the ague. Also he bought an unbound volume of poetry from Sedgmoor and Milton's. And of necessity, he bought a second-hand coat, of good blue broadcloth with pinchbeck buttons. It cost him eight shillings, and was richer than anything he was accustomed to. It was not often he gave much thought to his appearance.

When the low roof of the cottage came in sight the sun was balanced like a ball on the lip of the horizon, its crown hidden in a skein of purple corrugated cloud shot with luminous threads. A heron passed overhead, its wing tips briefly fired, and gave its lonely croak into the emptiness. It was still cold and there were faint crusts of ice along the edges of the swollen dykes: but there was a wind, fluttering the reeds along the banks, and Luke doubted there would be another frost. After the floods of this unpredictable autumn they could do with a spot of kinder weather, he thought. Though they should manage no matter how cruel the winter turned. He had cut and dried enough peat for the fire to last them till spring, and he had been up on the roof mending the thatch with pond-reeds only last week. And there was always a living to be had from this ghostly, watery land, if you knew it as he did. He was whistling as he unsaddled Royce in the outhouse that was both stable and store-room: the turf was stacked here and his fishing-nets and snares hung from the rafters.

Before going into the house he paused to check the hen-coop and to look at the flat land surrendering itself to darkness as the last embers of light receded. The expanse of black earth and water was uninterrupted except for the spiky tops of a few pollard willows by the dykesides. It was a stark, forbidding, and, to Luke, entirely beautiful sight. The wind was rising, and when it came strong from the north-east like this he always fancied he could smell the sea in it, keen and bracing, good to get into your lungs. She had been like that, the strange girl whose face had been before his mind's eye all the time as he rode home: fresh and vital, and unique.

At the same time he felt a vague dissatisfaction, an elusive sort of longing, and turned to go into the house.

There was a fire burning in the long stone-flagged room that was both parlour and kitchen, but no candles, and Sam was not in his high-backed chair by the hearth. Luke took a spill from the fire and lit a candle and mounted the ladder stair.

Sam's form lay huddled in his wooden bed. Luke thought at first he must be asleep, but the old man stirred as the light from the upraised candle brushed across him.

'Luke,' he said faintly.

'It's rare for you to be abed before cockshut, owd 'un,' Luke said.

'Had a hard day, have you?' At the same time he saw Sam's face was pasty, his usually ruddy cheeks drawn and hollow.

'I'm sick, Luke,' Sam said. 'I looked to be pickin' up today, but the chills just wun't leave me.'

'That's only the ague you got. You belong to be used to that, living out here. See, I brought you some physic from town, that'll set you up.'

'Can't seem to stop shivering.'

Luke had not heard that piteous tone in Sam's voice before. He held the candle a little closer and saw the violent trembling, the rag-work cover pulled close around the old man's shoulders. He had never known a father, but he felt for this roguish old fenman the same affection. Trying to keep anxiety out of his voice, he said: 'You did ought to have a doctor see you.'

Sam made a weak movement with his hand. 'There's only Dr Villiers in these parts. And he's only concerned for the rich folk in Peterborough. Besides, I've no faith in doctors wi' their leeches and potions and all their clat.' He made an effort to sit up in the bed. 'What about you, Luke? Did y'sell?'

'Aye.'

'And spent, I'll be bound. But I were the same when I was a younker.'

'Coming twenty-five, Sam, you forget. Not so young.'

'Young enough.' Sam coughed, and kept coughing. When at last he was done he said: 'But you've never a thought for the morrow, Luke, thass your trouble. Living from day to day. Though I've not been a good example to you in that regard.' He smiled wanly.

The illness was making Sam serious. The absence of his usual wry jokes and colourful curses troubled Luke more than anything.

'You'd be better off down by the fire,' he said. It was cold and draughty up here, with the bare plank floor and the sloping thatch above.

Sam shook his head. 'I'd rather be in my own bed,' he said. 'You go down, boy. Have you eaten? I'll sleep and mebbe I'll be better come morning.'

'Can I get anything for you?'

'No.' Sam turned over, pulling the covers in a cocoon about him. 'Hark how the wind's rising! Be sure and fasten the shutters, Luke.'

Luke turned to go down the steps. 'If you're no better tomorrow

21

I shall fetch surgeon. We can pay him in kind if need be. You shout, now, if you want anything.'

He heard Sam shiver again in the bed.

3

It sounded as if they were in for a real fen-blow. The wind made a muted, musical note down the chimney: at intervals it rose to a piercing shriek and the fire glowed red, scattering sparks. Outside it tore round the corner of the house and nearly snatched the shutters from Luke's hands, and he heard Royce in the outhouse whinny and shuffle uneasily.

At last he sat by the hearth and cut himself some cheese and bread, keeping an ear cocked for any sound from Sam.

He would have liked to tell the old man about the girl he had met in Stamford: Sam was past sixty but he still had a lively interest, and an endless store of salacious tales from his own youth. But on second thoughts, even if Sam were well Luke felt he would prefer not to mention it. For what Sam had said about him held true there too. There had been women in Luke's life, but they had been part of an exciting, amusing game, soon over and soon forgotten with few regrets on either side. If he had any regrets, it was that his various involvements had always shared – or perhaps been a symptom of – his restlessness, and latent dissatisfaction.

The girl in Stamford, with her fearless vivid eyes, had in one brief meeting stirred him in a different and profound way.

Luke Taplin had led an active, and in some ways unconventional life. He could match at wrestling any man in the fens, and his quick temper had meant the point had been frequently put to trial: yet sometimes he would go into a deep abstraction for hours, even days, lost in a cheap volume of ballads, or in his own thoughts. Amongst the fenmen he slipped naturally into their way of talking: but everyone, whilst accepting him, knew he was not really one of them. His childhood, as far back as he could remember, had been spent as a boarder at Mr Godman's Classical, Commercial and Mathematical Academy in Stamford. He had been told – at an age when he was hardly able to understand the information – that he was somebody's natural child, and that his education had been paid for, so that he might be raised in habits of industry and discipline, and ultimately make his way in the world.

That was all he had been told, and he rarely hankered to know more. He learned from boyhood to disregard the circumstances of his birth and rely entirely on himself, and liked it. But his lowly position at the school meant he was partly a kind of errand boy for the master and his wife: and some time after his twelfth birthday, the sight of the busy world going on beyond the dreary stained windows of the schoolhouse became too much for him, and he ran away.

An interval of casual jobs at inns and livery stables and farms, and of some hardship and rough handling, had ended with his meeting Sam Toft. Sam was a widower and his only son had been drowned in the Nene a year before. It was meant to be a temporary arrangement: Sam had a fit of the rheumatics to which fen-dwellers were so prone and the young Luke did the heavy work of punting the boat through the sluggish streams and laying the clap-nets for snaring ruff and reeve alive. In return he got his board and keep: but more than that. Though neither of them said it, or needed to, Luke replaced the son Sam had lost, and Sam became the father Luke had never known.

So Luke had stayed. He loved the fens, the true fens where you could see for fifteen miles, where cultivation had failed or never been started and there were only sheep fattening on the damp meadows: where you could get a good living amongst the misty meres and dykes, catching wildfowl and fish and cutting coarse thatch, enough to be self-sufficient and some over to send to market. The solitary and elemental nature of the life suited him, and he was happy. Still, there was a formless kind of anticipation at the back of his mind, a sense that his life must soon take some other turn.

Luke stretched his long legs towards the dwindling fire, pleasantly tired. Fair dowking, Sam would call it. Rebecca – that was her name and that he had called her, though it was little short of impudence and he knew it. Her clothes and her voice and her looks had all marked her as a lady, whereas he . . .

Oh, but she was no prim miss, forever on ceremony and afraid of a pair of breeches. That hint of mischief in her eyes convinced him of that. Besides, he wasn't ashamed of what he was. Well, they had arranged to meet.

He looked forward to market day.

 *TWO*

I

Mary and George Hardwick's first child was born at Morholm on Saturday December 6th 1777. In spite of the efforts of medical science, mother and baby were alive and healthy.

A year and a half ago she had miscarried at four months. Horrible as the experience had been, it seemed if anything to make this pregnancy easier. She was hardly ill at all, and remained busy and active right up to the last minute: and this conduced in her a feeling that everything would be all right when the time came.

George was less sanguine, and privately cursed the isolation of Morholm. There was only Dr Villiers, a good hour's ride away in Peterborough, and as George said, 'Likely to be out pandering to his overbred ladies.'

This problem of a doctor was a solitary sore point between the Hardwicks, who had had nearly two years of extremely happy marriage. Not even the financial straits of Morholm, the family home of the Hardwicks, a great Jacobean manor on the edge of the fen north of Peterborough, had yet overshadowed their content.

Old Grandmother Peach suggested an apothecary at Peakirk, whom she swore had removed the warts from her arm as if by magic: but George had seen him, a squinting man with a toper's purple nose and hands that shook, and politely declined the suggestion.

It would have to be Villiers. The man had a good enough reputation, though some said he was over-ready to resort to the knife when his treatments failed. He had built up a lucrative practice amongst the rich and fashionable of Peterborough and Stamford, and had prospered so well as to move with them socially. It was his boast that he had even been called in to give a second opinion to

24

Lord Burghley at Burghley House. But in the past he had made it pretty clear that he did not think much of the Hardwicks of Morholm, decaying squireens stranded amidst their damp acres with an inflated sense of their importance: and George thought him a pompous fellow and more covetous of his fee than even most doctors.

'If we had a house in town like the Wainwrights things would be simple,' George had said.

'If we had a balance at the bank like the Wainwrights' a lot of things would be simple,' Mary said. 'Don't fret, George. I would just as soon have old Meggy from the village. She has delivered more babies than St John Villiers, for all his talk.'

'Leave you to the tender mercies of an old dame who goes from a laying-out to a laying-in in one morning?' George said. 'No, indeed. You shall have the best, even though it be Villiers and his airs. It's a whim I have, my love.'

Then came the bad weather and the floods of autumn, and they seemed to strengthen Mary's hand. The road from Peterborough to Aysthorpe, poor at the best of times and running through the waterlogged fields, was a quagmire.

'Dr Villiers will hardly wish to stir for a seven-mile ride in these conditions,' Mary said, hopefully.

'Then he shall be fetched,' George said.

To this end, as the time approached, he had the servants on constant alert. At the first sign, Benwick, the groom, was to gallop off to Peterborough on the young mare they had bought last summer. The only other horse they had left in the stable, Monmouth, was now too old for any but the gentlest pace. If by some chance Benwick was unavailable, then Will Binnismoor must go.

It had been a great surprise for George and Mary when three months ago Mrs Reynolds, who had been housekeeper at Morholm for nearly fifteen years, came to them and said she was in a quandary. A man had asked her to marry him. It would break her heart to leave Morholm after so long: but Will was a rare good man and she didn't want to turn him down. (She had not been married before: 'Mrs' was a courtesy title.)

Will Binnismoor had been a strawhop – a flail-thresher – at a farm up-country near Spalding. He was a bald smooth-faced man of forty with a slow way of speaking and a reputation for sagacity. He had one finger missing from his left hand that he claimed had been eaten off by a pig: there was a scar on his behind from the same encounter which he was willing to show if anyone asked, which no one did.

With money tight, and getting tighter, George and Mary had decided Morholm must have an absolute minimum of servants: so the best arrangement seemed to be to establish Will Binnismoor, who was a willing worker, and his new wife, the former Mrs Reynolds, as a couple to keep the house, with wages of thirty pounds a year. Young Benwick slept over the stables and did farm work. A girl from the village came in as a day-maid.

Unless things improved she too might have to go.

The day before George met his new neighbour Mr Walsoken in Stamford, Dr Villiers had made a call.

The physician was at his most pompous: 'I have bled your wife, Mr Hardwick, to draw off the gouty humours that may rise at this time and threaten the infant. There should now be an intermission of fever.'

'She was perfectly well this morning,' George said, 'so I don't see the advantage.'

Dr Villiers frowned and thrust out his lower lip. 'As I have said, Mrs Hardwick is making good progress, and with – experienced medical attention, there will be no difficulty at the parturition. The child will present itself in a week or ten days, not before.'

So the next day, Friday, George went into Stamford, leaving strict instructions with the Binnismoors to be watchful over the mistress; and after a long and unpleasant interview with Thornton Wiley, the banker, raised a mortgage of nine hundred pounds on security of two hundred and fifty acres of land. Part was to go towards long-standing debts: the rest should see them safe until next summer. Beyond that he did not like to contemplate.

Dr Villiers' bleeding yesterday had made Mary feel ill, as was the usual effect: but when George reached home that afternoon she was feeling well again, and was in the stillroom where she had been casking the small beer. Quoshing the impulse to say she should be resting – it always irked her – he told her about his brief meeting with their new neighbours.

'So there are folk in the old Jarrett house again,' she said. She had her back to him and he could not see her face.

'Does it trouble you, love?' he said. 'I know the place has unhappy associations for us.'

She squeezed his hand and smiled. 'No, it's only a house. The people in it are what matter. Come, what are they like?'

'Well, I saw but little of them, though old Wiley told me what he knew. There are three sons, one quite young, the others grown and away. Walsoken was born local, apparently, and went to Norwich and built up a fortune in worsted from nothing. He is prodigious rich, and now he wishes to become a landed gentleman. There are a hundred acres or so, mostly derelict, that go with Bromswold; but he has been buying up more land from smallholders who have had to sell out because of the flooding. If I had known I might have been disposed to sell him some myself.'

'Don't say that, George. We will manage, won't we?'

'Well, we shall not suffer like some of the poor wretches on the fen this winter.' He put his arm round her. 'Yes, we shall be all right – the three of us.'

2

The fen-blow raged throughout that night, rattling like a madman at the leaded casements of Morholm, and in George and Mary's bedroom cold draughts whipped through the heavy curtains. But at dawn the wind had spent itself, and for an hour or two the sky was pale and gentle. Then as if nature were showing off her versatility, a fleet of dark clouds rolled over the horizon, and the rain came again.

It caught George as he was setting out on foot north-east to the Etton farm and by the time he got there water was coursing off his hat and his boots were caked with mud.

He had come to inspect the fields where the tenants of the farm had sown wheat; hoping to find that the wet autumn had not entirely blighted hopes of a good crop. The land here was drained, but Peterborough Great Fen was just to the east, and the Long Ditch to the west was swollen. And years of paring and burning had lowered the level of the soil. His heart sank as the rain increased and the clouds massed together to form a great indigo dome over the land.

The tenants of the farm were a young family, strong, eager and hard-working: and they put a brave face on it when George arrived, telling him how they were clearing the dykes of silt, and there was

27

hope yet. Last spring they had discussed the possibility of digging a new cut across to Car Dyke. At the last George had decided against it. Now staring out from the shelter of a barn across the black liquefying soil he cursed himself for a faint-heart.

Gambling: so much of farming, especially in this country, was gambling. When it came off – when a sea of yellow wheat came under the scythe and the wains groaned beneath the weight of harvest – there were rich returns, high rents, a prosperous country-side. Other times there was disaster, and the harvest might even have to be gathered in by boat. This year had not been that bad – but bad enough. The home farm seldom failed them: it was on the upland, and they grew wheat, beans, oats, turnips: it was their safeguard. Away to the south and east where Borough Fen began the farmlands were unreliable again, susceptible to flood. Matthews, the home steward, had suggested turning over part of the east closes to sheep. Huge flocks could be seen fattening on the fen commons beyond Peterborough. But then in time of flood they were liable to sheep-rot.

Over all the sky brooded and the water crept up and receded across the earth. Gambling.

Five years ago, as a callow young man lounging about London with money to spare, George Hardwick had had a taste for gambling. But then his father had been alive, a symbol of older, more settled times. Now he had lost the taste. Or perhaps the stakes were too high.

The Dutch gables of Morholm, solitary at the north end of the village amongst bare elms, were in sight. George wondered whether to turn towards Helpston Woods and call on John Newman: it was only a quarter of a mile, and it wasn't as if he could get any wetter. Newman, a former tenant, had an extensive knowledge of the land – and, more importantly, an instinct for its humours and peculi-arities – and he was always worth listening to.

The wind, having spent and rested itself, was gusting again, snatching up the rain and letting it go in stinging handfuls. George pulled his hat brim over his eyes and struck the path to Newman's farm.

Grandmother Peach had fallen asleep by the fire in the winter parlour: Mary, listening to the rain pattering on the windows, felt tempted to do the same. To stretch out her slippered feet towards

the fire and be fat and fudgy till dinner time ... She thought of
George ploughing out into the rain, and reproached herself. She
ought to turn out the room adjoining their bedroom: she had been
telling herself she would for weeks. She went upstairs, pausing for
breath on the landing-step as George had insisted.

The connecting room was originally a dressing-room: but in these
frugal days such a thing had seemed inappropriate, and it was cosier
to just use the bedroom, so it had gradually filled with lumber.

The room would be ideal for a nursery. There was a serviceable
Turkey rug and a good fireplace; and the window faced south-east,
so it would be light and cheerful.

Some of this stuff could go in their bedroom: a broken boot-tree
that could be mended, a Chinese fire-screen, out of fashion now but
attractive. She carried them through and then noticed George's
watch where he had left it on the chimney-piece, forgotten as usual.
When he did remember to wear it he forgot to wind it. She touched
it fondly, thinking of the happiness they had had these past two
years. They must hold on to it. They had had their storms, but she
could not imagine life without George. She well knew the restive,
indocile spirit in George, that made him kick against the traces of
fate with its indifference and its cruel absurdities. She knew that he
was being sorely tried now, with Morholm deep in debt, the country
impoverished, the old easeful times gone. But they must hold on to
their happiness, keep it inviolate, sturdy through whatever vicissi-
tudes the future might bring to shake it. That was the important
thing.

Downstairs she heard the bang of the outer kitchen door, away at
the back of the house. The wind was rising and had probably taken
it.

She went back and looked again at the Turkey rug. In fact it was
rather less worn than the one in their bedroom: she could try a
swap. She gave the edge of the rug a gentle tug, and it did not move.

One corner was pinned underneath the trunk. Without thinking
she bent and shoved at it. The trunk shifted a few inches and she
fell on one knee, really surprised at the sudden pain that lanced
through her as if a sword had sprung up through the floorboards
and transfixed her. She rested an arm on the top of the trunk, taking
careful breaths, gathering her strength to get to her feet again.

She found she needed all the breath she had – and more – just to
contain the pain. Not enough to stand. Not enough to shout.

*

'Matty Farren, him as married me sister-in-law's sister, over to Crowland, he woke up one morning and found the watter lapping at his window-sill. Like Noah's flood he said, in one night.' Will Binnismoor laid his armful of kindling down on the kitchen flags and paused for reaction.

'There now,' his wife said.

'Ah. Course, this is nowt compared wi what I'm seen in my time. Hardly enough to get your feet wet, this ent. I mind years ago at Lolham Bridges: a wagon and driver and hosses got swallowed up, the whole boiling, trying to cross the ford in winter flood. Thought he could get across, see. Took a chance. The watters closed uvver his head and he was never heard of more. Like Pharey's armies in the Red Sea.'

'Fancy,' Mrs Binnismoor said.

'Ah. Course, Matty says, he wouldn't live or anywhere else. One time the river bust its banks, the rain come down, and he saw the muck in his garden heaving up and swelling and turning to slub before his eyes, like as the watter were coming up from the bowels of the earth.' Will wiped his forehead. 'Seeping,' he said.

Mrs Binnismoor, with great labour, lifted the big stewing pan on to the fire. 'There now,' she said.

'Ah. Mind, up in Spalding I'm see the river rise in one night so as – '

'Dear life, what was that?'

The crash, and the splash, had come from the outhouses across the yard. Mrs Binnismoor hitched up her skirts and ran across the cobbles, her husband loping after her with the rain drumming on his bald pate.

Inside the cowshed the four calves were kicking up a tremendous fuss. There was a big hole in the roof above them. The roof was nearly flat, and the gutters were blocked: under the accumulated weight of water the slates had given way. The calves were unhurt, but drenched and startled, and when Will opened the stall door one of them burst out and ran with skittish panic into the yard.

'Catch hold of him!' Mrs Binnismoor cried. 'I'll see to these. There, I told you them gutters wanted clearing.'

Will, in his unhurried way, went after the calf. 'I'm only got one pair of hands,' he said. 'Better shift 'em all into the stable for now. This rain's holding.'

'Go and tell mistress, shall I?'

'Nay. She's not to stir. Mr George'll likely be back soon. Ah, damn you, beast, come you here!'

It was the habit of Mr Joshua Walsoken to say a short prayer before beating his children.

On this occasion he omitted the prayer before laying the rod across twelve-year-old Paul's back: for he was really administering the punishment in an outburst of plain bad temper, which was unusual for him, a man of almost frightening composure.

'You must learn, sir, that this ungovernable spirit,' Mr Walsoken said, perspiring a little, 'is Satan himself mastering you. When I beat you I beat the devil.'

There had been no peace at Bromswold all morning. Workmen were still in the house, putting in sash windows on the second floor, and tearing out the old decayed wainscotting in the front parlour. Dust and splinters and flakes of plaster were everywhere. Mr Walsoken had somewhat underestimated the alterations and repairs the house needed. The roof leaked, the kitchen was running with damp, and the back staircase was perilous: Nancy, the maid who had come with them from Norwich, had twisted her ankle on it last night. Mrs Walsoken, still in black for her deceased father whose fortune had helped buy the estate, had taken to her bed with a chill. Sarah had been wailing that half the best crockery had been broken in the move. Paul had been running about trying to help the workmen and getting in their way, until his father's patience had snapped.

Rebecca snatched up a cloak and slipped out by the back door, putting her finger to her lips at Nancy's inquiring look. Even the rain and wind were preferable to the atmosphere in the house today.

She was meant to be helping unpack the plate, which was still in crates in the scullery, and she knew she would be reprimanded for leaving the house without permission: it was clear already that a change of establishment did not mean any change in the austerity of her father's rule over the family. The last time she herself had been beaten was well over a year ago, when she had said she did not want to go to church. Her father said she had a rebellious spirit that must be broken.

It had not been: but she had learnt to keep its manifestations hidden from him. That she should have to live in this way did not strike her as strange, for she had no means of comparison. But she

31

perceived that now that her father was seeking to convert his wealth into standing and launch himself into local society, some things would change inevitably. It was an exciting thought.

The house looked bigger from the outside, especially next to the low thatched cottages of the village, but it was a place without beauty. A hundred years ago it had been a farmhouse: but successive owners had added to it and embellished it until it was a bulky lopsided manor with an illogical collection of slate roofs and chimneys. Compared with the mellow Jacobean stone of Morholm at the other end of Aysthorpe it was a poor thing.

She met few people as she followed the twisting street that was the village: a milkmaid with her twin pails tripping deftly among the puddles, a carter carrying a broken wheel on his shoulder, two old women returning from the common with bundles of sticks held in their aprons. They peered at her uncertainly and gave her vague nods, not sure what her station was: with her cloak whipped about her and her long copper-dark hair streaming there was something unfamiliar, almost gypsy-like about her.

Little to see in the village: low cottages of good Barnack limestone with the characteristic long sloping dormer windows, the Seven Stars Inn, the Rectory. Her father had already called on the Rector, Mr Medhurst, and had not been favourably impressed. ('A mild little creature,' he had said. 'Not, I fear, a vigorous churchman.') Her steps took her to the gates of Morholm, and for a time she gazed across the acre or so of unkempt lawn at the house, her hair heavy and dripping.

She was lonely, but it was a feeling that had always been so bound up in her way of life that she hardly noticed it. Her own wayward thoughts and impulses had often been her refuge from the stifling air of home since her twin brother Peter had gone to study at law. Pale and slow-speaking like her father, with none of her own volatility, there was yet something sympathetic and vital in him that emphasised the bond between the two of them, a bond she felt for no one else. Her mother lived a devoted semi-invalid life in her father's shadow. Sarah had the rigid piety of her father and the temper of a child. The eldest son Jeremiah, Mr Walsoken's favourite, was at Cambridge. Being alone was entirely natural to Rebecca.

So when her thoughts constantly returned to and lingered over

32

market day in Stamford and the young man with the black hair and the impudent expression, she found nothing unusual in having no one to express them to. And in fact she could scarcely have articulated these troubled, turbulent feelings even to herself.

She wondered how young Paul was feeling after his thrashing. It was her father's code that you should not use ointment or anything to heal yourself afterwards, for it showed you did not sincerely repent of your sin. It was, he said, the code in which he had been brought up. Rebecca would wait until he was out of the way and then find some ointment for the boy.

Her father must have noticed her absence by now. A pair of rooks croaked overhead, making for the tall elms that surrounded Morholm. Suddenly, partly prompted by curiosity about the house, she decided to call and enquire after Mrs Hardwick's health.

When no one answered at the front door she hesitated and then went round the building to the back where the stables were. There was no one about in the cobbled yard but a door leading into a big kitchen was standing open. She stepped inside and called out 'Hello?' A pan bubbled over the fire on a chain: two capons ready to be plucked lay on the long oak table.

Somewhere in the house her ears caught the sound of a woman's voice calling out.

'Will! Bridget! Someone, please! Mrs Peach! Please!'

Her cloak was sodden. She threw it off and went down the passage to the big panelled hall. The voice was coming from upstairs.

She grasped the banister and sprinted up.

3

George, returning to Morholm across the fields, arrived at the back and saw at once the damage to the cowshed roof. He found the calves, shivering and upset, in the stable, old Monmouth regarding them with a neutral eye. The young mare was not in her stall. He went into the kitchen.

Mrs Binnismoor's face was flushed. 'Oh, sir, I'm that sorry, but – '

'Oh, that couldn't be helped, Mrs B. At least the beasts came to no hurt.' He took off his coat and shook it at the door. Then he looked at the housekeeper's face again.

'Will's gone to fetch surgeon, sir, for young Benwick's away mending the meadow fence where the sheep broke through. We didn't hear her calling, sir, it was that roof going and them calves – ' George was gone.

Mary was lying on their bed. Her face was shiny with sweat but she gave a painful smile when he burst in. He scarcely noticed the girl sitting in the chair beside the bed.

'Have you fallen? What is it?' He gripped her hand. 'Is it – ?'

'It's all right, George.' Her breath was coming short. 'Dr Villiers must have miscalculated.'

Earthquakes of love and concern moved in him. 'Damn him for an incompetent . . . And him so sure.'

'No, George. I overtaxed myself. It's all right.' She raised herself a little on the bed. 'The servants were outside so they couldn't hear. Luckily Miss Walsoken here arrived. She helped me to bed. She's been very kind.'

George looked at the girl for the first time. 'Forgive me. Miss Rebecca, isn't it?'

Mary patted his hand, and he could tell she wished him gone. He was helpless here. 'Let me have Mrs B up here, and you go now, love. Go and get Miss Walsoken a glass of something to warm her.' Her hand lightly touched his face and his wet hair. 'Please, George.'

Mrs Binnismoor was still tearful with apology when George came down but he said: 'Never mind. All's well. Go to your mistress now. Stay, when did Will set off?'

'Oh, not ten minutes ago, sir. Rode off like the wind, without his hat. He say the rain rolls right off his head.'

George, struggling to control his agitation, seated Rebecca in the winter parlour. He raised an ironical eyebrow at the sight of his grandmother Peach, snoring sturdily by the fire as if nothing had happened, and then fetched the girl a glass of canary.

'This has been an informal beginning between neighbours, Miss Walsoken,' he said. 'We owe you a great debt of gratitude.'

Her father frowned upon anything stronger than small beer for his daughters, but she accepted the drink gratefully. 'It was quite by chance that I came, to ask after Mrs Hardwick's health.'

'We have not always been so ill-organised at Morholm, but our fortunes are not what they were, and we have had to make economies. I fear the work is too much for so few servants.' George walked up and down restlessly. 'This picture of tranquillity, by the way, is my maternal grandmother, who if I could rouse her might make room for you by the fire. You are wet and must be chilled.'

'No, no, don't disturb her.' Rebecca had finished the wine quickly and it had warmed her. 'Is it difficult to get a doctor here, Mr Hardwick?' ·

'One must send in to town,' he said, sitting down and getting up again immediately. He refilled her glass. 'Or make do with some clumsy apothecary. Physicians are reluctant to settle out here. I wonder if Bridget's here yet . . . Will you excuse me?'

While he was gone Rebecca's eyes took in the slightly shabby comfort of the parlour, the old heavy chairs with gilded legs, the walnut bureau, the spinet in the corner, a needlework bag on the settee. She liked it and was a little envious. It was a place that spoke of ease, and affection; so unlike her old home, and, she was afraid, her new.

George was back. 'I've sent the maid to fetch old Meggy from the village,' he said. 'There's no telling when Villiers may get here, and it may be just as well . . . Is there anything I should be doing, do you know, Miss Walsoken?'

Both times when she had met him Rebecca had thought George looked somewhat older than his years: but now as he stood in the middle of the room rubbing helplessly at his hair he seemed very young. 'I have no more experience than you, Mr Hardwick,' she said, 'but I believe one should have water on the boil. That will be a start.'

'Of course, of course. Thank heaven you're here, Miss Walsoken. And I ought to fetch Benwick in too. He'll do no good out in this rain.' He looked at Rebecca with a sort of appeal. 'I imagine you should be getting back to Bromswold soon . . .'

She smiled. 'If I can be of any use, I'll stay.'

So Rebecca stayed, and did what she could to help, whilst George burst from room to room like a jumping-jack. Old Meggy came, a fat capable woman with a pair of spectacles and a pair of strong arms, and said all was well with the maid and all she needed was a tot of brandy and no potions poured down her to upset things. George began to wonder if Mary had not been right after all.

At half-past one Dr Villiers arrived, in no very good humour. When Will Binnismoor had come knocking at his door in Cross Street in Peterborough he had been in private consultation with Sir

Hugh Woodhouse. The baronet had wanted to know why his wife had still not given him an heir: he became loudly unpleasant at the physician's evasive answers. Villiers, if he had dared to be frank, could have told him what the trouble was in a couple of sentences; but Sir Hugh was too powerful for men like himself to offend. Then this fellow had turned up, very insolently insisting that Mrs Hardwick had started when it was sure to be a false alarm, and taking no denial, and he had had a filthy ride and a thorough wetting. He exchanged a brusque greeting with George and setting his face into its most pompous expression mounted the stairs.

Within a short time he was down again.

'Really, Mr Hardwick, I must protest. As a qualified doctor, licentiate of the Royal College of Physicians, I attend my patients on the condition that it is my medical knowledge and mine alone that they seek to engage, and this has always been accepted by my patients, who number amongst them several members of the aristocracy.'

'What's your complaint, man?' George's face was hard and dangerous.

Dr Villiers swallowed and said: 'There is a person in attendance on your wife – not a nurse, that would be quite proper – but a person, who would describe herself as a midwife, as any ignorant harridan may do – and it is quite foreign to my professional standards to co-operate with such a person at a confinement: even to countenance that such a person should – '

'Your professional standards are not at issue,' said George, whitely, 'but your professional competence is. My wife is in labour, the woman was willing and on hand, and it seemed a better notion to send for her than sit cooling my heels while you dance attendance on your powdered fops.'

Dr Villiers swelled. 'Sir, these are not the words I expect when I have – '

'Listen!' Rebecca, who had sat disregarded all through this, jumped to her feet. 'Listen . . . I think I hear . . . a cry . . .'

Dr Villiers coughed and patted down his lace stock, and his face was suddenly serene. 'As I was going to inform you, sir, if you would allow me, I administered an emetic to your wife, which has had the encouraging effect I anticipated. Now, I shall return to my patient, and – '

George pushed him aside and ran up the stairs.

4

The baby was a boy, and they named him Charles Joseph. Grandmother Peach, poking her whiskered face into the cradle, declared disgustedly that he was a true Hardwick. Mary and George were delighted to concur. They decided to postpone the christening, and hold a large party for it at Christmas.

Rebecca stayed long enough on the day of the birth to go up and see mother and baby, at Mary's insistence: but then she had to go home to face her father. Fortunately, the Hardwicks sent a letter round to Bromswold, expressing warm thanks for Miss Walsoken's help; and her father was so far mollified by this good beginning with his high-born neighbours that he forgave her disobedience.

Dr Villiers, very much on his dignity, stayed overnight at Morholm, and the next day pronounced no danger of the childbed fever. George, light-headed with relief, regretted his harshness to the physician and tried to be conciliatory before he left: but it was clear that Dr Villiers was not a man to forget a slight.

By Friday the weather had cleared, and Mr Walsoken himself called to offer his good wishes. Sarah was with him, but not Rebecca. They were still lacking certain essential purchases for the house, and Rebecca had volunteered to ride into Stamford market, with a servant as escort, to buy them.

THREE

I

The London–Stamford coach had been making slow progress since Alconbury. The last few days' rain had left the road ridged and potholed and in places like quicksand so that one or other of the wheels would sink and stick fast, the coach heeling sickeningly to one side and the driver urging the weary horses forward with curses. A parson and his wife had got out at Eaton and now, though there were several passengers on top huddled against the growing cold of evening, there was only old Horace Hardwick and a young man inside.

Horace groaned as the coach slowed to a crawl, stopped, and then with a rattle and a screeching of the swingle bars gave a great lurch forward again. 'This is not a journey for a man of my age to make too frequently, if he wishes to see another summer,' he said, groping at the leather strap by the window-sill, and struggling to sit upright.

'Nor a man of any age,' said his companion. He drew back the velvet curtain and peered out, but the sun had gone down half an hour ago and all that was to be seen was a faint phosphorescent line marking the horizon. 'The roads seem very bad here.'

'Winter floods. They'll be better when we cross the river. The coach road between Wansford and Stamford was improved a few years ago. I think we must be near to Stilton now: we'll get fresh horses there.' Horace drew out a scarlet handkerchief and blew his nose. 'I hope when we do reach home my man has remembered to air the bedrooms. My garden reaches down almost to the river, and the house is liable to damp.'

Horace was the oldest of the Hardwicks, great-uncle to the Morholm family, a prominent citizen of Stamford who had made a large fortune in the mercantile. He was a bachelor of dour and frugal habits, habits reflected in his foxy, fleshless face.

At the Bell Inn at Stilton the passengers stretched their legs and took some refreshment in the coffee-room and when they went out to the yard again there were fresh horses stamping in the traces and eager to be off. On retaking their places inside the coach Horace and his companion were joined by a third, a tall man of twenty-six or -seven with a scholar's stoop and a pale bony face and light hair tied in a queue, a bundle of papers under his arm.

'Mr Hardwick, how do you do,' he said, laying the papers on the seat and extending a hand. 'You are travelling up from London?'

'Mr Milton. Yes, I have been there some weeks. Much changed since my last visit,' Horace said in his spare fashion. The coach gave a jolt and rumbled slowly out of the cobbled inn-yard and then began to pick up speed.

'I heard James had returned to London a while ago.'

'Yes. I have been to help establish him there. He had had thoughts of taking up the law again, but it is not a study that may be lightly interrupted. I have certain acquaintances in the East India Company, and have helped him to a commission there. He sails for Bombay next week.'

'What of his sight? I fear that would be a disadvantage.'

'That has partly been my business also. We went to consult with the best surgeons in the capital, such as they are. As you may know, James had limited vision in the right eye but the left was useless. We visited several puffed-up boobies who talked Latin and did nothing, before quite by chance we met my companion here, Dr Christopher Kesteven. The only physician I have ever met who is not a complete humbug. Kesteven, this is Henry Milton – a relation of sorts – married to my great-niece Julia.'

'I'm glad to meet you, sir,' said Milton. 'You had some success with James, then?'

'Great success,' said Horace. 'And the fellow has gone some way to curing my gout also.'

Dr Kesteven smiled and flushed at this praise. He was a soberly dressed young man in a black frock-coat and white waistcoat: he had a very youthful face and fresh complexion but there were flecks of grey at his temples. 'A mild case, and – easily treated,' he said diffidently.

Horace shook his lean old head. 'Hm. But not so James. I never thought to see such an improvement.'

'It was chiefly a matter of diagnosis,' said Dr Kesteven. 'In fact the aqueous matter of the eyeball was little affected. It was the ulceration of the inner lid that was the chief trouble, and to operate on that, though uncomfortable for the patient, was a far less serious matter . . .' He stopped suddenly, as if struck by shyness.

'The fact is James can see well enough to pass muster now,' said Horace. 'It's a blessing, for he made a poor invalid, and I knew his talents and energy should not be denied. Twice the astuteness of his brother George, but that can't be helped.' The old man stroked his chin with the head of his malacca cane.

'You have been practising in London, Dr Kesteven?' Henry Milton said.

'I have practised nowhere as yet,' said the young man with an innocent frankness. 'I studied at Oxford, and qualified at the University of Leyden in Holland this year. I have been continuing my studies with Dr Lettsom in London – perhaps you have heard of him – he has been working to establish inoculation.'

'Your name is from this part of the country,' Milton said. 'Do you have family here?'

'My parents were from Lincolnshire.'

'I have persuaded Kesteven to come and try his luck here,' put in Horace. 'The country is ill supplied with skilled physicians. He is to stay with me until he can find a lodging somewhere.'

'It will have to be modest,' the young man said. 'My parents are dead, and my inheritance was all but spent on carrying out my studies. I must begin work immediately, in however small a way.'

'You will find ample occupation among the poorer folk,' Milton said. 'I fear you come to a depressed country. There is much hardship in the fen districts. But Mr Hardwick, I had forgot – you perhaps have yet to hear the news from Morholm.'

'Aha!' said Horace, narrowing his pale eyes. 'Don't tell me. The old ruin has an heir, eh? Or is it an heiress?'

'It was a boy. A week ago.'

'Is the brat well?'

'Yes, and Mary too. It was an easy delivery, so I hear. I have been too busy to visit yet, but Julia was going over today.'

Horace nodded pensively. 'A son,' he said. Milton noticed the old man's hands, vague and weak and restless as he toyed with his stick.

'My great-great nephew . . . Morholm, by the way, Kesteven, is the ancestral home of the Hardwicks. Of whom I am but a minor branch. And . . . a somewhat withered one,' he added, with a mordancy Milton did not expect from the incisive old man.

'You are in good health for one of your years, Mr Hardwick,' Dr Kesteven said soberly.

'You think so?' Horace said, jerking his head up with his old keen look. 'Well, it may be. But old, sir, it can't be denied, and you medical fellows are yet to boast of a cure for that. And there is the mind, too, you know: if it does not fail, it begins to dwell, to brood, to – to remember.'

The coach gave a great bone-shaking jolt as the left-side wheels plunged up and over a hump in the road and there were thumps on the roof as the outside passengers struggled to stay on.

'Well, if I can survive this journey . . .' Horace said, settling his wig. 'Milton, you are a good way from home at this late hour. Have you had business in Stilton?'

'Of a sort. Something of a fool's errand. My partner and I are getting up a scheme to launch a new newspaper in this district. A Mr Babbage, at Stilton, was formerly the proprietor of the *Northampton Mercury*. He offered advice and even expressed a tentative interest in joining the project. I have been to visit him, only to find he had backed down, and the only advice he could give was that we should not even attempt the venture.'

'Well, he must have good reason,' Horace said. 'Our friend here is a partner in a printing and bookselling business in Stamford,' he added to Dr Kesteven. 'Does it not show sufficient profit, Milton, is that why you seek to expand?'

'It will not make us rich,' Milton said, 'though it is secure. Broadsheets, pamphlets, religious tracts and so on are always in demand, and we have had some success in publishing famous works in a cheap serial form – *The Whole Duty of Man*, for instance.'

'But, Milton, this newspaper,' Horace said. 'Is there a demand for it? The *Stamford Mercury* has been established for sixty years. You will be hard put to compete with it.'

'We believe there is room. Peterborough, after all, has no newspaper. We think to call it the *Stamford and Peterborough Courant*. The chief aim is to ensure a wide distribution. After all, carriers bring the *Northampton Mercury* as much as fifty miles from its place of printing. The only problem for myself will be the extra work. I am from home too much already.'

'Well, wait till you have a squalling infant in the house, like Morholm, and then you will be glad to be out of it,' Horace said with sour humour.

The muscles of Milton's jaw tightened a little and he looked away. 'I shall certainly be glad to see my home tonight,' he said. 'I have two miles to walk from Alwalton. I would have made this whole journey on horseback, but my horse has gone lame. The farrier in the village fears I may get no more service from him.'

'Have a care, Milton,' Horace said. 'I have heard the woods about Longthorpe are a favourite haunt of footpads.'

'Oh, I doubt my proofs would be much of a prize.' He looked out of the window. 'The moon is nearly full. I shall keep to the field-paths.'

2

Henry Milton left the coach at Alwalton and tramped across frosted country to Longthorpe, a village on the western edge of Peter-borough. He and Julia had rented a house here just over a year ago. Earl Fitzwilliam of Norborough, Viscount Milton, was their land-lord, as he was of the whole village and much of the city. Milton House lay hidden amongst its parkland not far to the north, but Henry had never seen his illustrious namesake.

They were close to the river here, and a cold mist was curling up from the damp meadows at Gunwade Ferry. He was thoroughly chilled when he reached home, and was glad to see the light burning in the front parlour window. The place had formerly been a farmhouse, and was full of inconveniences; but his spirits were always lifted on returning to it, not least because so much of his time now was spent at work.

Julia made him take off his boots and sit by the fire, for he was shivering, and mixed him a brandy and hot water. 'You will take cold if you're not careful,' she said. 'Mrs Dawes was telling me there is much fever abroad on the fen. Have you supped?'

'Yes, Babbage gave me a meal, if nothing else.'

Julia bent and lit another candle at the fire, and as she straight-ened it threw a crescent of light over her strong serious face. 'He was no help then?'

'He was full of words, none of them encouraging. I doubt he ever meant his offer seriously. Well, a third partner with experience would have been an advantage, but we shall manage. Francis is very confident.' He passed a hand wearily across his face: only now that he was warm and comfortable did he realise how tired he was. 'I met Uncle Horace in the coach, returning from London. He seemed rather strange. I wonder if he may be turning senile, from some of the things he was saying.'

'What things?' Julia came and sat with him on the oak settle.

'Oh, morbid things, about regrets and memories and how he can't rest. I can't imagine what he may have to regret, unless it be a life spent getting money and never enjoying it.' He clasped her hand and she leaned against him. The candle on the table guttered, displacing the shadows in the room, picking out a glint of polished wood here, pewter there. He breathed in and savoured the companionship that was the signal grace of their life together. 'So tell me. The newest Hardwick. Our nephew. Does he resemble George, or Mary?'

'Well, he resembles nothing so much as a small greedy animal in night-clothes, that lives for food and sleep. George says that in that at least he is a thorough Hardwick. No, seriously, he has George's eyes. Very little hair at present. Oh, Henry, you should see how happy George and Mary are now. They still have all sorts of difficulties to face with the estate – but somehow the child has made all the difference.'

There was a moment's silence. A tassel of smoke lifted from the guttering candle.

'As it would to us?' he said quietly.

Julia did not answer, but played with his long fingers restlessly. She sighed. 'This newspaper project . . . it means you will be more from home, doesn't it?'

'Francis deals with the business side of things,' he said. 'There's plenty of work that I can do as well here. But, yes, I'm afraid it does.'

Mrs Dawes, who kept the house, put her head round the door. 'Will you be wanting me any more, ma'am?'

'No, Mrs Dawes, you go to bed,' said Julia. She got up and stirred the fire, and stayed crouching there, her heavy black hair drooping.

'Henry, do you know what I did yesterday?' she said, staring into the flames. 'I helped Mrs Dawes dip rushes. I fed the hens. I sewed

43

a little. I went for a walk as far as the Park. On the way back I met Gaffer Brough from the village who told me about his rheumatics and said the weather was turning and wished me good day. I came home and baked a rabbit pie. Then I sat by the fire and waited up for you.' She pushed back her hair impatiently. 'That was my day.'

He looked at her unhappily. He knew Julia's occasional restlessness, her acute critical mind: and knew that she was never one to carp or be petty, to pick at grievances. But in his tired, preoccupied state he thought he detected a hint of accusation directed at himself, and said: 'Well, I can tell you what I did yesterday too, if you like: I worked in the printing-office till noon, I checked two hundred pages of proofs, I visited the paper merchants at Wansford, I went back to the office – '

She put her hands on his knees, shaking her head. 'No. I don't mean it that way. That's part of it too. That we . . . that there is so little that binds us together.' With a sudden passionate movement that was typical of her she reached up and held his face and kissed him.

'There is our love,' he said, looking into her grey eyes.

She kissed him again, and then rested her cheek against his knee. He stroked the tresses of thick hair and there was silence except for the crackle of the fire.

'I wish,' Julia said, her voice muffled, 'I almost wish I had not been to see them and – and the baby today.'

'They would have been hurt if you had not,' he said gently. She did not raise her head. 'Julia, my love, it isn't so very rare for couples . . . My mother didn't have her first child till she was near thirty, and you are but two-and-twenty. It is – '

'How long had your parents been married then?'

He sighed. 'A year.'

'And we have gone two years.'

'I know it,' he said. 'It pains me too, Julia.'

She pressed his hand and said: 'Grandmother Peach kept asking me today when I was going to follow Mary's lead.'

'She's an ill-natured old woman.'

'She said I was to put tansy and motherwort and clove under my pillow and that would do the trick.'

'I don't see how. With the smell of all that I should be reluctant to come near you.'

They laughed, but with unease, and on her side certainly the laughter was dangerously near tears.

'In the coach this evening,' he said with an effort, 'there was a young man with Horace – a doctor, coming here to settle. He seemed keen, intelligent: I wonder if perhaps – '

'Oh, doctors.' She made an impatient gesture. 'No doubt he would say the same as Villiers – that we are perfectly all right and must simply be patient.'

'Well, so we must.'

'But it's *easier* for you, Henry. You have so many other concerns to occupy your mind. Here – alone – I can do nothing but think and brood . . .'

He looked at her in the fitful light, her full lips and dark introspective eyes, gleaming a little wet. He was oppressed with a sense of his own powerlessness, and a renewed appreciation of the elusive depths in the woman he loved: the impenetrable mystery of this other person, with whom he shared his life, whom he knew – and who knew him – better than anyone living.

Theirs had been rather a whirlwind, unexpected marriage. Julia Hardwick, George's younger sister, had had an unhappy life: at Morholm as a girl she had been withdrawn and plain and sullen, and when she was nineteen, after a disastrous affair, she had briefly drifted into a miserable life of prostitution in London. Henry Milton, George's friend, had just got over an unhappy affair of his own, and was working in Grub Street. He and Julia had suddenly come together with a vivid passion that has surprised them both. Plenty of folk had said the marriage would never work. But it had . . . so far.

He said: 'Perhaps your impatience is with me also.'

It was a weak thing to say and immediately he disliked himself for saying it. But she simply shook her head and said: 'No, I think it is you who will have to be patient with me.'

3

It was over an hour after Milton had left the London coach that it finally rumbled into the inn-yard of The George at Stamford. Ostlers ran out with lanterns, and yellow lights appeared in the latticed windows. The outside passengers, swathed to the ears in cloaks and scarves, climbed stiffly down, more dead than alive. Frost sparkled on the cobbles and the breath of the snorting horses was like thick mist in the cold air.

Horace Hardwick leaned heavily on his stick as he led Dr Kesteven over the river bridge and down St Mary's Street to St George's Square. It was after ten o'clock and there were few people about: though when they passed the Black Bull the windows were all lit and there were lively noises from within. The square tower of St George's Church bulked razor-edged in the blue moonlight.

They had been travelling since dawn, and Christopher Kesteven, who was twenty-two and had led an active life, was dead tired: and he was concerned for Horace, past seventy and becoming frail. But once inside the gloomy townhouse the old man seemed to rally fresh energy, rounding on his servants and setting them hither and thither lighting fires and bringing candles. Kesteven was more than ready to go straight to bed, but Horace pressed him to a chair in the parlour facing the square and busied himself at the fire.

'You may be the doctor, but I have my own prescription for taking off the chills, and that is an egg-nog,' Horace said, presenting the young man with a steaming glass. 'You may go to bed presently, but for a while you must humour the whims of an old man who finds sleep comes less and less easy.' He sank into a Windsor chair, wrapping the tails of his old snuff-brown coat around him.

Dr Kesteven took in the spare furnishings of the room, the dark wood panelling everywhere, a heavy clock ticking, a single portrait on the wall. There was a fusty closed-up smell about the house and an atmosphere of both frugality and wealth.

'It is quite natural for a man to need less sleep as he gets older, sir,' he said.

Horace seemed to take no notice of this, and stared into his glass. 'I must see Wainwright tomorrow,' he said. 'He was telling me about a property of his in Peterborough for which he is seeking a tenant. It was attached to a river warehouse, but he has closed the warehouse now. It is little more than a cottage, mind you, but I think I could persuade him to let you have it for the repairing, for a time at least.'

'You are very good, Mr Hardwick,' Kesteven said. 'I – hope I can justify your faith in me.'

'Well, I have had little faith in your profession in the past, young man: but what you did for my great-nephew James impressed me, and I shall be glad to see that pompous Villiers and his like suffering a little competition. They were unable to help James. I have a certain bond with James, almost alone among my family. I shall miss him . . .'

Horace's face was drawn and pensive. Kesteven felt uncomfortable. He was almost painfully sensible of his obligations to the old man, but he did not know what to make of the fits of brooding into which he kept falling. He was glad when Horace stirred and said in an altered voice: 'So! With luck we shall find you accommodation. You know Peterborough?'

'I have been there as a small child, as I have to Stamford: but all my memories are vague.'

'Both are fine towns. Stamford has the more elegance and fashion, if you want it,' Horace said. 'It is hampered insofar as the Earl of Exeter – we passed Burghley House as we came in, you recall – seems to consider the whole place his private property. The borough corporation, of which I was formerly a member, can do little to oppose him. His placemen are everywhere in office, the lawyers are his agents, his nominees sit for the borough in Parliament. Edward Wainwright, of whom I spoke – perhaps the richest man in the town – is trying to break the stranglehold. However, there is power and prestige in Peterborough too: you will be well situated. Of course it is the country that predominates here: the wealth lies in the land. You had better invest in a horse, for the farmers will be the bulk of your patients.' Horace stretched his long thin legs. 'Ah, how I wish I was your age, just starting out in the world again. I was in a similar position to you, then, you know: well, perhaps not quite, for my father was Sir Robert Hardwick of Morholm, whose portrait you see there, and at that time it was a great family and a great house. But I was the youngest of three sons, and had to make my own way. I was apprenticed at a firm of wool merchants when I was fifteen, and I was a merchant in my own right before I was thirty. That was the path I chose, and I have made a success of it. I have had little time for anything else. Folk have no doubt thought me a dry grasping sort of fellow, but it is a regrettable part of human nature that a – a harsh judgement is the inevitable consequence of an ignorance of the true facts of the case.'

There was pride in Horace's voice, but Dr Kesteven also detected a plaintive note of self-justification that he could not account for.

'Do I talk like a cynic, Kesteven?' Horace said. 'Well, perhaps I have been. But then perhaps I have reason . . . Who can say? You can't. There is no one who can, unless – well . . .' He laughed softly, almost inaudibly, shaking his head and gripping his glass in a covetous fashion.

In London, when Kesteven had been called in by Horace to examine his great-nephew's eyes, his impression had been of a great alertness and vigour about the old man despite his years: now he thought of the aged people he had seen in the private asylums during his studies, put away because a rambling turn of mind had suddenly affected them, restrained in chains and straps and mumbling their grievances and regrets. But Mr Hardwick did not seem –

'D'you believe our actions are irrevocable, Kesteven?' Horace said suddenly, throwing him a sharp glance. 'Don't worry, I am not casting you into some theological debate, I am no canting Methody. I am speaking practically. If there is – some radical change to make, some wrong to right, should one do it no matter how long it has been postponed, no matter how short a time in this world one has left to repair it – or should one leave well alone and be thankful to have lived this long and be damned to the rest? Come, you are a physician, you have seen life at its end and at its beginning. None of your equivocations.'

'Mr Hardwick, I confess that I do not understand you, and – '

'And you want to go to bed. So you shall. I realise it would be presuming on so slight an acquaintance to burden you with confidences. Even supposing I should want to.'

Kesteven hesitated. 'If . . . if there is anything, any advice I might be able to offer, I am quite ready to – '

Horace gave a short, sceptical laugh. 'Advice. How old are you, Kesteven, two and twenty? D'you know anything of women, for instance?'

Dr Kesteven coloured. 'I cannot say I do.'

Horace waved his hand, still smiling sourly. 'You meant kindly, I know. I intend no disparagement. Anyhow, I must rely on my own self in this matter, as I have always done. Go on to bed now. Pull the bell. Forrest will show to your room.' The old man sighed, settling himself deeper in his chair and shading his eyes. 'I rather think I shall get little sleep again tonight . . .'

4

The next morning Kesteven found himself breakfasting alone: his host was already closeted in the office at the back of the house.

'I must leave you to your own devices today, young sir,' Horace said, 'for I have much to do. Take a turn about the town. But have a care about your purse: Friday is market day, and there are always rogues about who are glad to relieve you of it.'

The livestock market was busier than ever, for it was a fortnight before Christmas. Kesteven's eager professional eye noted many well-fed laughing faces, but also he saw many haggard and drawn, and scarred by smallpox; and children with the stick-like limbs and pot-bellies of malnutrition. The situation, he thought, was not unhealthy; the town was built on limestone, which gave it an advantage over the moist country to the east and north, where there would be poisonous miasma, and probably malarial fevers such as he had seen when studying in Holland.

In High Street he noticed the sign *Sedgmoor and Milton*, remembering the man in the coach last night. A little further on at the corner of Ironmonger Street he saw an apothecary's sign pointing across a yard. The old man in the little one-storeyed workshop was at first sycophantic when he thought Kesteven was a customer, and then guardedly hostile when he said he was a physician and merely here out of professional interest. But the young man's sobriety and bearing obviously convinced him, and then he began fishing, saying how he supplied drugs and did locum-duty for the best physicians in the county, and the young gentlemen could do no better, if so be as he was to practise here, might that be the case . . . ?

Kesteven looked at the bleeding-bowls, the feeding-cups, the ill-smelling brew bubbling over an open fire, and the drugs stored in Delft jars. They looked clear enough, but one often found they had been adulterated, and a bad druggist could mean half your work wasted. He knew doctors who had had patients die on them because their prescriptions had been mixed with chalk or alum.

He was sniffing a jar labelled 'Balsamic Cordial', and deciding that it was simply peppermint water, when the door burst open. At first he did not heed the conversation going on behind him.

'I've a shop to mind,' the old man was repeating. 'You keep giving him them powders I prescribed, that's all. They need time to act, see. Besides, I can't ride out there, it was enough for me last time. I got a shop to mind. Now if you was to bring him into town – '

'But he's mortal sick, I tell you!' A young man's voice, very agitated. 'I've been to surgeon Marcus' house in St John's. He's from home. I'll pay you. God's life, I'm afeared he's going to die!'

Kesteven straightened. 'Can I help? I'm a physician.'

The young man was tall, well-built, roughly dressed. He looked startled, then radiantly hopeful. 'Oh, sir, if you but could – it's Sam, he's old, he's got the ague – he's had it before many a time, but he took it bad and now he's got so he hardly knows me, and – '

'I am a stranger here. Where does he live?'

'Where I do, sir, it's on Holme Fen. A tidy way – fifteen mile – but he's that bad – '

'I would be glad to come, but I have no horse, no means of . . .'

The young man, distraught but plainly also near fury, turned to the apothecary. 'You've got that old nag out back. If you won't come, you can at least lend her to this gentleman.'

'Now, wait a minute, Taplin, I can't go lending my Bess to all and sundry.' The apothecary glanced at Kesteven. 'Leastways, not to anybody, without – '

'But you know this man, obviously, know his place of abode,' Kesteven said. He had taken something of a dislike to the shifty little druggist, and the young man was clearly sincere. 'It cannot be so much of a risk.'

'Mebbe I do know him. And mebbe I know he's more'n a bit wild. And begging your pardon, sir, I don't know you, though I shall be glad – '

'I see,' said Kesteven. 'Well, it looks as if when I begin my practice I had better look elsewhere for a druggist.'

The apothecary perspired and looked from one young man to the other. 'Now, sirs, no call for high words. Perhaps we can come to some arrangement.'

Ten minutes later Luke Taplin and Dr Kesteven rode out of the town at a canter. As they turned on to the Barnack Road Kesteven noticed his companion glancing back. 'Is something wrong?' he said.

'I was meant to be meeting someone,' Luke said. 'Can't be helped, but – '

'Could you not have left a message?'

Luke shook his head.

It had not been easy for Rebecca to get permission to go to Stamford this Friday. She had seen suspicion in her father's glance at this sudden helpfulness in his wayward daughter. The articles she proposed to buy, he said, could just as easily be ordered. And it was not convenient for her to go: she should be helping Sarah with the sewing for the door curtain: Ford the manservant would have to accompany her, and he could ill spare him: besides, he did not think it a good thing that a girl of her age and position should be so frequently exposed to the vanities and vulgarities he had seen there ... It was her mother who had settled it, complaining that all her combs had been lost or broken in the move, and she must have new ones immediately. Grudgingly her father allowed her to go, with strict injunctions to be home well before dusk.

Her heart was beating fast as she rode past the walls of Burghley Park. There was the problem of getting rid of Ford who, silent and morose, seemed to be sticking close to her.

Even supposing the young man turned up ... In intervals of excitement she was feeling nervous and defensive, and indignant – as if he had somehow trapped her into coming today. Their meeting at all was improper to the point of madness. He should never even have suggested it. So went an intermittent voice in her head – a voice speaking in the accents of her father.

But why then was she descending St Mary's Hill today with this wonderful lifting sensation at her heart?

Often in Rebecca's young life her own motives had been obscure to her: yet never more so than now, when all the dictates of propriety, duty, upbringing (not that these had struck so very deeply on her independent spirit) and simple reason pointed to one plain course of action. All through the week she had revolved the scene of her meeting with Luke Taplin over and over in her mind: one minute scarcely able to wait for Friday to come, the next bitterly repenting her promise and on the verge of pouring the whole thing out to her father and putting an end to it. Yesterday she had fully determined that she would break her promise, stay at home at all costs, not go within a mile of Stamford: and here she was, dismounting in the yard of the Black Bull, tipping Ford a sixpence and telling him to have some beer and meet her here in an hour's time, adjusting her hat and the double-breasted riding-habit of blue velvet – her father's parsimony did not extend to his children's clothes, for they reflected his own status – and her mind still an arena where warring impulses clashed.

The watch at her waistband said twenty to twelve. The visit to the haberdasher's to buy her mother's combs took ten minutes. She paced up and down in front of the theatre. Debilitated sunshine filtered from a cold sky, lightening St George's Square ahead. People hurried by, with baskets, with parcels and packs, muffled against the damp chill in cloaks and scarves and muffs. A butcher's boy with a pole of hares on his shoulder. Horses clattering on the cobbles, riders in greatcoats and boots. A man selling pies from a tray round his neck. A woman driving a dozen geese.

Rebecca rubbed her thinly-gloved hands to warm them and thought of the pair of earnest brown eyes that sparkled into laughter, the musical confident voice, the shaggy hair, the long-legged rangy grace, like a half-tamed cat.

Well, at least she knew virtually no one here and stood little chance of being recognised. She experienced a frisson of pleasure at doing something secret and clandestine: suddenly felt free and complete, felt she had made the right decision. She scanned the market-day crowds for a mop of black hair.

A wagon rumbled by loaded with barrels of water containing live fish, pike and tench and eels, bound for London markets. A messenger hurried with fresh sheets of the *Stamford Mercury* strung on a cord. Twice a beggar, blind from syphilis, stretched out a hand in her direction, but she had no money left to give him.

A sharp wind was blowing from the east, tugging her hair. Bells began ringing in St Mary's Church.

It would be a long and fruitless wait.

5

It was Horace Hardwick's custom, in defiance of the modern fashion for late dinners, to dine prompt at three.

He postponed the laying of the mutton chops until four, and sent a servant into the town to look for Dr Kesteven: but when there was still no sign of his young guest at half-past four, he gave in to his hunger pangs, and sat down alone.

Kesteven arrived at five, cold and tired, his hair wild from the wind.

'So there you are!' said Horace, who was still at the table with his port. 'Forrest, bring Dr Kesteven his dinner. I was beginning to think you had been set upon in some alley and left for dead.'

'I'm very sorry,' the young man said. 'I did not expect to be away so long. I found myself making my first professional call.'

'Indeed? Well, that is a good beginning. You may soon make your fortune at this rate.'

Dr Kesteven smiled slightly. 'Oh, I took no fee.'

Horace raised an eyebrow.

'It was all quite by chance.' The servant brought in a covered dish and Kesteven sat. 'A young man was seeking a physician for the man with whom he lodges. A very remote place, right out on the fen. I borrowed a horse from Salter the apothecary. Those foggy distances seem endless.' He shivered. 'The man was far gone with a malarial fever and had taken the pneumonia. He had been wandering in his mind all night, the joints stiff, the throat parched. He was beyond the power of any doctor . . . he died while I was there.' He looked up at Horace. 'I'm sorry, this is not a subject for the dinner table.'

'I'll agree it gives no great relish to the meat,' said Horace dryly. 'But no fee, Kesteven? You attended the patient. Every sawbones that I know charges whether his patient recovers or not. Makes out it's your own fault if you die on him.'

'Well, this was little more than a cottage, you understand. The young man could probably not have afforded much, though he offered to pay. Name of Luke Taplin, an unusual sort of man to find out there, I would think: obviously with some education, and articulate: though they tell me fenmen are a breed apart from the rest of England. The old man was no blood relation of his, but he was very much distressed. There must be a great prevalence of ague in those districts. An unhealthy clime.'

Horace mechanically refilled his glass, but did not drink. His face was stony.

'I assure you, Mr Hardwick,' Kesteven said a little uncomfortably, 'I shall have no qualms about taking my fee, I am not such an idealist as that. But in this case it seemed – '

Horace waved his hand. 'Yes, yes,' he said shortly. 'Forrest, bring Dr Kesteven some wine, man, don't stand there dreaming.' He took a sip of his port and rubbed his forehead. 'I – by the way, I saw Wainwright today. He called earlier.' He stopped.

Kesteven waited. 'Is there some difficulty with the house? Pray, Mr Hardwick, don't trouble, for I can quite well seek for something on my own account.'

'Eh?' Horace looked at him vaguely. 'Oh, no, no, the place is yours, it is all fixed. Wainwright was quite agreeable.' He picked up his glass and set it down again untasted.

'Sir, I am extremely grateful. You have been – '

'Kesteven.' There was a quaver in Horace's voice. 'Do you – This fen-cottage you went to today – can you remember exactly where it is?'

FOUR

I

Mr Edward Wainwright was no enthusiast of architecture, but he was always grudgingly impressed when his son-in-law's mansion came into view at the end of the long drive between dripping lime-trees. Built in severe white Palladian style, Deenecote Hall, the residence of Sir Hugh and Lady Woodhouse, formerly Elizabeth Wainwright, had a formal grandeur that the rambling homesteads that passed for great houses to the east lacked. His daughter had certainly done well for herself, in that respect.

Whether in other respects was a moot point, and one on which Mr Wainwright wanted to satisfy himself.

The coachman and the postilion who got down to open the carriage door were in livery, and the horses in the traces were fine greys: but Mr Wainwright, stepping nimbly out, cut no figure to match this finery. Past fifty, small, spectacled, in a plain bottle-green coat and a dusty wig, he looked more like a moderately respectable tradesman who had been given a lift by an indulgent patron than one of the richest men within fifty miles.

A footman showed him into a large room as chilly as a vault and went in search of Sir Hugh. Mr Wainwright walked round studying the richly damasked walls divided by painted pilasters, the marble chimney-piece, a satinwood Pembroke table, a bureau and chairs in the Adam style. Several pieces he had not seen before: the new ormolu clock alone must have cost a pretty penny. It had ticked away fifteen minutes before he heard his son-in-law's booming voice down the hall, and the door was flung open.

'Damn the man, he's put you in here, has he? And not even a fire. I'll have it lit directly. I've just this moment got in. Phoo, it was a poor morning's hunt. We drew a fox at long last at Woodnewton, but we lost him before Willow Brook. Van Druyten took a tumble and complained his back was broke. Cock's life, the fellow's a lily. Then my Zenith cast a shoe. Ah, well, it was lively country. You ought to hunt, father-in-law, it would put new blood into you.'

Sir Hugh Woodhouse, a large heavy porcine man of thirty, threw down his gloves and crop and sprawled on the sofa in red coat and muddy breeches and boots.

'Is Lizzie not here?' Mr Wainwright said, taking a seat at last.

'Oh, she's took to her bed with the megrims again. This place don't suit her in the winter, she says, but I say it would be a shame to miss all the hunting. Come New Year we'll go up to London, that always cheers her. I suppose you are going out to your country place for Christmas?'

'For myself I would better prefer to be in town where I can keep an eye on things.'

'Keep your interests warm, eh?' Sir Hugh said, mixing his drink. 'You've subordinates to sit on 'em, surely?'

'I like to keep a tight rein on my business, however far it extends.' Mr Wainwright took a tiny sip. 'Indeed it is partly about such a matter that I have called.' He took off his spectacles and began to polish them on a handkerchief, carefully not looking at his son-in-law.

'Business? Oh, debt-collecting. Well, you may search all my pockets and take what you will, but it won't come to anything near a thousand.'

Mr Wainwright allowed himself a small smile. 'I am not here to repossess your furniture.' With an economy of movement that typified him his eyes slid to the Pembroke table. 'Though I believe I am right in saying that piece is new, is it not?'

Sir Hugh looked at him dumbly, caught in mid-belch. 'What of it?'

'I – understood the loan was advanced to ease a temporary financial distress. On such a condition I was more than happy to make it. I can hardly believe the distress was of the sort that arises from an inability to lay out money on expensive new furniture.'

Sir Hugh shook his shoulders. 'Damn it, you have my word that the debt will be repaid in January, what more do you want?' He glanced round, and turned to the fireplace again. 'Unless, that is, the word of a gentleman born is insufficient for you, and you crave a pound of flesh.'

Mr Wainwright looked without pleasure at his son-in-law's broad back. 'As I said, Hugh, I am a man of business. My reason for inquiring is simply that I am taking stock of my assets at present.'

Sir Hugh stared at him. 'You don't mean to say *you're* in trouble?'

'Not at all. But there is change in the air. This war in America. You've heard the news of Burgoyne's defeat at Saratoga, I take it?'

'Oh, that. Only a setback. England's strength is not half tried yet.'

'That's as may be. But I see no early end to it, whilst the King is given his head and North goes unopposed. There are many among the mercantile who are worried for the effect a continuance will have. Whatever happens, I wish to secure my interests.' He looked narrowly at Sir Hugh. 'I am the more isolated in that I have no son to aid me.'

Sir Hugh shrugged, his dull eyes lidded. 'Pooh, I don't believe you'll be in any danger, dear father-in-law. Not while you have the brewery and maltings. There'll never be a drop in demand for beer. God knows our servants consume enough of it.'

'That is simply a foundation. Besides, there are these taxes North is levying. A tax on manservants now. More to come, I'll wager. So it is a time for taking stock. I have your assurance, and that is all I required.' Mr Wainwright got up and went to the window. In summer this would be a fine view across the park sloping south to the river Nene: but now the great trees were bare but for huddled clumps of rooks, and the scene had a melancholy tinge. 'In fact, I have thoughts of extending my interests in another direction. You know, of course, that I have a controlling share in Wiley's Bank.'

'You're going to buy him out?'

Mr Wainwright shook his head. 'I doubt he would come to any such accommodation. He is a good enough man, but not adventurous. No, I plan to start up banking on my own account. It is a prospect, you understand. I have told no one else of it.'

Sir Hugh sniffed. 'I'm honoured by your confidence. I suppose then you could start charging me interest, eh? Well, one would fancy that at your age you would want to rest up a little rather than expand.'

'I am fifty-three,' Mr Wainwright said matter-of-factly. 'There will be all the more need for secure credit facilities in these times. I think it will do well.' He turned from the window. 'As I say, I have only daughters to inherit, no sons. It is up to me to put my affairs in order.' He left a second's pause. 'Of course, I did not consider myself unreasonable in supposing that my son-in-law might come to play some active role in the business.'

Sir Hugh had just taken a pinch of snuff, and a stillborn sneeze enhanced the expression of surprise on his face. 'I don't recall that clause in the marriage contract,' he said. He sneezed at last. 'A tradesman is a tradesman, and 'twould stick in my craw to become one. You had better find a husband for your Wilhelmina, someone more amenable to the counting-house. I suppose mother-in-law is past producing the necessary son, eh?' He gave a short rumble of laughter. 'Nay, no offence meant. You'll stay to dinner?'

Mr Wainwright inclined his head. 'Thank you. I – presume that means the end of the subject.'

Sir Hugh pulled the bell and it sounded somewhere down the cold corridors of the house. 'Eh? Oh, well, no doubt you'll try again. I'll go and change now, and see if Lizzie intends coming down.' At the door he stopped. 'Never mind, father-in-law. You may not have an heir, but at least you have daughters.'

'I don't follow you.'

'Come, don't tell me you haven't wondered when you're to be presented with a grandchild.'

Mr Wainwright hesitated. It was a point he had not been able to bring himself to raising: perhaps because it seemed to carry a brood of even more delicate questions with it. 'You are both young,' he said finally. 'There is plenty of time.'

Sir Hugh grunted. 'Not *so* young. We'll have been married three year next April, you know. Damn me, I swear people are beginning to talk.'

Mr Wainwright hesitated again. It was on his lips to mention just what talk he had heard about Sir Hugh; but he knew his son-in-law's temper. And there was Elizabeth to consider. 'Nonsense,' he said.

2

Elizabeth, Sir Hugh announced, was rather better and would be coming down soon: she said they were to begin dinner without her. The winter afternoon had gone quickly dark and there were many candles burning in the huge dining-room where four footmen hovered in and out of the shadows. The glittering polished silver cast a bloom on the high moulded ceiling.

For the first course there was carp and trout, calf's heart and a couple of ducks boiled with green peas. Mr Wainwright, who was a martyr to dyspepsia, ate sparingly.

Sir Hugh motioned impatiently for more wine. 'How long will you stay out of town?'

'I must be back in Stamford the second week of January,' Mr Wainwright said. 'A meeting of the corporation.'

'Burghley-baiting again, no doubt. The Earl is a fine man. What do they suppose the town would do without him?'

'That is not at issue,' said Mr Wainwright. 'Certain abuses of privilege are. The right to grind corn in mills other than his, for example. Oh, we don't seek to set ourselves up in opposition to him. But when the borough's Members of Parliament are his relations and placemen, as now, then we who represent the true interest of the town are denied a voice. If we could field a Parliamentary candidate of our own – '

'Oh, really, father-in-law,' Sir Hugh snorted. 'I thought you too big a man now to involve yourself in these petty alderman quarrels.'

He had touched Mr Wainwright on a sensitive spot. 'It may seem to you – ' he began.

'Ah, here she is,' Sir Hugh interrupted him, rising clumsily to his feet. 'You rescue me, my dear, your father was reading me a lecture.'

Mr Wainwright studied his daughter's face as she came round the table to kiss him. 'Elizabeth, this is sad news, you poorly again.'

'It was nothing. I'm better now. Rest was all I needed, I think.' Elizabeth, Lady Woodhouse sat opposite her husband, a tall, very fair young woman richly dressed in a silk flowered polonaise, whose exceptional beauty had never helped her to an easeful manner. Mr Wainwright was too subtle to continue his scrutiny for long; but he detected if anything a greater aloofness in his daughter, something closed about her pale fine-boned face.

'Take a little heart, my dear, and you will be quite set up again,' said Sir Hugh noisily. 'No? What do you say to a little cold tongue? Steels, take this away and bring the cold tongue. And the game pie.'

'Your mother and Mina send their love,' Mr Wainwright said. 'We leave for the country soon. Have you seen a doctor?'

'Villiers came and talked some stuff last week,' Sir Hugh said.

'A mild depression of the animal spirits, according to Dr Villiers,' said Elizabeth. She took a small helping of tongue and refused the

59

wine. 'He prescribed a lowering course of treatment. Light food, a little Theban opium each evening.'

'It's the damp air of these winter nights, it is full of poisonous humours and breeds fever,' said Sir Hugh, filling his sizeable mouth with veal. 'Steels, tell Mrs Jennings these veal collops are fit for nothing. I have ridden horses younger than that meat. Is the women trying to poison us?' He pushed the dish away and motioned the footman to the game pie. 'I have a tender stomach and must treat it with care, father-in-law, as Lizzie will tell you. Come, my dear, have you still no appetite?'

'No, really, Hugh – perhaps I will take something at supper.' Elizabeth got up, and Mr Wainwright wondered if he was imagining that she avoided his eyes. 'I believe I will go into the drawing-room now.'

'You see,' said Sir Hugh after she had gone. 'It's no wonder she don't keep in good health. Don't you think she has gone thin?'

'She was always slender.' Mr Wainwright watched as Sir Hugh attacked his pie. 'Hugh, excuse me, I can eat or drink no more.' He got up.

'Must be hereditary,' said Sir Hugh, lifting his head from his plate for a moment. 'I'll join you shortly.'

Mr Wainwright found Elizabeth in the drawing-room.

He smiled uncertainly at her as she handed him his tea, aware for the first time how superficially he knew his twenty-three-year-old daughter, whose beauty was celebrated in three counties, for whom he had planned so much, who had indeed by her marriage given him connections that as a starveling youth apprenticed in a counting-house he had never dreamed of: and he was aware too that in his own fashion he loved her.

It all made it very difficult to broach the subject that was troubling him.

'I hope you are prospering, father,' she said, to his surprise speaking first. 'I have heard there is some anxiety over this war. They say when the French join with the Americans we will be hard pressed.'

'You are well informed,' he said, a little nonplussed.

She gave him an odd sort of smile. 'All the news comes here eventually, father.'

He looked at her a moment and then with puckered, exaggerated interest examined the miniature portraits on the wall above the fireplace. Sundry ancestors of the Deenecote Woodhouses, a branch who had risen at the Restoration and since then had been always wealthy and seldom useful. 'Well, I can't complain,' he said. He blew on his tea. 'I hope you and Hugh are prospering, Lizzie.'

Elizabeth stared at her work-basket and at last drew out a coloured thread. 'We have a great deal of company here. Last fortnight we received an invitation to join Lord and Lady Fitzwilliam at the theatre in Peterborough. Though Hugh refused, as he is no friend to Lord Fitzwilliam's Whig notions, as he calls them. And I do a lot of calling on my own account, now I have a carriage of my own always ready. We are really very busy here, though as you know I prefer to be in town.'

Her face was calm and composed. Of course, he thought, Letty Townsend was known as an incorrigible gossip, and if there was no scandal to tell she might well invent some. He would probably have taken no notice of her twitterings at that supper-party last week, when he had overheard her mention a rumour that Sir Hugh Woodhouse had been seen about with another woman, if it were not that in his heart of hearts he believed his son-in-law perfectly capable of such a thing. He said with difficulty: 'Are you often – Is Hugh much from home?'

'Well, you know his passion for hunting. And he has a taste for a little gambling, which he indulges at Mr Van Druyten's. I have joined him there on occasion, but I find it vastly tedious.' As she bent over her embroidery the bright colours of the silks cast a faint reflection on the curve of her cheekbone. 'I think it must be universal for men and women always to differ entirely in their amusements. I remember when I lived at home, often the only time mamma and I saw you was at meals.'

'That was business, not amusement,' Mr Wainwright said absently. 'But I wonder whether you – '

'Well, that's a cheerful fire,' Sir Hugh said, marching in. 'Regrettably I must leave you to enjoy it a while. I have a fancy to check on Zenith. That shoe he cast was badly fitted, and I'm uneasy that the hoof may be damaged.' He patted Elizabeth's arm. 'Mind you don't strain your eyes doing that, my love, and bring on your megrim again.'

Mr Wainwright watched his daughter's face closely as she smiled up at her husband. 'All right, Hugh. Don't take cold in those stables. Father, more tea?'

'Thank you, my dear.' He sighed inwardly as he passed his cup. There was nothing he could say: there really seemed no concrete evidence of anything amiss. All those years of wrestling with commerce and finance, with power and prestige, with the heavyweights of life that came at you squarely: he wondered whether he had not lost entirely the ability to tackle the more intimate, elusive problems, and whether they were not after all the most formidable ones.

3

Her father left at eight, and just over an hour later Elizabeth, Lady Woodhouse went upstairs and prepared for bed.

At her dressing-table, which was draped in silk from mirror to foot, she sat in her peignoir, examining, and acknowledging, her own beauty. This was one of her few unmixed pleasures, and she excused its vanity on that score.

Her fine blond hair, which in the day was dressed high off her forehead, she took down and began to brush. The regular motion of the strokes soothed her, and the undeniable beauty of the reflection pleased her. But the unhappiness was lodged in her like a canker, to be forgotten occasionally, to be purposefully ignored sometimes, to disappear never.

Perhaps that beauty was at the root of it all. Consciously or not, she had come from an early age to see it in the light of a commodity. The atmosphere in her parents' house had scarcely discouraged that. From the age of sixteen she had been the most sought-after heiress for miles around, with suitors of wealth and nobility at her heels. Only the most stridently aristocratic voices had raised themselves in demur to point out that the Wainwrights' gentility was only one generation deep. It had been quite simply the business of her life to make a good marriage.

It was doubly impossible to admit even to herself that she had made the wrong choice.

As if for reassurance she touched the lacquered powder-box, the gold ring-tray, the ivory comb, for the darkness had swum in on her for a moment. She forced herself to think of their season in London last year, when she had sat in a box at the opera, when she had been presented to the Duchess of Devonshire, when she had been a success wherever she went. That was what this marriage had promised, and had in full measure provided. It was that which Hugh Woodhouse had seemed to embody, and seeing him thus she had bound herself to him.

She glanced with a helpless flicker of alarm at the watch on the dressing-table. He would be up soon.

Perhaps, she thought, she was naturally a cold woman and doomed to be so. Certainly all her life she had been guarded in her emotions, as her family had steadily risen in the world and studiously regulated its behaviour so as never to make a false step. But then at first the experience had not been actively unpleasant, the strangeness of the act mitigating it and fitting in as a piece with the novelty of being married. And at first Hugh had seemed overwhelmed anew at her beauty in its complete revelation: his lovemaking had been tremulous and reverential, and it had rather gratified her to be the idol, granting favours that were received with such delighted humility.

That had not lasted long. With familiarity had come, not contempt, but concupiscence, and a bullish insistence.

Involuntarily she thought of the latest demands he had made, and a wave of sickness hit her. She clutched at the brush and closed her eyes, fighting it down, pushing away the memory with its humiliation and nausea.

It was unlikely, she thought, that the rumour of Hugh's seeing another woman had reached her father's ears, although he seemed to have been watching her closely today. She herself was used to the fact that her husband had a roving eye. If she could believe it was anything serious – that might even be preferable. For as it was she lacked one vital weapon against him. Always it came back to the fact that she had given him no child. Always he could cast that at her, turning the wrong to her side by a ghastly logic to which somehow she submitted.

And as she still gave him no child, his attentions – attacks, more correctly – grew more and more frequent, and more and more they expressed conquest and crudity and vengefulness.

The footstep along the passage was unmistakable. She stared with beating heart into her mirror, willing her face to be pale, to be drawn, to show even to him that it was out of the question tonight.

She heard him yawn in his dressing-room and throw down his

63

coat before appearing, reflected in the glass, at her door. His face was flushed, but he was not drunk: he was by no means abstemious, but generally knew where to stop. He smiled and came in, loosening his stock.

'Well, Zenith is not lamed, thank heaven. I'll have words with that smith when I see him though.' He unbuttoned his striped waistcoat. 'Wind's up again. Horrell tells me there's a young lime down, close to the summer-house. I think we should have planted elsewhere. The soil there's poor and thin.' He yawned again, and then came over and placed a hand on her shoulder. 'My poor dear, having to entertain your father all evening. Did he talk to you of balances and prices and accounts? I always think he looks rather lost without your mother. Still, it was pleasant to see him.' He was in a good mood tonight.

Seizing at the faint chance she said: 'Well, yes, it did rather tire me – ' but he forestalled her. 'But you had a good rest this afternoon, so no harm done,' he said. His arm was round her shoulders now, and he bent to kiss her.

Her lips were quiescent against his while her mind struggled. Perhaps this was all, and in a moment he would bid her good-night and go to bed.

Then she knew it was not.

'Hugh,' she said, disengaging herself, 'I – I have not been well . . .'

'And now you are better.' There was still the remnant of a smile on his face, but his eyes were pale and watchful.

'No, I – '

'No? What then? Tell me what is wrong, my dear.' As she hesitated he went on: 'What? No, it cannot be that time again, unless the moon is running a very peculiar course. Come, my love, you must not begin to fancy yourself ill when you are not.' His hand stroked her arm.

She was unable to disguise her shiver. 'That's not fair, Hugh – '

'Now, let's not have any talk of fairness.' His voice was still soft, but it was a tone she recognized. 'You are my wife, Elizabeth. You chose to be so. Unless you are regretting – '

'No, I – '

'Good. And as my wife you have certain obligations. Now, is it fair in you to behave as if your husband were repulsive?'

Her peignoir was closed, but he could see the rise and fall of her small white breasts and the lines of her long slender legs. He tried to control his noisy breathing. He had been affable today, he had been patient. He was prepared to remain so: but he felt he must have his reward. He mumbled an endearment as he pressed his lips to the soft skin between neck and shoulder and his hasty hand groped along her thigh.

'No, Hugh. I said *no!*'

She pushed him away. He took a step back, more from surprise than from the force of the push. The colour had mounted to her face and her eyes were fierce, as he had never seen them before. And to his surprise again, he found this by no means cooled his desire.

As his hand touched her shoulder again she screamed out. '*No,* Hugh. I *forbid* it! Do you hear me? I *forbid* you to!'

His mouth had dropped open. The sight of his young, beautiful, reserved wife, her fists clenched and her yellow hair thrown back, her face a mask of wild desperation, seemed at that moment bizarre and almost unearthly. He glanced around, as if fearing she would produce a knife or a gun. 'I think you are out of your senses, Elizabeth! You cannot mean – you must recollect yourself – '

'I am perfectly in my senses, Hugh, and I tell you I forbid you my bed. I will scream if you touch me, scream and fight. I am in earnest!'

Sir Hugh had gone crimson. 'By what *right* . . . by what *right* do you threaten to deny me – to deny me *my* rights as your husband – to deny your duty as my wife – and so deny me the child that it is your duty to bear?'

In her frenzy this appeal did not affect her. 'You have heard what I have said.' She spoke low now. 'I swear to God I mean it.'

He stared at her, wishing to disbelieve her, wishing to recover the situation somehow, but so taken aback by her vehemence that his mind and tongue felt frozen. He turned at last and flung into his bedroom and slammed the door.

She found she was shaking violently. She heard him throw off his shoes, heard him subside heavily into bed. Then silence.

She did not cry. She knew whatever he was feeling it was not acquiescence. Surprise had won her a victory: what it meant for her future life she could not tell. It seemed impossible even to look to the next sunrise.

A tenacious draught from the curtained window blew out the guttering candle on the dressing-table before her. She was glad of the darkness, so that she could not see her face in the mirror as she pressed her hands to her temples and the words were forced between her clenched lips: 'Oh, *God*, I wish I were dead . . . Oh, God, help me . . . I wish I were dead . . .'

FIVE

I

Christmas Day 1777 fell on a Thursday. On the Monday morning before, Will Binnismoor arrived at Bromswold with an invitation to the Walsoken family to a christening party at Morholm on Christmas Eve.

Mr Walsoken was at work in the room in the wing of the house, formerly the still-room, that had become his study. Rebecca took the letter in to him and waited while he read it. Spread about on his desk were yellowing papers that had belonged to the last owner, old Nathan Jarrett, and had lain mouldering in the house for years: leases and deeds, and maps of the parish and the estate in faded ink. The room was very dark, with a single high window the size of a handkerchief, but there was only a frugal taper burning on the desk.

'Well, daughter, this is gratifying,' he said. He always called her 'daughter' when he was in a good humour. 'We are invited to the christening of Mr Hardwick's son on Christmas Eve, and afterwards to a seasonal dinner at Morholm.' He nodded his large leonine head judicially. At such times there was about Mr Walsoken's appearance something of the classical bust, the grave face of the distinguished senator: only the weak indrawn mouth detracted from the impression. 'This is gratifying. That we who are still strangers here should be shown such attention by our – eminent neighbour.'

'Shall we go?' Rebecca said, shortly.

He lifted his head. 'Certainly we shall. I shall write an acceptance forthwith.' He drew a clean sheet of paper towards him. 'Oh – has the man gone away?'

Rebecca nodded.

'Well, I shall have Blythe take it over tomorrow.' He put the invitation carefully in a drawer. 'Why do you ask?'

She was idly scanning the books that he had stacked on a shelf below the window: guides to agriculture and estate management. 'Why do I ask what, father?'

'Whether we shall go.'

She looked blankly at him a moment, then turned away again. 'We have hardly ever been out socially in the past.'

'I think you exaggerate,' he said. 'Besides, a father has a duty to his family to ensure they are not led into giddy and vain paths.' He looked with some perplexity at his daughter's graceful figure bent over the books, the rich auburn hair pushed impatiently back. For a week or more, after signs that she might be conquering her wilful disposition and becoming the helpful child that he wished, she had been back in her old enigmatic ways. In fact her mood seemed an entirely new one, and quite incorrigible. He constantly felt that at any moment she might say something shockingly free – he did not know what, but something – so little did she seem to care for his approval. Or care for anything, come to that.

His reaction would have been the more severe were it not for the fact that he had vague, but definitely high, hopes for his youngest daughter. Sarah, of course, was a good child, dutiful and pious, if a little prey to nerves: but already at twenty-four she was a hopeless old maid, her fitting place by her mother's side. But Rebecca with her intelligence and striking looks must surely play a part in the greater things he had planned: if her spirit could only be conquered.

'Rebecca,' he said carefully, 'it is not only our place of residence that is changed. No doubt in Norwich you felt we led a plain and retired life, though lacking in no comforts: but you must understand I was a busy man, working and devising so that we might attain just such a position as we are now in. And now, of course, your mother's inheritance has improved our prospects further. We are in a position to launch ourselves in the best society – always keeping in mind our first duty to God. Rebecca, are you attending to me?'

She turned with an absent smile. 'Certainly, father.'

'Well. As I say, great things may lie ahead of us. And I – I am sure I can rely upon you to do your part.' He searched his pockets for a pinch of snuff. 'It is something of a pity that Jeremiah will not be coming down from Cambridge for Christmas – I would have liked to introduce him at Morholm: but he writes me he is to spend the season with a friend he has met at the university: a most distinguished family, the Boscoignes of Cornwall.'

'Father, I thought to take a walk in the village. Shall I take your acceptance over to Morholm myself?'

He looked at her as if expecting a trick. 'Hm – well, it might be more seemly to send a servant. But then you might pay our respects to the Hardwicks, and ask after Mrs Hardwick's health. Very well. A moment while I write a message.'

At Morholm Bridget, the maid, showed Rebecca into the winter parlour and said she would fetch the mistress. It was some minutes before Mary came in. She was in an old dimity frock with an apron that was spotted with dirt, and there were streaks of grease on her face.

'Miss Walsoken, I'm sorry to keep you, George is from home. Grandmother Peach has took to her bed with the chills . . . How are you? You must let me get you some tea . . .'

Rebecca was so surprised at seeing the lady of the house like this that she found herself stiffly holding out her father's letter. 'I – I've brought father's answer to your kind invitation.'

'And you're coming? That's marvellous. There will not be a large party, of course, but – ' Mary took the letter and struggled to open it: Rebecca saw her hands too were covered in grease.

'Mrs Hardwick, I'm afraid I've called at an inconvenient time. Let me go away again and – '

'I won't hear of it.' Mary abandoned the attempt to open the letter. 'I was in the middle of dipping rushes, so I'm not in the cleanest of states.'

They compromised, and Rebecca went into the kitchen with her. On the big table was a pile of dried bullrushes, and a steaming pan of hot fat. Mrs Binnismoor was there too, her long face shiny with grease. 'I'm afraid the air's not very sweet in here just now,' said Mary. 'But we're nearly done, and I don't want to let the fat go cool.'

'Could I not help you?' Rebecca said.

'It's kind of you. But you'd spoil that gown for certain, and I'd never forgive myself.'

Rebecca looked down at her long polonaise of pale blue velvet. It was nothing ostentatious, but in here it suddenly seemed absurdly impractical and frivolous, and she blushed.

'Please sit down,' Mary said, indicating a wheelback chair, 'and we can talk as we go. And I promise you, when you come to dinner on Wednesday you will not be dragged into the kitchen to help cook it!'

Rebecca laughed. 'How is little Charles Joseph, Mrs Hardwick?'

Mary drew out a rushlight and laid it to cool with the others on a stone slab beneath the window. 'He's thriving, thank you. There is much infant colic about in Peterborough, but I think out here, with luck, he should escape it. George dotes on him, though he still seems to fear he will break him when he picks him up. I hope you've settled in well at Bromswold, Miss Walsoken.'

'It was something of a shock at first, for the house was very run-down, but father is doing wonders with it. But I have been surprised how different the country here is from Norwich. People speak so different, and the land is so flat and wide and empty.'

Mary smiled. 'Some folk find it gloomy.'

'Oh, no, I like it. I like the great distances, and the way you can see the sky, and see the sun come up and go down.'

'Well, we are comparatively civilised here, for Aysthorpe is only on the edge of the true fens. Beyond Peterborough it can seem like a land apart. And the men there are a race apart too, they say: fiercely independent and defiant, caring for nothing – '

'Indeed.'

Rebecca had spoken curtly, and Mary wondered if she had said something wrong. 'And – have you been to Peterborough yet, Miss Walsoken?'

'No, not yet. The weather has been uncertain for riding.'

'Well, it is a handsome place, and the cathedral is a sight worth the journey. George has gone in this morning – a meeting of the magistrates. I wish it were something else, for they always put him in a bad humour for the rest of the day.'

'Does he not like serving on the bench?'

Mary tipped the pan to collect the last of the fat. 'Well, it's difficult to say. Today I believe the meeting is only about the repair of the Nene bridge or something. But you see . . . George has never been of a – peaceful disposition himself. There is a rebellious spirit in him that he has never lost. When his father died he was appointed magistrate in his place almost immediately: there has been a Hardwick on the bench for a hundred years or more. But it has never sat easy on him. In a bad winter like this, when there is much distress abroad, when people are brought forward for taking fire-wood or a hare from private land to keep themselves alive – well, he is inclined to disagree with his fellow magistrates, who are often set on strong sentences, and he was never one to mince words. More than ever now that we are somewhat pressed ourselves. There.' With Mrs Binnismoor's help she lifted the empty pan off the table and into the basin beneath the pump. 'Now, I promise you you shall have some tea, and a little comfort.' She pushed her dark hair back from her face with her forearm, a tired, pretty young woman with a generous smile. She had quickly become slim again after the baby. 'I shall just go and tidy myself up and check on Charles Joseph.'

As they took tea in the winter parlour Mary thought her visitor seemed ill at ease: she tapped her shoe and several times her face set into an abstracted frown before she at last burst out: 'Mrs Hardwick, you have made me feel so useless.'

Mary smiled at her quizzically. 'I'm sorry, Miss Walsoken. How – by not letting you get covered in grease and spoil your frock?'

'Oh, it's not that.' Rebecca ran a hand through her hair. 'But – at home I think I am meant to – to sit with mother and Sarah sewing samplers of texts from the Bible. Because I am a young woman I am supposed to be made of eggshell, and – ' She frowned again. 'And I have the impudence to come here and complain to you of how idle I am when you would be glad to sit and rest – '

'Pray don't feel guilty about that. There is nothing worse, I know, than to be filled with energy and unoccupied. Especially if the mind is unoccupied too.'

'That is precisely it,' said Rebecca decisively. 'You see, we have come here to be – well, father is passing rich, and means to make the most of it at last, and move in society, and – I feel there should be something I can *do*.'

Mary studied her, considering her answer. She did not really seem a discontented girl and she wanted to say the right thing. 'Well, Miss Walsoken – '

'Please call me Rebecca.'

'Well – Rebecca – I mentioned there is much hardship this winter: what with the bad harvest and the floods; and here in the village there are many families who will have but a poor Christmas of it – '

'But there, isn't that what is expected too? For a young lady to – to flatter her self-importance by going round and being gracious to the poor?'

Mary hesitated, liking the young woman's frankness but somewhat at a loss. 'It depends how it is done. As you say, it can be merely patronising. But folk in these parts will soon spot an intention to play the lady bountiful, and have nothing to do with you. If you really want to help – '

Rebecca lifted her head. 'I do.'

The cottage was one of the last few in the village. All the houses along the main road were built of good Barnack Ragstone, and even the meanest looked sturdy enough, with their thick walls and low eaves like beetle brows: but the cluster that followed the stream towards the distant rim of Helpston Woods were considerably older and much poorer. Rebecca saw decayed timber and gaping thatch, and two half-naked children who had been playing in the frozen mud scuttled away at her approach. Across the fields a grim lead sky lowered: it seemed to have drawn all the colour from the earth, gathering the hardening winter to itself and leaving the ridged land below to stiffen and die till it should relent.

The name of the old woman she was going to see was Mrs Gedney. From her high reputation in the village she had become known as Goodwoman Gedney, and then Goody Gedney. She was nearly eighty, Mary had said, and there was now only a young granddaughter to support her.

Rebecca well knew this mood she was in, though it had never afflicted her quite this badly before: it drove her restlessly from unfathomable introspection out into fitful action and back again, searching for some salve for her mental itch: it made her difficult to live with, and she did not like herself very much. Her twin brother Peter was due to arrive from London tomorrow: but even to unburden herself to him was impossible.

Partly she blamed the young man – she would not even think of his name, for what did he matter to her? It was simply the shame of being left waiting on a street corner for him like some silly girl in the throes of calf-love. She felt nothing for him and no doubt would have seen him only to send him about his business; the whole thing was impossible, and she wondered how she could ever have brooked such impudence.

She had waited that day in Stamford for nearly an hour.

Partly she blamed herself, for even allowing . . . She had been too familiar. She was vividly angry at the thought of him: felt she could fly at him, punching and kicking, if she ever saw him again.

Not that she would. It was a foolish little episode that must be forgotten. He had not turned up when he promised, and that was that. Perhaps a belated sense of decency had come over him and he had deliberately stayed away from the town. Perhaps he had found some other naïve young girl, one of his own sort, with whom to have his sport. Good. Forget it. Look to the future.

Perhaps he had been in an accident, or sick or thrown from his horse or drowned in the endless dykes and streams in that misty tableland where he lived . . .

Rebecca knocked twice at the cottage door before a thin, sawing voice said: 'Come you in, I can't stir.'

She blinked as she went in, for the cottage was almost dark as night. As her eyes adjusted she saw that the one room had an earthen floor and a single unglazed window, the damaged shutter crammed with rags to keep the draughts out. There was a ladder-stair leading to the loft in the roof. Against the wall was a bed with a straw mattress and a couple of wooden forms, and there was a rough-hewn table in the centre of the room on which stood an old cloam teapot and some pewter dishes. A black pot stood on an iron trivet over the cold grate. The only other furniture was the high-backed chair in which the old woman sat. She wore a patched serge gown and cap: on her lap was a basin in which she was washing potatoes with rigid arthritic hands.

'You'll have to come closer,' she said mildly, 'for I can't see you yet.'

'Mrs Gedney,' Rebecca said, 'you don't know me. I'm Rebecca Walsoken, from Bromswold.'

She came closer. There was time meanwhile for agonised self-reproaches: self-reproaches for brooding over some half-fledged infatuation, for complaining of boredom: not least for sailing in here in her rich dress as if she owned the place, acting just like the lady bountiful she did not want to be. In confusion she said: 'We've but recently moved in, and – and Mrs Hardwick was telling me about you, and I've come to see you and – and wondered if there was any help I might offer.'

'Ah, Bromswold. Deborah do tell me there was folk there again.' Her eyes, lost amongst puckered wrinkles, searched Rebecca's face. 'You must find yourself a seat, for I can't stir. Do you sit down.'

Rebecca sat, part wishing she had never come: but it was the old lady who calmed her misgivings with a natural dignity. 'I don't get across to see Bromswold now, I can't walk so far,' she said, laying

73

the basin on the floor. 'Thass stood empty for nigh on three year now, I reckon. I hope you'll find a comfortable welcome here, miss – you're not from hereabouts, I can tell . . .'

In this way, talking pleasantly and asking questions, she quietly put Rebecca at her ease, at the same time bringing it home to her that to offer help was all very well, but to abruptly fling it down like halfpennies for a street-beggar without first making acquaintance was simply bad manners. Rebecca was grateful to Goody Gedney, and did not mind at last saying: 'It's very cold today. If you haven't enough wood for a fire, will you have some of ours? Father would be glad to send you some from the pile we have in the yard. He sends his respects, by the way.' She was pleased with that improvisation. 'As you know, Mrs Gedney, we are strangers here, and – and we would wish to be neighbourly.'

The old lady smiled. 'Thass kind of you, dair, and I'll be glad owv't. I'm gone past feeling it, you know, at my age, but thass my granddaughter I think on. Deborah. Brave gel. She'll be home soon.'

Things were not so easy with the granddaughter.

She was about Rebecca's age, a strongly built girl with black hair and brows and an oval face from which flashed strikingly green eyes. She looked at Rebecca but did not speak when she came in: and when Mrs Gedney explained her presence she was silent for a moment.

'We're obliged to you for the thought, miss,' she said at last. 'But I wasn't aware we'd begun begging.'

'Well, Mrs Hardwick was telling me your grandmother hadn't been well, and – '

'Nor hasn't she.' With gentleness the girl kissed the old woman's head. Then she turned and cast a glance over Rebecca's clothes and then looked away again. 'I've got a bundle of wood out the back, grandma. Some I think will be damp. But Nat Royle found me some scraps from his yard that'll make rare good kindling. His Betty's near her time, he say, and so swelled thass like to be twins. We won't keep you, miss, good day,' she went on in an unaltered voice.

Rebecca stood, unable to speak. She looked at the old lady, but she seemed as helpless as herself. To hand them money would be the worst thing . . . 'I didn't come here to be a busybody,' she said indistinctly. 'I wanted to help.'

Deborah Gedney looked at her critically, here eyes lambent as a cat's in the gloom of the cottage. 'Then you can help me chop that firewood,' she said. 'Less'n you're scared of spoiling that dress.'

The challenge was the perfect outlet for her feelings. 'Of course not,' she said.

The bundle of wood was piled against the back wall of the cottage. There were fallen branches and twigs and sticks, lumps of rotten bark, leavings of carpenter's timber and shavings, tangled brushwood. Parts of it, where there was damp and moss, were good for nothing, as Deborah told her abruptly.

Rebecca had never used a bill-hook or hatchet in her life. Within a few minutes her hands were raw and her thumb was bleeding. The air was cold enough for her breath to turn thick white but she found she was sweating as if she had a fever. But nothing could have induced her to stop: and Deborah worked on beside her, silent and grim and practised. There was no sound but for the crackling and snapping of rent wood.

So absorbed did she become that for a moment she did not notice that Deborah had stopped. She was leaning on the shaft of the axe, regarding her with a kinder eye.

'That'll do,' she said.

Rebecca tried not to show her breathlessness. 'How long will this last you?' she said.

Deborah shrugged. Dressed only in a short coarse frock and apron, her head and arms bare, she yet seemed untouched by the bitter cold. 'Depends on the weather,' she said. 'Might eke it for a fortnight.'

'When it's all gone,' Rebecca said, 'I hope you will let us send you some wood from Bromswold.'

Deborah's eyes were a little mocking, but she smiled gently enough. 'That I will. That's good of you.'

Rebecca suddenly felt too weary to be bothered about the making of points, on either side. She turned to go when Deborah said: 'No doubt you think me very proud.'

'Well, aren't you?'

Deborah mopped her hair back with a brown arm. 'It's a good thing to hold on to. Grandma's never lost her pride and I don't mean to either.'

'Even if it means letting her shiver by a cold hearth?'

Deborah looked hard at her, but she did not seem displeased. 'Help, kindly meant, we'll take and willing. Christian charity. Not gentlefolk-charity. Oh, there's a difference. When I came in and found you setting there wi grandma, I thought: I know this game. Being inspected. Make sure we're deserving. As if, just because it's a poor moiling little place, tis open house for ladies to come poking and prying and seeing how we get on.' Her face suddenly shone with a smile of great good humour. 'So I thought, *I'll* do the testing, and see if the *lady's* deserving.'

'I hope I can skip the test in future,' Rebecca said, smiling too. 'And if I'm not poking and prying, how do you live?'

Deborah took a length of string from her apron pocket and bent and began to tie the sticks into rough faggots. 'I do milking up at Castle Farm, over to Maxey. Summer I work in the fields, tis easier then: winter it has to be anything I can turn my hand to.'

'How far is Maxey?'

'Two or three mile.' She held the cord in her teeth for a moment. 'Bless you, it's not for ever. I'm promised to be married next year. Mark Upwell, whose father's got the farm over towards Marham. We s'll have grandma to live with us. I don't mind when I've that to look forward to.'

There was a maturity about her that impressed Rebecca, and made her feel slightly sad. 'I wonder – are you handy with a needle?'

Deborah dusted down her apron. 'I am that.'

'At Bromswold my mother wants curtaining up at all the doors. It is a big job. If I were to put that work in your way, could you do it, at home?'

'Right enough.' Deborah's eyes were piercing again for a moment. 'Now, this is real work, that's truly wanted? No charities, you understand? All right then.' She smiled. 'I'll be glad to think of you as an employer.'

'Perhaps,' Rebecca said, 'you might think of me also as a friend.'

2

After the magistrates had met in Peterborough that morning they adjourned for a dinner at the Talbot. George Hardwick, who would have preferred to go straight home, was seated next to Sir Samuel Edgington, and endured his talk on the treatment of farcy in horses until the old man at last slid into a fat port-soaked sleep with his forehead resting on the table.

George left the city at three and was in Aysthorpe before four.

The days were at their shortest and when he turned his horse in at the drive to Morholm, after stopping off at the gatehouse to speak to Matthews the farm manager, the last light was bleeding from the sky and the flat horizons to the north behind the house were receding in layers of sickly mist. He spared a glance for the half-ruined gateposts. Extraneous at the best of times, as the stone wall that had once surrounded the property had long disappeared, and the gates were never closed: but handsome and worth repairing. Perhaps, he thought, one day he might be prosperous enough to do it.

They were in the winter parlour, a small room facing west and the warmest in the house: Grandmother Peach, who had tottered down to crouch and wheeze by the fire, Mary, and Charles Joseph in the cradle.

George looked down at his sleeping son whilst Mary mixed him a hot toddy. A dark-lashed and sturdy-looking baby: an expression of the intensest concentration on his face. What, George wondered, would be his inheritance – supposing he should survive the hazards of infancy, avoided the swinging scythe that cut down so many when their stake in life was barely established: a great house, rich land, wealth and respect – or a clutch of debts and mortgages?

Mary came to join him, and he put his arm round her and kissed her, trying to dismiss his gloomy thoughts. 'I hope you have been in no fights with the justices today,' she said.

'Oh no, it was all quite routine, though very tedious. There was so much I could have been doing here.' He looked at her face, thought he detected something oddly abstracted about it. 'Is anything wrong, love?'

Mary shook her head. 'Not wrong . . . The strangest thing has happened. There is a letter from Great-Uncle Horace, saying he will be coming to the christening-party on Wednesday.'

'I'll agree he is not often so sociable,' said George. 'But why so strange?'

Mary shook her head again. 'You must read it.'

From the chimney-corner Mrs Peach muttered: 'Old Horace. He were always a close one. But after all these years . . .'

Mary brought him the letter and they read it together standing by the cradle.

Dear George and Mary,
I write to tell you that I shall be happy to attend the Christening of

young Charles Joseph: also, as I have not yet offered my Congratulations on the event, to do so. He prospers I hope.

I wish also to acquaint you with some News which I have no doubt will be surprizing to you in the Extreme, and must of Necessity be here announced somewhat baldly.

You must set another place at your table on Christmas Eve. I shall bring with me to meet you my own Son. The History of his birth and bringing-up is not a happy one, and its Relation is best postponed. Suffice it to say that he is twenty-four years of age: that he has lived under the name, which I gave him, of Luke Taplin, the latter being as you may know the maiden name of my mother. He had never seen me or known of me until ten days ago. My Reasons for acknowledging him at last I can scarcely articulate even to my own Self: but it is my hope that your own recent Joy will aid you, if not to comprehend, then not to judge harshly: and that his Reception at the family home of the Hardwicks will be such as he would have expected as a matter of course, had he come into the world as little Charles Joseph has done, instead of entering it under the blight of Bastardy, and of a father's Cowardice in refusing to own the Consequences of his actions; a wrong which I seek late but sincerely to right.

HORACE HARDWICK

3

Mr Walsoken did not join his family for dinner that day but worked in his study till three, taking a bowl of broth and a slice or two of chicken breast at his desk. Then, feeling a little cramped and stuffy, he went out to take a turn around the garden and outhouses.

The former owner of Bromswold had been a wool merchant and had no interest in either the gardens or the land, both of which he had let go. The garden was not much more than a walled paddock of knee-high grass and a few old contorted apple trees. The stable was a tumbledown shed of timber and thatch: it was poor accommodation for their four saddle-horses, and as he hoped to set up a carriage soon it was best knocked down and rebuilt completely. But there was a good stone barn and a buttery and brewhouse, all of which he intended repairing when the weather was more favourable. Something might even be done with the derelict mill that was on the property, half-hidden among trees at the far end of the long field behind the house.

The cold did not affect Joshua Walsoken. Always a man of spartan tastes, his wealth had never caused him to modify them. It had always been his habit to rise at dawn, to eat and drink in moderation, to dress soberly, to work tirelessly, to set aside time in each day for study of the Bible and rigorous prayer. His family must of course have only the best, as befitted the station to which it had pleased God to elevate them, but for himself his personal wants were modest.

His puritanism was however of a limited kind. He had an intense dislike of Methodism, which he considered a dangerous levelling movement, its aim to undermine the authority of the church. He had spoken of it in strong terms to Parson Medhurst yesterday after the service. Mr Medhurst had said there was a small group of Methodies in the village: they had their meetings at Seth Upwell's farm. To Walsoken's disgust, the little cleric had been mild about them, saying he did not entirely approve of the sect, but they always attended his church and were very decent people. Walsoken was for no such tolerance. The Vicar's Warden at Aysthorpe Church had always been old Dr Milton, but he was too frail to attend now and Walsoken hoped for the position himself. He would be glad to have any influence to use against those levellers and enthusiasts. He had had to be very firm with his wife on that score in the past: Patience had heard Wesley preach at Norwich when she was younger, and he suspected she had caught a little sympathy for the movement.

The short day was guttering like a candle, and while there was still some light he took a walk down past the ruined mill to view the prospect of the house from the south. To the west of the paddock lane was common land, but the rest was his, as far as the stream and down to Marham Woods.

Well, the house would never be a noble sight, but with the new windows, and the new roofing when it was complete, it was highly respectable. When the garden was improved it would be a place fit for inviting company to: high company.

There was enormous satisfaction for him in savouring the fact of his ownership of land, modest though it was as yet. Norwich was a city of merchants, and there he had been one – though a rich one – amongst many. This was entirely different. This was the realisation of his dreams.

Joshua Walsoken was fortunate in combining in his character both ambition and patience. His father had kept a small livery

79

stable at March – only just kept, for he was an improvident man and a drinker. Young Joshua had been the scholar of the family, diligent and serious, and inheriting a devout temperament from his mother. He had also been thought rather dull and sullen, a fact which troubled him not at all. He had gone to Norwich at fourteen as an articled clerk to a firm of wine merchants, where a dealer in worsted had spotted his application and talent for business, and lured him away with an offer of a higher wage. His rise to a partnership by the time he was twenty-five surprised no one – for there was really no one to surprise. He had no friends, no social life to speak of. By the age of thirty he was a prospering merchant in his own right. In the meantime he had further advanced his prospects by meeting and marrying Patience. She was related to the Gurneys, one of the richest and most powerful families in Norwich. She was also a timorous, naïve young woman, an only child, whose days were spent in reading a Bible from which her doting parents had excised the improper passages. Considerations of birth were less pressing in the highly mercantile atmosphere of Norwich: and Joshua had seemed quite eligible, especially with his sobriety of manner and sincere piety: and Patience worshipped him. He was also then – as he still was in some respects – a handsome man, with a sturdy figure but a grave, pale face and delicate hands, and a skin of feminine softness that bled at the slightest scratch. The softness was lacking in his personality. His religion and his acumen were branches on the same tree of severity.

So he had established his new bride in a small house in the Cathedral Close: and time passed and children came – seven, including two who in the way of things died in infancy – and the house was exchanged for a large elegant one on the outskirts of the city. The girls attended a genteel day-school where they would learn nothing that would disturb them, the boys the Cathedral school. And so came 1777, and Jeremiah the eldest son prepared to go up to St Johns College, Cambridge, and Peter went to London to study at law: and Mrs Walsoken's father died, and as the inheritance of a married woman immediately became her husband's, Joshua Walsoken the rich merchant found himself in his forty-eighth year richer by twelve thousand pounds.

It was a history that he liked to contemplate as uniting the rewards of industry and temperance with the blessings of inscrutable Providence.

Walsoken strolled on, and startled birds rose with a flutter from the ragged grass by the path. Plans still to be made. Paul's interrupted schooling must be attended to: he had thoughts of sending him away to a public school. The boy was highly-strung and needed stiffening. Harrow was a possibility. Work still to be done. He puckered his eyes in the failing light at the farmhouse a quarter of a mile away to the south. Upwell's, he thought, casting his mind back to the old map he had in the study. One of those Methodist agitators.

His foot slipped a little as he happened on the edge of an overgrown ditch. He perceived that the earth on the other side was fenced from the common and had been ploughed. He looked about him, thinking of the map and trying to get his bearings. The honking cry of a moorhen came thin and rarefied from the direction of the stream to the west. Darkness had formed in the sky in great masses, shouldering aside the last patches of cold pink light. With a puzzling thought half-grown in his mind he turned back to the house.

The next day, the twenty-third, the sun rose out of mists into a bleak white sky that seemed to strip it of its warmth like a cloak. The temperature plunged down, and when at six John Newman set out from his farm at Helpston to walk the mile and a half to Seth Upwell's, the ground underfoot was hard as stone and the land was powder-blue under a paring of moon. John shivered and quickened his pace. The old coat he was wearing was thin stuff, and with a few acres of field that this year had proved unproductive and two babies to feed there was small chance of getting another this winter.

The prospect of the meeting cheered him. After an early conversion his Methodism had waned until last year when Mr Cradock Glascott of Lady Huntingdon's Connexion had preached at the Butter Cross in Peterborough. John, amongst others, had been fired anew with the conviction of salvation. As yet the meetings at Seth Upwell's were informal; they were only six, and not a proper Class; though Seth, who had been converted when hearing Whitefield preach twenty years ago, was acknowledged as the leader, and the brethren in Peterborough were building a chapel in Wood Street. Jenny Newman had never been converted and though she made no objection to his going to the meetings John sometimes thought she suspected him of humbug.

There were candles burning in the window of the squat slate-

81

roofed farmhouse, and John saw the table pushed back and the chairs set in a row: but there seemed to be no one there yet. Seth's only son Mark opened the door to him.

'Reckon I must be early tonight, Mark.'

Mark, a slender, lively young man who suffered from a weak chest, shook his head gravely. The fun that was usually in his eyes was not there.

'Come you in, John, and git warm,' came Seth's voice.

Seth was smoking his pipe in his high-backed chair by the fire, and he looked up at John in a vague lost way. The Bible was closed on the table. 'There – there'll not be a meeting this even, John,' he said. 'I've sent the others back home.'

'Something wrong, Seth? You sick?'

Seth shook his head, and motioned John to the wooden settle opposite him. 'Not sick, John. Leastways, not ill. But I hadn't the mind for a meeting today. I'm sorry I fetched you all this way on a cold night. But mebbe as you can help me.'

Mark bolted the door again and came and sat down, patting the dog that lay mournful-eyed under the table.

'How long have I been here, John?' Seth said.

'What, at this farm? Well . . . long as I can remember. Since I were a little tacker. Why?'

'Forty year,' said Seth. He was a big man of great strength, but his voice was coming out small as if he were going to cry. 'My father's afore that.' He cast his eyes round the room: stone floor, deal furniture, polished pewter on the dresser. 'Not much of a place, but it belong to me.'

'Nobody'd say nay, Seth,' John said.

Seth looked into the fire, pulling at his sparse beard. ''Twas a poor year. We scarce got a price for our corn. I don't reckon the taters'll be up to much.' He stirred with an effort to marshal his thoughts. 'I had a visitor today. Walsoken, him as has moved into Bromswold. You know him?'

'I seen him at church.'

'You mind old Nat Jarrett? 'Twas of him that my dad leased the fields running down to the old mill. This house was his own holding, see, and the yard, and then there's corner of common in front. The rest he leased, all proper and written down, from Nat Jarrett. The lease to last till the end of his life. When he died I renewed it, fair and square. Good land, only fifty acres, but always drained well –

till this year – and took to barley. Kept us well. I was always thinking of young Mark, and how he'd be set up when he was grown. Then when old Jarrett went bankrupt, the house and effects was all sold off, the place was empty . . . I carried on. Naught else I could see to do.'

'Does Walsoken doubt you? Ye've the deeds – '

'Aye, that's all right. But I've been working on a dead lease, see. The property's his now, all Bromswold land.'

'You can renew it again – '

Seth shook his head. Mark was watching him solemnly. 'He say no. He want to claim the land back. Y'know Jack Dutch, as had a freeholding at Northborough. He sold out to Walsoken when he came here. Oh, that were all fair dealing. Walsoken wants his own estate, see.' He swallowed. 'And he say I owe him a quarter's rent. He bought the property in September.'

John frowned. 'I don't know as that's right . . .'

Seth shrugged. 'He say he'll bring a lawyer out from Peterborough to prove it if I want.'

'Can you pay it?'

'Mebbe just. We'd have to sell stock – the pigs say. But what's to do after?'

'But the house is yourn. And the corner field.'

'Thass flooded. And that can't keep us.'

There was a bloodless despairing look about Seth that John found disturbing. 'Surely – surely he'll leave you carry on till spring? Ye've sown the land. Tis only sense – '

Seth shook his head weakly. The big man seemed drained of strength even to draw on his pipe. 'He don't see it. When we set foot on that land we're trespassing, he say. He can prosecute us. He's in the right of it.'

'Mebbe, but it seem hard, too hard.' John looked from father to son and back again. A twig snapped in the fire. 'What do you mean to do?'

Seth stared into the flames. 'There's young Mark hoping to be wed next year an' all,' he said softly. 'I don't know . . . we'll have to pay the back rent and – manage as best we can . . .'

'Don't fret about that,' said Mark. 'Deborah won't complain, you know her.'

'I'm sorry about the meeting, John,' Seth said. 'Tis shameful to own it, but I – I'm not in the mind for praying tonight.'

83

SIX

I

Early on the twenty-third, while her father was presenting his unpleasant news to Seth Upwell, Rebecca rode in to Peterborough, accompanied by the manservant Ford and an excited Paul, to meet her twin brother Peter off the coach at the Swan Inn in Midgate.

In view of the uncertain weather Peter Walsoken had elected not to risk the twelve-hour journey in the Peterborough Diligence from Holborn: instead he had broken the trip, sleeping the night at the Sun in Biggleswade. He was expected about two o'clock. This gave them ample time to view the old city, and indeed part of the reason Mr Walsoken had allowed Paul to go was so that he should see and be suitably impressed by the noble cathedral of St Peter.

Approaching the city from the west she saw the giant gables rearing above the low houses and damp pastureland, incisive against a bitter cadmium sky: they seemed to brood on a memory of a past more heroic and more terrible.

It was a sight to match her own spiritual visions, that in silent rejection of her father's narrow piety had been turned outward to embrace the passions and mysteries of life: so that she thought with a kind of horrible wonder of the forgotten labours of the hundreds of men who had raised those stones, of the shadowy lives and deaths of the first monks among its cold corridors, of the torchlit procession bearing the murdered body of Mary Queen of Scots from Fotheringhay to be buried.

Below, the town hurried about its business: carriers' carts from the villages thronged the narrow streets, wheels crunching in the frozen mire of the gutters: prentice boys crammed the doors of the Angel, eager to see the cockfight that was advertised in a bill pasted to the door: a quarrel began as a maid hurled the slops down from the steps of a townhouse and splashed a potman rolling empty casks. After they had stabled the horses at the Swan they crossed the Marketstede to Goodman's, where Rebecca thought to buy a christening present for Charles Joseph Hardwick. There was a rank smell here from the eels being skinned at the pump on the corner. When she emerged from the shop, with a little riding-crop inlaid with silver, she found Paul joining in with some boys who had made a slide, and with difficulty persuaded him to come with her through the stone gate to the Cathedral. He got few outings and when he did his high spirits got the better of him.

The pleasant anticipation of seeing Peter again, and – despite the fact that Christmas was only observed in her father's household with extra devotions – the atmosphere of the season, seemed to have laid the ghosts of confused longing raised by the young fenman. Ghosts of another kind were more likely here, as she wandered by the mossy Monks' Cemetery behind the building. There was no market bustle now: the only sound was the cawing of rooks in the bare trees around the Infirmarer's Hall. At Norwich the cathedral was soaring and airy: this was a quite different place, dark and secretive, a gaunt holiness.

She emerged at last from the cloisters to see Paul, who had strayed away from her again, whizzing along a slide he had made on the well-kept path in front of the Abbot's Gate. He had made the slide too well. As she opened her lips to call him his feet flew up into the air: he put out an arm to save himself and the crack was audible as he went down.

It was natural, though she reproved herself for it, for one of her first thoughts to be 'What will father say?'

She helped Paul to his feet, and saw he held the arm out stiff and trembling. He was trying very hard not to cry in front of his sister, but he was not succeeding. She asked him if he had felt the crack, and he nodded, the tears running over.

'There must be a surgeon in the town,' she said, and thought: the arm will have to come off. Dear God, don't let him see me cry too.

An old sexton had seen the accident and came running. 'Please,' Rebecca said, 'is there a surgeon or a doctor at hand? I think the arm's broke.'

'We-ell,' the old man said slowly, 'there's Dr Villiers over to Cross Street. But I seen him riding off on his white hoss an hour since.'

'Is it far? We can try. Will you help us?'

'I can walk,' said Paul through his teeth.

It was clear that each step jarred through him, and by the time they had emerged into the Marketstede he was crying openly. 'How much further?' Rebecca said in despair.

'Past St John's there,' the sexton said. 'Like I tell you, I don't reckon he's in.'

A crowd had gathered about them, partly from morbid curiosity: but one plump woman with a brood of children at her heels said. 'There's a new surgeon moved in, up by the bridge. Young strip of a feller. Send off for him, shall I?'

Rebecca nodded, not trusting her voice, and the woman sent her eldest child off up Narrow Bridge Street at a run.

The crowd lessened, but a few onlookers remained, offering comments and advice in the see-sawing, guttural accent. One of the farmer's wives who sat under the Butter Cross selling eggs gave Paul her chair. Rebecca remembered her father's overseer in Norwich who had broken his arm falling from his horse: the surgeon had sawed it off at the shoulder in a twinkling. She began to dread the arrival of the young strip of a feller.

The smallest of the plump woman's children was offering Paul a bite of his gingerbread, which Paul with some grace was refusing, when the young man in the black coat shouldered his way through. 'That's him,' the woman said in a satisfied tone.

'Fell on the ice, eh?' the young man said, laying a small leather bag on the ground, and without further preamble began to feel Paul's arm with long white fingers. Rebecca waited for a cry of pain, but it did not come. 'So . . . what's your name?'

'Paul – Paul Walsoken.'

'You must take more care, Paul. Where are your parents?'

'Home. That's my sister.' Paul gestured with his good arm.

The young man's eyes flickered to Rebecca and lingered for a moment. 'Well, your brother has sustained a fracture – Miss Walsoken.'

Feeling as if she were choking, she said shrilly: 'What does it mean – what are you going to do?' A couple of the onlookers drew a little closer. 'Linseed poultice,' the plump woman said knowledgeably.

The young man did not reply but straightened and looked around him. 'It's quite a long walk to my house,' he said. He pointed across the square to the Talbot. 'I'm sure the innkeeper will not mind if we use a room there. Will you help me bear him?' he said to the old sexton. 'Now, Paul, keep very still and try to relax your body if you can. Give way, please.'

The young doctor's manner was quietly authoritative, and the innkeeper hurriedly cleared a way through the tap-room to a private room. 'What do you need, sir?' he said. 'Water, bowls, bandages – '

'Thank you, nothing,' Dr Kesteven said. He settled Paul in a chair, quietly closed the door on the onlookers hoping to sneak in, and turned to Rebecca. 'Pray don't be alarmed, Miss Walsoken. I think there will be no danger to Paul's arm. Now, Paul, can you lay the arm out with the palm upward. And the muscles must be completely relaxed. Relax the arm completely, now.'

Paul did as he was bid, with one frightened glance at Rebecca. Regretting her hysterical outburst, she tried to give him an encouraging smile. A murmuring was audible from the tap-room outside.

The young man pulled back Paul's sleeve and began to feel along the arm again. Unable to watch, Rebecca studied his face instead. A lean face but very boyish, which contrasted oddly with the premature grey at his temples. At least he had not reached in his bag for any instruments.

'How old are you, Paul? Twelve? Well, I remember myself at twelve. It's not so very long ago.' He talked on in a low soothing voice. 'I remember once I fell off the ladder in the orchard and hurt myself, but I was afraid to tell anyone because I wasn't supposed to be taking apples. I think my father knew but he never said anything, perhaps because he thought – '

'Oh!' Paul gave a yelp and jumped in his seat, but more from surprise than pain.

' – Perhaps because he thought I'd learnt my lesson already.' His fingers, having stopped for a moment, continued their exploration. 'Now, Miss Walsoken, if you will call the innkeeper in again: see if he has some stick of wood, anything light and strong, with which to make a splint. And a sheet of cloth, anything will do, for a sling. I have bandages.'

'Is – is it all right?'

'That feels easier,' said Paul, whose long hair was damp with sweat.

The young man smiled for the first time, a grave but warm smile.

'I have set the fracture,' he said. 'Now the arm must be supported and kept very still.'

'Set it so soon?' Rebecca said. 'What about – ointments, or things like that.'

'Presently, perhaps.'

The innkeeper brought some sticks of kindling and an old apron: and the onlookers from the taproom, some a little disappointed that there was no blood, were allowed to watch in the doorway while the young man fitted the splint and sling.

'You have been lucky, Paul,' he said at last. 'It is a simple fracture, I think: and though you must keep it like that for several weeks, and it will give you pain, it might have been much worse.'

Paul, rather proud now that the worst of his ordeal was over, stood up to show the sling off.

'I can't thank you enough,' said Rebecca. 'I feared the worst – I thought you might . . .'

Dr Kesteven shook his head emphatically. 'Some cases perhaps. The important thing is to set the fracture immediately. It is quite a new idea. I came across it when studying earlier this year with Mr Percivall Pott, the author of *A Treatise On Fractures and Dislocations*, at St Bartholomew's Hospital in London. A brilliant man. Now you must take care to restrain Paul. I imagine he is of an active disposition.'

'I don't know your name – we are quite new here, and a woman just said to fetch the young surgeon.'

He smiled. 'Well, I am a physician, which is different from a surgeon. I'm sorry, that sounds rather pompous; I'm afraid it was drummed into me when I qualified.' He extended a hand. 'I am new here also. My name is Christopher Kesteven.'

'Rebecca, what about Peter? We should be meeting him,' said Paul, now growing restive under all the attention.

'Of course . . . And how are we to get home? Paul was to ride in front of me on my horse – it is some miles.'

'That will be all right, if you go very gently,' the young man said. 'Make sure he rests when you get home. A simple salve, and perhaps some Theban opium if the pain lingers – your own physician will see to that if you require it.'

She noticed how he tended to avoid her eyes. 'We have none,' she said. 'Besides, father will surely wish to thank you, and to have you attend on Paul yourself, if you will. The house is Bromswold, at the south end of Aysthorpe.'

He flushed slightly. 'I shall be glad to.'

'And there is your fee – '

'Perhaps when I call. If Friday would be convenient?'

She nodded; and after a word or two to Paul about the arm he was gone, edging his way out hastily. The authority he showed when called upon professionally seemed totally to desert him, and leave only unease.

When at last, after Rebecca had thanked and pressed some money on the innkeeper for his trouble, she and Paul walked down the Long Causeway to the Swan, they found the coach already in and Peter Walsoken waiting for them under the inn's leaded shell-hood. He was a tall young man with the slight stoop of asthma and short hair a shade redder than his twin sister's. Amongst the explanations, and Paul's own account of his ordeal, there was little time for greetings. Only when they were jogging slowly out of the city, passing the gallows on the turnpike road north, did Peter say: 'I have been remiss in writing of late, but I expected you would be too busy to reply. So now, tell me all the news since you came here.'

'Well, where to start?' Rebecca said. 'We have met our neighbours, I have assisted at an accouchement, Nancy slipped on the back stairs . . .' And I fell in love? She pushed the thought down. There must be no more of that.

Peter was looking at her quizzically.

'I'm exaggerating, of course. I just happened to be there at the time. No, we have been very quiet . . .'

2

Christmas Eve was the coldest day so far, and there was ice in the font at Aysthorpe church where Charles Joseph Hardwick was christened at eleven o'clock. The Rev. Mr Medhurst, Rector of Aysthorpe-with-Ufford, who was getting up in years and in poor health, blew on his fingers and went through the service at a canter so that he could get back to the parsonage and play at piquet with his sister by a warm fire.

The little church, which dated in parts to the thirteenth century, was damp and draughty, and the breath from the small congregation hung like a veil of mist in the air. The godparents were Julia and Henry Milton, and Francis Sedgmoor, Milton's partner and a family friend, who was here with his wife Kate. The Amorys from Barnack were here, and the Walsokens: Joshua and his wife, delicate and leaning on his arm, Sarah very solemn, Rebecca and Peter, both tall and copper-haired. Paul had stayed home. And in the Hardwick pew Grandmother Peach gripping her stick, and old Horace next to her, standing straight as a man of forty, his lean face alert and critical. And next to him, Luke Taplin – Luke Hardwick as he must learn to call himself – his dark curling hair combed and tied, in a new blue double-breasted frock coat and striped waistcoat.

And Luke thought: this is my family. This, now, is my world.

By rights he should, he knew, have been transported with joy to discover that his parentage, so long unknown and disregarded, linked him with one of the oldest and most respected families in the district: and placed him as heir presumptive to one of the richest men in Stamford. Instead he felt only numbness: it was as if his emotions had received a blow such as, if not to kill them, then to render them unconscious.

He looked at them, the parents of the baby, the godparents, and even the gaunt old man beside him who was his father. They were strangers to him, utter strangers. And She was here too, the girl whom he had met – years ago it seemed – in Stamford. That had been a pleasant sort of dream at the time, fitful and in all probability doomed to come to nothing. This was reality – she was here, as befitted her, friend and neighbour of the Hardwicks of Morholm. His family. His world. As strange to him as if it were one of the new lands at the other side of the world: but as exciting also.

He and Rebecca caught each other's eye once across the church. She looked away.

At first he had felt he would have given it all to have old Sam alive again. Young, vigorous, and unattached, Luke for all the rough variety of his life had had no dealings with death. It had been a horribly vivid moment when the young doctor who had ridden out to the fen with him from Stamford had gently closed Sam's eyes. Sam had seemed as enduring an element as the water that welled over the dykes or the sun that dragged the day over the sharp rim of the horizon. Then the next morning had come the young doctor again, bringing with him a thin old man, exhausted from his ride, with tears on his sallow cheeks, who had taken his hand and said simply, 'Luke.'

He had lost a sort of father and gained one of another sort. It might have been a sick kind of joke.

The first disbelief was soon over: the old man knew all the details of the school to which he had been sent, the instructions as to his future. Beyond that, of course, nothing: but there could be no doubt.

But that *this* should be the man . . . If he had ever speculated, it had been to assume it was some tradesman clinging on to respectability, some farmer who had tumbled his serving-maid. He knew a fellow on the fen whose long-lost father had suddenly turned up: a miller who had the pox and was always drunk: he had wanted nothing to do with him.

But this man . . . The name of the Hardwicks was known to everyone in this country. And now it was his. The old man wanted it to be his.

When he came that day to the fen cottage he wanted Luke to come home with him there and then, and had seemed hurt when he refused.

'I want to give old Sam a proper burying. He's got nobody but me.'

'That can all be seen to,' Horace had said.

'Well, I can see to it myself. Besides . . .'

'Yes?'

Grief and shock blew up a wind of hostility in Luke. 'Why should I come wi' you? What's the use? This is my life out here, where I belong to be, where I chose to be. I'm content here. What do you mean coming round after all these years, calling me son and plaguin' me and – and telling me what I've to do?' He struck his fist against the wall, in his bewilderment wishing the whole world to the devil.

The old man watched him solemnly. 'I wish to make amends, Luke. Oh, late, very late, I know. But not too late. Will you – will you not give me leave to offer now what should have been yours these twenty years and more?'

'I – I don't understand it . . .' Luke had stared at his father. 'It's done now. You've seen me, and I've seen you. I don't bear no ill will. And I don't want no help. Leave me be here, damn you . . .'

All the certainties of his life had given way like rotten planks beneath him. All he could do was tramp across country, following the silver trail of mist on the dykes, through that sleepless night, struggling to come to terms with the past and the future.

The next day Sam had been buried in the churchyard at Ramsey St Mary's. Horace rode out again, and it was clearly a strain for the old man: but he stood beside Luke at the grave, flinching at the bleak wind that scoured across the fen. Luke had looked at him there, pale and shivering but determined, and had suddenly seen his father's courage. He respected courage: and his heart acknowledged that here was a claim that could not be denied on either side. Sam was gone, and this was his future: and he would embrace it.

The fen cottage had been rented by Sam, and though the landlord might have been willing to come to some accommodation with Luke, Horace insisted he come to live with him in Stamford: and Luke had made up his mind now. The furniture, the poultry, his rods and nets and snares, all were put up for sale. His old horse Royce, at Luke's insistence, found a home in Horace's stable.

'Your old life is over,' Horace said. 'Your new one is beginning.'

So he found himself in the airless townhouse with the office in the back and the view acros the busy Welland, dressed in new-bought clothes, feeling not clumsy but somehow too young and too large for the place, trying to get used to the footmen who stalked softly about the rooms and called him sir and asked if there were anything he required. His father talked almost constantly, with a nervous inconsequentiality. Luke did not know what to say to him: or rather, he did not know how to say it, and at last settled for 'Why?'

This was at dinner, and Luke laid down his knife and fork and looked his father in the eye. 'Why now?'

'It is not simply a case of *now*,' Horace said with some testiness. 'D'you not think – d'you not realise you have been in and out of my thoughts ever since you were born? I have that much conscience.' He wiped his lips fastidiously, and went on in an altered voice: 'I had a great-nephew of mine here to stay a while, when he was ill. Having him about the house . . . it invigorated me, for I have lived always alone. And troubled me. It made me think of the child I had wronged. Yes, wronged. I had made sure you would not want until you were of an age to fend for yourself, but no more.' He cooled his long fingers on his wine-glass, staring before him. 'And I am old, Luke. I am active and am not ready for the winding-sheet yet, but I know my span cannot be much longer. You cannot be expected to understand this, but with age comes a wish to – to settle accounts. I am not a praying man. There has always seemed too much to be done in this world to trouble myself about the next. But one comes to review one's life, and to wish to set things right. I think – I hope – that that is what I am doing. But I would be a fool if I did not realise that you must greatly resent your wrong, knowing at last what you have been denied.'

'Tisn't that at all. I've had a good life. I'd not change a minute. But . . .'

'But I am not what you expected, eh?' Horace smiled slightly, his face old and shrewd. 'Perhaps you thought yourself the product of some seedy liaison? Well, perhaps you were. I have not told you of your mother: it matters little, as she is dead some years since, and besides – '

'Whoever she was,' said Luke, an edge coming into his voice, 'if you're about to speak ill of her, I'd better prefer not to hear it.'

'Ill?' said Horace with a genuine surprise. 'No, not ill – unless to say she did not want you, and as for that neither did I. But that was merely the circumstance of your birth.' He pushed his plate away and passed the decanter to Luke. Outside there was a clop of hoofs and the rumble of a cart across the cobbles. 'She was a beautiful woman of past thirty. At least I thought her beautiful, though some felt she was haughty, intimidating. She was a widow then, of a rich husband. She had a taste for living, and the money to fulfil it. Men flocked round her. She came from London to Stamford one summer to stay with friends. You must bear in mind, I was then a man of almost fifty: prosperous, hale, well-respected, mixing with the best society of the town: but solitary and settled and neither expecting nor wanting to be anything else. From an early age I had rejected the emotions – rejected love and passion, as destructive things – and perhaps it may be said, chosen wealth and gain instead.' His eyes were on Luke. 'You cannot have lived the life of a monk, Luke. I hope you can understand what happened, the way – the way reason, prudence, all the foundations on which I had built my life turned to quicksand.'

'I understand.'

'I wonder if you do . . . It was all the more strange and alarming when I considered who I was. I was no catch – not that she needed one. But dry anyway, dry and dull, and I had never been handsome. The strangest thing is I think she despised men. She needed them, and they came to her like moths to a candle: but even at the time, captivated as I was, I felt deep inside that she despised them: and that she despised me.' He sighed. 'How easy everything is in hindsight! To be brief, this episode – an isolated episode for me, and I do not mean disparagement when I say it was not so for her – ended in the way you expect. She was outraged. That such a thing should happen to her, tying her down, restricting her gay brilliant life, bringing shame and disgrace . . . She wanted to return to London in the winter. What was she to do?'

The old man's tone had become almost unemotional now, as if relating a story in which he played no part.

'My own reaction was mixed. But I proposed that we should marry: not even sure that that was what I wanted, but I proposed it. She laughed bitterly at that. Marry me? She had had enough of that the first time. She felt nothing for me, she said. I was nothing but sport for her. She meant it, too. I remember her eyes, very dark eyes like your own, shining with pride and contempt.

'She was ready to go to one of the old hags who engage to bring on abortions: but I knew such things are more likely to kill than cure, and though I now had but little influence over her, I persuaded her out of it. I told her I would provide for the child: she need never have any communication with it or me after it was born. Have no fear of that, she said. So, she went to a discreet friend out in Lincolnshire, and retired there for the birth. Oh, Luke, do not be hurt when I say she returned to London as soon as it was over. She did not want you, only insofar as she did not want me, did not want anything to come between her and the breathless life she led. I never saw or heard of her again, until I read of her death in a London newspaper. She had lived as she wanted right to the end.' He passed his hand over his eyes, and Luke saw that it trembled a little. 'As for you, you were put out to nurse with a cottager family. I intended – I fully intended – that as soon as you were weaned, you should come here to live as my son, and be damned to the eyes of society. And so we come to my real shame. I prospered still, I was elected burgess of the town, my interests extended: and always I put off the reckoning with you. I was a coward. The longer I put it off, the more impossible it seemed that I should own you. And so you were placed at a school. I was, though I did not admit it to myself, washing my hands of you. I thought, let him have this start, and make his own way in the world as I did.'

'And weren't you disappointed when you found how I had turned out?' Luke said, moved but unable to keep a trace of bitterness out of his voice.

'I had deceived myself there too . . . thinking I had provided adequately for you. When I knew quite well that in this world, without family, without connections, you would be hard put to it. But I was trying to erase you from my mind altogether. A dangerous proceeding. If I had not found you at last . . . I think I would have gone mad.'

. . . And now here Luke stood in Aysthorpe church with his father, their relationship publicly proclaimed for the first time. The mother of the child, Mary Hardwick, caught his eye and gave him an uncertain smile. Trying to be encouraging, no doubt, and he was grateful. But he came here, if a little defensive, without fear. The Hardwicks were gentry, of course; small enough gentry nowadays, and according to Horace fallen on hard times: but they sprang from several hundred years of breeding and ease. Fenmen, however, were known for their lack of respect for authority. He would take them as he found them, and they could do the same or go to hell: he wasn't going to bow and scrape to anybody.

But he looked forward to the dinner at the great house after the ceremony with a certain tingling of nerves: because She would be there, the girl who, before, had seemed so far out of his reach.

Dinner at Morholm was early, for with the risk of frost or fog the guests, except for Horace and Luke and the Miltons who were to stay the night, would need to get home before full dark.

George and Mary had felt the occasion justified making an exception to the general rule of frugality. It was many years since sixteen people had sat at the long table in the draughty dining-room: and if anyone noticed that there were more vegetables than meat in the fowl pies, or that there was a surplus of fat pork and an insufficiency of beef, they did not complain. Mary privately dreaded what the kitchen must look like.

Julia and Henry Milton, as family, and the Sedgmoors as near enough had been told all about Luke: but for the rest there was no explanation of his presence beyond the fact that he was Horace Hardwick's son, and George and Mary hoped none would be needed. The Walsokens were strangers here anyway, and old Humphrey Amory was too preoccupied with his wife to take much notice of anything else. He lived at Leam House, a handsome square mansion set in a landscaped garden two miles to the west: and up until last year the neighbourhood had seldom seen anything of him, for he lived under the rule of a censorious and fearsome wife. Then she had died, and within three months he had taken a new wife twenty years his junior.

Humphrey Amory was a florid, garrulous man in his mid-forties. He had had a trepanning operation when young after cracking his skull in a fall from his horse. He was very proud of this, and was more than willing to whip off his wig and rap on his head with his knuckles to prove it, though some said it had sent him a little mad. The new Mrs Amory, Esther, had a violet satin Levite gown, small dainty hands and feet, and a pretty head that was obviously, George thought, well screwed on. Rebecca was seated next to Mr Amory – she had had a moment of panic at the thought that she might be placed next to Luke – and she noticed that he held his young wife's hand so much she could hardly get her food to her mouth.

Talk at the table presently turned to the war.

'They say that when the news of this defeat at Saratoga first arrived, Germain tried to deny it in the Commons,' Francis Sedgmoor said.

'The whole thing is a disgrace,' said Horace. 'But I knew it would happen. Fox has called for a debate on the state of the nation, and not before time.'

'Fox?' said Mr Amory. The word roused him from his uxorious attentions. 'What right has that man, that reprobate, to set himself up as the guardian of the country's morals? He is forever hock-deep in debt. They say he will lose five thousand pounds in a week at the gaming tables and think nothing of it.'

'A bad example,' said George dryly. 'But is not the same true of the King, who has confessed himself £600,000 in debt?'

Horace snorted. 'And what's more North, like a good lackey, engages to pay it off for him.'

'The probity of the sovereign can never be at issue,' Mr Amory said hotly.

'Nor ever will be, with a government who are his toadies,' said Horace. Age had not softened his combative nature.

96

'I wonder,' said Joshua Walsoken, who all the time had explored the company with his watchful colourless eyes as if committing each face to memory, 'can one place any confidence in these reports? One often has only the word of the newspapers, whether local or from London.'

'Do you have no faith in the Press, Mr Walsoken?' George said.

'I would not allow a newspaper in my house,' he said. 'Certainly not for my wife and daughters to see. It appears to me they are mere mischievous sheets, tricked out with all manner of venality and sensation, and calculated to appeal to the prejudices of the ignorant multitude.'

The second course was being placed on the table by Mrs Binnismoor: pork, roast duck with sweet sauce and peas, giblets, boiled rabbits with parsnips. George coughed nervously.

'I am afraid, sir, you may not know you have a couple of interested parties at the table,' Julia Milton said, indicating Sedgmoor and her husband.

Walsoken turned his unblinking gaze on Milton. 'Are you a proprietor of a newspaper, sir?'

'Not as yet,' Milton said. 'But my partner and I hope to be shortly.'

'God and the ignorant multitude willing,' Sedgmoor said lightly, to a general laugh.

'I would agree with you to a certain extent, sir,' said Milton. 'A newspaper, improperly directed, may be scurrilous and irresponsible. But we can only engage to say that ours will not be so. Much of its content will of course be local, but the provincial Press is also there to convey the news of the capital. And is it not the case, that such things as misrepresentation and prejudice arise out of the restrictions Parliament itself places on the reporting of its business?'

'If one believes that the high transactions of state are to be accountable to every ale-house agitator who can spell out the print,' said Mr Walsoken crisply. 'Are you not afraid, sir, that by disseminating such matters you will raise up a presumptuous and subversive spirit in those who cannot fully comprehend them?'

'Well, I don't know about that.' Luke was speaking for the first time. He was at the other end of the table and there was a general hush to hear him. 'For my part, what I've heard of the goings-on there makes me think it's a powerful lot of talk and not much else, and they're welcome to it. But tis only right that folk be given the chance of knowing what they're up to. If it's made out to be all a great secret they'll suspicion something's wrong. And if newspapers are the only way of doing it, then – then the more the better.'

'Hear, hear,' said Sedgmoor.

'But this rapscallion Fox, like that fellow Wilkes, simply uses it to his own ends,' said Mr Amory, his fingers playing an arpeggio along his wife's white arm. 'Heart, will you take a little more pork?'

'Is Fox a rapscallion?' said George. 'I don't know. Burke is with him against the war, and surely no one could accuse Burke of personal immorality.'

'I believe Fox alone can be the nation's saviour,' said Horace. 'The shortcomings of his private life are beside the point. We are none of us free of those.'

'I do not entirely blame him,' Mr Walsoken said. 'It is well known that the sins of luxuriousness and improvidence were instilled in him at an early age by a too lenient father. Fox has been quite simply spoilt: and that is what unfits him for office. Surely, sir, as a father, you yourself have had a care to ensure that your son's character is formed, for nothing so burdens a man in taking his place in the world, as retaining bad habits that were never corrected in his youth? It is a duty and a kindness to do so.'

Luke's face had darkened: but Horace was not at all discomposed. 'Indeed, sir,' he said. 'But my son and I have for long been – estranged: and I have not had the bringing up of him. I know, however, that he has not been spoilt.'

'Well, this is lively talk, but hardly seasonal,' said George. He looked across at Rebecca. 'Miss Rebecca, may I ask if you are musical?'

'I used to pick out some simple exercises on the spinet,' she said, smiling, 'but our spaniel used to howl so dismally when he heard me that I left off.'

'The reason I ask is we usually have the choir from Aysthorpe Church call on Christmas Eve to sing carols, and if you were musical I should advise you to stop your ears. They make a noise like Charles Joseph when he wants to be fed.'

'I believe they have never been the same since Gaffer Pode decided he was a tenor instead of a bass,' said Mary.

Rebecca laughed: but her father said: 'Is there no one in the district who teaches the choir, Mrs Hardwick?'

'Er – I believe Parson Medhurst's sister used to – but she is old and housebound now.'

Mr Walsoken nodded. 'My daughter Sarah performed just such a function at the church of St Giles in Norwich, did you not child? I feel sure she would be glad to do so here.'

'It will be quite a task, Miss Walsoken, but I'm sure Medhurst would be delighted if you were to undertake it,' George said.

Sarah, half pleased and half frightened at being singled out thus, fluttered something in reply and nearly choked.

Rebecca thought: how nice Mr and Mrs Hardwick are. I don't think they quite know what to make of father. He is so very serious. I suspect Mrs Amory is getting tired of her husband's attentiveness. Imagine being called 'Heart's delight' and 'angel mine' all day. There must have been some fine parties in this room in the old days. Dear God, he is sitting over there and smiling and talking as if everything were normal . . . God *damn* him!

Normally she had a very healthy appetite, but she could eat hardly a thing. The astonishment, the shock, of seeing Luke at the church, and of the brief introduction from George – 'Miss Rebecca, my great-uncle Horace Hardwick. And this is Mr Luke Hardwick, his son' – were still with her. Whatever was going on – and in spite of the fine clothes he did not seem entirely at ease here – it was still pretty clear she had been made a fool of. Luke Taplin – now you've met your first true fenman – I've sold me ten brace of fowl today . . . Had he been lying to her, playing some foolish joke? And not turning up to meet her that day in Stamford – was that part of the joke too? She didn't care how handsome he looked . . . the most frightening blazing anger was in her. She was glad there were so many people here to separate them. Yet she also wanted to face him, wanted to demand an explanation, to gain some revenge for the weeks of hope and disappointment.

Mr Amory was still on Charles James Fox.

'. . . And they say he had the effrontery to propose a toast to the rebel general Washington, in the house of an archbishop! He was ordered out, and quite right too. I would have had him horse-whipped. Nay, I'd have done it myself!'

'My dear,' said his wife, 'you halloo after this Fox as if he were a real one with brush and all! Spare us, please.'

'Forgive me, sweet. May I rot before I bore you again.' He gave a sudden short bark of laughter like the report of a gun. 'But she's a wit. Like a real fox . . . God damn me, she's a wit! Ain't she, Miss Rebecca?'

Mary said: 'Mrs Walsoken, this is sad news I hear about young Paul.'

'Oh, ma'am, I declare I near fainted away when I saw him yesterday,' said Mrs Walsoken. She was a small woman whose figure had been wasted rather than coarsened by much childbearing: the prettiness of her features had become so delicate and transparent she might have been made of eggshell. 'He is bearing up very brave: but he must remain quiet and still and he finds it tedious.'

'He was most fortunate in that a physician of some skill was on hand in Peterborough to attend him,' Mr Walsoken said. 'Rebecca, what was the name of the man again?'

'Kesteven,' Rebecca said. 'Christopher Kesteven. He told me he was come here to set up practice quite recent.'

'Is that the name of my protégé I hear?' said Horace, who had been talking to Julia, across the table.

'Your protégé, sir?' Mr Walsoken said.

'I exaggerate. But I discovered his talents in London. I meant to tell you of it, George. It was he who operated on James's eye. He is young, local-born, newly qualified; and I persuaded him to come here and begin his career.'

'I shall be glad to meet the young man when he calls,' Mr Walsoken said. 'Paul has praised him to the skies.'

'When I was young,' Grandmother Peach said, 'we used to have old Dr Tooke from Spalding. He used to prescribe urine for the palsy. Drank a pint of his own every day and swore it did him good.'

Luke grinned at her and said: 'And did he make tea in his chamber-pot?'

Mrs Peach grinned back with a show of salmon-coloured gums. 'Well, I don't know about that, young man. But I do know he lived to be ninety-one. Till the flying gout took him.'

The tail-end of Luke's smile rested on Rebecca for a moment. She examined her plate. Then the plum puddings were brought in, the apple and damson tartlets, mince pies, cream, oranges and nuts.

Horace was asking Milton about the projected newspaper. 'Will you become embroiled in Stamford politics like the *Mercury*?'

'We hope not. We aim for a broader approach. News from London can be simply culled from the London papers: it is a usual practice, but the effect is stale, and we hope to get despatches by the mail from contacts in London. Much of the paper will of course be public advertisements – notices of sale, auctions, prospectuses. Space will be at a premium, but we plan to include more learned and general articles after the manner of the *Universal Chronicle* or the *Gentleman's Magazine*.'

'It remains to be seen whether we are tempted into Prodigies and Phenomenons,' said Sedgmoor. 'Most small newspapers abound with mathematical pigs and those unusual women who give birth to litters of rabbits.'

'And we must arrange for copies to be taken out in the carriers' carts to all the villages: up towards Lincoln, down to Northampton, all across the fens,' said Milton. 'It will come out on Wednesdays, so as not to directly compete with the *Mercury*, which comes out on Fridays. It will of course be available at the inns and coffee-houses in Stamford and Peterborough, and at the shop.'

'Sedgmoor and Milton,' said Luke suddenly. 'I've been in there many a time. Well, when I could afford it.'

Milton looked expectantly at him.

'Cheap books of poetry I was usually after,' he went on. 'Oh, not all, for some of it is such milk-and-water stuff: but when I found some I liked I read till the pages fell abroad.'

'It can't have been Henry's!' Sedgmoor said with a laugh, in which Milton joined.

Luke looked startled at him. 'Do you write poetry?'

Milton smiled, discomfited. 'I used to, once,' he said. 'In London. It was simply hack-work for commission.'

'But tell me, Luke, what was some of the verse you enjoyed?' Julia said.

Luke glanced at the dark grave woman with the deep voice and smiled. He was not shy by nature and the wine had relaxed him. These folk were not so bad at all. 'Well, there's Goldsmith – "The Deserted Village" – I near enough got that by heart. But not much that's recent: tis all poor rattling stuff now. Shakespeare I read, of course: and Spenser, and the old sonnets: but what always pleased me best was the oldest ballads – Dowland's Ayres, or them that's passed by word of mouth and then written down, oft on plain broadsheets. There's no pretending about them, they speak always clear and fresh.'

Horace said with some approval: 'My son is fortunate in that the artificialities of modern taste have never had the opportunity of spoiling his native good sense.'

It was the first mention of Luke's background: and there was a barely perceptible silence at that end of the table before Julia said: 'Well, I think Henry is likely to be so busy with his newspaper that I may have to put a notice in it asking for his whereabouts.'

Rebecca, in spite of herself, was looking at Luke. He saw her and said across the table: 'Miss Rebecca, d'you – d'you have a favourite poet?'

With horrible pleasure she glanced away from him and said: 'You must pardon me, sir, I read for pleasure of reading, not to make a boast of it.'

Presently the ladies left the gentlemen to enjoy their port and smoke pipes and ease their breeches at the littered table. Some of the ladies visited the earth closet upstairs, about which Mary had had a brief panic this morning. It was unpleasant at best, and the whole household tended to use the privy that was outside by the stables and much healthier. It was so long since they had done any entertaining at Morholm the problem had quite slipped her mind. George was dismissive. 'Why, Julia will take no heed, nor Kate Sedgmoor: and I don't fancy the Walsokens are any better off at Bromswold. As for Esther Amory, she must take us as she finds us.' She had had some uneasiness too about providing a room upstairs for the ladies to tidy themselves in, for none of the spare bedrooms was very clean or light: but thankfully everyone seemed content as they were.

When she came back to the drawing-room after feeding Charles Joseph, and glancing in at the chaos in the kitchen, she found the seven women getting on well. Bridget had been in to light the candles, for it was past four o'clock. It was a front room and exposed to the east wind that was getting up with a soft moan off the fen, but a good fire had been lit here since morning. The candlelight tactfully made the best of the shabby furnishings, the faded carpet, the worn upholstery.

Kate Sedgmoor, the lively daughter of Thornton Wiley the banker, who had married Francis earlier this year, was asking Mrs Walsoken and Sarah about the shops in Norwich, and Julia, never one for small talk, was keeping Mrs Amory company in presenting a suitably attentive face to her Grandmother Peach's reminiscences.

Rebecca smiled when Mary came in, and joined her at the table where the tray with tea and coffee was set.

'I hope Charles Joseph is none the worse for his wetting this morning, Mrs Hardwick. I noticed he did not cry once.'

'Yes, he seems remarkable even-tempered already,' said Mary. 'In that regard at least he is not a true Hardwick!'

It was as good an opening as she was going to get, and Rebecca drew in a breath and mentally chose some words whilst Mary was handing out the tea and coffee. But when her hostess came back to the table she still hesitated.

'I – it's been a great pleasure meeting your family, Mrs Hardwick. Your husband's family I should say. I – '

'Mine also,' said Mary. 'George and I were cousins, Miss Walsoken – forgive me, Rebecca – though I was born at Wisbech, and we lived quite removed from the rest of the family. Of course you do not see them all here. Julia, George's sister, has of course married and lost the name – though only to a man who is our dearest friend. I have a brother, who I last heard was in King's Lynn: and there is George's brother James in London, and Aunt Catherine also, who married late in life. Old Daniel Hardwick died two years ago. And there is our cousin Kingsley, but where he is I don't know. That's our extent, I'm afraid. We have never been a prolific family.'

She passed Rebecca her tea.

'It's a great shame your brother Paul could not come today,' she went on. 'But I was glad to meet Peter. You had not told me about him. He looks very much like you – '

'Yes,' Rebecca said absently. She looked down at the teacup in her hand, unaware that she had taken it. 'Mrs Hardwick, I have met – I have met Mr Horace's son before.'

'Yes?' Mary's voice was light, as she searched for an answer, or a question.

Rebecca put down her cup, suddenly despairing. 'I have known you scarce a month, Mrs Hardwick, and you and your husband have shown nothing but the greatest kindness to me. And so I am using this as an excuse to poke and pry . . .' She stood up straight, as she did when ashamed of herself, and unconsciously looking tall as a man as she did so. 'And I wish you would give me a withering glance to stop my mouth.'

'In that month you have shown yourself a good friend to us, too,'

Mary said. 'And as I am to call you Rebecca please call me Mary.' She glanced at the others, spoke softly. 'It is our first meeting with Luke. He is Uncle Horace's natural son. Horace has never acknowledged him till now. But now he wishes to be a proper father to him, and to make him his heir and make no secret of his existence.'

Rebecca stared. Her mouth had gone dry. 'And – and has he never – never known his father?'

'No. He has been brought up quite different, as you may perhaps tell. For our part we are glad to see him, and want to make him feel comfortable, though it has been a surprise to us, and must have been a great shock to him.' Mary looked closely at Rebecca, whose face had drained of colour. 'You said – you said you had met . . . ?'

Rebecca licked her lips, trying to smile. 'In – in a very different situation. But I suppose that would explain it . . .'

'I think I shall like him,' said Mary. 'He is not quite at ease yet, but who would be? And what do the circumstances of his birth matter – the important thing, and much the best, is that father and son are reunited, however unfortunate their beginning. Though no doubt there will be plenty of folk ready to point the finger.'

'Yes . . . oh, yes . . .'

3

'Have you seen much of the county of Norfolk, Mr Hardwick?' Joshua Walsoken asked. Mr Amory passed him the port, and he poured a small measure and passed it on.

'The only part I know is around Lynn, which is at the western edge,' George said, trying to get his clay pipe lit.

Walsoken nodded. Whilst Mr Amory had taken off his powdered wig and even old Horace had settled back and stretched out his long thin legs, there was no relaxation of Walsoken's manner. 'In the body of the county there are many estates which by their running are of great interest to those with an interest in husbandry, such as yourself,' he said. 'I have visited several, notably that of Mr Curtis of Sommerfield. Some two and a half thousand acres. A comparable estate to Morholm?'

'Dear me, no. Well, once upon a time it was. It is not so much now. But go on.'

'The farming proceeds on scientific and experimental principles. The rational division of holdings, principally by enclosure, the use of rotation and various unconventional crops, turnips for example, the practice of marling the soil – all these are gone into most thoroughly and minutely. And good drainage of course, which is a most pressing problem in these parts.'

'My father introduced turnips, and we have had some success. But as for the rest, we are horribly old-fashioned.'

'It is a question on which I have had much thought, since becoming a landowner in my small way. I have two modest holdings to the north which I thought to combine in one farm after the Norfolk fashion. And install a tenant on a long lease who is competent to operate on the new methods. I am no friend to innovation normally, but in this matter I feel the spirit of commerce is the kind of injection that is vitally needed.'

George gave up on his pipe and accepted the port again. 'But I assure you, sir, that any suggestions that may enable the likes of me to – to get out of debt, in short – are very welcome.'

Walsoken knitted his formidable brows. 'This is distressing to hear. I hope, Mr Hardwick, I have not encroached upon – that in talking thus I have not been the goad of painful sensations.'

George, who had enjoyed the day, was not in the least put out, though he was a little amused by his neighbour's punctiliousness. 'You have encroached upon nothing that is not common knowledge. We have had two years of bad harvests and flooding. There can be no high rents where there is no money. In addition, long-standing debts were incurred when the estate was – temporarily administered by my brother, who was even more improvident than myself. We cling on and hope for better times.'

'Such close neighbours as we are, I feel we should live in a spirit of co-operation. Our prosperity, the prosperity of the parish, is in a way common cause.'

'I'm glad you think so,' George said. 'I should not wish, however, for you to take a share in our misfortunes.'

'No,' said Walsoken. 'But if there is any way in which I may help you out of them . . . This is of course a social gathering. But we must talk of it again. I believe there are always opportunities for the enterprising mind. Here especially. I have heard for instance of so much land on the fen, potentially enormous rich, being sold cheap for want of drainage. Land left to a few fishers that if properly drained would yield a profit of tenfold.'

'True enough,' said George. 'I have known many farmers make

great fortunes thus. But our fens have always been notoriously unpredictable, and those few fishers and fowlers can be exceeding difficult to deal with, especially when their livelihood is at stake.'

Walsoken lowered his eyelids, which gave his eyes a hooded appearance. 'They should be told what is good for them.'

'I should be glad to see you try, sir,' put in Luke from the other end of the table. 'Folk out there take a special dislike to being told what's good for 'em.'

Walsoken glanced at the young man without favour. 'The ignorant and ungodly always do,' he said quietly. 'Our Lord Jesus found it so, and I have also.'

'Well, I'm sure He would be gratified to know you agree with him,' said Luke.

George pushed back his chair rather noisily and rose. 'I think we are neglecting the ladies,' he said. 'Shall we rejoin them?'

The carol singers had been waylaid at the Seven Stars and would be late. Henry Milton requested that Mary play, so she sat at the spinet and gave them two old Christmas songs, 'The Virgin Unspotted' and 'Softly The Night' and then a piece by Scarlatti. It had not been a big meal by the standards of the age but everyone was well filled and happy to sit back and listen in the candlelight. Humphrey Amory's plump face wore a foolish tipsy smile and he softly beat time to the music on his wife's knee.

'We are making you do all the work, my love,' George said when she had finished. 'But do not ask me to sing. Our guests would never accept our hospitality again!'

Mary saw Luke moisten his lips as if to say something and taking a chance she said: 'Cousin Luke, perhaps you will be kinder than my husband and help me out.'

He had not been called cousin before, and it gave him confidence. 'Well, I've only ever sung to please myself, but – ' He glanced around, and his eyes seemed at once to light on Rebecca and to avoid her. 'Aye, I'll sing. If so be as you could find the tune, cousin.'

He came and stood by her at the spinet. ''Tis a daft little thing, but I think the air is well-known.' He hummed a few bars, and Mary smiled and nodded and began to play.

Luke had a clear tenor voice: he was shaky at first, but he grew more confident. With feelings incoherently mixed Rebecca watched and listened. Strangely he reminded her more now of the first time she had seen him in the Stamford street: tall, broad-shouldered in his fine coat, his black hair falling across one brow . . . And he was looking straight at her. As he sang he moved closer to where she was sitting. His eyes did not leave her face. She stared into her lap, burning, aware of her father watching the two of them.

'Now the winter is gone and the summer is come,
And the meadows look pleasant and gay;
I met a young damsel, so sweetly sang she,
And her cheeks like the blossoms of may.

I says "Fair maiden, how came you here,
In the meadows this morning so soon?"
The maid she replied, "For to gather some may
For the trees they are all in full bloom."

I says "Fair maiden, shall I go wi' you
To the meadows to gather some may?"
Oh the maid she replied "Oh I must be excused
For I'm feared you will lead me astray."

Then I took this fair maid by her lily-white hand
On the green mossy banks we sat down
And I placed a kiss on her sweet rosy lips
And the small birds were singin' all round.

When we arose from the green mossy banks
To the meadows we wandered away;
I placed my love on a primrosy bank
And I plucked her a handful of may.'

He smiled as they applauded, and made a bow with a tinge of mockery.

'Such a sweet old song,' Kate Sedgmoor said. 'It is very foolish of me, but those airs always make me want to weep.'

'That's the stuff to hear,' said Grandmother Peach, who had taken a shine to Luke. 'None of your fancy Frenchie modern nonsense.'

'And well sung, sir,' said Francis Sedgmoor. 'I am heartily glad we did not have George!'

Luke glanced at Mr Walsoken, who had not applauded. 'I hope my singing hasn't displeased you, sir,' he said.

Mr Walsoken shifted in his chair, his eyes lidded. 'Perhaps I am a little old-fashioned,' he said, 'and am not fond of songs so – secular at a holy season.'

'Not a season of joy?' said Luke.

'That has reminded me,' put in Humphrey Amory, not out of tact but because he could never stay silent for long, 'we never had a toast to our hosts' little younker. We can toast him with tea, eh? Charles Joseph. Long life to him.'

Amidst laughter, the toast was drunk, and then Mrs Binnismoor put her head round the door to say the carol singers had arrived. The party moved out of the drawing-room into the big hall to hear them. There was the sound of a viol being tipsily tuned. Luke put his hand on Rebecca's arm and held her back.

'Rebecca,' he said.

'Are you addressing me?' she said, realising they were now the last.

'Are you addressing me?' he mimicked her, and she shook off his arm. 'Leave me go,' she said.

For answer he closed the door quietly, leaving them alone in the room. Out in the hall the singing began.

'Miss Rebecca, then,' said Luke. 'Is that better? Or what have I to call you before you'll speak to me?'

'Perhaps I should call you Luke Taplin,' she said. 'Is that it? Or are we to make a rendezvous somewhere so you can tell me who you *really* are – and then you can stay away again and find it all *so* amusing!'

'When I met you I *was* Luke Taplin and nobody else!' he said. 'I didn't lie to you, say what you will! This is the first time – '

'I know that now,' she said, turning away from him. 'I know that. Mrs Hardwick told me. Your father's claimed you. You're Luke Hardwick. Very well. That has nothing to do with anything. If you'll let me go – '

'Yes, I'm Luke Hardwick, and I didn't know that when I met you! You accept that. So what more have I to say to – '

'What *more?*' A tide seemed to swell in her, uncontrollable. 'Perhaps something about why I came to meet you in Stamford that day and you weren't there . . .'

They were silent a moment: something new.

'Sam died that day,' Luke said quietly. 'The old 'un I lived with.

I couldn't come. I had to look to him. That's the only reason. If I – '

'Oh, what does it matter!' she cried, only aware that she must keep up her indignation.

'I reckon it does matter,' he said. 'I reckon it matters that you went to Stamford that day. To meet me. I reckon that matters, Rebecca.'

She looked at him coldly, and he said, shaking his head, 'Well, I must have been wrong. When I met you that time I thought, there's a girl wi' no nonsense about her. No airs. Speaks to you straight out, don't give a damn.' He shook his head again, his dark eyes glinting and faintly sardonic. 'Must have been mistook.'

'No doubt you were,' she said curtly. Her pride smarted like a wound. She was in an impossible position, and she had put herself in it. She moved to go past him, but he held her arm.

'Mebbe I was,' he said. 'But I reckon I had good grounds. I reckon I had good grounds for thinking you wanted to see me again like I did you. Else why should you go in to Stamford that day to meet me? Ye've said it yourself!'

She shook off his hand and flared at him. 'God damn your impudence!'

'Aye, and God rot it and cess on it too, if there's cursing to be done.' She saw then that he was angry too. 'Mebbe then you didn't think of me at all – except as some rough fenman who give you a hand. *Far* beneath you, m'lady. And now you don't like to mix with me. Reckon I ought to be sent out to eat with the servants, is that it?'

It was this savage portrayal of herself that stung her into daring. 'Very well,' she said, flinging her hair out of her eyes, 'it can make no difference now, so I'll tell you what I really thought. How after I saw you that time I couldn't stop thinking of you all week. How I wondered what you were doing, and whether I would see you again. And how I wondered what it would be like to be kissed by you, whether I should like it or hate it, if you must know. There. As I say, it makes no difference now, so if you will get out of my way – '

She pushed past him, and was pulled back. She felt his lips pressed on hers. She put up a hand to free herself, touched his hair, his shoulder. In the hall the first carol came to an end. She drew away and they stared at each other: it was he who looked suddenly uncertain, his face immobile and startled.

She wrenched open the door and hurried out into the hall to join the others.

The guests who were not staying left at six. The Walsokens were the last to go, and Joshua stopped in the big hall to examine the portraits under the stairs.

'They are not a distinguished collection, I fear,' George said. 'Most were painted by local journeymen. The best is the oldest, of Geoffrey St John Hardwick, who built Morholm in 1603.'

Mr Walsoken pursed his lips. 'I had thought the family of greater antiquity.'

'So it is,' said Horace from behind him. 'The land estate was inherited by Anne-Margaret Warboys and passed to Geoffrey St John on their marriage. The Hardwicks had been till then established in Huntingdonshire. A Hardwick fought with Henry VII at Bosworth. Before that another in orders was chaplain to Edward III's queen Philippa.'

Horace spoke informatively, unemphatically, but Rebecca was aware for a moment of a little grating of temperaments in the air. Then it was lost in the general goodbyes and good wishes for the season as they all went outside to where Will Binnismoor had brought the horses round. A bright slip of moon was riding among a few shavings of cloud and the lawn in front of the house was crisp with frost. As she went to her horse she found that Luke had come up close behind her: but he did not speak. He bent to make a step for her foot, and after a moment's hesitation she complied. A fleeting contact, and then she was on her horse and gathering the reins, suddenly breathless. His eyes held hers for a moment as he straightened.

There was little conversation amongst the family as they trotted the quarter of a mile through the village to Bromswold: but her brother Peter moved his horse up next to hers and kept beside her, as if instinctively aware of the turbulence within her.

4

At Bromswold Peter had the room next to Rebecca's, and before they went to bed he came in and they talked for a time, their first chance to do so alone.

He told her of his life in London at Gray's Inn, the long dry hours of study, the atmosphere of the courts and character of the law, part grave and learned, part crude and bawdy. After a while he looked at her quizzically.

'It seems longer than six months I have been away,' he said. 'You seem to have changed, sister.'

'In what way?'

'Perhaps changed is the wrong word. Grown perhaps.' Peter had a melodious voice, pitched lighter by asthma. 'You seem to have become a woman very quickly.'

'Do I?' She hoped he could not detect her flush. 'Well – sometimes I feel like a woman. Sometimes like a child of ten again. But there is something about coming here, the effect it has – something in the smell of the air.'

'I even wondered when I first saw you whether you were in love.'

Her heart seemed to give a double beat.

'But that can hardly be,' Peter went on. He smiled. 'It's a pity we are so far apart. Perhaps some time in the future you may come to stay with me in London.'

'Oh, I would dearly like that!'

'But who knows,' he said. 'Father was talking of the possibility of taking a house in town for a season, not this year but the next perhaps. He may wish to take you into society himself. He is still severe, I know: but I believe he has great hopes for you, sister.'

Rebecca smiled, and her mind strayed to her own hopes – unformed and dormant and barely acknowledged by herself – and wondered if they could ever have any place amongst the great ones of her father.

BOOK II
March 1778

# ONE

I

Mr Edward Wainwright had spent the last few days in a round of activity that would have taxed the strength of a younger man and wearied the spirits of a less ambitious one.

Monday, the twenty-third, had seen the burgess elections in Stamford, and as he was one of the twelve Capital Burgesses and the centre of the cell of opposition to Lord Burghley's control of the town he had a natural interest in the outcome. The next day was spent in the last arrangements for the launching of Wainwright's Bank, to open its doors on April 3, at 15 St John's Street, Stamford.

Wainwright's Bank: just that. No partners, sleeping or otherwise. His attorney Mr Quy had at the last moment meekly suggested bringing in a partner, perhaps someone with a – a more ancient name, just to lend a little weight . . . ? Mr Wainwright had coolly refused. What mattered was large capital reserves, and everyone knew he had those.

Yesterday he had made the journey by carriage to King's Lynn, there to take stock of his interests. His wife had her entertaining mood on and he preferred not to go back to Barn Hill until it was strictly necessary. Not that Jane's passion for social and fashionable life actively displeased him: it performed a valuable function in affirming their status in the town and the district. The higher aristocracy might be yet out of their sphere – but the gentry of the area, though some might affect to despise the Wainwrights, were always glad enough to be entertained at their expense. For himself he preferred being behind a desk to exchanging compliments with powdered boobies most of whom he could buy ten times over.

But his wife was different: and she was planning a ball to be held at the Assembly Rooms in St George's Square. It was to be a

'Patriotick Assembly': the news had come through that the French, as was expected of them, had joined with the rebel Americans and were at war with England. Quite how the assembly was to help the war effort was unclear, but it was a gesture and might, he hoped, be an opportunity to canvass custom for the bank.

So he went to the counting-house – the bank as it soon would be – and turned over some accounts in the plush back room where he intended to receive his more distinguished depositors. He was a man at peace with his world.

Until the door burst open again and Sir Hugh Woodhouse marched in.

'I suspicioned I should find you here!' his son-in-law boomed. 'I went up to Barn Hill, and Mina said no, he ain't here, he should be home soon, and I said to myself, I'll wager I know where he is. Your wretched little rabbit of a clerk was going to announce me, but I said no, let me surprise the old Hebrew in his den, and so I have!' Sir Hugh threw down his gold-trimmed tricorne hat and fawnskin gloves and paced up and down the room, bulky and high-coloured and looking as if he might knock over the frail elegant furniture.

'This is a great surprise,' Mr Wainwright said. 'I had thought you still in London.'

'Got back yesterday. Damned jolting ride we had of it. Very nearly overturned outside Huntingdon, and Lizzie as sick as a dog.'

'Dear me. I hope she's well now?'

Sir Hugh sank into the chair opposite, which creaked at his weight. 'What? Oh, she's right enough. So, this is where you will turn the screw on your debtors, eh? You had better put down some oil-cloth to mop up the blood.'

Mr Wainwright raised an eyebrow and went to the bureau and took out a bottle and glass. His son-in-law continued to gaze round him in an aimless way and his boot tapped restlessly, shedding mud on the carpet. He seemed in a decidedly odd mood.

'Your stay in London was not long,' Mr Wainwright said.

'Eh?' Sir Hugh gulped his wine. 'Oh, we had three months of it, but the town was deadly dull. Nothing but talk of politics and the war. Still, we have come back in good time for mother-in-law's assembly, eh?' He gave a mirthless chuckle, then leaned over and picked up a handbill from the desk. It was a printed circular advertising the bank. 'Cock's life, you'll not fail for want of advertisement,' he said, tossing it back again. 'Of course, you'll have my account. I dare say most folk will shift with you, rather than stick to old Wiley after you've left him in the lurch. Think you he'll go under, without your backing?'

'I have not left Thornton Wiley in the lurch,' Mr Wainwright said carefully. 'I was the chief partner, though my name wasn't publicised. The partnership is now dissolved, and Wiley's Bank will continue to trade. We shall be rivals in a way, but there is room for us both . . . Hugh, did you perhaps have some particular purpose in seeing me?'

Sir Hugh stared down at him. 'If you mean you're busy, I'll go.'

Mr Wainwright shook his head. 'I do not mean that at all. But if there is some matter you wish to speak of . . .'

Sir Hugh frowned at his empty glass. 'Well, it's Lizzie.'

'Her health?'

An unpleasant expression passed across the baronet's face. 'Her health is perfect, father-in-law. Unless one counts her temper, her – her disposition.'

'To what are you referring?'

Sir Hugh opened his mouth, stopped, swallowed. 'You want a grandchild, don't you, father-in-law? Same as I want an heir. Eh? Well, it's never going to happen, the way things are.'

'You say Elizabeth's health is perfect – and yet now – '

'The point is she just won't perform her duties. A wife's duties. Just refuses.'

Mr Wainwright's breathing was audible. 'I – Hugh, I hope I misunderstand you – '

'What's to misunderstand?' said Sir Hugh loudly. 'She's refused me her bed, and it ain't right.'

Mr Wainwright polished his spectacles. He was not a prudish man, but sometimes he found the manner of the upper class amongst whom he now moved offensive. 'You're telling me . . . you and Elizabeth's marriage – '

'Our marriage is all right enough,' said Sir Hugh. 'Leastways, we get along. She enjoys the life we lead, she enjoys society. But there's more to a marriage, father-in-law, there's duties involved – '

'I am acquainted with the marriage vows,' said Mr Wainwright harshly. He stared at Sir Hugh. 'So this is why you have had no – '

'Oh, no, no. She was never – eager. But that's because she's a lady, quite rightly,' he added hurriedly, seeing his father-in-law's frown. 'But it's only since – oh, a few months ago, she got *this* notion in her head. I thought, she's a bit high-strung, a London trip will do her the world of good, bring her round. And so it did. But not that way.'

Mr Wainwright stared at the ledger in front of him. It was a highly distasteful subject and he had half a mind to tell Sir Hugh to be gone and never speak of it again. And yet – and yet . . .

'Why do you come to me?' he said.

'You're her father. She's fond of you, respects you.' Sir Hugh puffed out his chest. 'I thought you might remind her of her duties.'

'I?'

'Well, why not? She's got no rights in this matter. We do well enough as a couple apart from this. It shouldn't be allowed to spoil things, jeopardise our marriage. Now I know you don't greatly love me, father-in-law, but I'm not without my uses, am I? Who was it introduced you to the Duke of Bedford? And now you're moving into banking, you'll be more in need of contacts than ever. In the fullness of time, who knows – I may be of use to you, in all sorts of ways.'

Mr Wainwright glanced at his son-in-law and then away again. The unsubtlety of Sir Hugh's arguments did not blunt their pertinence.

'What of your own conduct, Hugh?' he said.

Sir Hugh sniffed. 'Meaning?'

'I mean that this temporary – I trust it is temporary – difficulty between yourself and Elizabeth may be – in short, that certain rumours may have reached her ears.'

Sir Hugh's colour mounted, and in his effort to speak a little spray issued from his lips. 'I'm surprised at you, father-in-law, giving credit to scabby tales and gossip – and tittle-tattle cooked up by – '

'I did not say I gave any such credit. But rumours there have been.'

Sir Hugh stalked across the room and glared out of the window. Then he half-laughed. 'I don't pretend to be a saint, father-in-law. Moving in the circle I do, there's always flirtations, temptations. It means nothing. Leastways, it *should* mean nothing. But when a man's *wife* denies him what it is her *duty* to provide, then perhaps he – '

'Enough.' Mr Wainwright held up his hand. 'I wish to hear no more, Hugh. Not from prudery but because there is no point. And I honestly believe there is nothing I can do. It is up to you to heal this breach, such as it is. I do not believe my daughter to be an unreasonable creature, and I believe that, with the right attitude, you will not find her so. Women are strange in many ways, and it is up to men to adapt themselves to them. If there is any cooling between you, then you must restore the – the warmth by natural means. Not by invoking rights and duties.' It was strange for Mr Wainwright to find himself articulating this, but he became convinced of its rightness as he spoke.

Sir Hugh looked at him with disdain, and then swept up his hat and gloves. 'Ecod, father-in-law, so you are a man of sentiment beneath the money-bags. That's your advice, is it? Well, I'll think on it.' He put on his hat. 'In the meantime you go without a grandchild. As you like.'

2

There had been sunshine earlier but the March afternoon was grey and cold when Sir Hugh stepped out into St John's Street. He was glad of it, for as usual when he was angry he had grown extremely hot.

An insufferable meeting! It was bad enough having to talk about such a thing; and then to find himself hinting those little concessions he was prepared to make about involving himself in his father-in-law's wretched trade . . . And then to stand there and receive a lecture from that jumped-up little brewer with his burgher's morals! It was too much. It was all Elizabeth's fault for putting him in this monstrous position.

The worst thing was he still wanted her, badly.

London had seemed at first a success. She had blossomed, as she always did, responding to the fashionable life and coming out of herself. They had got on well, talking and laughing together. Even then he had bided his time, with what he thought commendable subtlety and patience, before making his overture. And again the refusal – the downright *refusal*. She had no right to do it. But she was so fearfully in earnest . . . They had come back to the country barely speaking to each other. Only his frustration could have driven him to seek help of her father.

He stumped across the road in the fading light to the George Inn, where he found a seat in the tap-room and drank morosely. The

Truth and Daylight coach had just got in from Cambridge and he scowled at the noise made by the chattering passengers as they passed through. He started with shrub but soon changed to neat brandy. He found a handbill on the table advertising Wainwright's Bank, and crumpled it and threw it on the fire. The old lickpenny's damned notices were everywhere.

He continued drinking, but ordered a plate of beef and caper sauce as well. He had no inclination to go back to Deenecote yet, cold and unwelcoming with the dust covers hardly off and Elizabeth colder still. He drank and nursed his grievances.

When he finally left the inn it was dark, the stars retiring behind smudges of cloud, and there were few people about in the streets. With seemingly casual steps he walked across to Water Street, a narrow thoroughfare of warehouses and quays and a few seedy cottages backing on the river where an unhealthy skein of mist lurked. A thread of self-justification ran through his mind. It was Elizabeth's fault: it was she who brought him to this. Denying him his rights. Marriage was ordained so that this sort of thing could be avoided. The gall of it. She had failed to give him a child, and now denied him the opportunity. If his attentions had become – well, pressing, who could blame him? And it was a wife's duty, if not to enjoy it, then to be gratified – no matter what . . .

He hunched his face in his velvet coat collar as he picked his way through the refuse. Wouldn't do to be recognised. He was a figure in the district and well known. Somewhere a rat scratched, and the cobbles were slimy underfoot.

He had been to this house once before, but that was years ago when he was fifteen and his father had given him some money and told him to go and get blooded: but clearly the same trade was carried on. The woman who admitted him to the damp ill-lit cottage was old, her pox scars insufficiently covered by white paint and patches. There were two girls, one the old woman's daughter, the other about sixteen and fresh-faced. No doubt some country girl who had got caught out and had taken the inevitable path down: he could hear a baby crying somewhere in the house. Unusual to keep it: often they dropped the brat down a handy well. He chose the daughter, who was slim and fair-haired. He stifled the thought that it was because she reminded him of Elizabeth.

The upstairs room was not very clean, but there were bunches of herbs hung everywhere to ward off diseases, and a scented pastille was burning on the mantelpiece. And he was not in the mood to be put off now. He clinked out some money on the rickety table by the bed while the girl mechanically undressed.

Sir Hugh's preliminary caresses were cursory in the extreme, but the girl was used to that, and when, breathing stertorously, he got up from the bed and began to take off his shirt she settled herself more comfortably and prepared to get it over with. He was a very hairy man with powerful shoulders and a thickening waist. At least he didn't stink like some of them did. She watched as he hung his fine cambric shirt with fussy care over a chairback. A lot of them, the rich ones, were like that.

When at last he turned back to her, face flushed and grey eyes heavy, her expert eye fell on the flap of his breeches and observed that he had gone small again. Well, that was common enough too. A few postures usually did the trick. In a listless way she stretched out her legs and ran her hands through her hair and over her breasts. It was all part of the routine.

What was completely unexpected, however, was what happened next, as Sir Hugh knelt up on the bed and with an expression of feverish enjoyment urinated all over her naked body.

3

Rebecca had called at Morholm this morning but had not stayed long: the twenty-fifth being Quarter Day, George was visiting his tenants, and Mary was busy and worried over Charles Joseph who was fretful with teething.

There was no sign of spring in the air and it was chilly, but she was reluctant to return home yet and set out for a ride across the common. Paul Walsoken had been sent to school at Charterhouse – Mr Walsoken had decided it would benefit him to be sent away, but he would be close to Peter in London and could see his elder brother for half-holidays and the like – and Rebecca missed the young liveliness he lent to the house.

She had never hunted: her distaste was personal and by no means a product of the intense religion of her father's household, for there were clergymen aplenty who enjoyed nothing better: but she sat a horse well, and though her father would have disapproved if she had told him, she went on long gallops across the common and heath towards Helpston, a semi-wilderness of thick grass and furze and tangled copses, empty but for a few sheep and the odd cottager's cow. Though the sight of her, skirt splashed with mud and long hair whipped back, might not suggest it, she found these rides helped her to think.

To think . . . To think sometimes – often – chiefly – always – of Luke Hardwick.

They had not met since the Christmas at Morholm. In a way she was glad of it. She had grown used to thinking of him as a Hardwick now, was reconciled to who he was. But that he should have kissed her as he did . . . She should have struck him: no squealing lady's slap but a good swinging blow. The arrogance of the man . . . Yet she had responded – she could not quite deny that to herself: and it quickened her resentment.

And she could not deny, also, that she was constantly thinking of him: whether in terms of anger, or – yes – wishfulness, her thoughts were of him. Often she wished she could drive him out of her head: or at least, impose some rationality on these rioting emotions.

But then there had never been anything rational in their short association. They had seemed drawn together – though even now, especially now, she could not admit it – by something quite beyond and outside the dainty limits of propriety and reason. It frightened her. The only hope seemed to be that she would not meet him again – that their paths would not cross . . . But that was the greyest, bleakest, most dissatisfying idea ever to go by the name of hope.

Cold sunlight was falling in pools across the furze and picking out a few primroses and crocuses and the damp heads of toadstools. A flock of wild geese arrowed across the sky north towards the Welland. Rebecca made out the figure of Deborah Gedney amongst the osier-holts by the stream and turned her horse towards her. Then she saw that a young man was with her, and Deborah was handing him something. They kissed, and the young man turned and struck out across the heath southward.

Deborah was smiling and shielding her eyes with her hand as Rebecca came up to her and dismounted.

'Tis a fine day.'

Rebecca greeted her uncertainly. Deborah had done the sewing for the curtains and done it well and been paid: so far so good. But she could still be defensive where she thought she was being patronised.

'You've just missed Mark,' she said.

'I thought it was him. Is he well?'

'Right enough. Seen the flowers about, have you? Spring'll not be slow now.' Deborah gathered her shawl about her, bare arms brown and strong. 'I'll be late to Castle Farm, I reckon.'

'Deborah, wait,' Rebecca said. 'Tell me. Did you give Mark money?'

She thought for a moment the girl would flare at her: but she sighed and nodded. 'I got a bit to spare – and he needs it.'

'I thought the Upwells – '

'Mebbe you didn't know. I thought to spare you.'

'Spare me what?'

Deborah looked uncomfortable. 'Seth Upwell leased most of his fields off o' Bromswold. And when your dad came, he made him pay back rent on the nail, and took the land back. He say he want to combine it in a big farm. Seth had to sell near all his stock, and now his milch cow's dead of the tympany, so they're scrattin' about to live . . .' She noticed Rebecca's expression. 'Oh, it was fair dealing, I suppose. All right by the law. But it seem hard, for tis Seth and Mark who've worked that land. He could've left 'em be while harvest.'

'I – didn't know.'

'I thought not. But it makes no odds between us, now does it? And Mark and me are still going to get wed so soon as we can. Now the evenings are getting lighter I can do lace-making again. Rebecca, I don't want there to be any trouble betwixt you and your dad.'

Rebecca swung herself into the saddle. 'No, no trouble,' she said, and smiled briefly before cantering away.

Joshua Walsoken had amassed a sizeable collection of books on husbandry and improvement. He had a standing order at Sedgmoor and Milton's for anything in this line: Norden's *Surveior's Dialogue*, Dugdale's *History of Embanking and Draining*, *The English Improver Improv'd*. Methodically he made notes in his precise hand, collating facts and opinions, as he methodically collated acres of land. Last week he had arranged to buy a hundred acres from Humphrey Amory, who was laying out money on his pretty wife with a free hand and was feeling the pinch: and this morning he was composing a letter to him, asking advice on the best way to go about stocking the grounds with game. He himself had no interest in shooting, but there were plenty of influential people who did and whose friendship he was eager to enlist.

He was not pleased when he was interrupted in his study by Nancy, timidly announcing that there was someone who wanted to see him, Newman by name.

'Newman? What manner of man is he?'

'If you please, sir, he'm a farmer I b'lave. He do say he ask the favour of a word.'

John Newman, tall and tow-headed and smiling his gentle smile, gave Mr Walsoken good day and waited patiently while he read over the letter he was writing.

'I don't believe I know you, Newman,' Walsoken said at last.

'No, sir. I farm over towards Helpston.'

'What business can you have with me?'

'It's – well, I'm taking the liberty of asking a favour of you, Mr Walsoken. Not on my behalf alone but on behalf of a group of us.'

Walsoken's face was a study of repose, not hostile, not friendly. John might not have been there.

''Tis about the old mill building, sir. Thass on your land – '

'I am aware of that.'

'Well, thass been a ruin for twenty year now, and we was wondering if we might use the stones. For building a meeting-house. We thought to take a spot on the common and – '

'A moment. A meeting-house for what? Who is this "we"?'

'Us as do follow the Wesleyan way, sir. There's me and Seth Upwell and Betty Pooley and the Gowts from Peakirk – '

'I think I must misunderstand. You are proposing – you are proposing to remove part of my property in order to set up a so-called meeting-house – '

'Not remove without your leave, sir,' John said. ''Tis a ruin and we thought you might be glad to be rid of – '

'To set up a *meeting-house*,' Walsoken went on, 'where your subversive sect may broadcast its doctrines of levelling and enthusiasm.' Anger made his face still paler rather than reddening it. 'As if it were not enough to attempt to suborn the authority of the church you ask me to connive at it! You make a great mistake there, fellow.'

'We go to church same as anyone,' said John composedly. 'We don't seek to overthrown no authority. All we seek is to live the whole of our lives in the joy of Christ, and it is to share that joy that we meet, no other reason. Mebbe if you could tell us the worth of the stones we could try and raise the money?'

Walsoken stared at the young farmer, blue-eyed and handsome, cleanly dressed in leather waistcoat and holland breeches. There was no actual insolence in his manner – but something that smacked of presumption to Walsoken, a lack of proper humility that was typical of the wretched sect he belonged to. 'You speak to *me* of Christianity – as if it were the possession of your canting Methodys,' he said, trying to control his voice. 'I can scarcely believe your effrontery. But I tell you you shall have neither stick nor stone from my land. And I shall do everything in my power to ensure that you never build your meeting-house in this parish.'

John was not an aggressive man, but he felt a sense of keen, and shared, enmity in the room. 'I'm sorry that's how you feel, sir,' he said. ''Twas a simple request, and I meant no harm. I'd heard you were a Christian man yourself.'

They stared at each other.

'. . . And I somehow doubted it then,' John said.

Walsoken pulled the bell with an unsteady hand and Nancy appeared.

'Have this fellow put out,' he said.

4

He found he was too overcharged after this encounter to continue with his letter to Humphrey Amory: so he ordered Nancy to bring him a mug of milk and went out to inspect the progress of repairs to the outhouses. The new byre was almost finished: soon they would be able to move in the young heifers he had bought at Peterborough market. He had been reading recently a report published at Norwich on the improved breeding of stock. In Norfolk he had seen animals of prodigious size that dwarfed the creatures one saw here grazing on the heath. So much could be done with a scientific approach.

He paid the labourers who were working on the outbuildings their day's wage of one and sixpence – he always paid good wages and expected the very best service in return – and when he went back into the house his temper was restored. He disliked becoming heated: it implied a loss of control, it was wasteful. He did not return to his study but sat in the parlour with his wife and she read out from the Bible. This, quite separate from the formal prayers which he himself read to the family before mealtimes and at night, was his chief relaxation.

On this scene Rebecca burst in. It was not a favourable interruption.

He listened to her story in silence. When she had finished he took out his snuffbox.

'Are you suggesting, child, that – I hardly know how to put this – that I have acted in some way unjustly?' he said. His voice was softer than ever.

'I think – you seem to have shown no consideration for the people amongst whom we are to live.'

'Rebecca!' her mother said plaintively.

'My dear, I must order you to be silent.' Mr Walsoken delicately held a pinch of snuff between his fingers. 'Quite apart from the fact, Rebecca, that you seem to be on terms of quite inappropriate intimacy with people of this station, you also, it appears, are ready to listen to their half-imagined grievances and to take their part against that of your father. Is this not the case? That you have rejected your first duty to me?'

'No, father.' Rebecca felt her breathing constricted. 'But I think you were too harsh. You have taken away most of the Upwells' livelihood, and – '

'The land is mine, to do with as I please. Their lease was expired and I chose not to renew it as I have other plans. Regrettably they have been long confirmed in habits of sloth and negligence while the administration of this property lapsed, and they must adapt them-selves to a more modest style of life. I may employ them as labourers on the land in time. I have acted within the law.'

Rebecca looked at her father. She was alarmed at the resentment and dislike that was rising in her.

'There is such a thing as goodwill, father,' she said. 'And behaving so severely with folk in hard times will not create it.'

Mrs Walsoken looked from her frightening daughter to her frightening husband with pretty, helpless eyes.

'As for the goodwill of these Methodists and – and subversives, I hardly think we need or desire that. I am disgusted that you, who have been brought up to follow strictly the precepts of the estab-lished church, should even associate with them. But the point is, daughter, that it is flying in the face of your filial duty to speak to me thus, to attempt to – to take sides against me on such a matter. My interests, my values must be yours.'

'No father. No. Not if they are shameful ones.'

Mr Walsoken drew in a long breath. 'You will take that back and apologise to me immediately.'

'Rebecca, consider!' said her mother.

'Why? I speak the truth. If you intend behaving in this ruthless fashion then I will not be identified with it, father or no father.' She was beyond restraint now, could feel the hairs rising at the back of her neck.

'You will take that back and apologise to me immediately,' said Mr Walsoken again.

'I will not! Am I to end up a frightened mouse like Sarah? Of course, if I were Jeremiah, or even Peter, the case would be quite different – '

'Do you see this?' her father exclaimed with sudden violence, grasping the wooden rod he kept by his chair.

'I see it,' she said. 'And no doubt I shall feel it. Perhaps, father, you should take it with you next time you go out into society, to show how extremely refined we are.'

A twitch passed across Joshua Walsoken's face – what in a less self-controlled man might have been a flinch. The ormolu clock on the mantel struck one into the silence.

'Go to your room, Rebecca,' he said. 'This conversation is at an end.'

The door slammed behind her.

Rebecca did not go to her room. She slipped out by the scullery door. In her haste she had left her horse tethered to a post in the yard, and now she remounted and dug in her heels.

Where she was going she did not know at first. She let the thunder of the hoofs drown out her thoughts as she hit the road out of Aysthorpe. Two little children playing in the mud scampered out of her path.

A strong wind was blowing, throwing her hair in a clinging net about her face, and swiftly shunting herds of clouds across the sky that unrolled giant shadows on the fields. She would ride to Peterborough, lose herself amongst busy strangers, even board a coach that would take her elsewhere, London, anywhere. The thought of returning to Bromswold seemed impossible.

A flock of sheep driven by a small boy blocked the lane ahead: she heard his high unbroken voice counting them across the ford with the strange old number system: 'Yan, tan, tethera, pethera, pimp, sethera . . . goo on – methera, hovera, covera, dik, yan a dik . . .' She turned her mount off the road and across the fields. Once she set him at an old stone wall and she felt a savage exhilaration as he lifted and sailed over. On the horizon to the east a line of windmills, sails turning in the endless effort of drainage, marked the edge of Borough Fen.

She joined the road again at the village of Dogsthorpe: by luck rather than judgement she had avoided the turnpike at Walton, for she suddenly realised she had not even a penny to pay the toll. As she pounded south out of the village with the spires of Peterborough cathedral etched in the distance she was aware of the sound of another horse behind her, catching her up, and she faintly caught the words 'Miss Walsoken!' on the wind.

With difficulty she reined in her foaming mount and turned to see Christopher Kesteven. He was very out of breath.

'Miss Walsoken . . . are you – are you all right?'

She patted her horse's neck, trying to calm both him and herself. 'Should I not be?'

'I thought . . . I saw you fly past at the crossroads and thought your horse must have run away with you.'

'He's done nothing I do not want him to do, Dr Kesteven.'

'Oh . . .' He took off his hat hastily. 'Are you – unescorted?'

She glanced around at the bare fields. 'It would appear so,' she said. She was no longer in a passion, but found herself venting the remnants of her anger on him. 'I took a fancy to ride alone just as I pleased, Dr Kesteven. That's all. Not so strange, surely? Do you never do such things?'

'My horse is only serviceable,' he said, 'and I have too much to do to ride for pleasure.'

'I am reproved,' she said.

He coloured, and she felt a pang of regret. He said: 'I'm sorry if I gave the impression – '

'You spoke very rightly,' she said. 'I am in a bad humour.'

'I – ' He hesitated, and his horse – in fact little more than a pony – tossed its head. 'I hope Paul continues well?'

'He has gone away to school.' Kesteven had called twice at Bromswold after Christmas to observe the progress of Paul's arm, and had been well received by her mother and father. 'But we have had one letter from him, and he seems happy enough, and says the arm gives him no trouble. I – hope I have not diverted you from an urgent visit, Dr Kesteven.'

He smiled a little constrainedly. 'I was just coming from one. Perhaps you have observed the gibbet, outside the city near the flour mill? Well, it was in use today. One of my less palatable tasks as gaol surgeon is to attend on hangings. When the victim is cut down I must examine him to pronounce life extinct.'

'Oh God . . . What had he done?'

'He was a cutpurse. Apparently he had a previous conviction, for which he was burnt in the hand. He would be a couple of years younger than yourself, Miss Walsoken. No sooner had I pronounced life extinct than the body was chained and hung up again, to be left there as an example. Certainly a sight to give anyone pause.' He fiddled with his crop, his face grey and vulnerable. 'Hanging does not leave a peaceful-looking corpse . . . But I distress you.'

Rebecca had a hand to her mouth. 'No . . . But what a dreadful duty for you . . .'

'There are few fees I would be so loath to take. The laws of the land are not my concern . . . but for one whose occupation is meant to be the preservation of life it is not a pretty business. Well, I have one more call to make at Paston. If that is on your way, may I . . . ?'

'In truth I am not going anywhere in particular,' she said. 'I will ride that way with you.'

The village of Paston was handsome, with its ancient church and rectory: but the cottage Kesteven was visiting was little more than a shack, built on the Ridings near the old almshouses and almost crumbling into the stream behind. He told her about the family he was attending and she volunteered to go in with him to help. After a hesitation he said firmly she was to come no further than the doorway.

Smallpox was the scourge of the day; and it had left its mark on this wretchedly poor household. One child of four lay on a straw bed beneath the window: he was covered in pustules but not feverish and would probably recover. Another child scarcely weaned lay covered with a cloth on the floor: it had died that morning.

Rebecca turned helplessly away from the scene at the door, Kesteven talking quietly to the distraught mother, and stared out across the bleak Ridings until he rejoined her.

'It was not a pleasant sight,' he said. He spat on the ground and wiped his mouth with his handkerchief. 'I had suspected the baby would die, though sometimes there is a sudden recovery.'

In a choked voice she said: 'I – I wish there was something one could *do*.'

He looked at her in some surprise. 'So do I,' he said. 'It is a common feeling in my profession. In this case, of course, there is.'

'Go on.'

'Well, in the first place they need better light, better food, more heat. Of course the disease strikes rich and poor alike, but the chances of recovery are never helped by such poverty. But inoculation, I believe, is the real answer.'

'I have heard of it, I think . . .'

'It is some years since the idea was first touted. It has gained a limited acceptance in London, where I became convinced of its efficacy. One introduces a mild form of the disease to the body by incision: it is quickly got over, and thereafter the child is in no danger. It is of course a preventive, not a cure. But I believe it would prevent tragedies like that – if what happens every day can so be called.'

They walked to their horses, which they had tethered to a tree.

She said: 'Is it difficult to do – dangerous?'

'It's very easy, and safe if done properly. But that family, for example, would probably not have consented to the operation. Who can blame them? When a surgeon produces the knife, they think he is going to chop them up and they are likely to die. And an inoculator, who it may appear is actually introducing the disease to a place, may be hounded out of town.'

His face, normally closed and even dull, became animated when he talked like this. Rebecca stroked her horse's soft nose and said: 'Well, I think if I had children I would have them inoculated. After what I have just seen . . . You have made a convert, Dr Kesteven. I will tell everyone I know.'

He smiled, flushing with pleasure. 'I'm grateful.'

'I had better start for home now.'

He helped her mount: and she did not observe the way his eyes kindled as he looked at her. 'Miss Walsoken,' he said, 'are you certain about riding home unescorted? I can easily – '

'It's all right, thank you. But please call when you have time.

Mother speaks so well of you, and she has suffered much recently from sick headaches. Although . . .' She stopped.

'Go on.'

'I was going to say she fancies it half the time, but that is perhaps uncharitable.'

'Well, maladies can often be the creation of the mind – but that does not make them any less real or painful.'

'I am reproved again.'

She had smiled as she said it, but she saw from the discomfort on his face that he was not an easy man to joke with. 'Anyway, please call.'

After she rode off he did not remount but stood by his horse watching her graceful figure until it was out of sight.

5

Evening was coming down as Deborah Gedney stood in the ruined mill and waited for Mark Upwell.

Though Joshua Walsoken would have been shocked to know of it, the old mill building on Bromswold land, standing like a rotten tooth a couple of hundred yards from the house amongst stunted willows and gorse, was sometimes used as a trysting place by lovers in the village. The door had long since been ripped away for firewood: but the roof was virtually intact, and inside the earth floor was dry and there was nothing to disturb but the rustlings of an owl that nested in the high eaves above.

From the doorway Deborah had watched the brilliant sky fade in tints of orange and yellow and turquoise growing ever more delicate and shadows creeping like a tide across the land: she had seen the thousands of starlings rise from the fields and sweep overhead in a black whirring mass towards their roosts in the reed-shores of the Fen to the east: she had heard the hollow boom of a bittern somewhere near the stream and the whistling wind that ran like a comb through the coarse grasses of the commons.

Mark came round the building unexpectedly from the other side, making her start.

'Sorry,' he said, 'have you bin waitin'? Reuben Phypers' sheep have started lambin', and I give him a hand.'

Mark's eyes were bright in the glowing dusk as he took her hand. His was a keen mobile face that seemed too thin. Along with his weak chest that was what made some folk fear a consumption in him, though there was no history of it in the Upwell family.

'Leaving me here,' she said, smiling, drawing him into the mill, 'while you clat about wi' Reuben's sheep. I don't know, Mark Upwell. I've a mind to go marry someone else.' She kissed him, holding his face in her hands.

'Ye never will . . . And then I had to call in and see if dad were all right.'

Her face was serious for a moment. 'How is he?'

Mark shrugged. 'Things seem to hit him hard just now. The cow gooing like that . . . He don't seem to be able to bear up. I tell him we s'll be all right. We s'll be on taties and little else, and most o' them's rotted, but it'll be better come summer.'

'Course it will.'

'And – he do say he's let us down.'

'Us?'

'Well – he were lookin' forrard to us gittin' wed just so much as we were.'

'Tell him not to whittle over that.' Her hands were firm and cool and strong as she stroked his hair.

'Course, he say we could come an' live wi' him: but you can't leave Goody.'

'She say the same – that we should live wi' her. There's precious little room in our cottage . . .' She kissed him again with a sudden hot fierceness, pulling him down to the ground. 'Never fear, my lover, things'll turn up come summer.'

He smiled, his face vivacious and youthful beside hers. 'And it's not as if either of us is gooin' to run away in the meantime, is it?'

Up above the owl made a flutter of soft wings as it set out on the hunt. Mark could feel her heart beating where his slender hand lay lightly on her breast.

'No,' she said, 'I'm not running away.'

TWO

Neither George nor Mary being of a religious turn of mind, they only made an appearance at Aysthorpe church a few times a year: and grandmother Peach only went when she had her devotional moods, which were infrequent: so the Hardwick pew was empty on the first Sunday in April, when a restless congregation waited for half an hour for the Rev. Mr Medhurst to arrive and begin the service. He never came: for that morning, after several times complaining to his sister of indigestion, he was reaching up to a cupboard where he stored a sheaf of old sermons when he gave a quiet groan and fell down dead with an expression which Miss Winifred Medhurst later tearfully confided was one of 'serene beatitude' but was really of vague puzzlement.

The news was at last brought to the church by a servant from the Rectory, and it was given first to Joshua Walsoken as, in the absence of the Hardwicks, the senior person there. He at once went to offer consolation, sending his wife and Sarah and Rebecca home.

A subdued Rebecca. After the clash with her father over the Upwells, relations between them had stiffened to icy composure. It did not disguise the real antagonism underneath. She was aware that he was more watchful over her, more jealously inflexible in attitude than ever. As for herself, it seemed that mutinous feelings, once let loose, were difficult to rein in again. Sometimes her very blood seemed to surge, pressing her to seek some avenue of release. Though what that avenue could be, she did not know.

The news of the Rector's death was brought to George and Mary by Will Binnismoor, from the village grapevine, on the Sunday evening.

The next morning George had business in Peterborough: so Mary walked over alone to see Miss Medhurst, and when she came back Mrs Binnismoor told her the carrier had been and left a letter for her and George.

With Charles Joseph on her knee she read the invitation, keeping it out of reach of his fingers, which were beginning to wander to any tempting object. Neither she nor George had got on well with Mrs Wainwright in the past: but apparently they were still of enough consequence to warrant an invitation to the Patriotick Assembly. She doubted they would be able to go – there was the baby, leaving aside the fact that they had nothing suitable to wear – but it was pleasant to be asked.

When George returned just after one it had been raining heavily for an hour, and his dark hair was plastered to his head and he was muddied to his knees: but true to his unpredictable temper, this made him laugh, especially when he caught sight of himself in the glass over the chimney-piece. It was quite some time, after Mary had rubbed his head with a towel and he had pulled her on to his knee and kissed her and got her wet too, before they had stopped laughing and she was able to tell him of their invitation.

'Our existence is not entirely forgot, eh?' he said. 'Let me look at that invitation again. Are you sure she is not engaging us to wait on the tables?' He looked at his wife. 'Would you like to go, love?'

She shrugged, smiling. 'It would be nice if it were possible. It's long since we had an outing. But with Charles Joseph . . .'

He nodded. 'If it were summer, a ride to Stamford and back in one evening might not be such an undertaking. It's a pity. We are still young yet, though often it's hard to keep in mind.'

'Uncle Horace was always on good terms with the Wainwrights. I wonder if he – and Luke – have been invited?'

George turned his steaming coat in front of the fire. 'It can't be easy for the young man. Bringing him to Morholm is one thing – taking him out before the prying eyes of Stamford society is another.' He felt in the coat pocket. 'I had forgot – I picked this up in Peterborough.'

It was the first issue of the *Stamford and Peterborough Courant*. Mary turned over the four pages with their densely packed print. 'So here it is at last! Let us hope it prospers.'

'Let us hope Henry prospers under the effort. I met Francis Sedgmoor at the Talbot, and he tells me it is Henry who has to write virtually every word. Also he had a piece of news that you will not find in those columns. Kate is expecting a child.'

'Oh, that's brave news! When is it to be?'

'Around October, Francis said. He's delighted, of course.'

'I – wonder if Julia knows yet.'

George looked at her.

'Something she said, last time she was here,' Mary said. 'It – it seemed as if her and Henry's failure to have a child is putting a strain on them. She didn't say in so many words, but . . .'

George stared into the fire, serious now. 'I've sometimes felt of late that Henry is like a man driven – always working, always taking so much on himself. I wonder if I could speak to him.'

Charles Joseph was stirring in his cot.

'What can you say?' Mary said. 'I don't think we'd do any good to interfere.'

Charles went over and picked Charles Joseph up and peered into his small round face. 'You have a plaguey troublesome family, Charles Joseph Hardwick,' he said. 'A plaguey lot. Sometimes I wonder what is going to become of them.'

2

The next day Henry Milton went into the Angel at Peterborough, having walked from Longthorpe, to pick up some books that had arrived by the London mail. There was a letter too from Matthew Bedford, his old friend in London who had sent the books, a retired publisher with whom he had been in frequent correspondence since the setting up of Sedgmoor and Milton's. He drank a tankard of porter while he read the letter. The noise from the cock-pit next door was loud, but here there were only a couple of farmers haggling at another table.

Mr Bedford concluded by asking after Julia's health. Milton wondered about that himself. She had taken the news of Kate Sedgmoor's pregnancy better than he had feared – or it seemed so, outwardly, for she was difficult to read. This morning he had left her vigorously raking out the oven preparatory to baking bread, and that at least he understood: with Julia a sudden frantic exertion was the sign of unhappiness.

The news that should have been so happy – and indeed he was happy for Francis and Kate – had taken something of the savour out of the satisfaction of seeing the *Courant* become a reality. For a brief space it had seemed as if they would not get the first issue out on time. They had two slightly dilapidated presses and their journeyman printer and his apprentice had worked far into the night setting up the type and inking and pulling the great wooden beds. The result was four pages of folio size with four columns per page. About half was advertisements, for which they had to pay duty, as well as paying the stamp-tax, which had increased with the war. The rest consisted of foreign and domestic news, local news, lists of farming prices and stocks, marriages and deaths, and an essay each week on some current topic.

For the essay in the first number he had taken the subject of the American war and the commissioners who had just been sent to the colonies to report. He was opposed to the war, but had been circumspect in the essay: it would not do to alienate any section of opinion so early.

So now it was launched. It remained to be seen how it would hold up against the *Mercury*. Advertisements were helpful, but the chief profit was in a large circulation. As the *Mercury* was oriented towards Lincolnshire, the *Courant* would be towards the south and east. There was a possible market in five counties: and there was money to be made, if not a fortune.

And yet – although they had earnestly worked and planned for this for a year – was there not another sort of dissatisfaction in him? His words would, with luck, be read by a large circle of people: but he still wished for something else. His life in London as a hack-writer a few years ago had rid him of many illusions about the literary life, but he had never stopped writing. He had sent some poems recently to his old publisher Isaac Carey, and Carey had cautiously asked to see more. Though this newspaper business promised to be both remunerative and time-consuming, there was a corner of his mind that always sheltered a hope of grander things.

He finished his porter and stood up to go. Unnoticed by him, a young man had taken a seat in the corner and Milton saw he was reading a copy of the *Courant*.

On impulse he stopped by the young man's table and said: 'Pardon me, is that the first issue of this new newspaper?'

The young man looked up. 'Yes, so I believe. I picked it up from a hawker in the square.'

'Might I ask you – how do you find it?'

The young man smiled and laid the newspaper down. 'Oh, these sheets are all pretty much alike, are they not? It's well enough presented, but as for the news, I might as well have saved my threepence and hired a London paper. As for the rest . . .'

'Go on.'

'Well, this essay or whatever it is: very worthy, no doubt, but such stiff, formal stuff, no liveliness or wit. But please, take it and judge for yourself, I have finished with it.'

Milton hesitated. 'I – confess I had a different reason for asking. My name is Milton. If you observe the by-line . . .'

'"Printed at Sedgmoor and Milton's, High Street, Stamford",' the young man read out. He stared at Milton a moment and then burst into a shout of laughter. 'God's life, you are a proprietor? And here have I been damning it to your face! Well, sir, you must excuse me; you should have told me who you were first, and then I would have known the right reply to give you.'

'A candid answer is much more valuable,' said Milton with a smile, and lifted his hat.

'Stay, sir, will you not allow me to make some amends? Take a drink with me, and I will try to give you some more considered opinion, or keep it to myself, just as you please. Landlord!'

The young man had an engaging manner, and Milton accepted. He was about twenty-two, with fair hair fashionably dressed: he had a slightly hawkish profile but intelligent dark brown eyes and a humorous mouth. His clothes – a turquoise cutaway coat with striped revers and large gold buttons, and on the seat beside him a hat of a new fashion, round with a tall crown – suggested the dandy, but there was a hint of self-mockery here too.

The landlord brought more porter, and Milton said: 'Perhaps I should forestall further embarrassment by saying that the piece you so dislike – indeed virtually the whole paper – is from my pen.'

The young man put a hand to his forehead. 'I hope you are not a good pistol shot, sir.'

'Nothing so serious. I just had a fancy to see what an unprejudiced observer thought of the enterprise. I only get automatic praise from my friends.'

'Amongst whom I fear I will never be numbered . . . But in truth, you have put a different complexion on things: to write the whole paper is an achievement in itself, Mr Milton. Is this prodigious feat to be repeated weekly?'

'Well, I suppose so. It is a small enterprise, just my partner and myself.'

There was a great roar from the cock-pit, and a little skinny man burst into the tap-room and ran for the door, presumably defaulting his bet. A couple of men came shouting after him and dragged him back.

'Is he a spectator or a bantam, one wonders?' the young man said. 'Well: an unprejudiced observer is right in a way, sir, for I have been away from this dear barbarous part of the world for some time, and am just accustoming myself to its peculiarities once again. My name is Robert Landless, Mr Milton – the name of my father is perhaps familiar to you?'

Milton thought, frowning. 'Not the Dean of the cathedral?'

'Late Dean, alas. You have launched your paper just two months too late to print his obituary.'

'I didn't know . . . I'm sorry.'

'I am too, rather, though I imagine my father was not. He used to talk so much about meeting his Maker that I cannot but think he hurried gladly to the appointment at last. I have been nearly two years on the Continent, and though I hurried back when I heard of his impending dissolution I was not in time to be present at it.'

'And – are you to follow his calling?' Milton asked.

'Dear, no. Father despatched me to Oxford with, I think, hopes that my thoughts would turn serious, but they never did. My chief time was spent compiling lampoons and squibs and satires – which is partly what gave me the conceit to criticise your piece just now. Then I went abroad and contracted more bad habits, and now the question of a calling has become academic. I find I have a large dusty house in Priestgate and a large dusty fortune that I hardly know what to do with. So you see, my impudence in disparaging your efforts is compounded.'

Landless sat back and grinned. There was so little of vanity or self-satisfaction in his manner that Milton could not help but like him.

'Now, the question is,' the young man went on, 'are you going to reward my impudence with the appropriate challenge?'

Milton hesitated. 'To prove you can do better?'

'That's it! Let me submit something to your sheet, as I was unkind enough to call it. God knows I have leisure on my hands. Then you will satisfy yourself as to what a humbug I am.'

Milton laughed. 'Very well. But let me encroach on your leisure further, and invite you to visit our printing-house. When you see our presses you will be ready to forgive a lot.'

They shook hands, and Landless called to the innkeeper again.

The house in Longthorpe was full of the smell of the new-baked bread that stood cooling in the kitchen, and Julia was in their bedroom from where she saw Henry approach down the lane. The sun was beginning to edge down the sky through pockets of welted cloud, and his figure trailed a long shadow. She waved to him from the window and turned to go down and tell Mrs Dawes to begin dinner. Then she checked herself and went to the bureau in the corner where she had been writing. She gathered up the sheets of paper and placed them in a drawer and locked it before going downstairs.

The ink on the top sheet was not quite dry, but it had not smudged: and it read:

On A Primrose, found in a Barren Place

What profits thee, to lurk beneath
These Boughs o'erspread with sequinn'd Dew,
And ope thy Eye on Brake and Heath
Where e'en thy sister Weeds are few?

Dost thou in Gloom thus feebly shine
To cheer – is such thy modest Part?
Or is some sterner Lesson thine
To lay to my unfruitful Heart?

For, moor'd in Shades, thy Sweets are waste:
And bless'd by no approving Eye,
Thou must, by Nature scantly plac'd,
Unmourned wither – thou as I.

3

'Are you to attend the Patriotick Assembly this Saturday, Mr Wiley?' Joshua Walsoken asked.

There was a brief pause while the banker searched the enquiry for motives. 'I think so, sir. For myself I am not a social man, but my wife and daughters are keen to go.'

They were in the upstairs parlour of Mr Wiley's house in Stamford, above the bank office, and were drinking mountain. Mr Walsoken had come for – well, Thornton Wiley was not sure what he had come for. His first, unpleasant thought – that Walsoken had come to withdraw his money and move it to Wainwright's, like so many others – had proved to be wrong. Wiley was greatly relieved, for Joshua Walsoken, though a relative newcomer to the area, was perhaps his richest depositor: and so he was glad to offer his visitor a glass of something in private, and chat for a while. Unfortunately, business kept calling him downstairs, and Walsoken did not seem to take the hint, but sat stolidly there sipping his wine and awaiting the banker's return every time.

'. . . I beg your pardon, Mr Walsoken?'

'I was asking you, if there is a very varied class of depositor in this country?'

Thornton Wiley swallowed a belch. He was plump and gouty from overeating, which together with tetchiness was his besetting sin. 'Not – not greatly. Landowners, farmers, in the main. Our wealth lies in the land. As you know. Various merchants, lawyers. And of course small traders. Sir, will you again excuse me a moment?'

Wiley hurried downstairs to where his chief clerk was waiting in the passage.

'Well? What does he say?'

'He says, sir, he wants it all,' the clerk said. 'He says it's nowt to do with Wainwright's – he reckons he's got to make urgent repairs to his barns, and – '

'A likely tale,' Wiley snapped. 'I wish they'd just be honest. Very well, give him his damn money, and I hope he rots with it.'

Wiley paused at the foot of the stairs to wipe his plum-coloured face with his handkerchief. That was another, a farmer from Wiggenhall St Germans. A balance of just over a thousand. Oh, not enough to break them – as long as the trend did not continue. It was not a run – quite – but since Wainwright had withdrawn his shares to set up on his own a steady trickle of Wiley's customers had closed their accounts and, though few admitted as much, moved to Wainwright's.

It was Wiley's practice to keep a quarter of his deposits in his safes, and the rest was loaned and invested. So far he had met the demands . . . but if the trend continued, he would have to call in loans, to sell stock . . .

Sweating afresh, Wiley started up the stairs again. It didn't help having to exchange small-talk with this fellow, with his bloodless piety and his endless questions. His balance was welcome but his company was not.

Joshua Walsoken was standing at the window. 'I hope I do not intrude on your time, Mr Wiley?' he said.

'Not – not at all.'

'We were talking of land, Mr Wiley. As you know, I have been investing in land myself. In a small enough way so far. But I understand there are great fortunes to be made. Vast tracts of fen uncultivated, that would yield enormous returns if proper drainage and enclosure were undertaken.'

'Indeed. Indeed.' Wiley poured himself another glass of mountain with a fat, unsteady hand.

Walsoken watched him. 'Of course, my investments are not confined to land. A man must diversify, especially in these – expanding times. I have retained several interests in Norwich, and am always alert to the potential of others, in my new home. I have, after all, a large – very large – balance with this bank.'

Wiley sat down, fidgeting again for his handkerchief. 'Large – very large – indeed.'

There was a knock and the chief clerk put his head round the door. 'There's a Mr Humphrey Amory wanting to see you, sir.'

Wiley swallowed and stared at him. 'In – in a moment.'

'Mr Wiley, before I make the proposition that I am going to make – '

'Yes?' said Wiley, plying his handkerchief vigorously.

'Before I make it, I should first of all admit that my name is not well known in this region.'

'Perhaps – perhaps.'

'And, of course, I have no experience of banking, though naturally my mercantile career has given me a fair knowledge of the workings of credit, of investment . . .'

'Quite so,' said Wiley. 'Surely.'

'But what I hardly need point out is the fact that I have large capital reserves and substantial interests in the eastern counties, and – '

The clerk appeared again. 'Mr Amory says, sir, if you're busy he'll step out and come back when you're ready.'

Wiley licked his lips. 'Tell him – tell him I shall be free in half an hour. I have some – some very important business to discuss . . .'

THREE

I

Luke had spent five months in the house of his father. In that time he had acquired a wardrobe of new clothes, a few refinements of speech and habit, money, a genuine if reserved affection for the gaunt old man, and a little core of defensive hardness.

His generous, ardent, quick-tempered nature had not changed. He went about with his father, or on his own, expecting no deference and ready to take everyone as he found them. Horace's business associates, in the main, met him with the same openness of mind. It was all one to them whether he was a lofty duke or had been born in shame and dragged up in the gutter.

But there were others; the rich and fashionable who lived or congregated in the town, who thrived on gossip and intrigue over the tea-table and the card-table; and Luke had heard the whispered comment, the stifled squeal of laughter behind the fluttering fan, seen the half-amused, half-contemptuous glances . . .

An evening at the Warrens' in High Street St Martins: several card games going on, and Luke, who knew how to play none of them, uneasy on the sidelines. One of Mr Philip Warren's dogs, frisking round, nearly upset a table: a gentleman cried: 'Damn it, Warren, can't you keep your infernal mongrels out?' and Warren said, in a low voice, but plain enough for Luke to hear, 'Mongrels of all kinds are allowed in drawing-rooms now, Sims, didn't you know?' A snicker from somewhere, and the game went on.

Luke had felt the warning pressure of Horace's hand on his arm: had swallowed and mastered himself.

Horace counselled him to ignore such things – they would cease in time. But it was easier for him, Luke thought, he had a lifetime's respect and respectability behind him. No matter what happened, the old man was secure in his position and his consciousness of what was due to him. Luke had no such assurance: and in its place something guarded and resentful had grown and stiffened within him.

Partly because of this, partly because he had been accustomed to a life of activity, he involved himself with keen interest in the affairs of Horace's business. Horace Hardwick's prosperity had been built on his taking over a firm of wine merchants: and though he still imported and sold wine and spirits, with a wharf and warehouse in Stamford, he had many other financial irons in the fire. As he grew old he had been content to leave the day-to-day running in the hands of factors: but he found Luke an eager, quick and useful learner. The young man was given a generous allowance every month – which he hardly knew what to do with – but last week Horace had also made him a gift of a thousand pounds.

'I have placed it in your own account at Squire's Bank in Peterborough,' Horace said. 'The money is yours; you may rush out and spend it all if you wish: but what I hope is to see you invest it in some way. Don't be in a hurry – and don't tell me how you use it at first. I think you have a sharp brain; and I would like to see what you make of it.'

The invitation to the Wainwrights' Assembly was addressed to 'Mr Horace Hardwick and Mr Luke Hardwick'. Horace said they should go. 'Lord knows, I am no follower of fashion myself,' he said, 'but you must become accustomed to such things, Luke. It is your destiny to belong to this world, to take your place amongst these people.'

Luke stared out of the window at the dusty square and said nothing.

The Patriotick Assembly was to begin at eight o'clock on Saturday 11th April: but some guests were invited to the Wainwrights' townhouse first, to take a cold buffet and then go on from there. So by dusk Stamford was a concourse of carriages and saddle-horses from every direction and the innkeepers and ostlers of the town were looking anxiously at their stables and hoping there would be room for them all.

Mrs Wainwright had spread her net wide. On the fenland itself there were few gentry: those who had estates there preferred to live in the towns – Peterborough, Huntingdon, Spalding, and of course

Stamford, the centre of fashion – or in the greener, kinder country of the fen edge and upland at the borders of the hunting shires. So it was a fair proportion of the wealth and gentility of five counties that was to disport itself in the handsome, recently-built Assembly Rooms in St George's Square.

George and Mary Hardwick found themselves going after all. Mr Walsoken, whose private carriage was not yet finished, had hired two post chaises for the occasion: and insisted that the Hardwicks travel to Stamford and back with them. He did not keep late hours, he said, and could positively engage to have them back at Morholm before midnight, to save uneasiness over their child. On these terms they were happy to go – George, Mary perceived, chafing a little at being under such obligation to their new neighbours; but she was of a more practical nature. 'Pride is all very well,' she said, 'but I had rather lose a little, than we should sit at home getting grey hairs before our time.'

They rode in the second carriage with Rebecca, which suited them all. Rebecca noticed that George's green coat was a little shiny at the sleeves, and Mary's gown too tight at the bust: but she thought they made a handsome couple – George with his wry, slightly raffish good looks, Mary with her green eyes and elfin face looking younger than before the baby. They had no need of finery.

George and Mary, meanwhile, had exchanged an amazed glance when they joined Rebecca in the carriage. The warm, impulsive girl they had grown used to welcoming at Morholm at odd times, like one of the family, more often than not wind-blown and glowing, skirts stained with mud, was transformed. This was a different Rebecca: the auburn crown of hair lifted to frame her clear oval face with its deep brown eyes and olive skin. Her gown was cut below the shoulders, of emerald green silk with an open figured bodice. The effect of colour was entrancing.

She herself was chiefly aware of the unaccustomed discomfort of having her hair up and the stiffness of the new gown: and the sensation, also new to her, of extreme nervousness. She had never been to such an occasion before. Her father had had a genteel milliner at Bromswold to dress the ladies' hair: she had powdered her mother's and Sarah's, but had taken one look at Rebecca's rich red-brown profusion and put her powder-box away – it would be criminal to whiten such hair. The dress was certainly a marvellous thing, but she wondered that her father did not think it indecent. She had a very feminine figure, and the gown took careful note of it.

Mary had casually remarked that Horace and Luke would be there. The spring evening was only mild, but Rebecca began to feel suffocatingly hot.

She had never met Mrs Wainwright: and it was as much as she could do to stifle her smiles at the sight that greeted her in the drawing-room at the townhouse in Barn Hill. Mrs Wainwright was in fact no great eater: it was perhaps her greed for power, status, opulence – and sheer people – that was responsible for her huge size. She was corseted till her black button eyes bulged: her face was dead white with lead paint: her eyebrows, long moribund from excessive plucking, were replaced with a false pair, made of mouse-skin, and stuck on halfway up her forehead: and she wore a wig two feet high, powdered red, white and blue, with a British Lion on top encrusted with pearls and surrounded with ostrich feathers and fresh flowers, so she had to bend at the knees to get through doorways. Rebecca's father greeted her with his usual equanimity: but her mother looked terrified at this apparition.

The sun was spreading pink over the roofs of the town, and the doors to the garden were thrown open so that the company could wander at will on the smooth lawns, whilst liveried footmen carried round trays of refreshments. Rebecca, being assiduously introduced by her father, was surprised how many people he already knew.

This part was easier than she had thought. It was clear that most of the women only wanted complimenting on their dress, and the men only wanted their own compliments to be graciously received. Some, however, looked at her with a keener interest that was not at all unpleasant. But then she found herself looking round expectantly at each male voice – in case – and it might well be misconstrued.

One of the noisiest and most elegant groups included an exceptionally fair and beautiful young woman who Rebecca understood was the Wainwrights' eldest daughter Elizabeth, Lady Woodhouse, though she was adding little to the conversation. Here Rebecca found herself briefly monopolised by Sir Hugh Woodhouse and his close friend Mr Philip Warren, a short unprepossessing man in silks whose late father had been a judge and who now lived beyond his income by astute sycophancy.

'You *cannot* be Miss Walsoken,' he said, bowing over her hand. 'I have had the pleasure of meeting your father, and he is from

Norwich: but you must be London: I cannot believe otherwise – such elegance is only found – it is not possible – '

'I have never been in London in my life,' she said, amused at his little fastidious bows, and the thinness of his legs which he had tried unsuccessfully to disguise by wearing false calves in his stockings.

'Never been in – But it is town's loss. That is all there is to say. Can you believe it, Hugh?'

'It will be town's gain, in due course, I feel sure,' Sir Hugh boomed. 'Miss Walsoken cannot be allowed to – to waste her sweetness on this desert air.'

'Is it such a desert? I have found it charming.'

Warren narrowed his eyes in a smile. 'We do our best – we put up a show. Miss Walsoken is kind enough to be indulgent. Indeed, madam, you have encouraged me – emboldened me to ask the favour of the first two dances.'

'Have I?' Rebecca said. 'I didn't know it. Surely, sir, such a request should be made when we are actually at the ball? One can't put in a bid before the auction's started.'

'Ha! She has you there, Warren,' barked Sir Hugh. 'Before the auction – well said!'

Warren, smiling, but not entirely pleased, said: 'But when the prize is so beyond price, one feels one is justified in using any stratagem to gain it. But as you say, madam: I shall put in my bid again, when the auction starts. That is surely my right.'

'Certainly it is,' she said, smiling sweetly, 'as it is my right to refuse.'

George and Mary, having been hugely patronised by Mrs Wainwright, found themselves accosted by a young-middle-aged man in a clerical collar and wig and a red coat. George introduced him.

'This is the Reverend Doctor Emmonsales, my love. Sir, my wife Mary.'

'Charmed, ma'am. I imagine your husband has spoken of me. We are fellow magistrates in Peterborough, and often come to disagreements when he's too soft with sturdy rogues.'

'Yes, indeed, sir. I confess I sometimes fear you will lock George up in gaol with your other felons.'

The Rev. Dr Emmonsales gave a loud hard laugh. 'Not so bad as that, ma'am. Not yet. Now, Mr Hardwick, I heard of the decease of the incumbent of your parish quite recently.'

'Medhurst?' said George. 'Yes, it was a sad loss.'

'I understand it is a wealthy living,' said Dr Emmonsales, taking a glass of wine from a passing footman, 'and have written to the Bishop. I already have the livings of Northborough and Coates, but they are barely enough to maintain my family and establishment. I have two young daughters, ma'am,' he said, turning his sharp eyes on Mary again, 'and their mother is dead. I am told the Rectory is a good building, is that so?'

'Yes, it is quite large, in good repair.'

Dr Emmonsales nodded decisively. 'Well, I have high hopes. Perhaps we may be neighbours in the near future, Mr Hardwick.'

Mr Wainwright, having made a tour of the guests, consulted his watch and wished the time away. It would be better when they got to the ball proper: he was not expected to dance, and could retreat to a card-room and talk business. He watched Thornton Wiley stumping fatly around the lawn with Joshua Walsoken. Wiley had greeted him oddly just now. There had been a little bad feeling over the dissolution of their partnership and the setting up of Wainwright's Bank – but nothing to speak of. Yet there had been a most unpleasant gleam in Wiley's eye when they met today.

Rebecca, having detached herself from Mr Warren, was talking to her hostess with her father in the garden when she saw old Horace appear at the French doors. Her heart seemed to stop and then judder to life again. The unmistakable figure of Luke stepped out after his father. She watched him go over and greet his host, while Mrs Wainwright's talk flowed on, blurred and meaningless.

'. . . Bromswold I remember in the Jarretts' time,' Mrs Wainwright was saying, 'and it was sorely neglected. I must say it is kind of you, Mr Walsoken, to carry the Hardwicks here – sad to see such a decline in that quarter – but between ourselves the rot set in long ago.' She noticed Rebecca's glance towards the house and with difficulty looked over her shoulder. 'Well, I declare – there is another of that family – our old friend Mr Horace Hardwick. You have met that gentleman, sir?'

'I have,' Mr Walsoken said. 'At Morholm.'

'Of course it is all most unfortunate about this young man he has chosen to acknowledge at last,' Mrs Wainwright said in a lowered voice. 'One sympathises, of course – but it is embarrassing having to meet him.'

'Indeed,' said Mr Walsoken. 'It would have been a better action to have left the young man in the station to which he is fitted. One must show a basic civility, in view of his relations – and the stained circumstance of his birth is no doubt something for which he cannot be blamed. But,' he said with deep severity, 'there is an indelible coarseness and vulgarity in that young man, as is to be expected. I have seen it myself.'

'Have you, sir?' said Mrs Wainwright, looking interested. 'Well, I am not surprised. The vulgars will always show themselves, dress them up as much as you will.'

Her father had not moved his gaze, but Rebecca felt his words resound as if he had addressed them directly to her. Then she saw that Horace and Luke were coming across the lawn towards them.

'Mr Hardwick, how d'you do?' Mrs Wainwright said. 'And – Mr Luke. So glad you could come.'

A whirlwind passed through Rebecca's mind as father and son bowed. Why, why did they ever meet in the first place? Why was it all so complicated, so impossible? Why did he have to turn up tonight, when she was quietly enjoying herself, destroying her peace of mind again and looking at her with his dark eyes? Why was he the most beautiful young man in the world?

Mrs Wainwright adddressed herself exclusively to Horace – clearly as a snub to Luke – and her father, after the barest nod, did the same. They were soon joined by Mr Wainwright: and the result was that Rebecca and Luke found themselves talking alone.

The snub roused Rebecca's sense of injustice. Whatever she felt about Luke, it had nothing to do with his origins.

'Miss Rebecca,' he said. 'I hope you're well.'

'Yes, thank you.' She had an empty glass in her hand, and did not know what to do with it.

'I thought perhaps to see you here. And you're going on to the Assembly? Yes.' He was the first man to make no compliments on her dress, and after the first keen glance he had fixed his eyes slightly away from her. She thought him somewhat changed – still tall and straight and clean-limbed, with the strong line to his jaw and cheek, the black hair unpowdered in a simple pigtail, smartly dressed in a navy coat with high collar and striped waistcoat – but there was a certain reserve, even a kind of guarded hostility in the way he looked round him at the laughing, chatting guests dotted about the garden. He looked high-strung, dangerous. She suddenly perceived him to be in his way a proud man, and as suddenly warmed to this fact.

'It's a long time since we met,' he said rapidly.

'Four months.' She wished this glass were full instead of empty: she needed courage.

'Christmas at Morholm.' All at once he was smiling, warmly and intimately, and she could only respond. 'I reckon I didn't behave well that time,' he said, looking into her eyes. 'Did I?'

'Didn't you? I don't think I remember.'

'That could be taken either one of two ways.' He took the empty glass from her hand, stepped away to place it on a garden table, was back at her side.

'Let's forget about that anyway,' he said, low and urgent. 'And that time we met in Stamford. Pretend it didn't happen. What d'you say? And we've just met here, as folk do. Nothing more natural. And we've just been introduced. Eh?'

'Very well.' She smiled at him. 'I'm very glad to know you, Mr Hardwick.'

'I'm glad to know *you*, Miss Rebecca,' he said. 'More than glad. Proud. Happy, honoured, delighted . . . I don't know the words.'

A footman approached them with a tray, and she accepted another glass of wine gratefully. He moved on to Mr Walsoken, a few yards off now, and was waved away.

'I don't reckon your father approves of me,' Luke said.

She looked at the ground, stung as if with a personal shame.

'Ah, well, there's plenty of folk hereabouts who don't.'

She saw with surprise, and a little hurt of her own, the pain in his eyes.

'My father's views are his own,' she said, rather breathless. 'But of course I am expected to share them.'

'And do you?'

Her eyes travelled up his broad chest to his face. She found herself smiling. 'What do you think?'

'I think . . .' He gazed at her for several moments, an unborn smile on his lips, and then said: 'I reckon tonight's going to be wonderful. I've got a feeling . . .'

'I've been looking forward to it,' she said, 'so much. At least, I've been hoping – '

'Hoping I'd be here. That's what you've been looking forward to, eh?'

'Indeed I've not,' she said, drawing herself up. The trace of arrogance was in his face again, mixed with humour. 'You're a conceited man, Mr Hardwick.'

'Who wouldn't be?' he said in a half-whisper. 'Who wouldn't be standing and talking with you, Rebecca – you alone out of all these folk? You alone. That's enough to make a man shout out loud.'

She was, unusually for her, stuck for an answer. She seemed abruptly to have arrived, through a jungled passage of resentment and flippancy and anger and attraction, to a precipitous chasm of emotion down which she peered uncertainly. It was then that George appeared beside them.

'Well, here's cheerful company,' he said. 'Cousin Luke, I am glad to see you.' They shook hands. 'I hope the two of you are feeling full of patriotism. Is that what we are meant to do? I notice, though, while we are supposed to be hating the Frenchies, there is plenty of French wine on hand.'

'How's your little younker, George?' Luke asked.

George noticed it was the first time Luke had called him by name. 'He grows fat, makes a lusty noise, and generally thrives. I think Mary is more anxious at being away from him for an evening than she cares to admit, however.'

'Are you looking forward to the ball, Mr Hardwick?' said Rebecca. 'Do you dance?'

'After a fashion,' George said. 'We saw a dancing bear recently in Peterborough, and though my wife refrained from comment, I think she was irresistibly reminded . . . How about you, Luke?' he added, wondering at the same time if that was tactful.

Luke smiled. 'I can manage a few steps,' he said. 'I shall dance the first pair at least, for Miss Rebecca has promised them to me.'

George raised his eyebrows and looked from one to the other.

'So I have,' Rebecca said.

2

When the time for the ball came, most of the guests at the Wainwrights' chose to walk the couple of streets to the Assembly Rooms: the weather had been dry and the roads were pretty clean. Mr Walsoken, however, insisted they use the carriage: he did not choose to have his family parade before the eyes of the vulgar.

There were lanterns and patriotic ribbons around the doors of the Assembly Rooms: and opposite in the square Mr Wainwright, who at least did not wholly share in Joshua Walsoken's contempt for the vulgar, had arranged for a bonfire and fireworks later. Inside, the ballroom, card-rooms and refreshment-room were similarly decked out in red, white and blue, and the musicians on their platform were scarcely visible behind masses of rosettes and flowers. Many other guests were arriving, and the room was already very warm.

Mrs Wainwright had grown too fat for dancing, so the honour of leading off the first dance was delegated to her daughter Elizabeth, statuesque with her crown of fair hair, and Sir Hugh, a coarse figure beside her.

Rebecca's father had seated his wife and daughters and then moved away with Mr Wiley: but he would surely notice when Luke came to claim his dance. Well . . . he had asked her, hadn't he? And he had been invited, he was here, mixing with the rest – what was to prevent her dancing with him? She held this imaginary conversation in her mind – a habit of hers – whilst the band were playing 'God Save the King'.

Then Luke stepped through the crowd to claim her. His hand was cool around hers. As she walked on to the floor with him she saw the surprised face of Mr Warren from the corner of her eye.

'H'm, young Miss Walsoken is quite the belle,' said Mrs Wainwright to Horace, lifting a jewelled quizzing-glass. 'Your – young man is most favoured. I wasn't aware he danced, sir.'

'My son is lacking in nothing that befits his station,' said Horace.

'One respect excepted, of course, you would add, but what does that signify in these times?' said Mrs Wainwright. 'Naturally, as an old friend, my dear Mr Hardwick, you will permit me to say how much I admire your courage in claiming him.'

'Luke has given me no cause to regret that,' Horace said crisply, 'and I do not anticipate that he will.'

In the soft light of the candles ranged along the walls the dancers, powdered and ribboned in satins and silks, bowing, turning, pointing toes, crossing and re-crossing, made a shifting patchwork of pastel colours.

'Please,' Luke said, 'don't look so serious.'

'Was I?' Rebecca smiled. 'I'm sorry. I'm not really. Just afraid I'll forget my steps.'

'That's the spirit. We're here to enjoy ourselves, aren't we? Not just here, but on this earth. Isn't it so? A light heart, that's what Sam used to say, always bear a light heart. We meet, we talk, we dance. What's to say us nay? What more can we ask at this moment?'

She smiled again, almost convinced, and warming to his mood. 'True. We shouldn't take life too serious. It's – the cause of half the trouble.'

They separated, and when they came together again Luke said: 'You look – d'you know how beautiful you look tonight, Rebecca?'

'That's not light-hearted,' she said soberly.

'Mebbe. Well, shall I say you're looking ugly, then? Or quite plain – or just moderate pretty?' He laughed softly. 'But no, 'twouldn't be true, Rebecca. Twouldn't be true . . .'

Henry and Julia Milton had just arrived, and with them Robert Landless.

Milton and Landless had struck up an immediate friendship. The young man, true to his word, had dashed off a scribbled, smudged copy for the *Courant* that was far more concise, witty and readable than anything Milton could have done: but any resentment was impossible, for the same careless vivacity informed Robert Landless's character, and it helped to take Milton out of the labours and worries of his recent life. There were many eyes turned to the young man as he came in. He cut an elegant figure with his aquiline profile and mop of blond hair and his cutaway coat of spotted silk.

'Why, here's a lively scene,' Landless said. 'Is your husband in the habit of leading young innocents like me into dissipation, Mrs Milton?'

'Only if he can make them work for him,' Julia said. She was looking rather sallow tonight, her arresting features a little grim: her looks had the quality of altering with her moods.

'Oh, well, that is a pleasure. Though whether he will be able to keep me at it . . . my nose has a fancy to turn up at the grindstone. Now, tell me, which is our hostess?'

'Here she comes,' said Milton, as Mrs Wainwright threaded towards them with a smile of welcome. Ever since Milton's youthful infatuation with Elizabeth Wainwright, years ago, Mrs Wainwright had seemed to have, in her own way, a soft spot for him.

'Good heavens, all sails filled and guns blazing,' said Landless in a low voice.

Milton introduced him.

'I'm most honoured to be here, ma'am,' Landless said, bowing over her hand, which bristled with rings. 'I'm always glad of the

153

opportunity to be patriotic. Ah, it's comforting to be at war with the French again, isn't it? Life always seems so dull on those rare occasions when we're not. Whose turn is it to win this time, I wonder?'

The first minuetto was over. The assembly rooms were nearly filled with close on a hundred people dancing, talking, drinking: and the strong scents of pomade and perfume were already insufficient to obscure the smells of bodies that were in many cases strangers to soap and water. When they got to the country dances later there would be a fine old sweat, as Humphrey Amory remarked to his wife while his fingers played on her pretty shoulder: but by then everyone would be too merry to notice.

Rebecca, taken back to her seat by Luke, saw that Mr Warren was with her mother.

'Ah, now here she is!' he said. 'Miss Walsoken, you have used me cruelly. You as good as promised me the first. Admit it, now.'

'Really, I did no – '

'I had engaged the lady beforehand,' Luke said pleasantly.

Philip Warren glanced at him. 'Is that so? Yet when I tried to do so I was rebuffed. You have a hard heart, madam. But surely you won't refuse me the second: Mrs Walsoken, I appeal to you, is that not fair?'

Rebecca, about to say something, felt a light pressure of Luke's fingertips on her arm. 'Yes, that's surely fair,' he said. 'Excuse me, I must go and see my father settled.' He gave Rebecca a smile before moving away.

Joshua Walsoken, having regarded the whole company with his watchful eyes, refused wine and went in search of Mr Humphrey Amory, who had promised him an introduction to someone he wanted very much to meet.

This was a man named Bellaers, a youngish landowner from Lincolnshire. Walsoken lost no time in coming to the point.

'I have been hoping to meet you, sir,' he said. 'I have heard from certain quarters that you have a large tract of fen-land that you are anxious to dispose of.'

'Indeed? My affairs seem to be common knowledge.'

Walsoken looked apologetic. 'I have offended. Forgive me. I would not have mentioned it if – '

'Oh, it's of no consequence. Yes, I do. I'm sorry, it's just the thought of the damn place that makes me irritable.'

'Bicklode Fen is the name, I understand?'

Bellaers nodded. 'The bane of my family for generations . . .'

Rebecca found it irksome having to dance with Mr Warren. His affected twirls and gestures would have made her laugh out loud if she had not been so preoccupied with thoughts of Luke.

'Aysthorpe, my dear Miss Walsoken, has I'm sure its charms,' he said. 'But upon my honour, you must not lie buried there. You must move in the best circles in the district, you must join our set.'

'Oh? Whose set is that?'

'Why, mine, and dear Hughie of course. We lead, you know. Others follow.'

'I notice dear Hughie is not dancing.'

'Isn't he? Well, after all, he's an old married man now.'

'Not old surely. Or no older than you. And aren't you a married man?'

'I, madam? No, indeed.' Warren laughed with a show of prominent yellow teeth. 'I've never been landed. I always take the bait, madam, but never get caught on the hook. That way I get all the pleasure, none of the inconvenience.'

'Dear me.' The wine was beginning to take effect. 'Well, of course, it's always the littlest fish that no one cares to catch.'

'. . . Tell me, Milton,' said Robert Landless, 'who is that – I can't describe her – that incomparably beautiful woman sitting over there?'

'That? The Wainwrights' eldest daughter, Elizabeth. Married to Sir Hugh Woodhouse of Deenecote Hall.'

'Is she indeed? But how – how can that Gorgon with the parti-coloured wig be the dam of such a creature?'

'I used to wonder that myself,' Milton said.

Julia said: 'Henry was an unsuccessful suitor in that direction once, Mr Landless. But she married someone else, and so he took me as a last resort.'

Landless looked at them with a little alarm, but the Miltons laughed: they had been distant acquaintances then, and the subject was quite without pain. 'I was one of many in a state of green-sickness for that lady, years ago,' Henry said.

'That I do not wonder,' said Landless. 'But this husband of hers – where is he – why is he not in attendance – how can he bear to leave her side for one moment?'

'Oh, knowing him, I imagine he does it quite easily,' Milton said.

The one remnant of bitterness in him about that long-dead affair with Elizabeth was the man she had chosen to marry.

Landless turned to him, his face animated. 'Introduce me to her, Milton.'

'Me? I don't think I have spoken twelve words to her in as many months.'

'But I hardly know anyone else here. Please, I beg you. Else I shall only stare at her the whole evening.'

'Oh, very well . . .'

Luke, after paying his respects to Mary, who was with the Amorys, took his first drink of the evening and watched the dancers. The turbulent feelings that Rebecca had reawakened in him he had tried to control: he had tried to be circumspect and civilised. He had, he hoped, acted like a gentleman.

Mrs Wainwright, with her son-in-law Sir Hugh Woodhouse, passed by him: then she stopped and turned.

'Mr Luke – Mr Hardwick I should say – I wonder if I might prevail on you? Hugh needs someone to make a four at whist, and as you are not dancing . . .'

Luke hesitated. 'I should be glad, ma'am – but I'm afraid I don't know the game.'

'Such a pity!' Mrs Wainwright's false eyebrows rose right up to the hairline of her wig. 'But I feared it would be so.'

Refusing to be nettled, Luke said: 'I'm very sorry. Perhaps if it doesn't take much learning – or if there is some other game I could –'

'Oh, don't trouble yourself, sir,' said Sir Hugh, who had been looking him up and down. 'Whist is not a game the uneducated mind can quickly apprehend – and I know no fen-sports.'

Unruly anger welled up in Luke's chest: but George was suddenly at his elbow. 'Cousin Luke,' he said, 'Mary is already mortified at my dancing, and rather hopes that you will do her the honour of the next so that her toes may be spared. Ma'am – Sir Hugh – a delightful assembly, is it not?'

Mrs Wainwright's eyes glittered. 'Indeed. We were just asking your cousin, as you say, sir, if he would join Hugh at cards, but he confesses himself unequal to the task.'

'What about you, Hardwick?' Sir Hugh said.

George smiled without warmth. 'No, I fear you will be laying stakes; and with my money I have become like a jealous father with an only child, and keep it close-confined in my pockets.'

'Oh, but what is money for, but to spend?' said Sir Hugh in a tone of amusement.

'Yes, surely, Mr Hardwick, you place too high a value on mere money,' said Mrs Wainwright. Old enmities were stirring.

'Perhaps I do,' said George pleasantly. 'A shortage of it has that effect. As does a surplus, as you know, Mrs Wainwright. But I assure you there are things I value more.'

'Birth, breeding, perhaps?' said Mrs Wainwright, looking at Luke.

'Oh, what is birth, without good manners?' said George. 'And all the money in the world cannot buy those. Come, cousin, shall we find Mary?'

Mr Wainwright, standing by the fireplace with Horace, said: 'Tell me – have you seen much of Wiley lately?'

'No, I get about less and less: and I am training up Luke to carry much of the responsibility. He is a keen pupil.'

'Aye, you've done a good thing there. Wish I had a son to help me . . . But Wiley: he seems secretive – up to something.'

'D'you think Wiley's Bank may have to close, is that it?'

'No . . . no, I doubt it. There was some trouble just recently, but he weathered the storm somehow . . .' He watched as Elizabeth got up to dance with the fair young man.

'Your daughter has a party with her I do not recognise,' Horace said.

'Eh? Oh – them. Just some London friends of Hugh's.'

'I do not see young Kesteven here yet,' said Horace.

'Well, I sent him an invitation, as you asked. I've a mind to call him in to see Wilhelmina. She walks in her sleep and goes around breaking things and last week tried to set light to the curtains . . .'

Rebecca was being made much of: and though somewhat perplexed, she had to admit she was enjoying it. Having expected to come to the assembly and talk to the few people her family knew in local society and perhaps dance a couple of dances and then sit beside her mother and sister, it was rather overwhelming, as the fourth dance began, to find no less than five men competing for her hand and none of them willing to take a denial. Mr Warren was there again and Sir Hugh Woodhouse who was trying to win through physical presence and volume of voice, and a clergyman called the Reverend Doctor Emmonsales who clearly did not let his cloth interfere with his pleasure, and a man called Yeatman from the Woodhouse party, and even Humphrey Amory whose wife had temporarily deserted him to gossip with some old friends. In the end she stood up with Humphrey Amory, whom she at least knew and whose attentions were likely to be less personal: and as she danced she resolved to sit the next one out. Who did these men think they were? There wasn't one of them she would look at twice with Luke Hardwick in the same room.

'I am the most miserable of men,' said Robert Landless.

'Why?' Elizabeth said. 'Because I have consented to dance with you?'

'Not *that*. Great heaven, no. In that respect I am a man blessed. But in another I am cursed, doomed: insofar as – as – it cannot be said.'

'Perhaps then, Mr Landless, you had better not say it.' Elizabeth's voice was cool: but her face, which for long had been growing more and more pale, was tinged with colour.

Henry Milton had been drawn aside by his partner Francis Sedgmoor, and Julia was left sitting with Kate Sedgmoor, who was full of conversation, fired off at a rapid rate.

'Our husbands have their heads together over their wretched journal again,' she said. 'Francis talks of nothing else. You should have seen him when the first copy appeared! – he was actually caressing it with a little smile on his face. There was I feeling jealous of a sheet of paper. I declare I sometimes think men love mere *things* more than they do people. But there is one person – future person – whom I know we shall both love.' She glanced down at herself. 'I hardly show at all yet, do I?'

'Hardly at all,' said Julia, her deep voice very low. 'I wish you joy, Kate. It is wonderful news.'

'Of course, what I don't look forward to is becoming fat and frumpy and unable to go out. Francis says he will not mind me a bit, but I swear I shall hate to see myself in a mirror. Well, I hope this *Gazette* or whatever it is called does prosper, for we shall have an extra expense when baby comes, and Francis already says I live too extravagant now. How lucky you and Henry are having just the two of you to keep, Julia . . . !'

3

There was an interval for the first loyal toasts of the evening. Joshua Walsoken, who had drunk nothing and been in constant consultation with the landowner Bellaers, took the opportunity to speak to Rebecca.

'You have not wanted for partners, daughter.'

'No, father.' She looked at him. 'Does that displease you?'

'Not at all. It is right we should make a large acquaintance, as long as due propriety is attended to. There is one partner, however, of whom I cannot approve.'

She wrestled with her tongue: the last thing she wanted now was a quarrel with her father, especially when Luke himself had tried to make things so easy. 'He – he would not have been invited here if he were not a completely decent young man, father, whatever – '

'Allow me to be the judge of that. He was invited no doubt out of deference to Mr Horace Hardwick, but to anyone who is alive to the finer distinctions it is quite clear he does not belong here. Certainly it is impossible that my family should be on any terms of familiarity with him. Remember who you are, daughter. I will say no more. You know my feelings.'

Luke, after dancing with Mary, had looked across the room to Rebecca and seen her coppery head at the centre of a gaggle of suitors. At the same time he had overheard Esther Amory behind him muttering to Mrs Wiley: 'Yes, that's him. Oh, I could tell immediately – all the fine clothes in the world won't change that.'

He went to find a glass of wine, aware of a tightness at his chest. At the door of the refreshment-room a fan tapped his shoulder and someone spoke his name and he turned in irritation, prepared for another snub.

'By God, it *is* you!' the woman said. 'I've watched you for half an hour trying to make up my mind. Luke Taplin! What the devil are you doing here?'

He stared at her. 'Kitty . . . ?'

'Kitty Du Quesne, as ever was!' she said, with a hoarse attractive laugh. 'Well, there must be a story behind this. Come, there's seats in that alcove, away from all this posturing.'

She certainly looked different from when he had known her – five years ago it must have been – when she had lived on the fen, daughter of a smallholder who was drinking himself to death. The exotic name was deceptive: the Du Quesnes were descended from the Huguenots who had settled in the fens long ago, and Luke remembered them as poor if not poorer than their neighbours in the watery lands. Kitty then had had only the coarse frock and apron she stood up in: but now she was exquisitely dressed in a crimson polonaise with a jet choker at her throat, though she still had the same bold eyes and voluptuous figure.

'So tell me,' she said, looking him up and down with appraisal, 'did you have a winning lottery ticket? Or have you turned highwayman and robbed your way to fortune? Unless you're a footman here, and I'm mistook.'

Luke, in as few words as possible, told her his story.

'The devil's own luck!' she said when he had finished. 'Hardwick, eh?' She considered him shrewdly, the corner of her small red mouth curving. 'Well, I'm not so very surprised. Twas always clear that you were a shade – different. But a Hardwick . . . Strike me, you're set up for life, ain't you!'

'You could call it that,' Luke said. 'Sometimes the luck don't seem – entirely good. But what about you? Don't tell me yours is the same story.'

Kitty Du Quesne laughed, white teeth glinting. 'Nay, quite different. There's other ways for a woman to make her way in the world – as you should know, Luke. You was never a monk, if I remember right. I left the fen to go work as a seamstress in Deeping, but I soon found that didn't suit. Too much work and not enough play, and scarce two farthings to rub together. No, I chose to use my other talents.' She pointed with her fan. 'See him? The old warhorse there, half-asleep – Sir Samuel Edgington?'

Luke grimaced. 'I see him.'

'Oh, he's just the latest with a taking for me. Nothing more. He makes me some pretty presents and squeezes me now and then and I keep him at arm's length. I don't reckon he'd be up to the job if it came down to it . . . But I had a right good gent who was buried only this winter. Kept me in style for two years, and never any of the troubles and jealousies folk take on when they marry. Left me a tidy nest-egg, God bless him – though I don't reckon that's who he's gone to meet – he was too much of a rogue.' Kitty yawned.

'You always had a way wi' the men,' said Luke, noticing the rise and fall of her breasts as she stretched.

'Didn't I just? Course, there were few worth bothering with on the fen. Present company excepted, of course.' She narrowed her eyes at him. 'But you always kept just out of reach, didn't you? Always the dark horse . . . But what's this stuff about your luck? You don't regret what's happened to you, surely, you great lug!

Why, all that money to spend just as you will, take what pleasure you like.'

'Nay, you're right. I'd not change back now,' Luke said. 'But mebbe I don't think the way you do, Kitty . . .'

'Well, you should,' she said, tapping his chest with a finger. ''Tis the *only* way to think.'

Mary had seen Julia get up abruptly and go into the ladies' cloakroom ten minutes ago, and she had not returned. She went in search of her and found her sitting unattended with a handkerchief pressed to her mouth.

'Julia, are you unwell? What's wrong?'

Julia shook her head with a tight movement. Her thick unruly hair was coming down. 'This is a pretty spectacle,' she said huskily. 'I pride myself on never having feminine vapours . . . I just – had to get away for a minute.'

Mary drew up a chair beside her. 'Has something upset you?'

Julia twisted the handkerchief in her fingers. 'Oh, it is so foolish . . . But Kate – Kate Sedgmoor – she means no harm, but you know how she talks on . . .'

'Kate?' Mary frowned, and then suddenly everything was clear. 'Oh . . . Oh, Julia, but she cannot help but talk of it – '

'I *know*.' Julia took a deep breath. 'I know. As I would, God knows. But it – oh, you can't have failed to notice, Mary, it has become – like an *obsession* for me, this – this failure – '

'There's no *failure*,' said Mary. 'It's just one of those things. Every woman is different. In time – '

'But it *feels* like a failure,' Julia said vehemently. 'I feel empty, dried up, useless . . .'

'But Henry – surely he does not make you feel – '

'Oh, Henry is kind, thoughtful, everything. It hurts him too. But he has his work, which occupies him so much – more and more – and besides, it isn't possible he could ever entirely understand how it feels.'

Mary stroked Julia's hand, not knowing what to say.

'I shall be better in a moment,' Julia said. 'I thought, I shall have to leave, I shall have to go home. But that's so weak and hysterical – I *won't* become like that. Mary,' she said, suddenly fierce, 'don't mention this to Henry. I shall go out there again and be my normal self. We've got to keep up appearances. Though I wonder sometimes if those are all that's left . . .'

Christopher Kesteven arrived just as the toasts ended and everyone was reassembling for the dancing. Immediately he made for Rebecca.

'Dr Kesteven, I did not know you were here! How do you do.' She covered her disappointment: when the young man had appeared beside her she had thought for a moment it was Luke.

'Miss Walsoken.' He shook her hand. He was in his plain black frock coat, and looked as if he had been through some exertion. 'I hope I am not very late. It was no part of my plan – I arrived in Stamford in good time – but something quite surprising happened, in the pleasantest way.' He stopped, short of breath: she had never seen him so animated, and it made him look very boyish.

'Come, sit down and tell me,' she said.

'I had stabled my horse at the Red Lion,' he said, accepting a glass of canary but not drinking it, 'when a man in livery asked whether I was a surgeon – someone who recognised me had told him so – and he had been sent out to find one. A surgeon for Burghley House, no less.'

'You mean – you have attended the Earl of Exeter?'

'It was the Countess who was the patient. Their own physician is himself ill and the Earl was very concerned for his wife, though she said not to send for anyone. She was in a lot of pain from a tooth – the gum below had swelled and was suppurating; and I think she was fearful of having it pulled, as who is not.'

Rebecca shivered. 'I remember a barber in Norwich who pulled teeth. The screams one heard from his shop made me blench ... But go on.'

'Well, I was conducted along vast corridors to the Countess's bedroom. Burghley House I had seen from a distance, but the size of it when one is there is astonishing – it's like a town in itself. So ... I examined her in a palatial but very chilly bedroom – great tapestries, portraits – with Lord Burghley peering over my shoulder. An imposing man, gruff but not unfriendly. I was in some fear that the tooth would have to come out – sometimes one cracks the jawbone. You may imagine my gratification when I saw the answer – nothing so serious.'

She watched him take a sip of wine. 'Yes? Dr Kesteven, you are deliberately keeping me in suspense!'

He smiled. 'A sharp sliver of the skin of an apple had become deep embedded in the gum, so that it could hardly be seen. Almost by chance I detected it, and was able to remove it before the swelling grew worse. And so no need to lance, you see. Relief was almost immediate. I thought then I might be thanked and sent down to the kitchens to be given a glass of something. But the Earl himself took me into a vast drawing-room and pressed brandy on me, full of gratitude.'

'This is a feather in your cap indeed!'

Dr Kesteven licked his lips, his self-consciousness returning. 'I'm afraid I lapped up his praise, though any apothecary with a sharp eye would have noticed what was amiss. One should not, I know, feel any more gratified at this, than if it were a successful attendance on the poorest weaver. But it – it is a feather in the cap . . . As you say, Miss Rebecca.'

. . . 'In what do I offend?' said Robert Landless. 'In professing myself the slave of the most beautiful woman in the room – in the county – in England?'

Elizabeth, who had been sitting with downcast eyes, biting her lip, looked up at his earnest fine-boned face, and in spite of herself said: 'So you have seen every woman in England, Mr Landless?'

'I wouldn't care to now,' he said. 'You destroy all competition, Lady Woodhouse.'

Elizabeth looked away, hesitated. 'Whatever you choose to profess yourself, Mr Landless . . . I have no choice but to profess myself a married woman – and that for me to stand up with you again would be – '

'Improper? No, surely not so, not in these times. And where is this husband?' Landless raised his head, made a dismissive gesture. 'When he returns to his rightful place – beside you – I shall make way; but until then may I not repair his omission?'

Milton, who had had a hard day and was really ready for nothing but bed, watched them from a distance, his mind straying back to the time when he had played just such a part. She had been a different Elizabeth then, though – not just by the fact that she was now married. She seemed somehow tense and hard. But of course she had grown older, as they all had. The music began again, and people lined up for the gavotte, a new dance that was becoming popular. A miscellaneous collection, thin, fat, elegant, dowdy, beautiful, plain, young, old. An inescapable melancholy crept over him like a chill, as he thought of Elizabeth Wainwright as he had first seen her, of the young who would be old, the beauty that must fade.

. . . So, Rebecca's talking to the young surgeon fellow, Luke said to himself. So what then? And with great interest it seems . . . but why should that matter? He was determined to be a gentleman, wasn't he? In action and thought.

Kitty Du Quesne was amusedly receiving the gouty attentions of old Sir Samuel Edgington, and he had lost the other Hardwicks. He noticed Miss Yeatman from the Woodhouse party sitting alone. He had heard she was a stranger here on a visit, and she was looking bored and left out. He walked over and in his best manner asked her if she would care to dance.

She looked up, smiled, accepted. He stood aside to let someone pass. As she bent to gather up her fan Warren, who had observed him, leaned over and whispered in her ear.

She stood up, averting her eyes from Luke, said 'You must excuse me, sir,' and moved away.

. . . 'You see, Mr Walsoken, once the drainage failed so disastrously, my grandfather lost heart. Indeed I would say it broke his heart,' said Bellaers. 'I will be frank with you – Bicklode Fen is a wilderness. Most of it I cannot get any rent for at all. Those folk who do eke out a living there are hybrid creatures, I believe, more fish than man. Of course, if it could be reclaimed, its value would increase ten, twenty fold.'

Joshua Walsoken stroked his hairless chin. 'One hears these kind of figures.'

'It is true, I assure you. For my part I want no more to do with it. I sometimes wonder if one can ever really tame the fen. It has a way of always – mastering you.'

Walsoken smiled. 'I have never been mastered yet, Mr Bellaers.'

Luke watched the second gavotte with eyes that seemed to have lost the power of detail. All he saw was powdered heads and patched faces and lace cuffs and high clicking heels and pinched fastidious noses, merged as if part of one monstrous, supercilious creature at eternal enmity with him. Rebecca was dancing with the young surgeon. He watched and waited for the dance to end. There was only one thing he wanted here, he thought. Only one thing in the world. Be damned to the gentleman stuff. All that nonsense about a light heart had been an attempt, he now realised, to deceive himself.

Christopher Kesteven did not dance at all well: Rebecca suspected he had only asked her because he was afraid his medical talk had bored her. She had not been bored all evening; and she liked the young man and had not wanted to refuse him. But the wine that had made her a little tipsy earlier had worn off, and now she thought of Luke and the reels that were to come and whether he would dance those with her. She had last seen him talking, for some time, to a young woman in startling red, but bearing in mind what he had said earlier she tried to take no heed of it. There was the question, of course, of disobeying her father ... but deep down she had already made up her mind on that.

A light heart ... She did not feel light-hearted. Luke disturbed her in a tumultuous, alarming way. She felt – *vulnerable* before him. A light heart ... All at once the thought came to her of Luke dancing the reels with the woman in red, smiling his mocking smile.

Sir Hugh Woodhouse was enjoying the evening. It was all so much more jolly since his London friends had arrived, taking his mind off his dreary miserable deadlock with Lizzie.

In the meantime he had met a very agreeable fellow called Landless, who talked knowledgeably about shooting, a subject close to Sir Hugh's heart, and had some interesting tales about hunting and how it was done on the Continent. Must remember to ask him to come over and join them at Deenecote while there was still some hunting left.

Outside in St George's Square it was full dark and Mr Wainwright had given the signal for the bonfire to be lit and the fireworks set off. The cheering of a small crowd could be heard in the ballroom above the orchestra: and there were flashes of colour at the curtained windows as Luke walked towards Rebecca.

Mr Warren had stopped her to say something: and though she smiled as she turned to see Luke he was unable to stop a great festering bitterness that rose in him and made him say: 'Finished wi' your fine fancy friends, have you? Got a moment for me?'

'Don't be silly.' She was hurt, but he interpreted her expression as haughtiness.

'Oh, forgive me. I wasn't well taught. Well, if tis not beneath you to speak to me – '

'This is a ball,' she said whitely. 'So I talk to people and dance, if that's not too strange for you – '

'Aye, to be sure you do.' He could not stop himself: all the snubs, all the strain, all the impossibility of his position seemed to bear down on him, sending the fury racing through his veins. 'There's always folk who'll sniff round at the right encouragement.'

'How dare you!' she said. 'I suppose it would suit you if I sat meekly in a corner waiting for *you* the whole night.'

'Well, you seem to have been nice and comfortable in my absence,' he said. 'Your nice young surgeon. "Oh, Dr Kesteven, sit by me." "Oh, Dr Kesteven, how nicely you dance." Dear, dear, what a to-do.'

She glared at him with the pure heat of rage. 'Go on,' she said quietly. 'Go on, Luke. I'm so anxious to learn from you how to behave.'

'Where I come from there's only one word for your sort of behaviour!' he stormed.

'Where *you* come from! Oh, I wondered when we would get to that. That's it, isn't it? Where you come from everyone is a perfect saint and full of country virtue. Perhaps your little friend in red's like that, eh? Or is that different? Is there a different standard of behaviour when it comes to *you*?' She laughed bitterly. 'Now I know what you mean with your "light heart".'

'I don't have to answer to you for every damn thing – '

'And I'm not accountable to you! Perhaps you'd better go back to her – perhaps she's more amenable to what you really want in a woman.'

'What big words you use, m'lady,' he hissed.

'You'd prefer it if I didn't use any.'

He made a hopeless gesture, shook his head as if to clear it. 'All this crowd . . . it gets on my nerves. I got to speak to you alone. Rebecca . . . Come outside a minute.'

'Why?' Her throat was tight: a great fount of misery was already welling in her, but for the moment her pride and her temper still blazed. 'Why should I – I'm enjoying myself here. Why should – '

'Miss Walsoken, is this man bothering you?' Philip Warren was suddenly beside them. 'I can soon have him turned out, if he's getting above himself.'

With an economical movement, such that hardly anyone noticed it, Luke struck him in the face. Warren went down as if poleaxed.

Luke grabbed her arm and said, 'Come outside – Rebecca, ye've got to . . .' but she shook him off. 'I *won't*! Or what will you do – strike me too and *drag* me out? I don't *belong* to you! Nor my father nor anyone!'

'Then be damned to you!' said Luke in a clenched voice.

Warren's lip was bleeding but he was otherwise unhurt. By the time he was on his feet Luke was gone and the music was starting again. One of the few people who had witnessed the incident was Joshua Walsoken, who firmly steered Rebecca across to the other side of the room. 'Only what I expected,' he said. 'Talk to me now of that young man's decency.'

I won't cry, she told herself. I won't cry.

Outside in the square the bonfire was blazing: some little children were dancing round it and a man was roasting chestnuts in the flames. Smoke curled and rose and was lost in the deeper blue of the cold night sky. Fireworks cracked and whooshed and women squealed and drew back, pulling their skirts close around them.

Luke was covered in prickly sweat. His breath came in great hurt gasps and he stood and stared at the bonfire with the heat of the flames on his face.

A hand touched his arm, and he spun round. Kitty Du Quesne, a satin cloak about her shoulders. Her face was an enigmatic oval in the half-light, the eyes glittering and intense.

'That was the best entertainment of the evening,' she said.

He shrugged off her hand, turned from her irritably.

'Got the mulligrubs, have you, Luke? Me too. These gentlefolk don't know how to enjoy theirselves. Tis all flowery talk and bowing and scraping. I've had enough.'

'Aye,' said Luke. 'I've had enough.'

From out here the music came thin and rarefied, blown on the air like a scent, unbearably delicate. A spray of orange sparks flew out from the fire, hissing on the cobbles.

'We don't belong wi' that world, you and me, do we, Luke? We take what we can from it, but we don't belong, deep down.' Her voice was lazy, hoarsely soothing. 'Where are you going, Luke? Not back in there. Home?'

He licked his lips, looked away again. 'Nay . . . I don't know.'

'I'm for home,' Kitty said. 'I got a place up in Scotgate now. Moved in last month. Few rooms above Mistress Erith's. My nest-egg, see. Tis a cosy berth. Like to see it, would you?'

She watched his broad shoulders, tense with indecision. He cleared his throat, seemed about to refuse, then abruptly took her arm.

'So,' she said as they walked up St Mary's Street, 'perhaps the best part of the entertainment's not over after all . . .'

Just after eleven the Walsoken party, with George and Mary, made ready to leave, but the ball was going on. There had been more toasts and a patriotic song or two, and the hardiest dancers were still footing it. Humphrey Amory, who had hardly been off the floor all night, was still twirling and leaping, his wig slipping down over his eyes, while his wife yawned behind her fan. Old Horace Hardwick was still there, talking to Dr Kesteven. Mrs Wainwright had tried a few fishing remarks about Luke, but Horace refused to be drawn. He had resolved from the start that with Luke he would never moralise or lecture: let the young man take responsibility for his own actions.

George and Mary, riding back to Aysthorpe in the chaise with Rebecca, pretended not to see the tears that she impatiently wiped from her cheeks. They just kept coming unbidden. Before they left Mrs Wiley had made an admiring remark about her being the belle of the evening. But it was all dust and ashes. She stared out of the window at the darkened fields and thought: it's all over.

Kitty Du Quesne had some fiery smuggled gin in her cramped apartments over a shop in Scotgate: and Luke drank enough of it to feed the bitterness and turmoil inside him. When at last Kitty snuffed one of the candles and he slid her shift off her shoulders to reveal her uplifted breasts his lust was of the same kind, charged and grim, and desolate.

The silk gown and petticoat slipped rustling in a crumpled pool at her feet, and her eyes, hard and glowing above the milky nakedness of her body, watched him as he undressed. A feeble light from the window outlined him, taut and muscled, as he came to her. His hands were large and gently rough, thumbs chafing her elongated nipples and then sliding down her flanks and across the tight knot of tawny hair between her thighs.

They subsided on to the bed, and she arched her back and buried her fingers in his black shaggy hair as his lips and bristled jaw probed along her neck and breasts. 'Luke,' she said. His tongue travelled down her stretched torso, warm, moist, never still, while her breath came in shorter and shorter gasps.

His lips were on her face again and she reached down, touched powerful thighs and stroked his burning flesh. She groaned, drawing him into her, legs encircling his broad back.

The candle on the table was almost gone: at the last it was just enough to show her, as his hands gripped her buttocks almost lifting her off the bed and she choked and clasped him, that the light in his eyes was anything but holy. Her teeth grazed his shoulder before they were still.

Some time later clouds were dispersing in the night sky and allowed a little moonlight to filter into the room, showing up the bottle and glasses, the clothes, the shabby pieces of furniture in a mild, impersonal way. Kitty was quickly asleep, one arm thrown across the pillow, her breath faintly rattling. There was no sleep in Luke. He sat up and stared into the silver-blue shadows, with hell in his heart.

FOUR

I

One evening in August 1778 six gentlemen were seated round the rosewood table in the small panelled dining-room of Bromswold.

The six men were Mr Joshua Walsoken, at the head: Mr Thornton Wiley, now his partner in what had become the Wiley & Walsoken Bank: Dr St John Villiers, the Peterborough physician: a Mr Stead, who was there not in a private capacity but as the land agent of Lord Fitzwilliam of Milton House: Mr Abraham Quy, solicitor and notary for oaths: and Mr George Hardwick of Morholm.

They were Adventurers, in the old sense of the term as applied to those who undertook the drainage of fens: though it was only George Hardwick who fitted the term in its more usual sense, in that he still had at twenty-six an unquiet look about his lean face – and had, moreover, the most to lose of all the company.

They had dined well, and now the port-bottle circulated. Talk became optimistic, expansive, and even fanciful: the drier details of finance and planning had been gone through both during dinner and the previous few months, and this was really by way of a celebratory occasion. Dreams of riches and success were freely aired.

Mr Walsoken and Mr Stead had just returned from London, where they had successfully petitioned Parliament for the act enabling the drainage and enclosure of Bicklode Fen in Lincolnshire. Bellaers, the former owner of the majority of this great tract, had been happy to get rid of it at under four pounds an acre. The intention of the partners in the new scheme – led by Walsoken – was to drain the fen by making new cuts to the main outfall and erecting windmills to pump the water away, and when the land was reclaimed to divide it into holdings where, it was hoped, would flourish arable and sheep farming of huge productivity. Work was already under way in delimiting and enclosing the area, and the Commissioner had given the signal to begin hiring labourers to work on the new embankments at Michaelmas. Spurred by the energy of Joshua Walsoken, things had moved very fast. There were even hopes that the land would be under cultivation next summer.

The scheme meant an initial outlay of five thousand pounds for the four smaller partners – Walsoken and Lord Fitzwilliam being the major shareholders – with further calls on their purses to come, dependent on the number of pumping-mills that would have to be erected. George Hardwick was the last partner to join.

No one was more surprised than George himself that he should be one of them. Two turns of fortune were responsible for this: the third, and perhaps decisive element, was the gambler's streak in his character.

Wiley's Bank had very nearly folded in the spring. When it was relaunched as Wiley & Walsoken George's feelings had been mixed – his neighbour was now effectively his banker – but not for long. One of Mr Walsoken's first actions as partner was to review George's long-standing loan with the bank and drastically reduce the interest. It was an extremely handsome gesture – and even improvident – and George had at first been reluctant to accept it.

'My dear Mr Hardwick,' Walsoken had said, 'it is already done. Say no more of it, please. I am a man of business, but where I can mix it with pleasure I do so: and it gives me pleasure to lessen the difficulties of a deserving neighbour and friend.'

The second stroke of luck was even more unexpected. Two years ago, when the full extent of his brother's mismanagement of Morholm had become known, George had raised a loan of a thousand pounds, with high interest, from a Wisbech moneylender in the form of a promissory note. Last month the moneylender had written to him that the bill had been bought by a Mr Luke Hardwick.

George's first thought was that it was actually Horace who had done it: but a letter from Luke, whom they had not seen for some time, confirmed that it was he himself who was in possession of the bill – and he was not merely reducing the interest, but discounting it altogether. George was absolved of the debt.

It was heady wine for George. With Morholm surrounded by an ocean of wheat that promised one of the best harvest for years, a warm dry summer, rents back up to normal level – suddenly he had the prospect of actually being free of debt in the near future. It was almost too much to believe.

His decision to take a share in the Bicklode Fen venture was all the more inexplicable to Mary.

'For the first time since we were married we find ourselves almost free of debt,' she had said. 'And so you go and plunge into *new* debt. Oh, George, I don't understand. It just seems like borrowing from Peter to pay Paul.'

George had raised his share by a second mortgage on part of the estate. 'But this is an investment, my love. Laying out money in order that more money will be returned in due course. This land when it is drained will yield like the horn of plenty. It will make our fortune – real riches, instead of just ambling along as we would otherwise. You know what a keenly man Walsoken is – he knows a good investment when he sees one. You know it goes hard with me to – oh, to be humble, to just muddle along. To see you patching old clothes instead of buying new ones. In a year or two this will change all that.'

'I suppose Mr Walsoken would not be rash in such a matter. But he is very persuasive . . . and, George, he is *rich*. He can afford to take risks.'

'And so shall we be rich. And does not the taking of risks add a savour to life?'

Lawyer Quy, a small round rosy man who concealed an astute brain behind fluttering effeminate mannerisms, was proposing a toast to the success of the venture. George drank with the rest, and for the first time a bat of doubt flitted across his mind. Well . . . the die was cast now.

The ladies of the Walsoken household, whom Joshua had always insisted be kept out of the sphere of business, had taken their meal in the back parlour. Rebecca, tired of the prosings of her mother and sister, took the spaniel out into the garden.

With the dog frisking round her she strolled in the peach-coloured light of dusk, admiring in spite of herself her father's improvements.

She took an interest in her father's ventures, and last week had persuaded him to take her with him when he went out to Bicklode Fen. The carriage was useless there and they had gone on horseback.

Bicklode Fen lay fifteen miles to the north, not far from Spalding: but it might have been a different world from Aysthorpe, which was on the edge of the upland. It was different too from the fenland to the south. The Bedford Level, though always unpredictable, had been partly tamed. Here man's efforts had been feeble, fraught with failure. The horizon sliced the sky like a razor at a throat. Their horses picked a perilous path between reeds and pools, and after a time could not or would not go further. Clouds like mountains and castles of vapour converged above, throwing miles in and out of shadow in the space of a few seconds. She saw dykes choked and lost, a derelict windmill with sails like picked bones. There was a rich, ancient smell of peat and moss and rot, and the cries of strange birds, borne across the dwarfing distances. Here and there were stretches of deep green pasture where sheep and geese wandered at will: the rest was bog and dyke and mere. The few, scattered dwellings were virtually huts, lonely and squatting as low as the fen itself.

Partly it was beautiful: the fen-droves were broad swathes of colour, covered with meadowsweet and forget-me-not and marsh-orchis and lilies. Partly it was sullen, alien, a place that would not yield its secrets easily nor lightly. It made her think of the tales she had heard about the wild fens: of the men who lived there who swallowed opium as unthinkingly as she did tea to keep the ague and the 'horrors' away, of the will o'the wisps or 'corpse candles' that led you to your death, of the floods that descended like the one at Holland Fen eight years ago which George Hardwick had told her about, sweeping away the efforts of man in one stroke like a gesture of contempt. It made her think of the man who had flashed in and out of her life like those sudden flourishes of sunlight on the fields.

Her father saw it quite differently. It was land that was not being used properly: it was a potential source of great profit. She made an effort to share this attitude. To be impersonal, that was the secret. All else led to complication and frustration. But it was not easy.

She had been out and about a lot lately, chiefly helping Christopher Kesteven, who was attempting to introduce inoculation into the area. As her father's circle of acquaintance widened she became known at many of the houses of the gentry, and had gently bullied several families in Peterborough to have their children inoculated by Dr Kesteven. Once the idea was established others would follow. She had gone with him on other visits too, often to houses of the poor to reassure those who were half afraid of the doctor, suspecting he would experiment on them. It was activity, which was what she needed above all, and it was worthwhile: and her father saw sick visiting as proper for a young lady, as long as she did not go near infection. This she often did, but did not tell him.

From the garden she saw a figure go up to the servants' door and knock tentatively. She shaded her eyes with her hand. Deborah Gedney. Rebecca had not seen her for a long time: she wondered if she had been avoiding her.

Nancy had just opened the door when Rebecca came up. 'It's all right, Nancy,' Rebecca said. 'Hullo, Deborah.'

She saw immediately that Deborah was pregnant. The girl had flushed slightly on seeing her, muttered that she wanted a few words if it was convenient.

Rebecca took her in the music-room, which was seldom used, and made her sit down. Deborah's skin was buttery brown from the summer and she looked healthy, but her belly was already very big.

'Is it Mark's?' Rebecca said.

'Aye,' Deborah's green eyes flashed. 'Who else would it be?'

'I didn't mean it that way.'

Deborah frowned, rubbed her hands down her apron. 'Nay, I know. It's – it's your advice I come to ask. See, we was plannin' on getting wed come the autumn. Wi' Mark working on harvest – his dad's got no work for him – and me as well, we reckoned to have a mite saved up by then. Then Mark could move in wi' me and grandma – we could mebbe add another room on back, or a lean-to anyway. Mark's handy like that.'

'When's the baby due?'

'November-time. I can carry on working for now – but o' course I'll have to stop sometime. If – if I have it . . .'

Rebecca was puzzled for a moment. 'If you – Oh, no, Deborah. Not that.'

'They d'say a little turpentine will bring it off.'

Rebecca stared at her. 'Would you?'

Deborah grimaced. 'Nay. Nay, I couldn't. But it's come at an awkud time. Oh, tis our own fault, I know. But folk don't tek much heed round here. Some say tis best to happen before the weddin', for it shows the woman can have children . . . I just don't know what to do for the best.'

'What does Mark say?'

'He want for us to get wed straight away.' Deborah smiled faintly.

'And so does his dad. Trouble is, old Seth's not so well as he were – and when Mark has to support me he'll not be able to help his dad.'

'Get married,' Rebecca said. 'Right away. You love each other, don't you?'

'Oh, aye . . .'

'And then the baby will have Mark's name and you'll be together. Think of the other problems then. I'm sure that will be best.'

Deborah considered her a moment, then smiled broadly. 'I hoped ye'd say that. I just wanted to hear it said . . . I been worryin' and frettin' so long – but it's not a thing to be gloomy about, after all, is it?'

'You and Mark and the baby,' Rebecca said. 'That's what matters. And you know if you need help – '

'Now, don't say it,' said Deborah. 'Y'know how I feel about that.'

'Yes, I know,' said Rebecca. 'And you know the offer always stands. So there. Now tell me, when can I come and see you married?'

Deborah counted on her fingers, her face lit and cheerful again. 'Well, me and Mark can go see the new parson about callin' the banns – '

She broke off. Joshua Walsoken was standing in the doorway.

'Oh, father,' said Rebecca, 'have your guests gone? I – '

'What is this person doing here?' His eyes travelled over Deborah's figure and averted themselves.

'Deborah came to ask my advice.' She met her father's intolerant stare.

'I'll be going now,' Deborah said quietly, rising.

'You will not in future allow such persons in the house,' Mr Walsoken said.

After Deborah had gone Mr Walsoken began to talk of the Bicklode Fen scheme, pacing up and down and jingling the money in his pockets. '. . . Of course, I anticipate certain disagreements. Villiers in particular is a cautious man and all future expenditure will have to be – You have no interest in this, Rebecca?'

'Not at the moment. I can only think of the way you spoke to me in front of Deborah just now.'

'What? A common slut – '

'She is nothing of the kind. But that is hardly the issue.'

'I think it is. That you associate yourself with such shameless, brazen – '

'It does not matter who it is!' Rebecca said. Mr Walsoken perceived she was really angry. 'If you are so anxious to show you are better than such folk you will hardly do it by speaking to me in that manner in front of them! The worst drunken tinker who lays about him with his belt could do no worse.'

He stared at her. For the past few months there had been an uneasy truce between them: but this new defiance was doubly alarming. It suggested that there was someone – could it be? – in his household who was no longer afraid of him. And always she could hit home, undermine his authority by these cutting references to his pretensions to gentility. She deserved a beating, and he would have given her it – but for that last remark.

'I have strong views on morality,' he said, choosing to turn the point. 'In remote country districts such as this there may be different – traditions. But I cannot countenance them. I hardly need remind you of your Bible . . . Medhurst was too lax. I believe our new parson, Rev. Emmonsales, will have a beneficial effect. As for you . . .' He studied his daughter's face. No, she was not afraid – not afraid of anything. 'We – we will say no more on the subject.'

The skirmish was over: but the war might break out any time.

2

George Hardwick might never have had the chance to thank Luke for freeing him of that thousand pound debt: for Luke had come near to freeing himself of everything.

His father, often acidulous and crotchety with other people, loved him: but coming so late, it was by nature an unconditional love: the silences that fell between them, whilst not unfriendly, spoke of a huge gap of common experience. He made no comment as to where Luke had gone on the night of the Patriotick Assembly.

Kitty Du Quesne had turfed him out early next morning: she had Sir Samuel coming. They had met by chance since, as was inevitable in a town of five thousand souls. It was clear how little that encounter had meant to her: it was clear also she would not be averse to a repeat if the opportunity arose.

She soon found him out, however. Her eyes narrowed with slightly malicious pleasure as she said: 'Why, you're still pining for that red-headed streak of a girl – the one with the rich father who dresses like a parson! Well, well, who'd have thought it – Luke Taplin –

sorry, Hardwick – acting like a moonstruck calf. God's shite, I thought you'd more sense.'

He had heard of George Hardwick's bill from a business acquaintance when he was at the corn exchange in Wisbech. Horace had thought him mad. 'Family feeling is all very well, Luke ... but upon my soul, I hope you'll not make a habit of such things.'

'Tis a personal matter,' Luke said. 'Something it pleased me to be able to do. Business is different – you needn't worry on that score.'

But he felt a great emptiness inside. One day in August he rode out to Holme Fen to spend a day with his old cronies, punting and fishing amongst the streams and dykes. They were glad enough to see him: but they stood back from him a little, treated him with a deference he did not look for, as if awed by his fine clothes and altered manners. A glorious sun bathed them, warblers sang in the sedge, the horizons shored away on all sides in layers of vaporizing colour. But the old heart-freeing pleasure was no longer there, nor in the names that used to be so evocative – Bevil's Leam, Glassmoor, Ugg-Mere, Popham's Eau. He left his old friends early, with vague promises to meet again, and walked by himself on the shores of Ramsey Mere. It lay flat and smooth as polished steel: snipe and dabchick scored their reflections across it. On the dry marsh across the far bank were purple grasses, stroked like flock by the wind.

It was a lonely place, and Luke suffered a clouding of the spirit, such as he sometimes felt in the small hours at the silent townhouse in Stamford. But much worse.

A path led him into the edge of the reed-shore beside the mere. The reeds were very high here, twelve feet or more, screening him from sight. There was a marshy stink, and a whine of gnats like a mad vibration in the head. Half-consciously he decided to turn back and, twisting, found his foot sunk into the mud by the path. He pulled, and found himself in danger of losing his boot. He bent to hook his fingers through the boot-strap and tug. His other foot, taking his weight, slid with a plop even deeper. Within a few moments he was sunk up to his waist. And he was still sinking.

Stories of men, horses, carts lost this way spun through his mind. The smell was suffocating – old, rank, greedy. He sank slowly, slow as age, slow as death. He opened his mouth to yell as the mud reached his chest, and in the same moment his feet touched solid clay and the sinking stopped.

Gnats hummed. The sun was a genial ball, remote in an empty sky. The solid ground of the path was a couple of feet away – he could reach out and feel it with his fingertips – but there was nothing with which to grasp and heave himself up. The reeds towered on either side like a wall. The pressure of the mud restricted his breathing, and he took desperate gasps and there was a tic of panic in his brain.

And he knew he wanted to live. God forgive me, I even thought I wanted to die . . . But I want to *live*.

The sun watched him for several hours, at last growing dimmer and sliding down the sky as if losing interest. He conserved his breath for shouts, every few minutes.

Who lived around here? No one. Living with Sam they had often not seen a soul for days on end. Think. Ramsey a good way away. Drained fields to the north, sheep meadows. The odd cottage . . . But it was *harvest*, for God's sake! Labourers *everywhere*. Yes, on the wheatlands. Not on the shores of the mere . . . I want to live . . .

The little boy did not have the face of an angel – though Luke blessed him as such – but a firmly mortal face, streaked with dirt and rather frightened by the sight of the truncated man calling to him from the mud. He was going home after a day's work bird-scaring in the bean fields, and knew all the safe spots in the reed-shore. When he scampered away Luke had a moment of fear that he would not come back, but he did in a few minutes, bringing his father and brother who carried a length of rope and with much laughter dragged Luke out of the mud. They thought it very amusing the way this town gent in his fancy clothes had wandered into the reed-shore like it was a garden.

Luke saw the joke, and laughed too: could not stop laughing, for relief and joy at the life that was his again and that he knew for sure he wanted.

3

Elizabeth, Lady Woodhouse, was experiencing something like happiness for the first time in many months.

The stimulus of company at Deenecote was partly the reason for this: the London party were staying all summer. They were young and lively and noisy: their voices broke the silence of the long pilastered corridors, their entertainments roused her from her listlessness: and although she and Hugh still had separate bedrooms and were barely polite with each other, the presence of their guests made life infinitely more supportable.

When the days were fine, as they nearly all were that beautiful dry summer, they made parties out to attractive spots in Northamptonshire, for picnics, for boating on the river, for the races at Peterborough and Huntingdon, or they practised archery and played bowls on the smooth lawns behind the Hall: and then there were card-parties and billiards and suppers and once amateur theatricals in the library. Others of their acquaintance came regularly: the Van Druytens, Warren, the Bellaers. And Robert Landless.

Sleeves rolled up above pale forearms, propelling the punt through the water with graceful ease: one dark-lashed eye puckered as he took aim at an archery target: his sharp profile animated across the dining-table as he told a comic story to Hugh, who always bellowed with laughter: his erect figure on horseback, slim as a wand, buttery yellow hair lit by the sun: Elizabeth watched him, and tried not to, and tried to persuade herself that this happiness – this sickly sweet, out-of-place happiness – was not chiefly because of him.

They performed scenes from *As You Like It* in the library. Landless was Orlando. She was Rosalind. She could not act and knew it: but it didn't matter. His eyes were frank and without dissembling as he took her hand and said, in a voice scarcely meant for the spectators, ' "Then love me . . . Rosalind." '

Hugh liked him: he was a highly entertaining companion with ample leisure. But she knew what Landless really thought of her husband: she knew who was really his object in his visits to Deenecote.

Once, on an outing to Castle Ashby, she and Landless became a little separated from the rest of the party – the sort of accident that could not occur without some half-acknowledged design on both their parts. He seized her hand and pressed it to his lips, kissing it again and again. Neither had said a word, and in a few moments had joined up with the rest of the party. She could not have spoken: she was choked, dizzy, ecstatic, desolate, numb: and lost.

It was all hopeless of course: but there was a kind of delicious suspension about that summer, a sense of possibilities, and of unreality. It carried her along, heedless.

*

The Yeatman party were to move off at last for Scotland to be there in time for the beginning of the shooting season. Sir Hugh at the last minute announced his intention to go as well. The thought of losing that congenial company, and the prospect of the long dull months at Deenecote, was too much for him. He did not invite Elizabeth to go, and she made no demur. 'You rest up here, my dear,' he said. 'Take things quiet. You know how I fancy grouse-shooting – but it would be poor entertainment for you. Of course, you'll have plenty of company here. Good Lord, what with the Bellaers and the Van Druytens and your mother and Mina – I don't suppose you'll be alone for a minute. And the steward can always be relied on, if there's business about the estate.'

Deenecote Hall was indeed quieter and Elizabeth much relieved after the party had set off for Scotland. As Sir Hugh said, there were still many callers to while away the days. Not the least frequent of them was Robert Landless.

4

Virtually the whole of Aysthorpe was at work over the harvest.

George was out all day, either at the home farm, or at the outlying farms where to the delighted surprise of both him and his tenants, a record crop was in the offing despite the floods of the last autumn. The three big open fields of the village too, he was glad to see, were a patchwork of ripening crops: there was a better year in store for his small tenants and the freeholders. For everyone in fact: the largesse of the land could never be entirely appropriated, which was as it should be.

The new Rector of Aysthorpe-with-Ufford was – as the gentleman himself had predicted – the Reverend Dr Arthur Emmonsales. He had moved in with his two small daughters and several servants in June.

A cold wind had blown through the rectory and the musty old church. Rev. Emmonsales's Christianity was of a vigorous, horse-riding kind, with humility low on its list of tenets. George did not much like him, and the feeling was mutual. But Mr Joshua Walsoken of Bromswold was a man after his own heart.

The first banns of the marriage of Deborah Gedney and Mark Upwell were called on Sunday August 23rd. Rev. Emmonsales had stared hard at Deborah's swollen belly when they went to see him one evening after work in the fields, but had made no comment.

Mark Upwell was a light-hearted, quick-witted young man who took few things in life seriously. He was devoted to Deborah, and after the first shock of her pregnancy he had taken a sanguine view: so, all the better, they would marry, he would work all the hours God sent, things would work out all right. Come Michaelmas he would go to the hiring-fair at Peterborough where labourers were taken on for the winter: his father, old Seth, said he could manage what little was left to him.

But though Mark knew it was common enough for a pregnant girl to work in the fields right up until the baby was born – and be back at work the next day – he was not happy about it. Every day it took more of a toll on Deborah – and he knew she did not eat enough, for not only was she trying to put a bit by from her harvest earnings, but she gave the best titbits to her grandmother. Her only trouble was she was too kind: he didn't want the child to suffer.

He had heard that Joshua Walsoken had stocked the grounds of Bromswold with partridges: so one moonless night, though he was dog-tired from harvest, he took a net and left Seth sleeping soundly and walked over the fields to Bromswold and climbed Mr Walsoken's new fences: just to see how the land lay.

It was so easy. A plump bird almost fell into his hands. Bromswold, screened by trees, was in darkness. He supposed Walsoken had engaged no gamekeeper yet: the grounds of the old place, after all, hardly amounted to a park. Surprised at his own luck, he slipped back home across the fields.

He told Deborah that the bird had been caught straying on the common. She looked doubtful. But he could tell how much it was appreciated. Probably the first scrap of meat she had tasted in weeks. It did his heart good to see her eating well.

A week passed, and with it the second calling of the banns. The corn stood in fat drunken stooks in the fields. Mark spent his free time at the Gedneys' cottage, knocking up a few improvements that would make life easier when he moved in with Deborah. He was looking forward very much to the wedding. The brilliant sun continued to shine, and Mark's thin face was tanned nut-brown. Then there was a day of showery rain, and by night the clouds, though turning ragged, were still in the sky and obscuring the stars: and Mark decided to have one more foray on to Walsoken land.

There was, perhaps, a piquancy in lifting the odd bird from the grounds of the man who had treated his father so shabbily: but it was to see Deborah well fed again that he chiefly took the risk.

And once again there seemed hardly any risk at all. He crossed the hay fields – fields that his father had once worked – that lay to the south of the house, came up among the scrub and bramble of the derelict land round the old mill, and hopped over the wooden fence. There were bushes and young trees here where the partridges roosted: plenty of cover. A hundred yards ahead the trees thinned and there was a stretch of new-laid lawn and a path amongst flower-beds: then more shrubs and trees and a herb garden and beyond that the unshapely bulk of Bromswold.

He netted one bird almost immediately, and spotted another. He hesitated. No – he only wanted a good meal for Deborah, no more. How was he going to explain this one, anyway? Well, it would be the last one. To continue would be pushing his luck. He turned to retrace his steps, and a twig snapped underfoot. He froze, cursing himself for being clumsy. Then he realised it was not he who had made the sound. A shape loomed out from the thicket ahead.

He ran in the opposite direction, at right angles to the house, dodging amongst shrubs and saplings, low to the ground. He was fast and light on his feet. So Walsoken had engaged a gamekeeper. Or else it was a manservant keeping watch. Keep your head, make for the trees to your left. Get out there, where the barn and brew-house were. But his pursuer had guessed, was running parallel, heading to cut him off. Mark swerved, slipped, found himself in a shallow bowl overgrown with brambles, dropped and lay flat. Probably an old filled-in cesspit. He could not be seen if he lay absolutely flat and still. There were cracks and rustlings nearby. He held his breath as a pair of heavy feet passed just in front of him. The man carried a shaded lantern, a stave. No gun. Mark heard a low curse, and the figure turned back the way it had come, towards the mill.

He lifted his head cautiously. No way back to the hay-field. He could cut across to the north, where a few old elms marked the edge of the common. But it meant running right across the lawns, in full view of the house, before reaching the shrubbery at the other side. Still, his watchful friend had wandered off the other way. A short run, a few seconds. He gathered his sack under his arm and launched himself.

He had reached the other side of the lawn when the light flared in his face, almost blinding him, stopping him dead for a moment before he attempted to swerve. It was just too long. His boots slithered on the smooth damp grass, a hand groped at his shoulder, lost him, then seized his coat collar, pulling him back with a jerk so that he slipped and fell. A shout. 'Got the bastard! Over here!'

Mark lay winded, looking up at the lantern and the man's face looking down at him. Footsteps were coming from the other direction. Of course, he thought: he should have known: there would be not one but two on the watch. He should have known.

Mark was taken to Peterborough gaol and committed for trial at the next quarter sessions. Rebecca went to see Deborah the next evening.

Old Goody Gedney was rocking herself by the hearth and weeping. Deborah was not: she looked ashen and hopeless.

'What did he want to go and do it for?' she said. 'I'd rather go without. Oh, I was glad of it first time, but if I'd known – I swear I'd rather go without. I was going to come see you, but I thought your father . . . Oh, Rebecca, is it any good you speaking to him?'

'I'll try,' Rebecca said. She made an effort to smile encouragingly. 'You rest and try not to worry. Remember there's two of you to keep well, for Mark's sake.'

'Father. About – about Mark Upwell.'

She had found her father alone in his study with his Bible. She tried to hope that this meant he would be in charitable mood.

'What about him?' Mr Walsoken closed the book but kept a finger in his place.

'You know he was – is to marry Deborah Gedney next week.'

'Of what concern is that to me?'

She took a step nearer, trying to keep her voice soft and conciliatory. 'I wonder if – if you might reconsider.'

His gaze was steady, unmoved.

'I can't believe Mark is really a bad young man. Oh, I know he's done wrong,' she said hurriedly. 'But suppose you were to – to withdraw the charge – '

'Are you mad?'

'I don't mean to let him go free,' she said agitatedly. 'But it would be disastrous if he were to go to prison now, just for this – '

'Just for this?' Mr Walsoken opened his Bible again. 'The fellow is a common thief.' He waved his hand. 'Go.'

'But there must be some other way,' she cried, trying to master herself. 'Some arrangement. All the work still to do on the outhouses. You could make Mark do that for you – something in recompense. If you withdrew the charge and told him he must – '

'Enough!' Her father slammed his hand down on the desk. 'The fellow is a thief, and the creature he associates with a common trollop. She has put you up to this. I've instructed you before to have no truck with these people – '

'I'm just asking you to show a little mercy!'

'I shall press for the strongest sentence,' Mr Walsoken snapped. 'He shall get everything he deserves. And you, daughter, who seem infected with the same insubordinate spirit – I order you to go to your room at once and never mention – '

'And leave you to read your damned Bible and think yourself a fine Christian!' she shouted, and snatched the book from his hand and threw it on the floor. 'You're no more a Christian than some painted savage! You're doing this out of petty vindictiveness, out of *spite*, and you're too much of a hypocrite to admit it!'

Her father leaned quickly over the desk and struck her across the face.

She put a hand up to her stinging cheek, glared at him through her hair. Then she bent and picked up the Bible and laid it on the desk.

'There's something in there about . . . turning the other cheek, I think,' she said indistinctly. 'But I'm not going to do that, father. I'm not going to do that. If you ever strike me again I won't answer for what will happen.'

She turned and ran out.

Dinner was just over at Morholm when Rebecca arrived, and the Hardwicks invited her to a glass of port in the parlour.

'Mr Hardwick, have you heard that Mark Upwell was taken poaching in my father's grounds last night?' she asked. She kept her face at an angle so he should not see the mark on her cheek.

George shook his head. 'I have been up at Northborough all day. Poaching, you say? Caught in the act?'

'Yes. Servants caught him.'

'Hm. And – I suppose your father wishes to press the case against him?'

Rebecca looked down, nodded.

'Young fool,' said George. 'I wouldn't have thought it of Mark, however.'

Rebecca explained about Deborah.

'Wouldn't that – extenuate the offence, George?' put in Mary.

'It certainly might. It depends . . . He is to appear at the Michaelmas sessions, you say, Rebecca? Well – I've been served notice to be there, so I'll do what I can. Of course there are my fellow-magistrates . . . But you understand there can only be one verdict.'

'I understand. So, I think, does Deborah.'

5

The Michaelmas Quarter Sessions for the Soke of Peterborough were held on Tuesday 29th of September beginning at ten o'clock. The chairman of the justices was the Rev. Dr Emmonsales: the others were George Hardwick, Sir Samuel Edgington and Mr Matthew Wyldbore, an elderly man who was one of the city's two Members of Parliament.

Joshua Walsoken chose not to be present – the two servants who had apprehended Mark were the witnesses – but Rebecca rode to the city in company with Mary Hardwick, to sit in the Talbot coffee-room and await the verdict. Deborah Gedney, seven months pregnant, could not make the journey: Rebecca's was the task of taking back the news of her fiancé's sentence.

The Butter Cross which housed the courtroom stood in the centre of the market square. The lower storey was open, with the second storey supported on pillars. Above that was a smaller storey where the constables and prisoners were housed and the jury could retire.

It was stuffy in the courtroom, with a feeble light sloping through the dirty leaded windows and showing up the dust on the floor-boards. On the raised desk that faced the bench the Rev. Dr Emmonsales had placed a bunch of herbs to keep off infection.

The jurors had been sworn, constables of various villages had made their presentments: a couple of cases of vagrancy were dealt with, the landlord of the Cock Inn at Werrington bound over for keeping a disorderly house. Mark Upwell was the last case. Sir

Samuel Edgington, fat and dewlapped and half-alseep, surreptitiously consulted his watch and looked forward to dinner.

The two servants gave their evidence. There were no defence witnesses. Mark, standing in the box, looked haggard from the darkness of the gaol. When Rev. Emmonsales said: 'Has the prisoner anything to say?' he looked bewildered and helpless.

George leaned forward. 'Mark, you have admitted you took a bird from Mr Walsoken's land some days earlier. Why did you do it?'

Mark stared at George. He knew Mr Hardwick, as did everyone in Aysthorpe: but for the moment he was changed, just another of the stern faces on the bench. He licked his lips. 'Sur?'

'Did you sell the bird?'

'No, sur.'

'Did you eat it?'

'No, sur . . . I give it to Deborah. She don't get enough to eat, her and old Goody . . .'

Rev. Emmonsales was looking at George with raised eyebrows. George leaned over and said: 'I have some acquaintance with this man's character. I just wish to bring attention to the fact that he committed the crime not for profit but, misguidedly of course, to feed his fiancée, who – '

'Is she unable to support herself?' put in Mr Wyldbore.

'She is heavily with child,' said the Rev. Emmonsales crisply. 'I also am acquainted with certain facts of this case. The prisoner has now compounded that immorality with felony. Is that not so, Mr Hardwick?'

An unfriendly glance passed between them. 'But, in view of his previous good character, which I can vouch for,' said George, 'and considering this is a first offence . . .'

'An offence against property, wilfully committed,' said Emmonsales. 'Mr Wyldbore?'

Wyldbore coughed. 'Nay, I take your point, Hardwick, but the man's been caught red-handed, and it's shameful the amount of game that's lost this way.'

'Sir Samuel?'

'The worst kind of rogue,' the old baronet grunted. He was a hunting man and considered the poacher as the devil's own kin.

'I am inclined to agree,' said the Rev. Emmonsales. He sketched a flourish on the piece of paper before him. 'But as Mr Hardwick urges us to be lenient, I think we might settle on – twenty months in prison?'

The others nodded. Sir Samuel patted his stomach, as if reassuring it that dinner was on the way. George stared from face to face. He felt he could not breathe. 'For – for a first offence?'

'To ensure it will be the last,' said Emmonsales. 'I take it you are in disagreement, Mr Hardwick?'

'I am,' said George. 'But it would appear I am outnumbered.'

Rev. Emmonsales glanced at the others. 'I am afraid so. The prisoner is sentenced.'

Mark was removed. The court was adjourned, the constables and jurors clattering down the winding stairs, the clerk making a final scribbled note on the rolls. The Rev. Dr Emmonsales, gathering up his papers, noticed George's silence and said: 'Come, Mr Hardwick, I hope you understand that personal feelings must be left outside when we enter this courtroom.'

George took up his hat and riding-crop with an unsteady hand. 'So, it seems, must mercy,' he said.

Emmonsales's strong chiselled face hardened. 'I would remind you that we are, as it were, mere arms of the statute book. If the laws of the land – '

'Aye, the statute book.' George looked at Sir Samuel's gouty, somnolent face, at Rev. Emmonsales's clerical collar. A great disgust rose in him like sickness. 'One would have thought, Dr Emmonsales, that a certain other book should be uppermost in your mind, one in which the virtues of mercy and charity get more than a passing mention.'

'Nay, steady, my boy,' said old Mr Wyldbore peaceably.

Emmonsales had gone pink. 'I do not need reminding of my duties to the cloth, least of all by a layman,' he said.

'Do they include sitting in judgement on your fellow-men and dealing out savage sentences like some petty provincial Dracon?'

'You are insulting, sir,' said Emmonsales whitely. 'We are all under the commission of the peace: I assume you knew the responsibilities when you took the commission: if you find them so very irksome – '

'Irksome to the conscience,' said George. 'But they will be so no longer. I resign my commission here and now, Dr Emmonsales. Perhaps you will convey my apologies to Lord Burghley.'

'Hardwick, my dear fellow, there's no need for this – ' said Wyldbore, but George had turned on his heel and clattered down the stairs.

Mary and Rebecca were waiting at the Talbot. He told them the news in a few short sentences.

'Deborah's child will not see its father for another couple of years,' he said grimly. He sent a potboy to fetch him brandy.

'So long . . .' said Mary. She saw and recognised the darkness in George's eyes. 'Surely – '

'Three months I would have said,' George muttered. 'He has already spent a month in that noisome gaol. Well, I have done with it. If these game laws are to continue I would rather not have to dispense them.' His brandy came and he drank it quickly.

'You did right, George,' Mary said, touching his arm.

He raised an eyebrow. 'I did nothing, except probably make Mark's sentence all the severer by interfering.'

'I must go,' said Rebecca, 'I must go back and tell Deborah . . .'

'Stay, Rebecca, ride with us. We shall be going home soon. George, I – '

The landlord was at George's elbow. 'Begging your pardon, sir – there's a gentleman upstairs asks a word with you.'

'What gentleman?'

'If you please, sir, tis Lord Burghley.'

George frowned. 'Tell his Lordship – ' He glanced at Mary. 'Oh, very well.'

He followed the innkeeper upstairs and was ushered into a private room, where Lord Burghley sat at a small table with a bottle of port and a plate of game pie.

'Ah, Mr Hardwick. Forgive me, I have almost finished. The Talbot's provisions are so very good, I can never resist them.'

Brownlow Cecil, the 9th Earl of Exeter, of Burghley House, was a man of enormous wealth and prestige. It was his redoubtable ancestor, Elizabeth I's minister, who had built the enormous mansion outside Stamford, and he who had gained control of much of the powers of the Bishop of Peterborough: the present Earl was Lord Paramount of the Liberty and Keeper of the Rolls, which meant that it was he who nominated the justices, though he seldom sat on the Bench himself.

He was fifty-three, a heavy grave-faced man in a curled tie-wig and an unostentatious grey coat. George Hardwick was small fry beside him: he knew him only via the Bench. The Earl poured himself a glass of port and took another mouthful of pie. He did not offer George a chair. George, in no mood to be deferent, took one anyway.

'Well, we have had a fine summer at last,' the Earl said, chewing and swallowing. 'An exceptional harvest in the county, I would think. Did you have such at Morholm, Mr Hardwick?'

'A good year indeed, my lord,' said George, tapping his riding-crop restlessly.

Lord Burghley lifted his glass, looked at George coolly. 'I hope I don't trespass on your time, Mr Hardwick.'

'Not at all, my lord . . . but my wife is with me and I know will be anxious soon to return home to our child. I cannot think – '

'Ah, your child, I had forgot. I hope he prospers. Let me see, he would be . . . ?'

'Almost a year old.'

'Yes. He must be a great joy to you. It is a joy, alas, I myself lack.' He took a piece of cheese. 'You were about to say, Mr Hardwick?'

George hesitated. 'I was about to say, my lord, that I cannot think you summoned me here to talk about the weather.'

'No.' Burghley chewed ruminatively. 'No. I came in to town, Mr Hardwick, to observe the progress of the sessions. As you know, I do not act as magistrate myself very regularly, but I like to keep a watch on things. The clerk has just told me that you have resigned your commission as justice.'

'My colleagues insisted on a sentence that I felt was far too severe.'

Burghley raised his eyebrows. 'Is that a sufficient reason to resign your commission?'

George drew in a breath. 'In itself, perhaps not. But it seemed a – a culmination of something I have felt increasingly of late. As it seems such sentences will continue, I thought it best to resign and forestall any further arguments which, I am sure you will agree, my lord, cannot reflect well on the dignity of the Bench.'

'The fellow was a poacher, I hear.'

'Yes. I know him – not a tenant of mine, but he lives in the district of Morholm. Given his character and circumstances, and the nature of the offence, my own inclination was to be lenient.' I've had all this out, George thought. What's the point in going through it again?

Lord Burghley sniffed. 'The nature of the offence? Trespassing, thieving, acting against the inalienable rights of property? Is this a trivial matter, Mr Hardwick?'

George sighed. 'My lord, I have already got at cross with three gentlemen today, and I do not wish to do the same with you. For right or wrong, my decision is made, so if you will allow me – '

'Don't be so hasty, Mr Hardwick.' Lord Burghley cut himself another piece of cheese and ate it with the leisure of a man accustomed to having his words waited for. 'The game laws have attracted some unfavourable comment. Perhaps there may be flaws. But we do not carry out our responsibilities in order to create the perfect world, Mr Hardwick. That does not exist this side of heaven. Unless you are one of those restless after change, who prate of reform and all the rest of it?'

'I am a squire of a small estate which has a tendency to flood and requires constant attention,' said George. 'I have little time to think of anything else, my lord, least of all politics.'

The Earl smiled thinly. 'A pretty answer.' He took out a gold snuffbox. 'But tell me this – if a man is entrusted with the administration of the laws of the land, and feels that in some cases they are interpreted with too great a severity, which is the wiser action – that he continues to shoulder his responsibilities, and so be in a position to moderate what he considers the excessive zeal of his fellows, and perhaps carry his point occasionally – or throw up those responsibilities altogether, and so forfeit his chance of doing some good?'

'You argue with an eloquence I cannot command, my lord,' said George, impressed in spite of himself. 'But my mind is made up.'

Lord Burghley poured the last of his port. 'You are a stubborn man, Mr Hardwick. It is a quality I admire, but one can have too much of it. Of course, I have no power to prevent you, if this is what you have really resolved on. A replacement will have to be found, naturally. The gentleman who brought the action against this poacher – Mr Walsoken, is it not? A neighbour of yours at Aysthorpe?'

'That is so.'

'He was clearly anxious for the prosecution of this young fellow.' Burghley looked at George, shrugged. 'Well, he is of course a likely candidate to take your place, Hardwick. I'm not entirely fond of these new men myself, but if the old families choose not to perform the service . . .'

George's face was stony. 'As you say, my lord.'

'I'm sorry you take it this way, Hardwick.'

'I'm sorry I have to.'

Lord Burghley closed his snuffbox, drew some papers towards him. 'Your wife no doubt will be waiting. Pray give her my compliments.'

George, considering himself dismissed, bowed and left.

FIVE

I

Seven hundred years before the fens had been the last corner of resistance against the invading Normans: and though since then drainers and enclosers had intermittently tamed and ordered stretches of that great sullen basin, there were still parts, like Bicklode Fen, where men of an uncouth, fiercely independent and unique character lived an isolated life in its misty fastnesses, beholden to no one, and pretty well a law unto themselves.

In squat huts of timber and lath, with windows of horn, they bred up large families that were depleted by malaria and scrofula and chronic rheumatism: they fished and eeled and caught fowl and cut reeds, they grazed sheep and great herds of geese on the wet commons – and often set aside half of their dank cottages for the geese, roosting them in wicker racks against the walls six deep. In hard times they ate sparrow-pudden and even water-rats. In the depths of winter they were as remote from the world as Laplanders, surrounded by miles of crusted ice that could be heard shifting and cracking in the vast silence of night, where if an unwary horse wandered it was likely to lose its footing and be screeved – split from end to end.

The changes at Bicklode Fen had already begun. The commons were being fenced. Gangs of labourers worked ant-like at cleaning and widening and embanking the dykes, and cutting and blasting a new cut through to the main drain. There had been no local people to be seen – the fen might have been uninhabited beneath its great ribbed roof of sky – but the smoke of a chimney or two could be made out on the horizon.

One of the inhabitants was a man named Feast Holbeach.

He came to Aysthorpe on foot, with two companions, one evening in October. John Newman, together with Ned and Billy Gowt and old Seth Upwell, were putting in some work in the fading light on the meeting-house just outside the village – a few stones now stood above the foundations – and they saw the procession walking towards them across the common.

'Strangers,' grunted Billy Gowt, staring, for the three men were very different in appearance from folk here on the fen edge. The oldest stood well over six feet, a bulky man of forty with a face seamed and brown as old leather and brows that met in the middle. He wore a broad-brimmed hat and a patched coat and moleskin breeches and gaiters made of eelskin, which was said to keep away the ague. He had a peculiar high-stepping walk, as if he were always mentally wading. The other two, similarly dressed, were well-built but smaller, both in their late teens, and one had a grinning face with slanting Mongol eyes.

'Day to ye, mates,' said the older man. 'Working late, I see. Master keeps you at it, does he?'

'What's it to do wi you?' Ned Gowt said suspiciously.

'It's work for no master, friend,' said John Newman, in his peaceable way. 'We're raising a meeting-house for ourselves.'

'Methodies,' said one of the youths, with a snort.

'And what if we are?' Billy Gowt said. ''Tis no business o' yourn – '

'Nay,' the older man said, lifting a blackened hand. 'No call for that. Tom, you hold yer clack. Thing is, mates, we're looking for someone name of Walsoken. He lives hereabouts, don't he?'

John Newman pointed in the direction of Bromswold. 'Aye. The big old house there.'

'Ah.' The man screwed up his eyes. 'Know this gent, do ye?'

'Aye, don't we just,' Seth Upwell said with bitterness. He was sitting on the ground, exhausted: since Mark's imprisonment he had worked himself beyond his strength in an effort to forget his grief.

The fenman looked at him sharply. 'What sort of man might he be, then? Not popular? Not liked?'

'Not by Seth here,' blurted Ned Gowt. 'He went and turned him off his land, and then he went and sent young Mark off to prison just for the taking of a partridge.'

Old Seth shook his head wearily. ''Twas all right enough by law,' he muttered.

'Nay, Ned, I know what you mean, but we cann't take it that way,' said John Newman.

'Christian charity, eh?' said the fenman, smiling crookedly at John. 'You've nowt against this Walsoken, then, friend?'

John hesitated, lowered his pale blue eyes. 'I've no love for him,' he said. 'He hates us Wesleyans, and when I – ' He stopped.

The fenman regarded him keenly for a moment, and then said: 'Well, I got business with that gentleman, and I'm not of a mind to like him myself, less'n he changes a few of his plans. My name's Feast Holbeach: this here's my son Tom, and this is Jud, my nevvy.' The slant-eyed youth grinned harder. There was probably some inbreeding somewhere. 'Heard of Bicklode Fen, have ye? We've come all the way from there, so I hope our Mr Walsoken's in.'

The three strange figures, with the giant Holbeach leading, went on towards Bromswold, and John Newman watched them until they were out of sight.

Nancy poked her fluffy head round the door of the drawing-room where Mr Walsoken and his daughters were. 'If ee please sir, there's someone – someone – ' she quavered, and was then elbowed aside by Feast Holbeach, followed by the two youths. 'Go yer ways, ole dear,' he said. 'We ent about to be denied now. A few words wi yer master's all I'm wanting.' He swept off his hat, revealing a close-cropped skull, and replaced it again. 'Mester Walsoken, is it?'

Sarah had given a little muffled scream, but her father closed his book quietly, and did not rise. 'What is the meaning of this intrusion?' he said.

Feast Holbeach glanced at Rebecca and Sarah, showed his decayed teeth. 'Ladies. Mebbe as you'd step out so's I can have a word wi yer pa.'

'You do not order my family about,' said Mr Walsoken. He glanced at the clock. 'State your business. You have two minutes.'

The giant fenman made a gesture to his son and then said: 'Holbeach is the name, Feast Holbeach. From Bicklode Fen. You're the man behint all this drainin' work, these fences, this tekkin' away of a fenman's living, ent that so?'

'I am the chief shareholder in the Bicklode Fen venture,' said Mr Walsoken precisely. 'What is your interest in the matter?'

Sarah was white with terror, and Rebecca kept a hand on her arm. She was glad her mother was upstairs.

194

'Like I say,' Holbeach said. 'My livin'. And others like me. If your plan's what I've heard. To drain the whole fen proper – fence it all off for some damned upland farmers – is that it?'

'All interested parties were allowed to attend a public meeting held by the drainage and enclosure commissioners some months past,' Mr Walsoken said. 'Do you have a dispute over a claim under the enclosure act? That can be – '

'I'm disputing everything you're doing,' said Holbeach. 'I seen it before. All the fishing, all the wild duck, all the goose commons, all gone – you wi yer banks and yer windmills. There's me – and there's others – who won't stand for it.'

'It is a settled thing.' Mr Walsoken looked at the clock again and opened his book. 'You had the opportunity to present a counter-petition to Parliament when the act was mooted. Notice was given. Now you will get off my property.'

'Parliament.' Holbeach hawked and spat on the floor, but Mr Walsoken did not look up. 'You're not from these parts, I reckon. So mebbe you don't recollect what happened when they did the same to Holland Fen a few years ago. Fen-folk turned a mite wild. There was more than one man ended up wi a knife in his throat. They had to call the soldiers in to Boston to stop the town being burnt down. Get my drift, do ye?'

Rebecca watched her father. Still he did not raise his eyes. 'Your threats do nothing,' he said, 'except confirm my opinion of your kind. The sooner you and all your idle, lawless, godless kin are swept off the land and made to work or starve the better.'

Holbeach blinked, shrugged. His son looked expectantly at him, and he nodded. 'Wop it about, boys,' he said.

Immediately his son turned and knocked over a Chippendale table on which stood a tea-tray. The other youth gave a tug at the window-curtain and yanked it off its rings.

Mr Walsoken stood up. 'I warn you what will happen if you continue,' he said calmly. 'There are eight servants at present in this house. My gamekeeper is of course armed, and will not hesitate to shoot you.'

'Ye've had yer warning, Walsoken,' said Feast Holbeach. 'Friendly-like. Thass not the end of it. Fenmen'll not stand by and see their world took away wi'out a by-yer-leave. Next time you hear from us, mebbe it wun't be so friendly.' The broad hat was off and on again. 'Ladies.'

With a clump of boots, and a sour fishy waft of dirt, they were gone.

2

As she descended St Mary's Hill into Stamford Rebecca was reminded of the first time she had come here, almost a year ago, and the town had looked as if it were in riot. This time, however, the great boiling of people surging across St Mary's Street were not simply noisily marketing: there was real mischief afoot.

'Looks like trouble, ma'am,' said Ford, nudging his horse close to hers. 'Turn back, shall us?'

'I don't know . . .' The crowd, mostly prentice-boys but with a fair mixture of men and women of all sorts, were pushing somebody in a handcart, cheering and yelling. Many were obviously drunk. Some waved sticks. She had come to do some shopping for her mother, and then to meet her father who had a meeting at the bank and ride home with him. 'They look to be going to the square,' she said. 'We can turn left and go by way of Maiden Lane. That should be safe enough.'

'If ee say so, ma'am,' said Ford.

They reached Broad Street without trouble, but could hear the shouts growing louder in the direction of Red Lion Square. In the haberdasher's she asked the shopman what all the commotion was about.

'Oh, ma'am, I been feared out o' my wits.' He scratched beneath his wig in agitation. ''Tis the bull-running today. Or meant to be. Have you not heard? They set a bull loose and chase it down with dogs about the streets. All manner of rough lawless folk. A wicked custom. Many's the time they've tried to put a stop to it. Well, this time the magistrates put an order out against the butcher who advertised his bull for the running, and stopped him doing it. Breach o' the peace. They set him in the stocks for it, but that mob broke open the stocks and set him free and now they're chairing him round and threatening I don't know what.'

Rebecca thanked him and went out. Ford was across the street, helping an old lady who had dropped her basket. A sullen November drizzle was beginning to fall. Suddenly there was a thundering whirlwind of noise and motion as the cart, with the butcher joggling about on top, came hurtling past her propelled by half-a-dozen

196

prentices. Behind like a flood came the rest of the crowd, with an incoherent screaming from which she picked out the words 'We want our bull! Give us our bull!' She pressed herself back against the wall of the shop, caught a glimpse of Ford's alarmed face across the street, and then someone collided with her and the next moment she was lifted a few inches off the ground, borne along like driftwood in the tide of jostling, feverish humanity.

For a few moments she was completely startled: then she began to struggle, to fight, for breathing-space in the press of bodies and for a way out. The crowd squeezed harder, fiercer into the narrow bottleneck of Red Lion Street, and she could hardly get air into her lungs. There was a sweaty excited smell and a few makeshift flags were waving above the sea of heads. The tumult and riot that lay always beneath the decorous surface of the age had broken out. The bull-running was a hugely popular occasion: the unruly emotions it channelled were not to be denied. Then the crowd spilled into the square, and she found herself with room to move. She lunged, gasping, into a doorway beside the Red Lion Inn and flattened herself against the door as the stream of people continued to flow past her.

She could not see Ford anywhere. The mass of people filled the square, cheering and chanting: 'Give us our bull!' Someone was standing on the trestle of a market-stall in the centre of the square and trying to make himself heard. It was the town bailiff, and he was warning them to disperse. A great jeering noise rose up and then the bailiff was plucked off his perch as if a hand had seized him. Rebecca, with a flutter of panic, left the doorway and hurried across towards High Street. As if they were pursuing her, the crowd began to move after her, the bailiff struggling in their midst. They were going to throw him in the river.

Rebecca began to run, desperately, as one would run before a tidal wave that would sweep all before it. She lost her hat and mud splashed up her skirts and stockings. In St Mary's Street another wave of people came hooting from the opposite direction. She saw an old man knocked down on the cobbles, disappearing under tramping feet. She turned up St Mary's Hill, her eyes flickering back and forth, looking for an alleyway or something she could duck into, and realised from the sounds behind her that she was not running fast enough.

A hand grabbed her arm, pulled her to one side. She screamed. She was pressed against the doorway of a cottage.

'Rebecca!'

She knew the voice. She saw Luke Hardwick's face, and then he turned his back to her and placed his arms across the doorway, shielding her.

The stream of people seemed to go on for ever. They passed within a few inches of the doorway, colliding with Luke, jostling him, seeming at any time about to bowl him over or suck him out into the maelstrom. But he stood firm and at last the stragglers went by and the noise died down.

'Thank God I saw you,' he said, and she clung to his arm, panting, frightened and relieved. His eyes feasted on her face, and for a moment the impossible complexities of the past were gone and they were just two people. Then his eyes clouded, he stiffened, and said: 'This is a bad time for you to visit Stamford, Miss Rebecca. Are you unaccompanied?'

'Ford . . . he . . .' Still she clung to him. 'Luke, I was afraid . . . really afraid . . . I couldn't stop . . .'

He hesitated, looked out of the doorway towards the river. 'There's no controlling them now . . . Miss Rebecca – our warehouse is across the way. I've just come from there. I can give you a seat there, at any rate, and you'll be safe . . .'

She nodded, her face pale. She held on to his arm as he led her across. The crowd was on the river bridge and the far bank, and the figure of the bailiff could be seen bobbing about on their shoulders.

Luke opened the warehouse with a key and led her in, seated her on a chair by a desk, closed the door on the din. 'I've sent Jack home,' he said. 'We've no shipments today. Tis as well I'm here anyway, to guard the place. No telling what they'll do. I shouldn't be surprised if the dragoons are called in if this goes on much longer.' He talked on, uneasily, standing at the little high window that looked out across the wharf. 'I'm sorry I can't offer you nothing – anything. Well, daft, isn't it, we've gallons of port, ale, what have you, in here, but not for – '

'It's all right.' Rebecca felt normality returning, driving away the panic. She shivered.

'Are you cold?' Luke turned, his face vulnerable with concern. 'Mebbe you'd better go – where's your horse? I'll go with you. It should be all right enough now, if we . . .' His words faded away.

The warehouse was chilly, high-ceilinged, with big doors on to the wharf: barrels piled against the walls, crates, sacks: a couple of sparrows had got in and were living in the rafters . . . Rebecca saw none of these things, or saw them without recognising them, for she could see nothing but Luke, his tall figure, nervous and irresolute, his dark beautiful face. And when she wrapped her arms around his neck, when she felt his kisses on her cheeks and lips and brows, it was with a sensation like that of coming back to a dearly loved home – yet also a newness, the brink of an adventure: his touch sent the rest of the world, the past, the future, all spinning away into a void of irrelevance. All was contracted into the space occupied by their two bodies, a universe girded by the limits of his arms.

'Luke,' she said, and his hands caressed her hair, scattering droplets of rain.

Everything was suddenly, wordlessly, acknowledged and understood.

Then they drew back from each other, her hand in his. Outside the noise of the crowd by the river was audible again, like the sound of the world pressing in on them once more.

'Rebecca,' Luke said. 'I'm not dreaming, am I? No, no, I'm not dreaming. My love, my only love . . .'

Her cloak had fallen to the wooden floor, and he bent and picked it up, restored it to her shoulders gently. It was an unwise contact, for immediately they were in each other's arms again.

'All these months never seeing you,' he said. 'Working, eating, sleeping, always you've been in my mind. And now you're here . . . I can't hardly believe it.'

She ran a finger along the line of his jaw, down his chin. Her vision was suddenly obscured by tears.

'What is it? Rebecca?'

'I've thought of you too, Luke,' she said, her voice thick. 'Always, always – oh, how could it be otherwise?' She lowered her eyes, her hands playing restlessly with his stock.

'Rebecca, look at me.' He lifted her chin. 'What – what happened last time . . . I – '

She shook her head, impatiently. '*That*,' she said, 'it's nothing – less than nothing. But – '

'And d'you know, know how I feel, how much you mean to me – '

'Oh, *yes*.' She made another impatient movement, and his face hardened.

'Does it mean so little to you, then?' he said. For answer she seized him, kissed him fiercely. 'It means everything,' she whispered. 'There's no question about that . . . never has been, in truth. But don't you see – nothing's changed, Luke, has it?'

'I love you, Rebecca.' His voice was low, deep, softly accented, just as she had heard it in her dreams. 'That's never changed, nor never will. It's deep in me, like something I were born with, that I can't cut out no more than I can cut out my own heart. But you're right – nothing's changed. I'm bastard born, rough in most of my ways: these clothes can't make me a proper gentleman, and perhaps even time never will: your father thinks I'm low as dirt. Tis all wrong, a mess. I know.'

In tearful confusion she said: 'The time – I'd better go . . .'

'I shan't stop you, my love . . . All wrong, as I say. But right *here*.' He put a hand to his chest.

'I – I've got to go and meet my father.'

'So you must.' He nodded, released her hand, but still gazed at her. 'We've both got – responsibilities. To the world. But there's another responsibility – to what we *feel*. Right or wrong. That can't be denied, just so much as all those other things. You're all to me, Rebecca, sky and earth and water, all that life is. You're my night and day. There's no denying that.'

She was silent, wrestling with a great weight that seemed to labour and swell in her breast.

Luke dropped his arms to his sides. A weak shaft of sun slanted through the high window, breaking itself on the dusty floor between them. 'So . . . you'd better go, my love,' he said softly.

'Not yet, Luke . . . not yet . . .' She took a step towards him, her eyes filmed, weak with distress and love. 'No, not yet, dear Luke . . .'

2

Elizabeth, Lady Woodhouse, lay in her large curtained four-poster bed, watching the cold November dawn lightening the tall windows, aware of the warm space that her lover had left beside her, and trying to come to terms with the fact of being an adulterous woman.

Adultery . . . the word slipped from her mind, dull, colourless, meaningless. Such words could have nothing to do with her shining happiness.

He had left her a few minutes ago, to steal back to his own room, for the servants would soon be about. Before he went he had kissed her and looked down at her and said she looked like a mermaid, resting on the pillows with her golden hair spread loose around her.

Happiness . . . She shifted in the bed, to lie in the warmth where he had lain, to inhale the scent of him. Soon she would have to get up, to dress, to assume the face and demeanour expected of her: but for the moment she could laze and dream, and simply be a woman who loved and was loved by a man.

Could she ever have imagined that this would happen, a year ago – a few months ago even? Impossible to say . . . To look back at that past Elizabeth was to look at a different person.

He had made her come alive, as if she were seeing the world for the first time. Nowadays she found she was always laughing, humming to herself, talking; *interested* in what life had to offer. The old reserve that had held her, half-willingly, in a cage, was gone. Her mother, her friends, all remarked on the change in her spirits, without knowing the real reason.

Without knowing . . . that was certain. It was amazing how easy it had been. She was a rich elegant woman, and with Hugh away it was not expected that she should go into purdah. Friends still came to Deenecote Hall throughout the autumn, for cards and parties, and more often than not, as they were in the country and the roads were poor, to stay the night. Nothing more natural.

There were nearly twenty servants at Deenecote: but she was sure it was only her own maid Betty who knew, and she was devoted to her mistress and detested Sir Hugh.

The last day of August – she remembered it so clearly. Sun shining brilliantly, as if in defiance of coming autumn. They had been walking in the gardens, she and Robert Landless and Mr Warren and Emma Van Druyten. Warren and Emma had gone to the stables, with a common adoration of horses, to look over Hugh's hunters. Left alone together, she and Landless had strolled a little further, talking little, scarcely looking at each other. She had gathered some roses and was nervously arranging and rearranging them in a bouquet in her hands. Then he had suddenly stopped and one by one taken them from her fingers and laid them on a bench and then taken her hands in his.

'You must tell me to stop this,' he said, and she thought he was simply bantering as he often did, but his eyes said otherwise. 'You must tell me to stop coming to Deenecote altogether.'

'Wh – why?'

'I've worshipped you since the first time I saw you. No, don't speak. I have told you so and danced attendance on you all this lovely summer – and it has seemed, no doubt, like some pretty game, fit for the season and the company, fit for some decorous play at the theatre. A little midsummer madness. But it's true, my darling Elizabeth. No flippant sallies now. No lightness of heart. There is no lightness in what I feel.'

She had heard the drone of bees and smelt the richness of the grass, mingling into one sensual symphony of summer. She could not speak.

'So I must go away,' Landless said. 'I can't bear to keep seeing you . . . looking at you . . . wanting you always. When there can be no hope.'

A terrible chill had passed over her, blowing away the summer at one breath, at the thought of seeing him no more: she realised at that moment that he was all, all that mattered in her life.

He was about to release her hands: then looked down and saw that a thorn from the roses had pricked her finger, and there was a bright blob of blood there. He raised it to his lips, gently drew out the blood. His lips were soft and warm. Deenecote Hall behind him had swum and danced and risen in her vision like something from a fairytale.

That night she had undressed and sat in her robe at her dressing-table and waited. He had come to her room at last tentatively, almost fearfully, as if really expecting final rejection.

But it had not been so . . .

The first time during their lovemaking she had experienced a sudden stiffening, to her own surprise, as if it were her body rather than her mind that were recoiling in reflex, with its own memories of Hugh and his grossness. But it was over in a moment, as she touched again the mop of fair hair, recalled that it was Robert Landless, slender and gentle with his dark brown eyes that were usually full of laughter but were now earnest and tender. The ugly demon of Hugh's lust and cruelty that she had thought was lodged permanently in her body was exorcised.

He was no innocent, but she guessed that his experience of women was limited; and they discovered each other without haste and with growing delight, as if they were the first man and woman in the world. For Elizabeth, it was a revelation. Her body, which she had been used to hurriedly covering with clothes whenever she left her bed or bath, as something that spoke only of misery and degradation, became something as new and exciting to her as it was to her lover. When his tongue and lips explored her nakedness, it was as something endlessly beautiful and responsive, not a dead thing on which to vent brief passion. His hands caressed her breasts as part of her self, Elizabeth, not as abstract instruments for arousal. And the part of her that seemed to fill Hugh with a mixture of disgust and gloating he touched and kissed with the same honest love.

And when at last, feeling him inside her, their kisses growing desperate, endless, stabbing, her legs closing about him and her fingers raking his hair; when at last she had let out a great gasping cry, it had been a sound of shock as well as pleasure – for she had never dreamed of such an experience, never known she could be racked by this giant, life-sapping, drowning thrill that left her dazed and tingling.

Into the misery of her married life fate had tossed an unexpected garland. And there was more. The seventh of September: another date carved in her memory. A letter from Hugh, with a covering letter from the Yeatmans. Hugh had been injured in a shooting accident.

It was not serious. On the grouse-moors some damn idiot who couldn't handle a gun, as Hugh put it, had let off a wild shot that had fetched up in Hugh's left foot. The Yeatmans were happy to have him stay with them as long as was necessary, though Miss Yeatman said in her letter he was in a fearful temper and kept throwing his cushions at the surgeon who was attending him.

Elizabeth had laughed at that, not just at the picture but in a burst of heart-free relief and delight. A reprieve. More time, more precious time to enjoy her stolen love . . .

She yawned, sat up in the bed, coming fully awake: and the edge of a shadow fell on her mind which she had tried to keep at bay. It was November: the chill in the room, the greyness of the day outside proclaimed it. The season when Deenecote was virtually open house, the season of parties and company which had connived at their meeting, was pretty well over. Soon the roads would be very poor, their friends going into town residence for the winter ... and it would be that much more difficult for her and Landless to meet.

She tried to push the thought away again, but a coppery taste of despair had filled her mouth and her heart beat fast. No ... they must continue to meet. Somehow, they must find a way.

Robert Landless left Deenecote late that afternoon, and rode breakneck to Stamford, where he had promised faithfully, after several times putting it off, to meet Henry Milton at the *Courant* office. Halfway there rain like vengeful bullets began to fall from a black sky and by the time he reached the town his hair was plastered in a yellow cap around his face.

As well as writing for the paper Landless had recently invested five hundred pounds in the business: an appreciated gesture of faith, though as he admitted to his new partners, the fact was he had money and he hardly knew what to do with it.

Behind the shop was the room that housed the two old handpresses, the guillotines and drying-racks, and a stairway led to the office above. Here Landless found Milton, combing through a batch of London newspapers that had arrived that morning.

'So here you are, snug and warm, whilst I brave the fen weather,' Landless said, clapping Milton on the shoulder. He hung his riding-coat before the little fire that burned in the grate. 'Is that a flask of brandy I see there?'

'It is,' said Milton, 'and you are just in time, for I was just thinking of finishing it off myself.'

Landless grinned and poured himself a drink. 'Now,' he said, 'you may begin upbraiding me for my absences.'

'Nothing of the kind,' said Milton, lighting a second candle as the day died outside. 'But I wanted to see you, for I shall be leaving tomorrow for London.'

'Eh? No, no, don't tell me. A knighthood at last. And thoroughly deserved, sir.' He shook Milton's hand gravely.

Milton laughed. 'No, it's only the old story. Dreams of literary glory, I'm afraid, the old nonsense.'

'Never mind this false modesty, sir, speak out,' said Landless.

'I heard from Isaac Carey this week – my old piratical friend in the trade. He wishes to publish the set of poems I sent him – months ago, I had almost forgot them. Called *The Open Field, or the Country-Man's Ephemeris*. Not in anonymous sheets, Robert: a quarto volume, an edition of five hundred. So I am to go and see him at once: I should be away for four days, and – '

'My dear fellow!' Landless lifted the brandy flask. 'Well, there is just enough left for a toast – you have had quite enough already – but we cannot let this pass unmarked.' He slopped the last of the brandy into Milton's glass. 'And you sit there as if everything were normal, instead of dancing a jig around the room – !'

'Well, it is a little early to be – '

'Pah, you're a pessimist, Henry,' Landless said. 'I wouldn't abide it in anyone but you. What does Julia say? She is delighted, of course.'

'Yes, I think – '

'And so we shall soon be coupling your name with that other Milton.' Landless sat on the desk. 'As long as you never become as infernal dry as him I wish you well ... I almost hate to bring matters down to earth, but how are sales of the *Courant* faring?'

'Good in Peterborough and the Soke,' Milton said. 'Less so in Stamford and Rutland. The *Mercury* is well established.'

'Well, when you are swapping table-talk with Dr Johnson at the Turk's Head all this will seem like so much small beer.'

Milton smiled absently. In fact the news did not have quite the savour it should have had. He was thinking of a few weeks ago, when he and Julia had gone to dine with the Sedgmoors – and of course to see the new baby. Julia had been adamant that they should go: but she made the visit with something of the grim determination of someone going to the barber-surgeon to have a tooth pulled. Kate Sedgmoor, in her cheerful unthinking way, had several times put the child in Julia's arms.

'Henry ... Are you not going to ask me where I've been?' Landless's face was serious for a moment. 'Or is your silence one of disapproval?'

Milton shook his head. 'You know me better than that. I – hope Elizabeth's well.'

'More beautiful each day,' Landless said. 'More charming, more sweet-natured, more delightful ... You see, I am running on again. When I cannot see her I must talk about her.'

Milton stared at the page in front of him. 'It's a dangerous game you're playing, Robert.'

'Dangerous perhaps ... But no game, my friend. I love Elizabeth. Oh, I know at first it may have seemed a typical piece of young man's folly. Playing at being in love, the unattainable object and so on. But I am in earnest, Henry. I hope you believe that.'

'I would not be listening to you now if I did not.' The fact that Landless had taken him into his confidence over his affair with Elizabeth Woodhouse did not actively displease or disturb him. Indeed there was an enjoyment in it, in that he thus relived by proxy his own young agonies and joys – now so long ago, it seemed. There was no jealousy or envy of his friend – Elizabeth for Milton had been a superficial calf-love. But the element of engaging irresponsibility in Landless, which made it impossible for the young man to keep mum about his happiness, troubled Milton a little.

'She's miserable with that fat-headed horse-and-hounds husband of hers,' Landless said, frowning and running his hand through his hair. 'She won't talk about it, but I'm sure of it. When I first saw her it was that – that expression of hidden sorrow about her that fascinated me. Oh, but she is so much more lovely smiling, laughing. Henry . . . do you think badly of me?'

'My liking for Hugh Woodhouse is about as great as that of the King for George Washington,' Milton said dryly. 'And I don't suppose either you or Elizabeth are in a way to think rationally. It is . . . like a fever of the blood, I know.'

'Old graveairs,' said Landless affectionately. 'I knew you would understand. I would entrust no one else with such confidences – but it's as if I've known you all my life.'

'I'm honoured,' said Milton. 'But . . .'

Landless raised an eyebrow.

'Well, I can't help wondering . . . what will happen . . . in the end?'

Landless got up and rearranged his steaming coat in front of the fire. 'What will become of us all, in the end? But no . . . I know what you mean. How old are you, Henry?'

'I'm nearly twenty-eight,' said Milton, 'and don't you say I look older.' It was said lightly, but he knew he did. Always slightly solemn in appearance, he had of late grown pale and gaunt.

'Twenty-eight . . . well, you have six years on me. Not much, perhaps, but – the way I feel now, it's somehow impossible to look beyond tomorrow. The present is so intense, so marvellous, that the future just becomes a kind of phantom . . . Does that make any kind of sense?'

Milton smiled. 'No less than most of the things you say.'

'H'm, I hope that doesn't refer to my writing.'

'Speaking of which,' said Milton, 'and speaking with the authority of my great age, I have to remind you of a certain promise.' He picked up a proof of the *Courant*. 'This week's essay . . . ?'

'Damn it, I did promise, didn't I! Have I got time?'

'Well, we have to print tomorrow.'

'Ah, plenty of time. Have you got last week's copy there? Let me remind myself what stuff I wrote then. Good God, did I really write these supposedly comic verses about General Howe? "The Lesson plain, from this to draw, / Is thus: *Howe* Not To Win A War." I must have been drunk. Well, I think we'll leave the war alone this week. It's not as if England is ever going to win.'

'D'you think so?'

'Of course. We may have victories, this year, next year, but sooner or later we will lose America. It will be better for us if it is sooner, but there we are. Now, Henry, get up from that desk and go home to Julia. I shall send for a jug of ale and sit here until the piece is written.'

Milton left Landless a few minutes later, crouched at the desk in his shirt sleeves, a tankard of porter by his side, scribbling away at a furious rate as if he were trying to outrun time. That, Milton knew, was the way he was living at the moment. Sir Hugh Woodhouse would not stay away for ever.

SIX

I

Under cover of legitimate trips to Stamford or Peterborough, to shop or make calls, Rebecca managed to meet Luke. Such meetings were not easy to arrange: they were snatched and uneasy and clandestine. They were also completely improper by any standards. But such standards were blown away at one touch of his hand. She had to see Luke, just as she had to draw breath into her lungs.

Meetings, to talk, to look, to kiss: to let their love come blinking into the light, and reveal its awesome power. While she was with Luke, life was bathed in a brilliant light: beyond that, all was dank obscure mist. He dominated her thoughts, her feelings, her senses. All the stifled responsiveness of her being burst out when she was with him.

She was learning too that the notion of there being two sides to a person was an absurd simplification. The facets of Luke the man surrounded her, as infinitely varied as the world itself. But she was conscious of a certain duality in him. There was the bright, impudent, impulsive Luke she had first loved – the Luke who came running athletically to meet her, who could make her laugh with one droll look, who would suddenly buy ribbons from a street-seller and admiringly place them against her hair: who would draw her gently into the shadow of an inn-yard or the arched cloisters of the Cathedral and tenderly take her face in his hands and kiss her eyelids and the tip of her nose and then her lips.

The image of Luke in her mind had always been characterised by this warm openness and generosity. And so it remained. Except now and then she came upon a hardness in him, like a vein of barren rock in good dark earth: the other Luke.

Walking together in Peterborough market – dangerously in view, of course, but she was past caring – he had bought a paper of roast chestnuts. 'Thank ye, *surr*,' the vendor had said when he gave him the money. She had seen Luke give the man a hostile, suspicious glance, as if he feared he were being mocked. The truth was the man simply had a strong see-saw country accent. And in narrow Cross Street he had stepped aside to make room for a lady in a satin cloak and voluminous skirts: and once again, though the lady nodded graciously, the hardened, defensive look came like a shadow over his eyes, as if he were bracing himself for a snub.

Several times he made slighting remarks about 'fine ladies and gents looking down their long noses': half-humorously: yet there was the prick of real malice and resentment in his tone. Conversely, he mentioned business with dogged respect. His father entrusted most of it to him now, he said. He enjoyed the work. When it came to money, he said, you knew where you are. He even asked her several questions about her father's banking activities, searching technical questions, which she had not imagined him interested in.

Since Mark Upwell's imprisonment she had seen little of Deborah Gedney. Deborah, though not actually hostile, had drawn back from her somewhat. Perhaps it was inevitable, Rebecca's father having not only taken back the Upwells' land but sent Mark for trial: but it saddened Rebecca. Deborah had given birth to a baby boy on the fifteenth of November: but Rebecca had only heard of it from the servants, and had not seen the child.

She told Luke the story of Deborah and Mark, and he listened. 'Aye, well,' he said. 'It's a sorry tale. But then . . .'

She looked at him. 'Then what?'

'Well, folk should take responsibility for their own acts, shouldn't they?' he said. 'That's the way things are in this world.'

She had begun to say something at this, and then fallen silent. She felt suddenly cold. It was the vein of rock again: she was aware, in this man whose very presence overwhelmed her with feverish love, of something alien.

But the worst chill came in Peterborough one cold clear day at the end of November, when they walked down to the river by the meadows where St Matthews fair had recently been held and threw crumbs for the swans. Luke had been a little late for their meeting: he had had some business in the city in Cumbergate.

'We own a couple of properties down there,' he said. 'Always used to be the woolcombers' quarter, but the trade's dying out now.

Old fellow there, one of the last ones, hasn't paid his rent for months. Says he's sick and can't work his loom. Had to give him eviction notice. C'mon beauties.' He clicked his tongue to the swans, who came with an elegant absence of haste to the reedy bank.

Rebecca looked across the river at the mist gathered round the skirts of the willows. 'You mean you're going to evict him?'

'Rent's for paying,' Luke said.

'But if he's really sick . . .'

Luke grimaced. 'If he is, *I* cann't make him better, can I?' He smiled and took her arm. 'But you don't want to hear me chunter on about business, my love. Tis us we should be talking about . . .'

So it had ended: and she had soon put the subject from her mind, losing herself again in his eyes and his voice and his electric touch.

But that was not the end of it.

She met Luke at the Nene bridge, and they took the same walk by the river again. He rubbed her chilled fingers in his hands, talked to her of winter on the fen when you could see the fish moving about under the cat-ice and the cry of birds broke the silence of the sky like a shout. In an access of love she took his face in her hands and kissed him and they leaned against a willow while he stroked her hair.

At last they made their way up towards the bridge again. Her skin was tingling, not only with the freshness of the air but with a kind of heightened sensitivity: everything, every sight and sound and scent, seemed keen and large.

'Yes, it is a little exaggerated, but I think being in love is quite moderate. Quite moderately pleasant,' she said.

He held her arm closer. 'No more than that, m'lady?'

'Well, perhaps. Very agreeable. How does that sound?'

He grunted. 'It sound to me like you don't realise how lucky you are.'

'Don't I indeed?'

'No. Being in love may be like you say – but being in love with *me* is something quite different. There aren't any words to describe that.'

'Oh, you think I'm lucky, do you? Think you're something remarkable?'

He narrowed his eyes judicially. 'Quite moderate. Quite moderately remarkable.'

She raised his hand, bit it gently, kissed it. 'It was this time last year when I first met you,' she said. 'D'you remember?'

'Nay, I forgot that the very next day. Hullo, what's going on here? Another bull-run?'

They had crossed the bridge to the end of Broad Bridge Street, where Dr Christopher Kesteven's house stood beside the closed warehouse. A knot of people, twenty or more, were gathered in the yard in front of the house. Dr Kesteven's young servant was at the door, his face very white and shining with sweat, and trying to make himself heard.

'. . . I dun't know when he'll be back, I tell you, no more'n I know wheer he's gone. He went out to mek a call, thass all I know, doctoring like you'd expect.'

'Doctoring!' someone yelled. 'Murdering, thass what he does!'

'It's Dr Kesteven's house,' said Rebecca. 'What can they want with him?' She did not notice that Luke seemed reluctant to follow her.

Some of the crowd had simply collected as they would at a raree-show, a bear-baiting, or a simple street-fight: but clearly it was the young man who had his foot in the front door who was the leader. Rebecca saw him grab the servant by his neckcloth. She elbowed her way through.

'Why do you want Dr Kesteven?' she said. 'Is somebody ill?'

The man released the servant and turned to look at her with a frown. 'Who might you be?' he said.

'I'm a friend of Dr Kesteven – '

A muttering went up. The young man, a farmer from his clothes, glared at her and said: 'You'd best go yer ways then, mistress. We're not of a mind to be friendly with him.'

'What's he done?'

A woman who was leaning on the arm of the young farmer said: 'Noculating. Twas him as started it. Tellin' folk twould make their children safe agin the smallpox.'

'Broft it in, he did!' said a voice from the crowd. 'Only meks it wuss!'

Rebecca saw that the woman's cheeks were stained with old tears. 'I don't understand,' she said.

'Our littlest,' the farmer said in a strangled voice. 'We had him 'noculated, for our first two suffered terrible when they took the smallpox. This 'ere surgeon reckoned twas safe.' He drew in a great hurt breath. 'It killed him.'

'I – I don't believe it . . .' Rebecca said. She felt Luke touch her arm and heard him say, 'Come away, Rebecca. It's no concern of yours.'

'Twas the apothecary, Clews, who done it,' the woman said.

'Well then . . . !'

'But it were surgeon Kesteven who showed him how,' the farmer said. 'Same as he's been spreading it all round the Soke. We already bin to see Clews. He won't go doctoring for a while.'

'Broke his head!' shouted a delighted voice in the crowd.

'We're not after no revenge,' said the woman. 'Twon't bring my Davy back. But it's Kesteven who started it – '

'Tis murderin'!' cried the farmer. 'No less!'

'Aye, and what about Deeping?' someone said. 'There warn't no smallpox there – not till surgeon broft it wi' his 'noculating!'

'Rebecca, come away!' said Luke more loudly, over the growing noise.

'Here he is! Here he is!' screamed a child's voice.

Christopher Kesteven was riding up Broad Bridge Street on his mare. He dismounted when he saw the crowd outside his house and led the mare up to the yard. His servant, with obvious relief, came hurrying through to take the horse. 'Thank God, sir, I thought they were gooin' to tear me abroad!' he said.

Kesteven patted the mare's neck. 'Give her extra feed, Yelland, and then go on into the house.' He drew off his gloves and looked at the crowd. In his black high-collared coat, with his sober young face framed by greying hair, he was a dignified figure, and the shouts had died down at his approach. He was still the surgeon.

'Who wants me?' he said. 'Is someone ill?'

There were confused cries, a shout of 'Murderer!' From somewhere a stone flew through the air and struck Dr Kesteven's shoulder.

'Twas you who started this 'noculating, weren't it?' the farmer said, stepping up to him. Rebecca saw that his rage was mingled with tears.

'It was,' Kesteven said, 'but I – '

There was a roar, a surge towards him: the farmer's wife spat in his face, another stone was hurled, and then they drew back as Rebecca threw herself in front of the young doctor and faced them.

'What do you think you're *doing*!' she cried above the noise. 'You call this man a murderer, when it wasn't even him who did the operation! Have you no sense?'

Kesteven's pale blue eyes were startled and oddly flat as he looked at her. 'Miss Walsoken . . . please, you had better – '

'Experimenting!' someone shouted. 'That's what he do . . .'

'Leave me come at him, mistress,' the farmer growled. 'This ent your quarrel – '

'I shall damned well *make* it my quarrel,' said Rebecca. 'Folk have short memories. What did Dr Villiers ever do for you? Did *he* ever treat folk who couldn't afford to pay him?'

'All that won't bring my Davy back!' the farmer's wife said, sobbing now.

'Nor will attacking a man who's done so much good!' Rebecca said. 'You'll have to strike *me* first.'

This tall auburn-headed slip of a girl fearlessly shielding the surgeon was such a surprising sight as to defuse the situation. Some of the onlookers began to move away. The farmer and his wife stayed, but their anger had almost wholly given way to grief. Dr Kesteven talked to them quietly. He was to blame, he said, for allowing clumsy and inexperienced apothecaries to administer the operation: clearly this couple's child's blood had been poisoned. There were a few more upbraidings, a last stone tossed by a departing onlooker, but the danger was past.

And Luke, who had stood aside through all this, watched Rebecca and Dr Kesteven as the young man stammered out his thanks to her. Then he turned and began to walk up Broad Bridge Street.

She caught him up in front of the Cross Keys Inn.

'Luke, wait for me.'

He turned, half-smiled. 'I – thought it would be conspicuous if we came away together,' he said.

'I'm sorry about all that,' she said. 'I made a proper spectacle of myself . . . but Dr Kesteven's been a good friend – '

'Has he?'

'Yes.' She stopped in her tracks, so that he had to stop too. A brewer's dray rumbled past them, spinning out mud.

He muttered something, turned again. 'I'd best be going, Rebecca. I've business to see to.'

'Luke.' She held his arm. 'What was it you said?'

The hardness was in his eyes, as instantly recognisable and

213

ominous as a rash on the skin. 'Folk should learn to live their own lives,' he said. 'Interfering never does any good.'

'What was I supposed to do, then – just ignore it?'

He shrugged. 'He should have sent for the constable. Have that damn fool rabble put down.'

She gazed at him for a long moment. 'That's not you talking, Luke.'

'Aye, it is me. Me, Luke Hardwick. Not your precious doctor.'

She watched his retreating back in disbelief: then stirred and hurried after him.

'Luke, *wait*. You can't go like this.'

He sighed, passed a hand through his hair. People passed to and fro on either side of them. 'I don't want to quarrel, Rebecca.'

'Neither do I, Luke. But he's not my precious doctor.'

He looked at her, breathing heavily through his nose. 'Like I say – I got business to see to.'

'What business?'

He did not answer.

'You're going to turn that comber out, aren't you.'

He made an impatient gesture. 'It's nothing to do wi' you – it's business, I tell you . . .'

'Business be damned, if this is what it does to you!' She shook off his restraining hand, was gone.

She had reached the yard of the Angel and had ordered the ostler to saddle her horse before Luke caught up with her. The driver of the Lincoln coach yelled at him to get out of the way as it lurched under the arch and out into the street.

'Rebecca . . . I'm sorry, I'm sorry if I sounded hard – '

'Maybe you are,' she said, trying desperately not to cry. 'But does it change anything?'

'Change what?' His face was grim and dark, close to hers. 'Oh, if you're still harping on about that damn comber . . . You just don't understand, girl. That's the way the world works. The world isn't a kind place, Rebecca – I've found that out this past year. Having a good heart's all very well, but other folk are like to wipe their feet on it. So you have to beat 'em to it. You have to be hard, that's the only way to get on. If a man don't pay his rent then out he goes. I'm no fen fisherman now, for better or worse. I look to my father's firm. That's my way of livin' now. And you can't change that.'

'Sometimes I feel I know you all through like my own skin,' she said quietly. 'And then I come to this – this wall – '

'I run my business in my own way,' he snapped. He gripped her arm and said with great bitterness: 'I suppose your doctor friend wouldn't act like this.'

She said deliberately, trying to hurt him back: 'No, I'm sure he would not.'

They stared at each other. The ostler had brought out her horse and stood at a distance watching them under lowered lids.

'Well, that's pretty straight, isn't it?' Luke said. He turned to go.

'Oh, *God*, Luke, *listen* to me,' she cried, pulling him back by main strength. 'Dr Kesteven means nothing to me. If you won't believe that – '

'Haven't I got reason? To see you there siding with him against that rabble and saying what an angel he is! And painting me some kind of shite-begotten monster – '

'It's you I love, damn you!' she shouted, banging her fist on his chest. 'Yes, let everyone hear it, if I can convince you! I love *you*, Luke, and nobody else. What else can I say?'

He gazed at her, his lips trying to form words. He lifted a hand, let it fall and touch her wrist. 'Nothing . . . I know . . . Rebecca, I can't help it. To see you there with him . . . I'm a jealous man. Just to know – ' He held her shoulders. 'Tell me you won't see him again.'

'Would you believe me, trust me if I did? I help him sometimes. Getting patients. That's all. I'll not stop doing that.'

He made an angry gesture. 'You claim you love me – and now you say – '

'If you can't give me your trust there's no point in my saying anything!' She brushed away her tears irritably: she did not want him to think she was using them as ammunition.

Luke put his hand up to her wet cheek. 'Rebecca . . . I'm sorry. I'm sorry.'

Instinctively they held each other a few moments, wordless and frightened.

'So . . . you'll be going,' he said.

'I'll have to,' she said.

'But not – not in anger?'

She shook her head, patted his stock. 'No. No, Luke. I'll write you . . . when we can meet again . . .'

The storm, it seemed, had blown itself out. But it was not peace she felt as she rode away from the Angel with Luke watching her go from the yard, his eyes burning into her.

2

On Bicklode Fen the windmills were turning, and tons of water had foamed and thundered through the new sluice at Merith Old Drain. Now the darkness of the December afternoon was rendered darker as smoke rose in a billowing brown mass from the burning of the first of the great reed-beds.

From the shelter of a derelict hut three of the adventurers – Joshua Walsoken, George Hardwick, and Mr Stead for Lord Fitzwilliam – watched the burning.

Things were going well. The soil would be ready for planting next season, and Mr Walsoken had already put out an advertisement for tenants to take charge of the new enclosures. The opposition of certain local fenmen had come to nothing. Even the cautious lawyer Mr Quy was optimistic.

Things were going well . . .

George stole a glance at Mr Walsoken standing beside him, watching the burning with serene interest. He was suddenly struck, with a certain unpleasantness, by how much he was indebted to this man. The cost of the mills had been more than expected, and George had raised another loan on top of his mortgage from Walsoken's Bank (people had few illusions about the extent of Thornton Wiley's influence now). Not a high rate of interest, again . . . but the business of Mark Upwell's conviction had created a coolness between them. Walsoken had made no secret of the fact that he would have favoured an even stronger sentence. Of course, there was no outright hostility between Walsoken and George, or between Bromswold and Morholm, but it made things a little less relaxed, a little more complicated. And Mary had heard a rumour recently that Rebecca Walsoken had been seen with Luke Hardwick. There was no doubt what Mr Walsoken's attitude to that would be if he heard.

George fixed his mind on the future; the land dry at last, the banks secure, the black rich soil turned and marled and ploughed and planted, the spiralling rents and the countless acres of crops, the returns on his investment doubling and trebling and doubling again . . . Morholm restored, a great house as it was in its heyday instead of a draughty manor with half its rooms closed up . . . Yes . . . it was a good thought.

The burning went on throughout the month, and was completed before the hard frost set in just after Christmas and winter clamped on the land like a merciless fist. At Morholm Charles Joseph Hardwick casually tried a few words and a few steps, and looked startled at the delight this occasioned in his parents. At Bromswold Paul Walsoken came back from Charterhouse for the holidays, his voice half-broken, and inclined to be restive under his mother's caresses; and Peter Walsoken came from London for a week, and thought his twin sister Rebecca seemed secretive and abstracted.

In Stamford old Horace Hardwick, now seventy-five and feeling it in every inch of his body, seldom stirred from the house and watched his son Luke going indefatigably about his business and wondered if he should tell him to let up a little. And in the same town Elizabeth, Lady Woodhouse, spending Christmas with her parents, shrugged off her mother's enquiries as to whether she was off-colour, for it was impossible to tell her that she had missed her period.

And in Longthorpe Henry Milton returned from London quietly triumphant – having seen his work go to press and been taken to Drury Lane by Mr Carey and there introduced to the famous playwright Sheridan – and kissed the cheek that Julia absently offered him and had a strange feeling that his wife was not really there at all. And in Peterborough Dr Kesteven sat down to a solitary dinner on Christmas Day and silently, privately toasted a young lady. In America the English took Savannah, raising hopes that the war could be fought and won in the south.

And Bicklode Fen lay black and frozen, as if in hibernation.

BOOK III
1779

ONE

I

The former incumbent of Aysthorpe, Mr Medhurst, had frequently arrived late at the church for the Sunday service. Such a thing did not happen with the formidable Rev. Dr Emmonsales, however, until the third Sunday in January 1779, when he was delayed by a sudden illness of one of his small daughters at the Rectory.

The cold was dry and bitter and enveloping, as it had been since Christmas. A knot of villagers stood around the church porch, stamping and blowing on their hands, as Joshua Walsoken and his wife and two daughters arrived.

'Parson ent here yet, sur,' said Will Binnismoor, at Mr Walsoken's inquiring look.

There was some removal of hats amongst the villagers, and chat became quieter. With the Hardwicks seldom coming to church, the seniority of Mr Walsoken was grudgingly deferred to especially as his influence and prestige in the country grew. But he was not popular, Rebecca knew.

'It's a proper shame,' Seth Upwell said. 'Thass never happened before.'

'Dr Emmonsales must have been unavoidably delayed,' said Mr Walsoken.

'Tisn't that, sir,' Will Binnismoor said. 'We can't go in, for the church door's locked.'

'Never happened before,' said Seth again. The events of the past year – especially the loss of his son Mark – had hit the big old farmer badly: his patched coat hung in folds about his once broad shoulders. But he spoke with a bitter truculent edge in his voice. 'Not once when parson Medhurst were here. Church were never locked. Tisn't right.'

Mr Walsoken turned his deceptively sleepy eyes on Seth. 'A regrettable necessity in these times, I imagine, Upwell,' he said. 'With thieving so common.'

Seth stared, his lips moving, and then looked away. But John Newman, with his wife Jenny, blonde as himself, was close by, and he said, without looking directly at Mr Walsoken: 'Nay, tisn't right the church should be locked. It's not a granary or a warehouse. It's the house of God, surely, and should be open to all every day.'

'As your so-called meeting-house will be, no doubt?' said Mr Walsoken, to Rebecca's surprise rising to the bait.

'Yes, sir,' said John. 'Anyone can lay hold on the blessing. There's no place nor favour in Christ's brotherhood.'

'No place and favour,' said Mr Walsoken. 'And no place for the consecrated houses and ordained ministers of the Church, either, h'm? We are all to be one in the sight of the Lord – and all as one on the earth too, perhaps?' Rebecca saw the colour coming into her father's face as he spoke. Somehow between him and the gentle fair-haired young farmer there was a grating antipathy as instinctive as that between cat and dog. 'There we have it, do we not? In seeking to overthrow holy doctrines you levelling renegades have also in your sights degree and authority and all the due order of society!'

'We don't go against the authority of the parson nor his church,' John said. 'But we can read the Bible for usselves, right enough, and see what it say about charity and loving-kindness. And we can see worldly authority for usselves. Aye, and judge it. And respect's worth nowt without it's deserved. It just comes to fear and hate and envy.' Jenny Newman was tugging at his sleeve – she adored her husband but was of a sturdily practical nature – but John could not stop. 'You're a Christian man, sir, you'd say – but Christianity don't start and stop wi' the church door and the pages of the Bible and the chastisin' rod. Fair dealing, and goodwill, that's what it mean to me. I don't reckon I'm no leveller, but if that's what it makes me then so be it.'

There was an enthusiastic murmuring, not quite a cheer: and then the Rev. Dr Emmonsales came breezing up, full of loud apologies and explanations. His arrival put an end to further argument; but Rebecca suspected that her father in fact had no reply ready. A man with a particularly immobile face, it was perhaps clear only to her, who had an extreme sensitivity to his moods, that he was lividly angry.

It was the fact of the appreciative audience of villagers which, she suspected, really rankled. Mr Walsoken was now a figure in this country. Yet it was as if, Rebecca thought, the memory of his low birth and beginnings in trade attended him always like a hollow mocking echo, driving him onward to further and further efforts of self-aggrandizement. Lately, when he had spoken of the Hardwicks of Morholm, she had detected a faint note of pinched contempt in his voice, as if they with their lineage and breeding and their graceful shabby manor represented all that he both aspired to and secretly despised.

In the church she noticed Deborah Gedney, and as they were leaving after the service tentatively approached her.

'Hullo, Deborah. I – hope young Ben's well.'

Deborah glanced at her, nodded. 'He's with Grandma.'

'Deborah, I – I don't know if you know Dr Kesteven, from Peterborough, but I see him quite often, and he acts as surgeon for the gaol there – '

'Oh?' Deborah's eyes were suddenly alarmed.

'Oh, it's all right – what I mean to say is, with him making calls there, I could ask him to bring word from Mark and see that he's well, and – '

'Could you? Oh, that'd be wonderful if you could, Rebecca – just to have word of him and know that he's all right – twould make all the difference . . .'

Rebecca smiled. 'I'll do it. D'you – d'you worry a lot about him?'

Deborah shrugged. 'I try not . . . When I'm feeding and changing Ben, I talk to him about his dad, and what a good man he is, and how he'll soon be home . . . He'll be walking before Mark sees him,' she added harshly.

Rebecca nodded miserably. 'I don't expect you can think of me as a friend any more, Deborah.'

Deborah shrugged again, then put a rough hand on Rebecca's arm. 'Nay. I'm not so daft. But I can't think of your pa as a friend, Rebecca.' Her eyes narrowed. 'Never.'

Rebecca understood and was grateful. She reproached herself for not thinking of her more often: but there was only room for one thought at the moment.

She had managed to meet Luke last week: though as the winter hardened it became more difficult. They had made no mention of the stormy scene between them in Peterborough, or of Dr Kesteven.

It was as if they were cautiously groping back to firm ground: they had been quiet and tender.

Whatever happened – and she felt this with a curious chill – she must see him somehow. That was everything. To know that she was not to see Luke again would be like knowing there would be no dawn to follow the night. It was the fact of Luke that made her feel she was part of life, opened a vista from the narrow constraints of her father's world. It was this compulsion that shut out thoughts of the future . . . of her father . . . of their meetings being discovered . . . Thoughts that must be kept at bay. She must feel that the daylight would come.

One person who suspected that something was going on was Mary Hardwick, for in spite of the cooling relations between George and Mr Walsoken Rebecca was still a frequent and welcome visitor at Morholm. But Mary was too prudent to mention it to Rebecca: and moreover she had worries of her own. The Bicklode Fen venture was running to more expense than George had expected, and he had had to raise a further loan. She would never have dreamed of upbraiding him about this: but there was a sort of tension about him that suggested he was always prepared for a reproof.

The day after his clash with Mr Walsoken at the church, John Newman came to Morholm to see George on business: and after George had left to go in to Peterborough, John stayed talking with Mary.

He came out to help her feed the two pigs they had in the pen behind the stables. Though 1778 had been a good enough year for them to be able to take on two more servants, she had got into the habit of doing such work herself.

'Well, I think it was perhaps not a good thing to do, John,' she said. Will Binnismoor had told her what had happened yesterday. 'Oh, not wrong, not wrong by any means, but – not wise. Mr Walsoken, for good or ill, is now an important man here, far more than the Jarretts ever were at Bromswold. He has a lot of influence.'

John emptied his pail into the pen. The pigs foraged back and forth with complacent grunts of satisfaction. 'Aye, I know, mistress. Leastways, I know now. At the time I – I couldn't stop myself somehow. Jenny reckons I've lost my senses. It was just – oh, everything he stands for, everything he's done since he come here – it seemed to boil up inside me, like.' He smiled, passed a big hand through his hair. 'Twas no way to behave. Least of all for someone reckoning to be Methody.'

Mary put her pail down and rested her hands on the fence. 'Well, I don't like Mr Walsoken, John. There is something in him – something hard and ruthless – that I could never like. I certainly don't like George being so indebted as he is to him.' She looked at John, smiled. 'But you and Mr Walsoken are chalk and cheese, anyway, John, I'm sure. If I were you I should forget about it. You owe Mr Walsoken nothing.'

John smiled too. Between the Newmans and the Hardwicks there was a relationship that went subtly beyond that of landowner and tenant. John's father had known George's father: and years ago, at an unhappy and lonely period of her life when it seemed that she and George were torn apart for ever, John had been a faithful and much-needed friend. It was a friendship she still valued deeply.

'Well, I suppose I shouldn't have nothing against him,' said John. A shadow fell across his blue honest eyes, like a memory of old strife. 'But you've only to look at old Seth Upwell now . . . Mark did wrong, I know, but . . . well, that wouldn't have been the same if it had been Mr George, would it? Mr Amory over to Barnack, he caught Ned Gowt after a rabbit on his land . . . he lit into Ned like the devil, and made him mend his buttery roof for nowt, and what have you, but – tis different somehow . . .' John straightened, smiled with an effort. 'I'd best go. Give that younker of yourn a buss for me, mistress.'

Mary watched him go, tall and butter-haired and slightly stooped, and then, feeling cold, went into the house.

Two letters had arrived by the carrier this afternoon along with the *Stamford and Peterborough Courant*. One was addressed to George and Mary, in a handwriting Mary recognised. Aunt Catherine Hardwick had lived a fretful spinsterish life at Morholm until well after her fiftieth year, when she had married – if not for love, then something pleasantly near it – Mr Hector Finlayson, a Scottish barrister, and gone to live in London. The letter promised – or, in Aunt Catherine's characteristic style, announced – that she and Mr Finlayson would come to Morholm for a visit in the spring. The other letter was addressed to Mr George Hardwick, in a flowing script that Mary did not recognise.

It was a short note, but George studied it for a long time. 'Well,' he said at last, 'I'm honoured by his confidence, but not quite sure what is behind it. It's from Lord Burghley. To tell me, he says, that he has appointed Ephraim Spolding to the vacant place on the bench. The place I vacated.'

'Who is Ephraim Spolding?'

'Oh, a solid citizen, used to be a brewer. Must be over seventy by now. A pleasant enough man.'

'Didn't Lord Burghley suggest that Mr Walsoken would be a natural choice?'

George nodded. 'That's just it. And of course, Walsoken would have been even more severe a justice than the Reverend Doctor.'

Mary lit another candle against the gathering gloom. George admired the youthful grace of her figure as she stretched to pull the curtains closer. She might have been seventeen. 'So is this not – well, a sort of friendly gesture to you?' she said.

'We certainly did not part friends that day,' George said. 'But – well, that's the only interpretation I can put on it.'

Later, over dinner, Mary told George about John Newman and Mr Walsoken.

'He will never make himself popular with the local people – not that he cares to do so,' said George. 'He was speaking to me the other day of petitioning a bill for the enclosure of Aysthorpe.'

'Really? What did you say?'

George sipped his wine. 'He had lots of very convincing arguments in its favour. But in the end I did not find them – convincing enough. And while I am still the chief owner in the parish it depends on me. Some would benefit, including ourselves: it makes for more efficient farming, and higher rents – but some would not benefit, indeed would be materially injured . . . I think he thinks me a very backward fellow, still living in the dark ages.'

'Dark ages, indeed,' said Mary, as the wind shook itself and howled outside and the old house seemed to creak with its own long-drawn shudder.

There was no thaw the next day, and it turned even colder. George rode out early to the Peakirk farm, and after giving Charles Joseph his breakfast Mary made a quick despondent tour of her beloved garden, a dispiriting sight under the rigour of January. When she came shivering back to the house she met Will Binnismoor crossing the yard with a feed pail.

'See the Noah's Ark there, mistress?' Will said. He scratched his bald head and pointed up to the sky. A great dark cloud shaped somewhat like an anvil and stained with cadmium yellow bulked at the horizon like a distant mountain. 'Means floods on the way, that does. Never fails.'

Mary shivered. 'That's the last thing we need, Will.'

Whatever the merits of Will Binnismoor's folk meteorology, what the cloud brought that night was snow. It came from the east on haphazard flurries of wind, and was drifting by morning. For two days it fell, pretty and inconsequential, from a terrible black sky, and the fens were an endless white canvas interrupted by a few charcoal-strokes of trees. Then frost set in again, freezing hard the drifted snow and slush into striated agonised shapes, and making the carriage-roads a bone-rattling nightmare for all but the stoutest in heart and limb. The meres were solid, wrinkled and stuck about with brittle reeds sharp as needles: the wild geese and ducks made question-marks against the whiteness and sent their stricken cries into the silence. Sheep lay dead on the fen commons, humps of ragged yellow in the dazzling snow.

Dr Christopher Kesteven was busier than ever. It was as if the winter was making up for the rich kind summer, and people were unprepared. Pneumonia was common. Smallpox too, he noted bitterly, was rife. He had given up inoculation, chiefly because since the death of that child no one wanted it done. Rebecca aided him whenever she could, though she seemed to have less time these days. He noticed she went into infected places with a recklessness that alarmed him.

2

A letter from Sir Hugh Woodhouse to Elizabeth arrived at Deene-cote Hall on the twenty-fifth. He was coming home.

Elizabeth wept over the breakfast table. The footman stared at her until she sent him out of the room.

His foot was healed, Hugh said, and the moment the weather was halfway favourable he would be on his way. He had been away from her six months, he said, and was missing her very much and couldn't wait to see her again. His tone was fond and possessive.

Elizabeth ran to her dressing-room and was sick: sick at the thought of his coming, sick with fear, sick because she was pregnant and Hugh was not and could not be the father.

Because of the weather she had not seen Robert Landless for a week: but even then, though she had known, she had not told him. She didn't know why. Perhaps it had seemed absurd, wrong, out of place in their lovely unreal affair – this *thing*, this terrible, inevitable, inescapable thing.

But it could not be denied, could not be ignored. At night she cried and prayed and willed it not to be so. But it was.

It was Monday: Landless was usually at the *Courant* office on Mondays. She had to see him. He might not have got there today with the weather as it was, but she must try it. And she could not go to his house in Peterborough. It would be too conspicuous.

The groom and the coachman were amazed at her determination to go out in the carriage, and raised objections about the state of the roads. She cut them off with a brusqueness foreign to her.

It was a filthy ride until they got on to the turnpike road at Wansford, and twice the carriage got stuck and she had to get out while the horses strained to pull it free. But they reached Stamford at last, and placed the carriage at the George Inn stables, and she took a sedan chair up to High Street and got out at the door of Sedgmoor and Milton, Booksellers and Printers.

'You don't understand, do you?' Elizabeth was almost in tears. 'He's coming back, Robert. He could be here any day. My husband is coming back home and I am *pregnant* and it cannot be his! We have not – it has not happened between us for a year or more . . . And soon I will show – it cannot be *hid*!'

'So he is coming back,' said Landless. He was on his knees beside her, clasping her hand. 'Well, we knew he would. We knew! It was only a matter of time. But when he comes back to Deenecote you will not be there.'

She looked at him, her grey-blue eyes vague with tears. 'What do you mean?'

'I mean what I say. You will be with me. We love each other, Elizabeth! That's all that matters. And you are carrying my child. And you don't love Hugh. So there is only one thing to do.'

'Robert, you're not listening – '

'I am, my love, I am. And what I hear tells me there is only one thing to do. Leave him. Leave him and come to me.'

'Robert, I'm *married* . . .'

'Of course you are. And marriages have broken before. Leave

Hugh and live with me and have your child – our child – and we'll be happy and be damned to the eyes of the world!' Landless snapped his fingers. His eyes were fixed devotedly on her face.

'Oh, you *say* this . . . It's easy to say . . .'

'Easy to do. What's to stop us? We need not stay here. We can be off to London, to Europe. It doesn't matter. I have money enough. Oh, folk will talk. They always talk. But they'll soon get tired of talking. And what does it matter, so long as we are together?'

She looked at him through her wet lashes, seeing him slender and handsome and ardent beside her. And the visions he conjured up swam beguilingly in her mind . . . to run away . . . to live with him . . . to be free of Hugh, free of unhappiness, with one blow . . .

And a vision appeared also, strangely, of her parents: of all they had hoped and worked and planned for her: the brilliance, the desirability of her marriage and the life it granted her. Lady Woodhouse of Deenecote Hall . . . the London seasons, the wealth, the position, all the things she had been trained up to aim for . . . To throw it away, for a hole-in-the-corner gypsy life, to surrender all she had achieved . . .

And she was weak. She buried her face in her hands and sobbed out: 'I can't . . . I can't, Robert, I can't . . .'

He stroked her hair gently, thinking this meant she had capitulated. 'Yes, yes, you can, Elizabeth. You are a courageous woman, I know, and I know you can do it.'

'Courage?' She looked up at him stormily, her face white and hair-streaked. 'But there would not be courage in that. The real courage would be . . . He is my husband, Robert! We are joined . . . my life is bound up with his – it cannot be brushed away in a puff of air. We have been living in a – a *fantasy*, a beautiful fantasy – but he is the real world returning.'

'But *love*,' Landless said, his voice rising with a note of desperation, 'we love each other, for God's sake!'

'Oh, *love*. And it conquers all and we can ride on clouds and feed on kisses and make the earth spin a different way . . . Don't you understand, Robert? The dream's over. It's over.'

'I don't believe it,' he said brokenly, standing and gazing down at her. He looked very young and helpless, almost a boy. In sudden frustration he swept the inkstand and candlestick and paperweight off the desk and on to the floor with a crash. 'All – all we had together – '

'Stolen,' she said tonelessly. 'We knew it was stolen. And now we have to pay. *I* have to pay.'

His breath was coming in painful gasps, like a hurt child's. 'You don't love him,' he said. 'Elizabeth! Tell me you don't love him.'

She shook her head slowly. 'No, I don't.'

He stared at her for several moments, blew out a long breath. The hushed patter of a fresh fall of snow could be heard on the window-pane. 'Then what are you going to do?' he said.

'I am two and a half months forward,' she said, in the same deadened voice. 'It should not be difficult . . . there are ways . . .'

His hands went out, as if he were going to shake her. 'Oh, no. Not that. I won't let you do it. I won't let you!'

'You cannot *stop* me! You still don't see, Robert! You have no rights in this – we neither of us have any rights. It had no right even to be conceived!'

He saw utter, desperate determination in the coiled tension of her figure and the wildness in her eyes. His arms slumped to his sides. 'You really mean it,' he said.

She nodded, stood up, collected her muff and shawl.

'And – am I never to see you again?'

'Oh, I am Lady Woodhouse of Deenecote,' she said with a final festering of bitter wretchedness. 'We have a large circle of acquaintance, and no doubt we may see you about . . .' Her hand was on the door handle.

'Elizabeth, you can't do this!' he cried, and seized her at the door, tried to touch her tear-stained face. For a fraction of a second she hesitated, then wrenched the door open. 'It's *over*,' she said. 'We can't cheat the world any longer . . . it's over.'

She was gone. Her footsteps echoed down the stairs. The shop doorbell tinged. Landless, like a man drugged or beaten into stupefaction, walked unsteadily to the window and watched her figure hurry off down the snowy street, out of sight, out of his life.

TWO

Jeremiah Walsoken, twenty-one years old, eldest son and heir of Mr Joshua Walsoken, came to Bromswold in February. He had come down from St John's College, Cambridge, though without a degree: he had simply got tired of his studies, and his father accepted this without demur, just as he had accepted and redeemed the long tailors' bills and wine merchants' bills and occasional usurers' bills that Jeremiah had run up.

'To be sure, there are a few fellows who stick at their books as if their lives depended on it,' Jeremiah told Rebecca. 'Measly nashed little creatures, all of 'em, afraid to step beyond the college gate. But most are of my mind, sister: studies are a minor necessary evil, and the serious business of life is the punch bowl and the card-table and a good nag that rides easy and takes a jump when you dig your heels in. And a wench that does the same, come to that. And besides, my tutor and I had a disagreement. He called me a lazy good-for-nothing dog.'

'And what did you call him?' Rebecca said.

'I called him out.'

'You did what?'

'Don't believe me, eh? It's true. I said he was a spavin-shanked dried-up old whoreson crow and probably a mollie to boot.'

'What's a mollie?'

'Dear Rebecca, don't you know?'

'. . . I can guess.'

'Well, I threw that in, and then demanded satisfaction in the college grounds with pistols or swords, it was up to him. Of course he went white and bleated like a sheep, and so I left him there quivering amongst his damn dusty books.'

Jeremiah was very tall, very thin, long-legged like his younger sister and with something of her quick vitality. But he lacked the openness of feature that was part of her attraction. He had narrow eyes with long lashes very black like his hair, which was curled *en papillotte*, and a lean vulpine face and lips which sardonic nature had twisted into a permanent curve.

He brought with him an array of clothes that filled two trunks and two wardrobes. 'I shall have little chance to cut a figure in these barbaric regions, alas,' he said. 'But then, one should dress well for oneself, not for the eyes of the world.' Rebecca looked on without comment as he flourished before her the French frock-coats with embroidered button-holes, the riding-coats with layers of cape collars, the striped and flowered waistcoats of Italian silk, the buckled shoes cut low like slippers.

'You must be, let me see, nineteen now,' Jeremiah said. 'Has father no husband lined up for you? Some useful connection for him?'

'If he has, he has not told me of it.'

Jeremiah eyed her up and down. 'Well, you have certainly blossomed out of the harum-scarum girl I remember. Always climbing trees, I recall, or standing on your head. Always cuts and grazes on your legs. Tell me, has no man put a graze between 'em yet?'

'D'you think I would tell you in either case?'

Jeremiah smiled, an attractive smile marred by superciliousness. 'Maybe not. Perhaps my talk shocks you, sister.'

'Isn't it meant to?'

Jeremiah's eyes crinkled with amusement. 'Pretty answer,' he said. 'I'll wager you give the men lots of pretty answers. And men like 'em. They add relish to the pursuit. But they won't do for ever, of course – or perhaps you know that. Well, I'm sure mother doesn't know what to think of me. I'm sure I frighten her half to death, but then what doesn't?'

Jeremiah wanted to know all their neighbours.

He called at Morholm, with Rebecca and Sarah. 'Now this is more like it,' he said in the drive. 'Why couldn't father have found a place like this?'

George and Mary were surprised that this should be Joshua Walsoken's son: but they had to admit a certain spiky charm about the young man. He told them what delightful reports he had heard of them from his sisters, and hoped they would be good friends: and when he left he kissed Mary with a bold admiration that was more carnal than respectful.

'Country-squire folk, of course,' was his verdict afterwards, 'but well-bred, and Mrs Hardwick has a trim figure.'

Riding back through the village, they overtook Jenny Newman on her way back to the Newmans' small farm. She and John had two small children, but Jenny was as lovely as ever, with her masses of ashen blond hair and cream-coloured skin.

Jeremiah, with a glance at his sisters, reined in his horse beside Jenny and doffed his hat.

'Here's a neighbour I haven't had the pleasure of meeting,' he said pleasantly. 'At least I hope it's a neighbour.'

'Hullo, Jenny,' Rebecca said. 'This is my brother Jeremiah.'

Jenny looked up with her faintly sleepy expression and smiled. 'Jenny Newman, sir. From the farm over to Helpston Wood. How d'you do.'

'Well,' Jeremiah said to Rebecca as they rode on, 'so there are a few beauties amongst these thick-legged country hoydens. Perhaps I shall like it here after all.'

2

On Friday the 26th of February a gusty wind blew up from the south-east and for once did not sting the face into paralysis. It was the start of the thaw: though it would take time for the great crusts of frozen snow that lay across the fields like splintered glaciers to disperse.

Rebecca rode into Peterborough, to help Dr Kesteven at a sick household. Her father had recently begun to question these sort of visits: when the family concerned was a genteel one, there was nothing more proper, but he suspected she might be going into low and unwholesome places. Rebecca simply assured him she was not. It was a double deception, for sometimes she used these visits as pretexts for meeting Luke. She was, she knew, living precariously.

Dr Kesteven made an early call at the Bishop's Gaol by the Minster Gate in order to give Rebecca a report on Mark Upwell, as she had asked. Even for the age it was a foul place. There were three damp unheated stone-floored dungeons with only an iron grating above the doors: the prisoners slept on board beds with a covering of straw, and had only a small court to exercise in, where there was a pump and a stinking cesspit.

Mark Upwell was thin as a scarecrow and his face was covered with a straggly beard. He looked twenty years older. But he seemed in reasonable spirits, and asked the young surgeon to convey his love to his father and Deborah and the little 'un that he had never seen.

The family Rebecca came with him to visit were a labourer's family living in a two-roomed cottage in Boongate: a place her father would very probably have labelled low and unwholesome. But their predicament was desperate. The wife was laid low with influenza, a virulent strain that Kesteven had seen all over the fen district this winter; the husband had it too, but less badly, and was continuing to go out to work. A daughter of twelve also had it with complications of infection of the lung; only the five-year-old son was healthy. Dr Kesteven prescribed tincture of Peruvian bark and a goose-grease poultice on the chest, and plenty to drink to encourage spitting, which he said was necessary to relieve the infection of the lung.

Rebecca engaged to stay throughout the morning, to change the poultice and give the medicine, until the husband could come home at noon. Kesteven left her there to make another call. He paused at the top of the wooden stairs to look back at her, sitting by the girl's bedside, in the ill-lit single bedroom that the family shared, and was filled with admiration and something else that caused a tightness across his chest and seemed to threaten the impersonal equilibrium that governed his life.

He made a call on old Mr Sedgmoor the lawyer in Westgate – one of his richer patients, who had gratifyingly switched allegiance from Dr Villiers – and visited the druggist and then walked up to the river to his house to wash and change. There he found a servant who had ridden at speed from Deenecote Hall. Dr Villiers was not to be found, he said, and his mistress was in terrible need of a surgeon. Lady Woodhouse of Deenecote Hall, he said – fifteen miles or more, but it was dreadful urgent.

Kesteven said he would come at once, and had Yelland saddle his horse. But he made a detour to Boongate to see Rebecca.

The man of the house had returned, and Rebecca was just leaving. At the door he shook her hand and explained his errand.

'Let me thank you again, Miss Walsoken,' he said. 'You are – an invaluable assistant. I think the fever may be abating – thanks to your ministrations.'

'I'm glad to be of service,' Rebecca said. 'And thank you for seeing Mark. I'll call on Deborah this evening and give her his message. She'll be so pleased . . .'

She put on her gloves, and Kesteven thought she swayed slightly. He touched her arm – it was an unusual gesture for him, and his hand, normally so capable, trembled a little. 'Miss Walsoken, are you quite well?'

'Well? Certainly.' She smiled, reassuring him. 'You had better go to your patient now, Dr Kesteven. Goodbye.'

She watched him ride off, then walked across to the Swan, where Ford was waiting for her. There was slush underfoot and the icicles on the leaded hood of the inn-porch were dripping: there was even a smudge of sun in the grey sky above. But she thought it seemed colder than ever.

When she reached Aysthorpe after two the clouds had parted further, and the sun was stronger, dredging the stream with an oily radiance and gilding the bare twigs of the willows. But she was shivering.

She found Deborah at her lacemaking, seated at the open door of the cottage for better light, with the cushion fringed with its bone bobbins on a stool before her. Goody Gedney was nursing little Ben.

Deborah's face lit up at the message from Mark. 'Oh, thank you, thank you! D'you hear, grandma? Mark's all right enough. That young surgeon's checking on him. Oh, perhaps the time won't seem so long now!'

'He sends his love to Seth,' Rebecca said. 'I'd better go and tell him.'

'Nay, I'll do that,' Deborah said. 'You're looking tired. Ent she, grandma?'

Before she left the Gedneys' cottage Rebecca was presented with little four-month-old Ben to kiss. Deborah noticed with puzzlement that she only kissed the top of his head, lightly, and then was gone.

3

Earlier that day Jeremiah Walsoken rode out on his black blood mare.

Galloping past the old ruined mill he noticed the figure of John

Newman driving his cow towards the common. He smiled to himself and turned the mare in the direction of Newmans' farm.

Jenny was in the small earth-floored kitchen. Her mother had taken her two little ones off her hands this morning. Jenny was churning butter by hand in a great stone basin, and humming softly to herself.

The butter would not turn. Gaffer Pode had some charm that he would recite to make butter turn, but she didn't believe in that nonsense. It was just a question of persistence . . .

A shadow fell across her from the half-door. Jeremiah Walsoken was standing there, gold-laced hat in hand, saluting her with his riding-crop.

'Good morning to you, Jenny,' he said.

She straightened abruptly, pushing back her yellow hair with a hand that was damp with buttermilk.

'Ah – I've spoilt the picture, damn it. You looked so charming in your concentration – it was like an old Dutch painting.' Jeremiah smiled, his eyelids crinkling.

'I – can't get the butter to turn,' she said uneasily, wiping her hands on a cloth. 'Sometimes it go like that . . . they reckon some folk can say a . . .'

He waited. 'Yes?'

Jenny frowned, brushed down her apron. 'Mr Walsoken – '

'Jeremiah is my name,' he said. 'Save your Mr Walsokens for my father, who likes to be sirred and kowtowed to. I'm not at all like him. Am I, now?'

Jenny said nothing.

'Are you not going to ask me in?'

'Well – you can see I'm – '

'You're busy?' Jeremiah opened the door, closed it behind him, laid his hat down on the wooden settle. 'But the butter won't turn. Better leave it, I think. Be neighbourly for a while. After all, I'm a newcomer in these parts. I enjoy coming here, to your quaint little farm – '

'But not when my husband's here?' Jenny said, looking sidelong at him.

Jeremiah perched on the deal table, one booted leg swinging. 'That's not fair. How many times have I been? Twice? Coincidence, surely, that your husband has been out on both occasions. Am I responsible for his movements? Besides – ' he flicked an imaginary speck from his lace cuff – 'honest John – no, I mean no disrespect – might not understand the nature of my admiration. He is a husband and husbands are a jealous species. He might not understand if I were to tell him that I have known and enjoyed many delicious women, but none were as enticing as his lovely wife.'

Jenny bit her lip.

'I've no wish to be rude, sir,' she said. 'But if you think to make a game of me – '

'A game – but that is precisely it! What is love but a game? The most pleasurable game of all! And without rules. Without rules.'

Jenny looked at him coolly. 'Isn't what you're talking about not really love at all?'

Jeremiah shrugged. 'Call it what you will.' As she bent to move the stone bowl he reached out and curled his fingers round her bare arm. 'But I have never had a woman refuse me, Jenny.' As she shook him off he went on calmly: 'Now I know what is wrong. You think I would disparage John? Not a bit of it. He is a handsome young fellow in his way, and a good husband I'm sure. And you are a good wife. But must that be the end of it? There are refinements to love, Jenny. Does honest John know of those, I wonder?'

'Get out,' said Jenny.

'Now, I'm afraid I don't quite believe that,' Jeremiah said lightly. 'The outrage of the virtuous country girl. When I touched you the colour rose in your face and neck. It looked delightful. And I don't think it was from revulsion. I think your body was acknowledging what your mind will not. I think we should try the experiment. I am quite gentle, I assure you. Up those stairs is the bedroom, I suppose? I think I am right, Jenny.'

'You are *wrong*!' said Jenny. Her voice rose. 'Now *go*!'

Jeremiah slid off the table and regarded her interestedly.

'Do you cry out like that when John takes you?' he said.

Jenny slapped him full across the face, and in the same moment he seized her in his arms, surprisingly strong arms for his slight figure.

'So there is some passion in you after all!' he said, his words hissing through a triumphant grin. She struggled, managed to get a hold of his left wrist, twisted it up and sank her teeth into it.

He gave a gasp of pain, pushed her back against the settle. 'So that's how you like it, is it? Well, it can be enjoyable – '

'You *bastard*!' she screamed, drawing her nails down his cheek. 'You filthy *bastard*!'

Jeremiah pressed her down on to the settle, one soft hand clawing down to her crotch. 'No, my dear,' he said, '*gentleman*. You'll find it so . . .' She was pinned down, his lips on her breast.

John Newman came into the room like a bull at a gallop, slamming the half-door back against the wall so that its hinges screeched. He had heard Jenny's cry a hundred yards from the house, seen the black horse tethered outside.

With a bellow he lifted Jeremiah by the scruff and tossed him like a doll against the far wall. The impact knocked all the breath out of Jeremiah, and he could only slump there as he saw a great golden-haired fist swing towards him.

Unluckily for Jeremiah, Mr Walsoken arrived back at Bromswold that afternoon a few minutes before he did, so there was no chance for repairs to his appearance before meeting his father in the hall.

'Great Heaven! What has happened?' Mr Walsoken went white. 'You have been thrown – that horse – we must send for a surgeon – '

'I have been thrown by no *horse*,' said Jeremiah, irritably avoiding his father's outstretched hands. 'Have we brandy in this house, for God's sake?'

In the winter parlour Jeremiah slopped brandy in a glass and drank it with difficulty. His lip was split and a purple bruise like a ghastly flower was spreading across his face: his shirt-front and cravat were torn.

'Then what happened?' cried his father. 'Some thief – you were set upon – have you been robbed? Jeremiah, tell me!'

Jeremiah touched his face gingerly, wincing. 'I have been getting acquainted with our neighbours, father,' he said. 'One John Newman in particular.'

There was a moment's silence. Two pink spots appeared on Mr Walsoken's cheekbones and then vanished. 'That . . .' He flung down his gloves. 'We'll have him. We'll have the canting scoundrel, my son. Assault. Plain as day. Nancy shall bring water and lint and I shall go to Parson Emmonsales and have him committed this moment – '

'*Father!*'

Jeremiah's hand shook as he set his brandy glass down and slumped into a chair. 'I do not think that would be wise . . .'

'What do you mean – if *he* did this – '

'There was a lady in the case, father. At least, a woman. Newman's wife.'

Mr Walsoken stared at his son.

'Stupid slut.' Jeremiah reached for the brandy bottle again, brooding and saturnine. 'She has given me the glad eye several times. These idiot country girls – flatter them beyond their wretched worth and they bridle like colts . . . but then when the time has come for their just desserts they pretend to remember their damn yokel virtue. It's soon conquered and soon over and then they beg for more. I was unlucky in that that great chuckle-headed booby turned up when he wasn't wanted.' He raised an eyebrow and looked at his father with almost neutral interest. 'So you see, father. Having the law on him is not really the question. I fear the name of Walsoken would come off much the worst – '

'Good God! Then I am to let that insolent Methody insult me once again?'

Jeremiah watched his father's cold fury. 'I wonder, father, whether your concern is over my beating or your own hatred of this fellow.'

Mr Walsoken threw Jeremiah a black glance that suggested he might be about to turn his anger on him. At that moment, however, Sarah Walsoken came running down the stairs and flung open the door to tearfully announce that Rebecca had collapsed.

The story of Jeremiah and the Newmans was soon round the village. One garbled version, among a few spiteful souls, had it that John had given the same beating to Jenny: but mostly it was the truth that was passed on and whispered over.

But at Bromswold, the household revolved around Rebecca, who lay in a torrid fever that was like a whirlpool, sucking her down, down, down, each time she tried to struggle up with clawing hands and sweat pouring from her burning face. Every now and then a demon joined her in the whirlpool, demanding that she cough, poking his long fingers into her lungs and tickling, telling her to cough though she cried and begged him not to because the cough would shake her whole body with a rasping pain that each time seemed too much to bear.

4

It was a great surprise for Dr Kesteven when he was summoned that day in Peterborough to go to Deenecote Hall to attend Lady Woodhouse. He knew her only by sight: his small circle of rich patients had certainly never included her.

Two days earlier another letter had arrived for Elizabeth from Hugh. He was setting out for home, he said, immediately, weather notwithstanding. He would be there within a week.

Elizabeth read the letter twice, and then went upstairs to her dressing-room and stripped and looked at herself in the mirror. She had not been sick this morning. But her belly, that had always been slender and flat, was rounded like a small child's. The area around her nipples was darkly coloured and prominent.

She saw her eyes in the mirror, blobs of hollow dark anguish.

She dressed again, carefully, and then sent for Betty, her maid.

Betty almost certainly knew about Robert Landless. But she had been with Elizabeth since she was fifteen, and was devoted to her. So it was Betty that Elizabeth despatched to Cotterstock, the nearest village, to see the old woman there who kept a frowsy little shop. She sold a mixture there, did she not, Elizabeth said – a kind of mixture of turpentine and aloes?

Betty's face was round and terrified. But she said yes, and she went to buy it. Well, the maid could draw her own conclusions now. Elizabeth would just have to trust her.

The stuff came in a little earthenware bottle. It had a bitter pungent smell.

She poured the mixture into a glass. It was cloudy. She drank brandy with it: the more poison in the system the better. The stuff tasted foul and metallic.

At half-past seven she vomited painfully. With determination she washed her face, poured out the rest of the bottle, and drank it.

She felt sick and dizzy, but did not vomit again. Some time after nine she lay down on her bed, aching and weary.

She slept. She slept through the night, waking at dawn with a furry taste in her mouth, fully clothed on the bed. She felt bleary but not unwell. She had to use the close-stool.

That was all. It had not worked.

She went about that day in a daze.

She ate nothing: nor did she change her clothes or brush her hair.

It came loose in blond tendrils. When Betty came fussing and primping round her she sent her away.

There was no possibility of sleep that night. She had a big fire banked up in her bedroom, changed into her peignoir, and drank port. She had never had much taste for liquor but now it slipped down unnoticed. In the small hours she took a candle and roamed around the draughty passages of the house, opening the doors of spare bedrooms, looking in at the shapes of furniture shrouded in dust-sheets, glowing white in the darkness.

She was a girl again in the townhouse in Stamford. Fashionable people came and went in the gilded rooms. Her father pushed his spectacles up his nose and coughed irritably. Young Mr Milton who liked her – but his father was only a retired country physician . . . Card-parties and routs, steered around and protected by her mother . . . the assembly rooms . . . Mother, Hugh Woodhouse has asked me to be his wife and I have accepted him . . . My child, this is the happiest day . . .

She had finished the port. She crept downstairs, to the library where she knew Hugh always kept a bottle in the bureau. Up the stairs again, unsteadily, clutching the bottle to her.

Hugh, I'm going to have a baby . . . of course, it can't be yours, but it doesn't matter, does it? You can have your heir and . . . Hugh, don't look at me like that –

She came back to her bedroom. The embers of the fire spat at her. She sat in the chair by it and watched the dawn smearing itself milkily against the window.

Some time after seven o'clock she stood up. She felt her belly, its swelling roundness.

She walked out on to the landing. Her eyelids were heavy and she swayed a little. She looked down at the staircase. Portraits on the wall; Hugh's family of course; no Wainwrights had been painted yet. Twelve steps to the turning. Or was it thirteen? She tried to count again. She kept getting a different answer. They danced before her eyes.

She leant forward. She found her arms coming out, instinctively, to stop her fall. No . . . just fall forward, into the darkness, shed the burden . . . Still her arms came out. She undid the band of linen from her hair, looped it round her wrists, struggled to tie it with her fingers and teeth. It was not tight. But it kept them together.

With a pleasantly swooning sensation she toppled forward.

Steels, the head footman, came running from the kitchens at the noise, and found his mistress lying on the stair-turning, at the bottom of the thirteen stairs down which she had thrown herself.

He carried her fainting form to her bedroom and laid her on the bed. She was moaning. He roused Betty from her room down the passage.

Betty looked at her mistress on the bed, and her hand flew up to her mouth. She shooed Steels out of the room, and hissed at him to send for a surgeon. She let no one else into the room until Dr Kesteven came.

Elizabeth felt as if she were floating in some viscous liquid: but when she swooped out of unconsciousness she found she was in bed, and there was a young man standing beside her. For a delirious moment she thought it was Robert Landless . . . but this man had dark hair greying at the temples and a solemn face.

'Is it . . . ? Your name . . .'

'Kesteven, ma'am. Dr Villiers was unavailable. Rest easy, please, Lady Woodhouse.'

She was happy to do that, buoyed up on the opiate he had given her. There was a memory of terrible pain and revulsion somewhere, but it had faded away in a cottony well-being.

'Have I – ' She licked her dry lips. 'The time . . . ?'

'It is a quarter past three, ma'am,' said Kesteven. 'You fell down the stairs this morning. It's all right. I have given you a draught to make you sleep.'

Knowledge nibbled horribly at the edges of her mind: but sleep was stronger. She surrendered to it.

Kesteven watched her, a slight cleft between his brows. She had lost the child, of course. Should he have said something then? But it would come back to her when she woke again. She had had a very bad time. There was still a lot of bleeding, and he had fears of a puerpural infection or even a rupture of the tissues of the womb. It was a dangerous situation. Lady Woodhouse's husband, he was told, was away . . .

He would need to talk to her when she was awake: but he had already picked up signs of something strange in this business. It was a long way to fall so heavily; and he had smelt liquor on her breath. Her maid was acting oddly too, insisting on doing all the work of fetching and carrying and washing herself, letting no other servants into the bedroom, staring earnestly into his face.

Elizabeth woke in the early evening. The candle by her bed showed up her face as very pale, the skin stretched like parchment. It also showed she remembered.

Dr Kesteven made a further examination. The excitability of the tissues had lessened and he thought there was not much danger of infection. He could be more certain tomorrow. He sat down by the pillows, smiled encouragingly. 'Lady Woodhouse – I hope you have rested well.'

She nodded.

'You know you have lost, I'm afraid, your child. But now we must concentrate on having you better for when your husband returns. Do you know when that will be?'

'In – in a few days.'

'Ah. Well, it will be a little while yet, but I shall explain to him that you – '

'Dr Kesteven.' Elizabeth raised herself a little. 'My husband was not – is not aware of my pregnancy.'

'Well, you were only about fourteen weeks forward, I believe? I'm sure he – '

'He is not aware – because the child was not his.'

Kesteven was silent. The young woman looked at him, with an unflinching gaze, of one who knows she is powerless.

'I see,' he said. The fall, then, he thought, was probably a deliberate attempt . . . He glanced back at Betty, sitting staring by the fire; but Elizabeth waved a weak hand. 'It's all right. Dr Kesteven – I will not be well when he arrives,' she said, half-questioning.

'. . . No. Recovering, I hope and believe, but – '

'He will want to know what is wrong with me.'

A single tear was running down her cheek. Kesteven was moved, struggled for words. 'I am under Hippocratic oath, Lady Woodhouse – '

'What precisely does that mean?'

He smiled. 'It means my first responsibility is to my patient. And to the patient's confidence. When I see your husband I need tell him nothing of – the child.'

Her hand gripped his wrist above the sheet: a surprisingly strong grip. 'Do I have your word?'

'You have my word. But it is important, in order that you may recover the more quickly, that you do not agitate yourself. I shall return tomorrow if I may, and I expect to see a great improvement.'

A long sigh came from her throat. 'Thank you. I shall be – greatly in your debt.'

Kesteven smiled uncomfortably. 'Let us have you up and about again before we talk of such things,' he said.

He left her lying in the bed, a white troubled face crowned with fair hair, the maid staring mutely from the fireside.

# THREE

I

For two days Rebecca lay prostrated by the influenza. Her fever was high, and the coughs racked her until she fell into exhausted sleep, from which the tickling would suddenly rouse her again, until the tears ran down her cheeks.

Then on the third morning the fever seemed to abate. She sat up in bed and raked her teased hair with her fingers and asked for a drink of water. Dr Kesteven, whom her father had called in on the second morning – he had had a high regard for him since his setting of Paul's arm – smiled and nodded while his eyes were still watchful. She was for getting up – she had never liked lying in bed – but he said they must take care yet awhile. He prescribed milk to drink and a salt solution painted on the throat and complete rest, and said he would return tomorrow. He was very tired himself, having made another visit to Lady Woodhouse, who was still weak but recovering well.

That night Rebecca slept heavily. She woke just before dawn to find herself covered in sweat. And the demon was with her in a new and terrible form.

There was such a pain in her head . . . It felt as if it were made of thin glass, and it was about to shatter. Even her hands were burning. She laid them outside the coverlet and they seemed enormous and swollen, like hoofs, but when she rubbed her fingers together they were the same size.

The cough was changed. It sat on her chest, a great heavy malicious beast, and pressed down and down. It put its claws round her throat and choked her. Then it got bored and simply shook her, again and again, and she was almost deafened by the sound of her own barking.

The dawn stole in, a cruel conjuror: it made all the familiar contours of her room look strange and horrible, the curtains at the end of the bed, the books on the bureau and the ormolu clock, the wicker chair and the sewing basket. They were all alien, pointed, menacing objects that did not belong to her.

There was rain beating against the window . . . beating inside her head. Presently the objects in the room included people. Her mother by the bedside . . . or was it Sarah? Or was it her mother pretending to be Sarah? Why was her mother playing this trick?

There was stuff in her lungs but she could not cough it up. The demon would not let her. Her nightdress was sodden. It twined round her like a damp winding-sheet.

The rain in her head grew harder, louder. There was a man in the room. Or was it the demon? He had his fingers round her throat, tightening . . . She tried to scream – no, they were thin cool fingers. It was Dr Kesteven. His lean kind face looking down at her. Thank God . . . but he was fading away. The demon had got him. No, he was back. He was saying something to her, but she could not hear him. He was talking from the other end of a long tunnel.

'. . . Miss Walsoken, when you cough you must try to spit. No matter how much it hurts. Bring up the sputum and spit it out. It will hurt but it will relieve you. You must try . . .'

A spoonful of brandy was trickling down her throat, then a spoonful of something else. At first it soothed, then it burned . . . *They're trying to poison me* . . . The nightmare dragged her down again as the room got darker, the candlelight threw garish shadows into her mind. The rain was outside her now . . . *she* was outside, there was a great baleful sky above with moving ranges of cloud. It was Bicklode Fen, stretching away to the ends of the earth, wild and flat and empty . . . They were after her, but there was nowhere to hide here. It was Feast Holbeach and his fenmen, with staves and torches . . . *'Tekkin away of a fenman's living!'* There were lots of them chasing her . . . they were pushing someone in a cart . . . *'Give us our bull!'* There was no bull. They wanted her instead. Deborah was there too. *'Twenty months in prison!'* She couldn't run, the mud was sucking her down. She was floundering in a stinking pool with no bottom, clutching at the reeds which came away in her hands . . . It was so cold, she was shivering and shivering. *'Noculating – tis murdering . . .'* Then a hand was gripping hers, a strong smooth hand, and Luke was looking down at her, pulling her up, smiling. 'You want to be careful, Rebecca . . . Come you up here to me . . .' But her father was there too. 'Let go of her!' he said. He was making Luke let go: she was slipping back: her father was standing watching her with the rod in his hand. *'Take the consequences of our own acts . . .'* he was intoning. *'Rabble . . . bastardy . . . Methodies and agitators . . . low and unwholesome places . . .'* Luke watched her as she was sucked under . . . his dark eyes . . .

No, it was Dr Kesteven. His face loomed out of the fog. She was lolling half out of bed, and he was restraining her. She was coughing up some dark sticky stuff. The candlelight had become daylight. The furniture of the room looked dusty, and familiar.

She lay with eyes closed, a beating in her head becoming duller and softer. There were no frightening visions behind her eyelids. She felt as if she had run a hundred miles. Weariness like a warm bath engulfed her. When she opened her eyes again the candlelight was back.

Her mother was there, sewing.

Rebecca moistened her cracked lips.

'What – ' Her voice was hardly there. 'What time is it?'

'Ssh,' Mrs Walsoken said. 'It's seven o'clock.'

Rebecca thought for a while.

'What day?'

Her mother put a damp flannel to her forehead. 'Wednesday.'

Rebecca struggled; her mind felt as weak as her body. 'Have I . . . am I . . .'

'Hush. You must rest.'

Soon afterwards Dr Kesteven came again. He felt Rebecca's pulse, listened to her chest. She lay flat, watching him, her eyes large and distended, the only movement in her exhausted body. He announced that the crisis was past.

Joshua Walsoken shook Dr Kesteven's hand warmly when the young man left, with a promise to return next morning. Mr Walsoken was experiencing the strange sensation of being light-headed. Such was his relief that he could not even settle in his study to offer up a prayer of thanks: he could only go pacing about the house, clenching and unclenching his hands, picking up objects and setting them down again. Another man might have wept, laughed, leapt up and down, kissed his wife. Unfortunately, Joshua Walsoken had not only sought to curtail the emotions of his family: he had done the same with himself.

At length he wandered into the kitchen, where he inspected the cupboards absently. Nancy was just leaving with a tray for Rebecca. There was a bowl of broth and a cup of milk: also a letter.

Mr Walsoken stopped her.

'What is this?' he said, picking the letter up.

'Oh, ef ee please, sur, thass a letter for Muss Rebecca, come yest'day. Usually when – when she's well, sur, she always goes to meet the carrier herself – but what with the poor maid so sick an' all, I had to take it. I thought now she's on the mend . . .'

Mr Walsoken weighed the letter in his hand. 'Take the broth up, Nancy. We won't bother Miss Rebecca with this just yet.'

In his study he stared at the direction on the letter. A strong clear hand. Suspicion crept over him like sickness.

He read the letter several times, though it was short. His mind could not take it in. Luke . . . arranging another meeting . . . Luke Hardwick . . . *When can we meet again?* . . . Luke Hardwick . . . *My own dearest love* . . . Luke Hardwick.

2

Two days later Luke came on horseback to Morholm.

George was out, but Mary was there to greet him. They kissed, warmly but a little uncertain of each other.

'Cousin Luke, this is a surprise! We've not seen you for so long.'

She seated him in the winter parlour, where Charles Joseph clambered on his knee.

'This younker's getting nice and fat,' said Luke, giving Charles Joseph, squealing with pleasure, a pretend bite. 'You're looking well, too, cousin.'

Mary smiled. 'You must have had a cold ride of it.'

'Oh, I don't notice that,' said Luke. 'Wish I could say the same of father.'

'Horace? Is he not well?'

'Oh, not really. A bit short-tempered, but then he always is. Reckon I take after him. But he gets the rheumatics bad, and these days he don't hardly stir from the house . . .

'Mary, I wanted to ask – ask if you've seen Rebecca Walsoken just recent. Oh, I know – ' he went on before she could answer –

'tisn't fair – but I reckon maybe you've had your suspicions. And you and George, you're not only family but my best friends and so I've no call for secrets . . . She should have been in touch,' he said, taking Mary's hand. 'Tisn't like her – I can't understand it. She'll always get a note to me, find a way to – And I've been trying to think if it's something I've done – or if maybe something's happened.'

'Luke, Rebecca's been ill. No, wait. I sent Will to enquire this morning and I think she's on the mend. She's been very sick, but – '

Luke was already at the door. 'Sorry I can't stay for the tea, cousin.'

He had never been to Bromswold before. As he hammered at the door and tried to control his panicked breathing he looked up at the rambling house. This was where she lived. *Lived* . . .

He snatched off his beaver hat as a maid answered the door.

'Day to ye,' he said. 'I come – I've come to enquire after – '

'Who is that, Nancy?' Mr Walsoken's voice.

Luke slipped past the maid into the hall. Mr Walsoken was standing at the door to the parlour.

'Mr Walsoken,' Luke said. 'I've come to enquire after Miss Rebecca – I heard she was some sick and I thought to enquire – '
He glanced around for something to defend himself with: because it looked as if Mr Walsoken was about to fly at him and kill him.

'Nancy. Go and fetch Ford.' Mr Walsoken spoke with a kind of racked shudder, as if he were in agony. 'You can leave now,' he said, pointing an unsteady finger at Luke, 'or be thrown out.' Mrs Walsoken's small grey face appeared behind him. 'A choice.'

'I want to know how she is,' Luke said. So, it was out: Walsoken knew. 'I want to know. Then I'll go.' He must control himself – for Rebecca's sake.

'It is no concern of yours!' roared Mr Walsoken. '*Nothing* to do with my daughter is any concern of yours! That is my last warning. Now get out!'

Luke looked at the staircase, wondering if he could manage to slip past and sprint up and find her. 'Whatever you think of me,' he said, 'it can't be any harm just to tell me she's better – that's all I – '

'If you had come to me,' Mr Walsoken said, taking a step

forward, his voice choked and guttural, 'if you had come to me to ask to pay court to my daughter I would have sent you smart about your business. Immediately. Because you are a common and vulgar and insolent misbegot and so *beneath* my daughter that it is a presumption even to suggest . . . But I might have credited you with a grain of proper respect. But to know that you have been *skulking* behind my back – leading my daughter astray, leading her into God knows what filth – cheating and conniving like the impudent scum you are – and now you have the gall to come here and *demand* – '

'You're wrong, Walsoken,' Luke said. 'Oh, so wrong. Rebecca is a woman. Her own woman, with a mind and heart that's hers alone to give. Not yours. If there's been any skulking, as you call it, it's because you're such a damn petty tyrant – '

'How dare you!' Mr Walsoken yelled. 'I'll see you never go *near* my daughter again! Ford, put this ruffian *out!*'

The manservant approached Luke, not relishing the prospect. 'You may try it, friend,' said Luke. 'It's not your head I'd wish to break, but I will.'

He was fierce and determined. Luckily for Ford, it was then that Mrs Walsoken spoke up, emerging from the self-abasing shadow world where she lived. 'Rebecca has been very ill with the pneumonia following a fever,' she said. 'But the crisis is past and she is lucid now and eating – and Dr Kesteven tells us all will be well. But this is still a house of sickness. So now, will you go?'

Luke let out a long breath. 'Thank you, ma'am. I will.'

'Remember what I said to you, Hardwick!' Mr Walsoken cried.

'Oh, I will.' Luke's eyes were hard and black as coal as he opened the door. 'I'll not forget it, depend on that.'

Mary was waiting anxiously for Luke when he arrived back at Morholm.

'How is she?'

'She's recovering. She's going to be well and fine.' In his relief he hugged her.

Mary said, struggling for breath as he released her: 'You mean you saw her?'

'Oh, no. But at least I didn't come to blows with Walsoken. Not quite, anyway.'

'There's no love lost, then, Luke?'

He smiled grimly. 'No love lost. But she's *better*. That's all that matters.'

'So – your heart's taken, cousin.'

He nodded. 'Aye. It is.'

'I – I'm glad.'

Luke laughed. 'Well, you might sound it.'

'No, no, I am. But it's – it's not easy, is it?'

'No. It's not easy.'

Mary walked to the window, frowning. 'Luke . . . could you come and stay here at Morholm for a few days? I mean, would Uncle Horace mind?'

'Nay, I'm sure he wouldn't. And there's nothing I'd like better. But when – ?'

'Well, I was thinking – soon Rebecca should be up and about again. And George and I will of course want for her to come and see us. And if you happened to be here – '

He hugged her again, lifting her off the floor. 'Bless you, Mary. You're a wonder. When do you think? Next week?'

'Perhaps,' she gasped. 'I'll write you when she's up and about.'

'Bless you again, cousin,' Luke said. 'I hope George appreciates what a wife he has.'

'Oh, I hope he does too,' she said, with a nervous laugh.

The first time Rebecca got out of bed and tried a few steps around the room she panicked. Her legs were hollow tubes: her heart went into a gallop at the effort and she floundered back to the safe haven of the bed. 'I shall never be able to walk!' she said querulously to her mother. Later, ashamed of herself, she tried another circuit of the room alone. Shuffling like an old woman, clinging on to the furniture, she began to feel the vacuum of her legs filling up. In exhilaration she did a trembly jig and then rushed back to the bed. The next morning it seemed impossible to stay in bed a minute longer, and leaning on her father's arm she came downstairs.

Mr Walsoken watched his daughter's progress carefully, almost obsessively those first days of March. The revelation about Luke Hardwick, coming on top of his fear at her illness, had tuned his jealous possessiveness to snapping pitch.

He was in a dilemma. The association must be ended: it would be ended, for he would see to it: she would be watched, questioned, all her letters intercepted – given not a moment's freedom if necessary. But there was the question of what to say to her. She had betrayed him: she had acted with guile and mendacity and all the wilfulness of which he had suspected her capable. A beating . . . Yet she was still not strong. He must be prudent – moderate even.

But she must bend to his will. She must know she had gone far enough.

'Rebecca, I'm so glad to see you better,' Mary said the following Monday, greeting her at the door of Morholm. 'Come in, come in and get warm. And you have walked here by yourself?'

'I feel as if I could walk a hundred miles, let alone one,' Rebecca said.

'All the same, you must come in to the fire. We don't want you getting chilled.'

Mary showed her into the winter parlour. Rebecca took off her cloak and turned to find Mary gone.

A man was standing, silhouetted, at the window. For a second she thought it must be George. Then he spoke.

'Rebecca . . .'

They met in the centre of the room. She hugged and squeezed him with all her strength and more.

'Rebecca . . . you're well. Thank God, thank God . . .' He examined her upturned face, his eyes roving over every inch as if to reconcile it with memory.

'I'm well now, Luke. Oh, never better.'

3

They sat together on the settle and he held her hands, caressing and chafing them as if to infuse her with his own energy.

'I was so afraid,' he said. 'So afraid when I heard. Mary told me – '

'And did she arrange this?'

Luke nodded. 'God bless her. And bless you, my love.' He stroked her face. 'Mortal sick, and she comes out lovelier than ever, if that's possible. Are you warm enough? Shall I get – '

'I'm quite all right,' she laughed. 'You just keep holding me, Luke. That's all I need.'

'And are you eating well? You must keep strong. You mustn't slip back.'

'Dr Kesteven comes to see me every day. He prescribes me strengthening food and exercise. He's been very good.'

She saw his expression darken a moment.

'He helped save me, Luke,' she said. 'He treated me and now he's treating my convalescence.'

Luke winced, shook his head. 'Aye. I know it's . . . But you know how I hate to think of him – '

'Please, Luke. Please don't spoil it. We're together, aren't we? So everything's all right.'

His brow cleared at last. 'Aye. And you're better. God, I was so afraid . . . When I wrote to you. Did you not get my letter?'

'Letter? No, I . . .'

'I thought not. I came to Bromswold. To find out how you were. Your father . . .'

'Does he know?'

Luke nodded.

'What did he say to you? No – I can guess.'

'He hates me,' Luke said, clenching his fist. 'I'm lower than dirt to him.'

'So he knows about our meeting . . .'

'Aye.' Luke got up abruptly and walked to the fire. 'And he'll stop it. We've been living in a dream, haven't we? A dream world. Not the real one.'

She looked at him. 'I want to live in that dream, Luke.' She joined him at the fire and held his shoulders. 'Listen. He's my father. I'm just turned nineteen – I'm not of age. A woman. I've nothing. I've no power. Hopeless.' As he frowned she went on: 'But I want to live in that dream, Luke. Even a little while spent in that dream – like this – is worth it, if that's the way it has to be. All those nights lying there when I was ill – I was thinking, thinking, I want to see Luke, I'll be all right if I see Luke.' She stopped him as he moved to kiss her. 'Wait, love. So, my father forbids it. But he can't lock me up in a cage and – and feed me through the bars, can he?'

Luke made a wry face. 'Can't he?'

'What I'm trying to say is it's up to us. I love you and nothing can change that. Nothing can hurt us as long as we have faith in each other. We've got to keep our love strong, just like I've got to build myself up after the fever. Oh, Luke, don't you see I'd give a year of that damned real world for one moment spent in this one with you? But you've got to trust me, Luke.'

He sighed and touched her hair. 'But your father. You know how he feels. What can you do?'

'He'll try to stop me. And perhaps it will seem as if he has. I'll lie to him and deceive him if I have to. Make him believe I'm obeying him. But I need your trust, Luke.'

'You have it, my love,' he said. 'You have it. Anything that's in my power to give is yours. It's only because I feel for you so deep . . . oh, so deep that sometimes . . .'

'I know. There's a dark side to you, Luke, I know. And I love it because it's part of you. And as long as there's only my father that we have to fight . . . Then we'll find ways. We'll find ways.'

It was that evening, when Rebecca had gone to her room to prepare for bed, that her father came up to see her.

He smiled gravely, and at last he said: 'God has been merciful, daughter.'

She did not know what to reply, so she smiled and went to draw the curtains closer.

'Yes. God has shown mercy,' he went on. 'I have offered thanks for that. I wonder if perhaps it is also a sign, an indication. A sign that I too should show mercy.'

Rebecca looked at him mildly.

'Your – your providential recovery,' Mr Walsoken said, 'is in a way a new start. Do you not think so, daughter? A kind of purging.'

'A purging of what, father?'

Mr Walsoken's hooded eyelids came down. 'I am telling you, daughter, that there is something in your conduct which must cease. Which will cease. It may well be that this sickness was in a way a punishment.'

Rebecca felt angry colour suffuse her cheeks, but she stayed silent.

'Yes, a punishment,' he went on. 'And sufficient as such. And hopefully it has impressed on you the error of your ways. And thus purged, you may start anew on the paths that I choose for you.' He glanced darkly at her. 'Have you nothing to say, daughter?'

'What are *you* trying to say, father?'

He stared. 'You know. You know very well. You are extremely fortunate, Rebecca. At any other time you would have felt my wrath. As it is, I have found out in time. I am even prepared to lay most of the blame to the – the other party, in the light of your inexperience. But what I am saying is we may start anew. Because the association is over.'

'Oh, is it?'

'You presume too far,' he said hoarsely.

'How? For asking a question?'

'You trade on your weakness!' he said, raising a shaking fist.

'Oh, no, father. I am quite strong enough now to take a thrashing. But I wish to be quite clear. You are forbidding me to have any communication with Luke Hardwick?'

'You know that!' he said. 'And you knew it before! But I am not simply forbidding you, Rebecca, oh, no. I am informing you that it shall not be. I shall prevent it. I *can* prevent it. You have betrayed me once. That must lie on your conscience. But it will not be in your power to betray me any more.'

He glared at her, while she adjusted the coverlet on her bed.

'Have you still nothing to say?'

She looked up with seeming surprise. 'What is there to say, father? I am not to have anything to do with Luke Hardwick ever again. That is not a request but a statement. You will prevent me. So what can I say?'

'You won't win, Rebecca,' he said. 'You won't win.' He turned and stalked out.

She sat quietly a while on the bed, her head lowered, as if cowed and dutiful. But there was a look in her eyes that was not the look of defeat.

4

Whilst Rebecca Walsoken was feeling her strength returning after recovering from pneumonia, another victim of that cruel winter gave up the unequal struggle for life in a small gabled house in Church Lane, Stamford. The seven-month-old child of Francis and Kate Sedgmoor died a quick and meaningless death from smallpox.

Henry Milton was the first to be told the news, when he arrived at the *Courant* office one morning to find Francis at the desk staring into space whilst a kettle on the fire boiled dry. Milton's partner was completely stunned.

The funeral was held at St Martin's Church, Stamford on the seventeenth of March. The chief mourners included Henry and Julia Milton and George and Mary Hardwick. Robert Landless was there too – the first time Milton had seen him in several weeks. Landless had told him no details, but he gathered that it was all over with Elizabeth. Landless had written nothing for the paper in that time. Whatever suspicions Milton might have had at first about the light-heartedness with which Landless had entered into his affair with Elizabeth were gone now. He looked thin and unkempt and a little wild as he stood at the graveside, a man haunted by grieving phantoms of his own.

The Miltons and the Hardwicks rode out of the town together after the ceremony, the sky growing more ragged and the wind and rain more crazed as they went. The Welland was foaming and thundering through the arches of the bridge, and the Castle Meadows were flooded.

They were a constrained foursome. Mary, George could tell, was thinking of Charles Joseph, who they had left at Morholm in the care of Mrs Binnismoor bursting with health and life. Julia had been quieter than ever all day.

'God, this weather,' George said, trying to break the silence, edging his horse up to Milton's. 'I had to go out to Bicklode Fen with Walsoken yesterday. The dyke we had cut to the Forty Foot Drain was overflowing. The mill couldn't cope with it. I wonder if we built the banks high enough.'

'Is your association with Walsoken – does it still prosper?' Milton asked.

'What do you mean?'

Milton glanced at George's frowning face. 'Just – something Mary was saying,' he said uneasily.

George was silent for a moment. That he was regretting his involvement with Joshua Walsoken was something he could not admit even to his oldest friend: pride, foolish though it was, got in his way. 'I've got at cross with him more than once,' he blurted. 'Not wise, perhaps, considering the debts I owe him. Oh, he is the man of the future, I've no doubt. Richer than I'll ever be . . . so anything I say against him will sound like envy. But it's the way he goes about things, an impersonality, a ruthlessness. But tell me, Henry, when is this volume of verse of yours to appear?'

'Last week, I understand, though I have heard nothing from Carey yet, or seen a copy. I mean to go to London again shortly. There is talk of a second volume, if all goes well.'

Milton tried to sound enthusiastic, but it all meant nothing. The sight of the little coffin today had filled him with an oppressive horror, a sense of futility that was like a sick coppery taste in the back of the throat. The faces of the parents, Kate's tearstained and anguished, Francis's grim and set but for a tic below the eye, were etched on his mind's eye.

The two couples parted at the turnpike outside Burghley Park, the Hardwicks to strike across country to Morholm, the Miltons to follow the Great North Road to the Nene. The raving wind snatched away their goodbyes.

'I forgot to tell you, George,' Mary said as they bent their heads into the rain. 'There was another letter from Aunt Catherine this morning. She says she and Mr Finlayson are coming to Morholm the first week in April.'

'Is that so? Well, I shall be glad to see her, though she sometimes irritated me to fury when she was here.'

'She says she will be bringing Mr Finlayson's nephew. He is a captain in the Scots Greys. He was wounded in the American war, and has been staying with them. Do you mind?'

'Mind? No, the more the merrier.'

It was not a question she would have asked him even a few months ago. But there was an increasing preoccupation about George that seemed of late to have driven a wedge between them. She knew that the Bicklode Fen venture had driven him into further debt, and suspected that he was always nervously on the *qui vive* in case she should in so many words say 'I told you so'. She would not have dreamed of doing such a thing: but as a result, she could not even mention the subject, because it would seem that she was doing just that.

They said little for the rest of the journey home, and the rain fell more heavily.

A letter was waiting for Henry Milton when he and Julia arrived at Longthorpe. Mr Carey said *The Open Field, or the Countryman's Ephemeris* was out and had made an immediate impression: he enclosed a favourable notice that had appeared in *The Universal Visitor*. He would send a copy of the book with the next mails. In the meantime, he urged Milton to 'cobble together some more of the same – we must strike while the iron is hot'.

Milton put the letter down and went to fasten the parlour window where the rain was spraying in. Julia came back from the kitchen, wiping her thick heavy hair with a piece of towelling.

'Kate and Francis were very brave today, weren't they. At the church.'

Milton stirred. 'Braver than I would be,' he said. 'I wouldn't – I couldn't bear such a thing.'

Julia looked at his hunched shoulders. 'This day doesn't make things any better,' she said. 'I wish the spring would break through so we could – '

'One good thing to come out of it,' Milton said harshly. 'Thank God we can't have children. At least we'll never be put through that. In a way I'm glad we saw that today. Better to have none than raise them to suffer and die and be swallowed by the epidemics. Better to have none.'

'Henry – '

He turned restively, looked at her without seeing. 'I'm soaked to the skin,' he muttered. 'I'll go up and change.'

Julia stayed where she was on the settle, listening to his footsteps going up the stairs and the drumming of the rain on the window.

He had spoken in a burst of bitter melancholy. But his words did not leave her. They bit like acid into her mind and remained there.

5

Just beyond the lip of the fen horizon there must have been a colossal furnace that was manufacturing the endless clouds. They kept on coming, sailing across the sky in jostling numbers, rent and shaped by the wind into every conceivable shape. Warships with bellying sails and heavy purple keels, fantastic crenellated towers, blue drifting mountains that had broken free of the earth, they massed themselves monstrously across the sky and scattered rain like pounding shot over the fields and into the swollen rivers and dykes.

On the last day of March a shrieking wind attacked the sails of a windmill on the bank of Bicklode Fen. Labourers who had been sowing the first seed in the newly reclaimed fields nearby were called in to try and anchor the sails down. But the wind was too strong, and with a gleeful whoop it tore the spinning sails apart, leaving the plucked bones slowly, uselessly twirling. It was only the beginning.

At Morholm the same wind plucked the roof from the home barn like a wig from a gentleman's head. George was not there at the time: he was in Spalding at a meeting with the other Adventurers, discussing the disturbing news that a small breach had appeared in the east bank of the new cut on Bicklode. The hard frost of February had fissured the soil of the banks, and though it could be repaired there were fears of greater damage.

By Good Friday, the second of April, there were problems on the roads. In the Nene valley many were under a foot of muddy water: in places the wind had torn down trees to block the way. Henry Milton, returning from a visit to Northampton, found the bridges at Thrapston and Oundle had been smashed down by the course of the swollen river. On Holland Fen the spring flowers that had begun to appear on the dykesides were lost, their brief lovely message cut short as the water welled up above the banks.

Bloated bodies of sheep and new lambs floated in the murky tides. Folk in the lonely squat cottages jacked up their sheepskin beds on bricks and looked out on a drizzling lake interrupted only by the ragged heads of drowned pollard willows and the distant shapes of the fruitless windmills.

And on Bicklode Fen, in a squalid cottage a few hundred yards from the river, where there was a rank smell of tallow and the earth floor was slippery with goose-droppings and fishing-nets hung from the ceiling as if to drag the roof even lower, the giant fenman Feast Holbeach, with five cronies, smoked a pipe and spat and waited for darkness to fall. The rushlight picked out the whites of truculent eyes, the glint of the silver earrings that guaranteed long sight. They had been drinking gin spiced with penny opium all day, and now there was a heightened, febrile wakefulness about them.

At last the six men went out, walking in single file across the newly-drained commons, hopping over the new fences, guided by a few stars that wavered into view behind the clouds. Three of the men carried bundles under their arms, and Feast Holbeach held a storm-lantern. They might have been ghosts of a fenland past as they trod noiselessly across the acres of spongy silt; the fierce peasants who had rallied to Hereward, or the cut-throats who had harried Vermuyden and his labouring Dutchmen, descending on the drainers in the fen emptiness and leaving them dying at the dykesides with sharpened eel-glaives buried in their backs.

The new cut that the Bicklode Adventurers had built with so

much labour and expense from the Forty Foot Drain to the river was a faint glistening line to the horizon. At its brimming bank Holbeach halted the five men. The silence of the empty land was broken only by the hissing of the rain in the dyke. Two windmills were a vague vertical suggestion in the distance.

The three with the bundles, at a word from Holbeach, went trotting softly away to the left and right. Holbeach climbed up the bank, stood for a few moments gazing across the dyke. The storm-lantern outlined his seamed cunning face. He was grinning as he descended from the bank again.

There was no one to hear the explosions, to smell the acrid whiff of gunpowder, to see the bright blue flashes that sprang up at hundred-yard intervals along the dyke or the clouds of blacker smoke that lifted into the black sky or the glimmer of the water that snaked in slow gushes from the breaches in the bank. Nor to hear Feast Holbeach as he hoarsely cried: 'We s'll have our old fen back, boys! We s'll tek it back! Old Captain Flood! Old Captain Flood's let in again!'

By the tenth of April the sky was clear and blue and looked as if it had never known anything of wind or water. But by then the damage was done.

Around Aysthorpe, on the upland edge, the fields were water-logged, but the damage was negligible. Morholm land, except for the farm on Borough Fen, would suffer little come harvest. But away to the north Bicklode Fen, into which George Hardwick had poured his hopes of prosperity and the money that he did not have, was drowned.

Only a few stretches of lush green sheep meadow were dry. The fen had returned in the space of a few days to the condition it was in before the drainage work – a huge boggy morass for the wild duck and fish and reeds to claim once more.

There were long inquests after the event: but George had only half an ear for them. The Adventurers met at Lawyer Quy's house in Stamford. Mr Walsoken cited evidence of sabotage – breaches in the new bank ten yards deep that must have been caused by interference – possibly gunpowder charges.

George let them talk on, while figures ran mockingly through his head, the tantalising figures that had beguiled him into digging himself into debt over this venture. Land let at twenty shillings an acre: yields of twenty sacks of corn and forty bushels of oats an acre: the riches that were to come swealing off the land like fat from a roast . . . When talk turned to the future, and to the fact that the floods had set the venture back two or three years, he could not prevent a bitter laugh escaping his lips. That was time he simply could not afford.

He thought of Charles Joseph, and Mary. Well, it's ruin this time, my love. The Hardwicks of Morholm have pretty well had their day. But then you told me so, didn't you? You told me so.

6

Something peculiar had been going on: Sir Hugh Woodhouse was sure of that.

He had arrived in triumph at Deenecote Hall on the first of March, delighting in the sight of his white pillared home at the end of its drive of lime trees – so much more civilised than those damn draughty gloomy old Scottish piles – alighting grandly from his carriage with the stiffness in his injured foot quite gone and his body bursting with vigour, sending the servants scurrying hither and thither and falling over each other to greet him. (They missed the firm hand, he reflected.) His hounds were barking in the stables as if they had recognised his arrival: a large basketful of presents for Elizabeth was unloaded from the carriage.

And there was Elizabeth, coming out to the portico, leaning on her maid's arm, to greet him. How beautiful she looked, the perfect adjunct to his splendid house and his renewed consciousness of his importance. He had been away too long. He kissed her with relish.

She had been ill. He might have known.

But such was his pleasure at finding himself at Deenecote again that he was genuinely solicitous: and she certainly did look frail. A young stripling of a surgeon came out the next day to check on her, and talked some high-sounding physician nonsense. Some damn woman's trouble again, anyway. The fellow said she was on the mend.

So that was all right. Sir Hugh had consoled himself with various ladies of the town at Edinburgh; but on seeing again his wife's fair fragile loveliness he realised what he had been missing. As soon as she was on form again he would claim his rights. Silly the way it had become such a terrible issue between them. The break had done them both good, he thought: Lizzie seemed much more sociable with him, asking all the details of what he had done the last few months, telling him how she had passed her time.

Then the suspicions began.

It was poor hunting weather, with the rain and wind getting worse every day: but this did not stop Sir Hugh riding out with his old cronies. They were sorry to hear Elizabeth had been ill: she'd been, they said, in exceptional spirits till just recently.

Then . . . something Steels the head footman said, when Sir Hugh was talking to him about knocking a new window through at the end of the east wing passage, which was too dark. They could do with more light upstairs, Steels agreed: he shouldn't wonder if that was partly why mistress took a tumble down the stairs –

Sir Hugh confronted Elizabeth with this. He knew nothing of any tumble down the stairs.

'Oh – I didn't think it worth mentioning, Hugh,' she said. 'I – it was my illness. It came over me – made me faint. I wasn't really hurt. It was just – my illness.'

Sir Hugh grunted, as if to dismiss the subject. But he did not dismiss it from his mind.

He called on the Wainwrights in Stamford. How had Lizzie been while he was away? Very well, they said, as far as they knew. They had seen little of her just of late.

Without telling Elizabeth he rode too into Peterborough to see Dr Kesteven. He was not impressed by Kesteven's house – a measly place by the river, stuck on to one of his father-in-law's pesty warehouses: it lowered his opinion of the young fellow immediately. Kesteven's answers to his questions did nothing to modify that impression. Lady Woodhouse had been suffering from a fairly common female disorder that had caused her some discomfort and weakness. He was not at liberty to divulge any more details.

'Not even to her husband?' said Sir Hugh, staring him down.

'In such cases the only thing needful for the husband to know is that his wife requires loving care and consideration,' Dr Kesteven said.

The gall of this tuppenny-halfpenny sawbones to speak to him like that! Sir Hugh told Kesteven his services would no longer be required at Deenecote and they parted coldly.

It wasn't right. Something had knocked her up badly, and he was being left in the dark about it.

He hit on Betty, Elizabeth's personal maid, as the person to enlighten him. She was always very thick with her mistress, and ever since he had come home she had been watching him with her little scared rabbity eyes. She must know something.

Of course, it wouldn't do to frighten her. He made his approach subtly, waiting till one morning when Elizabeth had gone calling in Cotterstock and Betty was alone in her mistress's dressing-room tidying her toilet-table. Sir Hugh burst in from the connecting room, called out 'Ho, Betty!' and cut a few dance steps on the carpet.

'There, what do you think of that?' he said. 'Not bad for a man who's been shot in the foot so it swelled like a bladder but a few months since, hey?'

Betty, after the first start of alarm, curtseyed and said: 'Oh, indeed, sir. I'm glad you're recovered. We was all that worried when we heard about your accident.'

Sir Hugh cut another step. 'Strong constitution, that's what does it. All the Woodhouses have had a strong constitution. Worth more than all your physicking. Only wish your mistress had it. Eh? Bit of a weakly sort.'

'Yes, sir.' Betty turned back to the toilet-table.

'Still, I shouldn't wonder if she doesn't fancy it half the time. Isn't that so, eh, Betty? This latest business. I rather wonder if there's been anything amiss with her at all.'

Betty turned again and said vehemently: 'Oh, sir! You wouldn't have said that if you could have seen her – I was that afraid – '

'Eh, eh? Afraid of what? When were you afraid? What's the matter?' Sir Hugh stepped nearer to the maid, so she could not move away. 'When was this? When she fell downstairs?'

Betty, red with confusion and fear, said: 'Yes, sir – at least, when mistress fell ill – '

'Fell ill, fell downstairs, which is it to be?' Sir Hugh's voice grew loud, strident. 'What business had she to be falling downstairs? Come, Betty, you must have been with her. Did she faint, eh? Is there something I should know?'

Betty trembled and her eyes filled with tears. Sir Hugh was an expert bully and many of the maids were frightened of him. 'I – I really can't say, sir.'

'Can't say? Or do you mean you won't say? Is that it? You're keeping secrets from me, is that it, from the master of the house who pays your wages and could have you turned out and thrown on the parish if he wanted to!' Sir Hugh was shouting now, the veins standing out on his florid face. 'You'd better explain yourself, girl, or there'll be trouble!'

It would have taken a stronger vessel than Betty to resist. She had a mother and sister on poor-relief and the oppressive horizons of her life were gratitude for her position and fear of losing it. Under the bullying of Sir Hugh she broke down in hysterical tears and said her mistress had been going to have a baby and had lost it.

Elizabeth arrived back at Deenecote in time for dinner. She had been visiting a friend and while she changed she hummed a little to herself, feeling more cheerful. Perhaps it would be possible to get her life on an even keel again after all. Hugh seemed in a reasonable mood since his return, and she had to admit the house was less silent and gloomy with him there.

He did not appear for dinner: a footman said he was in the library and did not wish to be disturbed. Nor did he join her that evening, and at last she went up to bed.

Hugh had been drinking: but when finally he took a candle and went softly up the stairs he was not drunk. Somehow he had not had the taste for it: it threatened to dissipate his rage rather than concentrate it, and he did not want that.

Elizabeth was brushing her long fair hair when he came into her dressing-room. She smiled at him uncertainly but not without warmth. His head began to thump as if it would explode; but he closed the door quietly, congratulating himself on that restraint.

It was the last restraint he showed.

Down the passage Betty lay cowering and wretched in her narrow wooden bed and squeezed her eyes shut and tried to ignore the sound of the raised voices from her mistress's room. Soon they became shouts. Then they stopped.

Who was the man? That had been Hugh's first demand. The buzzing madness in his head told him he should know, though somehow it seemed less important: that could be dealt with later. The name Landless, that she at last spat out with weak defiance, hardly registered. Hugh did not really care who it was.

Once Elizabeth ran for the door and he pulled her back. He called her a whore and a cock-tease and a slut. The row tossed back and forth, in empty words. There was really nothing to say. Once or twice he hit her, across the face, leaving a bruise: but he found no savoury sting of revenge in that. Not in that.

At last the words, the accusations and recriminations, were at an end, and Sir Hugh stripped his weeping wife and made her kneel naked before him and urinated on her before raping her.

# FOUR

I

It was Dr Christopher Kesteven who had brought Rebecca through her illness, and he who attended her during her convalescence, part as physician, part as friend. She was full of gratitude to him, though he shrugged this off and said it was her own will to fight that had saved her. He called regularly to monitor her progress. But his manner, never easy, was subtly changed. She asked him about his work, about his patients, many of whom she knew, and often he answered distractedly or was painfully tonguetied. Sometimes it seemed as if he had absolutely nothing to say to her, but he was always slow to leave; and she found him looking at her in an intent way that made her restive until she caught his eye, at which he would look away.

She liked and greatly admired Dr Kesteven: but she hoped she was mistaken in what she read into those looks.

She took her walk one morning to see Deborah Gedney, and met Mary Hardwick returning through the village.

They talked of the floods and the blighted spring. Rebecca thought Mary seemed a little constrained with her. She wished she had taken more account of recent events. 'Is there trouble at Bicklode Fen, Mary?' she asked. 'My father has said little about it to me. Is the scheme – '

'All the drainage work has been undone,' said Mary flatly. 'George is – very disappointed, needless to say. He has gone to Spalding for a meeting about it today, with your father and the others.'

'I didn't really know – I've been – well, I've been pampering myself, I suppose.'

'And rightly,' Mary said. 'You've been ill, and weren't to be worried about anything. Anyway, we shall know the full extent of the damage soon.'

Mary had spoken to Rebecca with a lightness she did not feel: not least because she feared trouble between George and Mr Walsoken.

The other day John Newman had come to Morholm to tell them that he thought he was being persecuted. This was so completely unlike him that they thought at first he was joking.

It was no joke, however. Someone had been to the meeting-house, which he and the other Wesleyans had almost finished building, and broken down the rafters and smashed the casements. And someone had tried to poison his drinking water at the farm by throwing dead rats into the well: and there had been an attempt to block the ditch that drained his strip of wheat land.

'But you haven't an enemy in the county, John, surely?' Mary had said.

'Unless one counts Walsoken,' said George.

John looked uncomfortable.

'But this – this is so *petty*!' Mary said. 'Surely he wouldn't – '

'There's that son of his, Jeremiah, don't forget, who can do no wrong,' said George. 'And Walsoken has a long memory and a long reach. There are servants, employees . . .'

'Well, what I come t'ask is, should I go Bromswold and speak to him about it?' John said. 'I don't want no trouble, but it's gettin' Jenny down, and ever since that – that Jeremiah – she's not been herself.'

'No. No, that wouldn't be a good idea,' said George. 'He might well throw you off his property. Leave it a day or two, John. It may just be some mischief that will cease of its own accord. Perhaps I could have a word with Parson Emmonsales – he's a magistrate – though as you know he's no friend to you Methodies himself. If not – well, we'll see.'

So Mary waited anxiously for George's return from the meeting in Spalding.

He was late and tired. He poured himself a brandy before his dinner was put on the table. Mary could tell he had had some drink already that day, but not how much. His face was at its most heavy-lidded and unquiet: at such times the strong Hardwick bones were very apparent, marking his resemblance to his sister Julia.

Mary removed George's plate and brought the apple pie she had baked earlier. She had begun to cut it when he looked up and shook his head. 'No more for me. Thank you.'

Mary stopped. She suddenly felt, absurdly, like crying. 'I baked it specially,' she said softly. She was always afraid of appearing to reproach him of late.

He looked up, smiled and patted her hand. 'Ill humours,' he said. 'Cut me a big piece.'

She sat at the table, smoothing the cloth nervously with one hand, and watched him eat.

'The Bicklode Fen venture is to continue,' he said. 'Walsoken has made a full assessment of the damage. The banks are to be repaired and made higher, and two new windmills to be erected, and the drainage will begin again. The crops that had been sown are ruined, of course, and one or two of the tenants have given up, but most are for carrying on. It will, naturally, be at least two years before there is any return. So, that was the conclusion of the meeting today.' He glanced up at her. 'Are you eating nothing?'

'We had ours earlier. George – '

'Is Charles Joseph abed?'

'Yes . . . he was a thought over-lively today . . . George, I don't understand. Do you mean – '

'Perhaps I've given the wrong impression.' George pushed his plate away and reached for his brandy glass. 'The venture is to continue, but without me, of course. It has left me hock-deep in debt and I would not plunge further even if I could.'

'So you will sell your share?'

'It's already done. I arranged it today. As the fen stands, the share is almost worthless. I cannot afford to wait, so it is to be bought out by the other adventurers.'

'That will lessen your debt, then?'

George shrugged. 'A spoonful from a lake.'

He got up and went upstairs to change his muddy breeches and boots. When he came down to the drawing-room Mary was mending one of his shirts by the firelight. He sat down with another glass of brandy.

'Aunt Catherine will be arriving next Thursday,' Mary said, not from a wish to change the subject, but because George seemed to consider it closed. 'I thought we could give her and Mr Finlayson the west front bedroom. I don't know about Mr Finlayson's nephew – perhaps the one next to Mrs Peach, though I'm afraid it's damp.'

'Soldiers are used to frugal living,' said George. He swallowed his brandy. 'God knows, we shall have to get used to it again.'

Mary peered at the darn she had made in the shirt sleeve. 'George – I know the great hopes you had for this venture. But now it's – well, finished, for us at any rate – it means we will be no worse off than before, doesn't it?'

'If only it did. The point is, we have all been hit by this setback. Even Walsoken, with his great resources, is smarting a bit. The reason I joined in the first place was the hope of a quick return. Now that that is not to be . . . Walsoken naturally wishes to recoup some of his own losses. I had hints from him today that this will mean calling in loans made to me by his bank.'

George took his pipe from the mantel and lit a spill from the fire.

'Go on,' said Mary.

'The sale of my share will still leave me in debt to the bank for a loan on a note of hand for eleven hundred pounds at interest of ten per cent. In addition part of the land estate is mortgaged for another thousand or so. If Walsoken decides to foreclose immediately, then I have nothing with which to meet it.'

Mary stared into the fire. 'But surely he can give you time – '

'He could, but I misdoubt whether he will.'

'There must be something . . . some way . . .'

George shook his head gently. 'We must face it, Mary. I'm a bad risk. If Walsoken chooses to withdraw credit, then I must take the consequences. I have nobody to blame but myself.'

'That's not true, George, not true.' She watched the workings of his sensitive face, hollow and drawn in the firelight. He was a man who took his failures, and his failings, very hard. 'What will happen?'

George suddenly snapped his pipe-stem in two. He threw the pieces into the fire. 'Walsoken must know he can't get blood from a stone – though he is probably just the man to try. I have an appointment with him at the bank tomorrow, when all will be revealed. But he will wish to foreclose on the mortgage, that's for sure. The land will have to go. Oh, it's not the outlying farms: that really would be the end. But in effect it will mean making over our holding in Aysthorpe itself. We shall have the home farm, but the village property that has been Morholm tenure for generations will be the bank's. Joshua Walsoken's, in other words – he will not leave it as bank stock. In itself it's not much. Small tenancies, holdings in the parish fields. But there's enough old-fashioned Hardwick blood in me to feel sick at the thought. Not just the diminished consequences in folk's eyes, though I can't pretend to like that. But the failure of – responsibility.'

'Are you quite sure that this is what Mr Walsoken has in mind?'

'I wish I was not. Not only is it not in his interest to give me time; foreclosure will mean a useful fillip to his ambitions. He will be the chief landowner here.' George leaned his head back and stared at the moulded ceiling. 'As for Morholm – well, it will continue to stand crumbling here . . . an overlarge anachronism . . . a great vault for the deceased glory of the Hardwicks.'

Mary reached out and held George's hand. It lay unresponsive in hers. 'And the rest of the debt?' she said quietly.

'That depends on the goodwill of Walsoken. Not something I am in any mood to court.' He got up and moved away from her. 'So you see, my love. You were right about that venture. I hope that's a satisfaction to you.'

Mary watched his back. 'I didn't want to be right,' she said.

2

The next day George had his interview with Mr Walsoken at the bank in Stamford, after being kept waiting in an ante-room for fifteen minutes.

Joshua Walsoken looked like a man enjoying his power. His appearance was much the same: whey-faced, dark-browed, with a powdered tie-wig: but George noticed the fine Ghent lace at his cuffs and the row of pearl buttons down his waistcoat. Flamboyance might be beyond him, but he was obviously bent on advertising his wealth.

Their business was soon got through, pretty much as George had predicted it. Walsoken was anxious to emphasise that George was not being singled out. 'In view of the situation I thought it prudent to call in a good deal of long-term credit, you understand, Mr Hardwick. Wiley & Walsoken is, I believe, the safest bank within three counties: but Mr Wiley and myself had both put a great deal into the Bicklode Fen scheme, and in order to carry on we thought it wise to shorten credit. I am only sorry that one of the sufferers should be one of our fellow-adventurers. The psalm says "Let the floods clap their hands", and so I am afraid they have. As for the transfer of land, that may be simply arranged, though it is not a common proceeding, except in cases of bankruptcy, which is not the case here, of course.'

'Not yet, at any rate,' said George.

Mr Walsoken pursed his lips. 'Mr Hardwick, I hope you harbour no bitterness about this transaction. I may remind you that you joined this scheme, and raised these debts, of your own free will.'

George held up his hand. 'My only wish is to have it over and done. There is the other matter of the loan I raised some months ago. If you intend calling that in – '

'Now, Mr Hardwick.' Walsoken smiled thinly. 'I said no such thing. Let me see, the sum is eleven hundred pounds? Without security?'

George nodded impatiently. 'As you say. It was meant to be a short-term transaction.'

'Quite so. But Wiley & Walsoken does not wish to gain a reputation for cutting off credit entirely. Besides – '

'Besides, if you were to call it in I would not have the money, and there would have to be a forced sale of most of my property, and you would be an unconscionable time waiting for it.'

Mr Walsoken did not like being interrupted so much. 'As you say,' he said quietly. 'But I think we need not talk in those terms.'

Yet, he might have added, George thought.

Soon afterwards George left the bank and walked up to St Paul's Street to see Mr Abraham Quy, the solicitor, to arrange for the transfer of the mortgaged land in the parish of Aysthorpe to Mr Joshua Walsoken of Bromswold.

At last, the unpleasant business over, he headed for the Black Bull Inn for some dinner.

After the warm spring sunshine outside the inn was dark and cool. George squinted up with annoyance when he saw a figure moving over to his table. Then he recognised Luke.

They drank and talked together with pleasure. Luke, George thought, had grown in assurance: he looked what in effect he was, a prosperous young merchant with a busy life. George found himself envying him, though without rancour. Luke was only a year or so his junior, but to George he seemed much younger.

'I was at King's Lynn yesterday,' Luke told him. 'Got back this morning. We're looking to change the business. Selling up the warehouse here. Lynn's a keenly place, with money to be made.

271

What I plan is to set upon the quay there, with a ship of my own. Maybe to export – though p'rhaps just a coaster would be wiser to start.'

'What does Uncle Horace say to this?'

Luke smiled. 'Well, father gives me my head these days. He says I've a sharper wit than he has now . . . There's modesty for you! But he's old, you know, and likes to take life easy-like.'

'Tell me, Luke – do you ever miss that old life of yours?'

Luke considered, stroking the rim of his tankard. 'No . . . No, truly, George, I can't say as I do. I think of it sometimes – when I'm journeyin' about, and you see them sunsets like you can't see anywhere but the fenland . . . But that's all over now. I couldn't go back even if I wanted to. No, that's all done with.'

They left the inn together, and came upon a circle of spectators watching a fight between two carters in the middle of the street.

Luke and George stood at the edge of the ring of onlookers, watching the two men scrabbling and kicking in the mud. Luke tapped George on the arm and nodded. Mr Walsoken and Jeremiah were coming up to them.

Mr Walsoken gave Luke no greeting or acknowledgement. He frowned at the struggling carters and the hooting, laughing crowd. 'At such times one trembles for the state of men's souls,' he said to George.

'I agree,' said George grimly. 'But I always think the right to call one's soul one's own is the main thing.'

Mr Walsoken glanced at George and said: 'I hope your meeting with Mr Quy was satisfactory.'

'The business was done, if that is what you mean. I found small satisfaction in it.'

'Come Mr Hardwick,' Walsoken said, 'you must not make the mistake of taking this personally. That would be most unbusinesslike.'

'Personally . . . No. No, Mr Walsoken.' George looked at the pinched, authoritarian man before him, at the foppish figure of Jeremiah, who was watching them with interest. 'But while we are on the subject, might I not ask whether you are doing the same in regard to John Newman?'

Mr Walsoken's lips went white. 'To what are you referring?'

'Only to the fact that someone is making John Newman's life

uncomfortable. And if I have any influence left in Aysthorpe I shall use it to find out who.'

'I think you overestimate your influence,' said Mr Walsoken. 'And if you mean to suggest – '

'No, wait, father,' said Jeremiah, touching his shoulder. He regarded George with feline good-humour. 'We must remember Mr Hardwick's rather old-fashioned feeling for honest John and his kind. Country fellows with their praying-feasts and their supposedly virtuous maids. I think the trouble with you, Mr Hardwick, is you're sentimentally inclined – from the best of motives, no doubt – to believe their fantastic grievances.'

'I think the trouble with you, Jeremiah,' said George, 'is you cannot take an honest beating when you deserve it.'

'Sir, you are insulting!' said Mr Walsoken, but Jeremiah, his face crimson, stopped him again. 'No, father, no, Mr Hardwick clearly chooses to believe these fables,' he said, 'and I think we should humour him.' He reached in his fob pocket, pulled out two gold guineas. 'These supposed persecutions of the young Methody. What do they amount to, hm? This should make it up, should it not? More money than he and his wife have ever seen, I imagine. Perhaps you will give it to them, Mr Hardwick, as you are on terms of such intimacy. At least then I may clear the Walsoken name.'

He put the coins into George's hand. George looked at them and then flung them in the mud at Jeremiah's feet. 'Save it, sir, to pay the doctor next time you have to repair your beauty.'

Walsoken put a restraining hand on Jeremiah's arm. 'Steady, my son. I think Mr Hardwick is taking the tone from the company he is keeping. We must make allowances.'

'If you've anything to say to me, sir, say it straight,' said Luke.

Walsoken did not even look at him. 'I have nothing to say to you,' he said, 'except that if you were ever to dare to come sniffing round my daughter again – '

'Your daughter has a mind of her own, sir,' hissed Luke. 'You've yet to beat that out of her.'

'I'd see her dead before a misbegotten guttersnipe like you should touch her!'

'I would remind you, Mr Walsoken, that you are addressing my cousin,' said George.

Walsoken raised his eyebrows. 'If you choose to acknowledge such a relationship – '

'I do.'

Just then the fight broke up: the defeated carter made a run, and the victor went after him, with the onlookers streaming in their wake: and the four men, Hardwicks and Walsokens, who had been ranged against each other with enmity in the air sour as the smell of blood, were separated. When the crowd and confusion had dispersed the Walsokens had turned their backs and were moving away up St Mary's Hill.

Luke had calmed down by the time the cousins said goodbye, but George was still stiff and shaking with anger as he rode out of the town. Luke watched him with misgivings. George was in no position to antagonise Walsoken, he knew, though he did not know the details. As for his own antagonism, that would never die – ever.

He walked back up to St George's Square to his father's house, his mind running once more over his plans for King's Lynn. By keeping his ear to the ground he had come to know of the imminent sale of a warehouse and stone wharf near Purfleet Quay, in sight of the lanterned Customs House, in good repair with a remnant stock of grain. Aside from the rich profits to be made, the atmosphere of the port excited him. The spring floods had gone down, and scores of ships thronged the wide Ouse; sails billowing white in the tangy salt wind, brass glinting on the decks, tall masts pricking the bellies of the clouds and tangling them in a lattice of rigging. On the wooden jetties of Fisher Fleet catches of white fish and shrimps were swung from the little blackened fishing-vessels that came in from the Wash: on the bank of the Nar there were blubber-houses – wrapped in a rank, chest-seizing smell – for the Greenland whale boats. On the quays stood hills of shining blue-black coal from the north and pyramids of timber from the Baltic, and in the boatyards the sculptured skeletons of new vessels on the stocks: seagulls screamed in the sky and watermen, swarthy and foul-mouthed, rolled barrels down narrow planks on to the wharves and swung great loads of grain onto the weighting-tripods as if they were sacks of feathers.

It was a scene that made his heart pump faster, as if quickening in response to the abounding life that beat there.

He tried to communicate his excitement that evening to old Horace, who nodded and screwed up his pouchy eyes and put in sharp little questions.

'Wasn't there some concern about the silting up of the river a few years ago?'

'Aye, there was,' Luke said. 'But the Lynn corporation's called in an engineer to improve the harbour. I was thinking of a brig to export direct, but with this war growing worse they reckon there's no telling which way Holland will jump. Safer to stick to coastal trade for now and see how things go.'

'What about the distance to Lynn?'

'Well, we've got a good overseer in Purvis, I reckon. And I don't mind the travelling. Some time soon I could maybe rent a cottage or a few rooms in the town. What do you think?'

Horace had no real objections: his son had obviously thought it all through. Presently he composed himself to sleep in his wing-chair, his feet resting on a charcoal footwarmer. He felt the cold very much these days, even on a mild spring evening such as this. But his head did not nod and after a while he stirred and said: 'Luke, I make no criticisms of anything you have done. I am, in all respects, proud of you, proud to own you as my son. But there is more than pride – there is affection – love. And it is out of that love that I speak when I say – be on your guard. Be on your guard against becoming too absorbed in the pursuit of wealth. No, let me finish. You have industry and imagination, and you employ them well – and not, I think, merely for gain for its own sake. Which perhaps I did. Folk have called me a miser. I do not fear that in you. But if you go on simply living and breathing commerce every day – '

'It never did you no harm,' said Luke defensively.

'I think it did.' Horace hunched in his chair, sallow and ema-ciated, his eyes pale and watery with age: but his voice was as dry and authoritative as ever. 'That was why I chose to seek you out at last. Because I looked back over my life and it was written out like the pages of a ledger, ruled in narrow lines. And you – you are young, comely, warm-hearted.' Horace gestured impatiently with trembling fingers. 'I express myself poorly. All I mean is, I do not want to see you – '

'I know what you mean, father.' Luke walked to the window and stared out. 'I know what you mean. And all I can say is I'm not made of stone – nor brass and copper and notes. But there's problems that – maybe I can't tell you about. The feelings – they can be more complicated and difficult than any amount of accounts – more difficult to balance . . .'

# FIVE

I

A tardy spring came apologetically in with May, and from the Norfolk hills to the Rutland lanes, from the Lincolnshire wolds to the Huntingdon coverts, the fenland dried itself beneath warm cloudless skies.

Rebecca was now strong enough to ride again: but where she could ride to was a different matter. Her father surrounded her with a fine net of prohibitions. He had the convenient excuse of continued concern for her health – but both of them knew the real reason. She went nowhere alone. All her movements were strictly vetted. Whilst apparently leading the life of any young country lady with a protective father, she was effectively imprisoned.

Sometimes she felt she would scream aloud at the maze of dead ends into which her father's watchfulness channelled her life. Yet she knew she must forbear, use time as an ally. Even allow him to feel that he had won. In her heart the flag of mutiny was still raised, and he could not assail that.

But no one regretted more than Rebecca the cooling of relations between the Walsokens and the Hardwicks of Morholm. George and Mary were her first and best friends here, and in that there was sadness enough. But it also meant another avenue for communication with Luke was effectively closed.

But the greatest source of unease was Dr Christopher Kesteven.

Now that she was fully fit again there was no reason for him to continue to make his calls; and at last Kesteven admitted this himself.

'I am pleased to say you have made a complete recovery, Miss Walsoken. I was fearful at one time that there might have been some hepatizing of the lung, but I am convinced this is not so. So, I shall tell your father that my services are no longer needed.'

They were in the music-room, an airy room that opened on to the garden. Lion was chasing bees on the lawn, and Sarah was sitting with her sewing in the shade of an apple-tree.

'It feels wonderful to be strong again,' Rebecca said. 'Of course, Dr Kesteven, you know you will always be a welcome visitor at Bromswold.'

'You are very kind. I – ' Dr Kesteven fell silent, looked at Rebecca, looked away. He got up and went to the spinet, stood there tall and bowed, turning over some sheets of music. Outside in the garden notes of bird-song and the colours of spring flowers made random patches of sweetness.

'Yours was a very distressing condition,' he said abruptly. 'Distressing of course for the patient, but also for the observer. Experience may accustom a man of my profession to viewing such things, but never to the extent of remaining entirely unaffected. However, in – in this case, I must confess there was a further reason for – for my emotions to be less than objective.'

He was perspiring. I must stop him now, Rebecca thought with a rising panic. I must stop him, because otherwise I'm bound to hurt him. But her tongue was frozen.

'You are not ignorant of my position, of my prospects,' he went on. 'You have, through the generous – the estimable aid you have given me in my work in this district – gained a fair conception of my life and what it entails. In itself it does not, I have good reason to infer, repel you as it might – as it might repel some young ladies.' He paused to search in his pockets for a handkerchief, could not find one, wiped his brow with his fingers. There was something about his manner of speaking that suggested a speech that had been continually gone over and rehearsed. 'As regards what I am about to say – to ask – these are secondary considerations, that I realise. But I thought it best to – '

'Dr Kesteven,' she burst out, 'please believe me that I do not mean to be unkind when I ask you to say no more. Please, consider – '

'Miss Walsoken, I must finish.' His eyes had a sightless, half-wild look. 'I have nerved myself to speak out thus, and I must go on. I – '

'What's this, a tête-à-tête?'

Jeremiah barged into the room, flinging down his beaver hat. 'Phoo, one works up a sweat riding in this sun. Pull the bell, Becky, and we'll have some tea. My tongue's like burnt paper.' He sprawled in a chair, crossing his booted legs. 'How goes it, Kesteven? It's like my addle-headed sister to offer you no refreshment. Will you have some tea?'

'I – thank you, no.' Blushing, Dr Kesteven picked up his gloves and crop, almost dropping them in his haste. 'I must be going. Pray give my compliments to your mother and father.'

He was gone in a moment.

Jeremiah yawned vastly and tapped some dried mud from his boot on to the rug. 'He's a stiff-necked sort of fellow,' he said. 'What were you two hatching up? Discussing your precious paupers and their endless ailments, no doubt. I hope you'll not begin that nonsense again, sister. You caught a nasty dose going in their stinking hovels – that should be a warning to you to leave 'em alone and let 'em live or die. They're all pickled in gin anyway. I declare that surgeon fellow has a quite cadaverous face. I was reading of a case of body-snatching at Ely just recent – does our Dr Kesteven dabble in that for his researching, one wonders? A lot of these sawbones do, you know. Ha! Cadaverous is the word!'

Rebecca left him laughing at his joke and went out into the garden. Jeremiah had been in high spirits of late. There was a fairly well-founded rumour in the village that he was carrying on with Ellen-Maria Hurn, who was a maid at the Rectory, a loud laughing girl with striking dark Spanish hair and eyes. He certainly seemed happy to be at Bromswold, drinking and hunting and dressing extravagantly, and there was no reason to suppose that he was not indulging his other favourite pleasure also.

Rebecca strolled through the green-tipped trees in the direction of the ruined mill, sunlight slanting across her path, Lion trotting at her heels.

She did not love Christopher Kesteven.

That much was certain knowledge. But it was a certainty without satisfaction; for now she knew how he felt about her, and the inevitable end was that she would hurt him badly.

So. The conclusion was made. But there was no pleasure or relief for her in making it. She might not see him for a long while . . . perhaps he would think better of what he had been about to say today . . . But no. Some time it must come, and she would have to hurt him.

She bent down to stroke Lion, wiping her eyes as she did so.

2

Aunt Catherine Finlayson, *née* Hardwick, finally arrived at Morholm in May, after a fortnight's delay. It was the first time she had been back to her old home since her marriage to Mr Hector Finlayson four years ago, and she burst into a flood of tears on seeing it.

Aunt Catherine had never been a handsome woman, and this allied with an impatient temper and a rather shallow mind had led to her becoming the type of an old maid who, keeping house for her brother Joseph, George's father, grew daily more fractious and discontented. Then had come her sudden marriage at the age of fifty-three to Mr Finlayson, a Scottish barrister, now retired, of placid habits and a weakness for the female sex: and somewhat surprisingly, it had flourished. Marriage, and London, had suited Aunt Catherine. She brought with her a formidable array of trunks and boxes containing clothes and hats, and was looking forward to making quite a stir in this backward provincial society from which she came.

If she noticed anything tense or restrained about the atmosphere of the old family home, over which hung a Damoclean sword of debt and foreboding, she was too full of her own news, of inquiries after old friends, and of delighted admiration of Charles Joseph, whom she was seeing for the first time, to make any comment.

'And you have neighbours now at Bromswold, of course!' Aunt Catherine said. 'That must be a comfort to you – especially after the Jarretts turned out so badly. Walsoken was the name, I think?'

'It is,' said George shortly.

'Are you on good terms with them? Are they agreeable? What kind of people? Very genteel? I noticed the house and grounds have been much improved.'

'Mr Walsoken is very genteel, certainly,' said Mary hastily. 'And extremely wealthy. He came from Norwich. He's also a very – devout turn of mind.'

'What's that line about the Devil citing scripture for his own purposes?' muttered George, leaving the room.

The first week in June was the week of Stamford Races, and was accompanied by assemblies, plays, parties and concerts in the town; so the Hardwicks had little difficulty in entertaining their guests. George did not often accompany them, preferring to tend to his diminished estate: so, on their trips and outings, with Aunt Catherine and Mr Finlayson almost inseparable, Mary found herself often paired with Mr Finlayson's nephew.

Captain Alex Finlayson of the Scots Greys was in his late twenties, a tall, erect, soft-spoken man with cropped black hair and a suntanned face. He was slightly short-sighted, and this gave an extra intensity to his eyes, Celtic eyes which were so dark as to be almost black and relieved the austerity of his looks.

The wound that had kept him in England was in his hand, and one morning as they walked in the garden Mary noticed how he held it and asked him if it pained him.

'In truth it does not, Mrs Hardwick,' he said, flexing his fingers. 'The ball entered at the wrist and the wound was clean. But it is still so weak and stiff beneath the elbow as to be almost useless. The army sairgeons have given me an extended sick leave and believe it will recover with use. I have had to make shift to write with my left hand, y'understand. I confess I grow impatient for it to heal. I would dearly like to retairn to my regiment while there's still some fighting to be done.'

The garden at Morholm, often windswept and unpredictable, was heavy with blossom. Captain Finlayson lifted a dripping white branch for Mary to pass under.

'Do you think the war will soon be over, then?'

Captain Finlayson screwed up his eyes at the strong sun. 'I cannot think this business with the Americans will continue very much longer. We shall see it through, of course . . . But it is no longer a simple quarrel, y'understand. Now the Spanish are hoping to pick up scraps from the table. The Dutch may not stay friendly . . . and there's no telling what the Irish may do, if they take heart from the American example. These are not peaceful times.'

'Should that not please you – as a soldier?'

He looked at her and laughed. 'Well, I am trained up to be a soldier, ma'am. My father – Uncle Hector's brother – was not rich, and was able only to buy me a commission in the army before he died. It was my estate, so tae speak. So in a sense my life is bound up with war as your husband's is with the land. But that is not to say I am a bloodthirsty man. I have seen many bloody sights in America, and I think no man could be pleased by them.'

They came to the wicket gate that led on to the home farm. Captain Finlayson shaded his eyes with his hand to look out across the fields where there was already a patina of green. 'Aye, this is a handsome spot,' he said, turning back to look at the house with its Dutch gables and old stone the colour of burnt ale. 'I envy ye living here, Mrs Hardwick.'

'Do you?' Recent events had led Mary to cease to appreciate it.

'Och, yes. It has a genial feeling – a settled feeling. Something I have always lacked in my life, from necessity.'

'It's perhaps a deceptive feeling,' she said. He glanced at her, and she said, with a nervous laugh, 'You ought to see it in the drizzle of November, Captain Finlayson,' and changed the subject. She was strangely glad to see Aunt Catherine coming out from the house to join them.

A letter had arrived for George that morning, and he was poring over it in the library. Mr Finlayson – portly and grizzled, a man who never allowed life to break into a trot – ambled in there to see him. George, after a few words of explanation, showed him the letter.

Dear Mr Hardwick

Now that the transfer of land in the parish of Aysthorpe under the terms of your mortgage with the bank of Wiley & Walsoken has been completed, I feel it necessary to inform you that I intend, as largest single proprietor within the parish, to petition for a private Act of enclosure for the village, to ensure a rational division of holdings in the fields, currently open, and to bring the common and waste towards Helpston into cultivation. In this endeavour I have the support of several of the smaller freeholders, of Mr Amory whose estate shares certain rights of common with Aysthorpe, and of the Rev. Dr Emmonsales. Please call upon me at the bank or at Bromswold if you would wish to add your name to the petition.

Yours, &c.,
Joshua Walsoken.

'It's his tone that galls me,' George said. 'He only just refrains from adding that it makes no difference whether I agree or not. I have only the home farm here now, which is little enough.'

Mr Finlayson scratched beneath his wig. 'H'm, well, you could present a counter-petition if you were set against it. There are sure to be others also, small men who stand to lose out from enclosure. Though your chances of success would be very small.'

George dug his hands in his breeches pockets and stared moodily out of the window. 'I can't go against him at any rate, and he knows it. I owe him too much money to dare to thwart him anything.'

Mr Finlayson looked uneasily at the brooding figure by the window. The man was like a coiled spring. 'Aye, it's a pity. But you know, George, you shouldn't take this too serious. It won't affect you very much. Morholm still has those tenant farms eastward, does it not? And they're what matter. I understand your feelings, but perhaps the idea of the squire, the old Sir Roger de Coverley, is a trifle old-fashioned, you know.'

'Oh, right enough.' George turned, his eyes lidded. 'But the Hardwicks have – used to have – a responsibility to the folk here. And to see the growing influence of a man like Walsoken . . . There is something about him that sets my teeth on edge.' He smiled without humour. 'All of which sounds, I'm sure, like mere envy and sour grapes.'

'Well, I haven't met this Walsoken fellow,' Mr Finlayson said diplomatically.

'I imagine you will be spared that pleasure,' said George. 'We are no longer on visiting terms.'

The last day of Stamford Races was the grandest and most popular occasion, and this time Mary prevailed on George to come with them. Julia and Henry Milton also joined the party.

The Races were held on Wittering Heath to the south of the town, and the spectacle was a brilliantly colourful one under the June sun. The wooden stand was surrounded by canvas booths and marquees for refreshments, with flags and pennants rippling in the breeze, and a great convoy of carriages of every description was drawn up around the track: open barouches and landaus, gigs, wagonettes, post-chaises, chariots, carriers' carts, pony-traps. It was an occasion for the mixing of classes, and ladies with high coiffures and parasols seated in their open carriages peered over the heads of farmers' wives and milkmaids out on a red-letter day. The gin booths were doing good business, and nimble little children were darting amongst the crowd looking for dangling purses and pocket-flaps left imprudently open. There was music from hurdy-gurdies and fiddlers, and a constant passing and re-passing of servants going from carriage to carriage arranging bets between ladies and gentlemen who wished to back their fancies.

Not the least colourful aspect of this scene was Captain Alex Finlayson, in his red coat with gold braid and epaulettes, and more than one young lady cast an admiring glance in his direction. He seemed impervious to this, however, and watched the races with quiet reserve, turning to listen with great attention whenever Mary spoke.

The Walsoken family was here today also. Jeremiah was riding a horse of Mr Philip Warren's in the fourth race, for a silver cup and twenty guineas.

It was inevitable that the Walsoken and Hardwick parties should meet. They exchanged a few words, introductions of the Finlaysons were briefly made, and then they passed on.

One frantic glance had been enough to tell Rebecca that Luke was not here; but she was in a state of constant alarm lest she should see Dr Kesteven, though she knew it was unlikely he would be here today: it was an altogether too frivolous occasion. She lived in dread of their next meeting. She had even thought of writing him a letter, explaining that she understood what he had been trying to say at their last meeting . . . that she was flattered and proud but she must say no . . . But it seemed both cowardly and subtly unkind.

Sir Hugh and Lady Woodhouse were here too, part of a very elegant party. Henry Milton, passing close by Elizabeth who was seated in a barouche, looked up and raised his hat. Her eyes as she turned and inclined her head were remarkable. Blue as ever, but entirely flat and lightless, like a doll's, or a corpse's.

'Henry, whatever became of your friend Landless? I haven't seen him in an age,' George said.

Milton started, as if George had been reading his thoughts. 'Oh – he went away to London,' he said. 'Tired of doing hack-work for the *Courant*, I expect, as who wouldn't be.'

Robert Landless had left the day after the Sedgmoors' baby's funeral. He had come to Milton at the office to tell him so. He was closing up the house in Peterborough for the summer and going to London. He couldn't bear to be in the same country as Elizabeth, he said – now that it was all over. He was pale, dishevelled, more fitful and mercurial in his speech and movements than ever.

Melodramatics, Milton wondered? But no . . . He would probably get over it quite soon – as he once had – but for the moment he was genuinely distraught. And it looked as if Elizabeth was taking it hard too, though Landless had told him it was she who had made the break. Well, Milton was not surprised at its end. Now Sir Hugh was back, and the Woodhouses would continue their aimless fashionable life.

Sir Hugh laid a five-guinea bet with Humphrey Amory for the second race. As good as won – that fellow had no eye for horseflesh. Sir Hugh was enjoying today immensely. Fine sport, fine company, plenty to eat and drink in the warm sunshine . . . and his wife lovely and quiescent beside him.

Elizabeth was his again in soul and body. All it had taken was firmness: should have done it sooner. It was with women as with children, with dogs and horses – you had to break their spirit.

Elizabeth flinched slightly as the horses of the first race thundered past the stand. With their rolling eyes and stretched necks and straining veins they were threatening, obscene, grotesque. Facets of her present life.

She was a prisoner with her husband. A prisoner not only of his constant jealous surveillance but of his vengeful suffocating lust.

She remembered seeing a stuffed linen dummy in Mistress Bourne's dress shop. Patched and battered, stuck with innumerable pins, grubby from being dressed and undressed and twisted about and altered . . . Her own body felt like that. A passive, abused object. (Last night he had taken her from behind. He bit her, grunting. Sometimes he drew blood.) The lifelessness that Henry Milton had seen in her eyes was a reflection of the numb wound that was her mind. She was becoming as unresponsive and unreflective as an animal – for that was the state that life with Hugh was reducing her to.

'I've just realised what it is about Jeremiah Walsoken that I don't like,' George said to Mary as they went into the refreshment marquee for a glass of wine. 'He reminds me of myself at that age.'

'George! You were never like that!'

'You don't think so?'

'I would never have married you if you had been. Jeremiah is a *fop* . . .'

'So was I.'

'But not – seriously.'

'No. I hadn't even the integrity for that. But the seeds were there.'

'Of what?'

George sipped his wine, his face restive and intractable. 'Well, the spendthrift, the wastrel. Not so terrible in a youth . . . Come home to me, has it not? Or come home to us, more to the point. Not content with having an estate, with being a dutiful Farmer George, I manage to go and make myself a near-bankrupt.'

'George, I wish you wouldn't say these things.'

He licked his lips. 'Sour truths, but truths nevertheless. Walsoken is only biding his time, after all . . . Aunt Catherine did well to marry out of this damned family.'

Mary could find nothing to say. There was a darkness about him, and she could not reach him.

'Well, sister, aren't you going to lay a wager on me when I ride?' Jeremiah said. He and Rebecca were in the ring, where Mr Warren's horse was being saddled.

'If you like,' she said. 'As long as you promise not to cheat.'

'Cheat? Cheat? What put that in your carroty head?'

'It would be like you. You always cheated at games when we were little.'

Jeremiah made a wry mouth. 'True. But how could I cheat at a horse-race, I ask you?'

'Bribing the other riders, perhaps.'

He narrowed his eyes. 'You have a wicked mind, Becky. Not a bad notion though . . .' He straightened from examining the horse's fetlock and gazed toward the stand. 'I say, that young Scotch soldier is making a devil of a fuss of pretty Mrs Hardwick.'

'Is he?' Rebecca shaded her eyes with her hand.

'I suppose she gets scant attention from that impecunious husband of hers.'

'But Mr and Mrs Hardwick have always struck me as the happiest of couples . . .'

Jeremiah grimaced. 'No such thing, m'dear. No such thing.'

'On the subject, Jeremiah, do you think you were quite discreet today? Remember father's here.' Parson Emmonsales's maid, Ellen-Maria Hurn of the saucy black eyes, was at the races on a half-day outing, and Rebecca had seen Jeremiah giving her an intimate squeeze behind a gin-booth.

Jeremiah laughed. 'What a toothsome piece she is . . . But you must remember, sister, that dear shockable father is strangely unshockable when it comes to me.'

When the time for the fourth race came, the Hardwick party found themselves standing at the rails close to the Walsokens.

'Mr Hardwick,' said Mr Walsoken, 'as you see, my son is a rider in this race. I can hardly refuse to lay a little wager on him, though in the main I do not approve of gambling. What do you say? Will you back against me?'

'No, you must excuse me, Mr Walsoken,' said George. 'My objections to gambling owe less to sanctimony and more to a chronic shortage of money.' He bowed and turned away.

The fourth race was run, and Jeremiah came in second. The fifth race was the last, and after that the gentry began to drift away. The party of villagers from Aysthorpe, however, who had come on a carrier's cart, stayed on to make the most of the day, to drink and laugh and enjoy the impromptu fair that collected around the stand.

There was John and Jenny Newman, and old Seth Upwell, and Gaffer Pode and Ned and Billy Gowt and Widow Pooley and Ellen-Maria Hurn. The latter had soon become popular in the village, for she was lively and full of fun. The ribbing about her dallying with Mr Jeremiah Walsoken was given and received in good heart, though Widow Pooley, whose Methodism had been grafted on a strong tree of censoriousness, thought she was no better than a hussy. Certainly she was sailing close to the wind, for the Rev. Dr Emmonsales was known to be very strict about his staff.

As the afternoon waned and the light blushed pink across the heath, they sat on the grass with mugs of small beer, and talked turned to the news that there was a move to enclose the village.

'Thass Walsoken's doing,' said Billy Gowt. 'He's got hold o' land that used to be Morholm's now, on top of all. Reuben Phypers, his tenancy's bin took over by Walsoken. Upped his rent straight away. It's Walsoken who's behint it.'

'I reckon we're all right as we are,' said Gaffer Pode. 'They'll be tekkin' away the commons and fencing everything off – I seen it happen – and 'tis only them wi' money who stand to benefit!'

'Well, I can see the reasoning of it,' said John Newman, chewing a blade of grass thoughtfully. 'Like Nat Royle – he's got a fair few acres nowadays, but they're all scattered all over the shop, and he spend half his time draggin' from one strip to another.'

'Nat Royle's allus bin too mean to spit,' said Ned Gowt. 'And what about me and brother 'ere? We mek shift with our bit o' muck and a beast or two. Where we gooin' to graze our old milch cow if they tek the common away? Tis naught but robbery.'

'I'm agin it,' said Seth Upwell. He had drunk too much, and was slurring. The big old farmer was a sorry sight now, a shambling tattered disheartened figure. 'Not just on account of it's Walsoken who's behint it. Though I got reason enough to hate him. I mean, what's to do for my Mark when he comes out o' gaol, and his Deborah and the babby? There'll be no place for them if Walsoken has his way.'

'What's Mr Hardwick say to it, John?' said Widow Pooley. 'You've always been thick with him.'

'I don't know,' said John. 'Thing is, there's money troubles at Morholm, and I don't reckon there's much he can do. But mebbe it won't be so bad. Twill all be done legal and proper, I'm sure o' that.'

'Legal and proper,' said Gaffer Pode, scratching his yellow beard. 'That's just it, John. Seen lawyers, have ye, wi' their fancy clothes and fine houses? It don't cost nothing, bo'. All that surveyin' and measurin' and fencin'. You got a claim to a bit o' land, you pay your share o' the enclosin'. Prob'ly more than your land's worth.'

'Nay, it wouldn't happen like that, would it?' said Jenny Newman. 'Not when we're nice and settled. Can't we say nay?'

'Aye, ye can,' said Gaffer Pode. 'That'd cost ye, though. Tis the Parliment what decides – though blest if I know what they know about it. The rich folk like Walsoken axe 'em, see, wi' a special petition. They'd say to us, well, my good man, ye can make your own case agin it. Oh, ah. Reckon ye can manage that, John, dealing wi' Parliment?'

'Tis the small man who'll go under, and there's nowt we can do,' said Seth Upwell. He pointed a shaking finger at John. 'You'll see, John. Walsoken's done for me and Mark. He'll do the same to you and Jenny, and Ned Gowt, and all of ye.'

'Council o' war, is it, mates?' a rasping voice broke in on them. 'Why, we've met, ent we? Tis the young tow-head preacher! This don't sound like a prayin-fest!'

Feast Holbeach, with a stone jug in his meaty fist, grinned round at them with a show of sour teeth and levered his great body down on to the grass beside John. 'Remember me, do ye? I come on business wi' your friend Walsoken that time.'

'Aye, we remember,' said Ned Gowt, peering at the giant fenman suspiciously.

'Couldn't help overhearing his name again,' said Holbeach, settling himself with a belch. 'Still none too popular in your parts, ent he?'

'Mebbe,' said John.

'No mebbe about it.' Holbeach leaned forward into the circle, and there was an involuntary drawing back; none of them had tender noses, but the fenman's odour was uniquely powerful. 'Listen, mates, we're friends here, uplanders though you are. That time I come to Aysthorpe I were after stopping Walsoken and his schemes – schemes to rob a fenman of his living. Weren't I just. Drainin' and fencin' and meddlin'. Now I reckon he's plannin' on doin' the same for you, ent he? Ent that the gist of it?'

'It's no concern o' yourn if it is,' said Billy Gowt.

'Ah, I ent finished yet. Phoo, I'm swetten like 'oss.' Holbeach took off his broad hat and wiped his grimy brow. 'Know what happened out on Bicklode, do ye? Flooded. Hand o' God, ye'd say, preacher. Not all. Hand o' man too.' He clenched his fist. 'This hand. He built his damn banks. We broke 'em down and let the flood back in. Taught him he couldn't tek our living away. Stood up for usselves, see?'

Ned Gowt frowned, unconvinced. 'Nay. He'd have you in gaol.'

Holbeach shouted with laughter. 'Would he just! How could he know? A few powder charges in the dark. Twas easy.'

'But he's carrying on,' said John. 'Mr Hardwick told me. Walsoken's going to start the draining all over again. He's not give up.'

Holbeach took a pull at his jug. 'Aye. He's determined, I'll say that for him. But so are we. Soon as he build his banks and his mills agin, we'll destroy 'em, see? We ent gooin' to lay down and die. And if all that don't work, well . . .'

'But thass different for us,' said Seth Upwell, who had been watching the fenman with a strange fascination as if he were a snake. 'T'aint a question of floods – '

'It's a question o' standing up for yourselves,' said Holbeach fiercely. 'Else him and his kind'll trample you down. There's no place for you in his world, mates, 'cepting digging his ditches for him. You better think on afore it's too late.' He grinned at John. 'Your prayin-fests ent gooin' to help you, friend.' He stood up, clapping his greasy hat back on. 'You get any more trouble from

Walsoken, you remember my name. Remember I ent afeared on 'im. Fisher Bind Hole, thass where you'll find me.'

They watched him in silence as with his wading gait he disappeared into the fairground crowd.

3

It had been a long day. Mr Finlayson was almost falling asleep on his pony as the Hardwick party rode back to Morholm, and soon after dinner he went up to bed. They were due to leave tomorrow, and would need an early start to catch the London coach in Peterborough. Aunt Catherine, however, stayed up for another hour of solid uninterrupted gossip with Grandmother Peach.

'. . . I must say it has quite opened my eyes returning here, Mrs Peach, after four years of London! One forgets quite how rustic provincial society is – but it's a joy to see old family and friends again, like yourself, ma'am – I have piped my eye more than once. Such a surprise about Uncle Horace claiming a bastard all these years – though no surprise really – he was always close in his ways. I wish I could have met the young man, but he was not in when we called – but then, you know, I was afraid of a little embarrassment, for he cannot have been brought up genteel – but you say he is a fine young man, ma'am, so I believe it – and after all, the Hardwick blood will show itself . . . I must say poor Julia was looking dull today – not that she ever had much in the way of looks, but all the same . . . I wonder she and Mr Milton have had no children yet – I mentioned it to her, quite discreet of course, but she merely gave me a glance in that frowning dark way she has, so I held my peace . . .'

Mary was right to fear the effect of this on George's nerves. After the two old women had finally gone to bed, when George was offering Captain Finlayson a nightcap of brandy, the drawing-room door was pushed open and little Charles Joseph stood blinking there in his nightdress. He was too young yet to be taken to the races, but old enough to know something had been going on without him: he had been wakeful and fretful all day, and after Mrs Binnismoor had put him to bed had come inching his way down two flights of stairs.

Something snapped in George. 'God *damn* that child!' he stormed. He darted at him, gave his legs a stinging slap, scooped him up and carried the crying boy out of the room and up the stairs.

Mary hurried into the hall and was waiting at the foot of the stairs when George came down.

'George, what's the matter with you? He wasn't – '

'He could have broken his neck coming down these stairs!' Veins showed on George's forehead. 'He never does what he's damn well told.'

'He just couldn't sleep – '

'He's indulged too much, that's the trouble.' George's voice rose. 'We'd better not start accustoming him to luxury the way things are going here – that's the last thing we can afford!'

'Well, whose damn fault is that?' cried Mary.

They stared at each other a moment.

'I'll go up and see him,' Mary muttered.

When she had quieted Charles Joseph she came back down to the drawing-room. George had disappeared and only Captain Finlayson was there, still seated by the hearth, wearing the expression of someone who pretends he had not overheard something.

'Captain Finlayson. I'm sorry, you must excuse us . . .' In agitation she went to the table by his chair and began to collect up the tea things. Moisture filmed her eyes and her hands trembled and she upset the teapot. Hot tea spilled over his arm and hand and the pot and the milk-jug crashed to the floor.

'Oh, I'm sorry! What am I – That's the hand you injured . . . Oh, let me get you a bandage – '

'It's quite all right, ma'am, really,' said Captain Finlayson, who had jumped to his feet. 'Luckily it has less feeling than the other! Please don't trouble.' She had seized his hand in distress, and there was a moment of embarrassment as he disengaged it and wiped it with a handkerchief.

She knelt to pick up the teapot and jug, and the next moment he was kneeling beside her and taking them out of her hands. 'Let me,' he said quietly. She stood, put her hands to her burning cheeks, willing the tears not to brim over, while he carefully set the tray to rights.

'Thank you,' she said. 'Well, this is Morholm for you, Captain Finlayson . . . not such an abode of peace as you imagined . . . Things have been a little fraught of late . . .'

He stood up. 'My stay has been a most happy one, Mrs Hardwick. I shall remember it always with – the greatest affection.'

She was aware, as her tears ran over, that she had leaned back –

or he had leaned forward – somehow her body was resting lightly against his, and his hand was touching her arm.

A couple of seconds, though it seemed longer, and then they both drew away. She wiped her face with her hand, drew in a breath.

'I – think I should retire,' he said, his black eyes lowered.

'Yes . . . I – there is a candle in the hall.'

He went to the door.

She bent to pick up the tea-tray. 'Thank you for your help, Captain Finlayson . . . you've been very kind.'

'I want to say, Mrs Hardwick – if – if there's ever any sairvice I can offer you – I am yours to command . . . if ever it should happen that – ' He swallowed. 'Perhaps it is better not said.'

She stared down at her hands. Her own breathing suddenly seemed to have become terrifically loud. She nodded. 'Perhaps it is better not said. Goodnight, Captain Finlayson.'

He was gone.

 *SIX*

I

In August Christopher Kesteven attended at Milton Hall on Earl Fitzwilliam's pretty young wife Charlotte. Few local physicians could boast of attending on both Burghley and Fitzwilliam, the powerful aristocrats whose opposing influence took in most of the area of the Soke, and it was a tribute to his growing renown. Dr Villiers had lost several wealthy patients to his young rival, whose manner was less overbearing and whose treatments were both less drastic and more successful; and Kesteven often found himself addressed as 'Mr', a more prestigious title than 'Dr'. As his practice became more lucrative he was able to engage another servant, and to exchange his old mare for a handsome grey that took him about the country at a mettlesome pace.

But his mind, formerly so trained and methodical, was in a constant fever, a fever his own skill could not cure.

Always conscientious, he now threw himself into his work with desperation in the vain hope of driving away the very thought of Rebecca Walsoken. Having once wound himself up to speak out to her, and then been thwarted at the last moment, he had suffered a reaction, a return of his shyness and reserve, and attempted to put the whole thing from his mind. She had tried to stop him speaking that time – he ought to draw his conclusions from that. Forget it. Forget her.

The land bore its age-old burden of creamy yellow wheat: half-naked bodies laboured in the fields to the age-old rhythms of harvest. The sun was hot and brilliant, and in the towns miasmal fevers were rife. Dr Kesteven was out from dawn to dusk: in the evenings he worked at giving elementary training to Yelland with a view to his becoming his assistant.

And all the time he was distracted, half-mad with love. The more he achieved, the more his achievements seemed to mock him and jeeringly proclaim the dreadful weakness at his heart. And he did see it as weakness: kind, sympathetic and generous as he was, he had for long fenced his innermost self about with prohibitions that made of it something grim and relentless, something that once unfettered gave him no rest and no peace.

An extremely abstemious man by the standards of the age, he now sometimes drank himself to sleep.

There was no reason for him not to call at Bromswold. Mr Walsoken thought very well of him – certainly as a physician, probably as a man. As a husband for his daughter was a different matter . . . but he feared there was a nearer obstacle than that. And so he put off going to Bromswold. Until one morning, when he had only a routine visit to the Peterborough Gaol on his schedule, he faced the fact that the cure for his fever must be attempted again now or never.

He had half a notion, as he rode down Bridge Street towards the Cathedral, to miss out on his call – there were only three prisoners in the gaol at present. But conscientious habit got the better of him.

The smell hit him as soon as the gaoler unlocked the great creaking door under the gate. Stepping from the sweet sunshine into this darkness and stench was like descending into hell.

The gaoler held a handkerchief to his nose. 'Didn't know whether to send for you yesterday,' he said. 'Jenkins had been feeling slight for a day or two, but it didn't look like gaol fever to me, and I've seen plenty of it . . . Upwell reckoned he was all right enough. I – I can't be their nursemaid . . .' The gaoler's voice trailed off. He spat into his handkerchief, avoiding Kesteven's eyes.

The body of Mark Upwell lay in the third cell, covered with a piece of sackcloth.

'Fount him dead this morning,' said the gaoler. 'It were so quick-like . . . I couldn't . . .' He fell silent, hawked and spat again. 'I've notified the parish officer. It were so quick . . .'

Debilitated as he was by a year in the foul prison, Mark had been unable to fight the first attack of fever. His weak chest had given up. He was skeletal thin and white as paper but for the red blotches round his mouth. He looked little more than a boy.

Dr Kesteven covered him up again. Mark would never see his and Deborah's child after all.

Kesteven scribbled out a surgeon's report and ordered the cringing gaoler to have all Mark's clothes and all the straw and bedding burned, the floors washed and everywhere sprinkled with camphor. His own clothes were by now so impregnated with the smell that he had to go back to his house and change.

Then at last he set off for Aysthorpe. He had a more terrible reason to go there now.

Rebecca stood at the parlour window with her back to him for so long that he thought she must be in tears. At last she stirred and said in a muffled voice, 'Thank you for bringing me the news, Dr Kesteven. I must tell Deborah . . . and Seth . . . straight away.' She turned to him at last. Her face was drained of colour. 'What – the body – '

'I imagine the burial will be arranged by the city feoffees.' He swallowed. He had waited so long for this meeting; but under these circumstances . . . 'There was nothing I could do, Miss Walsoken – please tell them that Mark's suffering must have been – mercifully short.'

Rebecca nodded. 'They were hoping he'd be out before little Ben was walking. And now . . .'

'Is the girl – very poor?'

Rebecca made a hopeless gesture. 'Oh, yes . . . Deborah – Deborah will be strong, I think. But old Seth – it will break his heart.'

The desire to reach out and touch Rebecca, so slim and graceful, her dark eyes misted over with sadness, was so strong in Kesteven that he thought he would cry out.

But it could not be. He mastered himself, and after a few minutes he took his leave.

Rebecca put on her shawl and went out to do her awful duty.

Seth Upwell began drinking that evening, and did not stop for two days.

He was eventually turfed out of the Seven Stars, and moved on to Ginger's, a seedy little beer shop on the Castor road, where John Newman eventually found him.

The news of Mark Upwell's death had sent a shocked frisson through Aysthorpe. Deborah, the widow in all but name, was bearing up well after the first breakdown at the news, and she was the object of much genuine sympathy. And feeling against Joshua Walsoken, the author of the Upwells' misfortunes, ran high. All the higher in many quarters, from another piece of news: that the Act of enclosure had been passed.

The baking weather – dazzling sun in the day, humid and airless at night – enhanced the atmosphere of charged tension. It was like the bitter smell of gunpowder; and there were sparks aplenty.

Ned and Billy Gowt and Gaffer Pode and Reuben Phypers and his wife Tess had rallied to old Seth's side. Their grievances found a focus in the wronged figure of the big farmer, who was red-eyed from drink and lack of sleep and a desperate tearless grief that could only find its vent in fury.

'Have a drink wi me, boy,' Seth called to John across Ginger's shop. 'I might as well spend my last penny. It don't matter now. I got nothing left.'

'No, thanks all the same, ole dear,' said John, patting Seth's shoulder. 'Reckon you should let up a bit, eh?'

Seth's large haired fist smacked down on the rickety table. 'Don't start tekkin' me to task, John,' he said. 'You're a good friend, but I won't swallow it. Ain't I got reason? Don't tell me the Devil's got in me neither. Mebbe he has. But he's in that Walsoken one if anybody.'

'Nay, Seth, I don't blame you. Not one bit,' said John. He sat down beside Seth, looked round at the grim ring of faces.

'Seen them new hayricks behint Bromswold, have you, John?' said Reuben Phypers. 'Thass the way the wind's blowing. This enclosure now. He's gooin' to do it, bo'. And there'll be no place for you and me in Aysthorpe when he's done.'

'When I think o' the time before that bastard came here,' said Seth, gripping John's arm, thrusting his bristly face towards him. 'Me and Mark managin' nice and steady. Mark plannin' on gettin' wed. Deborah . . .' The old farmer drew in a great shuddering breath. 'I can't bear it, John, I can't bear it – I swear I'll go mad.'

'Don't tek on so, ole boy,' said John. 'Mebbe things – '

'Nay, John, like Seth says,' said Ned Gowt, 'there's a time for prayin' and forgiveness, and this ent it. Poor ole Mark . . . We all reckon to listen to you when there's trouble, John, for you're a proper good man, and a thinkin' man. But there's a limit. Never tell me you've no bitterness in your heart yourself agin that Walsoken.

Think what's happened to you. Think what's happened to Jenny.'
He raised his mug unsteadily to his lips.

John looked away, his eyes more blue and translucent than ever
against the summer tan of his face. He ran a hand through his thick
strawy hair and nodded slowly. 'P'raps I'll have a drink after all.'

'Where's he gooin' to be buried, Seth?' asked Gaffer Pode quietly.

'That'll be in Peterborough,' said Seth. 'Not even near his home.
A pauper's grave.'

'We s'll all end up in them!' cried Billy Gowt. 'You see! Less'n
something's done about that bastard.'

'It's like that fenman said,' said Gaffer Pode. 'He warned us.'

Ned Gowt nodded. 'Don't let him trample all uvver you, he said.'
He raised his hand for more beer. 'But thass what we've done.'

Seth, staring at his tankard, his great shoulders hunched, muttered: 'What were the name o' that outlandish place he lived?'

'Fish-something,' said Ned, 'you might know it would be.'

'Fisher Bind Hole,' said his brother. 'I remember. Up on Bicklode
Fen. Tidy way.'

Seth's shaking hand extended towards his tankard, then dropped.
'I – ' He cleared his throat. 'I'm gooin' out there and see him.'

Silenced by the import of his words, they gazed at Seth.

'Anyone for comin' with me?'

Reuben Phypers wriggled in his seat. 'Well . . . can't say as I
know the way out there,' he said.

John Newman drained his mug. 'I know the way,' he said. 'I'm
comin' wi' you, Seth.'

2

Friday the 20th of August, three days after the death of Mark
Upwell, was another beautiful day. Scythes beheaded the wheat in
the fields and sheep panted and sought the shade of the sparse trees
and the encircling horizons shimmered and palpitated under a
fenland sky that made the eye ache with its concentrated essence of
blue. Evening came softly on a few subtle moments of breeze and a
lemon-coloured three-quarter moon that carved the landscape with
incisive shadows.

In Seth Upwell's dilapidated little farmhouse there was a glint of
fearless roguish eyes in the dusk as Feast Holbeach sat by the empty
grate and drank from a flagon of ale and grinned round at the

others. Seth. Ned and Billy Gowt. Reuben and Tess Phypers. Gaffer Pode. John Newman. The table at which Seth used to hold his Methodist meetings was pushed against the wall to make room. In the byre behind the house the wall-eyed nag on which Holbeach had ridden bareback to Aysthorpe whinnied and stamped.

'What about servants?' Holbeach said, with a rich belch. 'Got plenty, I reckon. Likes being waited on. Eh?'

'They come 'ere with him from Norwich mostly,' said Ned Gowt. 'But they're all abed early. He works 'em hard – never see any of 'em at the Seven Stars. He allus meks his rounds on his own, last thing. Feared even his servants are out to cheat him.'

'We'll cheat him,' said Holbeach. He chuckled low in his throat. 'We'll cheat him all right.'

'Give him a real fright, that's what,' said Reuben Phypers, his teeth showing in a nervous grin. 'Shake him up. Put a flame to his damn ricks, eh?'

'Break open his barn,' said Billy Gowt. 'Show him. Show him there's folk in the village wun't stand for it.' His voice was pitched high, a little forced. There was the smell of Dutch courage in the cramped kitchen, and a faint scent of something like fear.

'I don't care what happens to him,' said Seth Upwell. He was standing at the window, bulky and stooped, and his words were slurred with drink. 'Fix him proper, I say. He as good as killed my boy. Left me wi nothing . . .'

'That's the way,' said Holbeach. He upended his flagon, and beer trickled down his chin. His eyes swivelled to John Newman, sitting with his elbows on his knees. 'You're powerful quiet, preacher. Having second thoughts?'

John was a long time answering. He was thinking of Jenny and the babies. He had not told her where he was going tonight: he knew what she would have said. But he had made his decision. He was alarmed at his own vengeful hatred, as if there had been a great rending of the foundations of his nature, but he could not deny it.

'No,' he said. 'But – I don't want there to be any bloodshed.'

'Who said owt about bloodshed?' said Holbeach. 'Not me, preacher. But we're all of us agin Walsoken. We're gooing to let him know it, see? Persuasive, that's what you'd call it. Bit o' damage, bit o' fire. Bit o' rough handling. Works wonders.' He bent and patted Seth's dog. 'So cheer up, will ye, mates! It won't be long now.'

*

The Seven Stars Inn did not have much call for stabling, Aysthorpe being off the main road, so the ostler was surprised that evening when Dr Christopher Kesteven arrived and asked for accommodation for his horse.

'Someone sick in the village, is there, sur?' he asked, as he pocketed his tip.

'Eh?'

The ostler raised his eyebrows in surprise. The young surgeon, a familiar figure, was looking very strange. Normally immaculate, he was unshaven, and his cuffs and cravat were soiled. He looked, in fact, a little wild.

'Someone sick, is there?' the ostler repeated.

'Oh . . . Oh, yes . . .'

The ostler waited with good-natured curiosity to be told who; but Kesteven had gone.

It was Kesteven who was sick – sick with a desperate passion. He walked down the village road south with unsteady steps. He had been drinking again today. His hands were shaking, and his mouth tasted bitter as it sometimes did when he experimented with mild doses of emetics to test their properties. He was sweating inside his cloak.

At the Walton turnpike, on the way here, he had almost turned back. A last whimper of dying reason had spoken within him and told him he was mad to go there now. It was after seven: he could not possibly just 'call' at Bromswold. Even supposing he did, he would not see her alone.

Even supposing he saw her alone he knew, deep down, what the answer would be . . .

His obsession had almost ceased to be with Rebecca Walsoken the living girl. It was cast in fragmented and symbolic terms. The long-lashed dark eyes, the soft curve of her cheek, the spring and curl of her hair with its rich depths of colour. Her quick supple movements and the warm inflections of her voice. He dwelt on such things till they were almost grotesquely magnified. He had ridden helter-skelter to Aysthorpe like a man possessed. If it were only to stare at Bromswold, to study the lights in its windows and think of her somewhere there, it might be enough to stop him going mad.

He skirted the house from the south, round the walled garden with its formal shrubs, clambering over the fences of the enclosed grounds: a stubbly hay-field, a deep meadow. The black scrubby outline of the heath marked the horizon beyond the fences. He came upon a few lopped trees and half-cleared brambles, and the ruined mill traced its squat shape against the choked purple of the sky. He could see the back of the house here: the sloping roofs of the outhouses, the kitchen garden and privy. A chimney smoking. The smell of beasts from the new stone byres. One light burning downstairs.

He skirted the house again. He loitered at the gates, and longing tightened across his chest.

The front door opened, and a maid appeared. A spaniel frisked out on to the drive, and the maid stood there, hands on hips, waiting for it to return.

Kesteven flattened himself against the gatepost. Looking to his left he saw a little boy coming down the road in his direction, swinging a reed switch, whistling to himself.

The boy started when Kesteven stepped out, peered mistrustfully at him in the thick dusk. Even now the young man absently registered the smallpox marks on the child's face and the rachitic thinness of his legs.

'D'you know the maid there, at the house?' he said.

The boy gaped, and said slowly, with some contempt, 'Yi-is, I know 'er. Nancy her name is. She talks funny.' The Norfolk accent sounded bizarre in these parts.

'Will you – will you give her a note for me? I'll give you sixpence. A shilling.'

The boy's eyes widened at these huge sums. 'Goo on,' he said.

'It's for Miss Rebecca,' said Kesteven, fumbling for his pocket-book. 'Now – can you tell the maid to try to – to make sure she gives it to Miss Rebecca alone. It's very important. Can you remember that?'

The boy's brow wrinkled in a mental search for motives, gave up the effort. He shrugged. 'Yi-is, course I can.'

Perspiring, Kesteven bent and scribbled with the pocket-book resting on his thigh. He tore the sheet off and folded it and handed it to the boy. 'There. Quick now.'

The boy looked at him with old, watchful eyes.

'Oh – yes, of course.' Kesteven fished a shilling from the fob of his breeches. The boy snatched it with a calloused hand.

For a moment Kesteven thought the boy would simply run off: but he walked up the carriage drive to where Nancy stood at the open door, handed her the note, said a few words. He saw the maid look at the folded note, shrug, and put it in the pocket of her apron; and then the spaniel came trotting back and she shooed it in and closed the door. The boy turned and walked back up the drive.

'I done it like you said, mister,' he said.

'Good. Thank you.'

The boy still lingered. Obviously anyone who would give a shilling for such a simple errand was stark mad, so there might be some more to come.

'Here.' Kesteven tremblingly gave him a handful of halfpennies and farthings, and at last the boy went on his way, glancing back now and then at the haggard figure leaning on the gatepost of Bromswold.

Rebecca was in the parlour, with her parents and her sister, suffering the perennial dreariness of evenings in her father's household. Reading was her only escape, and that was subject to the censorious eyes of her father: she had to hide the spines of novels lest he spot them and frowningly replace them with something like Bishop Warburton's *Legation of Moses*. Paul, now fourteen, had gone back early to Charterhouse this summer, and Jeremiah was staying at Mr Phillip Warren's for a couple of days: so she was back to her father's silence as he worked at an account book and the quiet prosings of Sarah and her mother.

I shouldn't feel bored and impatient like this really, she told herself. Think of poor Deborah, poor old Seth Upwell. What troubles have I compared with that tragedy?'

Oh, but I shall be twenty in November, and still I'm trapped and helpless as a child . . . I long for something to happen, for life to become large and vivid and exciting . . .

Twenty, did you say? More like fourteen to hear you talk. And the life of luxury you lead! Compare your family's life now with that of the Hardwicks of Morholm . . . My best friends. But father has blighted that, blighted the feeling between the two houses. The two families. Luke . . .

The full weight of her father's oppression seemed suddenly to be borne in on her. And she had been submitting to it.

She wanted more than anything else to be with Luke, to be in Luke's arms . . . And that, of all the dreams she could dream, was the most impossible of realisation. But wasn't she afraid, afraid of her own love, afraid of its power to disrupt and master her life just as her father's did? Why should she be afraid? She should run away with Luke. Throw everything to the four winds and just be with him.

She shifted in her seat, startled as if the words had been whispered in her ear. *Could* she do that? She was not of age. She had no power, no rights. Her father could do what he wished with her. Drag her back. Ah, but that was the fear again! If she really loved Luke then they must run fast and far enough. It was courage, the courage of love, that she had been lacking.

She saw now that what she had been pleased to call being practical these last few months was cowardice. She had presumed to set limits to love. In doing so she might have damaged it. Well, no more. They would be together. Tomorrow. She would get a message to him somehow.

Nancy, the maid, hovered about the front parlour door for several minutes, crumpling the note in her fingers. It was all very well to say give it to Miss Rebecca alone: but Mr Walsoken had had strict rules about that sort of thing for some time. Apparently she had been carrying on with some fellow or something. But it was a shame the way he treated the poor girl . . .

Nancy tucked the note in her apron and barged into the parlour.

'Ef ee please, sur, missus, thass such a to-do in that ketchen,' she blurted, very Norfolk in her agitation.

'What is the matter, Nancy?' Mr Walsoken said.

Nancy looked at Rebecca, her face shining. 'Well, Mrs Blythe say Muss Rebecca told her to – to save the chicken for baking tomorrow, and Jane say noo, she dedn't, and now they'm got in such an argument and I can't make 'em see reason, so . . .'

Rebecca stared at Nancy in surprise. Then something in the maid's anguished look galvanised her. 'Oh, dear,' she said getting up. 'It's all right, father, I'll go and sort it out.'

Out in the hall Nancy scrabbled in her apron. 'Boy brought this hair noot,' she said. 'Said it was to be give to you alone, Muss. Tedn't fair I should have to do this . . . I done me best, Muss.'

'You did wonderfully,' Rebecca said, seizing the note. It must be from Luke: she *knew* it. They had been thinking identically . . . wonderful . . .

She saw the handwriting, and her heart plunged.

Miss Rebecca

You will think me mad, perhaps I am, I must see you, I have come to Aysthorpe for that purpose. Meet me at the mill behind the house, I will be waiting. I beg you. I must see you. Just for a minute. Grant me this if nothing else. I beg you.

Christopher Kesteven

'Will you be wanting me, Muss?' said Nancy, watching her curiously.

'No, no, Nancy . . . thank you . . .'

The maid was gone, and Rebecca leaned her head against the newel-post of the stairs. Courage . . . This too was something she had tried not to face.

After a few minutes she opened the parlour door again.

'Father . . . mama . . . I think I shall go to bed.'

Mr Walsoken consulted his watch. 'It's very early, child.'

'Well, I have one or two letters to write first.'

'To whom?'

'Well – Mrs Amory. She invited me to go and see the hothouse flowers at Leam House.' She blessed her tongue, which seemed to have acted independently of her mind.

'They have such a delightful hothouse at Leam House, pa,' said Sarah. 'All manner of flowers and fruit out of season. Could we not have a hothouse here?'

'It is possible, certainly, child . . .' Mr Walsoken embarked on an architectural tirade, and Rebecca gave her second blessing – to Sarah for unwittingly making this diversion. She said good night and closed the door.

She carried a candle up to her room, set it on her night-table, stared at the note until it seemed imprinted on her memory.

Perhaps she was staring at it in the hope that it would disappear. But it was there, tangibly real, and it posed the problem that she could no longer evade.

She knelt and put her ear to the floorboards. She picked out the familiar voices of all the servants in the kitchen below.

She blew out the candle and started down the stairs.

Half a mile away in Aysthorpe, at the Rectory the Rev. Dr Emmonsales was in the study which Parson Medhurst had hardly ever used and was composing a sermon for this Sunday on the text: 'Woe unto them that join house to house, that lay field to field, till there be no place, that they may be placed alone in the midst of the earth,' and, when inspiration ran dry, making calculations in the margin about the forthcoming enclosure of the village, when he hoped to exchange his tithes for a grant of land in the parish. He had always rather fancied himself as a landowner.

And in the Rectory kitchen, the head maid Ellen-Maria Hurn of the gypsy looks and persuadable nature, was in a quandary.

She was in a position of trust at the Rectory. She had a little education and was firm with children, so Parson Emmonsales gave her much of the responsibility of looking after his two small daughters. But she was high-spirited and had a taste for life, and a taste for men, and the attentions of young Mr Jeremiah Walsoken, she had to admit, had quite turned her head – him with his lovely manners·and hands as soft as a lady's. It was only a bit of fun, and she felt she had managed to be quite discreet about it.

On the other hand she liked the company of her own kind for a laugh and a drink, and she was popular in the village in a way 'strangers' – meaning anyone who came from more than five miles away – seldom were. Billy Gowt had quite a taking for her, though she kept him at arm's length. She didn't want to begin anything serious, as he seemed to want, though he was sweet in his way.

And here lay her dilemma. She had happened to meet Billy Gowt at Royle's shop this afternoon. He had seemed rather fuddled with drink. He had attempted to give her a squeeze or two, but that was nothing out of the ordinary. Then, when she had mentioned Jeremiah Walsoken, he had said something. Something about their being 'trouble in that quarter tonight. Your precious Walsokens are heading for a fall . . .' She had taken little notice, disengaged his wandering hands, and returned home to her work.

Now, the more she thought about it, the more what she had heard began to make sense, and to dovetail with various other signs and hints she had picked up in the village the last couple of days.

If it was true . . . If it was true it was horrible, dreadful. The 'gentry', as she called them, had been good to her and she had a glowing respect for them. It was her duty to tell the master of her suspicions. He would know what to do: he was a churchman and a magistrate and utterly fearless.

But these were her associates, her friends . . .

But young Mr Jeremiah . . .

She had already been into the master's study once to trim the candles and draw the curtains: and had hovered about, watching the busy wagging of his quill, and drawing in great breaths ready to speak, and had finally turned and gone out again. Now she stood in the passage, biting her thumb, staring at the tall clock by the staircase.

She knocked and went in.

'What is it, Ellen-Maria?' The Rev. Dr Emmonsales did not look up from his papers. A candle was smoking. A decanter of canary stood on his desk.

'Sir, I – ' She swallowed. 'Shall I put Miss Anna and Miss Rachel to bed now, sir?'

Parson Emmonsales put down his pen and drew out his watch from his fob. 'No . . . No, leave them for half an hour. They'll sleep the better for it.'

He took up his pen and settled his wig, then glanced round at her. 'Is something amiss?'

Ellen-Maria dropped a curtsey. 'No – no, nothing, sir,' she said, and with thundering heart left the room again.

Rebecca, a shawl about her shoulders, made her way through the thick grass and shrubs towards the stump of the old mill. The servants were still in the kitchen and she had had to leave by the front door, closing it as softly as she could, and skirt round the house. The sun had gone down and left only a few rags of pink light tied to the branches of the trees. Here, in the part of the grounds which her father had yet to improve, there was a juicy rank smell of weeds and silvery moths fluttered. One settled on her hair and she brushed it off with a shudder.

The doorway of the mill framed a deep blackness. She stood on the threshold, wishing she could have contrived to bring a light. A sudden rustling movement: she started. The owl that nested in the mill roof flew overhead on pale wings, demanding 'Who – oo?' into the sky.

She stepped into the mill, and something moved.

'Miss Walsoken?'

Dr Kesteven's face was a white oval in the shaft of moonlight that penetrated the mill. He took a step towards her, then stopped. 'Thank you – thank you, Miss Walsoken. I feared – '

'It wasn't easy to come, Dr Kesteven,' she said. 'Any moment I may be missed. I know what you are going to say and I – '

'Twice I've tried to speak,' he said, as if he had not been listening to her. 'Twice I've been on the point of telling you – of asking you . . . You cannot deny me now!'

She was alarmed, and moved, by the fluting rise of his voice. In the dim light she could see his chest heaving and a glint from the whites of his eyes.

She shook her head, a biting anguish at her heart. 'Dr Kesteven – it cannot be. What can I say to – '

'You have not heard me out!' She saw his hand go up and agitatedly claw at his hair. 'Can you begin to understand how much I have longed . . . how throughout our association I have loved and wanted you so devotedly, so desperately? It has driven me to such a pass that I think of you every moment – impeding my work, my rest . . . I cannot sleep at nights. I am not a man of strong passions – *was* not, till now. Do you think I would ask you to meet me thus if I were not – if my feelings had not become intolerable for my very peace of mind?'

Rebecca put a hand to her mouth. 'Dr Kesteven, please don't do this . . . I am not blind, I have realised. I tried to tell you, to prevent you from – '

'Does it mean nothing to you, then? Do I mean nothing? For God's sake, I beg you!'

His voice rose to a shout. Somewhere a disturbed mouse scuttered.

'It means a great deal to me,' she said. A flat, horrible calm had come over her, the unnatural calm of someone going through a long-anticipated and long-dreaded ordeal. 'You are a good friend to me and – '

'*Friend* . . .'

'A good friend, and a man I respect and admire and will always be deeply grateful to. You nursed me through a bad illness, you do so much good work . . . I am saying this because it is the truth. Not because I expect it to be any comfort. Probably the reverse. But it is the truth. And I will always feel so. But as to loving you and becoming your wife – '

He made an incoherent sound. 'What must I do? What must I do to convince you of my devotion?' He moved nearer to her, and she caught the whiff of liquor on his breath.

'You need do nothing,' she said. 'I know, I believe you are in earnest. If that were all – '

'Isn't it enough?' He lifted his hands as if to seize her. 'Miss Rebecca, I am in *torment!*'

'I am sorry, I swear to God I am,' she cried, 'but it's not in my power to relieve you. I *am* flattered and deeply honoured, but at the same time this gives me no pleasure, to – to hurt you like this. But don't you see, I – I cannot pretend to feelings I don't have!' she half-sobbed out in desperation.

'I wonder about that,' he said.

'What do you mean?'

He did not answer, but half-turned away and stirred the straw on the floor with his boot. She heard his breathing coming quick and hurt and constricted.

'I'm sorry you should take it like this, Dr Kesteven,' she said. 'If there were any other way – '

'Haven't I a right to take it like this?' he said sharply. 'Yes! I would never have come to this condition if – if I had not been led to believe that I had a prospect – from the way you behaved towards me – led me on – '

A prickle of responsive anger ran up her spine. 'Dr Kesteven, wait a moment! When have I ever given you reason to believe – '

'Led by the nose,' he said in a fierce whisper, not attending to her, pacing up and down. 'You have led me on, and I have followed. And now you refuse me. A pretty trick.'

'I have not led you on, Dr Kesteven,' she said in a shaking voice. 'No, I have not.'

He turned and stared at her, as if he had forgotten she was there. 'Ever since the very first day I met you I have wanted – ' he said.

She found her arms suddenly seized and pinned to her sides by his hands. 'This *can't* be the end!' he cried, his voice rasping. 'Reconsider, reconsider, I beg you! Forget what I just said – I was mad. Think of me as a friend, as you say – friendship may ripen, may it not? There must be hope – just forget what I said . . .'

'Leave go of me,' she said, her head drooping, unable to look him in the face. 'Please leave go of me.'

His bony fingers tightened on her arms for a second: then relaxed and released her. 'I'm sorry,' he said. He gave a great shuddering groan and passed a hand across his face and then swept past her to the doorway.

306

'Goodbye,' he said, and then was gone. She watched his figure from the doorway, running, half-stumbling across the hayfield towards the village. Then her dammed tears burst through, and they seemed to go on for ever. She sat on the gritty floor of the mill and cried in great noisy gasps like a child, rocking herself in her arms.

At a quarter to ten Mr Walsoken, as was his habit, descended through the kitchen of Bromswold, receiving the curtseys of the maids and the housekeeper and telling them to be off to bed, then went out through the back door with a lantern and a bunch of keys to make a last tour of the outhouses.

He tried all the locks of the coach-house and the brewhouse and buttery, went on past the herb garden to the stone cattle-byres and the pigsty, across the yard to the hayricks that looked snowy white in the moonlight and the big red-roofed barn and the new linhay.

His progress was observed from two places. From the ruined mill, where she had cried herself into wretched exhaustion and crouched as if paralysed on the earth floor for an hour or so, Rebecca saw her father rounding the corner of the buttery. She moved to one side in the doorway. In her misery she had not thought of how to get back into the house. Soon it would all be locked . . . and if he were to see her here . . .

And from the south edge of the grounds, where a few ragged hawthorns marked the fence from the common, eight figures moved out of cover and started towards him.

Mr Walsoken rattled the locks on the barn. A splendid harvest from the Tallington farm he was supervising on the Norfolk principle. When his land in the parish was enclosed he would be able to experiment further. He heard a scurrying sound, and listened intently. Rats, no doubt. He ought to get in a couple of cats. Someone in the village was bound to have a litter of kittens.

He heard a sound behind him that was too heavy to be rats, and turned.

A ring of faces, lit by a storm lantern and a burning torch. John Newman's fair head.

'Mister Walsoken – we're come to tell you – ' John Newman said.

'What the devil is this?' said Mr Walsoken softly.

'*You're* the devil, you bastard!' roared Seth Upwell, who carried the torch. He lunged forward and swept it along the edge of the largest hayrick. Flames crackled and leapt up.

307

'What in God's name ...!' Mr Walsoken stepped forward, stopped.

'We're giving you fair warning!' came the shrill voice of Tess Phypers. 'Folk won't stand for what you're doing here no longer!' There was a ragged answering cheer, and the hayrick sent forth a great belch of blue smoke.

John Newman was staring with a kind of appalled wonder at the rising flames. 'Mister Walsoken ... we mean – all we meant to do – '

Mr Walsoken glanced around him, licked his lips. 'You'll answer for this, Newman,' he said, and then with surprising speed ducked aside and ran.

'Catch hold of him!' cried Reuben Phypers, and in the same moment Seth Upwell flung his torch on to the second hayrick and then dragging an iron hook from his belt attacked the lock on the barn door.

The flames from the ricks flung red shadows of confusion over the scene. A potent chemical combustion of fear and fury and exultation at their own daring filled the villagers as they ran and stumbled after the fleeing Walsoken. Stones flew and smashed the glass in the coach-house windows. Seth Upwell, having burst open the barn door, grabbed handfuls of flaming straw, scorching his big hands, and tossed them inside, and then ran at the brew-house door, battering at it, tears streaming down his cheeks.

But there was no exultation in John Newman. From the moment Mr Walsoken had turned round to see them, he knew he wanted no part in this.

He ran after the others, yelling breathlessly at them to stop, but he could not be heard over their shouts.

'Catch him!'

'Ye'll not tek away our common!'

'Give us our rights!'

'Murdering bastard!'

Mr Walsoken, panting, pulled himself round the corner of the linhay, but Ned and Billy Gowt had anticipated him and headed him off. He glared round, surrounded. He pressed a hand to his side. 'I'm warning you!' he said. 'You're putting your necks in a noose!'

'And we're warning you!' said Billy Gowt. 'Now you know – now you know the small folk won't be kept silent for ever! We got rights and we'll claim 'em if need be!' There was a long cheer, and some shuffling of feet, as if no one knew what to do next.

Suddenly Mr Walsoken made another dart away from them, and this time only Feast Holbeach, who until now had kept in the background, lunged after him.

With three strides of his long legs the giant fenman was upon him. John Newman lurched after him, screaming 'NO!' and dragging at the fenman's coat. But already Holbeach had swung his cudgel high in the air and brought it down in an arc on the back of Mr Walsoken's skull.

'There's the reckoning at last, Walsoken,' he hissed. He grinned and flung his cudgel away and disappeared into the shadows.

A horrified silence fell on the others, and they stood still and watched as John Newman bent to gently touch the motionless figure of Joshua Walsoken. Tess Phypers began to cry.

In the ruined mill, Rebecca's scream had died on her lips. She could not believe what she had just seen. She jerked her frozen limbs into motion and began to run across the scrub, stumbling, tearing her skirts, towards the outhouses where the ring of villagers stood.

She was not the first to get there, however. The Rev. Dr Emmonsales, on his fine chestnut hunter, had galloped across the fields from the Rectory with a pistol in his hand and his manservant armed with a muzzle-loader following on a nag behind. Ellen-Maria had at last plucked up courage to tell him what she thought was afoot, and he had set out for Bromswold immediately. Now he cleared the paddock fence with a fox-hunter's speed and came thundering across the cobbled yard and cried in a lusty voice that was used to making the Cathedral echo: 'Stay where you are, all of you! Stay where you are in the King's name!'

BOOK IV
December 1779

ONE

I

In the Stamford office of Mr Abraham Quy, attorney at law, a large wood fire was blazing to keep away the chills of early December, and John Newman was frowning at some sheets of paper covered with flowing script.

'But this,' he said at last, replacing the papers on the mahogany desk in front of him, 'it – it makes out I didn't do nothing – like I was completely innocent.'

'My dear Newman,' said Mr Quy silkily, 'that is entirely the point. You are to plead innocence at the assize, and stand up and defend yourself against the charges. Now, you cannot turn about and say, well, I was a little guilty perhaps after all.'

John ran his hands through his hair and sighed. He looked too big for this stuffy room with its fragile ornaments and miniatures and cameos on the panelled walls. 'Mebbe,' he said. 'But I did go there that night with malice and vengefulness in my heart. I can't deny that.'

'Fortunately the devices and desires of the heart, as scripture has it, are outside the jurisdiction of secular law,' said Mr Quy, taking a sip of the sweetened chocolate that he drank hourly every day. A short rosy dumpling of a man with a frizzed wig framing a pink cherubic face, he looked like a dwarf opposite John. 'Our purpose is to prepare a brief for the assize that will establish what really happened that night, and establish your innocence of the charges brought against you.'

'He's right, John,' said George Hardwick, who was seated in the corner as far away from the sweltering fire as he could get. 'There's a time for soul-searching, and this isn't it. If you can't think of yourself, think of Jenny and the babies. They'll not want a gallows-bird for a father. The fact is you had no part in the rioting and you didn't attack Walsoken. We believe you and we've got to make sure the jury do.' He got up and patted John on the shoulder. 'There are no developments regarding the others, I suppose, Quy?'

Lawyer Quy shook his head. 'A most ticklish business. We have little to hope from Upwell, of course. Having confessed immediately to his riotous behaviour, he has simply kept silence and appears to be waiting for the trial and, ahem, little caring as to what becomes of him.'

'Poor old Seth,' said John. 'It was Mark's death that did it. Sent him mad.'

Mr Quy caressed the Ghent lace on his chest. 'Yes, well, that would not be an adequate defence, even had he not pleaded guilty. As for the others – ' he peered at a note on his desk – 'Edward Gowt, farmer, William Gowt, farmer, Reuben Phypers, shepherd, Teresa Phypers, labourer – they are, I surmise, to turn King's evidence at the trial.'

'What does that mean?' said George. 'They were rounded up fair and square at Bromswold that night.'

'It means, not to put too fine a point on it, my dear Mr Hardwick, that they will lay the blame on our friend here,' said Mr Quy. 'In a case such as this the Crown is usually concerned with ringleaders. Make an example, don't you know. I hardly need remind you of Mr Walsoken's deposition after his recovery – that it was Newman who led the attack, Newman who committed the criminal damage, Newman who assaulted him with intent to murder – '

'Tis *lies*,' said John with sudden ferocity, slamming his fist on the desk so that Mr Quy's china paper-weights shook.

'Quite so,' said Mr Quy nervously. 'So we shall seek to prove. But you see, quite apart from the – er – settling of old scores, as I believe is the case with Mr Walsoken and our friend here, the preferment of these charges gives the law a – more digestible mouthful to chew, as it were, ha ha! And the others may quite understandably seek to save their own skins thereby. If they can claim to be only principals in the second degree, incited and led by Newman, they will come off much more lightly. Your friends formerly, I know, but different now. Human nature, alas. Original sin and so on. There is also the question of, dear me, how shall I put it: interested parties in the prosecution, who may perhaps apply a little pressure on the other defendants to that end – '

'Walsoken,' said George. 'God, how it all stinks.'

'You could not, I suppose, Newman, produce any actual evidence of – enmity between Mr Walsoken and yourself?' said Mr Quy.

John thought for a moment. 'Nay. Not really.'

'No. A pity. But if anything does come to mind . . . Of course your counsel will advise you when you see him in February.'

John slumped back in his chair. 'Oh, Lord, sometimes I wish I'd just give myself up. I'm – I'm all at sea here.'

'Come, my friend, not so bad as that, h'm?' said Mr Quy, tickling his own chin with the feather of his quill. 'Think of your family. Think of Mr Hardwick, who, ahem, has put himself to some trouble and expense to help you.'

John swallowed. There were dark circles under his eyes as he glanced at George. 'Aye. I shouldn't have said that. I'm sorry, Mr Hardwick.'

'Forget about it, John,' said George. 'Just try and concentrate on proving your innocence. I confess I could feel easier about the whole thing if we could trace this Holbeach fellow. John says he's the guilty one. How can a man just disappear?'

'Quite easily, I think, in those dreadful fen regions,' said Mr Quy. 'I am not hopeful in that quarter. Clearly such a rascally rogue had no intention of facing the consequences, and as soon as the deed was done made his escape. These folk have a history of lawlessness. But when you face your erstwhile companions in court, Newman, you may be able to press them on this question. Can they deny that this fenman was there? Of course much will depend on Upwell's testimony. I wish we could have got more out of him. But think hard, my friend. Remember you must speak for yourself at the assize. Your counsel may only speak on a point of law.' Mr Quy beamed suddenly, like a bewigged baby. 'But there, I am inclined to take a sanguine view. You will be tried before a jury – decent yeoman folk like yourself, in the main. You have a, ahem, taking and honest appearance, and it all goes towards making a good impression in the court. I confess I would feel easier if such a case had not come up at quite this time. What with America and now trouble in Ireland, folk are inclined to be severe with anything that smacks of, ahem, insurrection. But we shall see.' He dabbed his lips with a scarlet handkerchief and went on, avoiding John's eyes: 'There is one little matter further for today, Newman. Question of a will. Best to draw one up, you know. Just a precaution. You have a small freehold farm, I understand? Quite so. A formality, no more. A brief document leaving your property to your wife – Jenny, I think? Yes, dear me, such a pretty name. Oh, just a precaution.'

A flurry of sleet was coming down when George Hardwick and John Newman left Mr Quy's house and walked to the Blue Bell to meet Luke.

It was both the Hardwick cousins whom John had to thank for being able to defend his case. George had managed to raise bail for John, with the help of Mr Humphrey Amory who knew him well, but his purse could go no further. But Luke's offer to help when he had heard the story from George had been free and open-handed. There had been a closing of ranks over the events of the 20th of August. George and Mary believed John implicitly against the word of Mr Walsoken, and that was good enough for Luke. The burgeoning enmity between the two families had solidified around the coming trial: the Hardwicks and the Walsokens were two camps now, irrevocably.

Luke Hardwick had just been elected to a place on the Stamford corporation, and his invigorating presence was just what the despondent John needed. Luke, handsome and commanding in the flush of youth and success, was full of confidence about the trial. The strong Hardwick bones seemed to have come into prominence in his face of late, and there was a set look about his mouth. Among his employees at King's Lynn, where he now owned the coastal ship *Minerva*, he was gaining a reputation for being a hard driver.

The trial of the rioters of that August night was set for the county Assizes at Northampton in February. Normally, serious cases in the Soke were heard at the Peterborough Quarter Sessions, which had all the powers of assize, but a decision had been made – probably by Lord Burghley, George thought – to transfer the case to the county assizes. George felt the assize court was more likely to be impartial, and if it was Lord Burghley who was behind it he was grateful to him.

Ned and Billy Gowt, Reuben and Tess Phypers and Seth Upwell were in Northampton Gaol, waiting to face charges of riotous assembly. Gaffer Pode, with an ancient instinct for self-preservation, had slipped away that night before any damage was done. As for Feast Holbeach, he seemed to have vanished completely. The squalid cottage at Fisher Bind Hole was empty and abandoned, and enquiries could not trace him.

Mr Walsoken's head wound had been a terrible one, and for two days his life had been feared for. Dr Christopher Kesteven had been fetched to tend him that night: a servant from Bromswold had overtaken him riding only a mile or two down the Peterborough road at Werrington, where, he said, he had been on a call. John Newman and the others had been confined in Peterborough gaol for a week, whilst Mr Walsoken made his slow recovery, until he had been well enough to make his deposition before the Rev. Emmonsales and Sir Samuel Edgington, the examining magistrates. Unhesitatingly he had named John Newman as the leader and instigator of the riot and as his attacker.

The law had moved swiftly then. John was to be tried for riotous and unlawful assembly, incitement to riot, criminal damage and assault with intent to murder. The others were liable to lesser punishments. John Newman faced hanging.

The Hardwicks had believed John's innocence from the start – Mary especially was in deep distress for her old friend – but John seemed to be sunk in apathy, and needed a good deal of rallying as George went about the very difficult business of raising bail for him so that he could fight his case.

Walsoken was determined to have his pound of flesh, that was certain. George knew he ought to keep well out of the whole business, being so heavily indebted to him. But there was such a thing as loyalty.

So a great deal depended on the outcome of the trial. Not only John Newman's life. A noose of another kind hung over George Hardwick and Morholm. Walsoken had only to call in his debts – like pulling a trapdoor away. Ruin. Bankruptcy.

2

One vital witness was missing from the list who were subpoenaed to appear at the Northampton Assizes.

Rebecca had been saved from reflection on the events of that night by the necessity of nursing her father. Her mother and sister were too squeamish to be any help. He needed her: their quarrels were overshadowed by this. The thoughts and plans she had formed that evening had to be abandoned. Once he was recovered, however, the agony of mind and conscience began.

In the confusion of that night, as the Rev. Dr Emmonsales rounded up the villagers in the grounds of Bromswold and she rushed to kneel by her unconscious father's side, there had been no reason to suppose she had not come from the house, roused by the commotion, as Sarah and the servants had shortly afterwards.

No one need ever know otherwise. Her knowledge could lie locked in her heart for the rest of her life. Her knowledge that her father was maliciously lying.

Nothing of the attack could have been seen from the house itself; it had taken place behind the outhouses. At the mill she had been uniquely placed to see the whole thing: and she had seen it.

Hers was a simple choice, then. Keep silent, and perhaps send an innocent man to the gallows. Or speak out.

But no, it was not a simple choice. Could she stand up under oath in a court of law and testify against her own father? Testify to his being a liar and a perjuror? And what was more, testify that she had been a witness to the event because she had stolen out to keep a secret rendezvous with a man?

It would mean the end of all relationship with her father. She would no longer be his daughter. But there was worse than this . . . the effect of her testimony on someone else . . . Someone she had not seen since the terrible night. She could not even bring herself to answer the letters he had written, such was the frozen torture of her position.

On Christmas Eve she went alone into Aysthorpe church in the dim afternoon and sat in the empty pew and prayed. It was something she had not done for years; the God of her father had become a kind of symbol of his own intolerance. But she sat there in the freezing church, her breath steaming, and begged for an answer to her dilemma.

But none came.

3

The household of Julia and Henry Milton, whilst untouched by these events, was riven by a startling event of its own that Christmas of 1779.

Milton, in response to his London publisher Mr Carey's request for more poems to make a sequel volume to *The Open Field*, had collected together another sheaf of verse, some old and previously discarded, some newly written, and hastily sent them off. In December came a reply from Mr Carey. Milton read it at the breakfast table. He was silent for a long time, and Julia said: 'Henry, is it bad news?'

Milton looked up at her, gazed at her with a strange expression for several moments. 'You had better read it,' he said at last.

In the parcel of poems Milton had sent off there had been one that was not by him: it was by Julia. It had got accidentally among his papers, despite her usual vigilance in hiding her writing, and as she sometimes wrote out fair copies of his work he had taken no account of the handwriting.

Mr Carey enclosed it in his letter.

Some of your latest pieces, my dear Milton, are quite plainly dashed off, he wrote. *But this untitled piece has struck me most forcibly. This seems an entirely new Voice in your work, and indeed outshines all the rest. Is it very new? If you can produce more in this Strain, then I would be heartily glad to have them at the earliest Opportunity: the want of Force, a certain Insipidity that I have sometimes marked in your work is most definitely not the case here – quite the reverse. A volume of these would I am convinced quite excel your* Open Field, *which by the by is selling quite moderate well, though I do not anticipate a second Edition.*

And so it all came out.

Julia was reluctant at first to admit that the stray poem was hers; but at last, with a kind of unhappy resignation, she showed Henry the bundle of writing that she had done at odd times in the last couple of years, hidden away in her bureau.

'But why did you never tell me?' said Milton. 'God knows, it's nothing to be ashamed of. Carey is a harsh critic – I have never known him enthuse like this.'

'I just scribbled them to please myself, when I had time on my hands,' Julia said with a grimace. 'I never intended it seriously in the way you do. It was living in the atmosphere of writing, I suppose ... I had the urge to try. They can't compare with your work, Henry.'

Milton raised an eyebrow as he leafed through the crumpled and blotted sheets. 'I wouldn't be so sure of that,' he said. He looked at

319

his wife, who was staring moodily out of the window and seemed acutely uncomfortable about the whole thing. He had a renewed awareness of the elusive depths in Julia, the strange and vivid personality that lay beneath her awkward reserve. 'My love, you must make fair copies of these and we'll send them off immediately. Believe me, Carey is in earnest. God, I had no idea . . . and to think they might have lain buried in that bureau. To have these printed – '

'No, Henry.' Julia turned from the window, her face agitated, her hands restlessly smoothing down her apron. 'They're just – personal things, they're of no interest really. I don't want to see them printed. They're – they're not good enough, anyhow, I'm sure. Please forget about it.' She pushed back a lock of heavy hair. 'You should be meeting Francis this morning. I'll go tell Jack to saddle your horse.'

When she had gone Milton, shaking his head, picked up and read again the poem that Mr Carey had sent. There was no title, and the writing was jagged and violent.

> *Of Woman's Arts how oft the Poet's Pen*
> *In Venom dipp'd, hath scribbled to complain;*
> *With stinging Darts of Rhyme her Front to score,*
> *Her Subtlety denounce, her Wiles deplore.*
> *The sturdy Scold who sighing feigns to faint;*
> *The Hag who Age repairs with youthful Paint;*
> *The Whore whose mantling Blushes claim her chaste;*
> *The Lady proud in Jewels made of Paste.*
> *All these the Wits their Skills employ to damn,*
> *And shew in Verse, that Woman's made of Sham.*
>
> *Yet Stratagems she has, unsung by Wit:-*
> *Her needful Guile – of this no lines are writ:*
> *Of when, perforce, she honestly deceives –*
> *And must appear contented while she grieves.*
> *When gnawing Sorrow battens on her Heart,*
> *With genial looks she must maintain her Part:*
> *Though Chains they seem, her homely Cares attend,*
> *And while she pines, to pliant Cheer pretend:*
> *Her Smiles renew, her Husband's smiles to win:-*
> *Thus feigning Life, when all is Death within.*

4

Deborah Gedney had had no part in the attack at Bromswold, but she certainly had no sympathy to spare for Mr Walsoken. When the news spread through the village that his life was out of danger her response was only a shrug.

But Seth Upwell had been her old friend and her only remaining link with Mark, and she contrived to send him some small gifts in Northampton gaol, until in January the carrier brought her a piece of news. Seth Upwell, with his life reduced to bitter dregs, had in a burst of lucid calm decided to end it in Northampton gaol. After scribbling with a piece of chalk on the snuff-paper that Deborah had sent him last week the words 'God forgive me', he had hanged himself by his neckcloth from the grating at the high window of his cell.

 *TWO*

I

The Northampton winter assizes were due to formally open on Thursday the 17th of February, all being well. Delays were possible because of the torrential state of the roads up to Northamptonshire, which might impede the stately progress of the circuit judges, the retinue of barristers and junior counsels and clerks, and all the paraphernalia of the law setting out for their twice-yearly ministration of justice on the Midland circuit.

John Newman, in accordance with the condition of his bail, presented himself at the gaol on Monday. On the Tuesday he met his counsel for the first time: Mr Richard Pemberley KC, a plump cheerful youngish man who breezed through his brief over a flask of brandy and mordantly remarked that the gallows in Northampton were situated on the racecourse.

Northampton in 1780 was a town of six and a half thousand people, a good proportion of whom were shoemakers, and their cottage workshops were scattered all around the narrow medieval streets. The many inns did good business during assize week, with witnesses and litigants flooding in from the county. The Walsoken family, father and mother, Sarah, Jeremiah, and Rebecca, arrived on Wednesday in their own carriage and put up at the George Inn at the top of Bridge Street. The Hardwicks, George, Mary and Luke, arrived later that day, bringing Jenny Newman with them, and put up at the Saracen's Head.

Though John had wanted Jenny to stay away from the trial, she had insisted on coming: but she was in a trance-like state that suggested utter hopelessness as she sat that night in the dining-booth, eating nothing.

'Never fear for your husband, Mrs Newman,' Luke said to her. 'We'll be bringing him home on Saturday, I promise you.'

Jenny made an effort to smile. 'Well – don't think we're not grateful for your help, Mr Hardwick – both of you. We'll pay you back soon as ever we can – that's if – '

Luke waved a hand. 'Don't trouble about that. I'll go call on John's counsel tonight if he's free. Hope he's a keenly man.' He stabbed at his beef with sudden violence. 'Walsoken's lying through his teeth. I know it. I'd like to see him well and truly shown up in that court.'

Luke himself was taut with tension. Rebecca was in the town too, and that was reason enough. Their enforced separation had begun to taste bitter to him. Resentment and suspicion had begun to rise coppery in his throat. Kesteven was here too – he had seen him in the street earlier. Jealousy and frustration formed horrible shapes in his mind that he tried to dispel. *You must trust me*, she had said. Now she seemed somehow to be withdrawing from him. Had the prohibitions to their love come as a welcome relief to her? An excuse? No. It couldn't be . . .

2

There were five cases to be heard on Friday, of which *Rex v Newman* was the third, so the court convened early. The doors swarmed with barristers and clerks, gaolers, witnesses and spectators, and vendors of pies and lemonade: one man was enterprisingly hawking broadsheets purporting to be the Confessions of the hanged man, into which the name *John Newman* had been clumsily inserted. The Hardwicks and the Walsokens passed close to each other in the entrance, but they took seats on opposite sides of the court.

The Sessions House was an elegant one-storeyed pilastered building. The Assize Court inside was a lofty room with elaborately decorative plaster ceilings. Over the empty judge's seat there was a fat plaster infant, representing innocence. On one side of this symbols of virtue, rich fruits of the earth, led to an angel. Opposite was a tangled tableau of evil, with thorns and thistles, and dire symbols of punishment: manacles, whips, ending in the fiendishly grinning head of the devil.

Rebecca's eyes wandered over these fantastic rococo details as the court filled up. The devil's head in particular magnetised her. It was full of ingenious, high-spirited wickedness: it intimately knew death and mutilation and agony and dwelt on them with insensate glee.

Jeremiah whispered in her ear, startling her. 'Fellow told me there's a superstition about that devil's head up there. Apparently the tongue wags if someone tells a lie in court. It would save a lot of bother, wouldn't it?'

Rebecca glanced at him and then resumed her staring at the ceiling.

It was cold outside, but already a malodorous fug was settling over the crowded courtroom. At the front, the robes and wigs of the barristers: behind them, a sprinkling of rich ladies and gentlemen from the town who had come for the diversion. Crowded in at the back, noisy and ragged but here for the same reason, were the common folk. There was a renewed hubbub as the clerk rapped with a gavel and called the court to order and then a hush as the judge, the Hon. Hesketh Trewin of the King's Bench, came in.

There was a long pause while the jury were sworn in: tradesmen and yeomen and merchants, looking very ill at ease. Rebecca studied the judge: a man of forty-odd with a long austere face. The power of life and death . . . well, his appearance suited it. But she had it too, though no one knew it. This lovely and unhappy young woman, sitting here as a spectator, had that power, but she could not use it. For she feared it would mean, if not her own death, then the death of all her hopes.

. . . The case of the Crown versus John Newman came on at half-past eleven.

Rebecca, feeling suddenly faint, looked across at her father. His white uplifted face might have been made of marble.

John was brought into the dock. He was slightly hunched as if in pain and he had gone thin, but in his best serge coat with his blond hair tied back he looked solid and respectable, and he gazed out at the rows of faces without fear. Mr Pemberley took up his station just under the dock.

Mary put a hand on Jenny's arm and kept it there.

The clerk stood up.

'Jonathan Samuel Newman, hold up thy hand. Gentlemen of the jury, look upon the prisoner. Jonathan Samuel Newman, of the parish of Aysthorpe in the county of the Soke of Peterborough, you stand indicted upon the charge that you did, upon the night of the twentieth of August in the year of our Lord seventeen hundred and seventy nine, not having the fear of God before your eyes but moved and incited by the Devil, unlawfully assemble with diverse others to the disturbance of the public peace, that you did when so assembled incite and commit riot upon the property of Joshua Walsoken of Bromswold in the aforesaid parish: that you did commit arson upon and did unlawfully and with force begin to demolish diverse outhouses upon the said property: and furthermore that you did with malice aforethought assault with violence and intent to murder the said Joshua Walsoken . . .'

There was an impressed hush as the charges were read out. Jenny Newman was biting hard on her lip. Mr Walsoken contemplated his hands. Then John said 'Not guilty,' and the trial began.

The counsel for the prosecution, Mr Lamb, was an elderly man with a rich voice that seemed to have been soaked in port and learning. His orotund phrases and dramatic pauses made of the accusations against John something operatically dreadful.

The prisoner, he said, was a man of known levelling and seditious sympathies. Under the cloak of enthusiastic Methodism he had for long made known his subversive disrespect for due authority, in particular behaving with truculent insolence towards Mr Joshua Walsoken, an eminently respectable gentleman of property, a banker and landowner, who had come to buy an estate in Aysthorpe some two years ago.

'A move to enclose the said parish, led by Mr Walsoken, to ensure a more rational and efficient system of farming, irrationally incensed the prisoner, and claiming various other grievances cooked up in his own discontented fancy, he incited and led a party of hitherto peaceful citizens to this vicious attack on property and life on the twentieth of August. His accomplice, a fellow enthusiast name of Seth Upwell, admitted his part in these heinous crimes, and a short time ago took his own life in his prison cell whilst awaiting trial. While it would be horribly improper, gentlemen of the jury, for a court of law to condone the sin of suicide, Upwell's action does at least demonstrate the workings of a conscience, however distracted, a conscience oppressed by the knowledge of wrong-doing: a conscience which, the jury may plainly see, does not dwell in this man's breast.' Mr Lamb sighed with great melancholy. 'Setting forth from Upwell's farm under cover of darkness the prisoner led his fellows to the grounds of Bromswold, Mr Walsoken's seat, where he knew

Mr Walsoken was in the habit of examining his outhouses and barns each night. Mark well, gentlemen of the jury, the fact that his companions – poor labouring country folk – were in the habit of placing trust in the prisoner – however misguidedly – on account of his reputation for devotion, and his smattering of education – his ability to read and write: and education which, alas, has only encouraged him to regard with malicious envy the establishment of his betters. Thus he came upon Mr Walsoken, seeing to his business on his own property like any good husbandman: and with dire and foul-mouthed exhortations threatened him and incited his companions to commit riot. He set a torch to the ricks of hay that had just been gathered in, he attempted to demolish and burn down the grain-store, all the time urging his followers with terrible curses and oaths. THEN – ' Mr Lamb shouted the word, holding up one trembling finger – 'as Mr Walsoken, naturally fearful for his life – though he is a gentleman of courage, and had plainly demanded of the rioters what they wanted of him – as he sought to escape to the house, from this scene of barbaric horror with flames leaping to the sky and the mad cries of the prisoner urging greater outrages – as Mr Walsoken tried to flee, the prisoner, imbued with all the viciousness of fancied revenge and simple bloodlust, lifted a cudgel over the defenceless gentleman and struck him senseless to the ground.'

Mr Lamb, KC, drew a deep breath, and it was as if the whole court drew breath with him. John's face was expressionless, but his knuckles were white as he gripped the edge of the dock.

'It was then that the Rev. Dr Emmonsales, Rector of Aysthorpe-with-Ufford and a magistrate of the Soke, arrived at the scene, having ridden there with great dispatch after being informed as to what was afoot by one of his servants; and with great resourcefulness he apprehended the culprits, and it was he who as examining magistrate took the depositions of witnesses and accused.' Mr Lamb suddenly executed a stiff little pirouette, sweeping the court with his eyes. 'With your Lordship's permission, I call the Reverend Doctor Arthur Emmonsales.'

There was a low throaty muttering from all round the court. Mr Pemberley scribbled something and handed it up to John. Mary continued to hold Jenny Newman's arm, but it was as much for her own reassurance. The prosecution's account, with all its cunning half-truths and surmises, had stirred something deep in everyone, not least the anxious sober citizens of the jury. A horrible certainty stole over her that John, her friend from girlhood, was going to be hanged. With a tic of panic she glanced around. Luke beside her, grim-faced and lean as George could often look. George was in the ante-room, as a defence witness. Across the court, the auburn head of Rebecca Walsoken. She seemed to be absorbed in staring at the ornamented ceiling.

Parson Emmonsales, quite at home, delivered his testimony in a loud confident voice. At the back of the court a pie-seller had got in and was doing surreptitious business. Then Mr Joshua Walsoken was called.

He mounted the witness stand slowly, kissed the limp old Bible, and then folded his hands before him and regarded Mr Lamb. With his black suit and long wig and chalky face he might have been the judge himself.

Rebecca stared at the mirthful devil's head while her father gave his testimony.

'. . . And you see the man who led this attack in the dock before you?' Mr Lamb was saying, his voice pained and melodic.

Mr Walsoken's eyes flickered to John and away again. 'I do.'

'And this is the man who assaulted you, who left you bleeding on the ground and wounded in a manner that was likely to be mortal?'

There was a twitching at the corner of Mr Walsoken's right eye. 'It is.'

Mr Lamb sighed. 'I have no further questions, m'lord.'

Mr Pemberley nodded to John, and John cleared his throat. Mary gazed at the young farmer, still not quite able to believe he was there in the dock and defending his life.

'Mr Walsoken,' John said, 'd'you – d'you recollect who was there that night, aside from me?'

Mr Walsoken would not look at John. 'I do.'

'You recollect a man name of Feast Holbeach being there?'

Mr Walsoken glanced at Mr Lamb. 'I do.'

The judge was peering at his notes. 'I have no record of this person among the accused,' he said.

Mr Lamb bobbed up. 'One of the prisoners' followers, m'lord, who made his escape on the night in question. Enquiries have been unable to trace him.'

'Prisoner, you must justify this line of questioning,' said Mr Justice Trewin. 'We cannot try a man who is not here.'

'My lord,' said Mr Walsoken, 'as I have said, this man Holbeach was present. He is a fenlander of lawless habits, who once threatened me and my family, when I was undertaking a scheme of fen-drainage that he objected to. He was there, and it was no surprise to me that the prisoner should be an associate of his.'

John hesitated and cleared his throat. 'What part did Feast Holbeach play in what went on that night, Mr Walsoken?'

'He joined in the general rioting,' said Mr Walsoken crisply, 'but it was plainly *you* who led.'

'Who was it who set light to the ricks?' said John.

'You did.'

'What about Seth Upwell?'

Mr Walsoken licked his lips. 'He also.'

John looked at Mr Pemberley, who shrugged his shoulders and doodled on his notes.

'Mr Walsoken . . . did you see the man who attacked you?'

'I did,' Mr Walsoken snapped. 'It was you.'

'Was it light enough to see?'

'It was certainly light enough from the flames of my burning property!' barked Mr Walsoken.

John swallowed. Sweat was clammy on his brow. 'But you was struck down from behind, so how was it you could – '

'M'lord, I protest,' said Mr Lamb. 'This is surely a matter for the testimony of the physician who treated Mr Walsoken's injuries.'

'So it is, Mr Lamb,' said the judge. 'And that we shall hear. Have you any other questions to address to this witness, prisoner?'

Mr Pemberley, with his back to John, was shaking his head vigorously.

'No . . . no, my lord,' said John.

Mr Walsoken stepped down. Rebecca saw him do so only from the edge of her vision. Her eyes were fixed on the endless rococo traceries of that ceiling. They could not stop roving over its twists and curves and shadows: and in her mind, as in a dream on the edge of sleep, she seemed to be travelling some parallel route, through a network of passages that led only to locked doors, and she knew she must find a door that opened or it would be her that would be hanged . . .

Her heart gave a jolt, as if she had received a blow to the chest. She realised the name of Christopher Kesteven was being called.

The young physician was blinking as he took the stand, as if he had just come out of some impenetrable darkness.

Mr Lamb was on his feet. 'You are Christopher Kesteven, a practising physician resident in the city of Peterborough, and a licentiate of the University of Leyden?'

'I am.' Dr Kesteven appeared not to know what to do with his hands, and eventually put them behind his back.

'You recall being called in to attend Mr Joshua Walsoken, late on the night of the twentieth of August last year?'

'I do.'

'Be so good as to tell the jury what you found that night.'

'I was called in . . . a servant from Bromswold came . . .'

'You must speak up, sir,' said the Hon. Mr Justice Trewin. 'You speak too faintly.'

Dr Kesteven looked distractedly around the court, and went on: 'I was overtaken on the Peterborough road by the servant from Bromswold – I had – had – '

'You had been out on a sick visit,' said Mr Lamb.

'Let the witness speak for himself, Mr Lamb,' said the judge.

'I – was told that Mr Walsoken had been injured, and rode with the servant at once to Bromswold. I found Mr Walsoken in the front parlour where he had been carried by the servants. He was semiconscious and in great pain. He had suffered a small fracture of the skull, with laceration of the skin and loss of blood. I administered two grains of opium and bound up the head. I considered the possibility of a trepanning operation but decided against it, surmising that there was no pressure from splintering on the brain, and that my best hope of success was to let nature take its course. There was also some light grazing of the hands, face and knees, consonant with a fall.'

Mr Lamb nodded. 'And this injury, Dr Kesteven – it was, clearly, the result of a savage blow?'

'Most definitely a blow, with a heavy blunt instrument.'

'A blow, in fact,' said Mr Lamb, with a sweeping gesture towards the dock, 'that could well have been administered by a strong young fellow such as the prisoner?'

Mr Pemberley was on his feet to protest, but Dr Kesteven was already speaking. 'It was a blow with a heavy instrument, as I have remarked,' he said. 'As such it could equally have been administered with similar result by yourself, sir, or indeed by anyone in this courtroom.'

Mr Lamb did not appear to like this answer. He settled his wig pettishly and sat down.

Mr Pemberley was motioning frantically to John. John nodded and leaned forward and said: 'Where was this injury, sir? On the head, I mean to say.'

'The fracture was a transverse one at the base of the occiput,' said Dr Kesteven.

John looked blank, and Mr Justice Trewin stirred and said: 'Perhaps you will translate that into laymen's language for the jury's benefit, Dr Kesteven.'

'The injury was to the back of the head, here,' said Dr Kesteven, putting his hand up to his own head.

'So – so this was like to be a blow from behind?' said John, with some excitement.

'Oh, without question. The grazing of the face and knees, from the resulting fall, would corroborate that.'

'So Mr Walsoken wouldn't have seen who did it?' cried John.

'M'lud!' protested Mr Lamb, but the judge shook his head. 'Let the witness speak.'

'I think it unlikely,' said Dr Kesteven. 'Even leaving aside the position of the wound, a direct frontal assault usually means some bruising to the forearms as the victim instinctively tries to defend himself.'

Mr Lamb sprang up like a jack-in-the-box. 'Dr Kesteven, you are a country practitioner, is that not so? You have never, I think, served as a surgeon to the armed forces, which might authorise you to speak so confidently as to this matter?'

Dr Kesteven regarded him. 'I have not practised with the armed forces,' he said. 'But I studied for a year at St Bartholomew's Hospital in London under Dr Percivall Pott, the foremost authority on fractures and dislocations, if that answers your question.'

Mr Lamb pouted and whisked back his gown and sat down again.

3

The evidence of Dr Kesteven seemed, Mary thought, to have introduced a hopeful doubt into the case that Mr Lamb had been presenting as clear-cut. Beside her Jenny was sitting up straighter, her eyes fixed on John. But the next witness was Ellen-Maria Hurn, and she was so overawed by the occasion no one could get much out of her: and then it was the turn of Ned Gowt.

He stooped in the witness box, as if expecting a blow: he was haggard and wore an old coat that looked to have been simply clapped on his shoulders as he came to the courtroom. He gave his evidence in a low monotone.

'. . . you have, of course, admitted to your riotous behaviour that night. You were under the influence of drink?' said Mr Lamb, with exquisite distaste.

Ned nodded. 'Took a drop too much.'

'And the prisoner?'

'Nay. He don't hardly touch it.'

'So he was in full possession of his faculties?'

'Please?'

'Newman was quite sober, clear in his mind?'

'Oh, yes, sur.'

'When the prisoner prevailed on you to go with him to Bromswold, what did he say were his intentions in going there?'

Ned moistened his lips, and fixed his gaze on the opposite wall of the court.

'He said he were going to burn down Walsoken's barns and ricks and – and give Walsoken something to remember him by.'

The judge tapped with his gavel to quieten the court.

'You are quite sure of this?' said Mr Lamb.

'Yes, sur.'

'Why was the prisoner going to do this?'

'Well – he'd never got along wi' Wal – Mr Walsoken. Then there was this enclosin'. He was agin it. He said he wanted to teach him a lesson.'

Mr Lamb made an open-handed gesture and sat down. John, from the dock, regarded Ned more with sadness than anything. 'Ned,' he said, 'what about Feast Holbeach?'

Ned wiped his hand across his mouth. 'Don't know what you mean.'

'Weren't it him as was behind it all? Really, Ned?'

Ned Gowt glanced all about him, as if looking for a means of escape. In a despairing voice he cried, pointing at John, ''Twas John Newman as fetched him from the fen! Him and Seth Upwell went to fetch him for their mischief!'

Mr Lamb bobbed up. 'So this was a premeditated and artfully

devised plan on the part of the prisoner, for which he took the trouble of recruiting his unsavoury cronies! Mark that, gentlemen of the jury!'

Mr Lamb sat down in triumph. Mr Pemberley shrugged at John and leafed through his papers, as if thinking of his next case.

Reuben Phypers next. The same story, almost word for word. Then Tess Phypers. The same. Mary began to feel sick.

Billy Gowt, the younger of the brothers, was last. Sweat was glistening on his face and his lips moved as if in prayer.

While he told his story Mr Pemberley scribbled something and handed it up to John.

'Billy,' John said amiably, 'what light was there to see by that night? On the way, I mean.'

'Bit o' moon,' Billy said faintly.

'Was that all?'

Billy's eyes flickered to Mr Lamb. 'A torch, I reckon.'

'Who was carrying it?'

'Seth – Seth Upwell.'

'So it was Seth who did the burning?'

Billy swallowed. 'Yis – no, I reckon you – you had a torch as well.'

'Two torches or one? Mek up your mind,' said John, a hardness coming into his voice for the first time. It was as if he had suddenly realised his life was at stake. He thought of Pemberley's instructions: *You must press . . . They're bound to slip . . . Shake them . . . The Crown's out for a conviction, dear fellow . . .*

'Two, I think – I – I don't recollect . . .'

'What else don't you recollect? Don't you recollect me yelling at Seth to stop? When Seth torched them ricks? Do you recollect that, or not? Didn't I yell at him to stop it?'

'Nay,' said Billy, his chest heaving, 'nay, I don't . . .'

'So it was Seth who was setting 'em alight? That's so, then, is it? You recollect that, then?'

'Yis . . . no, I dunno – '

'You reckoned to know a lot just a minute ago,' said John. 'What else don't you know? What about that fenman, Feast Holbeach? You recollect him, don't you?'

'Yis, I – '

'So you recollect him being there. What was he about? Burning, smashing glass, was he?'

'Yis, I reckon . . .'

'What was I doing, then? Don't you recollect me trying to stop him? And what about when Seth bashed in the barn door? Didn't I try to stop him?'

'No,' cried Billy weakly, 'you never did no such thing . . . you – you egged him on – '

'Did I? What about when Feast Holbeach went after Mr Walsoken with his cudgel and struck him down, didn't I go after him and pull him back?'

'No, you never did,' Billy half-sobbed, 'you never did . . .'

'So it were Holbeach who struck him down! Thass what you're saying!' cried John, his voice almost drowned in the great hubbub that went up from the court. Someone cheered at the back.

'M'lord!' Mr Lamb was on his feet and shouting. 'M'lord, I protest – this witness is – his testimony is surely not – he is plainly of limited intelligence and is not to be relied upon . . .'

'In that case, Mr Lamb, you should not have called him,' said Mr Justice Trewin with some asperity. 'Do you have any further questions, prisoner?'

John did not. Billy Gowt, trembling and tearful, was taken away. The noise was a long time dying. Jenny Newman gripped Mary's hand fiercely. 'That's something, isn't it, Mrs Hardwick? That's something?'

'It is, Jenny, certainly,' said Mary, trying to smile. Something. A little in a heavily weighted balance. She knew it would not be enough.

At last there was a hush, as Mr Pemberley called the first defence witness. George entered the witness box and was sworn in.

'A pretty defence,' Jeremiah whispered in Rebecca's ear. 'The only witness a near-bankrupt!'

Rebecca was not listening. She was remembering with garish clarity a summer day in Norwich when she was seven or eight. She had been playing in the summerhouse and had caught a butterfly there under a glass tumbler. She had been able to see its vivid colours so well as it fluttered in the glass. She had meant to release it again in a moment, but just then she had been called in to dinner. It was several hours later that she had remembered the butterfly, with a horrible jolt, and run back to the summerhouse. It was lying dead in the glass. Beautiful as ever but dead. And an unbearable realisation had flooded in on her then, a pain new and undreamt of, that she and only she was responsible.

Mr Lamb was addressing George.

'Where were you at the time of the incident, Mr Hardwick?'

'At home. That is Morholm, your lordship, which is at the other end of Aysthorpe, a distance of a mile or so.'

'A mile,' said Mr Lamb. 'So you were not in a position to know anything of these events.'

'No,' said George. 'But – I was aware of bad feeling in the village at that time. Not only over the projected enclosure, but due to the death of Mark Upwell, Seth Upwell's only son. He had just died of fever in Peterborough gaol, my lord, whither he had been committed for twenty months for the taking of a single piece of game from Mr Walsoken's land. I too felt that the boy had been much too severely dealt with.'

'Thank you, Mr Hardwick,' said Mr Lamb pompously, 'but I hardly think it within your authority to question the actions of the law.'

'As to that, sir,' said George mildly, 'I was a justice of the peace when young Upwell was committed.'

Mr Lamb had not expected that answer. He sniffed and said: 'You – er – you say you *were* a magistrate, Mr Hardwick? So you were relieved of your commission, I take it.'

'You take it wrong,' said George, staring him down. 'I resigned my commission in protest at this sentence. You may step to Burghley House and consult the Earl of Exeter if you doubt that.'

Mr Lamb coughed.

'As I was saying, there was much bad feeling, and Seth Upwell was, I believe, half-crazed with grief. I am convinced that, in this state, he was a prime mover in these events.'

'Mr Hardwick,' said the judge, 'do you then condone this crime?'

'I do not, my lord, but neither do I believe that John Newman was guilty, indeed I am convinced of his innocence. I have known him well all his life, and I knew his father. He was formerly a tenant of mine and I can vouch for his unblemished good character. I firmly believe that in any such disturbance as took place in August, John's only role, as he has testified, would be that of a peacemaker. His reputation in the district is as high amongst all classes as any man I know.'

'You say this, Mr Hardwick,' said Mr Justice Trewin, 'so why do

334

you suppose Mr Walsoken should make this very firm accusation against him?'

George took a deep breath, trying to be calm. 'I believe in the confusion Mr Walsoken was mistaken. I – must add that Mr Walsoken has never hidden his dislike for John. He has an antipathy that dates, I think, from John's attempts to set up a meeting-house in the parish.'

Mr Lamb frowned. 'You are a Methodist, Mr Hardwick?'

'I am not.'

'But you sympathise with the movement.'

'Not especially. I have a suspicion of most kinds of religious enthusiasm, whether it be Methodism, or the spectacle of church divines meting out savage justice from a secular Bench.' Be careful, George told himself. He clenched his fist and tried to concentrate and ignore a movement that was going on half-way down the court.

'So you opposed the building of this meeting-house?'

'No. I – helped them to a few building materials. Let me say,' George went on hurriedly, 'the Methodists in our district are very few, a small group who – who live their own lives quite peaceably . . .'

Mr Lamb was not listening. He had turned to the jury with a flourish. 'Dear me,' he said, 'gentlemen of the jury, this witness seems to wish to express his covert support of Methodism against the established Church, his sympathy with discontent, and has admitted to abdicating his social responsibility in the belief that the law is too hard on those who violate the law of property.' He smiled. 'No further questions.'

George was cursing himself as he stepped down. The wrong tone entirely. Didn't help John one bit. No use acting the arrogant squire here, you fool. You don't have the power for that now, anyway.

He looked across to where Mary was sitting. Luke was not with her.

The movement he had seen in the court was Rebecca hurriedly leaving. Luke had seen it too, and had followed her.

He found her at the outer doors, leaning on the wall and gagging as if she were going to be sick.

'Rebecca!' he said. 'What's wrong? Are you ill? What – '

She turned to him a white face, blurred with dragging tangles of hair. 'Yes – yes, I'm sick,' she said, and beat her fist against the wall. 'Sick . . .'

335

'Rebecca . . .' He put his arms about her.

'You'd better not do this, Luke . . . not until . . .' She could not go on, and clung fiercely to him and sobbed.

'What is it?' he said, holding her. 'Tell me.'

'I'm sick because – because I know the truth – the truth of what happened.'

He looked at her blankly. 'You haven't been called. Are you a witness?'

'I haven't been *called* because no one *knows*! No one knows but *me* and – I can't bear it . . .'

'Rebecca.' Luke regarded her soberly. 'You've got to tell them. You must. You've got to say what you know.' He stroked her hair. 'Be brave.'

She looked him in the face for the first time. She studied him as if she were seeing him for the last time. 'Shall I? Shall I, Luke?'

'You've got to.'

'All right.' She wiped her face. 'But if I do – oh, Luke, tell me you love me before I go . . . please . . . I need to hear it.'

'You know I do,' he said. 'Always. Now hurry, before it's too late.'

'Too late . . . yes . . .'

He did not understand the last troubled look she gave him as she turned back to the court.

'My lord,' said Mr Pemberley, 'I have another witness to call for the defence, if it please you.'

'I have no record of any other witness,' said the judge.

'I am aware this is most irregular,' said Mr Pemberley, 'but I assure your lordship that this evidence has just come to light and is of the most vital importance. With your lordship's permission . . . call Miss Rebecca Walsoken.'

The three steps up to the witness box could not have seemed greater to Rebecca if they had led to the gallows. As she kissed the Bible she was aware of uproar below her. Judge, prosecution, and spectators seemed alike at a loss.

'My lord,' said Mr Pemberley, shouting to make himself heard, 'this witness, the youngest daughter of Mr Joshua Walsoken of Bromswold, has just made known to the defence her wish to testify. The reasons for her delay, will, I think, become clear.'

Mr Justice Trewin was staring at her – everyone was staring at her. 'Madam,' the judge said, 'do I take it that you wish to testify against your own father?'

'Yes, my lord,' Rebecca said, and was surprised at her own voice. 'I – I was a direct witness to the events of the twentieth of August.'

The frenzied rapping of the judge's gavel was only a feeble accompaniment to the roaring of the court. The uplifted face of her father, a few rows down, swam into her vision like a gibbous moon.

'Any more disturbance and I shall have the court cleared,' said Mr Justice Trewin. 'Miss Walsoken, the depositions taken by the examining magistrates state that the family were inside the house when the attack took place. Remember, now, you are on oath.'

'I realise that, my lord,' Rebecca said. 'That is why I must speak. There – there is a ruined building, formerly a mill, at the back of the grounds at Bromswold. I was there that night, and it was from there that I saw what happened.'

The judge frowned at her. 'A *ruined* building?'

'Yes, my lord. Perhaps a hundred yards from the outhouses.'

'What reason could you have for being there?'

Rebecca's mouth had gone dry. 'Do I – must I – '

'You are on oath, Miss Walsoken.'

She was aware of the devil's head, cackling at her above the judge.

'I was there because I – I had kept a rendezvous with someone.'

A muttering below. She kept her eyes on the devil.

'A secret rendezvous, do you mean?' said the judge.

'Yes, my lord.'

Mr Lamb was on his feet. 'My lord, this seems to me a very dubious witness – '

'A moment, Mr Lamb.' Mr Justice Trewin leaned forward. He looked dry and powerful and pitiless. 'Miss Walsoken, you are under oath to tell the *whole* truth.'

Rebecca said, loudly, desperately, 'I had kept a rendezvous with Dr Christopher Kesteven, at his request. The gentleman is here and will, I am sure, confirm it. He had gone away, some time since, and I was still there when the rioters appeared, and I saw . . .'

The rest of her sentence was drowned out. Her father had jumped to his feet and was shouting. Mr Lamb was protesting. Mr Pemberley had half-climbed into the dock in his eagerness to speak to John.

At last the judge had the court's attention. 'Continue, Miss Walsoken.'

'I saw what happened – it was not John Newman who led them – he was there but he had no part in it – and it was the fenman named Feast Holbeach who attacked my father. I saw it very clearly. As my father made a run Holbeach went after him and struck him down. The prisoner shouted something and seized Holbeach by the tails of his coat. Holbeach had a cudgel. I had seen Holbeach before, the time he came to Bromswold to threaten my father; he is instantly recognisable. I ran out from the mill then and ran to my father . . . I swear to God this is the truth . . .'

All this came in a rush, like a glad painful vomiting of a life-threatening poison. For the moment there was only relief.

But her father was standing up and yelling as if the iron clasps of years of self-control had snapped and flown back. Mrs Walsoken and Sarah were trying to pull him into his seat but all eyes were on him as his shouts echoed round the court: 'You *whore*! You filthy slut! God *damn* you, you *whore*! . . .'

4

Eventually, when order was restored, Dr Kesteven was recalled to corroborate Rebecca's story. There were whistles and ribald shouts. The spectators, enjoying an extra whiff of scandal, were glad they had turned up today.

Mr Walter Lamb, KC, knew when the back of a case had been broken. He managed to quell Mr Walsoken's outburst and after a whispered consultation amongst the prosecution made a statement to the judge.

'Your lordship – most unfortunate – my witness, as your lordship may discern, is still I fear perhaps feeling the effects of the injury he sustained . . . Reflection on the part of my witness has – has, in short, convinced him that a mistake may have been made – ' he raised his voice above the swelling noise – 'a mistake quite natural, I am sure your lordship will agree, in the light of the confusion of the incident, the – ah – fitful light and the nature of the witness's injury – in short, the certainty with which he expressed himself as to the prisoner's culpability is perhaps – I am sure your lordship will understand . . .'

As the prosecution collapsed Mr Pemberley whispered urgently to John to forget about the long defence statement he had prepared.

'Just a few words, throwing yourself on the mercy and candour of your countrymen, nothing else needed. Nothing else, dear fellow.'

The few words took a few minutes. So did the laconic summing-up of the judge. The jury retired to the ante-room for an even shorter time.

Their foreman looked flushed and self-conscious, like an amateur actor, as he faced the clerk of arraigns.

'Jonathan Samuel Newman, hold up thy hand. Gentlemen of the jury, look upon the prisoner. How say you? Is he guilty of the indictments wherewith he stands charged or not guilty?'

'Not guilty.'

'You say he is not guilty and so say you all.'

Jenny Newman was crying. Mary gripped her hand and tried not to cry herself. She turned to Luke, and he mustered a smile. But Luke looked as if it were he who had been beaten and left for dead.

There was a great surge for the doors at the back of the court as the case was closed. Rebecca, moving like a sleepwalker, was propelled towards her family. She saw her father's face hysterically contorted. He was lunging towards her, his hands out like claws. Her mother was hanging on to him, trying to hold him back, weeping piteously.

Jeremiah had struggled to her side. 'Keep away, Becky,' he hissed. 'Get away. He'll kill you. I've never seen him like this.'

At last she burst like a cork into the open air, the grey chill noonday with the streets of Northampton full of unconcerned folk going about their business. She elbowed her way through the crowd, at last flattened herself against the wall under the portico of All Saints. She hung her head and let the tears fall.

She looked up through blurred eyes to see Luke standing a few yards away.

'Oh, Luke . . .' She longed to run to him, to shelter in his arms: in him was her only hope. Then she saw the expression on his face, and knew all her worst fears were real. It was as if the sun had fallen from the sky.

'Well,' he said, 'it was fortunate that you decided to tell the truth. Fortunate in all ways. Cleared a lot of things up.'

She took a step towards him, but he did not move. His hands hung limply by his sides. 'Luke, won't you listen to me, please,' she said.

'Oh, no, my lady,' he said. 'Seems to me I've done too much

listening to you. I think that's been my trouble. "Trust me." "He means nothing to me." "Trust me." God, how they trip off your tongue. We'll find ways, you said. Well, you certainly do. You've found ways to string two men along. At least. Or are there more? Very resourceful. Tell me, did you say the same things to Kesteven?' His chest laboured. His breath coming in great hurt gasps.

'What can I *say* to you? If you hadn't been always so damned jealous – '

'Oh! Getting things the wrong way about, aren't we? Turns out I had cause to be jealous. Turns out I was right. Well, I wish I could say I'm glad to be proved right, Rebecca.' His voice trembled. 'I wish I could say I'm glad. To be betrayed. To be lied to.'

'I've never lied to you, Luke,' she cried. 'Can't I make you believe that?'

'Ah, don't, Rebecca, don't.' He passed a hand across his face; he looked ashen, exhausted. 'Kesteven looked sick today. Had your little fun with him now? Thrown him over too, have you?'

'I haven't thrown you over!'

'No, my dear.' Luke grimaced, and said with a festering of monstrous bitterness: 'You must at least allow me that privilege.'

He saluted her and walked away.

She called his name, but he carried on, and was soon lost to view.

Choking, Rebecca turned and went at a run down Bridge Street, her skirts dragging in the mud.

Upstairs in the George Inn, to the room she shared with Sarah. Open her valise on the bed, throw in the clothes she had brought with her, shoes, money, pile them in anyhow. From time to time she had to hold in a great wrenching sob. Scribble a note to Sarah. Wipe her face. Everything was broken, ruined, hellish. Downstairs again.

'London coach, miss?' The ostler stroked his jaw. 'Naw, they've all gone by now. Talbot up the street you want – there's one goes about now. You'll have to go on top, miss,' he called after, 'that'll all be booked inside.'

She did not care. She would have been dragged on a hurdle as long as it meant she was getting away.

A few minutes later the Flyer rattled over the Nene bridge and headed south on the long journey to the White Bear in Piccadilly. Passengers in hoods and bonnets clung to the top, amongst them Rebecca Walsoken, just turned twenty and uprooted and alone.

THREE

'Well, you look much better than when you first arrived,' said Peter Walsoken with a smile, studying her beneath the coloured lanterns that hung from the trees. 'When you turned up at my door that night with your sad eyes like saucers I thought for a moment you were some abandoned waif. I imagine my landlady suspected I had come to bad habits at last.'

'I *feel* better,' said Rebecca, linking her twin brother's arm as they walked on. 'Like a completely new person . . . But why should your landlady expect bad habits?'

'Well, studying at law is reason enough. Most of the barristers and benchers drink to excess, and many keep mistresses. It seems to be the expected thing. Though it's also expected, if a man is elevated to be a judge, that he should marry the lady.'

'Very moral.'

It was a warm May evening, and they were walking in Vauxhall Gardens, which had just opened for the season. London's most popular place of entertainment, the gardens stretched over twelve acres in Lambeth. Entrance was a shilling, and this was one of the rare places where people of all classes mixed. Along its lamplit avenues of trees and its mock-Grecian arches and alcoves strolled tradesmen and their wives, young bucks in swords, beribboned aristocrats, and prostitutes; the young Prince of Wales was here tonight with his mistress, the scandalous Mary 'Perdita' Robinson, an actress at Drury Lane theatre. There was a singular atmosphere, of elegance and rowdiness mixed.

The orchestra in the Rotunda was just beginning to play, so they decided to stay and listen, and Peter went off to the refreshment-booths to get them some chocolate.

Rebecca, on looking about her for a chair, suddenly found a young gentleman, dripping with lace and powder, bowing and scraping before her. 'Madam, you seek a chair – you must let me find you one – indeed you must – I will not suffer you to trouble a moment longer – '

'Sir, I know how to get a chair for myself!' she said, almost bursting out laughing.

'I have offended – I am a boorish wretch – God strike me, I have offended.'

'Indeed you haven't, sir,' she said, smothering her smiles, 'but your bowing makes me giddy, and I know a chair when I see it.'

The gentleman's look changed, became a smirk. 'Rot me, but you're a country girl,' he said.

'Rot me, so I am,' said Rebecca. 'But you needn't fear, sir, I've left my cow and my milking-stool at the gates.'

She found a double seat beneath a tree at last – not before another beau had attempted to rescue her – and listened with pleasure to the starry lilt of the orchestra: not the usual Italianate stuff but a piece by the Austrian Mozart who was coming into vogue. Dear life, who do these men think they are, she thought. Peter, with his plain dress and gentle speech, cut twice the figure.

At the same time she admired the elegance of many of the company, the attractive new fashions: the men in bicorne hats with cockades, and high stand-up collars, the women in high-waisted *décolletée* gowns and jet chokers and huge tilted hats covered with plumes and ribbons: the tall stiff coiffures seemed to be going out and being replaced by a more natural flowing style with ringlets on the shoulders. (Surreptitiously last night she had been attempting to coax her own hair into this style with curl-papers.) A continual source of confusion to her in London, however, was the thin dividing line that seemed to exist between the highest ladies of quality and the prostitutes – one, it appeared, was trying to look like the other, but she could not tell which. She had often to admit that there must be more of her father in her than she had hoped.

Shocking, too, was the number of ragged creatures, barely recognisable as human, curling up to sleep on the Bulks, the stalls which projected on to the path from the shop-fronts. And there were worse sights to be seen in the anthill slums around Spitalfields, where Irish labourers lived in conditions genuinely worse than pigsties. Things like this took more getting used to than the conspicuous lechery.

London, while grander, was much dirtier than the compact, prosperous cities and towns of East Anglia that she had known. When she had arrived on the Northampton coach the shawl of coal smoke that covered the whole city apart from the dome of St Paul's had made her think there must be another Great Fire burning. When the wind was right the smell from the Fleet Ditch could make one gag in the streets: and from south of the river came an even more potent mixture of smells, emanating from the soap and gunpowder factories and the tanning-yards.

In fact it was only just recently that she had begun to venture out and look about her. At first Peter's lodgings in Portugal Street behind Lincoln's Inn had been a hiding-place for her, a bolt-hole to which she had fled from Northampton, feeling that her life was over. The details of what had happened came out only gradually, and Peter was too kind and patient to press her. He had let her simply stay in his rooms, looking after him and making him dinners as if under a kind of rule of penitence, and waited for her to open her heart.

Then he had been reassuring. 'Oh, at the moment, I am sure, father is livid and ready to beat the life out of you: but he'll come round. He's too fond of you, though it might not seem it. You probably did the best thing coming here to me. I'll write to him.'

Her own first letter to Bromswold had elicited only a curt reply ordering her to come home: but last week her mother had sent on some of her clothes, which Rebecca thought she could not have done without her father's consent. So she began to enjoy being in London, and being with Peter; overcoming, finally, the lurking guilt that said she should not be here simply enjoying herself after all that had happened.

Now Peter came back from the refreshment-booth bringing chocolate, and after they had sat listening to the music a while he said: 'Well, I shall tell you now. I had a letter from father today. Now, don't look so alarmed, sister.'

'What does he say? Don't be teasey, Peter, please!'

'He is not about to swoop down to London and drag you back to Aysthorpe by the hair, I'm sure of that. He has, moreover, arranged for a second allowance to be paid into my account at Coutt's, for your use. But as for forgiving you – I'm afraid he's as intransigent as ever.'

'Oh dear . . .'

'Now what's the matter?'

She grimaced at him. 'I think I'm going to start feeling guilty again.'

Peter laughed. 'No need for that, I think. It looks as if you have really only anticipated a general movement of the Walsoken family. Father thinks of coming up to London quite soon. Jeremiah has quite a circle of fashionable acquaintance, and has I think been tempting father with offers of introductions. I suspect he is also going to look for East India investments and the like. So you see. Reconciliation may come.'

Rebecca watched as a jewelled lady sailed by with her turbanned Negro page in her wake. 'Perhaps then we can put all that terrible time behind us.'

'Of course. By the by, how are your friends the Hardwicks, at Morholm? Father does not mention them.'

Rebecca shrugged. 'That's all part of it, I'm afraid . . . The part of it I regret most . . .'

They returned home after eleven, taking a sixpenny boat from the landing-stage at Lambeth Stairs to the Strand and walking through the narrow streets towards Lincoln's Inn, ignoring the shadowy figures in the alleyways, the women with bodices cut below their bare breasts, the strange surly youths with rouged cheeks and tight breeches.

'I envy you your life here, Peter,' she said before they went to bed.

'Do you? Reading in chambers with a bad-tempered barrister? Wading through Blackstone's *Commentaries* and Wood's *Institute of the Laws of England*?'

'No, well, not that. Though you seem to study much harder than most. But just – living your own life, going about as you please, not chaperoned and watched over.'

'As a woman cannot?'

'As a woman cannot. Unless she is some very grand titled lady.'

'True enough. But this city is, alas, not a safe place for a woman alone. More than ever just at present. I've never known such a seething atmosphere since I came here.'

Certainly London was no abode of peace that spring of 1780. The Catholic Relief Act had been passed some time ago with little comment: now it was on everyone's lips again as there were mass

344

meetings of the Protestant Association under the aegis of Lord George Gordon, screaming for the repeal of the Act. Gordon was an undistinguished Scottish member of Parliament, a tedious zealot who many said was more than half insane; but there was no doubting his charismatic effect in mobilising a militant anti-Catholic feeling. At the end of May thousands turned up at Coachmakers' Hall to hear his hysterical speech about saving the country from its Popish enemies, and at his house in Welbeck Street a huge Protestant petition grew hourly.

The next day Peter showed Rebecca an advertisement in the *Morning Chronicle*.

PROTESTANT ASSOCIATION

Whereas no Hall in London can contain forty thousand men; Resolved, *That this Association do meet on Friday next June 2 in* St George's Fields, *at 10 o'clock in the morning, to consider of the most prudent and respectful manner of attending their Petition, which will be presented the same day, to the House of Commons.*

Resolved, *For the sake of good order and regularity, that this Association, on coming to the ground, do separate themselves into 4 distinct divisions, viz. the London division, the Westminster division, the Southwark division, and the Scotch division . . .*

It went on, detailing the route of the procession, and enjoining supporters to wear blue cockades in their hats 'to distinguish them from Papists', and was signed 'By Order of the Association, G. Gordon, President.'

'But that Act about the Catholics hardly made any difference, surely?' said Rebecca.

Peter shrugged. 'A few concessions. Most notably it makes it easier for them to join the army, for the government is desperate for recruitment for the war. That's about it. When I qualify at the Bar, you know, I will have to take an oath in denunciation of the Pope. Oh, but it's always easy for someone like Gordon to whip up this sort of feeling against Catholics, the more so when we're at war with France and Spain. But it makes me uneasy. I have friends who are Catholic. A family living quite near here who were very kind to me when I first came to London: the Malones, as decent and patriotic folk as you could hope to meet. They will be uneasy, I know.'

The weather was close and humid that week. Across the street from Peter's second-floor rooms, in the gardens of Lincoln's Inn Fields, they walked in the relative cool of the evening, amongst the courtesans with their dampened frocks and the bewigged lawyers from the Inns, searching for a breath of breeze.

It was as if London had a hectic fever: and as if only a bleeding would relieve it.

2

After the Northampton assizes Aysthorpe settled into uneasy peace. John Newman was a free man, and plunged himself into work to begin paying off his costs: the four rioters who had turned King's evidence were given sentences of two to three months in gaol. Mr Walsoken was little seen about, either in the village or at the Stamford bank. He had come out badly. Suspicions of perjury, and vindictiveness, were slow in dying.

One of his first actions, however, was to foreclose on George Hardwick's debts. George had expected nothing less. Expecting this stroke, however, was different from having the resources to meet it.

One thing was for sure: Walsoken was not going to get his hands on another rood of his land. He would go to the debtor's prison first. But there was no more credit to be had. Wainwright's Bank would not touch him: Squire's Bank in Peterborough likewise.

The home farm stock, such as could be sold without giving up the home farm altogether, fetched a hundred pounds. Some plate that had lain in boxes of straw since Queen Anne's time fetched another thirty. Against his will, George raised the rent of the tenant farms, though that would bring in little enough. All the time as he went about these transactions he was more brooding and touchy than Mary had ever known him; and she soon learned better than to ask him, when he came home in the evenings, how the day had gone.

At Morholm – forbiddingly empty now with only two servants, the faithful Binnismoors, and Grandmother Peach, who had tremulously offered George a worthless brooch to sell – she racked her brain for further economies, and with bunches of wild flowers and make-do new curtains tried to cajole a little life into the chilly ghost of the great house. She found herself frequently wandering around its unused spaciousness, peering into the dusty drawing-room with its faded upholstery, looking in at the many cramped panelled bedrooms with their leaded windows that filtered the light like

346

water, examining the smoky portraits under the great staircase. And waiting for the collapse.

Occasionally, too, Mary looked at the second letter she had received from Captain Alex Finlayson. Not a formal letter enclosed with one of Aunt Catherine's: it was for her only. He had hoped to be rejoining his regiment and off to America, he said, as he was virtually recovered but he was stationed at Coxheath near Maidstone, where there was a great encampment in readiness against a French invasion. He got to London to see his uncle and aunt pretty frequently, he said. He hoped all was well at Morholm. It was a place often in his thoughts: he had spent a specially delightful time there.

It was an unexceptionable letter: no real reason to hide it. She did not know why she kept it hidden.

A remarkably beautiful spring flourished across the fenland, unnoticed and irrelevant at Morholm. In early May, one evening shortly after George had arrived home irritably shaking blossoms from his hair, they had a visit from Julia and Henry Milton.

The small bound volume, *Poems on Various Occasions by a Country Lady*, by Mrs Julia Milton, price two shillings, was admired and passed from hand to hand, while Julia ruffled little Charles Joseph's hair and looked uncomfortable to the point of sullenness.

'I never had any idea,' said Mary. 'When did you begin writing, Julia?'

'Oh, I used to scribble when I was living here as a girl,' Julia said, speaking to her lap. 'It – it wasn't anything, it just whiled away the time, and living with Henry I got in the habit of polishing and rewriting. I never meant them to be seen at all – I don't think they're worth it, I really don't understand the fuss, they're nothing like Henry's work.'

'You always did underestimate yourself, sister,' said George. 'So now there are two literary lions in the family. Who'd have thought it.'

'I don't know about *two*,' said Milton with a short laugh. 'My *Open Field* has rather quickly faded, and the edition is still not yet sold. Carey wrote us on Monday to say he had shown a first copy of Julia's poems to Mrs Montagu – perhaps you have heard of her, she rules literary London – and she was enthused, and said she wished to meet the lady.'

'Oh, couldn't you go to London, the two of you?' said Mary. 'If only for a while, to savour it properly.'

Charles Joseph, a dark charming child with the somewhat fine-drawn good looks of his parents, was passionately fond of his aunt Julia and had curled up comfortably on her knee. Julia beat time with his small fist and said: 'No, no, we couldn't – there's Henry's paper, and – and besides I doubt it will sell a single copy.'

'Do you and Francis still write the *Courant* between you?' said George.

'Pretty well. The last I heard of Robert Landless he was at Bath, with no intention of coming home,' said Milton. He poked the carpet idly with his toe, then stopped as he noticed it was wearing very thin just there. 'But I think I could leave it for a while. Francis often says I should take a rest.'

'I doubt it will sell a single copy,' said Julia again.

They managed to stretch dinner for their visitors. George was very silent throughout the meal and no mention was made of Morholm's financial plight. But later, as the Miltons were making ready to leave, Julia touched him on the arm and said: 'I have been paid eighty pounds for my book, George. Fifteen is already spent on a new mare; but the rest is yours, if it will help.'

George frowned, and then his face softened and he patted her hand. 'No sister,' he said. 'I would take it and willing: but even supposing it made any difference, there is the matter of my belated conscience. I must take responsibility for this myself. I have – averted my face too long.'

No more was said.

It was only that night, as they prepared to go up to bed, that Mary said: 'I know you don't like to speak of it, George, but you can tell me, surely. When Julia offered – is it really no use?'

She had snuffed all but the last candle in the great hall, and darkness was swarming in to reclaim it. George, his hand on the oak banister, did not answer for a moment.

'If Walsoken would allow me till next quarter day,' he said, quietly, 'I think we would be out of danger. Most creditors would take that as a matter of course. But there is a personal element, and it has gone too far for reason to intervene. Of course, I can begin to completely dismember the estate and soon get clear . . . But I'm not going to do it, Mary. Never. Not for him. I detest – hate and detest everything about him, everything he's done here, everything he stands for. Let there be a forced sale – let Morholm be stripped bare before I give in to him.'

She extinguished the last candle, and turned to reach out to him, to somehow convey to the tortured complexities of his nature her support; but he had already started up the stairs, and the greedy darkness had shouldered in between them.

3

On Friday June 2nd, about noon, Rebecca went out from Portugal Street to Covent Garden to buy a can of milk and some oranges. As she was about to leave the piazza by way of Russell Street some prentice boys began yelling that Lord George Gordon's procession had just come out of Fleet Street and was moving this way. Along with many other mildly interested folk she drifted down Southampton Street to view the Protestant Association marching past.

She had not expected to see so many. In lines eight abreast, with blue cockades in their hats, and flags and banners reading No POPERY, they came in orderly fashion – at the front, at least – down the Strand. The ranks of bobbing heads went on and on: as each rank passed St Mary's Church they gave a cheer. Towards the back, like the sooty tail of a comet, the crowd became noisier and less disciplined, its number constantly swelled by apprentices, beggars, cutpurses, prostitutes, all the flotsam of the streets drawn by the fuss and the attention: jugs of drink were passed from hand to hand and there were shouted obscenities.

The procession was still endlessly unwinding past when Rebecca turned to go home.

Peter was late returning from Lincoln's Inn that evening: Rebecca was beginning to feel worried for him when he arrived very hot and excited with his coat over his arm.

'Well, it's been defeated,' he said. 'Lord George Gordon's move for his petition against the Catholic Relief Act was overwhelmingly defeated. A hundred and ninety-eight to six. Mr Elliot sent two clerks to Westminster to see what was going on.' He looked out from the window on to the street, fanning himself with a newspaper. 'Such scenes there today. Tens of thousands of people cramming into Parliament Street.'

'I saw the procession when I went to the market,' Rebecca said. 'Passing down the Strand.'

'There was another that came by Westminster Bridge. All converging on Westminster. When the members of Parliament began to arrive in their carriages they could hardly get through the press. The peers and the bishops were pelted and their coach windows smashed. Apparently the Prime Minister's carriage came storming through at a gallop but they still slowed it down and some fellow reached in and snatched the hat from his head. Anyway, the debate went on at last, and finished at eight. Gordon's supporters were still outside, and it seems they're mad as fire, but the last I heard the justices were sending for the Guards to disperse them.'

'This must be the end of it, surely,' Rebecca said.

'I think so. Gordon's been discredited, and they say some who had signed his petition started withdrawing their names, because it had all degenerated into mere ruffianism. Well . . . it will make an interesting letter to send back to Bromswold.'

A light was still showing under Peter's door when she went to bed. She had drifted into sleep, and into a dream of the tread of thousands of marching feet, when he roused her again.

'I think there's trouble over at Lincoln's Inn Fields,' he said. 'Come and see.'

She dressed quickly and joined him at the parlour window that faced over the street. Lincoln's Inn Fields was a dark boiling mass of people. Torches and banners waved, and there was a great plume of flame in the centre. It was just after midnight.

'What is it? What are they doing there?'

Peter hesitated. 'I imagine they are attacking the Catholic chapel there. Chapel of the Sardinian embassy.'

The tumult went on all night. The next morning Rebecca and Peter joined a stream of curious sightseers in Lincoln's Inn Fields. The chapel was a charred shell. Bonfires still smouldered around it. All the sweepings of the unwieldy city seemed to have converged on it during the night, smashing the altar and the pews, leaving the building gutted before melting away again. There were flags and banners trampled in the embers.

Yet London seemed abnormally quiet. 'I suppose everyone is sobered by last night,' Peter said. 'I wonder if all's well with the Malones. Perhaps you'll come with me to see them later.'

Peter's friends were a gentle elderly couple of Irish descent who lived in a neat bow-fronted house in Cock Lane. They were not unduly worried by this trouble. They had heard about the riot last night, but they had also heard the ringleaders had been arrested. It would blow over.

Rebecca and Peter had tea with the Malones and then made their way home. At the top of Ludgate Hill they came upon a procession. The thirteen men arrested last night were being marched by sergeant's guard to Newgate. A crowd had collected around the soldiers, but in the main they were laughing and cheering them, and showed no sign of sympathy for the prisoners. It was a reassuring sight.

It was another hot and airless evening. They were sitting listless at the open windows when their landlady, Mrs Clay, came up flustered in her dressing-gown and said the footman next door had brought news of terrible riots going on to the east: chapels and Catholic houses set on fire, all manner of atrocities, and no one lifting a finger to stop it. Craning out of the window Rebecca saw a glow in the sky to the east.

'I think Mad Gordon has set something in motion that even he did not foresee,' Peter murmured when at last they went to bed.

On Monday morning Peter, before going to Lincoln's Inn, extracted from Rebecca a promise that she would not go out alone. She fully meant to keep it: but it was another beautiful bright day and it seemed absurd to stay inside. Daylight drove out the fear and replaced it with curiosity.

In the streets around Holborn she saw several houses with windows smashed and doors broken in. Incongruous objects, candlesticks, lengths of carpet, mutilated paintings, lay in the road. Knots of people, ragged and drunk and often blackened by smoke, roamed aimlessly, singing, shouting obscenities, waving blue flags, swigging from pilfered jars of gin. On Saffron Hill a youth ran up to her and grinningly handed her a blue cockade and said 'The Papishes are on the run, miss!' She smiled uneasily and after he had gone put the cockade in her pocket.

Somehow the town was going about its normal business, and she was not the only sightseer: but she suddenly felt that her curiosity was quite satisfied. She made her way back to Portugal Street trying not to hurry. Only her extreme casualness of greeting indicated how relieved she was when Peter came home.

He was agitated, and told her not to lay supper. 'It's starting again,' he said. 'There were crowds streaming down Holborn as I

351

came home. The stories I've heard of what went on last night don't bear repeating. Rebecca . . .'

He came and sat beside her, and she knew what he was going to say.

'The Malones have only two little serving-maids in their house,' he said. 'I wouldn't forgive myself if – anything happened. I'm so sorry. I ought to go – just spend this night with them – just in case . . .'

She nodded. 'Go, then. And take care.'

Peter kissed her cheek. 'I'll be back in the morning.'

She did not go to bed at all that Monday night, but sat wrapped in her robe, close to the front window but not so as to be seen, and listened to the tramping of feet, the cries and snatches of song, the thundering of troops of cavalry. Once she ventured to open the window and peer out, and saw the horizon ringed with fire.

That night the riots spread all over London. The great convulsion, with anti-Catholicism as its root, acquired a terrible dynamic of its own: the mob, that had been a disparate hotch-potch of zealots, rowdies, thieves, idle fops, urchins, whores, all the fragments of the dispossessed, the criminal, and the aimless, had become aware of itself as an entity. Houses and shops and warehouses were plundered and fired: troops hurried fruitlessly from one trouble spot to the next, uncoordinated and, since they could do nothing unless a magistrate was present to read the Riot Act, largely powerless. Some sightseers joined in the destruction: others, chastened, felt they had seen enough.

Rebecca woke with a start in the armchair. Noises on the stairs.

It was Peter. He burst in, looking grey and drawn, and gave her a tired smile. 'Up all night,' he said. 'No real trouble. Not in Cock Lane anyway.' He rubbed his unshaven face. 'Fires, looting, everywhere. Mr and Mrs Malone frightened to death.'

Rebecca blinked at the spears of sunlight. 'What time is it?'

'Half-past nine,' said Peter. 'Streets are still full of them. Have you been all right here?'

'Oh, yes . . . Shall I make you some tea?'

He shook his head. 'Bed for me. Dog tired. I won't go into Mr Elliot's today. Nothing's normal, after all. Guards all round the Inns.'

They both slept that Tuesday through till dinner-time. At dusk the distant sounds of disturbance all about the city swelled again.

Rebecca lit candle after candle, to press the darkness back, and at last turned to her silent brother and burst out: 'Peter – don't go to the Malones' again tonight.'

He sighed. 'They're old and frightened and alone and in danger, and they're my friends. Would you have me desert them now?'

She shook her head miserably. 'But at least let me come with you.'

'No, sister. You'll be safer here. I'm responsible for you, remember. Have Mrs Clay to sit up with you. And don't worry.'

She watched him go from the window, his stooped shoulders and red hair disappearing into the darkness.

Fires everywhere. The view from the windows was almost as light as day. Torches flared in the street below, more and more torches. Flags. Smash and tinkle of glass. Running figures: a man being pursued. He was caught; wriggled away, three strides, was caught again, went down under a hail of blows and kicks: did not rise again.

Renewed booms and whooshes as buildings went up in flames: the crack of muskets. She closed the window, dragged the curtains to. The sound of a long shrill scream still penetrated. She gagged on a sob.

Suddenly it seemed far worse to be imprisoned here, tortured by her own imaginings about Peter, than to get out.

Peter. He was too good, too honest. Even as a child he had been selfless. He had once been badly bitten, shooing away a dog that had frightened her.

Rebecca put on her bonnet and shawl, skimmed down the stairs, stepped out into the street. Black figures running in all directions. She felt in her pocket for the blue cockade and tucked it in her bonnet.

4

She was not the only one moving through the narrow maze of streets that led from Holborn into the City. She found herself part of a turbulent tide, sometimes jostled and carried along, sometimes almost bowled over. But their destination was not Cock Lane.

'Newgate' was the word shouted, whispered, laughed, sung to the accompaniment of thundering feet. Like the instinctive herding of beasts, they were massing towards the great prison at some invisible signal, some muezzin's call that triggered fierce springs of destruction and exhilaration.

Headlong, she passed several houses burnt and gutted, figures at the top windows hurling out goods: panting, she stumbled over bodies in the gutters, drunk to insensibility. One ragged man lay face down in a pool of dark blood where he had fallen from the roof of a sacked warehouse. Hastily-painted signs on walls, *This is a Protestant house, No Popery*.

Her own will seemed to have become enmeshed with that of the mob. Emerging into the Old Bailey she pressed herself into a doorway, mesmerised by the sight of Newgate under attack.

Popery was pretty well forgotten here. The mob wanted to set free the rioters who had been taken there on Friday night, but Newgate was a prize in itself. The huge prison with its elaborate stone facings was the largest in England, a grim citadel of misery and squalor, the source of a thousand tales of horror. On the periphery of the crowds teeming about the building were many spectators, well-dressed gentlemen, some in carriages, irresistibly attracted like Rebecca herself.

The adjoining Keeper's House was in flames, a landslide of furniture spilling out of the windows. Rickety ladders were being hoisted from the crowd and slammed against the prison walls. Scrawny blackened figures like wasted imps swarmed up, seemingly without a breath of fear, scrabbling for handholds on ledges and gutters. At the main gates hulking men, stripped to the waist and glistening red in the firelight, swung great hammers. Casks of gin and brandy had been brought up from the Keeper's cellars, and men and women were scooping it feverishly from buckets and hats.

Rebecca could feel the heat of fire on her face: she began to edge round to the next doorway, and just then a great plume of sparks shot out from the blazing shell of the Keeper's House, spattering on to the cobbles and on to the heads of the rioters. There were screams of pain, and laughter, indistinguishable. Then another perilous rain was descending, slates and timber from the roof of the cells, where the demon steeplejacks were working with axes and crowbars. Rebecca shielded her face with her arm as another molten roar shook the House. The flames were sending scorched shadows of themselves up the prison walls now; the forefront of the mob reeled back as they found the brickwork too hot to touch. All was bathed in a light intolerably vivid, hell's version of day, and the great curdled clouds of smoke were coating the rippling horde of rioters in black smut so that they looked like boiling tar.

Somehow the men on the roof had battered their way in, and a yell of pure animal delight went up as the first prisoners, struggling in chains, were hoisted out, flinching at the heat as the rafters of the prison itself began to smoke and smoulder. Rebecca, trying to shoulder through the onlookers to the corner of Skinner Street, saw one of the prisoners hobbling about in the crowd half-naked and weeping with shock and fear: another lay terrified on the ground as two men drunkenly hacked at the fetters on his leg with saws.

Suddenly the heads at the front of the crowd before the gates began to disappear as if the prison were sucking them in. The gates were down.

Wriggling tongues of flame were issuing from windows and rents in the roof of the prison as the prisoners came tumbling and limping out, cheered and accosted, some scooped up and tossed above the heads of the crowd. Others came screaming from deep parts of the building, blistered and almost baked alive by the encroaching fire. The whole of Newgate now was crawling with people, tearing down lumps of masonry and glowing bars, waving flags from the windows, tossing burning brands on to the roof, and strutting and posing on perilous ledges, their hands and feet charred and their clothes smoking on their backs: a youth with scorching hair perched on a sill and exposed himself and urinated on the heads below. The noise now shared the searing quality of the heat; a great screaming as of one throat scored with the deep bellowing of the fire and the crash of falling debris.

A child came bolting out of the crowd towards Rebecca, squealing and singed, his hair on fire, an undernourished rickety little creature. Rebecca screamed as he plunged past her. The scream seemed to break something down inside her: she remembered who and where she was, and remembered Peter: she realised that she had been clenching and unclenching her fists, her eyes greedily taking it all in, her mind beating to the same terrible rhythm . . . She turned her face away and began to run up Giltspur Street to Cock Lane.

Newgate was not the only fire: there were columns of smoke at all points of the compass. As she turned into the narrow slit of Cock

Lane, with its timbered houses leaning their foreheads confidentially together, she felt a sudden, absolutely certain premonition.

The Malones' house was gutted. There were still a few youths milling about, but the street was quiet. Half a dozen soldiers were drinking ale around the remains of a bonfire. She swallowed a bolus of panic and was about to plunge into the vaporous shell of the house when Mrs Malone called her name.

Behind the bonfire the Malones had a pile of salvaged goods that the soldiers had managed to protect. Here Peter lay flat on a straw mattress.

An apothecary was dressing his forearm which was singed from wrist to elbow. His face was blackened and grazed. His breathing was thick and laboured, his chest wheezing updown, updown, as it did when he had a very bad asthma attack.

'Smoke got on to his chest, dear boy,' said Mrs Malone tearfully. 'Whole house full of smoke. They set light to the roof. Someone must have told them – ' she dropped her voice – 'that we're Catholic.'

Peter smiled feebly up at Rebecca. 'Sister – you shouldn't be abroad tonight,' he said, snatching at breath.

'God bless him,' said Mr Malone, who had no coat and was shivering. 'Helped us get out from the back window, he did. Then he stayed in there, trying to save our few bits of things, till the last minute. Then the soldiers came. Sure, it's a fine brother you have, Miss Rebecca.'

Peter coughed and twisted round to see. 'The house – is it all burnt? Oh . . .'

Neighbours offered to lodge the Malones that night. Now there was the question of getting Peter back to Portugal Street. 'If only we could get a chair, a hackney – ' Rebecca said.

'There'll be none about tonight,' said Peter. 'I'm quite able to walk, sister.' The apothecary had bound up his arm and he stood quite steadily: it was that stertorous breathing that Rebecca did not like.

Holding his good arm, she began to lead him home through the tumultuous streets, but he was making slow progress, fighting hard for every shuddering breath. At the corner of Fetter Lane he had to stop. 'Sorry,' he gasped. 'That damn smoke . . .' The first time she had ever heard him swear. Tears of a kind of distressed rage came to her eyes.

She became aware that a chariot and pair had stopped beside them, and a young man was leaning out.

'Is that someone hurt there? Can I help?'

Thank God, thank God. She hardly took any notice of the young man as she stammered out where they lived and she had to get her brother home and thank you, thank you. Into the carriage, Peter half-dropping with fatigue. The horses were rolling their eyes in alarm at the fires and twitching to be off.

'This is so kind of you,' Rebecca said. 'I hope we're not putting you out of your way . . .'

'Not at all, not at all, just glad I can do some good this dreadful night. I have been flying hither and thither all night seeking out my friends. You have been hurt in a fire, sir? Forgive me, it pains you to speak.'

Peter grimaced, a stab at a smile. 'Asthmatic,' he said. 'Chest.'

Rebecca, in sudden horror, plucked the blue cockade out of her bonnet, but the young man smiled. 'A wise precaution, madam. I have been compelled to shout "No Popery" many times this evening. Though I fancy it has all gone beyond Popery.' He lowered the window and peered out. 'The way seems clear . . . You saw Newgate? Ah. Bridewell also, I hear. And Justice Fielding's house attacked. I was almost afraid the same would happen at the House this evening.'

'Your house?' said Rebecca.

'You misunderstand me. The House of Commons, where I am a Member. My name is Lovell Fitzroy.'

Peter's habitual politeness overcame his asthma. 'I'm honoured, sir. Peter Walsoken . . . my sister Rebecca.'

The young man, Rebecca at last took in, had a square decent face with a high forehead and light powdered hair; a broken eyebrow that gave him a quizzical look; clothes well-cut and quiet. 'The arm, sir,' he said. 'Has it been properly dressed? Will it need attention?'

'Oh, I can look after that,' said Rebecca hurriedly, not knowing quite why. The young man smiled at her, both kind and neutral, and then looked out of the window again. 'Here we are. Quiet down here, thank heaven. I hope you may get at least some rest tonight.'

It was nearly midnight, but the sky above the housetops was bright red as Rebecca descended from the carriage. Lovell Fitzroy helped Peter out and then said: 'Can I be of any more assistance?'

'No, thank you again,' Rebecca said with warmth. 'But – have you far to go home yourself? Will you be safe?'

'Grosvenor Square,' the young man said, shutting the carriage door. 'The opposite direction from the riots, I think and hope. Good night.'

Wednesday morning, and Peter was breathing easier. The arm, however, was blistered and painful, and later Rebecca proposed, quashing his protests, to go out to buy some ointment or salve to put on it.

She went only as far as Covent Garden, to a druggist there, but saw a city in a state of siege. And soldiers. Red coats everywhere, marching and riding, from encampments all around the country. Government had admitted at last that these were not 'disturbances'.

When she arrived back at their lodgings Lovell Fitzroy was there, chatting to Peter. He bowed over her hand in a very old-fashioned way and said he could not be easy this morning until he had inquired after his companions of last night.

After a few minutes of incongruously urbane small-talk he left them, with wishes on both sides to meet again. Whilst Rebecca smoothed the salve on to Peter's arm he said: 'Mr Fitzroy said it looks as if the mob intend to attack the Bank of England. The royal palaces too. But the King has taken matters into his own hands, and proclaimed martial law. Or what amounts to it, dressed up in legal phrases.'

'I heard rumours at the market that the King had been burned in his bed,' Rebecca said. 'How is Mr Fitzroy so well informed?'

'Well, he is a Member of Parliament, though it's not meeting today. Ouch. But also his uncle is the Duke of Grafton, so he is well placed to know such things.'

Rebecca stared at him. 'The Duke – '

'Of Grafton, yes, the former Prime Minister. We have been keeping higher company than we knew.'

'Good Lord . . .'

'What?'

She shook her head. 'I was just thinking of father – if he knew!'

Peter grinned. 'A step up from Jeremiah's foppish friends, is it not? Mind you, a Whig like Grafton, father would probably not approve. And I gathered that Mr Fitzroy is with the Opposition too.'

'A *Duke* like Grafton, that's what would impress father,' said Rebecca. 'Still – ' she dipped her fingers in the pot of salve again – 'I don't suppose we shall see him – Mr Fitzroy – again.'

'You think not? Well . . .' Peter smiled mischievously. '*I* won't, perhaps. But I think he may be more attentive in cultivating you . . . Ow, not so hard!'

Peter was much recovered by evening, and wanted to go out to see the Malones. Rebecca very firmly would not allow it. It looked as if tonight would be the worst yet. Mrs Clay, like many householders, had put out blue flags from her windows, but that was no guarantee of safety now. There was nothing to do but lock the doors and wait and hope while the two armies, the military and the mob, took the field of London.

Darkness never fell that night: it only turned a blazing orange. This time there was a continual crackle of gunfire: the rumour came through that the Bank was being attacked and wave upon wave of rioters shot down. From the very top of the house Rebecca and Peter saw a city aflame. Scores of fires were dotted everywhere, but on Holborn Hill there was a veritable volcano. Later they learned that Langdale's Distillery had been sacked and set alight, and ragged scarecrows had deliriously killed themselves gorging on the raw gin that coursed in a boiling stream knee-deep down the street.

In the unearthly quiet of Thursday morning Rebecca and Peter, with his arm in a sling, joined a general movement of sightseers calming their shattered nerves by a walk in the fresh air.

There were thousands of soldiers forming lines and barricades in the streets. Around the smoking ruins, of houses and chapels and shops, of all the main prisons, there were charred and stripped bodies, a few alive but drunk into a coma, most dead. A few shrunken wretches still in chains and fetters, sprung from the prisons and not knowing what to do, were limping about looking for someone to whom to give themselves up. Down on the wharf by Blackfriars Bridge there were more piles of bodies, grey and bloated, that had been fished out of the river. The word went round that the attack on the Bank had failed, that the King was alive, and that there were twenty thousand regular troops and militiamen in the city, some having come on forced marches from the Midlands and the West country. And there were whispers of French gold being found in the pockets of the rioters, of American spies urging them on.

'Yes,' said Peter bitterly, 'they will say it was French infiltration, or Spanish, or Catholics, or Protestants, or even it was all Gordon's doing, and so nothing will stop it happening again.'

They were both so tired they might have slept through anything that night: but there were only a few random shots to be heard, and a few bonfires that soon dwindled away. Friday, a week since the Protestant petition, dawned clear and cool, and the soldiers rounded up the escaped convicts at their leisure. The convulsion was over.

FOUR

The Gordon Riots, as they came to be known, had a chastening effect on the whole country. Only overwhelming military force had quelled them: the resources of a few constables and magistrates had proved totally inadequate. Lord George Gordon was imprisoned in the Tower awaiting trial, a saddened and despised figure: the Protestant Association withered away amongst the ruins of houses and prisons and chapels and the hundreds of corpses. But the Riots had done one thing that had seemed impossible: they made Lord North's government popular. Anything that savoured of insurrection, of associations and agitation and reform, was looked at askance.

The enclosure commissioners were in Aysthorpe that summer, surveying and measuring and examining title deeds. They were watched without pleasure, but no one interfered with their work. George had little time to spare for them. Most of the day he worked on the home farm himself, for any wage saved would help stave off collapse.

There was much talk of a highwayman who was to be hanged at Lincoln. George felt tempted to turn highwayman himself. Especially when he saw the coaches, with armed guard next to the driver, that plied between the Bank of Wiley & Walsoken and other banks up-country. Three hundred and ninety-five pounds, which was what his debt was reduced to, was not after all a large sum. But he had scraped the bottom of his credit. No one would consider a second mortgage on his property. As if in wry mockery of his position, the tenant farms were thick with blond tall wheat, no drainage trouble, a good year. The demesne of the Hardwicks. His inheritance. It had become a bitter one. The news that the Bicklode Fen scheme was prospering did nothing to lighten his mood.

On the first Wednesday in August he rode into Stamford on their one remaining horse. It was never Mr Walsoken who saw him at the bank now. Thornton Wiley, fat, gouty, oily, soured in temper by his own changed circumstances, had had his orders from the senior partner. Immediate repayment or they would be forced to begin proceedings. George banged his fist on the desk and shouted at the quivering jelly of a man. Time, give me time. Knowing it was no good. Typical boorish country squire, straw in his hair and not a penny to bless himself with.

He reached home sweating and grim. Well, there was a kind of relief in knowing. Will Binnismoor came to take the horse. He and his wife had volunteered to work without wages, until – until when?

'Where's the mistress, Will?'

'Upstairs, sir, bathin' the little 'un. He went and gotten in the pigsty. Young tinker.'

In the hall he threw off his hat and coat, suddenly missing Mary's greeting. He tended to forget that she was suffering with him. His tongue was so damn sharp these days. There was something prickly lodged in him like a burr, he couldn't help it.

Mrs Binnismoor was there, holding out a letter. 'This came for you, sir. Man brought it.'

A crested seal. George took it into the front parlour.

Dear Mr Hardwick,

I would be greatly obliged if you would wait upon me at Burghley this evening. I would hesitate to invite you at such short notice were it not a matter of extreme importance.

Exeter

A very lordly summons. George chafed while he swallowed a glass of ale and some cake and told Will to saddle up again. Assuming he had nothing better to do than come hat in hand to Burghley House whenever his Lordship snapped his fingers. Importance to whom, anyway? He left word with Mrs Peach where he had gone.

It was dusk when he turned in at the gatehouse to Burghley Park. The great house on the horizon at the end of the seemingly endless drive was like a small fortified town, turrets, cupolas, a spire. An extravagant, absurd and magnificent construction.

Servants in livery buzzed around him in the courtyard, taking his horse, and in the entrance hall, taking his hat and gloves. He was aware of being grubby and shabby and hot. Then he was being conducted down a cool musty stone passageway, up a flight of stairs, past paintings and trophies and tapestries and beneath spectacular carved and gilded and painted ceilings, and at last to a great parlour, where before a small fire in a gigantic marble fireplace Lord Burghley sat in an easy chair.

'Mr Hardwick. This is extremely good of you.' The Earl of Exeter got up to shake his hand. An old frogged coat and an unpowdered wig: at his ease. 'I very much hoped you would be able to come. I jsut came up from London yesterday. I've only just recovered from the journey.' He reached for the bell-pull in the wall beside the fireplace. 'My lady is still in town. I'm pleased to see a good harvest in readiness. You will have a glass of canary, Mr Hardwick? And how are you, my dear sir?'

'I find the heat trying,' said George. If his lordship expected deference he had chosen the wrong time.

'You must forgive my having a fire. An old man's foible.' Burghley was fifty-five. 'And Mrs Hardwick, and your young son?'

'All well, thank you, my lord.' A footman appeared.

'Bring a bottle of the canary,' the Earl said. 'Ah, a son. I have none, alas. As you know. My nephew Henry is my heir. I hear Aysthorpe is in process of being enclosed, Mr Hardwick.'

The Earl always seemed to know what was going on, George thought. 'It is, my lord. Mr Walsoken was the – guiding spirit behind it.'

'So I hear. A man, hm, very much in the ascendant. Our methods of agriculture must move with the times, of course. But I quite understand the opposition that is often experienced.'

George suddenly thought of the trial. 'My lord, I have not thanked you – at least, I believe I have you to thank. I refer to the case at the Northampton Assize. The case of riot and assault in Aysthorpe, which I believe you transferred from the jurisdiction of the Soke.'

Lord Burghley nodded. 'So I did.' The footman returned with wine, and another footman came with candles that valiantly tried to illuminate the big room, the high ceiling and dusty wall-hangings and the ponderous Jacobean furniture. 'Yes, I felt it was a case in which the assize would guarantee a greater measure of impartiality. Though impartiality is by nature absolute – but you take my meaning.'

'I do, and am grateful. That is, I – had an interest in the outcome, and was glad it was not left a matter for the Soke.' It was very fine canary, which he was drinking from a heavy old-fashioned glass.

'Of course,' said the Earl, 'if you had still been a magistrate, you would have been in a position to go into the matter yourself.'

'True, my lord,' said George. 'It is the only time I have regretted that decision.'

'The only time? Your feeling is still unchanged in that regard?'

So, this was what it was all about. Trying to keep weariness out of his tone, George said: 'It is. What I said to you at the time of my resignation, my lord, applies still. Perhaps more so.'

'You heard, of course, of the late disturbances in London, Mr Hardwick?'

'I read of them in the newspaper.'

'Of course, there has been talk of foreign agitators and the usual nonsense. It seems to me a simple matter of lawlessness and rebellion.' Lord Burghley looked at George sharply. 'But I must remember I am speaking to one of reforming tendencies, am I not? Perhaps you do not feel so strongly about these riots, have a certain sympathy even?'

'There is at Morholm only a rusty musket and a pair of pistols that I doubt would fire, my lord, but I would not hesitate to use them if someone tried to burn down my house. If that answers your question.'

Lord Burghley chortled. 'It was a very unfair question. I'm sorry. But what you said to me when you resigned your commission – the game laws and so on. You were quite plain. What about Fox with his annual Parliaments and all the rest of it? Does that have your sympathy?'

'You mean of what party do I consider myself,' said George. 'It will no doubt seem like equivocation when I say I don't know. I believe Fox is much maligned and has more talents than the whole of North's government together. But I cannot call myself a Whig. As for the war, I really don't care one way or the other. It seems to me that England will dig a grave for herself unless she spares a thought for the domestic problems. Unglamorous problems, no doubt. Folk not having enough to eat. Being unable to afford the good loaf their fathers ate, or keep the pig or cow that kept their fathers above subsistence. And forbidden to take so much as a hare off the land without the full weight of our clumsy laws crashing down on them. The gallows for every crime from stealing a handkerchief to passing a forged note. Parochial concerns, I know, but I can only speak as a country man, whose family, for good or ill, have been tied to the land for generations. To see my neighbours fed and with a fair measure of independence means more to me, I'm afraid, than what goes on in Quebec.'

'And, dear me, what is Fox's cry – equal representation? You would count yourself a supporter of this? Association Movements and so on.'

'Well, I rely on the newspapers for my information,' said George. 'But . . . as far as I can see, reform must come. And sooner rather than later, for everybody's good. There is, it seems to me, a too arbitrary concentration of power. Whether it be in government, or the appropriation of the land to the use of a few landlords who see in it only another page in the profit ledger.' Lord Burghley was looking at him shrewdly. George frowned at the fire and tried to collect his thoughts. The Earl might as well hear it all. 'We are rightly proud of our parliamentary system – but I wonder if our very complacency thereby endangers it. It is open to all kinds of abuses.'

'Oh, such abuses are nothing new, Mr Hardwick.'

'Indeed not, my lord. All the more reason that we begin to take notice of them. Dunning's motion in April – But I wonder whether you really wish to hear me prate like this, my lord.'

The Earl of Exeter made an openhanded smiling gesture.

'Given the corruption that goes hand in hand with our electoral system,' George said, 'it seems to me that Parliament cannot claim to truly represent the country. And so you see . . . I have condemned myself out of my own mouth. Equal representation. The reforming party. I had not meant to say so much.'

'Mr Hardwick, I beg you, don't consider yourself on trial,' said Lord Burghley pleasantly, refilling George's glass. 'I am most interested to hear what you have to say.'

'And must be aware by now, my lord, that I am not about to change my mind as to the question of the Bench.'

The surprise on Lord Burghley's face was genuine. 'I didn't suppose you were. It isn't that which I have asked you here to discuss. Or not exactly. As you well know, that venality you spoke of could very well find a perfect example in me. I control the borough of Stamford and nominate its MPs. My nephew is one of them. The borough corporation see me as a Tory tyrant. A perfect example, is it not, of the exclusivity and irresponsibility of the present system?'

'I hope I did not suggest – '

'You could not help but suggest. I led you on to doing so.' The Earl was breathing hard. 'But these classifications, these labels are not helpful. Fox started out a Tory, for example. And you should not assume that I have necessarily disagreed with everything you have said. My support is with the present government, but I am not blind to its shortcomings. However, this is the matter I wish to talk to you about. I have some confidential news for you. Parliament is to be dissolved in a few weeks' time, and a general election called.'

'Good Lord. I thought there was another year to go.'

'There was. But North has decided to go to the country now. And support must be quickly drummed up. What we need above all is to get a mandate for the continuance of the war. Stamford has two Members, as you know, both of them my nominees and supporters of the government – my nephew, and Sir George Howard. However, Howard has just made known to me that he does not wish to stand for the seat again. So I must find another candidate quickly.'

George nodded. 'I see your difficulty.'

Lord Burghley finished his wine. 'I'm glad of that,' he said, 'for I am offering the nomination to you.'

George could not help his gale of laughter, though he feared it had offended the Earl, who was smiling thinly.

'Perhaps, Mr Hardwick,' he said, 'you will share the joke with me.'

'I'm very sorry, my lord. The joke is against myself . . . You are naturally aware of the expense involved in standing for Parliament. I don't know if you have heard about my own financial situation. Walsoken's bank is demanding immediate repayment of a debt. Money I cannot raise.'

Lord Burghley shrugged. 'The borough of Stamford is controlled by me, Mr Hardwick. The price, the expense of returning my nominees to Parliament is borne by me. That is no obstacle.'

George frowned. 'But the obstacle remains, my lord, in that you would not, I think, wish to nominate a near-bankrupt. Certainly I have been in a comparable position of debt before. But my creditor is Joshua Walsoken, and there is a – personal element.'

'Oh, yes, I heard of some ill-feeling between you,' said the Earl. 'I wasn't aware it had developed in this way. What is the sum you owe?'

George hesitated. 'A little under four hundred pounds.'

'Good God,' said Lord Burghley. His tone said 'So little' rather than 'So much'.

'So you see, my lord. I hope you can now forgive my laughter. The idea of me standing for Parliament, now, seemed doubly absurd.'

Lord Burghley adjusted the fire-screen. 'Talking of the Bench, as we were. Have you heard that Sir Samuel Edgington is dead?'

'No, I hadn't.'

'Last week. It poses the problem for me once again of finding a new magistrate for the Soke. I passed over Mr Walsoken last time. He has, I know, expressed a very strong desire to be a magistrate, and will certainly be hoping to be chosen this time.'

George waited. Lord Burghley was examining his wine.

'It would be quite possible for me not to appoint him. Or, more precisely, to appoint him only on certain conditions. One of which would be that he does not foreclose on your debt.'

George gaped, and then remembering himself closed his mouth. 'I – I don't know what to say . . .'

'"Grant Mr Hardwick a reprieve, or I appoint somebody else." Yes. Not in quite those words, of course. I take it that given time, you could get clear of the debt?'

'Yes . . . yes, that's so. But would he give in to such pressure?'

'Oh, I think so. There are other pressures too. My estate agents do a lot of valuable business with his bank. Question of withholding favours. Yes, I can soon get you out of your financial difficulty. You will have to think of better obstacles than that, Mr Hardwick. Unless, ahem, you deplore aristocratic privilege so much that you would not accept this help?'

George smiled. 'I think you know my answer to that, my lord. But forgive me – you undertake to do all this for me, if I will stand for Parliament as your nominee. And yet you have just heard me – well, prate, is my own word – and show myself to be in complete disagreement with you over most issues.'

'Some issues,' said Lord Burghley judicially. 'As I say, what the government requires is a mandate to continue the war. I have engaged that the two Members I supply will always give votes of support. That is my only condition. These issues of domestic reform that concern you, for example: you would be free to vote as you wished, pursue these interests all you like. I am not a tyrant, in spite of what the Stamford corporation say. And there we come to my reason for choosing you, Mr Hardwick. The Stamford corporation have become unfriendly to me, resentful of my influence. They have made it known that next election they will put forward a candidate of their own against mine. They of course make great play of the fact that my nephew is one of the sitting MPs – proof of nepotism and corruption. But if my other candidate is Mr George Hardwick – that is a different matter. No family connection with the Burghleys. An independent country gentleman of good name, not a place-seeker. So this charge that I am the town despot will be much weakened. So you see, Mr Hardwick, I also have my own interests at heart in this. But I would not offer it to you if I did not think you were the right man for the job.'

George put down his wine-glass: he needed to be clear-headed. 'I am – deeply sensible of the honour, my lord. But – I would appreciate time to – '

Lord Burghley was brisk. 'Time is a luxury we must forego, Mr Hardwick. Parliament will be dissolved on the first of September. I shall ring for another bottle of canary, and while we drink it you shall give me your answer.'

There was only one answer to give, though George still felt as if he were in a dream and the cold light of waking would break in at any moment. After such certain despair, to know that he could be solvent again, free, his position suddenly reversed, the terrible cloud lifted . . . The Earl of Exeter, portly and gruff, made an unlikely Good Fairy, but that was what he was for Morholm.

So, the agreement was made, and toasted in a last glass of canary. Only as he was about to leave did George say: 'Do you have any idea, by the by, who the corporation is likely to put forward to oppose us?'

The Earl shook his head. 'Some tradesman no doubt. It doesn't matter. Whoever it is, my influence and your independent name will be enough. I guarantee.'

368

Parliament, as the Earl of Exeter had predicted, dissolved on the first of September. The same day a dinner was held at Mr Edward Wainwright's townhouse in Stamford, where the corporation's own candidate for the election was presented and toasted.

It was Mr Wainwright who had always led the opposition to the Burghley interest, and had proposed fielding a candidate when an election should come. Now that the time had arrived he had less joy of it than he had hoped. For one thing, there was Lord Burghley's choice of George Hardwick as one of his nominees. That was very astute. With Burghley's influence in the town so strong, it was unlikely the voters would dare to reject his nephew, Henry Cecil: but Mr Wainwright had hoped they could be persuaded to reject his other candidate in favour of the corporation's. But Hardwick put a different complexion on things – a man of more than nominal independence, a local man, a respected name, who could hardly be called the Earl's lapdog. An astute choice.

And then there was the candidate chosen by the corporation – this rather louche dandified young man at the head of the table who had been undressing the ladies with his narrow eyes all through dinner. Jeremiah Walsoken. Not quite the solid businesslike type they had envisaged. Oh, certainly gentlemanly, with many high-born contacts, for what they were worth. But really the choice had been foisted upon them. Stamford was a scot and lot borough, where everyone who paid a rate for the maintenance of parish affairs had a vote. Votes had to be bought. Mr Joshua Walsoken had great ambitions for his son, and was prepared to lay money out to further them. He had been all the more eager when he heard that Hardwick was one of the opposing candidates.

So, here they were. They had eaten well and now, the ladies having retired, were drinking well, Jeremiah Walsoken setting the table roaring with scurrilous jokes, his father watching him with a kind of baleful possessive pride. A witty young man, thought Mr Wainwright (not laughing, for he did not have a sense of humour). Perhaps he would do. It could have been worse. There had been some talk of persuading his own son-in-law, Sir Hugh Woodhouse, to stand. Thank God that had not turned out, though Hugh was here now, having come over with Elizabeth this morning and decided to stay. He was all got up in a yellow cutaway coat and striped stockings and a tight white waistcoat – he had put on a lot of weight – and he was laughing at Jeremiah's sallies with that great crack-jawed bray of his.

Mr Wainwright had little time for his son-in-law these days. He was tired of bailing Hugh out when he overspent: and whatever accord he and Elizabeth had come to over their marriage, it didn't seem a healthy one. They scarcely spoke to each other, and Lizzie never looked well, and what's more didn't seem to care, didn't dress to her best. It was as if she had lost interest in life.

In the drawing-room the talk was of the Prince of Wales and the enormous sums he was spending on his mistress and how it was breaking his father's heart. Mrs Walsoken, prettily faded and entirely innocent, listened in genuine shock: Mrs Wainwright, her voluminous flesh garnered up by a whole whale's-worth of whale-bone, adjusted her frizzed black wig and said tut tut while her eyes from their wrinkles of fat darted to her silent daughter. There was a mark on her wrist, she noticed, like a burn, most odd: the child seemed to be growing very sloppy and careless, her silk gown was creased and soiled. Perhaps she could speak to her . . . but she could never get anything out of her these days.

And Elizabeth, Lady Woodhouse, toyed with her coffee spoon, presenting an attentive face to the company, though her mind was no more present than if she had been a hundred miles away. She was aware of that mark on her wrist, but she had not bothered to cover it up. It had happened at Deenecote yesterday, when she had put her hand round the silver teapot to see if it were still hot. It was, but she had not removed her hand, just let it stay there. Didn't seem to matter. It was only her flesh, after all, the lowest and foulest of substances, that existed only for the periodic lustful assaults of her husband. There was a remission at the moment, for he was enjoying one of his occasional flirtations, but he would come back to her. Still hoping for an heir, of course, but she knew that could not be. Her insides were dry and withered and wizened, she knew, she could feel it keenly. It was about all she could feel.

She still had a couple of Robert Landless's old letters, yellowing now, and sometimes she took them out and looked at them. But it was chiefly a reflex: they occasioned in her a dumb bewilderment. Sometimes she murmured 'I love Robert Landless', but the words fell dead from her lips, dry rattling husks. Love – no, that was fevered flesh and grossness, sweat and clutching and pain. No. She didn't feel anything, didn't think anything: except, occasionally, that she was going mad.

3

'So, when do you leave for London?' George asked his sister.

'On Monday, all being well,' Julia said. 'Henry still has a little business to attend to at the *Courant*. But then we shall be off for three months or so.'

'Depending on how long Julia can bear being feted,' said Milton. 'There have been good notices galore for her poems. Carey wishes to talk to her about a second volume already.'

They were at the election dinner, in the dining-room of The George in Stamford. Tomorrow, the fifteenth of September, the poll would be held, and here had gathered Lord Burghley's friends and supporters and a number of voters who needed to be wooed with ample food and drink.

George looked at Julia and smiled. She was in good spirits, with a consequent softening of her strong features. With her piled mass of dark hair and full figure she did not look exactly the bluestocking of contemporary myth.

Henry Milton was excited at the prospect too, and their relationship had recovered some of its warmth. He had kept at bay, so far, the slightest tickling of resentment. It was unworthy and must be squashed. But he could not deny that it was Julia who was going to be the celebrity: the success had come unlooked-for to his wife, not to him, the success that had always been his cherished ambition. He was too honest not to admit what was now obvious, that he was a small poetaster whose work all the effort in the world could not lift above the ground, and that Julia's was the real talent, a talent as wayward and brilliant as a flower blooming in the weeds of a boggy fen.

'With any luck you will be joining us soon,' Milton said to George. 'What do you think are your chances, really?'

'Well, whatever happens, it will not be for want of expenditure on his lordship's part,' said George with a constrained smile.

'Oh, this is nothing exceptional, as borough elections go,' said Milton. 'Wainwright's party will be up to all the same tricks, naturally.'

'Naturally,' said George. He was finding it difficult to be relaxed.

Not only were the real implications of his decision to stand now coming home to him, but he was beginning to realise the extent of Lord Burghley's influence. The Earl was very frank about the way he purchased votes for George and his nephew. Many houses and shops were owned by the Burghley estate, and tenants knew better than to risk an eviction notice. Similarly, tradesmen and suppliers could find one of their biggest customers withdrawing his custom if they voted the wrong way.

It was, as Milton said, nothing exceptional, and George told himself not to trouble about it. He had, after all, benefited from the same influence himself: Mr Walsoken had indeed yielded to the Earl's pressure on his bank, and George was now out of the wood – he would be fully solvent by the time the new Parliament opened, whether he were elected or not. And there was an added spice in seeking for election when it was Walsoken's own ne'er-do-well son he faced. So, he should be thanking his lucky stars, not gnawing over his conscience like a dry bone. He would soon be free and independent again. Financially, at least . . .

Mary was at the opposite side of the table, next to Luke. He had with him a good-looking, lambent-eyed young woman with a circlet of pearls in her hair whom Mary thought she remembered. Luke introduced her as Kitty Du Quesne.

'George looks none too happy,' Luke said. 'Does he think he will lose? There's several on the corporation who will support him, not just me. The Walsokens aren't as popular as they like to think.'

'I think he can hardly believe it's all happening,' said Mary. 'I was astonished myself.'

'Is your husband not a man for politicking, Mrs Hardwick?' said Kitty Du Quesne, crumbling bread in her long sharp fingers. She had a marked fen accent still, but seemed quite at her ease.

'He has always claimed it bored him to tears,' said Mary, smiling. 'Though I must admit of late that – things have happened that have made him feel strongly.'

'What will you do if he gets in?' Luke said. 'Will you rent a house in London? I suppose Charles Joseph's old enough to go with you now.'

'I've hardly thought about it,' said Mary. 'We've grown so used to being at Morholm all year round. But I would like to see London again.'

'We'll have to get you into Parliament, Luke,' Kitty said, winking at him. 'I could fancy a jaunt down to London.'

'You have enough jaunts,' Luke said indifferently.

A strange couple, Mary thought, if that was what they were. Luke, lean, handsome, well set-up, and yet with a restive air, did not look like a man in love. He treated her with a mixture of impatience and confidentiality. Single-minded, that was the characteristic that best described him now; but it was a single-mindedness that seemed to have been embraced as a creed for want of anything else, and had become a narrow deepening groove, forcing his life into one channel that gave him no room to turn about and change.

After dinner the windows overlooking the street were opened and the supporters outside cheered as Lord Burghley and his nominees, Henry Cecil and George Hardwick, waved their hats and according to custom scattered hot coins from a pan.

Luke, standing beside Mary watching, said abruptly, 'What a rabble. Look at them grubbing there. As if they know or care who ends up in Westminster.'

His tone was full of contempt. Mary glanced at his sharp-etched profile and said: 'You sound very bitter, Luke.'

He smiled briefly. 'Well, are they not a rabble, cousin? Always worked up about something. There's been trouble at King's Lynn this week, with gangs of wretches complaining about the ships that go out to export wheat. Wheat that should be feeding them, is the cry. Do they think trade can stop altogether?'

Mary, about to say something, stopped and held her tongue.

Kitty Du Quesne was yawning behind him. 'God's my life, all this screeching gives me a pain. I think I'll be going home now, Luke.'

'Very well,' he said, without so much as a glance backward.

When she had gone he said to Mary: 'I don't suppose you have ought to do with Bromswold now, cousin?'

Mary shook her head.

'Rebecca,' he said. 'Rebecca Walsoken. She went to London, didn't she?'

'So I hear. To stay with her brother.'

'Hm. Well . . . reckon I'll get back and see how father is.'

Mary's surmise about Luke was not far from the truth: though it was with an aimless sort of drifting that he had been drawn back to

373

Kitty Du Quesne. Her old mentor Sir Samuel Edgington was dead, and she had no objection to taking a new one.

There were moments, in the small hours, in the flashes of wakefulness that light on the soul, when he was conscious of self-disgust. But why should he care? You took what you could get in life, and learnt not to cry for the moon. Otherwise there was intolerable pain and betrayal. That was his philosophy. There was nothing else for it.

On the morning of the fifteenth there was some excitement in Stamford at the prospect of a contested election, the first for many years.

The town hall chamber was full, but the returning officer, the mayor, had not yet arrived. George, with Lord Burghley and Henry Cecil, took a turn about the room talking to their supporters. At the other end of the hall was Jeremiah Walsoken, in a narrow-waisted coat and cockaded hat, smiling but nervously tapping his riding-crop against his leg: with him his father, in earnest discussion with Mr Wainwright.

George turned to see Great-Uncle Horace, leaning heavily on Luke's arm, making his way into the chamber.

'George,' he said, giving him a hand that was like a bundle of twigs, 'I have been a Whig and an opponent of Lord Burghley's all my life. You have placed me in a difficult position.'

George was shocked at the decline of the old man: normally so erect, his head was sunk down in his shoulders, his skin like parchment.

'You must vote according to your principles, uncle,' said George, 'and not from family obligation.'

Horace wiped his moist eye and grinned foxily. 'I shall try to do both, nephew,' he said.

It was time for the candidates to take their places on the platform. As they made their way through the crowd George found himself next to Mr Walsoken and Jeremiah.

'Ho, Mr Hardwick,' said Jeremiah, raising a yellow-gloved hand. 'I hope we shall have a fair fight of it, in spite of all that bribery can do. I must confess I am surprised to be standing against you. Whatever happened, I wonder, to that fine old Hardwick name and its reputation for independence?'

George shrugged. 'Reputations can be lost and gained,' he said.

He glanced at Mr Walsoken. 'A reputation, for example, for hypocrisy, for falsehood, for perjury in an open court of law.'

They stared at each other, then moved away and mounted the opposite ends of the platform.

The town clerk read the proclamation opening the poll, and the mayor was sworn in as returning officer and opened the great calfskin book on the raised table.

The speeches over, the first voters began to mount the platform. Among the first were Luke and old Horace. Luke for Mr Hardwick and Mr Cecil. Horace, in a quavering voice, voted for Mr Hardwick and Mr Walsoken. He shrugged at George as he tottered off the platform, and George smiled back.

The mayor's quill pen wagged over the great book. There were something like six hundred registered voters. It would be a long day.

4

As dusk was melting over the church spires of Stamford word went round the town that the poll was closed and a result was imminent. The street was jammed with people outside the town hall, and Mary, Luke and Henry Milton had to fight to get into the chamber.

It was hot and smoky inside, and groups of rival supporters were shouting slogans and coming to blows. On the platform Lord Burghley was offering snuff to his nephew, and George was standing with his hands behind his back, his eyes cast down. Jeremiah Walsoken was whispering in Mr Wainwright's ear: Mr Walsoken, to a few whistles and catcalls, was studying his Bible.

At last the mayor, a red-faced and uncomfortable grocer in a horsehair wig, rose to his feet and flourished a sheet of paper.

'The voting – ' He cleared his throat again, to renewed boos. 'The voting for election as Members for the borough of Stamford has been as follows.' He squinted at the paper. 'Henry Cecil, two hundred and nineteen votes: George Lawrence Hardwick, two hundred and seventy-eight votes: Jeremiah Matthew Walsoken, ninety-eight votes. I hereby announce Mr Cecil and Mr Hardwick elected as Members to. . .'

The rest Mary did not hear; it was drowned in the uproar, and she was being embraced by Luke and Henry. Some rotten fruit was being shied at the platform. Lord Burghley was shaking George's hand. Mr Wainwright looked as if he wanted to get down from the platform, washing his hands of the whole business. Jeremiah Walsoken shrugged. His father had dropped his Bible, and his lips had gone white.

Over the shouting Mr Walsoken said: 'You see? They put their faith in some damned bankrupt adventurer because he has a soft spot for beggars and criminals and subversives. And because he has an ancient name. The old gentry looking after their own, no upstart enterprise allowed.' He was trembling.

Jeremiah wrinkled his sharp nose and smiled, seeming to assuage his own disappointment by goading his father's. 'Popularity, father,' he said. 'If folk don't take a liking to you that's an end to it. Not gentry, ordinary folk. Have to please them. Which you have singularly and constantly failed to do.'

A sweat of relief had broken out over George's forehead. Well, he had done something right. In fact it had been a rout. The pleasure was undeniable. He saw Henry Milton had elbowed his way to the edge of the platform, and was holding out his hand.

'Well, George,' he said smiling, 'so you will be coming to London with us after all!'

BOOK V
September 1780

ONE

I

Richard Brinsley Sheridan, celebrated author of *The Rivals* and *The School for Scandal*, proprietor of Drury Lane Theatre and now – just seven days ago – Member of Parliament for Stafford, kissed Julia's hand and said: 'Mrs Milton, the literary world will be as delighted as I am at the proof of your existence. Rumours have been flying around that you were nothing but a pseudonym, and I hear one fellow has claimed to be the author of your poems.'

'Good God,' Julia said. 'And I was for having them printed anonymously. Perhaps it's as well I didn't.'

'And what did that rascally bookseller pay you for them? Too little, I'll be bound. If there is to be a second edition you must haggle with him, now that you have the fame. And how does it feel, then, to be a literary lion?'

'I feel I should ask that of you, Mr Sheridan,' Julia said.

'Oh, I have done with all that now,' Sheridan said with a laugh. 'I've exchanged the lions for the bear pit – and a pretty penny it has cost me. A thousand pounds to be elected for Stafford, what with ale tickets and subscriptions to this and that. Just the sort of corruption I have vowed to fight in Parliament, but one must use the tools that come to hand, I suppose.'

'Does this mean you are going to give us no more comedies?' said Henry Milton. 'Surely you don't mean to stop writing now.'

'Ah, my dear Milton, as I told you, I wrote for gain, no more nor less,' Sheridan said with a smile. 'I have never sat through a play in my life, not even my own. Especially not my own. A career in Parliament is what I have set my heart on, though I think Eliza – ' he glanced at his wife – 'fears it is not for me. I shall leave the courting of the Muses to you and your wife. They were sulky mistresses to me at best.'

It was the Miltons' third day in London. Henry had been introduced to Sheridan on his last visit, and flatteringly an invitation to supper had come almost as soon as they had arrived. Sheridan, who was a year younger than Milton, was very much the man of the moment. His plays had galvanised the theatre in a way not seen for a hundred years, and his personal life was equally prominent. He had married the famous singer Eliza Linley, who was seated next to Julia on the sofa, a woman of exceptional beauty who had been painted by Gainsborough eight years previously. Sheridan had undergone a stormy courtship with her, including an elopement and a duel with swords in which he had been badly wounded. His *School for Scandal* had made him £15,000 and at Drury Lane Shakespeare revivals had been booed off the stage in an attempt to bring it back. Milton surmised, however, from this house at 22 Orchard Street, that Sheridan lived at a rate that matched his income. The drawing-room was in expensive taste, with Chippendale furniture and one of the new instruments called 'pianofortes', manufactured by Broadwood's, with a deep sustained tone that struck very strange, when Mrs Sheridan played upon it after supper, on the ears of the Miltons, accustomed to the scratchy sound of the harpsichord. Sheridan himself was a good-looking man, tall and slim with a fair complexion and a curved sensual mouth and humorous eyes and a faint Irish lilt to his voice. Milton had heard he had a wandering eye for the ladies, though he found it hard to believe looking at Mrs Eliza Sheridan, which he had been doing all evening.

'So Carey is to take you to Mrs Montagu's the day after tomorrow?' said Sheridan after supper. 'I think we shall be there ourselves. You'll see a fair sprinkling of the literati – those that she has not antagonised. She has a somewhat fearsome reputation. It is a rule of her house that there shall be no card-playing or music: conversation only. A rule that you might think would produce nothing but embarrassed silence as everyone tries to think of something to say, but it seems to work.'

'Shall we see Dr Johnson there?' said Julia.

'My wife has a great longing to see the great man in person,' Milton said.

'You may well do, though I hear that he and Mrs Montagu have quarrelled.' Sheridan suddenly leaned forward and gazed at Julia. 'Mrs Milton,' he said, 'have you never been painted?'

Julia laughed. 'It has never crossed my mind, Mr Sheridan. At Morholm, my family home, we have a clutch of old portraits, but the custom seems to have died out.'

'All the more reason,' said Sheridan, jumping up and eyeing her from all sides. 'You've heard of Tom Gainsborough? A good friend of mine. He painted Eliza and her sister. He's the man to do you justice. What do you think, Eliza?'

'He will shout at you if you don't keep still,' said Mrs Sheridan.

'Mr Sheridan,' said Julia laughing, 'even if I were to have my picture painted we could never afford Mr Gainsborough. You must remember who we are.'

'All right,' said Sheridan. 'But there are portrait painters aplenty here, some quite as good as him, I'm sure. Try it. What do you say?'

Julia, eyes shining, turned to her husband, as if unable to speak. Milton covered her hand with his own. 'Whoever should paint her,' he said, 'he'll never be able to do justice to her.'

They had done the right thing in coming to London. Julia had stepped out of the shadows into which her complex personality seemed to have withdrawn. Her dark face with its lurking intelligence was newly lit, and there was an answering glow inside Milton: a keen awareness of how dear she was to him. In the boat that they had taken on their way to Sheridan's from their lodging in Southwark they had found themselves kissing like new lovers. The boatman, after the first surprised stare, had gallantly averted his eyes. Then they could not stop laughing. It was a warm night, and wonderful. The lanterns strung from the striped poles at the landing-stages cast gold plumb-lines into the murky Thames. Towards London Bridge the sky was held in an extraordinary palisade of masts, from ships of every nation, wedged into the river hull to hull. They were happier than they had been since the first year of their marriage. Happier than they had ever been.

The next day they explored the sunless courts and alleys around St Paul's where the booksellers' quarter was, including their own Mr Isaac Carey. Here too collected the last dregs of literary endeavour: broken-down clerks who scrambled a living as screevers, writing false testimonials, turning out documents for professional beggars attesting that they had been injured in shipwrecks and military campaigns.

They talked of this to Mr Carey, in his chaotic shop in Cheapside. 'Aye, it's a constant matter of wonder to me how some wretches will make shift to keep body and soul together,' he said. 'D'you know there are actually fellows in this great city who are reduced to going about the streets collecting dog-shite in sacks. They sell it to the tanners, who use it, if you please, in their manufacturing. Think on that next time you buy a pair of shoes, Milton.'

Carey was an elderly scarecrow of a man, growing more sardonic and misanthropic every day. But he was genuinely delighted with Julia's verse. He promised a second edition as soon as it could be printed.

That night they went to Sadler's Wells, a combination of spa, gardens and theatre about which hung an attractive odour of the not-quite-respectable. Here rope-dancing was the speciality, and they saw the renowned Isabella Wilkinson perform the art: though she was past her best and rather fat, so that the tightrope almost touched the floor.

As they were strolling by the lake outside the playhouse, Julia tugged Henry's arm and said: 'On that bench there – isn't that Miss Walsoken?'

'So it is. I heard she was staying in London.'

Greetings were exchanged. Rebecca, who had met the Miltons only a few times at Morholm, seemed delighted to see them. Of the two young men with her, they had met her brother Peter before: the other was introduced as the Hon. Lovell Fitzroy.

Rebecca had naturally heard about the Stamford election in a letter from Bromswold: but she wanted to know when George and Mary would be coming down to London. 'Mother and father and Sarah and Jeremiah are coming next week. My fear is that they will meet the Hardwicks on the road,' she said ruefully. 'I suppose this election has only made feelings worse?'

'It – hasn't improved matters,' Milton said.

The Miltons rode back to the river in a hackney-carriage. They talked of Rebecca Walsoken, and what a beauty she had become: a beauty perhaps not in the way of the doll-like creatures in feathers and silk who paraded, statuesque and corsetted, in Hyde Park – there was something too vital and restive about her for that – but in a way that drew the eye. Certainly, they agreed, it seemed to be drawing the eye of the Hon. Lovell Fitzroy, who while they had been talking of news from home had not ceased to gaze at her.

The meeting with the Miltons affected Rebecca strangely: they were part of a world and a past life from which she had been completely cut off. Now it was as if she became abruptly aware of herself, Rebecca Walsoken, again – and also aware of the earnest, gentlemanly young man who was now conducting her and Peter so courteously to his carriage. She was sure that the Miltons were making surmises – surmises that the Hon. Lovell Fitzroy was paying court to her. Something she had not really faced herself yet.

Fitzroy was twenty-nine years old. Both his parents were dead, and he had a large fortune of his own and a house in Grosvenor Square. He sat in Parliament for the borough of Thetford, a seat procured for him by the Duke of Grafton, his uncle, with whom he was very close. The Duke was at present at his country place, Euston Hall in Norfolk, but he would be coming back, Fitzroy said, for the new Parliament, and he hoped to introduce them to his uncle. 'I am most anxious that he should meet you – both of you – that is, I shall – er – be so glad to introduce you,' Fitzroy said with his diffident smile.

His face wasn't particularly handsome – long and rather pale, with the broken eyebrow – but it was a good face, a face that wore its expressions the way he wore his clothes, simply and without affectation. His hand, when he assisted her into his carriage, was very gentle and cool on hers. Sometimes he gave it an extra pressure, not much, but enough. Oh yes, he made his feelings known, though so subtly – kindly was the word she would use – that no one could possibly be offended, least of all Rebecca.

The odd thing was, she felt so at ease with him: even while she knew where it was heading. The agony of that terrible moment when Luke had walked away – that hellish day in Northampton that even now she could hardly bear to think of – had made her sensual spirit, that quick of her being that was so responsive, draw back like a snail into its shell: everything that touched it was to be avoided, all such entanglements were to be shunned. But it wasn't like that with Lovell Fitzroy. He was, of course, much associated with the reforming Whigs of the Opposition, but his concerns went beyond those of a narrow party agitation: he had interests in the reform of criminal law, of the treatment of insanity, of the iniquity of the slave trade in the West Indies: and he talked to her about these things, not as a figure of consequence spouting because he liked the sound of his voice, and not in the talking-down way of a man parading his large concerns for the benefit of the butterfly brain of a pretty woman, but as an equal.

As they rode away from Sadler's Wells in the carriage Fitzroy talked to Peter about his studies at the Bar. That was another thing – he and Peter genuinely got on well together; it was not simply a pretext. Peter knew, all the same, that he was not the chief attraction in Lovell Fitzroy's visits to Portugal Street, but such was his good nature that he felt only mild amusement at his unspoken role of chaperon – and allowed it to remain unspoken.

A few days ago Rebecca had gone out from their lodgings to Covent Garden to buy some butter, after dusk. She should have sent the young girl who waited on them, but the knowledge that she was really one of their landlady's servants had combined with her own irresistible attraction to the place. Evening darkness seemed to come more quickly to the lattice of streets and alleys around the Piazza, as if it knew its natural home, and when she made her way back she found herself being stared at, and found herself alarmed. Prostitutes, from young fresh girls just begun, to old women, slit noses showing they had been convicted, disguising their age with poisonous lead face-paint, to girls of nine or ten and boys even younger, loomed out from every doorway. A couple of elderly rakes who hung around the theatres gave her speculative looks. Signs reading 'Milliners' and 'Chocolate-House' feebly concealed the real purpose of various ill-lit premises from which came a stale hogo of spirits and perfume.

The shudder of disgust as she passed through was soon succeeded by something darkly and yet undeniably pleasurable: there was an exciting whiff of danger here. And that, she realised, was what was so strikingly absent in Lovell Fitzroy.

But the passions, did they not end horribly in painful ugliness? Wasn't the calm and rationality of the agreeable company of a man like Fitzroy preferable? Why should one seek the flame? It was warm and brilliant, but it could burn you up. The loss of her love, the wreck of hope, had made her cautious, stepping warily round the borders of life.

Her father had rented a house in Golden Square, and she was to join the family there next week. He had made this plan expecting

Jeremiah to be elected at Stamford, but he was coming for a season in London anyhow, and seeking to renew his acquaintance with the banker, David Barclay, whom he had met in Norwich. She could not deny to herself, in spite of everything that had happened, that she needed the reconciliation with him. Perhaps the acquaintance of the Hon. Lovell Fitzroy was in a way her own conciliatory offering . . . But that was a path of thought she did not like to pursue too far.

2

Mrs Elizabeth Montagu was the first of the blue-stockings. A widow whose husband had left her a large fortune, she had turned her mansion in Portman Square into a salon for the literary world. That literary world held a not entirely kind opinion of her own writings – her *Essay On Shakespeare* published ten years ago excited some derisive comment – but it flocked to her receptions: and she had often given practical help to struggling authors.

Her drawing-rooms were already full when the Miltons arrived the next evening. Mr Carey, their guide in this new world, made the introduction to their hostess and then went in search of the drinks.

Mrs Montagu was a woman of sixty in a silver turban and a sack gown, very short-sighted, with a hooked nose and a harsh voice. She immediately led Julia to a sofa, leaving Milton alone.

'Mr Carey will have told you how entranced I was with your book,' Mrs Montagu said. 'Immediately I said, I must have her here: I will have her. And I *knew* you were no man hiding under a *nom de plume*, as some have maintained. That's men for you: once they genuinely *admired* – without condescension – they became convinced it must be by one of their own sex. As for me, I knew it could be none but a woman who could draw the workings of the heart so precisely, and yet so without sentiment.'

'Of which men are always accusing us, ma'am,' said Julia. 'When it is they, in truth, who are the sentimental ones.'

'And we must never let them know it,' Mrs Montagu said with a smile. She peered at Julia. 'But you are so young! How old are you, tell me.'

'I'm twenty-five, ma'am.'

'So young . . . And have you had no instruction? Well, that is no question. You are a woman, and have probably been taught to sew and play a little and make a good marriage. Eh?'

'I hate sewing and am tone-deaf, I'm afraid,' Julia said. 'And the man I married is not rich or of great family. I suppose that is not a good marriage in the eyes of the world, but . . .' She smiled, and her hostess smiled also.

'Never care for the eyes of the world, Mrs Milton.'

Sheridan was here, and called to Milton across the room. Milton joined him gratefully.

'Your wife has already been snapped up, eh, Milton?' Sheridan's handsome face was slightly flushed with drink. 'Mrs Montagu has a voracious appetite.'

'As long as she doesn't spit her out again,' said Milton, taking a glass of wine from a liveried footman.

Sheridan gestured around him, at the damasked walls, carved ceiling, scores of candles in silver sconces. 'Have you a fancy to live like this, h'm? The rewards of literature. Well, no: Mrs Montagu married money, of course. Ah, money. Boon and curse. One is constantly thinking of it: the trick, of course, is to have enough so that one does *not* think of it.'

'But they say Drury Lane is a goldmine,' Milton said. He had just discovered that his wine was champagne.

Sheridan grinned. 'So it is. But mines must be maintained. If I were to tell you the expenses of the theatre – rent, coal, taxes; tailors, mantua-makers, bill-stickers, musicians, porters, lamplighters: even haggling over whether the dancers may have the candle-ends as perquisites . . . By the by, I do not see Dr Johnson here tonight. He spends a lot of time now with the Thrales at Streatham: we will see if we can get you invited there. But you are sure to see him sooner or later.'

Even if the great Dr Johnson was not here, it seemed as if everyone else was. The gilded rooms were crowded and noisy with laughter and debate: here was Georgian society at its most elegant, witty and vigorous. Milton felt the champagne going to his head, and Sheridan was high-spiritedly drunk. He pointed out to Milton an extremely ugly and pallid man who he was surprised to learn was Edward Gibbon, already famous for the first volumes of *The Decline and Fall of the Roman Empire*, and less so for his talents in Parliament. 'He's been in for six years,' Sheridan said, 'and has never said a word . . .'

*

It was after two o'clock when the Miltons arrived back at their lodgings in Southwark, and the gong-farmer, the man who went round with a cart emptying the cesspits, was already clanking about his nocturnal business.

Their rooms were on the top floor of the house, and those below were occupied by a crusty retired merchant; so they crept up the narrow stairs on exaggerated tiptoe, holding their breath and smothering explosions of giggles. They were fired with talk and excitement and champagne. Milton had been content to hover on the periphery, drinking it all in, and Julia had been made a fuss of by Mrs Montagu for much of the evening.

After much fumbling effort Milton found flint and steel and lit a candle and made a fire in the hearth to boil a kettle. He fell into a chair, weak with laughing, and Julia sat in his lap.

'Oh, Lord, I'm beginning to remember the things I said tonight,' Julia said. 'I just rattled away out of nerves, and said the first thing that came into my head, and Mrs Montagu said Indeed, indeed . . . oh, dear . . .'

'You were a triumph,' Milton said, kissing her scented hair. 'You were yourself, and so could not fail to please.'

Her eyes shone out at him in the candlelight. 'Oh, Henry, how I love you . . . London is lucky for us, don't you think? Remember how it was here, years ago, the first time . . .'

He traced her full lips with his fingers. 'I remember, Julia. How can I forget the day my life began?'

She kissed him. 'I remember something else also,' she said softly. 'What?'

'That you didn't bolt the front door when we came in.'

Cursing and laughing, he got up again and removed his shoes and crept down the stairs and crossed the hall and locked the door. When he got back Julia was not in the parlour, and the kettle was off the hob.

Another candle was burning in the bedroom, and Julia was sitting in the old wicker chair in her Ghent lace bodice and underskirt. A sheen of light fell on her shoulders. She sat still and straight, her posture almost prim. Though it was not prim. She tapped a finger on her lips. 'Kiss me.'

He did so, bending over her, a hand on her neck, no longer laughing.

She sighed. 'And kiss me here.' She slid the fine lace down, her

387

arms white, her nipples dark and enlarged. He was trembling. 'And here . . . And here . . .'

They were slow, and loving, and absolutely alone together in the giant city of so many thousands: and the candle had burnt low, and the counterpane was twisted in a tortured rope across the bed when at last she crushed him to her, her fingers tracing frenzied patterns down his spine and haunches, as if a pen of fire were scribbling their mutual release across his nakedness. She held him cooling inside her, stroking his sweatsoaked brow, and all the complex web of feeling resolved into a love sharp and bright as a point of light.

They drew the counterpane across them and looked at the square of sky in the high leaded window.

'The stars are all out,' she said, her voice husky.

'So they are,' he said, 'every single one.'

3

In the 15th Parliament there were 558 Members, and in St Stephen's chapel, the chamber of the House of Commons, there was seating room on the greencloth-covered benches for only about 400. George Hardwick thought this rather typical of a place full of paradox.

The chamber was lit by a huge chandelier, above which was a grill where newspaper reporters could peer down at the proceedings. The Strangers' Gallery ran along both sides, a balcony where visitors could stand – when it was open. At the far end of the chamber was the Speaker's throne with the clerks' desks below it. A carpeted gangway divided the five rows of benches, Government and Opposition, on each side. Here on Wednesday 1st November George took his seat to hear the King's message on the opening of Parliament.

He took his seat on the government benches, though this was really an expedient. Last night he and Mary had dined at the Earl of Exeter's townhouse in Grosvenor Street, and the Earl had expressed his misgivings about the political situation. The stability of North's government had by no means been strengthened by the election, and the war news was not good. For the moment, he said, George should vote just as he pleased: he would let him know if there were any issues on which he absolutely required his support.

This was a generous dispensation, and Mary – who was in the Strangers' Gallery – saw that it soothed George's chafing conscience.

His low self-esteem that had dated from his dragging Morholm into debt had threatened to become worse at the idea of being bailed out by Lord Burghley, of becoming the tame toady of an influential peer. But it was all right, so far.

They had made the long coach journey to London – she, George, and little Charles Joseph, now three years old, with Bridget the maid – last week. It was the first time they had been away from Morholm for some time, and in the beginning they were both chiefly full of worries – largely unfounded – about the estate. They planned only to stay until the new year: with Lord Burghley's reprieve, they were solvent again and out of Mr Walsoken's power: Grandmother Peach would be quite comfortable in the care of the Binnismoors: Mr Matthews the steward was quite capable of seeing to day-to-day affairs, and cousin Luke had promised to go over to Morholm regularly, and deal with any problems the villagers brought: and Charles Joseph seemed to enjoy every minute of the rattling journey. And they had taken pleasant lodgings in Buckingham Street off the Strand, where George had stayed before: and Aunt Catherine was more than delighted to look after Charles Joseph whenever they wanted. So, they had continually told each other to stop worrying as the coach had lurched through the straggling villages north of the city – Barnet, Finchley, Highgate – with their lime-kilns and market-gardens: and then excitement had taken over. It was a heady prospect for them; after so long in pinched and troubled circumstances, to be transported to a life of new glitter and prestige.

Below her, in the House, was a sea of hats – three-cornered, round, bicornes – and powdered heads. Some Members lolled, yawning, tapping riding-crops, chewing apples: a few were clearly asleep. She was unable to hear much of the King's address from the throne, delivered in a thick monotone: she caught something about military success in Georgia and Carolina, and about the perfidy of France and Spain. George III himself, with his florid face, reminded her of a gentleman farmer, dressed in incongruous robes.

As the debate turned into a stream of invective Mary's thoughts strayed to Charles Joseph, whom they had left with Aunt Catherine in Crutched Friars that morning. Already resembling his father, as Aunt Catherine had pointed out. Captain Alex Finlayson had been there. He had come in from the square of back-garden, where he had gone to smoke a pipe. He looked very big in his red coat and top-boots against the dark fumed beams of the old house. He had stopped dead on seeing Mary.

'Why, Captain Finlayson, I'm glad to see you again,' George had said, extending a hand. The young officer had stared for a moment before recovering himself, shaking George's hand heartily, Mary's briefly. 'You have not been packed off to America again, then, sir?' George said.

'No, no, Lord be praised, Alex is still at Coxheath,' Aunt Catherine fluttered, anxious as always to monopolise the giving of information. 'I had quite forgot to tell you – one thing drives out another – we have him with us for a short furlough – I wish he were with us all the time – I have never been easy in my mind since those dreadful riots in June . . .'

'Is – is your wound quite recovered, Captain Finlayson?' Mary said, forcing herself to speak.

He smiled warmly and flexed his fingers. 'Och, yes, I thank you, Mrs Hardwick. Once the sairgeons left off prodding it and blistering it it made better progress. I'm trusted with a gun again now without fear of shooting my colonel by accident.'

'Will you be shooting the French at Maidstone?' George asked. 'There were all kinds of rumours of invasion a while since. Or perhaps that's not a fair question.'

'Not at all, Mr Hardwick. There are always more rumours in the army than anywhere. For my part I think there was never any real danger. I expect to join my regiment in Ireland soon.'

'Such an unsettled life!' Aunt Catherine sighed. 'Sent from pillar to post, and little prospect of anything at the end. I continually ask Hector if some position could not be found for Alex in the City – anything I think would be better than such a life of danger and restlessness – '

'Bless ye, ma'am,' Captain Finlayson said, touching her arm, 'but I doubt I could settle for a sedentary life now, even if something were to come up. I assure you I am quite happy.' He glanced at Mary and took a deep breath. 'Very happy.'

When they left the Finlaysons' the Captain, having clapped his busby on Charles Joseph's head, was giving the delighted little boy a ride on his broad back. 'He's a fine young man,' George said. Mary had nodded.

... Mary craned over the balcony to look for George's dark head on the government benches. She suddenly felt a great need to be close to him. George, her only love ... there had never been, could never be anyone but George. She loved him and she admired and believed in him: it had never ceased to be so, even as they drifted apart during the trials of the last year or so. Now that lost ground must be made up again; the opportunity must not be lost. They must, she felt with an obscure urgency, be together as much as possible, she must keep him close to her, never allow the wedge to be driven in between them.

... It was time for the division of the House. George, after a second's hesitation, voted with the government side: he had been more sympathetic to the Opposition arguments, but he felt he owed at least this one gesture to Lord Burghley. In the resultant crush to get out of the chamber he found his hat knocked from his head. A gentleman next to him stooped to retrieve it and handed it to him. 'No damage done, I think,' he said. 'You must be a new Member.'

'Thank you,' George said. 'Does it show so much?'

The man laughed. 'Only insofar as you have not learned bad manners. One must use one's elbows here ... Besides, one gets to know the faces: memorise them, don't you know. Whiles away the boredom of the speeches.' There was a bottleneck at the chamber door, and they were obliged to wait a moment. The stranger extended his hand. 'Ranulph Powys. Member for Shrewsbury, for my sins.'

'George Hardwick. Stamford, for mine.'

'With the government?'

George hesitated. 'Independent, by inclination. As far as one can be with a patron, you understand.'

'Oh, of course. I'm in Lord Spencer's pocket myself. Farmer George was mortal tedious today, wasn't he? They say Prinny is breaking the old fellow's heart with his extravagance.'

They emerged at last into Palace Yard. 'Prinny?' George said.

'Prince of Wales, don't you know. See him now and then at Brooks'. Lays down a thousand guineas in one night and thinks nothing of it. Of course, Fox is the worst. He'll lay a bet on two raindrops running down the window. Speaking of which.' A cold drizzle was falling. Some gentlemen were putting up umbrellas, a thing George had never seen before: they had always been thought effeminate. Mr Ranulph Powys, George saw now, was a big man touching forty, with a fleshy tolerant sensualist's face, fashionably dressed with stiff curled hair and immaculate starched ruffles. 'Mr Hardwick, have you a carriage waiting?' he said.

'No,' said George, looking around. 'I'm seeking my wife. She was in the gallery.'

'She will be held up by the stampeding reporters,' Powys said. 'Sir, will you allow me to carry yourself and your wife home in my own carriage? I think the rain has a fancy to stay. You are more than welcome.'

This was kind. 'I shall not refuse, sir, thank you. Buckingham Street is our lodging.'

'You reside in the country, I take it?'

George smiled. 'Does that show also? Yes, my estate is just north of Peterborough. You do not, I take it, live at Shrewsbury.'

Ranulph Powys burst into a shout of laughter. 'No, indeed. I have been there only twice in my life – when it was necessary to tell the voters how much I loved them, and beg them to vote for me again – and both times I could hardly wait to get out of the place. I have a horror of the country. Whenever I have to drive through it I pull down the blinds of the carriage.'

'Well, I cannot afford such refined sensibility, as the country is my means of support,' said George grimly.

'Oh, I mean no disparagement, sir,' Powys said. 'The landed interest is the foundation of our prosperity. Please forgive me. I am not the worst. I know a man who has never been beyond Marylebone, and who feigns nausea if ever fresh vegetables are brought to the table.'

George laughed. 'I wonder if – Ah, here she comes – '

George was pleasantly surprised as Mary, ignoring his companion, ran into his arms and covered him with kisses.

'Well, daughter.' Mr Walsoken's smile was appraising and possessive, if not fond. 'We have had our troubles – tempests even. We have – both been sorely tried. It is not for us to enquire into the motives of divine Providence . . . So we must be simply thankful – in short, our lives are peaceable again, and – and great prospects are ahead of us, I think. Great prospects.'

His hesitancy was a measure of the emotion that he had allowed, as he so seldom did, to surface. Rebecca smiled, and was filled with

392

unease. Not only was there reconciliation, but she was for the moment the favoured child.

It was no coincidence that Lovell Fitzroy had called today and been invited to stay for dinner.

Her father was, as her mother admiringly expressed it, in full fig. He had a new gold-laced suit, very different from the old parsonical black, and a frizzed bag-wig of real hair: and this townhouse that he had rented for the family in Golden Square was of a sort that clearly did not come cheap. He was going to enjoy his first London season in style. Now he sat back in his easy chair and, unusually for him, drank a second glass of brandy. 'Yes,' he said. 'An eminently respectable young gentleman, Mr Fitzroy. Most complaisant and obliging of him, indeed, to offer us an introduction to his uncle the Duke.'

'Doesn't appear to have any of his uncle's habits, more's the pity,' put in Jeremiah, who was examining himself in the pier-glass prior to setting out on the nocturnal jaunts about which his father never enquired. 'I remember when he was Prime Minister fellows referred to him as the Racing Duke out of his fondness for Newmarket. Or the Whoring Duke – his other favourite pursuit.'

Mr Walsoken pulled down his brows. 'The private lives of the great are always subject to calumny,' he said, with a wave of his hand.

Besides, a Duke is a Duke, he might have added, Rebecca thought.

Lovell Fitzroy had been a success at dinner, adapting himself to her father's severity rather than being nonplussed by it as many people were. She could not deny that she wanted her father to receive a good impression – that somehow his opinion still mattered.

Fitzroy had talked of his interest in prison reform, and his work with the Society for the Relief of Persons Imprisoned for Small Sums. 'There are something like three thousand men imprisoned for debt,' he said, 'and most commonly for trifling sums. They languish in the Marshalsea and the Fleet, crammed in the most squalid conditions, and often their children are reared up there, side by side with felons. One may imagine the corruption that results.'

Rebecca had watched her father's face slowly puckering into a frown. 'But sir,' he said heavily, 'if a man cannot pay his debts, surely it is right and proper that he should be punished.'

Firzroy glanced at him, and at Rebecca. 'True enough, sir . . .

But where the sums are small, it is a most pernicious system that places a man in a confinement, where it is impossible that he should ever be able to extricate himself from the debt. The shoemaker, the sailor, the shopman who has run into a few pounds – a few shillings – of debt may find himself in prison for years: unable even to support himself, let alone pay off his debt; whilst predatory bailiffs and attorneys, the procedures of litigation and arrest, all consume more than the worth of the debt. The system is in fact a sad depletion of the country's wealth. The Society acts by discharging these unfortunates, so that they can return to their trades and manufactures.'

It was a good answer: calculated to convince Mr Walsoken, by appealing more to economy than compassion. Rebecca resisted the urge to applaud. But it was perhaps a measure of her feelings for Lovell Fitzroy that she observed the way he pleased her father with an objective interest rather than hopeful anxiety.

But now there was another factor, which had thrown her feelings into dark confusion.

A few days ago her father had gone into the City on business, and she had taken the opportunity to slip out and call on George and Mary Hardwick, whose address she had learned from the Miltons.

They were both in; but it was an uneasy meeting at first. Too much bitter feeling had grown up between the families. Then Charles Joseph had trotted into the room, recognised her at once, and run to show her a new chap-book he had got, *The History of Goody Two Shoes*, bound in horn covers with woodcuts on each page.

The ice had been broken. Talk flowed, whilst she took Charles Joseph on her knee and rubbed his curly head.

'And what's the news from Aysthorpe, Mary? Deborah, and her little boy? And Mrs Peach? I do miss it – I miss the sky – the sky here is just a little smear of smoke above the chimneys.'

'Mrs Peach is well, and Deborah Gedney, and her little boy is growing fast.'

'And old Mr Horace, and Luke?' There, it was out.

'Uncle Horace is very frail, and seldom stirs from the house,' George said. 'Cousin Luke is prospering, a shipowner now, very much the coming man. He's very thick with that Du Quesne woman, Kitty I think is her name – '

A warning glance passed from Mary to George, just too late.

Rebecca left soon afterwards. At the foot of the steps, as she waited for a chair, Mary said hesitantly: 'We've never properly thanked you for – well, what happened at the trial – John Newman I know was very anxious to thank you – '

'Oh, that.' Rebecca smiled painfully. 'Well, that's – that's all past now. Goodbye.' She turned and hurried across the street.

The day after Lovell Fitzroy came to dinner, Mr Walsoken proposed taking his wife and daughters to be fitted for new gowns at the elegant *salon* shops along the Strand and Cheapside. He was noticeably more insistent, in the gilded drawing-rooms where dazzling silks and satins were flourished for their inspection across plush benches, that the very best should be reserved for Rebecca. But she went along with everything he said.

TWO

I

It was late evening on the sixth of November, and Luke was drinking in the taproom of the Duke's Head Hotel at King's Lynn and staring with angry dismay into the face of his own personality.

He was tired, having been active since dawn, but his brain was revolving like a squirrel in a cage, and the drink did not seem to be stilling it. Someone was singing an endless ballad to an accordion, and the room was full of smoke.

He had lost a contract today. Not a large or valuable one. It was the manner of his doing so that was troubling him. The gentleman was a small dealer in wool from North Norfolk, looking into prospects of shipment from Lynn. They had met at the Corn Exchange and then Luke had taken him to the wharf near the Customs House to see the *Minerva*, which had just returned from London with a mixed cargo.

The gentleman was parsimonious, or did not have much money to spare, or both, and kept haggling over prices. Luke had found himself growing more and more irritated. Then, as they were talking in the warehouse, Luke's apprentice overseer had come to him with some footling question about where to store some fragile goods.

'Don't bother me, damn it,' he had said. 'Put 'em in the loft for now.'

'But, sur,' the youth said in a whining voice, 'yew said that was damp and we warn't to use it – '

'Don't tell me what I said!' Luke had stormed, and given him a heavy box across the ears.

The gentleman looked at him in some surprise. 'That seems a little hard, sir,' he said. 'Surely – '

'And don't you tell me how to run my business,' Luke snapped.

The gentleman stared a moment, then put on his hat. 'I wouldn't presume, sir,' he said. 'As for my own business, I shall take it elsewhere.'

'Go, then, and good luck to you,' Luke said, turning away.

. . . It was no way to run a firm, that was for sure. But it wasn't just that. It was the way he had become an alarming stranger to himself. The apprentice had been keeping out of his way all day, glancing at him with fear and resentment. He wasn't a bad boy at all. Probably little different from what Luke had been ten years ago.

He had allowed himself no inward reflection for a long time. (All that soul-searching nonsense doesn't get you anywhere – thus went the hackneyed promptings of a dour creed that was beginning to strike sour and flat on his inner ear.) But now the prickly questions – How did I get to this pass? Have I chosen to be this man that I find myself to be? – were forming themselves in his mind, and were running riot with their new freedom.

But this business that he had taken over from his father – taken over and expanded – it was what he had worked wholeheartedly at, investing in it not only money but selfhood. The wharfs and warehouses, the *Minerva*, the share in the iron foundry, the shops, the position on the Stamford corporation, the hefty balance at Wainwright's Bank that was ostensibly in Horace's name but effectually made his own name as good financially as any in the five fenland counties. It was a solid base, a very solid base, from which he could become a far greater force than his father. But as a base for a human life – as the foundation of a man, with all of a man's failings and strengths, all the flesh and feeling that marked him as human . . . ?

Yet if it was not enough, what then? There was no possibility of returning to the old life, a rough fenman eking out a living and not thinking from one day to the next. That would be a mockery, even supposing he should want it.

He ordered more brandy, and while he drank it thought of Kitty Du Quesne, and could not deny to himself her part in this new mood that came over him. For while he accepted her as his mistress and maintained an everyday indifference about this which suited her, she nagged at his mind in a way that seemed to crystallise his doubts about his life.

Lately he had begun to notice, or be aware of, or perhaps imagine, her perfume clinging about him. It was a sweet perfume, but it seemed to linger like – like onions, was all he could compare it with. Her touch was arousing, but mechanically so; practised, like the bored sure hands of the eel-skinners in the market. That they had nothing much to say to each other should have been a matter of course, but it disturbed him; and he should not have been surprised, when he had got a copy of Mrs Julia Milton's verse recently and spoken to her about it, that Kitty had burst into a peal of good-humoured derisive laughter.

In bed she took him, when the mood was on her, to a pitch of excited exhaustion, which seemed to satisfy neither of them. As dawn came they would still be awake, flung across her heated bed, their flesh gluey and chafed, the morning light gliding across their naked bodies like the jaded glance of loveless familiarity.

He was a man seeking the fulfilment of his desires (but that was a noble phrase – seeking to expend them rather, and have done with them) and she was an intelligent adventuress seeking, as was her only possible course besides outright prostitution or a life of grinding labour in the fields or in the seamstress' cellar, to gain a fortune out of such desires. They despised each other, for the role each was playing.

His was the more despicable role, for he had nothing to lose.

Last week, when Kitty had wanted some money to buy a pet monkey – a fashionable accessory – she had said so and smartly tapped his coat pocket. In a shard of bad temper – such as he had suffered today – he had snapped out 'No!'

They had been at Horace's house: his father was in bed. With a smile, her head on one side, Kitty had tapped his crotch just as she had his pocket. 'This says yes,' she said.

She had got her monkey, and they had despised each other the more.

Luke finished his brandy and left the Duke's Head. He paused in the cobbled market place, sniffing the cold air, disinclined to go back to the spartan rooms he rented in Old Sunway. He began to walk down King Street, past the chequered medieval merchants' houses with their warehouses reaching down to the river. The tide was in and was lapping softly at the quayside. A couple of dogs rooted amongst the coils of rope and rotten fish. Lanterns winked, swaying, from the decks of several ships: colliers, his own *Minerva*, a big levanter drawing a lot of water.

There was a strong streak of romance and honest sentiment in

Luke. It was a part of himself he had tried to strangle, but it survived, and now it was afflicting him doubly.

The recognition of his loneliness first made him feel better, then worse. There was noise and laughter coming from a little beer-shop down King Staithe Lane. He was drawn by the promise of drink, and human company.

It was hot and stinking in the one big room with the deal benches and brass-bound barrels piled to the ceiling. The place was full of merchant sailors and fishermen and stevedores with a few lank-haired doxies of the town. They were yelling jokes and snatches of song and calling for more beer: two had begun a half-hearted drunken fight. There was a reek of fish-oil from the lamps hanging on chains from the beams.

Luke drank more brandy on a bench in the corner and looked about him sourly. The sweepings of the port. Such a filthy, empty-headed, ridiculous rabble . . .

There was a sudden commotion at the door. A blast of cold air. A scream from one of the girls. Men began to scramble over tables and benches, spilling drinks everywhere. Luke stood up to see.

A group of six men in the doorway. Two uniformed officers. Four tars, with cudgels, one with a musket. Press Gang.

Luke was struggling, scrambling with the rest. An officer was shouting something in the King's name. One small window: a tar ran to block it. Yells and crashes of glass. A door behind the bar. Luke vaulted the bar, slithering on spilt gin. Cramming with three other men into a narrow passage. A hand grasped his sleeve, held. Pure panic. He wrenched, turned, struck out with clenched fist, plunged down the passage.

The door at the end of it was barred. Cellar steps, barrels. A small window on to the yard to the right. A fisherman was smashing it with his bare hands, then diving through. Slivers of glass everywhere. Uproar behind them. At the mouth of the passage a tar had hold of a youth by his shirt and the youth was trying to wriggle out of it.

The second man was through. Then the third. Luke hoisted himself up on the sill. His coat snagged on a jagged piece of glass. A shout behind him: 'Stop in the King's name!' Cool air was on his face as he tugged. Oh, God, freedom . . . Then the fisherman who had got out before him was grabbing his arms and pulling him through. 'Come on, matey. Thass it.'

He fell in a heap on the cobbles outside, gulping delicious air. The fisherman lifted him to his feet. 'Better run a bit, boy, lest they come arter us.'

They ran clattering through the mazy alleys of the quayside, but were not pursued. At last Luke stopped, out of breath, and leaned in a doorway. 'God, I thought I'd be taken,' he gasped. 'Thank you for helping me . . . a thousand thanks.'

The man grinned in the dark. 'You have to move sharpish, else they'll have you,' he said. 'Seen 'em afore.' He was a seamed, craggy man with a fishy whiff. One of the stupid rabble . . . 'Y'all right now?' he went on. 'What a night! Reckon I'll get home. You better look to them cuts, boy.'

Luke's coat was torn and his hands were bleeding, but he was laughing with relief when at last he closed the door of his lodgings. What an escape . . . It was an unpopular war that was being fought, and the Press Gangs were seeking more and more catches in the trading ports. He was young and strong and it was doubtful if his good clothes would have saved him.

And for a moment his loneliness had been scourged away. He had fought and scrambled and run with the rest, he was part of them. He lay down on his bed and laughed again.

He spent the next morning at the warehouse, tipping the apprentice a bonus before he left, and arrived back at Stamford in mid-afternoon. Fog had settled in the basin of the town and there were cold droplets on his hair as he opened the front door in St George's Square.

Forrest, the footman, was standing in the hall, staring. 'Oh, sir, thank heaven you're back. We didn't know when to expect you – '

'What is it? What's the matter?'

And immediately Luke knew.

Forrest had been with Horace most of his life. There were tears in his eyes as he explained.

'The master went into the study this morning, sir . . . he seemed quite well, at least, no worse, you understand . . . He didn't ring for anything, and eventually I went in to see him, and he was stretched on the floor – and I couldn't rouse him . . . Dr Marcus wasn't home, so we sent for Dr Kesteven, but it was no good . . . no good. He never spoke . . . just gone.'

They had lain Horace on the couch in the back parlour. Luke

went to see him. He looked small and weightless. He looked as if he had left the world quiescently, having seen what he wanted to see. Luke held his father's cold hand for a while. He wished he could have spoken to him.

I'm nothing now, he thought with a terrible calm lucidity. He made me what I am, lifted me up, made me feel I belonged. Now I'm less than nothing. I can't carry on alone.

Dr Kesteven called again before evening, and explained in a few stiff words that Horace had suffered a strong heart seizure, beyond the power of medical help. He was saddened at the death of the old man who had helped him get established, but he was a little surprised to see Luke so obviously desolated. But there was a profound contrast between these two young men. In the physician was a vein of genuine hardness, partly as a result of his profession, but also of his own temperament. The knock that he himself had received over Rebecca Walsoken had never touched this inner grain. He had gone on, expanding his practice further, experimenting, gaining experience, and would continue to do so.

As for Luke, he felt helpless as a baby. He had to be prompted by the servants to start making the funeral and legal arrangements, to write letters, to continue living himself.

Kitty came to see him that night. Her rattling cheerfulness, meant as consolation in her own way, was the last thing he wanted. But she stayed, and his loneliness was such that he could not prevent her.

2

The news of Horace's death reached his relatives in London a few days later, and shortly afterwards came details of the will.

Horace had been a rich man. The bulk of the estate, his thriving business concerns, went of course to Luke: but there were legacies for the Morholm family and for Julia. Despite the circumstances of its coming, it could not be otherwise than welcome for the Hardwicks. It was so strange for George and Mary to find themselves actually with spare money on their hands that they did not know quite what to do with it. One morning, however, George slipped out early, whilst Mary was still asleep, and while she was sitting over the late breakfast that was such an unaccustomed luxury in London

– they rose at dawn at Morholm – a messenger brought a small parcel to the door.

She unwrapped it, giving the coloured paper to Charles Joseph, and stared into the little box. She swallowed. 'Oh . . .'

The necklace was of emerald and jade, set in a filigree of gold on a gold chain. There was note in the box. *This, I think, is long overdue. I hope it will match your eyes, though it could never compare with them. All my love. G.*

She took the necklace into their bedroom, where there was a mirror, and held it against her throat. 'Oh,' she said again.

The maid Bridget came in. 'Is there anything wrong, ma'am?'

Mary's eyes were shining in the mirror. 'No, Bridget,' she said. 'There's nothing wrong.'

She was wearing this on Saturday the eighteenth, when she and George and the Miltons rode out early to visit the village spa of Hampstead.

'I wonder how Cousin Luke is managing,' Julia said.

'He and his father became very close, I think,' George said. 'Well . . . at least Horace had his son with him for a couple of years. It meant a lot to him. Perhaps Luke may think to marry and settle down properly now.'

'I don't think so, somehow,' said Mary quietly.

They dined at a tavern overlooking the bowling-greens, and a courtyard where there was an Italian *fantoccini* show, with marionettes almost life-size. London was a smoky mass to the south.

'How do you get on in that talking-shop at Westminster, George?' Milton asked. 'Have you made your mark as an orator yet?'

George grimaced. 'I have spoken once. In support of Mr Jonas Hanway's work for climbing-boys and other apprentices. They can be indentured to cruel masters with less rights than the West Indian slaves. The slaves are a much more interesting subject, of course, and I was heard with indifference, if I was heard at all, and soon sat down. Even the radicals who collect round Fox seem to care little about such things. The idea of talking about chimney-sweeps in Parliament seems to occasion amusement. By the by,' he went on, 'please thank your friend Sheridan for helping to secure me election to Brooks'. I haven't seen him in the House of late. He and my friend Powys have arranged it for me.'

'What would Lord Burghley say to you entering the Whig stronghold?' Milton said.

George laughed. 'He keeps me on a long leash.'

'Will you not have supper with us tonight?' Milton said. 'We can send out for some excellent steaks and porter from a cook-house down the street.'

'Alas, I'm engaged to go to Brooks' tonight with Ranulph Powys,' said George. 'But what about you, love? Charles Joseph will be quite all right with Bridget for a while.'

'I'd be glad to,' Mary said after a second.

Only Julia, always observant of the feelings of others, noticed that Mary would have been more glad if George had stayed with her.

3

George, as a very young man, had briefly been an habitué of at least the fringes of the London gambling world, and had got no joy of it: and he had sought election to Brooks' chiefly out of enjoyment of his new status. When he went along with Mr Ranulph Powys that night it was not with the intention of risking his new comparative affluence on the turn of a card. Powys had been kind to him in helping him settle in at Westminster, and he enjoyed the older man's company.

The club, in St James' Street, was the second home of many radical Whigs – the friends of liberty – but it was defiantly aristocratic. The gaming-rooms and supper-rooms were superbly furnished and lit like noonday. The finest wines were brought by slippered footmen to the green baize tables where piles of gold guineas were shunted and thrown like children's counters.

'H'm, not such a turn-out tonight as I'd hoped,' Powys said. 'Fox will be here later, of course.'

George was staring at the piles of guineas. 'Forgive me,' he said rousing himself, 'I was just thinking of those underfed faces we saw staring in the street outside.'

'Oh, I quite see what you mean,' Powys said. 'But it keeps the money in circulation, you know, which must be all to the good. Better than locking it up in vaults. Now, I see Townshend over there, so we shall be able to have a rubber or two of whist, I think.'

'Well, I hadn't intended to play – '

Powys smiled at him and handed him a glass of wine. 'You hadn't intended to play because you are a sensible fellow, and didn't fancy these high stakes – but whist is played in a small way: and because you are a very decent fellow, and feel that as a Member you should be diligent and worthy and so on – but you have already shown yourself very diligent, and have earned the right to play a little: and because you have a lovely and charming wife, and that if you spend your time gaming the night away you don't deserve her – but she is so lovely you don't deserve her anyway. So. Those are my arguments. Now let us play.'

They were partners at whist for an hour, and when the game broke up they had won fifty guineas between them. It was nearly eleven, and Brooks' was filling up.

'There, that wasn't so painful, was it?' Powys said.

'I confess I never expected to be going home with a profit in my pockets,' George said.

'Dear Hardwick, who said anything about home? Well, you just did, I know. But really you can't. Fox is here now, and is setting up his faro bank. Besides, if you go home to your wife *now*, at this in-between sort of hour, it will merely appear to her that you got bored and couldn't think of anything better to do.'

George raised an eyebrow. 'Rather than that I couldn't wait to be back with her?'

'My dear, you're a married man. Married men have more, not less freedom. Sweethearts, you see, have to be forever ramming their devotion down each other's throats, for they have no other ties. I mean, you wouldn't let your dog roam in the open sheep pasture, but he may sniff where he likes in the garden, for the gate is locked. You take life too serious, Hardwick.'

'I have but just recently got out of debt,' said George.

'And you have found an extra relish in being solvent again, is that not so? Contrast, dear man, contrast is the essence of relish. We wouldn't appreciate the sun if it shone brightly twenty-four hours a day all year round. We wouldn't appreciate pretty women if they were always accommodating . . . oh, I don't know, though.'

'Well, I would like to stand in the sun a little while longer,' said George laughing, 'but lead on, show me this faro game. I have never played it.'

'Easiest game in the world,' Powys said as they went to a large table in the corner of the subscription room. 'Pure chance. You stake your money on one card on the table. The banker, that's Fox of course, deals cards into two piles, a winning pile and a losing pile, and you wait for your card to come up. Win or lose . . .'

George, with perfect beginners' luck, won, and by midnight he was the richer by seventy guineas. Powys, who had lost, was mockingly indignant when George proposed going home.

'Aye, aye, the man who has won is all ready to slip away,' Powys said. 'His penniless companion is left to beguile the night away as best he can. Come, Hardwick, you're not deserting me now?'

This was said in good-humour: good-humour was a mark of everything the big genial man said, even in his cynicism: he seemed to underscore his whole life with self-mockery. It was doubly attractive for George after the troubled austerity that had recently been his lot. He was in high spirits, and not really ready to go home yet.

It was then he felt a tap on his shoulder. Jeremiah Walsoken was there, with a couple of curled and powdered cronies in tow.

'Hardwick, as I'm alive!' The young man's wolfish handsome face was flushed with liquor. 'So this is how our guardians of liberty beguile the time.'

George cautiously took the unsteady hand that Jeremiah offered, and introduced his companion. 'Jeremiah. I'd heard you were in town.'

'Aye, I'd had enough of that damned country barn, and fortunately so had father. I suppose Becky's been to see you? Yes, she would. So how do you get on at Westminster? Has North offered you a portfolio yet? Under-Secretary for Bankruptcy? No, no, no, ignore that, sorry. We two needn't be at daggers drawn like you and father are. Come, tell me what it's like.' Jeremiah drew him away from the faro table.

'There's a lot of talk, and I add little to it,' said George.

'Dreary place,' Jeremiah said, gesturing to a waiter. 'To speak truth, Hardwick, I'm glad you beat me to it. Don't think I would have got on there at all. Father was mad as fire, of course, but then you're pretty well *persona non grata* with him anyway.'

'How is Mr Walsoken?'

Jeremiah grinned. 'How I love that English country-gentleman courtesy! You know as well as I that you heartily wish my father at the bottom of the river.'

George smiled in spite of himself.

'And so do I sometimes, to speak truth again,' Jeremiah said. He brought his glass on a weaving path to his lips. 'He could buy fellows like *you* ten times over, of course, but I think he'll never be a gentleman. Sometimes I'm ashamed to be seen with him. The richer and more fashionable he gets, the more he resembles a grocer.' He belched.

'Well, how are the rest of your family then? I may ask that without hypocrisy.'

'Sarah is much as ever, her virginity unassailable, not that anyone wants to assail it. Peter studies in a quite horrifying way. Paul comes to us from Charterhouse once in a while, and dresses in silks and thinks himself a man and has a voice that honks up and down like a donkey's. Mother is enjoying herself swelling the coffers of every quack in town who claims to cure her ailments. As for Becky . . .' He drank deeply, and gestured to the waiter again.

'Well?' George said impatiently.

'Engaged,' Jeremiah said. 'Who'd have thought it? All quite sudden. Engaged to be married. Name of Lovell Fitzroy. Nephew of the Duke of Grafton, if you please. Father's rubbing his little grocer's hands, as you may imagine. He's seeing coronets and garters before his eyes.'

'The name's familiar,' George said.

'Member for Thetford,' put in Powys. 'I've met him at Lord Rockingham's. Whig, reforming type, quite young.'

'That's him,' Jeremiah said. 'Not my sort of fellow at all, a bit starchy. But right out of the top drawer, of course. Connections *and* money. Odd, I wouldn't have thought he was Becky's sort of fellow either, really: thought she had warm blood in her veins. Still, that's women. Like to preserve their mysteries. Thinks it makes 'em interesting. Just like when they say no when they mean yes. But how is it you're carousing so late, Hardwick? Don't tell me you've been awhoring with that pretty wife of yours at home.'

'I'm going home soon,' said George absently. He was still thinking of Rebecca. 'When is she to be married?'

Jeremiah yawned and belched and groaned all in one. 'Eh? Oh, don't know. It was all sudden, you see. I don't mean it's a shotgun wedding, of course. He's not that sort of fellow . . . So you've been gaming? I like to play myself. We must throw a dice together sometime. Eh? Let me get a little revenge for you denying me a seat in the House.'

'If you like,' said George. He was still thinking of Rebecca. The news was unexpected.

4

The news had a certain quality of the unexpected for Rebecca herself.

She had none of her father's veneration for titles, but all the same she had trembled a little at the prospect of meeting Lovell Fitzroy's uncle, Augustus Henry Fitzroy, the 3rd Duke of Grafton.

The Duke's star had waned somewhat since the heady years of '67–'70, when he had held the office of Prime Minister: but he was still one of the handful of leading Whigs and a power in the land. His passion for horseracing and women was said to be fading in favour of religion. He owned two country houses, 30,000 acres of land, and this townhouse in St James, where the whole Walsoken family had been invited to dinner to celebrate her engagement.

It was not such an ordeal after all. The Duke was a smallish, softly-spoken immaculate man of forty-five. He looked into her face, pressed her hand experimentally rather as a doctor would, and seemed to indicate that he was satisfied. He was a renowned judge of horseflesh, and she felt herself examined and approved in rather the same way.

There were several of the Duke's family at dinner also, so the table was well filled and conversation general and there was no pressure on her to shine. She was glad of the relief. The last couple of weeks had spun past her, scattered and fragmentary like the autumn leaves that whirled in frantic clouds across the fens, and as difficult to catch and hold.

Lovell smiled across at her, a reassuring smile that seemed to say that all this, the glittering silver, the scores of candles, the liveried footmen, the polite talk, did not really matter. It was a look both fond and respectful, intimate and gentlemanly. His was often a reassuring role. He was the sort of man you could rely on in moments of crisis: indeed, the sort of man whose very presence seemed to guarantee against such a thing as a crisis.

Her father was listening earnestly to the Duchess – the Duke's second wife – who was on his left. Rebecca had never been so much in his favour. She had lifted him with one swoop to the tables and the confidence of the great.

It was a good match. Her settlement from her father would not be small, and Lovell had a large personal fortune. They would live in style in London and at a lodge in Suffolk that Lovell rented from his uncle: though there would not be ostentation. There was a certain asceticism about him that matched with his pared fatless body. Jeremiah had twitted her – 'engaged to an Honourable, large fortune, carriage and pair – my, my, Becky, I confess I never saw you as a fortune-hunter' – but it was half-hearted raillery, even Jeremiah acknowledging that whatever were her reasons for marrying Lovell, that was not one of them.

. . . Perhaps it was Sarah, of all people, who had in some measure decided it for her. One morning when Sarah had been trying on her new lace tippet in her bedroom, and seeking reassurance from Rebecca that it was not too 'forward'. Lovell Fitzroy had been at dinner with them the night before, along with some of her father's acquaintances. The evening had ended with an impromptu dance, Mrs Walsoken playing at the spinet, the carpet rolled back: their father even keeping time with the music by tapping on his knee while he talked business in the corner. Rebecca and Lovell had danced. He did not dance well, as he cheerfully admitted. He was altogether too earthbound. It was rather endearing. They had laughed together a lot. Conducting her back to his seat he said: 'You must forgive me, or rather your toes must. Have I broken them all?'

'Well, no. But they have not had such a beating since my dancing lessons at Mrs Grimble's School in Norwich, where I had to dance with Fanny Bruford, who was the fattest girl in the school.'

'Mrs Grimble . . .' He smiled at her. 'I picture steel spectacles and a mob-cap and a back straight as a ramrod.'

'That's about right,' she said. 'She also drank, however. She kept her brandy in a cloam teapot. I'm afraid we drove her to it.'

'How I wish I could have known you then,' he said.

'I don't think you'd have liked me. I spent half my time standing with the other girls at the schoolroom window gazing out for a sight of the Norfolk militia in their uniforms. And giggling and falling in love with the drawing-master.'

He laughed. 'Well, at the time I would be, let's see, at Cambridge, wasting my time shamefully and forever having my hair curled and powdered and thinking myself a very fine fellow.'

'I don't believe that. I don't believe you wasted your time.'

408

'Well, now I consider all time wasted – ' he seemed to hesitate a fraction of a moment – 'that is not spent with you.'

It was an unusual speech for him. She was affected, and showed it.

It had been a delightful evening, and Sarah talked of it while she adjusted her tippet. Sarah was half in love with Lovell Fitzroy herself, and went on praising his manners and his kindness before suddenly saying: 'Becky, why don't you marry Mr Fitzroy?'

Rebecca looked at her own reflection in the mirror. Her face was very still.

The figure in the mirror said: 'He – he hasn't asked me.'

'Oh, I know, I don't mean that,' Sarah said impatiently, 'but he is going to, of course.'

'Yes . . . he is,' Rebecca said. Not with vanity, but simply out of a certain knowledge.

'Well, then? Why don't you?'

Rebecca stared at the reflection, as if challenging it to answer. And thought: yes, I will.

She enjoyed being with him so much; she looked forward to seeing him again, found a pleasure in his company and his conversation that went beyond anything in her family circle. She felt relaxed with him, unselfconscious. She warmed to his honesty and lack of affectation, which seemed to shine out the more brightly in the society in which he moved. She felt herself valued by him, in a way without possessiveness. And she thought: yes, I will, in the same clear-headed pleased way in which one would react to any good idea.

It would be a good life with Lovell Fitzroy. A public life, which she found an interesting prospect: and a worthwhile one. Without being priggish, it would be a life with a hope of doing some good in the world, with his various progressive interests: there would be action and involvement, rather than the enervating vacuity of lying in bed till noon and spending the rest of the day dressing and being fashionable and dreading the day the wrinkles should appear.

So, in this strange way, it was decided. Two days later he asked her to be his wife, and with something of the same strange lucidity she readily consented.

Her brother Peter, who had struck up a strong friendship with Lovell ever since they had met at the time of the riots, was delighted. So much so that she grew a little restive at his expressions of

409

pleasure. Her mother too. As for her father, he was as near to being in transports as his undemonstrative, rationed nature would allow.

And Jeremiah . . . Jeremiah, apart from the odd jest, had said little except something that disturbed her. He had looked her very closely in the face and said: 'Well, well. Little Becky. I'm just looking for the silly moony glow of romance in your face. I'd always associated you with romance. But I really don't see it.'

'I'm turned twenty-one, brother,' she said with an irritable half-laugh. 'Romance, as you call it, is for schoolgirls.' He had raised his slanting eyebrows and said nothing. She had been obscurely annoyed with him for the rest of that day. Though there was no reason to be. After all, never, ever, had she relied on Jeremiah's judgement against Peter's.

So, a few kisses, ratified by the engagement. It was a long time since she had been kissed by a man . . . Anyway, it was all very pleasant. He was a very tender man, in his way.

Something he had said, just previous to asking her to marry him . . . He had remarked that he did not perhaps know her well – 'at least, I know sufficient of you to be filled with the deepest affection and tenderness, Miss Rebecca – but what I mean is, we met in somewhat unusual circumstances, and I may be taking a liberty that I could not be aware of – that is, if there is some claim on your heart, some attachment that meeting as we have I could not know of – I beg you to speak now if so, and forgive me insofar as I was unaware – '

No, she had said, there was no claim. She felt a kind of relief in saying it. Saying things could make them true.

. . . And now here she was at the house of the Duke of Grafton, who would be, considering his closeness to his nephew, virtually her father-in-law. Her future husband across the table was attending to Jeremiah, who, loquaciously tipsy, was relating a long and improbable erotic narrative in which he was a protagonist. Lovell was listening with a glint of humour in his eye but without mockery. That was typical of him. He was an admirable man, she thought.

. . . Yesterday afternoon he had taken her out shopping in his carriage: such unchaperoned outings were a bonus of engagement. She loved to see the endless variety of London shops. They had walked down Cornhill, and within a hundred yards the signs had read Hodges, Shoemaker; Nicholas, Woollen Draper; Rainbow Coffee House; Cleeves, Pewterer; Mrs Carter, Milliner; Warner,

Stationer; Hare, Music Shop; De Veer, Toy-maker; Young, Teapots, Tea-Kettles, Chamber-pots &c; Strahan, Bookseller. At this last she bought a copy of Mrs Julia Milton's poems.

It had been a lovely time, and she should not have lost her temper, but she did. A shower of rain: Lovell's concern lest she get wet. A good-humoured exclamation from her that in the fens she had been soaked to the skin many times and not given it a thought. Repeated concern. Her own repeated assertion that it didn't matter. An admiring remark from him that she was so different from the town ladies who shrieked when a drop of rain touched them . . . and then another remark that the rain was really quite heavy, perhaps she should shelter here . . . And she had snapped at him, snapped at him not to be so considerate all the damned time, she wasn't about to run away and leave him just because he didn't possess an umbrella . . . She was immediately sorry – it was not the sort of thing to say to him however you felt – it could never be taken the right way. But there was no right way, anyway, it was unforgivable.

Still, they had driven home in equanimity, with darkness swallowing the city – the shops stayed open until ten. Along the main streets the lamps were lit, four-branched posts crowned the glass globes in which cotton wicks burnt in whale oil. Their light rounded off the corners of the grand squalid city, softening, and she was softened and said apologetically: 'I'm afraid you must think your future wife has a temper.'

'She has a mind and spirit of her own,' he said, 'and that's why I love her.' This touched her, and made her feel worse.

Her father had taken Sarah and Jeremiah to Covent Garden Theatre, and only her mother was there to meet her in Golden Square. She did not seem surprised when her daughter cast her head on her breast and started crying. Mrs Walsoken, who had a fund of sentimentality that the Old Testament had not scourged out of her, felt she understood. In fact she did not. It was a shudder of the past that had afflicted her copper-haired, lovely, confused daughter.

You could never get the past back, of course. It was unattainable – a quality it shared with the things that were never to be; and in this case they were certainly related.

# THREE

Bethlem Royal Hospital for Lunaticks, in Moorfields, was commonly known by the less euphonious name of Bedlam. For a penny
you could go in and tour the cells and stare at the mad people in
their chains and leg-irons, as Sir Hugh and Lady Elizabeth Woodhouse were doing. They had come to London on the twentieth of
November, a week ago, but this was their first proper outing
together. Perhaps an unfelicitous choice, but Hugh had made it in a
genuine reconciling spirit; and besides he always liked coming here
– the half-naked women sprawled on straw, grinning and fondling
themselves, the men strapped in the confining-chairs talking an
endless stream of nonsense, made him simply roar.

They had come up to London to stay till the new year. Rather
surprisingly, Mr and Mrs Wainwright, who visited town less often
nowadays, had come with them, taking a house close to theirs in
Welbeck Street.

Mr Wainwright would have preferred to be at home. However,
he knew why his wife felt they should go. It was not spoken, but it
was felt by both of them. The strains of Elizabeth and Hugh's
marriage were becoming obvious, though their exact nature was
doubtful. Lizzie wasn't right, that was certain. Her clothes – in
themselves expensive, of course, but she looked as if she dressed in
the dark. Her beautiful blond hair was lank and unwashed, her skin
was bad. Not long ago there had been a bruise on her cheek, and
cuts and grazes on her arm. Neither Mrs Wainwright nor her
husband made any comment. They did not need to. It was tacitly
accepted that they should keep their daughter and son-in-law in
sight, and that meant going to London.

Elizabeth had shrunk from visiting Bedlam before, but now it rather interested her, perhaps because, as she well knew, she was mad herself.

Two attendants were force-feeding a woman in a cell, one holding her down while the other spooned some grey mush down her throat. Elizabeth watched with interest. From other cells came screams and gurgling laughs and snatches of broken song. There were several sightseers alongside them: a little boy nearby, brought by his father as part of his education, was crying and asking to leave. Bunches of herbs hung in the corridors, to mask other smells for the benefit of visitors. But they did not succeed, at least not to Elizabeth: she could detect the other smells, the smells of humanity, scourged and reduced in the alchemist's pan of suffering and revealed as the foul dross it was.

. . . A terrible row the other night. It was as if a latch had been lifted in her head, as if light had briefly broken in on her catatonic spirit. She had screamed and spat at Hugh, thrown things at him, aimed punches at his broad body. She detested him, she said, he was repulsive, their marriage was a sham. She would leave him, she would run away, she would denounce him for what he was.

A frightening nightmarish scene. Their bedroom was always very dark, as one of the windows had been bricked up to avoid the window-tax, and there in the guttering shadows and the dark hangings they had wrangled and fought, their marriage poised above the abyss.

After the first shock, Hugh had hurled words back at her. Where would she go? What would she do? Her property was his. She was bound to him by the strongest ties of law and religion. If she left him she'd never get a penny from him. What would she do, go creeping back to her fat vulgar mother and her scrimshanked brewer of a father? A failure, a useless pathetic failure, tripping exiled behind her mother until she grew old . . . Lying, deceiving slut – what about that Landless fellow – didn't find it so repulsive with him, hey? Shall I tell the world about that? Go on, she said, I don't care, anything must be better than this . . .

They had been left wordless and exhausted. Hugh's blustering did not disguise his own alarm. But she had lapsed back into torpor, choked on the dregs of hate and despair. Even the fact that he had been considerate since then barely registered.

Yes, she was going mad, she knew. Her own actions were increasingly mysterious to her; some other person shared her body,

413

someone who mislaid objects, broke them, or just toyed with them for hours on end. The bruise her parents had silently noticed had indeed been caused by Hugh, but the others had not. She had found herself experimentally lacerating her flesh with combs and pins.

And she thought she had begun seeing things too, for on her second day in London, riding with her mother in Hyde Park, she had seen a figure that looked like Robert Landless. He was on a chestnut mare, riding around the Ring, where young bloods showed off their clothes and mounts. She recognised the mop of fair hair, the fine-drawn profile, the easy, erect posture. The figure had seemed to disappear, among the other riders, and so she thought she must be seeing things.

The day after their visit to Bedlam, they went to the Tower to see the lions in the afternoon, and in the evening to the Haymarket Opera-House, accompanied by Elizabeth's parents. Every appearance was of normality. They talked of the mild November weather, of what a dashing figure the young Prince of Wales had become, of the grand masquerade ball to be held at the Pantheon next week where the Duchess of Devonshire and Lady Bessborough would be present. This calm might have deceived: but Mrs Wainwright noticed, on greeting her daughter with a kiss when they met at the opera, that she seemed to shrink and recoil at her touch. From that moment her bright button eyes missed nothing.

The next day Hugh went out riding early. Elizabeth, in another interval of waking — there was no other way to describe it — took a hackney to see a lawyer at Gray's Inn, and giving a false name spoke to him in confidence of separation and divorce.

From the endless legal periphrases the bitter kernels of truth emerged. Separation — well, a matter between the two parties. As for divorce, that was the, h'm, prerogative of the husband. Proof of adultery required. Act of Parliament required. Vast expense. Names public, scandal. Distressing for both parties.

She returned to Welbeck Street, sunk again, an automaton.

Hugh did not come back for dinner that day. He rode out beyond Hampstead, tiring out his horse but not himself, and came back into the city in the drizzling afternoon, still reckless and explosive with fear and anger.

He dined at a coffee-house, with its curtained booths and hats hanging on racks above them. He paid his penny to borrow the newspaper, but did not read it. When someone attempted to share his booth he growled at them like a bear. The monstrous fact of the failure of his marriage capered all the time before his eyes. The tempestuous row, the screamed, unretractable words. Suddenly the earth on which he stood had rumbled and quaked. Elizabeth, his wife, so beautiful and desired, so estimable an accessory to his life. Hatred. It was as if one of his dogs had suddenly turned on him, a ravening wolf.

Occasionally brutish indignation stirred in him, the old indignation – she was his wife, he had a right, he must be firm, he must be master ... That he should be agonising like this, peering fearfully into an unimaginable future, on account of his wife – a woman – over an aspect of his life that he should control, was ridiculous: what would his father say? But it had become hollow, redundant in the face of their dire situation.

He went to Dr Dominicetti's Fumigatory Steam Baths in Cheyne Walk. He had always found this place invigorating. But he emerged more turbulently wretched than ever. And so, as evening was falling, he turned for comfort to the stews and gambling-houses and brothels of Covent Garden. The high-class establishments were to be found in St James's, but his tastes tended to run the other way, and tonight he was seeking the sordid.

At Mother Harrington's bagnio he drank 'usquebaugh', or whisky, which he had got a taste for in Scotland. He was soon drunk, and fired, his blood thumping. But he fancied none of the painted girls who were brought one by one into the upstairs room by the waiter – the ugliest first, so that the customer might tip him to produce a better.

He left, and fell in with a couple of young bucks just out of Eton who fancied themselves as Mohocks. They lurched from one drinking-den to another, yelling and laughing, darting out of sight of the Watch as he passed by with his bell and calling obscenities at him, throwing handfuls of coins at top windows to waken sober citizens. Hugh felt ten years younger: he felt a fine fellow. He had a cundum in his pocket, which he had carefully washed out after using it last time, and he was full of excitement.

They ended up in a bagnio that hid away in the darkest corner of Martlet Court. It was dingy outside but inside there was red damask on the walls and looking-glasses everywhere. There were flogging-women here – professionals, who left the business of intercourse to the ordinary girls, and had their own special parlour. Sir Hugh's companions headed for it immediately.

The liquor was dancing in Sir Hugh's head. He had plenty of money in his pockets, and the drink loosened it. In a bedroom with a brocaded four-poster he played, in company with an elderly gentleman in a clerical wig, the game of 'Money Chuck-Hole'. Two very obviously experienced women lay naked on the bed, their legs spread wide, and Sir Hugh and his companion took turns at tossing guineas into their vaginas. Sir Hugh's aim was the better, and he boasted of it. Sportsman, you see, sir. He called for more brandy to be brought, and then more. Later the women – for a libation of guineas more conventionally donated – obliged their audience with the 'Game of Flats'. Lesbianism was regarded as a rather quaint aberration; but the sight of women pleasuring each other excited Sir Hugh volcanically.

He forgot his cares and forgot Elizabeth: he drank so much he almost forgot his own name. It was past one when he left the place, congratulating himself on still having a couple of guineas in his pocket and blissfully unaware that his pocket had been picked as a matter of course as he left.

Elizabeth was asleep when he arrived at Welbeck Street. Or rather, she was not asleep but lying still in bed pretending to be so. He looked in at her, holding a candle, swaying on the balls of his feet, then went unsteadily into his dressing-room where he had a bottle of port in the bureau. He threw off his coat, loosened his stock, and swigged from the bottle. He did not feel like sleep: he felt like anything but sleep, or so he thought.

He went back into the bedroom, set the candle down clumsily, and drank from the bottle again. He looked at Elizabeth's too-rigid form. Her hair, its fairness faded of late, was spread across the pillow, fine and ghostly in the candlelight.

Sir Hugh began to undress, staring at her. He was a man who was genuinely the slave of his passions, but he was too conceited to see the pathetic in this. He put his hand on her shoulder, half a waking-up gesture, half a caress. Her eyes flicked open immediately, twin points of dread.

He was crouching over her, murmuring a mixture of endearments and obscenities, one hand pushing back the bedsheet and scrabbling up her nightgown. She began to struggle and protest, as she had done before so often, feeble against his gross strength. Her night-gown was wrenched up to her neck. His lips, slobbering, brushed across hers.

She could smell the drink, but that was nothing new. She could smell also, with particular keenness, the rank scent of the women he had been with, and she was retching.

He was looming over her, in only his shirt, one thick thigh straddling her, pinning her.

And his breath was coming in snorts, not of lust, but of frustration. The drink and the debauch of tonight had exhausted more than his finesse. He stared down at himself. He was as limp as a wrinkled baby.

Elizabeth took advantage of his outraged hesitation to try and wriggle from his grasp. But he caught her on the other side of the bed, and wrestled her down again. His face swelled like a mad red moon close to hers, and his lips sprayed. 'Now, now, darling, Lizzie – a drink – you like a drop of port, eh – goes sweet down the throat, eh – what about here – '

And he was edging the half-empty port bottle up between her clenched thighs, thrusting the neck upwards, the wine spilling redly on her pubic hairs, and the scream that was ripped out of her was wonderful rage more than horror, and she lunged out of his grip on to the floor, and managed with her bare heel a glancing kick at his face. Then she was up on her feet, alive as she had not been for months, and grabbing her peignoir from a chair and running down the stairs to the housekeeper's room on the second floor. She flung into the room, to the startled surprise of the old lady in the narrow bed, and turned the key in the lock. But Hugh had not followed her.

When dawn came she sent the housekeeper up to the bedroom to fetch her some clothes. Sir Hugh was sleeping like the dead on the bed, the old lady said tremulously. Elizabeth dressed and then leaving no word walked to her parents' house in Vere Street. She did not return.

The story carefully leaked by Mr and Mrs Wainwright for the benefit of inquisitive acquaintances was of a tiff between their daughter and son-in-law, nothing serious. They could get little more out of Elizabeth herself. But Mrs Wainwright thought it prudent, when Hugh had come calling at their door later that morning, to refuse him admission.

417

Captain Finlayson said: 'I hope I'm not intruding, ma'am.'

'I – not at all, Captain Finlayson,' said Mary, trying not to appear flustered and not succeeding. 'I hope all is well with Aunt Catherine?' She picked up a bonnet of Charles Joseph's from the back of a chair, laid it down again. The room suddenly looked untidy to her, though there was no reason why this should matter.

'Aye, she's in rudest health.' He cleared his throat. 'Mr Hardwick is not here?'

'No.'

She sat, but he remained standing, fiddling with his gloves. 'I hope your wee boy – '

'He's well, thank you.'

Captain Finlayson suddenly struck his thigh with his gloves. 'I'm intruding, surely,' he said. 'Pardon me, I'll – '

'Indeed you're not, Captain Finlayson.' How had her voice acquired that squeaky pitch? 'Will you – will you have some tea? Or a glass of canary – '

'No, nothing, thank ye, ma'am.' He sat down at last, his boots creaking, his soft dark eyes lowered. 'I hardly know what to do with myself, ye see, ma'am. I have my orders to embark for Ireland on the tenth of December. So I – '

'Oh!'

She could not help the exclamation, and felt herself blush. He looked at her with a sort of timidity that sat strangely on his big leanness, then looked away. 'So you see,' he said, 'I feel a sairtain restlessness. It's always the way when we have orders to move on. One feels one would rather go now than wait around, if ye see what I mean. So, this is my excuse for drifting aboot and imposing myself on all my acquaintances and – and friends.'

She was not properly listening. 'But that will mean,' she said, 'you will be spending Christmas in your new billet, in Ireland, with no comforts . . .' The idea made her strangely unhappy.

Captain Finlayson smiled, though not unkindly. 'Bless ye, ma'am,' he said, 'that's nothing new to me. And you'd be surprised how well soldiers contrive to live in their billets, when the occasion demands. Rough and ready it may often be, but convivial, I assure you. And you and your husband, ma'am, will you be returning home for the season?'

The word *home* afflicted her. 'Yes, we hope so. When Parliament closes for the Christmas recess.'

'I envy you,' he said. 'I've never forgot Morholm, Mrs Hardwick. The air so clean, and the sky and the earth stretching away . . . It's an image, a picture I keep in my head, so to speak, to enjoy when I need it.' He stopped, smiled. 'An ideal, no doubt. It has its troubles and disadvantages also, I'm sure.'

Mary smiled too, but said nothing. For Morholm had something of the same value for herself. Especially now. Now, as her hopes about the effect of their London stay on the relationship between herself and George were being overturned. Now, as he went, it seemed to her, as the moth to the flame, the flame of the gaming-table and the tavern and the brittle society to whom money meant nothing instead of – as it had been till recently for them – everything. He seemed to be purging his low self-esteem, which had haunted him for the last couple of years, in an almost frantic seeking of the rarefied worlds of prestige, with all their refinements of sensation and risk. She might have been able to live with that. But he was living on a plane where she could not, of necessity, follow, and it seemed to her where he did not need or want her to do so. He had spent only one evening with her this week. The rest of the time he was in a state both exhausted and stimulated, his mind still tangled in a buoyant cloud of gambling and high vinous talk. It went without saying that he had little time for Charles Joseph. Many wives, no doubt, accepted all this as normal. But she was not many wives. She had different ideas about the relations of a man and a woman. And sometimes just of late a blazing angry resentment flared up in her. And she was both afraid of and vengefully hungry for where it would lead her.

There was no telling when George would be back. There was a debate in the House on relations with Holland, and the possibility of war with a third continental power, which he wanted to attend: and he might well repair straight afterwards to the club and the tables with Ranulph Powys. She had made no plans to meet the Miltons: the day stretched empty before her.

Captain Finlayson was, at a pinch, a sort of relation, so there could be no harm in going out for a while with him. So it was decided.

They walked, in cool November sunlight, to Josiah Wedgwood's exclusive pottery showrooms in Greek Street, which she had a fancy to see. (She was to have gone with George last week.) There was no suggestion of *shop* here. It was like a grand house thrown open to the public. Dinner services were laid out on mahogany tables as if for a meal: vases and bowls decorated the walls and were arranged in corner cabinets. You could consult the pattern-books with Mr Wedgwood himself or his partner in a withdrawing-room.

Whatever darkness in Mary's heart might be lurking and feeding on her resentment, Captain Alex Finlayson was not simply a convenient object. An objective part of her acknowledged that she would still have thought him an attractive man, even in a situation without the danger inherent in this.

In some ways he was a mysterious man. He had a quality of self-containment, which did not, however, repel: it was rather the sign of a man accustomed to solitude, the solitude carved, as a preservation, out of the noise and press of the barrack and the battlefield. Yet looking at him she seemed to see, expressed on his person with particular clarity, the marks of his personality and his past, as it was on few people: he had about him no deception.

It was doubly dangerous, in her present mood, to look at him so much.

They went to St James's Park after Wedgwood's. As they walked he did not take her arm. It was somehow more significant than if he had.

'We have six tickets for the masquerade at the Pantheon on the sixth,' Mary found herself saying, staring across at the Palace. 'I wonder if, Captain Finlayson, you would care to be of our party – '

'Why, that's good of ye, ma'am,' he said. 'But I think I shall be there anyway. A brother officer of mine, Captain Bridie, is making up a party. I – had doubted whether to go, but – as you say you will be there . . .'

They walked on, in a strange burst of silence.

'I – I would like for you to meet Bridie,' he went on hurriedly. 'Och, he's a fine man, my dearest friend. Always laughing, full of cheer. A big red face like the sun itself. He's been some years in India, you understand, and has taken to it like a native.'

'George's brother, James, is in India, a merchant with the Company,' Mary said. 'He was always rather pale, but I suppose he will look like that now.'

'Aye, it's a harsh climate, and not many wives will stand it, though Mrs Bridie has followed him everywhere.' He paused. 'In truth, the army life is no life for a lady, wherever it be.'

She glanced up at him. 'Is – is that why you have not married, Captain Finlayson?'

He did not answer. Instead he said, after a moment, 'Are you cold, ma'am?'

She had not even thought about it. 'Do I look cold?' she said.

He did not look at her, but said brokenly: 'No . . . You look . . . Your skin . . . There's – a glow, a most beautiful glow. Like rose petals on snow.'

They were silent, and then walked on and talked of other things.

They returned to Buckingham Street in the dark afternoon, still strangely formal, polite, superficially relaxed. So, whatever might be her own feelings, there was in him nothing of the opportunist. He spoke with respect of George, and had looked surprised at a bitter little outburst of her own in the park when he had casually asked about George's work in the House and she had said he hardly spoke of such things to *her*. This made it all the harder.

They parted at the steps to their lodgings. He said: 'Mrs Hardwick, you are vairy kind to an idle dog of a soldier. I wonder if I may call again to see you . . .'

'If you would like – '

'It is everything that I hope for,' he said with a sudden vehemence.

'. . . Of course.' She turned, breathless, but he said – for the first time – 'Mary!'

Her head was spinning horribly as she looked at him.

'You know,' he said, 'you have only to say the word – '

'Captain Finlayson – '

'No,' he said soberly, 'hear me. You have only to say the word – to send me away. I will obey.' He put on his hat and was gone.

She was glad of the presence of Charles Joseph when she got inside. He came running from Bridget to embrace her, and she hugged him tightly.

'Mummy,' he said with interest, pressing his ear to her chest again, ''s going all fast.'

'Is it?' she said. '. . . It's because I've been running.'

She gave Bridget the rest of the afternoon off, and to occupy herself sat and wrote a letter to Luke. She did not know whether she was doing the right thing in telling him of Rebecca's engagement, but it seemed better than that he should learn of it some other way – supposing he was interested. But it was soon done, and then she played with Charles Joseph till he grew tired and leaned against her shoulder by the fire, eyes blinking and seeing nothing.

'Where's papa?' he said once.

'Oh, he'll be home soon,' Mary said, stroking his hair. And to herself she said: 'Yes, come home, George. Come home and sit here by the fire with us, and grumble about money if you like, and try to light your pipe and give it up like you used to . . . But come home, because I need you.'

However, he did not, until past two when she was asleep.

On the thirtieth of November, Henry and Julia Milton attended the official opening of the Finsbury Dispensary in Union Street, Southwark, in company with the Sheridans. Sheridan had been involved in the subscription, and had encouraged the Miltons to add to it.

While Julia and Sheridan were talking to one of the resident surgeons, Milton spotted, amongst the gentlemen and ladies who had subscribed being shown round the next room, the Wainwrights – she a great blob in coloured silks, he a comma, an afterthought beside her – and with them their daughter.

Elizabeth did not say a word while Milton chatted to her parents. Her eyes slid back and forth, restless and obscurely alarmed, like those of a confined animal. She kept her arm through her mother's all the time.

'How does your friend Hardwick go on in Parliament, Milton?' Mr Wainwright asked. 'Cost me a mint of money, that business. Wish I'd never got involved. I'll leave the fine folks to their own devices in future.' There seemed an extra drop of sourness in his usual vinegary tone.

Milton looked at Elizabeth, puzzled by her silence. 'Do you go to the Pantheon next week, Lady Woodhouse?'

She merely looked, frozenly, towards her mother, like a little child addressed by a stranger.

'As to that, we're not certain,' Mrs Wainwright said. 'We may not stay in town so long . . . These masquerades can have rather a low tone, I think, anyhow . . .'

Milton, about to say something, stopped. 'Well . . . I must rejoin my wife. Perhaps we shall meet again in town. Ma'am. Lady Woodhouse.'

As he moved away he found his arm taken by Mr Wainwright, who had followed him. 'Look here, Milton,' he muttered, 'we've known you a long time. I think you can be discreet. Fact is, spot of trouble between Lizzie and Hugh. She's staying with us just now. Want to keep it quiet – you know what this place is like. Just till it's sorted out. You know.'

'Oh . . . I hope I haven't been clumsy just now – '

'Not at all.' Mr Wainwright snatched off his spectacles and polished them furiously. 'Not at all. Wish I was out of this damned city,' he added in a hiss.

The Sheridans left soon afterwards, and the Miltons went with them. Sheridan said: 'Well, we shall meet at the Pantheon next week, I take it?'

'Yes, we shall be going with my brother,' Julia said.

'Ah, of course.' Sheridan paused. 'I saw him at Brooks' last night – at Fox's faro table. He seems to be going it a little, doesn't he?'

'In what way?' Julia said.

'Oh – well, stop me if I'm saying too much, but it's – well, easy to fall in a little too deep. Get a little dazzled. I should know. Not all of us have the bottomless coffers of Fox. Just thought I'd mention it.' The Sheridans' carriage was brought round to the front of the Dispensary. 'Can we take you home?'

'No, it's just a short walk, thank you.'

The carriage rattled off, and the Miltons turned to go. Milton was about to say something about George when they saw a procession of ragged women coming up the street.

The young woman in the lead carried a small bundle. Her face was grey and tearful. The others were patting her and urging her on.

She came up to Julia, and said: 'Please, ma'am, is this the new place where the surgeons are? Where they give physic?'

'Yes, yes, this is it,' said Julia, glancing at the bundle. 'Go in now, the surgeons will see you.'

'I can't pay,' the woman said pathetically. 'I've no money to pay.'

'It's free,' Julia said. 'Go in, hurry.'

The woman, followed by her chattering supporters, went in.

Henry and Julia had both seen the baby in the woman's arms; and it was plain to them, as it was to anyone who had lived in a town of the age, that the child was far gone with typhoid fever.

Julia took her husband's arm, but for the moment he was rooted to the spot. 'It won't live,' he said tonelessly. 'Not an auspicious beginning.'

'No,' she said. 'Come.' Gently, she pressed him to walk with her. His face was like chalk.

As they walked, and he was silent, she talked, in spinning coils of nervous desperation, of last night, when Mr Carey had at last taken them to dine at the Thrales' at Streatham, where Dr Johnson spent much of his time. Their hopes had been at least partly disappointed. The Thrales were Dr Johnson's greatest friends – Henry Thrale, a wealthy brewer, was a quiet reserved man, but his young vivacious wife Hester had made their house the resort of literary society – and he lived like one of the family with them. But on this occasion Dr Johnson had not appeared for dinner: Mrs Thrale said he was staying in the library reading.

'Oh, well,' Julia said as they arrived back at their lodgings, 'I dare say we would have been disappointed if we'd met him anyhow.'

They sat down to dinner of broiled beef and capers and tongue, but Henry ate little. Julia said, fingering her wine-glass, 'That was Elizabeth Woodhouse with the Wainwrights, wasn't it? Is she all right?'

Milton looked up, as if he had forgotten she was there. 'All right? I think so. Why?'

'She looked – strange. Distracted. Like a ghost.'

'Yes, she did.' Henry frowned at his meat, put down his fork.

'Henry – that baby –'

He got up quickly, his chair scranching across the floorboards. 'I saw Frank and Kate Sedgmoor's child all over again. God, the waste, the vile waste!' he said viciously.

'There wasn't anything we could do,' she said, hopelessly.

He stood at the window looking out. A man was ringing a bell and calling out for broken chairs to mend. Dogs were fighting over a bone in the gutter. 'That's what makes it so sickening . . . Thank God, thank God we haven't been put to that trial.'

Don't say that, her mind screamed, please don't say that. 'I know – I know how you feel,' she said. 'But – but it doesn't have to be. We're here, aren't we? We survived. It does happen. Little Charles Joseph. There's always – a fair chance.'

A crumb of bitter laughter fell from his lips. He was haunted afresh by a horror that chilled him like a physical fever, like the fever that baby was going to die of. 'The chance. Well, at least no child of ours is to be thrown into that lottery.'

'Henry – we can't be sure – '

'What?'

She drew back at the last moment. 'What I mean is – just supposing, one should come – '

'God forbid.' He wiped his hand across his mouth, as though he had been sick. 'I want no such thing. Almost as well to drop it in the river like the unwed country girls as offer a child up to the gods of the epidemics.'

He went off to speak to their landlord. She stayed at the table, with the congealing remains of the meal, and was paralysed. The cold crept up over her own spirit. For she had known for certain this morning that she was pregnant.

She had thought carefully about how to tell him, and planned to choose a good moment; but had foreseen nothing like this. She had been bubbling with delight all day, but now the unexpected riches that had fallen to her this morning had all turned to dross and clinker in her hands.

She did not weep easily, and could not now. Even that relief was denied to her.

4

Up on the fens, the mild winter was stiffening, and the fogs that had curdled across the levels for the last month were giving place to the first frosts. The sheep on the commons, in the mornings when the sky radiated winter colours like stained glass, cropped grass that was brittle as matchwood, their breath conjuring a second mist and their feet leaving crushed pockets in the crisp turf.

The commons at Aysthorpe, however, presented a different scene, for the work of the Enclosure commissioners was done at last, and the great rugged expanse between here and Helpston was being cleared by gangs of labourers, and the first fences were going up, as they were in the village, altering and defacing the land and changing, not exactly overnight but with startling suddenness, the patterns and customs of centuries.

On the third of December, a Sunday, Luke rode over to Aysthorpe, as he did every week, to check that all was well at Morholm.

It was a duty he enjoyed all the more since the death of his father: he felt a renewed consciousness of his link with the old family home.

Grandmother Peach was querulously glad to see him: the Morholm holding was little affected by the enclosure now, but a stream of villagers had come to the house with complaints and questions about what was going on which she could not answer. George ought to be here, she said.

John Newman turned up at the house, having seen Luke coming through the village.

John had conscientiously paid back Luke for his costs at the trial: and there had been a mutual respect between the two men since that time. They drank a mug of ale together in the winter parlour, and John told Luke that he was selling up.

'The enclosure?' Luke said.

'Aye. I'm not saying owt agin it, mind. Feeling in the village's changed a bit, now that the work of fencing and clearing's going on – that gives work to plenty of folk. Course, that won't last for ever . . . But anyhow, I can't carry on. Because I've got a bit o' land in my name, I have to tek a share o' the costs, and I can't manage. They're marking out my little parcel of land, fair enough, but it won't do. Wi' the common going, we can't graze the cow. I sold her at Peterborough market last week, but it's not the time for selling stock, so we din't git much.'

'What will you do?' said Luke.

'Oh, stay here. Git labouring work. There'll still be plenty o' that. Jenny was for moving to Peterborough, mebbe, or Wisbech, and gitting town work, but I can't see us leaving the land. We was talking to Mr Walsoken's steward the other day. It's Walsoken as has got the biggest parcel of land, you see, and he thought I'd get a price from – '

'You'd not sell out to Walsoken!'

John flushed slightly over his tan. 'I've no love for him,' he said. 'As you'd expect . . . But tis a question of surviving. It's like – fighting against a current, for men like me. Walsoken's settled here now, and his way of doing things, for good or ill.'

'God curse him,' said Luke savagely.

'Nay,' said John. 'I've no bitterness. There's got to be change, I s'pose, and he's just a part of it.'

'Whilst the smaller men go under and end up building his fences for him,' said Luke.

John Newman smiled uncomfortably. Luke smiled too. 'Still forgiving, John?' he said.

John finished his beer. 'Nothing else for it,' he said.

Luke rode back to Stamford in the afternoon. He found himself agreeing with Mrs Peach, that George should have been there. Perhaps he should write to him about John.

As if in response to these thoughts, he found a letter from London waiting for him in Stamford, addressed in Mary's handwriting.

He read and reread the letter – or more particularly the lines: 'We have some News about the Walsoken family, which is rather unexpected, and which I feel I should pass on to you. Rebecca is to be married, in a few weeks time. He is a Mr Lovell Fitzroy, an MP, and Nephew to the Duke of Grafton. I have met him once and he appears a pleasant sort of man, it is difficult to tell of course': and when he had finished the room had gone dark. It was as if his own darkness had swelled out to fill it.

Forrest came in with candles.

'Is everything all right, sir?'

'Yes . . . yes.'

The old servant coughed. 'Will it be dinner just for one, sir?'

Luke remembered that Kitty was supposed to be coming. 'Er – no, no, two,' he said.

When the servant had gone again he sat at the escritoire and smoothed the letter over and over with his hand. His body felt sapped, loose and light and helpless. But his mind blazed. It was as if a fundamental imperative of his nature were rearing up and declaiming *No*. Little flickers of resignation, of rationality, were swallowed up. Emotion, pure and elemental as earth and fire, was all.

Action. To remain, to do nothing, was death.

In his bedroom he rapidly packed clothes in a valise. Clean shirts, waistcoat, stockings. Comb and hair-ribbon, tinder-box, razor. Enough. He went down to leave instructions with the servants, saying he was going to London. A limpid calm was on him, he was curiously detached from all that had gone before and all that was to come.

Then Kitty arrived.

'What's to do?'

He barely looked at her, as he searched about the parlour for his pocket-book. 'I'm going to London.'

'What for?'

He did not answer.

'Lor, well, you can't go till tomorrow. Sit down and stop clattin' about.'

Luke looked up, as if this had only just struck him. Then he shrugged. 'I can get as far as Huntingdon this evening.'

She was silent a moment. 'What's the almighty hurry?'

'It's – ' He struggled with the impossibility of explaining and the impossibility of staying.

Kitty Du Quesne, however, had more than her share of intuition. She saw the letter lying open, and, as he made no protest, picked it up and glanced at it.

The look she gave him was shrewd, though not unkind. 'So,' she said. 'I suppose it's no use asking, what about me?'

He stared at her, and knew that, in spite of the cynicism of the relationship between them, he still had to grant her the power to hold him back if she wanted or set him free: honour demanded thus much, no matter to what degree they had used each other.

But Kitty said, in her ironical way, 'Well, I suppose it didn't have much further to run, anyhow, did it? It was nice while it lasted. I still think you should leave it till tomorrow . . . Sleep on it, eh?' She cocked a grin at him, then stopped and directed a wry smile at herself. 'No, that won't do.'

'Kitty, I want you to understand – '

'Oh, I do understand, Luke. Always have. Men aren't so mysterious as they like to think. I just hope you're – well, doing the right thing.' She picked up her shawl, and smiled again. 'Besides, I can't fight romance, can I?'

A coach left for Huntingdon from the George Inn an hour later, and Luke was on it.

FOUR

I

The masquerade at the Pantheon was to be held on Wednesday December 6th, and was to be a last flourish for London society before the Christmas recess.

The day before, Julia went for a sitting for her portrait, at the studio of a young painter they had found off Cheapside. Milton's black mood was fading somewhat, but she seemed to be sunk in a blacker one of her own, and had almost put off going.

Milton was standing at the window overlooking the muddy street that morning, and debating whether to go out himself, when he caught a glimpse of a fair head entering at the door below.

Delighted recognition dawned, and he ran to the top of the stairs, to meet Robert Landless coming up.

It was a warm reunion. Milton could have wished for nothing better to lift his spirits. Landless, smiling, held him at arm's length and said: 'Not changed a bit, by God. Old Graveairs.'

Landless was unchanged too. The same lively, humorous handsomeness, the dandified clothes worn with a spirit of self-mockery.

'I'd no idea you were in town,' Milton said. 'How did you find us? I've heard nothing from you, not a word, I never knew – '

'You forget, Henry, your wife is something of a celebrity,' Landless said. 'Saw a copy of your wife's poems – and what a talent she has. Why didn't we recruit her for the *Courant*? Made a few enquiries at the bookseller – simple matter. Is the authoress not here?'

'No, she's out . . . But how long have you been in town? Where have you been all this time? It must be a year and a half. I wondered if – '

'Three weeks for the first question, and as for the rest, have you a drink to offer me? We've a lot to catch up on, and a drink will oil the wheels.'

'Damn, we've nothing here – '

'Good! Then we shall go out. We shall go to Ashley's Punch House, and toast renewed friendship in their best punch, and become insensible.'

They took a boat across to Blackfriars Stairs, and walked to Ashley's in Fleet Street. On the way Milton told him of the success of the *Courant*, of the sudden revelation of Julia's writing, of what they had been doing in London. At Ashley's, among the parliamentary reporters and gossips, they ordered a bowl of punch and Milton said: 'Now, tell me, what you have been up to and where you have been.'

'You make it sound strangely unsavoury,' said Landless with a laugh. 'Well . . . since I left Peterborough I have been – well, where have I not been. Ireland, with friends of father's. Brighton. Bristol. Even, God help me, Scotland.'

'What did you do there?'

'Shot at numerous birds, for want of anything else to do, until I decided they looked better decorating the sky than in some slobbering dog's mouth . . . And then Bath. I was there for most of this season.'

Milton raised an eyebrow. 'Trying the waters?'

'Don't jest, sir. At Bath, sir, I was engaged to be married.'

Milton's expression was such that Landless burst into a shout of laughter. 'Well, very flattering! I'll admit it seems unlikely that any woman would have me, but you needn't look so surprised.'

'No, indeed, I – '

'Stop spluttering, dear Henry, and I'll explain.' He filled Milton's cup again. 'Her name was – *is* – Miss Amelia Hawkins. Her father, deceased, was a plantation owner in the Indies. I met her in the Pump Room, where she was accompanying her invalid mother. Well, Mrs Hawkins fancied herself an invalid, if you understand. Never mind that she was a good fifteen stone with a splendid moustache and could wrestle down an ox – there she was, each day, immersed in the King's Bath up to her neck, in one of those ridiculous caps, drawing water like a man o' war, pretending to feel the benefit, and sweating like a – I shall refrain from the comparison. Her daughter was left with little to do while her mother was thus submerged, and so our courtship began, watched, at ground level, by the basilisk eye of Mrs Hawkins . . . You gather, I think, that there was more than a touch of farce about the proceedings.'

'But you must have been serious at some point,' Milton said, between laughter.

'Oh, surely. I hope you don't fancy me a – *trifler*. Miss Hawkins was very pretty, and spirited, and bad-tempered. And I was bored and aimless and in a way to fall in love, or something near it. Also – I believe I was playing the fortune-hunter. The old negro-driver's plunder had made Amelia quite an heiress. And before you say, in your carping way, I don't need to be a fortune-hunter, well, that's why I say I was playing at it. Playing the role, if you like. Seemed as good as any other. There was a certain thrill of competition about it.'

'And what about the amphibious mother?'

'She rather liked me. Because my father was a Dean she seemed to look on me as a sort of member of the cloth,' Landless said with an expression of perplexity. He sighed. 'Drink about, Henry, we've hardly begun yet. Anyway, it all ended as amicably as such things can end. I didn't run off at the altar. Miss Hawkins and I began to realise that once we had left off singing duets at the harpsichord and writing each other little billets-doux and flirting behind her fan – am I turning your stomach? – we had practically nothing to say to each other. She began to yawn most charmingly in my face, and she elaborated her pretty habit of stamping her foot by stamping on mine. The Gorgon was happy enough to see the engagement broken off, for she began, if you please, to be courted herself, by an Italian singer – not, one hopes for her sake, a *castrato* – and she wanted her daughter as a chaperone.'

'You could work up a comic novel out of it,' said Milton. 'But . . . what now?'

'Now? Why, I'm in town with my best friends, the celebrated Miltons, and we shall go to the Pantheon together tomorrow, and you shall spare your wife's toes by letting me dance with her all evening.'

Milton was sober for a moment. 'Well . . . we shall have to go home come new year. Do you think of returning to Peterborough?'

'I see. You want me to revive the sales of the *Courant*.' Landless's smile faded and he examined the lace at his cuff. 'I just don't know about that. I suppose it's high time . . . But I left because I wanted

431

– needed – to get away from the area . . . its associations. And I don't know if I can go back yet.'

It was something that, despite the laughter, had been hovering at the margin of their conversation. Milton said diffidently: 'Well, you needn't stay – I mean, you could try it for a time and – '

'My dear fellow, we're both tiptoeing round the subject, aren't we? I left because of Elizabeth. I've been drifting in this ridiculous way because of Elizabeth. There, it's out now.' He frowned. 'Perhaps I've been playing another role – the jilted lover. But it doesn't feel like that. If I've been attempting a cure this past year, then the cure hasn't succeeded. Oh, it's very puppyish, I know, and I'm lucky to be able to indulge the luxury of such brooding, and all the rest of it. But I still can't face the prospect of – of being near her again. Not yet. I wish I could. However, to prove I'm not a complete fool over the whole thing, I shall ask you – as you no doubt expected – if you've seen her of late, and how she is.'

'I saw her last week,' said Milton.

'She's in London?' Landless's eyes kindled.

'Yes.'

2

Milton wondered momentarily what to tell his friend. Mr Wainwright had spoken to him in confidence – but this was different . . .

'Being squired around town by that lumpish Hugo, no doubt,' Landless said, with unavoidable bitterness. 'And being treated like one of his carriage-horses.' He drained his cup, and said in a rush, 'You didn't know, did you, that – at the end – when we . . . She was pregnant.'

'No.'

'She got rid of it. It was the finish . . . God knows how she did it. She wouldn't have anything to do with me then. I half-hoped she wouldn't go through with it, and that there was a child that was part of us both, even though I could never acknowledge it. But no.'

Two men in the next booth were quarrelling over politics, and the serving-girl came to take away their glasses. Milton and Landless looked at each other. All the fun had gone out of their meeting.

'So,' Landless said. 'Digging over old graves . . . All best left undisturbed, I know. But tell me. How is she?'

'She – she wasn't with Hugh. She was with her parents.'

432

'Well, that's preferable to him, anyway. Where is he, then, off with his – '

'Robert.' Milton touched his arm. 'I can't not tell you. From what I gathered, Elizabeth and Hugh are separated.'

'What? How do you – '

'I don't know any details,' Milton said unhappily. 'But they're living apart, in London. Something's gone wrong. That's all I know.'

Landless had gone pale. His mobile face was frozen, drained of expression, like that of a man who finds the basis on which his life is built cracked and overturned, suddenly confronted with a future of inchoate darkness from which anything might emerge.

'So . . . you spoke with her?' Landless said slowly.

'Well – not properly. I suppose I must tell you, she looked terrible. Each time I've seen her of late she's looked worse. Somehow lifeless, hopeless – I can't explain.'

The punch bowl was empty. Landless gestured impatiently for it to be refilled. He stared at the table. 'And all this time I've been thinking of her as lovely and smiling as when I knew her . . . Well. So much for peace of mind.' He grinned without humour.

'I didn't know whether to tell you. I thought – '

'No, no, no, no.' Landless patted Milton's shoulder absently. 'Of course, you had to. It's not that.'

The fresh bowl of punch came. Landless dipped his cup into it but did not drink. 'I'm glad,' he said. 'Oh, not out of simple jealousy – though I can't deny I'm pleased *he* will get no more of her. But I'm glad for her, glad she'll be free of him, for she didn't love him, I know that, and he never deserved her. And I'm glad you've told me, Henry. Forget what I said about peace of mind.'

The men in the next booth had come to blows, and two burly potmen were firmly escorting them to the door. Milton cast about desperately for some new subject. 'Julia will be home for dinner,' he said. 'Won't you come back and join us? I know she'd love to see you.'

Landless smiled, sadly and affectionately, and Milton knew what he was going to say.

'Tell me, Henry, where the Wainwrights are staying.' As Milton hesitated he went on: 'I can find out from someone else, somehow, if you won't tell me. And I know, I know, you are about to talk reason and caution to me, and you're right to do so, but this – it

433

goes beyond them . . . There are the imponderables of life also, you know – of course you know – and they go deeper and strike harder – and for pity's sake, you must tell me. I must see her!' His voice had grown to a shout, and his knuckles were white as he gripped the table and half-rose. 'God forgive me,' he said in a softer voice, 'but I must see her.'

'Vere Street,' Milton said, 'at the corner of Oxford Road.'

Landless was gone.

At the Vere Street corner a hurdy-gurdy man was playing, and being watched by a trio of Lascars, Indian sailors who came over on the East India Company's ships and were forced to wander destitute and despised around the foreign city until their ship should set sail again. They watched with dull interest as a hackney-carriage drew up and a man with yellow hair got out and ran up the steps of the first townhouse.

Mr Wainwright, a martyr to indigestion, had gone upstairs to lie down after dinner: Mrs Wainwright had gone out to call on a friend after trying in vain – 'you ought to be seen about' – to get her daughter to come with her. So Elizabeth was sitting alone in the small parlour, an open book lying unread in her lap, when Robert Landless was announced.

He came only a little way into the room, and they gazed at each other. She was a tall woman, but he thought she looked small as she sat there, her eyes two blue spots of absence in her oval face. She was wearing white, as she had been when he had first met her; and her hands that lay in her lap had no more colour than the gown.

'I had to come,' he said. 'I heard – I heard that you and Hugh . . .'

She turned her head, and he saw that she was trembling.

'Elizabeth.' He took a step closer. 'Please forgive me for – for appearing like this. God knows, I never meant to trouble you again. And have me turned out in a moment if you will. But I have to *know* . . .'

She looked up at him, her eyes puckered a little as if she were looking up into strong light. 'How did you hear? Is it rumoured all round the town?'

'*No* . . . it doesn't matter how I heard. But is it so? Are you to separate?' As she said nothing he flung his hat on to a chair and cried, 'I know I have no right to ask this. From the moment you sent me away I had no right to anything, and I accept that, Elizabeth, still I accept it. But – '

'Why do you want to know?' Elizabeth said.

He looked at her, and quicksands moved under him. Whatever intentions he had had of mastering his feelings were gone as all the bitter beauty of their love welled up afresh. 'God in Heaven, do you need to ask that? Why do you think I came here? I haven't stopped loving you, Elizabeth – all this time I've been trying to escape you and I can't – '

'Robert.' Her eyes were closed. 'Please, don't. Don't say another word.' She stood up, put her hands to her face. 'It's – it's all over between me and Hugh. Our marriage. In truth it was over a long time ago . . . but anyhow, that is it. But it doesn't change anything, Robert. It doesn't change anything.'

'What will you do?'

She shook her head, mutely, as if the question were unanswerable.

He looked in distraction at the objects in the room, the firescreen, the spinning-wheel, the china figures, banal everyday objects that struck on his consciousness as extraordinarily bizarre, such was the dreadful pitch of his emotion. He said huskily: 'And is this it . . . Are you about to send me away again, as you did that day in Stamford when Hugh was coming back and you were carrying my child?'

'You forget yourself,' she said, forcing the words out.

'No,' he said. 'I remember you, and the way we parted. I didn't believe – ' Impetuosity seized him. 'I didn't believe then that it was because you no longer loved me. And I don't believe it now, Elizabeth. I won't believe it until you tell me otherwise. I came here as soon as I heard – so quickly I couldn't examine even my own motives. I just had to see you. But I know, I admit that even then I must have hoped . . .' He made a gesture of helplessness.

'I – don't blame you, Robert,' she said quietly. She sat down again, stared at her colourless hands. 'Oh, God, it would be easy if I could just send you away – as I did before – and say I feel nothing for you. But it wouldn't be true, and I suppose you know that – '

'Elizabeth – '

'But what's happened since that time, Robert, don't you see?' she cried. 'There's no going back . . . Look at me.'

'You look pale,' he said. 'And thinner. And entirely beautiful to me, my darling.'

She winced, and shook her head. 'All this time – you don't understand – '

'Time, time is *nothing*,' he said passionately. 'Since I left you it's been a round of dead days, useless. Forgotten. It's only the thought of *you* that has lived during that time. And now, now I see you again, nothing's changed, we can throw all that time away.'

'No,' she said sadly. 'Oh, Robert – I've kept you in my heart all that time too, kept you there like a – last precious resource, oh, so precious. But – ' she held up a hand as he took a step towards her – 'it's not just a matter of the heart, or the mind, or the soul. We're enclosed in flesh – ' he did not see her tiny shudder – 'layers of flesh, turning everything to its foul uses . . .' She scrabbled for a handkerchief and pressed it to her lips. 'How can I make you see, Robert – I'm not whole any more, I'm not normal. If I could be for any man it would be you, Robert, you must believe me – but I'm sick . . .' Tears stood in her eyes but did not fall.

He reached out to touch her hand, and felt her flesh shrink. Love and a strange fear broke like clashing waves in him. 'My dear, forgive me. I know my coming has distressed you – '

'It's not *that*,' she said, going hastily to the window. 'But I can't make you understand – understand why you must go – why it can't be . . .'

'Don't send me away again, Elizabeth, not like this,' he said brokenly. 'All I want is to offer you my love, my life. If it isn't – if it isn't what you want then tell me – just tell me . . .'

She turned to him, part desperation, part appeal. The tears were on her cheeks. She let him take her hand, trembling. She inclined towards him, her feelings a tortured knot strained to breaking point. 'Oh, Robert,' she said weakly, 'it's no good . . .'

It was his touch – it was Robert, gentle and handsome and devoted – it was not Hugh, it was not Hugh . . . But the suffocation and nausea and the nightmare of flesh rose in her, the indelible wound flared, and she broke from him in revulsion, and he reeled back astonished and horrified as he saw the result of his tender embrace, as Elizabeth lurched and gagged and with a painful cry vomited.

She wept, her handkerchief at her mouth, her white gown stained. 'You see,' she gasped. 'He's – he's made me like this. I can't . . . not ever. Go *away*, Robert, go away, please – now you understand . . .'

He stood appalled. He reached out a hand to touch her, stopped, let it fall. He was a man in shock.

'Elizabeth – oh, my God, what he's done to you . . .'

She choked again, and ran from the room.

Landless picked up his hat and wiped his eyes and left.

3

The masquerade ball at the Pantheon the next evening was due to start at nine. It had turned bitterly cold by then, and the rutted London streets were treacherous with white frost. However, nothing was going to prevent the high society of the town getting there and enjoying themselves in their rather frequently low fashion.

Earlier that day Rebecca had tried on her costume, a gown in mock-Elizabethan style with a high ruff and panniers, and Lovell had called and with rather stiff laughter – he had no taste for this sort of thing – showed her his costume of Turkish cloak and turban.

And about the same time, a surprised Mary greeted cousin Luke at Buckingham Street.

He had been three frustrating days on the road, having set out on Sunday night and arrived only late last night, Tuesday. A chapter of accidents: a coach-horse going lame at Baldock, and then trouble with a wheel outside Stevenage. He thought he would have gone mad at the delays. But now a calm self-control had come over him. He kissed Mary briskly but warmly and hoisted Charles Joseph in the air.

'I'm staying at the Saracen's Head,' he told her. 'No time for finding a better lodging yet . . . Where's George?'

'At Lord Burghley's. There's nothing wrong, is there, Luke? I mean I'm delighted to see you, but it's so sudden.'

'No, there's nothing wrong, cousin. All's well at Morholm.' He smiled at her. 'I came as soon as I got your letter.'

'Well, I felt you ought at least to know. But, Luke – '

'Now, I'm not going to do anything foolish. But you must tell me where they are living. The Walsokens.'

She looked at him. An unusual man, bold and high-strung: but at the moment there was a quiet purpose about him. 'At Golden Square,' she said. 'But you can't go there, Luke. Can you?'

'Can't I?' He smiled obliquely. 'No. Perhaps not. But I'll find a way. I have to. Can you understand me, Mary?'

'I think so. But Luke – I don't want you to get hurt.'

Luke admired the drawings that Charles Joseph brought him. 'Bless you, cousin. But it seems to me – more and more since father died – that we can spend too much time trying not to get hurt. Afraid . . . so that we hide in a shell. Or build a shell for ourselves. Tell me, what is he like? This Fitzroy.'

Mary shrugged, watching him. 'Very polite, well-mannered. Soft-spoken. Luke, I hope you're not going to – '

'No, you misunderstand. It's just that I've been trying to picture him. I don't hate him or anything like that. How could I, really, when he has obviously admired and loved like me, and unlike me has seized his chance?'

Mary bent to poke the fire. She said suddenly: 'We are going to the masquerade at the Pantheon tonight. She – Rebecca – is sure to be there. And her fiancé.' She turned to him. 'Would you like to come with us?'

Luke smiled. 'Need you ask?'

Oxford Street was one of the broadest in London, and it needed to be to accommodate the great concourse of private and hired carriages bringing the revellers to the Pantheon that night. Around the carpeted entrance to the building link-boys with flaming torches ran, lighting the guests as they picked a path through the ordure of the street, fitfully illuminating fantastic costumes and jewelled masks.

The Hardwick party – George and Mary, Luke, and the Miltons – arrived at half-past nine. Mary had improvised a costume for Luke: a short cloak over one shoulder, with a laced collar, in the manner of a Spanish hidalgo. It suited his dark eyes and black hair. He was in good spirits, though Mary and George were silently speculating on what he meant to achieve by seeing Rebecca with her fiancé.

There was little of good spirits in their companions. Henry Milton was preoccupied by thoughts of Robert Landless, who had returned from Vere Street yesterday in a stony silence and had said they would meet at the Pantheon tomorrow and disappeared. Julia too was silent. She had been sick this morning – unknown to her husband – and was concealing a greater sickness inside now.

The Pantheon assembly-room was of huge size, with a high domed painted ceiling and arched galleries with seats running along the sides, and a stage at the end on which a professional orchestra, also masked, was playing. There must have been already more than a hundred people there when the Hardwick party arrived. Above the music there was a great hum as of giant bees, and the colour, beneath the huge glass chandeliers, assaulted the eye.

Some wore simple dominoes and masks over the eyes: some carried masks like fans before the face. A few, Rebecca saw from her seat in the lower gallery, had abandoned masks already, her father included. Others had thrown themselves into dressing-up with gusto. There was much anti-Catholic spirit – Popes covered with patches to represent pox, *décolletée* nuns: and gallows humour – a hanged man complete with noose and shroud and chalk-white face. There were many devils, with tails and horns. (No angels, she noticed.) Extreme Whigs provocatively wore American military costumes. Classical figures abounded: Bacchus, Venus, Vulcan, Helen of Troy, Arcadian shepherds, too – some with ravaged, decidedly un-pastoral faces, one with a live lamb.

There were more guests arriving constantly, and Rebecca did not see the Hardwick party come in.

'There's so much wealth here,' Rebecca said to Lovell. 'That lady – can those be real diamonds on her mask?'

'Oh, most certainly.'

'I would be feared lest they come off! Imagine grubbing on the floor for them in this crowd!'

'Well, I think that lady might well afford to buy new ones. She is Georgiana, Duchess of Devonshire.'

'Good God! I see why she is known as such a beauty.'

Lovell smiled constrainedly. He did not like her to use even mild oaths.

The Miltons had been joined by Sheridan and his wife, Sheridan very rakish in the costume of a cavalier. 'My sympathies tend to old Cromwell,' he told Milton, 'but the Royalists, alas, had the more flattering fashions.'

'I told Dick he looked absurd in that hat,' Mrs Sheridan confided to Julia. 'But there's no telling men anything, is there?'

'No,' Julia said, 'there isn't.'

'Mary, is Cousin Julia quite well?' Luke asked, a little way away.

'I don't know – I was wondering that myself,' Mary said. 'She's not an easy person to read.'

She observed Luke from the corner of her eye. He had refused

439

wine, and though he was scanning the room carefully she was struck afresh by his air of calm. The calm of a man staking all on his last card.

Milton missed what Sheridan was saying to him. He had just seen a big man walk past in Knight Templar costume, and was sure it was Sir Hugh Woodhouse. So he was not letting the wreck of his marriage spoil his pleasures.

Milton's surmise was right, though a savage desperation lay at the bottom of Sir Hugh's feelings. He had come with friends, and was determined to make a night of it. Let Lizzie go hang. Be damned to her. A mistake from the beginning. He could live without her – by God, he could live, he could start enjoying himself at last. He repeated such phrases in his head, to stave off the darkness, to douse the consciousness of the hardest blow he had ever received, a blow that had shaken the foundations of even his confidence and conceit, deep and mighty as they were.

The first minuet began.

Joshua Walsoken watched Rebecca take the floor with Lovell Fitzroy. Even without the mask, there was no sign on his square authoritarian face of the pride Mr Walsoken was feeling. Pride on his own account. He had risen, risen so high. His cup was full. And it was the daughter who had so often defied his will who was the agent of it. That was extra satisfaction.

'Father,' said Jeremiah, slim as a knife in a silver Harlequin costume, 'will they be happy, d'you suppose?'

Mr Walsoken frowned. 'Why should they not be?'

Jeremiah smiled at him unpleasantly. 'No matter.' He swallowed his sixth glass of wine. 'The Hardwicks are here, did you know? At least, I saw Mrs Hardwick a moment ago.'

Mr Walsoken drew in a sharp breath, then exhaled. It mattered little. He could forget the thwarting, the humiliations, at the hands of that hated family. He had risen beyond their circle now. He was out of their sphere. He had come out on top.

. . . 'I feel this evening will not end entirely genteelly,' said Lovell Fitzroy.

Rebecca lifted her eyes in surprise. She had thought for a moment (rather hopefully) that he was making an Improper Suggestion. But he was referring to the couple next to them in the dance, both tipsy, the lady in Greek draperies which made an open secret of her nipples, the gentleman dressed as Henry VIII with a jewelled codpiece that looked to be under some strain.

'Oh, you must be used to this sort of occasion,' she said.

'Not entirely,' he said. 'I – seldom go out in this way – er – normally.'

. . . 'D'you remember,' Mary said to George as they danced, 'when we first danced together?'

'The Bell at Stilton,' he said. 'A little band, rather out of tune. It seems a long time ago. A lot has happened since then. A lot has changed.'

'Some things don't change,' she said.

'I wonder if Powys is here yet,' George said when they came together again. 'D'you know he had me for fifty guineas last night? He'd better not deny me my revenge.'

'You plan to go gaming tonight?'

'Oh, just for a little while afterwards. Just to get my money back. You wouldn't have me retire a loser, surely?'

The dance separated again, before she could reply.

Luke had spotted Rebecca, though she had not seen him.

She was not easy to pick out in the great crowd of people. But she was for him. Once he saw her, he saw nothing else. The mêlée of brilliant colours, the bowing, turning, pirouetting dancers, were just a background for her, the setting of the jewel. Only she. Just as in his life, she was the bright centre of the shifting world, with its sometimes distracting peripheries, and only she could hold it together. She was the magnetic pole to which, though he might drift in sterile margins, he must inevitably return.

. . . After the minuet Mary was going over to speak to Julia, who was sitting in silence, when she heard her name called.

Captain Alex Finlayson – in uniform, not costume – introduced her to his companions, the Captain and Mrs Bridie of the burnished complexion, who unsurprisingly were in Indian garb.

'This is a splendid occasion, is it not, Mrs Hardwick?' Captain Finlayson said. 'Och, but I'm glad to see ye here. It's made the evening complete. I was afraid you might not be.'

For the first time it seemed he had had a drink, though he was certainly not drunk. Mary was aware of his eyes on her, lit and appreciative, bolder.

'Mrs Hardwick, are you engaged for the third?'

She hesitated, and turned to look at George. But George had spotted Ranulph Powys across the room, and was gone.

'I am now, Captain Finlayson,' she said, and a vile stab of bitter pleasure went through her.

Mary danced the third with Captain Finlayson, and then the fourth. And then the fifth. In the interim George did not rejoin her: he was with Powys and, of all people, Jeremiah Walsoken. And so they danced the next too.

The young Scot was in high spirits, but spirits that would suddenly soften into a wondering sort of attentiveness to her. His reserve eased by drink and enjoyment and by her own compliance, his eyes dwelt on her unashamedly. She wanted people to see. She wanted George to see.

There was an interval after the sixth. It was then that George appeared beside her. Her heart did an odd leap.

'Well, my love,' he said, 'you have more energy than I for this kind of work.' He wiped his brow. 'I didn't know it would be such a sweat in here. Mary – '

'A dance will revive you,' she said. 'Let's join the next – '

'Oh, an old man like me dancing,' he said laughing. 'I'll leave that to the young ones. You have four years on me, remember. No, I was thinking of slipping out of this press and going down to the club. I'm determined to have my revenge on Powys, and Jeremiah Walsoken's angling for another game.'

'What about me?' She hated herself for sounding pathetic.

'Oh, I'm not suggesting you leave, love. You're enjoying it, I see,' George said, smiling. 'Besides, you seem well attended.'

She looked for some irony, some resentment in those words, but could find none.

'Very well. If you must. You'll be losing heavily, I suppose. And not coming back till almost dawn.'

'I wasn't aware you'd been setting spies after me,' he said lightly, too lightly.

'I don't need to.'

He frowned. 'I lost the other night, certainly. All the more reason to – '

'No, George, less reason. Oh, it's all very well for Mr Powys. And Jeremiah, who has money from his father. But don't you see? Don't you really see what's happening?'

His face was stony. 'I'd be obliged if you wouldn't speak to me like a child, my love.'

'If you didn't act like one I wouldn't have to.'

The exchange had suddenly gone beyond their control; and both knew it, and both were too angry to retract.

'I see,' said George. 'Is there anything else?'

'No,' she said. 'Because there isn't anything that could stop you going anyway. But,' she added mutinously, 'you needn't think to find me waiting up for you.'

'I don't expect to,' he said, and turned to go. This was bravado, and bravado born of shame, for her rebuke had indeed stung him. But it would be compounding the shame to admit it: and, equally, she did not realise this in her hurt fury. So, he left. And she willed herself not to cry, and succeeded.

It was just as the second set of dances had begun that Robert Landless arrived.

Milton had been looking for Julia, and could not find her, when he saw the young man threading his way across to him. He wore no costume – and not even evening clothes, just riding-coat and boots – and had torn off his mask as soon as he came in. There was no smile or greeting. He looked like death.

'I expected to see you in something very flamboyant,' Milton said. 'I'm surprised you were admitted like that.'

'I told them I was a highwayman,' Landless said. Milton smiled, but saw no humour in his friend's face. Landless's eyes roved, smoky and haunted.

'Is she – she's not here, is she?'

'Who?'

Landless glanced at him impatiently. Dangerously.

'No. I haven't seen her. Did you expect her to be?'

Landless shook his head. He was silent for some moments.

'Woodhouse is here, though?'

'Yes. I just saw him go downstairs.'

'I thought – ' Landless's voice thickened, and he cleared his throat. 'I thought so. That is the chief reason I came.'

'I'm flattered,' Milton said with an uneasy laugh. A nameless fear afflicted him like a chill, driving away the heat of the ballroom.

. . . Lovell's uncle, the Duke of Grafton, had arrived. He was in the left gallery talking with his nephew and the Walsokens. Mr

Walsoken was waiting on the Duke's every word like a dog hoping for scraps at the table.

It might have occurred to Rebecca that she was, in fact, a little pushed out of the group; the Lady smiling submissive at the edge (it might have been her father who was marrying Lovell Fitzroy) – but another thought was occupying her. Not a thought . . . a feeling, an intimation. 'The shrims', her old nurse used to call this feeling.

For she was aware of a figure standing against the pillar nearby. The light from the chandelier was falling behind him, outlining the shape of a curly head, broad shoulders with a Spanish cloak. Perfect stillness.

She could not see the eyes, but she knew they were watching her.

And then the seventh dance was starting up, and the figure was moving towards her, and she felt that quicksilver sensation – so rare and elusive that in both hope and retrospect it seems a phantasm – of her life coming, from widely diverging angles, to a point sharper than a needle, a point sharp enough to explode into meaningless fragments the stretched bubble – seen for the first time for the superficial thing it was – in which she had sealed herself and tried to float. The shadows receded from the figure like the dawn peeling off the sullenness of the Fen, and Luke was there.

'Will you dance?' The voice, and the hand coming out towards her, the hand in which her own fitted as if it were a missing part that made a whole . . . There was no mistaking.

And no resisting – or should not have been.

But she was to be married to someone else. Who had turned, and was looking at them quizzically.

Luke said: 'Sir. You must be Mr Fitzroy. How d'you do.'

Rebecca found herself saying, 'Oh – Lovell – this is Mr Luke Hardwick – George's cousin.'

Lovell's face had changed, and he was shaking Luke's hand. She realised that now it would actually look odd if she did *not* dance with Luke.

So they went. He did not speak.

She said: 'Luke . . . I was sorry to hear about your father.'

Still he said nothing. She said, seeking for the urbane tone: 'I didn't know you were in London. Are you staying with George and Mary?'

'No,' he said. 'At the Saracen's Head. Just arrived.'

He was silent again then, and she burst out: 'Oh, Luke, what are you *doing* here?'

'I heard you were to be married. So, naturally, I came.'

'Yes, I'm going to be married.'

Luke shook his head. 'Not to him, Rebecca.'

She made a wrong step, recovered herself. 'Has my father seen you here?'

'I don't think so. But it doesn't matter. Nothing else matters. All these obstacles, difficulties, these distractions, all the things that have come into our lives since we met: they're just shadows. I've realised that, at last. I realised it when I heard of your engagement. And so I've come to stop it.'

'How do you suppose you're going to do that?'

'Rebecca – you can't marry that man.'

'*That man* is my future husband,' she said. 'I can and will marry him. It has nothing to do with you. And I can't listen to you speak disrespectfully of him.'

'But I don't. I've nothing against him. I dare say he's even worthy of you. More so than me. But it doesn't matter. I've come to claim you, Rebecca.'

. . . Robert Landless set down his glass of wine untasted and pointed across the room.

'That,' he said to Milton, 'if I'm not mistaken, is Woodhouse.'

Milton caught his arm. 'Robert – this surely isn't the place for – well – '

Landless smiled quite gently and shook off his arm.

Milton followed him, across the floor, to where Sir Hugh Woodhouse was standing in an alcove with a glass in his hand, listening to a bawdy story told by one of his friends.

Landless said clearly: 'Sir Hugh?' and the baronet turned.

Landless quietly took the glass from Sir Hugh's hand and threw it in his face. Then he took his glove from his pocket and struck Sir Hugh twice across the cheeks.

'When will it be convenient for you to meet me?' Landless said.

'*You*, you young puppy,' stormed Sir Hugh, wiping his face, 'I'll meet you in hell – '

'Very probably,' Landless said. 'But in the meantime I demand satisfaction.'

'Robert – ' Milton hissed.

Sir Hugh's face was crimson. 'Why, I'll thrash the life out of you – '

'That is what I hope to determine,' said Landless. 'That is why I ask you to meet me. Unless you wish me to noise it abroad that you are a coward – as you are – and refused the challenge.'

It was fortunate the four of them were in the alcove, and unattended. Sir Hugh's friend was watching him carefully.

'Robert, this is nonsense,' said Milton.

'This man,' said Landless, shaking, 'this man is the lowest scum that ever poisoned the earth with his filth. And I demand satisfaction.'

'Very well, damn you!' said Sir Hugh, his mouth spraying. 'If you're such a fool, I shall be glad to! I know all about you, Landless! I'm glad I shall be able to blood you at last, and give you what you deserve, for sniffing round my property. Tomorrow, what do you say to tomorrow, eh? At sunrise, hm?'

Landless wheeled round. 'You hear, gentlemen? I hold you as witnesses to this agreement.'

'I want nothing to do with this – ' Milton began. 'It's senseless . . .'

But Sir Hugh's friend was eager: and Landless was fierce. 'You can't back out on me now, Milton,' he said. 'I shall need a second.'

'Very well,' Milton said abruptly. 'If only so that I can find a way of stopping it.'

'There's only one way of settling this,' said Sir Hugh.

Landless looked at him coolly. 'Hyde Park, by Grosvenor Gate?'

'Any damn place.'

'Then it's settled.'

And it was, though Milton could hardly believe it. As they moved away he said: 'You can't seriously mean to go through with this – this archaic – monstrous – '

'I'm going home now,' Landless said. 'I'd advise you to do the same. We've to be up and fresh early in the morning. You will meet me there, won't you, Milton? I am in earnest. I am in deadly earnest. I can never explain what that bastard's done, Milton, not even to you. You must trust me.'

'I'll be there,' Milton said, 'God forgive me. Robert, damn you, Sir Hugh is a *sportsman*. He *lives* shooting.'

'Then he'll die shooting,' said Landless.

. . . The dance had ended, but Rebecca had not escaped from

Luke. In the shadow of a pillar he held her arm. 'You can't marry him. I won't let you, Rebecca.'

'Leave go my arm! You've no right to do this. You can't stop me doing what I want, damn you!' Indignation, to ward off other emotions. 'Let *go*.'

'Not till you tell me something.'

She struggled, her strength not quite enough for his. She glared at him through her hair.

'Tell me you love him. Look me in the eye and tell me you love him.'

'Very well!' she cried. 'I do love him! I love Lovell Fitzroy and I'm going to marry him. Not that it has *anything* to do with you, but if it means you'll let me go you might as well know it!'

He let go of her arm, but continued to gaze at her. 'I think you're making a mistake –'

'Oh! don't tell me – "I don't know my own mind". If *that's* all you've got to say –'

'No. You don't know your own heart.'

'And you do, I suppose.'

'Yes. Because it belongs to me.' She tried to turn away, was caught again. 'We're one, Rebecca. We meet like earth and sky, different elements that make the whole. I've seen that at last, though for so long my face has been turned elsewhere like yours now, seeking God knows what and believing in everything but the one true fact in this life. You think I come here out of some petty pique, when this is something that can't be denied any more than the wind or the sun or the rain? D'you think I'd do this to you if it weren't that every fibre of my being weren't crying out for love of you and saying *this can't be*?'

With a choking gasp she broke free of him, and was gone.

The Walsoken party left the Pantheon soon afterwards, for Rebecca said she was feeling ill.

The Miltons left shortly also. Julia showed no desire to stay, and Milton had his own reasons to retire early, though he decided not to tell his wife of what was to happen tomorrow.

Luke Hardwick left too.

Mary Hardwick, however, did not leave early, but stayed and danced almost the whole evening with Captain Alex Finlayson of the Scots Greys.

4

Sleepless nights.

For Henry Milton, who dozed and woke from dreams of mad slaughter. And Julia, who lay long wakeful with a hand at her belly.

For Luke Hardwick, who paced his inn room and saw nothingness. Brave words. I've come to claim you. Words that had failed, that he knew had failed even as he spoke them. The last card.

And for Rebecca Walsoken.

Who sat up in bed, in her cold grand bedroom in Golden Square, and hugged her knees and rocked herself, and tried to make sense of her life.

A little French clock ticked away on the mantelshelf. Hourly, it chimed, and shortly afterwards, as if to confine it, she heard the watch ring his bell somewhere in the streets and cry that all was well.

And her thoughts raced hectically around her mind, as if they were trying to beat the little clock. Sometimes she laid her head down, and wished aloud that she was dead. But she had never wanted to be dead. It did not convince. She wanted to be alive. The hands of the clock, at ten to two, formed a grin, as if to remind her of this. And she wondered if, these past months, she *had* been fully alive.

Hours till dawn. She felt almost as if she were at a sick-bed vigil. Her own.

Four o'clock and all's well . . .

Half-past four, and she punched her pillow, flung her head down, and resolved to sleep and have done with it. And then she sat bolt upright, with a wonderful feeling of clarity like someone who knows they have recovered from illness.

It was as if her circling thoughts had suddenly dropped through a trapdoor of her mind: into a region that was not dark and subterranean but bright, bright as day with the shining truth of the heart.

All's well . . .

She knew what she must do.

Without hesitation she wrote, sitting shivering at her bureau as the palest intimations of dawn gestured at the window: and without excuses either, she wrote the letter to Lovell that said she could not marry him, and that the engagement was off: '. . . It will surely make things worse to admit that I have lied to you – in saying I had no previous attachment: and it can be little more comfort to you to hear me say that, in that regard, I have lied to myself also. But this is the only attempt at justification I can make: and I must beg you – though I have no right – to believe that nothing short of this unanswerable claim could ever have made me do this to you . . .'

When she had finished the letter, she sealed it and directed it *For Mr Lovell Fitzroy*. Then she packed a bag, and waited for the morning to come.

# FIVE

I

It was late when Mary left the Pantheon, accompanied, at her suggestion, by Captain Finlayson. A demon of hurt and revenge drove her. Classic situation. The neglected wife. What's sauce for the goose . . . Oh, dear God.

You know where this is heading, she told herself in the carriage, with Captain Finlayson's lean head in profile beside her: you know where this is heading. But that was a road she still refused to look down, even though her feet were already treading it.

They had been observed tonight with some interest: she and George already had a circle of acquaintance, and in this society scandal was like twitch-fire, always ready to break out. She submitted to the scrutiny with an air of cold contempt. But that was only a mask. This part she was playing – the stuff of gossip and of melodrama – was one in which she took no joy, only a deathly gratification that burned like a poisonous drug.

They passed large crowds emerging from the theatres in Covent Garden, and Mary stared at them. Captain Finlayson was uneasy: ardent, certainly, and hopeful, yet perplexed by her manner. 'Mary. Tell me what you're thinking.'

She stirred. 'Oh . . . I was thinking of the first play I ever saw.'
'Go on.'

'It was at Morholm, when I was fifteen or so. A party of travelling players came and performed in the barn. The leading man was drunk and the lady playing the young heroine was past forty . . . Oh, but I loved it. I thought it was marvellous. I'd never seen a play before.' She shrugged, half-laughing. 'What a little fool I was.' A great desolation had suddenly risen up in her, threatening tears. She did not want that. She wanted to be hard and glittering.

'I suspect you don't feel at home in London,' he said. 'Isn't that so? When I think of you, it's of the country I think – the fresh air, and green trees, and sunlight.'

She swallowed something in her throat. He was perceptive, more than he knew. But she must not allow herself to think of Morholm either. No, at all costs. 'And you,' she said. 'Where do you feel at home, Alex?'

'Nowhere, in truth. That sounds a thought pathetic! I don't mean it like that.' He smiled, and then his smile faded. 'But as to where I feel happiest . . .'

He had taken her hand. She let it lie for a moment, and then found herself answering the pressure.

Well, this is what you wanted, isn't it? This is what you wanted.

Their hackney drew up at Buckingham Street. He handed her out, and she kept her hand in his.

'Will you not come in, Alex?'

Their lodgings were in darkness. Charles Joseph and Bridget were in bed. In the parlour a remnant of fire glowed in the grate. She took a spill and lit two candles.

This is what you wanted.

'Mary – will your husband not be retairning?'

She set a candle on the mantelshelf. 'Why do you ask about my husband, Alex?' Yes, that was the right tone. Heartless.

He had stolen up beside her, had placed his arm about her shoulders.

'No,' she said, 'he will not be home yet.'

'Mary . . . I never dared to hope that this could happen.' His lips were on her neck. She closed her eyes. Then he was kissing her.

Strange, almost objective, thoughts – a different man, different lips. Not unpleasant. But this isn't *me*, she thought. She no more felt she inhabited this body, this body being embraced, than if she had been a spider on the wall watching.

'Oh, Mary, you are so lovely.' His fingers stroked her bare shoulder. 'Lovelier with each moment. What I said about sunlight – that's you. You shine, you are all light . . .'

'Oh, I have my dark corners, I assure you,' she said. Even her voice did not seem her own.

'All beauty then. Night and day. Everything . . .'

She was aware of the powder in her hair, her jewels, her face-paint, and suddenly she wanted to rake them off and scream at him, *this is me*, I'm not this vision you are drawing.

There was a noise from the next room – Charles Joseph's room. She lifted her head, all alertness.

'What is it? Is it your wee boy?'

She nodded, listening. There was silence.

'It's all right,' she said.

She sat on the sofa, and he sat beside her, but did not touch her. 'Mary,' he said, 'you know I will be leaving for Ireland shortly. In a week or so.'

'I know it.'

'So, you see – what I mean to say – '

'What do the poets say? Gather ye rosebuds while ye may . . . Then come kiss me, sweet and twenty, Youth's a stuff will not endure . . .' She gave a brittle laugh.

'No. No, that's not it. I know it must seem to you – well, the old story of the soldier out for a lark before he goes back to his billet. But that's just what it is not, believe me. If I were leaving next month, or next year, or never – I would still feel the same.'

She could not breathe. Her voice said: 'And you would still like to make love to me?'

He gazed at her very soberly. 'I would like to make love to you.'

Then he was kissing her again, more confidently, and his hand was circling in firm gentle swathes up her stomach and over her breasts. And now the division in her mind stretched and threatened to break altogether, for one half was responding, quickening to his touch. And suddenly it was resolved, from the strength of her real feeling for him, that she must be truthful with him.

She disengaged herself.

'Alex – '

'What is it, my love?'

'I – have to tell you. I don't think . . .'

'Is it your wee boy? Forgive me, I – '

'No, no, it isn't that.' His hand was still on her arm, and she moved it: she must be free of that to speak.

He watched her. 'Is it George?'

'Partly.'

'I've been clumsy. I've hurried you, my darling. I'm sorry. But – '

'No, you haven't, it isn't that.' She hated herself. But the truth must come out. It would fester and corrupt otherwise.

He had moved to kiss her again. 'You said that George will not be home yet. Oh, I've wanted you so dearly tonight, Mary. Surely now is the time – '

She used more force this time, and got to her feet. He looked up at her in surprise.

'Alex,' she said, 'please listen to me.'

His face had changed subtly, as if with a dawning realisation. 'I'm listening,' he said, and at his tone her heart plunged.

'Oh, Alex,' she said miserably, 'what must you think of me?'

Something of the military stiffness of bearing had come back as he sat there. He dusted something from his sleeve. 'I think,' he said, 'that you have decided to be faithful to your husband.'

'I know how it must seem – '

'It seems rather late in the day, sairtainly,' he said. She saw he was wounded, and proud. 'Are you afraid of him, is that it?'

She shook her head in anguish, not trusting herself to speak.

'Well.' He stood up. 'I confess I thought you felt something for me. I confess I thought I had reason to do so. You tell me I'm wrong, so I must accept that.'

'And I do feel something for you. The deepest affection and – and – But George is my husband, and my only love.'

'Fortunate you remembered in time,' he said. His mouth was set. 'This is a poor trick you've played me, ma'am.'

She noticed the 'ma'am', and burst out: 'I don't expect you to forgive me. But if I can only explain. It's *because* I like you so much that I cannot – cannot go through with it . . .'

He raised an eyebrow. 'Well, that's the fairst time I've heard that excuse, at any rate,' he said. 'And I suppose if you had not liked me you would have been quite happy to – '

'Yes!' she cried. 'Yes! Don't you see, what I was looking for was just revenge, a horrible revenge for – for the way things are between me and George now. If he *had* found me in someone else's arms I would have been *glad*. But I wasn't looking for the love, the kindness you could offer me. To have taken that, knowing in my heart what my real motives were, would have been a – a travesty, a trampling on what was good in its own right. An insult to you, who deserve much better. And I'm not trying to fob you off with sweet words. I mean it. But there's only one man for me, I know it now – for better

453

or worse – and perhaps it *would* be better if that were not so. But that's how it is, and I'm sorry, so sorry . . .' She fought back her tears, for they too might seem to be playing for his sympathy.

'I'm sorry too, ma'am,' he said. He picked up his gloves and hat. 'Perhaps when I'm in a better mood I shall be able to appreciate your reasoning. It is all a very sorry business. But I hope at least in future you may solve your matrimonial problems without dragging in third parties.'

He went to the door, and opened it, and met George just coming up on the landing.

He passed George without speaking. George watched him go, and then came into the room and closed the door softly.

'Well,' he said. 'You have very late visitors.'

She covered her mouth with her hand. She wanted to die.

George picked up her sewing from the bureau, turned it over in his hands. 'This is rather interesting,' he said tonelessly. 'Tonight I caught Jeremiah Walsoken cheating at cards. I've suspected him before. His winning streaks seemed to occur with unnatural regularity. I watched him quite carefully, biding my time, and then got hold of him by the shoulder as he was reaching for his winnings and ripped his coat back. There was a pocket sewn inside with a couple of cards in it.' He put the sewing down quite gently. 'It made quite a fuss in the club. He was ejected, swearing copiously. I got all my money back, as did others who had lost to him. Apparently he had made quite a habit of cheating.' He looked at her. 'Rather a coincidence, is it not?'

They were silent. The fire sighed and went out.

There was a china vase on the bureau, and George edged it over with one finger and then with a savage jerk swept it on to the floor.

Mary blinked at the crash, watched the pieces scatter.

'It wasn't what you think,' she said huskily.

'Spare me,' said George. He moved towards their bedroom but she went after him and pulled him back.

'George, wait. It isn't what you think – I swear there's nothing – '

George shook her off. He was white. 'God, what a fool I've been! Under my very nose. We should have come to London during the riots. Then you would have had hundreds of soldiers to choose from.'

'That's a terrible thing to say!'

'It's a terrible thing to do. But that doesn't appear to have stopped you.'

Her tears began to fall at last, agonisingly.

'Tell me,' George said, 'did the presence of our son in the next room not trouble you? I, of course, was out of the way, but – '

'Oh, yes, *our* son now,' she spat back. 'I'm glad you remember him. Accuse me if you will but don't use him as a weapon, George, because it's the first time you've given him a thought in weeks.' A torrent rose in her. 'You were out of the way, yes. As you always are. Don't you see? But it wasn't because of that that I danced with Captain Finlayson all night. Or why I asked him in here tonight – yes, I did that. It was because I wanted you to know! I wanted you to see that someone thinks me worth attention. And if I had to go further, then I was prepared to do that. Oh, yes. But I have not – cannot. Never could. Because it's you I want, George, my husband – not him, not anyone but you. I've been losing you, watching you drift away, and there was nothing I could do . . . and I wanted you back.'

George stared at her. 'So this is it. You gnaw away on some damn grievance for so long, and then you face me with *this*. As an excuse for – '

'It's an excuse for nothing. Don't you think I would have gone off with him weeks ago if there were anything real between us? Of course I would! Rather than submit to your treatment, waiting for the odd word, for the odd moment of your time. But, God help me, I love you and I can never love anyone else.'

'Well,' George said, 'I wish I could admire your methods of finding that out.'

She said slowly, dully, 'I sent him away. I meant to go through with it, to get back at you, but I sent him away.'

'Oh, capital. And am I supposed to feel comforted by that?'

'I don't know what you feel, George. I don't know what you feel or think these days. You're like a stranger to me since we came here. Oh, George,' she cried in desperate appeal, 'all this – everything – Captain Finlayson, London, money, jewels and frocks, Morholm – don't you know I'd throw it all away just to be alive and with *you*?'

George was breathing hard. He paced to the window. 'This – is all very strange. I find my wife alone with a handsome officer who's been ogling her for months; and by some peculiar logic the blame is all turned to me. I applaud you, my dear.'

'Oh, damn you then!'

She ran into their bedroom, dragged her clothes from the closet and began flinging them on to the bed.

George had followed her. He stood in the doorway. He looked sick and drained. 'So,' he said huskily, 'I have been neglecting you.'

She shook her head mutely, unable to speak.

'Mary. What are you doing?' he said. And then: 'Where will you go?'

'I don't know . . . it doesn't matter. Julia's . . .'

'Not to him?'

'*No!*'

She struggled with the carpet bag. Its mouth was tied with string and she could not undo the knots. He took it from her hands and began to untie it.

'It's very late,' he said. 'I – contrary to appearances I care enough about you to – to not like the idea of you going out at this time. I care enough, Mary . . .' There was a tremor in his voice. 'I care . . .'

She suddenly put her hands up to her face, weak with distress.

He picked up her chemise from where she had thrown it on the bed. 'I told you about Jeremiah tonight,' he said after a moment. 'Ripping his coat and so on. It sounded very dramatic. Satisfying. But it wasn't, really. I thought afterwards – why shouldn't he win by cheating? It's all much the same after all. Easy money. A shadow of excitement. Nothing real. No one likes to hear the truth about themselves,' he said harshly. 'But perhaps you're not the only person to do that tonight, Mary. Perhaps I've been doing that myself.' He stroked the chemise gently. 'Perhaps that's what I don't like hearing. It – it bites deep.' He put the chemise down. 'Are you going to leave?'

'Do you want me to?'

He looked down, his breast heaving. 'I don't think I have any right to – to say yes or no. Perhaps I don't have any right to say – to ask you to let me try to make amends.' His voice was breaking. 'And certainly not to expect you to believe me if I say that I will. I can only beg you . . . beg you to believe that I don't want to lose you . . . ever . . . I don't want to lose you, Mary . . .'

Her heart opened to him. 'Oh, you haven't, George.' She held out her hands, her throat choked with tears. 'I'm *here*. Always will be.'

He looked up at her and then hugged her fiercely to him.

They were still like that when Charles Joseph in his night shirt appeared at the door, screwing up his eyes at the light. He saw the tears on Mary's face.

'Mummy,' he said unhappily, 'you're crying.'

She bent to pick him up. 'It's – it's because I've been laughing so much,' she said, wiping her cheeks.

'She's been laughing at me,' George said, patting his son. 'Because I'm a fool. Oh, I've been such a fool. But I won't be any more.'

2

Luke was up and dressed before the latticed window of his room had turned luminous with dawn.

He ran a comb through his tangle of hair, looked out at the inn-yard, where the ostlers were already leading stamping horses across the cobbles. A cold drizzle fell. He touched his chin, debated whether to shave. There seemed no point.

Where was he going anyway? What was there for him in London? Only the ruins of his hopes. Home? What was there for him there?

The mask he had worn last night at the Pantheon was on the desk. He picked it up, bunched his fist as if to hurl it to the floor. But no. There was no fury in him. No fire, only ashes.

He slumped at the desk, and bowed his head.

He was still there, holding the mask in his fingers, when the tap at the door came.

'Come in.'

The maid's voice. 'If you please, sir . . .'

'Set it down there, thank you,' he said, thinking she brought hot water. He did not turn round.

'If you please, sir, a lady to see you.'

He heard the door close. At last he lifted his head, and turned.

Her cloak was dripping wet, and she slipped it off and let it fall to the floor beside her bag. Her hair was loose and there were beads of rain on it too.

'Oh, my love,' he said. 'I'm not still sleeping, am I?'

'No, Luke,' Rebecca said. 'And neither am I, at last.'

A second passed, and she reached out her hand, and was taken into his arms.

There was both everything and nothing to say, and for a while they could only kiss and touch and laugh and weep and hold each other and look and then kiss again. There was only the one chair in the room, and she sat on his knee and he pushed back her damp sweet-smelling hair and said at last: 'How did you know where – '

'You said the Saracen's Head last night,' she said. 'Don't you remember?'

'Last night . . .' He shook his head. 'Rebecca, last night – '

'Was last night,' she said. 'And this is the morning. Our morning. Our beginning.' She stroked his face.

'I haven't shaved,' he said apologetically.

She laughed, hugging him to her. 'Oh, Luke. Oh, I do love you, my darling.'

His arms around her, his lips on hers. It was right. She was whole, made over again, a new person. The person she had always been meant to be.

'Does no one know you're here?' he said.

'No. I just left. I – there was nothing else for it. It had to be. Like you said.'

'But – what about . . .'

'Lovell?' She shook her head. 'I've hurt him for sure. And I'm sorry. And yet I'm not. For just as this is something that had to be, my marrying Lovell was something that was *not* to be. As you said last night. And even then I didn't realise it at first. Afraid of my feelings . . . afraid of the truth.'

Luke nodded, his eyes lowered. 'I know that feeling,' he said. 'Oh, Rebecca – that time in Northampton – what can you think of me? Can you believe me now, that I love you – and always have and always will and nothing, ever, can change that.'

His words were lost as for an answer she held him and kissed him with fierce tenderness, and the room, the inn, the city, the past and future were lost too.

It was about this time that Mr Walsoken discovered that his daughter had disappeared, leaving a letter for her fiancé.

3

Milton rose at half-past five. Julia was sleeping at last, her face grey and troubled. In the next room he dressed and washed by candle-light. It was cold, and he felt numb and stiff. He wished last night had been a dream. He hoped Landless or Sir Hugh would not turn up.

There was a faint phosphorescence in the sky when he reached the river at King's Arms Stairs. The boatman was still yawning. They crossed through a thick shawl of mist that was half drizzle. Upstream bulked the shape of a brig, and someone was ringing a bell on board. At Charing Cross he found a chair. The streets were just waking in the purple fore-dawn: a couple of street-traders about, a maid emptying slops from a window. As he rode it occurred to him that as a second it might be his duty to provide pistols. Was that right, or not? He had never possessed such a thing. Oh, but it was all so incredible. The stuff of cheap romances, of the sort of thing he used to turn out as a hack-writer.

But of course it did go on, though society frowned and the law was cracking down. His friend Sheridan had once fought a duel, and only just came out alive . . .

And Landless's face last night. Such hatred. Something about Elizabeth . . .

He got out at Tyburn Lane, paid the chairmen, watched them jog off. The glow was mounting up the sky and coldly firing the tops of the trees in the Park.

A brief hope that Landless had wryly thought better of the whole thing was extinguished as he came to Grosvenor Gate and his friend, in riding-cloak and hat, stepped out from behind the bole of a spreading oak.

'A cold morning,' Landless said. 'I was afraid you might not come.'

'I've come,' Milton said, 'to see if I can put a stop to it.'

He looked at Landless. No, his mood had not changed. The young man's nostrils were taut, his eyes naked and sleepless. He held a pistol-case under his cloak.

'Let's walk a little,' Landless said. 'I need to keep alert.'

Tiny mushrooms studded the crisp grass. From the trees came the sawing voice of a rook.

'An apology,' said Milton. 'Is that no use? Some formal apology is surely enough – '

Landless laughed shortly. 'Dear friend,' he said touching Milton's arm. 'An apology is not the question. No apology he could make could satisfy me. Only one thing can.'

They walked on. The darkness was evaporating like dew.

'I have made no arrangements, of course,' said Landless. 'I'm afraid I must burden you with that also . . . if need be. My lawyer is Mr Fellowes at Ely. It is all to go to Elizabeth.'

'To Elizabeth?'

'She may not need it. But it's all the better for her to have money of her own. More independence.'

'Very well,' said Milton miserably. He noticed it was full dawn. And he noticed, with a sinking heart, as they retraced their steps that two figures were standing in the clearing ahead.

Sir Hugh's friend, a florid military man named Rogers, carried his brace of pistols. Two horses were tethered to a tree, and Sir Hugh was booted and spurred. He looked very large.

The two parties met, in a semicircular clearing surrounded by chestnut trees.

Sir Hugh and Landless stood apart, staring across the lightening Park, whilst Milton and Rogers conferred.

'Is there no way of stopping this, for God's sake?' Milton said.

'Fraid not,' Rogers sniffed. He seemed to be enjoying it. 'Hugh's a man of his word. And your man seems to be mad to go through with it. A bit unbalanced, what?'

Milton bit his lip. 'What if – well, we need a surgeon?'

'It's each man for himself,' said Rogers. 'That's understood. Got to be the strictest secrecy, you realise, sir. You know the law. Sir Hugh and I will not hesitate to ride off after the event; and in – different circumstances – you and your man must do the same.'

Milton nodded. He looked from Sir Hugh to Landless. 'Gentlemen,' he said, 'it's a cold morning, and I'm sure we all wish to go home to a hearty breakfast. Can we not do so now and consider this matter closed?'

Sir Hugh patted down his lace stock. 'I have been insulted and challenged,' he said noisily. 'The responsibility is not mine.'

Milton said: 'But this quarrel – '

'Is between me and that bastard,' said Landless whitely. 'He knows why. Elizabeth knows why – '

'Don't you bandy my wife's name, you insolent puppy!' roared Sir Hugh.

'Gentlemen, gentlemen,' said Rogers, 'let us have no more. Mr Milton, I think the light is good enough now?'

Milton glanced around. He could make out the bare twigs of the trees in the distance, and the chimneys of St George's Hospital. One was smoking. The drizzle had almost petered out.

'Very well,' he said. He indicated the clearing. 'This ground will suffice?'

The two combatants nodded. There was pink at Landless's high cheekbones. His fair hair was immaculately combed and tied.

Rogers oversaw the priming and loading of the pistols. Milton felt useless: he knew nothing of this. There was a foul taste in his mouth.

Sir Hugh was slightly the taller of the two men as they stood back to back, pistols held upwards. Birds were piping in a thin wintry way. Sir Hugh's face was more than usually high-coloured, but he looked calm, as if he did this every day. He had fired his first gun when he was barely out of his cradle. Landless's jaws were working and Milton saw his hand tremble.

'Ready, gentlemen?' Rogers said. 'Mr Milton will count. Fourteen paces. At fourteen you will attend, present, and fire.'

Milton glanced at him, moistened his lips, began.

'One . . . two . . . three . . .'

He counted slowly, perhaps with some mad idea of never getting to fourteen. Impossible, of course. Like holding back the tides; holding back the dawn. Holding back death.

'. . . eight . . . nine . . . ten . . .'

The sun was weaving gold patterns in the trees to the east. A breeze lifted Landless's hair-ribbon. Colour was coming to life in the grass.

'. . . twelve . . . thirteen . . . fourteen.'

Two puffs of smoke and, almost simultaneous, two sharp cracks. Landless seemed to fire wildly, high. Space of a second. The left sleeve of Landless's coat had ripped apart above the elbow as if an invisible hand had torn it. He glanced at it in surprise, then up again, lifted his second pistol. But Sir Hugh had done a strange little half-pirouette, and he was on the ground and Rogers was hurrying towards him.

Landless dropped both pistols on the grass and touched his arm gingerly. Milton was beside him. 'Are you wounded? Let me see . . .'

The coat sleeve, and the shirt sleeve beneath, were in tatters where the ball had whizzed past. A smell of powder and scorching. But the skin of Landless's arm was scarcely grazed. 'Thought I'd been winged,' he gasped. 'Milton – go and see – Woodhouse . . .'

461

Startled birds were wheeling in the sky as Milton walked over to where Sir Hugh lay, mountainous and still.

Rogers rose from his knees as Milton came up. He had gone white.

Sir Hugh's lashes were fluttering, and his eyes were staring up, up into the sky with an expression of wonder. But they were not seeing anything. There was a splintery mess at his right temple that was matting his hair and staining the grass.

'Oh, my God – '

'This is a bad business, Mr Milton,' said Rogers. 'I – confess I never expected this.'

Milton stared at the great body, seemingly huge and swollen in death. 'What can we do?'

'Get away, and get your man away,' snapped Rogers. 'This won't be easy to hush up. I'll keep to the bargain, though I wish to God I'd never . . . Go on, man.'

Landless was there. He looked as if he was going to be sick.

Milton took his arm, steered him, half-dragged him away. He was like dead weight.

'We'd better leave by another gate,' Milton said. 'Come on, Robert, there's nothing we can do.'

Landless allowed himself to be led until they reached the edge of the park at the Corner. Then he shook Milton off and buried his face in his hands. 'Oh, God, I've killed him. I've killed him.' All the grim hate was gone: there was only sickness and horror. It had the effect of stiffening Milton.

'Yes,' he said. 'You've killed him. That's why you've got to get away. Come.' He dragged him on.

'Oh, Jesus Christ . . . Elizabeth . . . Henry, what will I do? Where will I go?'

Milton's mind raced. 'In such cases people often claim a shooting accident or something. God, I don't know how this can be covered up. If it comes out, it's plain murder, Robert. You know that. Now, I think Rogers will do what he can. But there'll be a coroner's report. Someone may have heard the shots. Someone may have caught what was going on at the Pantheon last night. Do you see?'

Landless slumped against the bole of a tree. 'I don't know,' he said brokenly. 'I can't think straight . . .'

'You've got to. Are you going to stay here and face a possible murder charge?'

'Perhaps I should. I don't care.' All of a sudden he looked very young to Milton. 'I did it. Perhaps I should just – '

'Now listen.' Milton gripped his arm hard. 'The only thing is to go abroad. For a time at least. You've friends in France, haven't you?'

'You forget we are at war with France, Henry,' said Landless with a sickly smile.

'Ireland then. That will have to do.' He pulled him on again. 'A hackney home. Change that coat and shirt. By coach you could be in Bristol tomorrow. A packet to Ireland. Out of the country till it blows over. It's the only way.'

They found a hackney-coach at the Corner, and Milton put Landless, unprotesting now, into it.

'Elizabeth,' said Landless. 'What about her?'

'I'll try to see her,' Milton said. He peered out of the window, almost fearing to find them pursued. 'She'll be all right. It's you we've got to worry about.'

There were tears in Landless's eyes, but they did not fall. 'How did we ever get to this pass?' he said.

Milton had no answer.

4

They were together. That was all that was important to Rebecca and Luke that day. It was all that had ever been important.

They had breakfast together in the coffee-room of the Saracen's Head. Even such trivial things as eating rolls and drinking coffee, in each other's company, were transformed. They laughed at each other across the table: they laughed at the serving-girl, and tipped her enormously.

'What shall we do?' Luke asked. 'What do you want to do?'

'I ought to be tired,' she said. 'I didn't sleep at all last night. But I'm not.'

'Me too,' he said.

'I just want to be with you, Luke.'

He raised her fingers to his lips and kissed the inside of them.

They were scarcely noticeable in the bustle of the great coaching inn: they were free, and alone. They went back to Luke's room.

A maid had been in to make up the fire, and Rebecca hung her damp cloak in front of it. She looked at Luke's things, shaving tackle, boots, hat on a hook. There was something special about those too, a wonderful intimacy.

She looked at him and smiled. 'What do you stare at, sir?'

'You.'

She reached in her bag for her comb. 'Well, I'll make myself half-way worth looking at, anyway.'

'I've no mirror in here,' Luke said. He leaned a hand carefully on the mantelshelf. 'Rebecca – they are sure to have another room here, if that would be better.'

'Wishing to get rid of me already?'

'You know it isn't that – '

'I'm not teasing you, Luke.' She came to him, kissed him. 'I want to be with you. That's all. Here. What you said last night – about realising at last the one true thing – oh, then I was too taken aback, too afraid to let it sink in – but now I've come to that knowledge too. Ever since we met it's as if we've been joined by some thread – infinitely long and fine, but strong, so strong, and wander where we might it would always draw us back together. And now . . . Always the world seems to have thrust in between us like a wedge. And yet we have our own world, my love. Ourselves. This room.' She waved a hand. 'It's everything, as long as you are in it with me.'

He stroked her neck, and her arms, slowly. She shivered at his touch, though not with cold.

'Your gown's still a little damp,' he said.

'So it is.' Her mouth had gone dry. 'Perhaps I should put it in front of the fire.'

She slipped out of the gown, and as she bent to hang it with the cloak the fire lit her hair redly and he saw the pale warm olive of her skin and the long clean lines of her legs in the white underskirt.

She sat on the bed. Her heart was pounding, as if it had never properly beat before.

He knelt beside her and began to say something about how he had always wanted to touch her and how –

'I've always wanted you to,' she said thickly. 'Oh, Luke, I've always wanted you to. God, I've wanted you so much.'

Her skin seemed to melt beneath his fingers as he slipped off her stockings and traced the delicate flue of her thighs.

He stood up and locked the door, and then undressed. She watched, and admired the lean muscled economy of his body, and reached out a hand for him, and suddenly they were lost. Lips, and tongues, and hands, and shifting planes of tingling skin, wove them together in a skein of passion, tangled, caught up, and lifted to a rarefied height from which the world fell away. The movements of an intricate dance wherein each step was invented and elaborated at each moment until the pattern was as complex and perfect as a tapestry of arabesques. Their fingers roved in perpetual motion, an endless exploration in which every place was discovered and rediscovered and made anew. She arched and gasped, and his lips inscribed curlicues of delight on the contours of her breasts and stomach. His tongue probed her wetness, and the quick of her self was transfixed, as if all the feeling in her had stood up like flock and a hand had passed across it. He tensed and groaned, and her palms moulded and created the sculpture of his body, smoothing out broad shoulders, tracing ribs and narrow hips and shaping the rigid member, delineating the muscles of the chest and conjuring with the help of lips and teeth the hardened nipples. He folded her into him, and he caught her sharp intake of breath and looked tenderly into her face, but she caressed his brow and eased herself beneath him. And they were lost again. Till presently she cried his name, and they were free of the tangled skein.

They lay still, a drift of flesh washed up by the tide of love, and the room began to take shape around her again.

Rebecca looked with dark drugged eyes at her lover, touching his black hair, filled with a sensuous lassitude. Then she smiled and said: 'Do you know what the time is?'

He put out a hand to his watch on the night-table, could not reach, subsided. 'Must be about half-past ten. Why, love?'

'Oh, I don't know.' She gazed up at the ceiling. 'It's just strange – half-past ten in an inn-room on a Thursday morning – with the carriages rattling about outside and the cooks turning the spits downstairs – and here we are . . .'

He smiled too. 'And no one knows. Our world, like you said. It has different rules.'

She glanced down at the two of them with a glint of mischief. 'It has *no* rules.'

Then they laughed together, long and soft and hoarsely. Then he touched her cheek and said: 'You know I love you, Rebecca.'

'Yes, I think I do.' She stirred lazily and said: 'And I think I'd like to lie here with you all day.'

'All day? Hm. What about food?'

She bit his shoulder. 'A minor point. You'll have to think of something better than that.'

'What about your gown?'

'My gown?'

'If it's not turned round soon it'll scorch.'

'Very well. You may do that.' But as he smiled and made a movement to get up she held him with soft strong hands.

'I don't think I'm going to let you go.'

At around noon that day, Mr Walsoken, irritated with his daughter Sarah's chattering, struck her – a thing he had not done for years. It was an indication of his feelings.

Lovell Fitzroy had called at eleven, and gone away a short while ago. His own feelings, after reading the letter, he kept well hidden. He did not say as much, but he found Mr Walsoken's ranting threats against Rebecca – alternating with anxious promises that she could not mean what she said, that it could all be sorted out – in bad taste and rather vulgar. As far as he was concerned it was all over, and he was not interested in pharisaic curses of revenge.

His disappointment was not unmixed. The manner of its coming was a shock, but he had just lately begun to suspect something of the sort. He had not felt secure of her, and he was a man for whom security was everything. Her rather too colourful language, and rather too revealing frock last night: he had tried to disguise from himself the suspicion that she was a little bold for a lady. It was a disappointment, it was unfortunate, but it was her choice, and he could not quite comprehend – and did not wish to – the blazing fury of her father.

For Mr Walsoken's self-control was gone. He was volcanic. For he had more than an idea where – or rather, to whom – Rebecca had gone. He himself had not seen Luke Hardwick in the crowded Pantheon last night, but Jeremiah had, and had told him so with relish this morning. The idea took root, and blossomed horribly.

The disgrace. The ruin of his great hopes; the match with the house of Grafton, the place in the highest society. Gone. And when this got out, he said to himself, he would be a laughing-stock. His triumphant first London season was wrecked. And the instrument of it – he was more sure of it with each passing moment – was that most insolent and detested of that insolent and detested family, the Hardwicks. No matter how he rose above them, with their pride and blood and damned arrogance, they cheated him and thwarted him and reduced him again to the ostler's son.

So he reasoned, and raged. But their triumph would be short-lived, he swore. His daughter might have disgraced herself and him, but she would not be allowed to go free. He had already sent servants and messengers out, to make inquiries all over the city, from acquaintances, from inns and lodging-houses and hackney-men and boatmen, from constables and watchmen. Somehow, he would find her. And bring her back. Better that she should be under lock and key than in the arms of Luke Hardwick.

5

It was about noon also that Henry Milton saw Robert Landless off on the coach that was to take him to Reading and Marlborough and Bath and Bristol and so to Ireland.

Though he was sure he was doing the right thing, there was no time to debate the question. Landless had to have everything done for him: he was still numb with shock. Milton had taken him to his lodgings, packed his bags, and booked his place on the coach. He had told him to write when he got to Bristol and again when he got to Ireland. If there were any inquiries Milton would try to parry them: and he would go to see Landless's lawyer in Ely and make arrangements with him about the house.

'It may soon all blow over,' Milton said again as he packed Landless's bags. 'This way we can be sure. I'll find out about the inquest, and when you have an address I can write you of any developments.'

Landless raised his head from his hands. 'I truly loved her, Milton, always. Everything I did I did for love of her. Believe me.'

'I know it.'

Landless's face was anguished. 'But how can it be, Milton? How can love, love the great healer, the goddess, that's supposed to be the blessing of life – how can it end in these horrors?'

Milton shook his head.

As they waited at the inn-yard in the Strand for the coach Landless had seemed to rally. He looked at Milton as if seeing him for the first time and patted his shoulder. 'Poor Graveairs,' he said. 'You have been involved in this ugly business under protest, and still you do everything to help me and don't get a word of thanks.

You must regret you ever spoke to me that day in the Angel in Peterborough.'

'No, Robert, I don't,' Milton said. 'If anything . . .'

'Yes?'

'I regret the day you first saw Elizabeth.'

'Ah, no. No, no. Nothing could make me regret that.' The young man winced, as at a twinge of pain. 'Watch over her for me, Henry.'

The coachman was blowing his horn, and soon afterwards Milton watched it struggle out of the inn-yard, bucketing on the cobbles, with a fair head leaning out of the window and a hand waving, it seemed somehow, with something of the old feckless irony. And then Landless was gone.

Milton dined, with little appetite, at a coffee-house in the Strand, and was back at his lodgings in Southwark by three. Julia was not there, but he remembered she had a portrait sitting today. Soon after he had arrived Mr Rogers, Sir Hugh's second, called.

'I thought it best to apprise you of what has happened, Mr Milton,' he said. 'After you had gone I found a link-boy and sent him for a physician. Hugh was dead, of course. I said he had been practising with his pistols and there had been an accident. It went hard with me, sir, I don't mind telling you. I've known Hugh on and off for years: not that we were ever bosom friends, you know, but to see him lying there . . . But, if a man fights a duel, this is what he must expect. As soon as he agrees to do it, he accepts these rules. So, we had the body borne back to Hugh's townhouse, and notified Lady Woodhouse at her parents'. Unfortunately, a pompous little constable got interested in the business on the way, and wanted to know all about it.'

'Will there be trouble?'

'Difficult to say. There'll be an inquest, of course. But I don't think anyone saw your man there this morning. Just as well you got him away like I told you. Is he still in London . . . ?'

'No, no. He's gone.'

'Sensible thing. Well, I must be away. I confess I've no relish for this business. But 'twas a fair fight. Hugh was always a rash sort of fellow. They who live by the sword, and all that. Goodbye.'

After Rogers had gone Milton realised he was very tired. He realised too how much he wished Julia were here.

He had fallen into a troubled doze in an armchair when he was roused by a knock. It was a messenger from the portrait painter, saying Mrs Milton had not turned up for her sitting that day and inquiring after her health.

Milton thought it was strange, and wondered if she could perhaps have forgotten: she had been very abstracted just recently. It was only as the swift winter twilight was falling, and he had been waiting for her to come home for hours, that he went into their bedroom and found her clothes were gone.

SIX

I

Julia had not returned. Milton had fallen asleep, eventually, in an armchair, and woke stiff and bewildered soon after dawn on the eighth. The room had a metallic smell of the brandy he had drunk last night, and the candle beside him had burnt to a stub.

Fragments of yesterday came to him uncertainly, as if his mind were picking them up and turning them over in palsied hands. The duel . . . Sir Hugh's great body sprawled and undignified on the grass. Soles of his shoes showing. Death had no dignity. Packing Landless off. Rogers.

Julia gone? Yes . . . that was the worst, most vivid memory of all.

He went into their bedroom and stared stupidly, as if expecting to see her lying there in bed, with her dark unruly hair and the intent expression she wore even in sleep.

Meanwhile he was pricked with unease, the peculiarly horrible unease of retrospect. Her manner of late . . . a thousand small signs of something wrong. Signs that would have been imperceptible – except to a lover or husband.

Except to a lover or husband. Yet he had managed to miss them – to disregard them.

A lover or husband. One should include the other. Had it been so? Had he failed in one of those departments? Or both?

But to just disappear – leave him like this. Clothes gone. No word. The most disturbing thing was that it was not *like* Julia. Julia – so reserved, and yet so open: Julia, who would never let anything fester, who would confront you in her hard, generous, vulnerable way, and never be a mouse. Her favourite term of disapprobation: 'such a mouse'; though in the attic at Longthorpe she had found a squirming litter of mice and swept them nest and all into a bowl and then managed to find the parent mice and taken the whole trembling family to the wood behind the house.

Mechanically he set the kettle on the hob. He was surprised to find he was near tears.

Where could she have gone? To George and Mary? But they would have told him. *She* would have told him. If she were going to leave him she would have said so. There must have been something terribly wrong for her to do this.

He made tea and drank it, though he could not eat. He washed, though his hands felt too uncertain to shave.

He began to think of that dark time all those years ago, when she had been used and jilted and had drifted alone in the seedy London underworld, drawn into a hellish life on the streets . . . No, no. Not that.

He heard a footstep on the stair, and jumped out of his seat. Then he recognised the flopping slippers and groaning progress of the maid from downstairs.

He opened the door. 'This come for you, sir,' she said through her lank hair.

He turned the letter over. No – not Julia's writing. He felt like throwing it in the fire.

He took it at last over to the window and frowned at it in the milky light.

To Henry Milton, Esq.

8 Bolt Court
December 8th, 1780

SIR,
You will pardon the liberty of my communicating thus with you, whom I have not yet had the pleasure to meet; but I write to inform you that Mrs Milton is at present staying at my house. She came hither yesterday in some distress of mind, which I have done my best to alleviate: but to restore the peace of mind of both parties, it is my cordial wish that you would wait upon me here at your earliest convenience.

I am, sir,
Your humble servant
SAM. JOHNSON

471

Dr Johnson's house in Bolt Court was a narrow four-storeyed building in a sunless corner. Milton, however, could not have been more surprised to find himself knocking at this door if it had been an enchanter's castle poised on top of a cloud.

A Negro manservant admitted him, and seemed to be expecting him. He conducted him up two flights of stairs.

Dr Johnson's house – untidy, bursting with books, and none too clean – a frequent temporary refuge for acquaintances who were sick or distressed or desperate, where they could retreat for a while in the shade of his discreet generosity. And here, spurred by a mental anguish that Milton had yet to comprehend, Julia had come.

The Negro servant showed him into a small parlour overlooking a walled garden. Here Julia sat at a tea-table, with Dr Johnson opposite her, in a half-broken chair, feeding oysters to his cat on the floor.

'Hullo, Henry,' Julia said softly.

'This is the man, is it?' Dr Johnson rolled himself clumsily out of the chair and took Milton's hand. 'I've been anxious to meet you, sir.'

'Dr Johnson.' Milton was so bewildered he allowed his hand to be shaken bonelessly, as a dog does.

The big stout old man before him wore a shambling suit of snuff-brown and an old grey horsehair wig. He was remarkably ugly, with a pock-marked skin and overlarge bulbous features: he peered into Milton's face with extreme short sight.

'Well, sir,' he said stertorously, 'are you not going to give your wife a buss, now that you have found her?' His accent was noticeably Midland.

Milton stared. 'I confess I am at a loss – '

'Never mind that, sir,' said Dr Johnson. 'Kiss the lady, else I'll take one myself.'

Milton did so, feeling as if he were in a dream.

'That's well,' Dr Johnson said, nodding. 'Now be seated, and we shall have some tea.'

Dr Johnson, who seemed never to stop moving – swaying from side to side, stamping his feet, fluttering his hands – sat in his broken chair again. 'Mrs Milton came to me yesterday, sir,' he said.

'Troubled, and asking advice, and clearly in need of a little respite. I offered her the protection of my roof. I had read your wife's admirable verses, sir, and met her at last at the Thrales'.'

Milton looked at Julia. 'I didn't know – '

'We met by chance in the library,' Dr Johnson said. 'I did not come down to dinner that day. I was feeling out of sorts for company, but I had a most pleasant conversation with Mrs Milton, and asked her when she went down not to tell anyone I was abroad. And said if ever she should wish to call on me I would be glad to see her.'

Julia passed Henry his tea. He took it, looked at it, did not know what to do with it. 'It appears,' he said, 'that I have been kept in the dark about a lot of things.'

'Now, my dear sir, don't take that tone, I beg,' said Dr Johnson, taking his tea, almost attacking it, in a stooping gurgle. 'I asked you to come here so that you two could be reconciled.'

'I'm obliged, sir,' Milton said, 'but I would suppose it nobody's business but our own.'

Dr Johnson smiled – a gentle and benevolent smile, that softened his uncouth face. 'I have been married myself, Mr Milton,' he said. 'It is the best of all states for man and for woman. But it has hazards that must be negotiated. Now, now, wait a moment, sir,' he said as Milton half-rose in irritation. 'Mrs Milton has confided in me – '

'A confidence she would seem unable to extend to her husband,' Milton said bitterly.

'That's just it, sir. She has been afraid to tell you. Now, sometimes a disinterested third party may be exactly what is required. As in this case.' Dr Johnson gulped down the last of his tea. 'Mrs Milton is with child, sir: most happily for you both: that is the long and short of it.'

Milton was spilling his tea. He put it down. His head was spinning. '*This* is what it's all about . . . with . . . And you didn't *tell* me?'

'Ah, consider what you are saying, sir,' Dr Johnson said. 'Recollect.' He looked at Julia. 'Mrs Milton?'

'I've known for a week or so,' she said, her head lowered. 'I was so delighted . . . I wanted to tell you. Then – you said – you said you didn't want it.'

'I said *what*?'

'Ever since the Sedgmoors' child died,' she burst out desperately, 'it's haunted you . . . and then the baby at the Dispensary brought it all back. You never wanted to be put through that, you said. You couldn't bear it to be born only to be a victim to a passing epidemic. And then I found I was pregnant – and all I could think was *he doesn't want it*, he doesn't want our child, and I knew I couldn't keep hiding it – and I had to get away . . . Oh, Henry, I'm sorry.'

'Nay, Mrs Milton,' said Dr Johnson, who was watching them carefully with his puckered eyes, 'don't apologise to the man.'

'A child . . . But – but I never meant – ' Milton could not go on. The grim folly of his own words afflicted him, stinging him with shame and confusion.

'If you do not *mean*,' Dr Johnson said, 'you should not *say*.' He bent with a grunt to stir the fire; then casting on Milton a look both stern and shrewd, said: 'Really, sir, what nonsense is this? We are all hostages to fortune. If a man were to never again eat a morsel of meat, because he had once known it poisoned, he would very soon starve to death. If a poet were always afraid to put pen to paper, for fear that the result would not match his aspirations, then he would never get anything writ. Children die, and parents are bereaved, very frequently: but the reverse is true also. And the human race would come to an end altogether, if everyone were to labour under such apprehensions as you have, sir. I never had a child: but I heartily wish I had: and it would have been an occasion of undiluted joy, as it should be. A man who troubles himself with fears that his child may not live, instead of rejoicing that the child does live, is his own tormentor: and if you will persist in being that man, Mr Milton, then I say you are undeserving of your excellent wife, and of the child she bears you.' He made a fierce face at Milton. 'Now, kiss her again, sir, and be content, the both of you, and let us have no more of it!'

They emerged together from the backwater of Bolt Court into the maelstrom of noonday Fleet Street. Henry carried her carpet-bag. They had still not spoken. A chill rain was falling and swelling the gutters.

'Henry,' Julia said. 'I left you. I deserted you. Oh, I felt I had to get away at the time, but now I see what I did. It was – so *cowardly*.'

'Julia – '

A wide brewer's dray was rumbling up the crowded street, and they had to press themselves into a porched doorway to make room. Julia had on a long grey cloak and under the porch he searched in its folds for her hands and took them in his. They were cold. He chafed them. 'Your hands are so cold,' he said, and the fact of this transfixed him with a sudden renewed and keen and marvellous tenderness.

'I should have told you,' she said miserably. 'And then the more I left it the more impossible it seemed. I don't think you can forgive me.' She frowned down. 'I've been a damn *mouse*.'

'Julia,' he said, trying to get her to raise her eyes, 'my love, my dearest love. If there's forgiving to be done, let's talk of my stupidity – my cruel, damnable, pig-headed folly all this time. My darling, if you couldn't tell me you were going to have our baby, if you had to hide and suffer and agonise over what should be the most wonderful thing to happen to us – then that is my fault, my most grievous fault, no one else's. All I can do is ask your forgiveness. And if you can do so, well, this is the happiest day – and I am the happiest, luckiest fool who never deserved his lovely wife . . .'

He could not go on. He did not need to. She gathered him to her, squeezing him tightly, the folds of the cloak enclosing him and sealing them together. 'My love,' she said. 'Oh, I'll never leave you again. Never, never.'

'What are we weeping for?' he said at last, laughing and wiping her eyes and his.

'I don't know! We love each other and we're going to have the child we've wished for so long. We should be laughing.'

And they were laughing, as they held each other under the dripping porch.

'So . . . we did get to meet Dr Johnson at last,' he said. 'Not in the way we expected. We have a lot to thank him for.' He kissed her, tasting her cold fresh skin.

'We'll write him,' she said, 'when the baby's born.'

'And if it's a boy,' he smiled, 'perhaps we could call him Samuel.'

The second morning of their idyll.

After breakfast Rebecca and Luke took a stroll down to the river, past the rebuilding shell of Newgate. Bitter cold was reflecting from a harsh winter sky. Horses trotted in clouds of steam: one had slipped on the frost and upset its cartload of leather.

They were quiet, content. Storms of passion there had been, but

475

their love could also take the form of companionable peace and silence, with no sense of restraint. It was a good sign.

'Will your father seek you out, d'you think?' he said.

He had read her thoughts. 'I don't know. I suppose I've been trying not to think of it.'

'Rebecca, do you wish for a reconciliation?'

She shook her head. 'It can never be, now. But no. I don't want anything from him. I've made my choice. I'm of age. He can do nothing more. But – '

'Yes?'

'There's Peter – and Sarah – even mother. *They* have nothing to do with what father feels, or should not. I don't want to be estranged from them. But,' she added as he seemed about to speak, 'they can *all* go hang, if it's a choice between them and you.'

He frowned into the distance, thinking. 'It doesn't have to be that way . . .' He suddenly turned to her, with a delighted and boyish smile. 'We'll get married.'

'*Now?*'

'Yes! Why not?' He laughed, and picked her up in his arms and spun her around.

'But, Luke, we – we – '

'Why, you're not turning me down, surely?'

She began to laugh too, her mouth against his cheek. They laughed till they shook, and people in the street stopped and stared. 'No, of course not, you great fool,' she gasped. 'Of course I'll marry you.'

They walked back to the Saracen's Head, talking excitedly all the way.

'Some sort of licence,' Luke said. 'I'm not sure how to go about it. I think someone has to stand bond . . . George would know. I'll go and see him. And he and Mary can be witnesses.'

'And Peter. I can send word to Peter.'

'But what about your clothes and things? You've scarcely any-thing – '

'Oh, I don't care about that if you don't. I'd marry you in my nightgown.'

'Would you?'

She glinted a smile at him. '*Especially* in my nightgown.'

'And we'll leave this place,' he said when they got back to the inn-room. 'No place to be married from. Find somewhere smarter. Nothing but the best. What do you think?'

'I think we're mad. And we'll do it.' She kissed him, then patted him on the seat. 'Go on, my lover. Go and see George. There, I'm ordering you about already. And I'll pack. And I'll bribe the landlord again for not minding our goings-on under his roof. Shoo.'

He kissed her, went to the door.

'Luke.'

He looked back.

'Don't be long.'

When Jeremiah had told his father, in a sulky undertone, that he had been caught cheating by George Hardwick and had been expelled from Brooks', it looked as if Mr Walsoken would have an apoplexy. Sarah and Mrs Walsoken stared at him like frightened rabbits. These last two days he had been more terrible than even they could remember. He had become an incarnation of the wrathful God whose precepts he had beaten into them.

Worse, he had been drinking. Never before. It was horrifying.

But it was shortly afterwards that one of the manservants came with the news that he had been waiting for. The scouring of the inns and lodging-houses had paid off. An ostler at the Saracen's Head in Snow Hill had said he thought there was a Hardwick there at present. The boot-black had confirmed it. With a young lady. He had done their shoes that morning.

'Effrontery indeed,' said Jeremiah, seeming as always to salve his own anger by taunting his father. 'Not even the decency to make an elopement.'

Mr Walsoken glowered at him, his brows bristling. He looked ill and dreadful with fury.

'I am going there,' he said quietly. 'Have the carriage made ready, Ford.' He looked at his son. 'Will you come with me, Jeremiah?'

'I think I will,' said Jeremiah, uncoiling himself from his chair. 'It would give me some satisfaction to break a Hardwick head this morning.'

'Joshua!'

It was so unusual to hear Mrs Walsoken speak so emphatically that her husband stopped.

'Think,' she said. 'Think of what you are doing.'

After a moment he averted his eyes. 'Come, Jeremiah,' he said.

The bags were packed: little to do, really. Rebecca looked around the inn-room. It was rather a shabby place, and there were cockroaches under the bed. Their little world . . . Such joy here. She would always remember it.

A maid put her capped head round the door. 'Please, ma'am, there's two gentlemen to see you.'

Mr Walsoken came in. 'Go about your business, girl,' he said to the maid. Jeremiah slipped in behind him, and closed the door.

Her father's eyes travelled over the packed bags, her body, her face.

'Where is he?' he said.

'Not here,' she said. She looked at him, and strained with an effort of memory to think: *This is my father.* But no. She did not know this man. 'Father, why have you come here?'

He stepped forward. For a mad moment it seemed he was going to take her hand. Daughter, you are forgiven. But instead he struck her hard across the face.

She cringed with pain. His eyes were grossly enlarged, the veins purple and ghastly on his forehead. She caught the whiff, unbelievably, of spirits. ' "Ye have ploughed wickedness",' he intoned, ' "ye have reaped iniquity. Ye have eaten of the fruit of lies." '

She stared, and he struck her again. '*Slut,*' he hissed. '*Whore.*'

She made a move to get past him. He caught her. His hands were like claws on her arms. 'Disgraced me,' he said, panting. 'Worse than the foulest trollop of the stews. Thrown your sin in my face – '

'All right!' she cried. 'So that's what I've done! So I'm not your daughter! I don't *care.* You've had your say, father, now it's over. If this is the way it has to be, then very well. Cut me off without a shilling, never see me again and all the rest of it. Don't you see, I don't *care.* That's all over. This is what I want. So just *go.*'

'Go? And let you traduce me in your sin with that godless bastard?' There was a shrill crack in his voice, like the fluting treble of madness. 'How weak do you think I am? Do you think I'll stand by, while my daughter turns and flouts the authority of her *father*?'

'I'm of age!' she screamed. 'You can do nothing!'

' "Their deeds do not permit them to return to their God",' he said, struggling with her. ' "For the spirit of harlotry is within them, and they know not the Lord." Help me, Jeremiah! "My father hath chastised you with whips, but I will chastise you with scorpions." I'll see you dead before you cleave to him. You shall be restrained until your sin is borne in upon you, Rebecca.'

The two of them were too strong for her. She was being led, weeping, to the door. A nightmare. 'You can't *do* this . . .'

' "Thus they were defiled with their own works",' her father shouted, ' "and went awhoring with their own inventions." You will thank me, daughter. You will thank me for saving you. From yourself. Till then you must be restrained . . . you must submit . . . you must learn obedience at last. We shall lead a retired life together, pray together. For forgiveness.'

A nightmare. He was going to take her away by force.

' "Thou shalt break them with a rod of iron; thou shalt dash them in pieces like a potter's vessel . . . A virtuous woman is a crown unto her husband: but she that maketh ashamed is as rottenness in his bones . . ." '

When Luke called at Buckingham Street he found both George and Mary there.

'We thought perhaps you'd gone home,' Mary said. 'After the other night . . .'

'Home, no! Not yet.' He suddenly burst into a shout of laughter. 'Well, which of you will congratulate me first?'

'Rebecca?' Mary said, and then hugged Luke and kissed him. 'Oh, cousin, I hoped it would be so.'

'This is all very sudden,' said George, shaking his hand.

'In a way,' Luke said. 'But in another way it's not. I reckon it had to happen, somehow, from the very day we set eyes on each other. She's with me now. And we want to be wed immediately. I wanted to ask you about that. We'd have to get a licence, wouldn't we?'

George nodded. 'Julia was married by licence, I seem to remember. I think that was got from the archdeacon of the Soke. I don't know about here. I've got to see Lord Burghley this afternoon. He'll know. You can wait another day, I presume?'

Luke smiled. 'Aye. I reckon so. And tonight – I want you two to come and dine with us. With your future cousin.'

'You're making her a Hardwick,' George groaned. 'Poor girl.'

'And what then, Luke?' Mary said. 'Will you stay in London?'

'Nay, I think we'll go back to Stamford in a day or two. Father's house. Old Forrest will be surprised when I bring home a new wife.'

'Perhaps then we can travel together,' George said. 'We're leaving soon, before Parliament closes. Christmas at Morholm.'

'You're not resigning your seat?'

'Oh, no,' George said. 'But – rearranging life a little.' Mary slipped her hand in his. 'A question of priorities.'

'We wish you both all the happiness in the world,' Mary said. Then, soberly: 'What of Mr Walsoken, Luke? I suppose he knows you are together?'

'It's got nothing to do with him,' Luke said. 'Rebecca's finished with him. That's the way she wants it.'

On the way back to the Saracen's Head Luke lingered at a little jeweller's shop in Fleet Street where the shopman tempted him with a tray of rings and necklaces. But it was mostly gimcrack stuff and he did not buy anything. Rebecca deserved better.

He ran the last few hundred yards up Snow Hill to the great inn. It was perhaps an expression of the bubbling spirits within him that made him constantly want to sing and kiss fat old gentlewomen in the street: perhaps simply because he could not wait to see Rebecca again. Only afterwards did he wonder if some uneasy premonition had made him hurry. Whichever way, it was fortunate.

When he saw the commotion in the inn courtyard, with its galleries running above, he thought it was some drunken disturbance. Then he saw the glint of auburn hair in its midst.

They were dragging her towards the waiting carriage. People were looking on, some laughing, most rather shocked.

Jeremiah got Luke's fist squarely on his pointed chin, and went down on the dung-spattered cobbles. 'Breaking Hardwick heads' seemed a sorry boast. But Mr Walsoken hung on, mulish and whey-faced and possessed, to his daughter's arm, and even her considerable strength could not break his grip.

'Let her go,' Luke said. Incandescent with fury as he was, he felt a flicker of alarm at Mr Walsoken's face, its demented zeal. It should have been absurd, but it was not.

'"Be sure your sin will find you out",' he cried. ' "I had rather be a doorkeeper in the house of my God, than to dwell in the tents of wickedness . . ." '

Strike him. This man, who so eminently deserved it, this hypocritical bigot who sought to own his daughters like cattle. Her father . . .

Luke hesitated. But someone was tittering – at Mr Walsoken. And Jeremiah was getting up from the ground, nursing his chin, and saying: 'Father. You are making a fool of us both.'

Mr Walsoken stopped, and stared, and must have relaxed his grip, for Rebecca wrenched herself away.

'Father,' said Jeremiah. 'It's done with. Finished. Let us just go.' He plucked at Mr Walsoken's sleeve.

'Your daughter and I are going to be married,' Luke said, holding Rebecca close to him. He felt a sudden need for some kind of normality – some rationality, somehow. 'You can't change that now. Your approval or your opposition don't matter. You've got to realise that. You don't like it, but you must accept it.'

The ring of spectators had closed in: they were enjoying it. Jeremiah was scarlet. 'Come *away*, father,' he said. 'You're making things worse.'

'Do as Jeremiah says, father,' Rebecca sobbed. 'It's over, can't you see?'

Mr Walsoken did not look at her. His eyes were on Luke.

'God damn you,' he said. 'God's curse on your marriage and all your life. God damn you and your blood to all eternity.'

Only then did he suffer himself to be led away to the carriage by Jeremiah.

Luke and Rebecca had gone back to their room in the inn, and held each other, sitting on the bed amongst the packed bags, in a strange mute need.

Luke feared for the effect of what had happened on Rebecca. But he had reckoned without her resilient spirit.

'And in a way I'm glad,' she said, when she had recovered. 'I can't feel any remorse now. No little faint hope for a reconciliation. Everything's clear now, settled.'

With a sudden urgency they made love on the bare bed. Afterwards he traced the curved line of her face with a finger and said: 'We've come a long way since that day in Stamford. When we first met. Remember?'

She sat up abruptly, naked, a hand to her mouth. 'Oh God!' she said.

'What's wrong?'

'Think – just think – if I hadn't happened to meet you that day. It might never have happened!'

He laughed. 'Well, don't sound so excited about it.'

'No, no, but think, Luke. How arbitrary it all is. Paths crossing. Say I hadn't gone to Stamford that day, or you hadn't ... It's frightening.'

'No, it isn't.' He caressed her smooth back. 'I think we were fated to meet anyway.'

4

Rebecca Walsoken and Luke Hardwick were married in London, at St Giles' Church, on Monday December 11th 1780. As the register showed, the bride was twenty-one, the groom twenty-seven.

Mr Walsoken had taken his family – wife, Sarah, Jeremiah, and also Paul from Charterhouse – back to Bromswold on the ninth – the day after his last attempt to restore his authority over his wayward daughter and to salvage something from the wreck of his ambitions.

But Peter Walsoken was still in London, at his studies at Lincoln's Inn, and he came to the wedding, and gave the bride away.

Her twin brother had never judged her or upbraided her, and he did not now.

'Surprised?' he said to her. 'Well, in truth, I'm not. I would be more surprised if you did *not* do something unconventional. And – you look happy, sister.'

'I am. More happy than I ever thought possible.'

'Then there's nothing more to say.'

George and Mary and the Miltons were there too. Julia and Henry were to leave London at the end of the week – Julia had one more sitting for her portrait – but the Hardwicks were to travel back to the fens together tomorrow.

George and Mary, of course, were returning to the home of their ancestors, though with a sense of freshness, a new awareness of it and of each other. But Luke and Rebecca would go to the house in Stamford: a beginning, a new home, a new life.

SEVEN

I

George and Mary Hardwick came back to Morholm late on the fourteenth of December. Charles Joseph had fallen into an exhausted child's sleep on the last horseback journey from Peterborough where they had left the coach, and they put him to bed straight away.

The house had been well enough looked after in their absence, but there seemed something cold and musty about it. They lit fires and candles and listened to the news from Mrs Binnismoor – one of the heifers had kicked a hole in the stall door but Will had mended it, Benwick was courting and thought to get married – and at last sat down to supper in quiet content, the content of peace recognised and savoured.

Then Mrs Binnismoor came back to tell them that Gaffer Pode was wanting to see them.

Gaffer Pode, wrinkled and sturdy as his old oak stick, begged their pardon for coming so late; only he saw the light burning . . .

And so his long story came out, about this damned enclosure going on – and everyone knew who was behind it and who stood most to gain . . . and there was folk who welcomed it, for what with all the fencing and marking and clearing of the common there was a lot of work to be had, and that was all well and good, but that was only temporary-like, and when it was done, what then . . . there was John Newman having to sell up, and probably end up working for Walsoken on day-work . . . and himself, now, what was he to do about his old mare, that he'd used to turn out on the common at night . . . A long story of grievance and lament, spun in confusion from his memory of Aysthorpe as it was and the strange new imposition that had fractured that old world. Part of that old world was his hope that Mr Hardwick could do something about it.

George promised him he would consult with the commissioners to try and ensure there was fair compensation, and Gaffer left seeming satisfied, perhaps chiefly from having got all this off his chest. But both George and Mary felt their powerlessness.

'This is bad about John,' George said. 'Reduced to a labourer. I'll see Matthews tomorrow, try and think of something to do for him.'

They found, without being aware of it, that they had sat together on the sofa to listen to Gaffer. 'George, I wonder . . .' Mary said. 'Mr Matthews is well in his sixties now, and his wife was wanting him to retire when he had the influenza earlier this year. Could there be room for John there, do you think?'

George nodded slowly. 'That's a good thought. Steward . . . he might not take to the idea – but still . . .'

'We can ask him,' Mary said. 'It can be borne in mind.'

Without noticing it also, they had been answering Gaffer Pode's questions as one. They had slipped into accord so easily. They found themselves smiling at each other at this. There was no need for words.

After supper Mary said: 'By the way, what did Lord Burghley say to you when you saw him yesterday?'

'Oh, just wanted to know how we were getting along. He seems content enough with me so far, and did not raise the matter of my voting rather often with the opposition. He wasn't in good spirits. The war in America will be over soon, he said, and we will not win it. It's as if he'd faced this idea for the first time.' He finished his brandy. 'Changes . . . and a new decade. I think we'll see many more changes.'

'Not all bad,' she said. 'Changes – they can be growing too, developing, moving forward. We needn't fear that. As long as there is a – a centre.'

Their hands had come to lie loosely together on the sofa between them. 'Julia and Henry will find that now, I hope, with the baby coming,' he said.

'We must have them here for Christmas,' Mary said. 'Julia and Henry and Rebecca and Luke. A Christmas like we used to have.'

'Rebecca and Luke. Changes again. New blood. A new Hardwick family.'

'I think they'll be happy,' she said. 'Turbulent, perhaps, knowing them as we do. But happy.'

George nodded. 'I think there's life in the Hardwicks yet.'

They were quiet again, content in the knowledge of each other's love. That terrible night in London they had found, without expecting it, that what they had feared might be about to break was far stronger, more deep and true, than either of them had realised.

Whilst Rebecca and Luke were settling into life together at Horace's old townhouse in Stamford, and becoming accustomed to a world larger than an inn-room, the town's most prominent resident, Mr Edward Wainwright, returned from London with his wife and widowed daughter.

If Mr Wainwright did not deeply mourn for his dead son-in-law, he mourned for his daughter. Hugh's estate was hers, of course: but the thought of her returning to that echoing Northamptonshire mansion, with every stone redolent of Hugh, oppressed her parents as much as it did Elizabeth. For the moment she should stay with them.

Hugh's death had been recorded as by misadventure. Elizabeth had her own suspicions – suspicions that were near certainties – but they could not be voiced. To anyone.

She could not feel grief at Hugh's death. Nor yet could she feel release, though that might come soon. Feeling, normality, were making little inroads on her consciousness, like scattered signs of spring in a dour March. But the time for the complete awakening was not yet. She had come through the dark corridor of the past, and the door had been closed upon it; but the corridor of the future was unlighted too, and she did not know what she would find when she entered it.

2

Rebecca, Luke and the Miltons came to spend Christmas at Morholm, arriving on the twenty-third. It was strange for Rebecca to feel herself linked to the Hardwicks – indeed, bearing the name – and to this ancient house where she had found a welcome and friends when she had first come from Norwich three years ago. And it was a delightful meeting. They were all young, and full of festive spirit, and the old rafters and panels of the house rang with laughter and seemed to stir and creak as if with memories of older times, almost but not quite forgotten.

On Christmas Day dawn came with tissues of dispersing mist draping the horizon and a sky variegated with patches of biting cold colour. Then from this swirling palette emerged a perfect pure red sun. The shadows drew back from the fields, and every blade of grass and every bead of dew on every blade stood out in crisp relief, as if the clarity of the sky were magnifying the flat world below.

After breakfast at Morholm the whole family stepped out into the gardens, enjoying the mild December sun with its light like old copper, leaving crushed dark footprints in the springy grass. Charles Joseph, who had been indoors a lot of late, soon ran away from Mrs Peach's side, going faster than his short legs could carry him, stopping only to admire the spider-webs that trembled on the hedges and looked as though they were made of spun glass.

'Do you remember,' Luke said to Rebecca, as they walked arm-in-arm, 'three Christmases ago, here? The first time I ever came to Morholm.'·

'I remember. And we spent almost the whole time staring at each other and never saying a word. And you sang that saucy song – what was it? Something about meeting a maiden – summer meadows . . . How did it go?'

'Oh, I can't remember it now,' Luke said.

'Don't you? You must do! Anyway, I remember my father didn't approve.'

He squeezed her arm and looked at her. 'Are you troubled, my lover? Thinking of him?'

'No,' she said. 'No, not that. But I think it's made me realise something. That *we* must never be like that. Intolerant . . . I don't know. I don't know the word. Hardwicks and Walsokens, at each other's throats . . . all that hate. But out of that *we've* come. Something new, a future. We can leave all that behind. What I mean is, we must always keep a – an open heart. Because love can turn small and hard and grim too, can't it? We know that, Luke, more than anyone. It's like Julia's child – and Charles Joseph – love has to be nurtured and cared for. So it can grow.'

They stopped at the paddock gate, to let the others catch up, and to look at the broad fields and the sun mounting above the bare trees. It was a quiescent landscape, bearing its nakedness with

486

dignity, brooding on its ancient knowledge of change and cycle, of decay and flowering.

Rebecca thought: I am alive, I feel the life pulsing through me. Perhaps it's this quietness that makes one aware of it . . . But then that is life too, not only excitement and passion and motion, but moments like this, Christmas Day 1780: with friends around me – George and Mary, who are quiet too, but in a profound contented way, and Julia and Henry – who not so long ago looked old and worried but now look younger than any of us. And Luke beside me. All the difference. The future like a great sea and us standing on the uttermost shore. Together.

Oh, it won't be easy. We both of us have a temper. There'll be storms . . . and we wouldn't have it any other way. I'd fight anyone to keep him. I'd fight *him* to keep him. Life is long and tangled and unpredictable. But as long as there are moments like this, when I can hold my happiness, like holding it in my hand and feeling its weight, then I can't ask for any more.

Beside her Luke began to sing, almost under his breath, softly and mischievously:

'Now the winter is gone and the summer is come,
And the meadows look pleasant and gay;
I met a young damsel, so sweetly sang she,
And her cheeks like the blossoms of may.'